THE BOOK AND THE
BROTHERHOOD

Iris Murdoch was born in Dublin in 1919 of Anglo-Irish parents. She went to Badminton School, Bristol, and read Classics at Somerville College, Oxford. During the war she was an Assistant Principal at the Treasury, and then worked with UNRRA in London, Belgium and Austria. She held a studentship in Philosophy at Newnham College, Cambridge, and then in 1948 she returned to Oxford where she became a Fellow of St Anne's College. Until her death in February 1999, she lived with her husband, the teacher and critic John Bayley, in Oxford. Awarded the CBE in 1976, Iris Murdoch was made a DBE in the 1987 New Year's Honours List. In the 1997 PEN Awards she received the Gold Pen for Distinguished Service to Literature.

Since her writing debut in 1954 with *Under the Net*, Iris Murdoch has written twenty-six novels, including the Booker Prize-winning *The Sea, The Sea* (1978) and most recently *The Green Knight* (1993) and *Jackson's Dilemma* (1995). Other literary awards include the James Tait Black Memorial Prize for *The Black Prince* (1973) and the Whitbread Prize for *The Sacred and Profane Love Machine* (1974). Her works of philosophy include *Sartre: Romantic Rationalist*, *Metaphysics as a Guide to Morals* (1992) and *Existentialists and Mystics* (1997). She has written several plays including *The Italian Girl* (with James Saunders) and *The Black Prince*, adapted from her novel of the same name. Her volume of poetry, *A Year of Birds*, which appeared in 1978, has been set to music by Malcolm Williamson.

ALSO BY IRIS MURDOCH

Fiction

Under the Net
The Flight from the Enchanter
The Sandcastle
The Bell
A Severed Head
An Unofficial Rose
The Unicorn
The Italian Girl
The Red and the Green
The Time of the Angels
The Nice and the Good
Bruno's Dream
A Fairly Honourable Defeat
An Accidental Man
The Black Prince
The Sacred and Profane Love Machine
A Word Child
Henry and Cato
The Sea, The Sea
Nuns and Soldiers
The Philosopher's Pupil
The Good Apprentice
The Message to the Planet
The Green Knight
Jackson's Dilemma
Something Special

Non-Fiction

Acastos: Two Platonic Dialogues
Metaphysics as a Guide to Morals
Existentialists and Mystics
Sartre: Romantic Rationalist

Iris Murdoch

THE BOOK AND THE BROTHERHOOD

WITH AN INTRODUCTION BY
Malcolm Bowie

VINTAGE

Published by Vintage 2003

2 4 6 8 10 9 7 5 3 1

First published in Great Britain in 1987 by
Chatto & Windus

Vintage
Random House, 20 Vauxhall Bridge Road,
London SW1V 2SA

Random House Australia (Pty) Limited
20 Alfred Street, Milsons Point, Sydney
New South Wales 2061, Australia

Random House New Zealand Limited
18 Poland Road, Glenfield,
Auckland 10, New Zealand

Random House (Pty) Limited
Endulini, 5A Jubilee Road, Parktown 2193,
South Africa

The Random House Group Limited Reg. No. 954009
www.randomhouse.co.uk

A CIP catalogue record for this book
is available from the British Library

ISBN 0 09 943354 0

The author and publisher gratefully acknowledge permission from Faber & Faber Ltd and Random House Inc. to
quote on p. 127 lines by W. H. Auden from 'Out on the lawn
I lie in bed...', in *The English Auden: Poems, Essays and
Dramatic Writings 1927–39*.

Printed and bound in Great Britain by
Cox & Wyman Limited, Reading, Berkshire

CONTENTS

TO DIANA AVEBURY

Introduction

In the autumn of 1983 Titian's late masterpiece *The Flaying of Marsyas* travelled from Kroměříž, in what was then Czechoslovakia, to the Royal Academy in London. Throughout the winter this work of astonishing cruelty presided over the 'Genius of Venice' exhibition, and drew lengthy commentaries from the leading art critics of the day. It became fashionable to be troubled by Titian's retelling of one of the less familiar tales from Ovid's *Metamorphoses*, in which Apollo exerts a terrible revenge on the satyr who had presumed to challenge his musicianship. This scene of bloodletting, painted with an old master's free brush and impatient finger-ends, became for a while a theatre of self-laceration for the art crowd of the metropolis: so this was what lay behind their social ceremonies and their urbane talk; this was the blood-dimmed tide that ran through their aesthetic enthusiasms; this was the dark craving that no emphasis on artistic form and executive address could ever fully disguise or deter. The simple fact that the canvas has been transported from the depths of Moravia, which at the time remained difficult for visitors from the Western fringes of Europe to access, enhanced the general sense of strangeness and singularity that surrounded its visit. A scandal was in town.

A haunting memorial to this visit is still to be found nearby, in the National Portrait Gallery, for a section of Titian's work was used by Tom Phillips as a background in the official portrait of Iris Murdoch that he began in the year the great Venice show closed. The section chosen by artist and sitter offers much more than a discreet allusion to one of her favourite painters, for Apollo's scalpel, at work upon his victim's skin, is poised over the right-hand side of Murdoch's head, while a bucket for the collection of blood dangles over the left. Her cool expression and even cooler open-necked blouse are overarched by a scene of horror; as a nimbus around her intelligent head Murdoch wears a picture of a picture of an unspeakable deed. The allegory is of course clear and need not be laboured: by this late stage in her career as a novelist, Murdoch was already famous for the demon lovers, black princes and Mephistophelian philosophers who populate her fiction, and had already, in her detached and quizzical way, contrived countless scenes of sacrificial violence. The Phillips portrait dramatises the split between the novelist and the moral philosopher, yet at the same time suggests something of the healing power that Murdoch's own creative personality possessed. If goodness and truth were the philosopher's everyday goals, and celebrated by her in her arguments, it was the novelist's business to make sure that these virtues were removed periodically from the cloister and tested in the real world of human enmity and wilfulness. The novelist must know about darkness, acknowledge it as her own, and be prepared to manipulate it by verbal art. The dangerous complicities between art and cruelty, symbolised by Titian in the person of a god who first plays well and then flays well, is one of those matters on which the novelist can be teacher and the philosopher her pupil.

The Book and the Brotherhood, which Murdoch began writing in the mid-1980s, with the shadow of Marsyas still upon her, is a problem novel in a number of ways. Although she herself was particularly fond of it, her admirers have generally been rather more reserved in their response. It has struck many people as excessively long and loose. It tells a profusion of criss-crossing stories and characters often seem to wander aimlessly from one of these to the next, as if new meanings could be found for them simply by changing the company they keep. And perhaps oddly in a book that moves with such leisure in its broad unfolding, the pacing within paragraphs is often constricted and spasmodic:

Jenkin had of course not divulged to anyone what Tamar had told him. Gerard, after a cautious enquiry, sheered off the subject which was evidently secret, and he said nothing to Rose about Tamar's extraordinary arrival at Jenkin's house. Rose knew that Tamar had been 'in a state', had run away from home to stay with Lily, and was now back with Violet. Rose had written to Tamar asking her to lunch, but had had no reply. Gerard and Jenkin seemed to have nothing to say on the subject of Tamar's troubles. Neither had Lily, whom Rose had rung up. Violet's flat was not on the telephone. Rose had been making up her mind to write to Violet, or else appear unexpectedly at her flat one evening, when the drama of Jean's accident took her to Boyars. On her return to London there was still no letter from Tamar. Rose had written to Violet but had had no reply. (p. 402)

Writing of this kind reads as the breathless synopsis of a still unwritten and only vaguely plotted play or opera. The novelist has projected herself to some distant imaginative outpost where the destiny of each character stands revealed, and then sent a series of perfunctory telegrams back to her reader: let him clutch at these straws and catch up as best he can.

Other stylistic features create a similar impression – of rapid verbal fire directed at fleeing targets. There is, for example, Murdoch's mania for adjectives, which are sometimes played out or reeled off as if the creation of a coherent fictional work depended on them alone, to the exclusion of all other building materials:

She saw Sinclair suddenly so clearly with his blond mane and his short straight nose and his luminous intimate dark blue eyes which were so like Rose's, and his jaunty roguish teasing air of a spoilt boy which was so unlike Rose's gentle patient withdrawn look.

You need more than characteristics if you want to make a character, one is tempted to protest, and unsupported adjectival strings have very limited power when it comes to the animation and mutation of characters over time. There is a graver difficulty, too, for if the supposed physical and moral attributes of a supposed person can become tiresome and point-less when they are simply sprayed into the fictional texture, clothing and other items from the props basket are likely to fare even worse as particularising agents:

Rose wore a long dark green jacket of heavy tweed, a thick high-necked brown jersey with a green silk scarf at the neck, knee-breeches and thick socks. Lily wore a white polo-necked skin-tight jersey, with a V-necked red jersey over it, a loose fluffy belted black cardigan of angora wool, and black woollen trousers tucked into red socks. Noting Rose's well-worn knee-breeches, she had remarked that tucking one's trousers into one's socks looked just as good and was easier. (She at once regretted this observation.) Both women, as they announced, had on their thickest woollen vests, Rose two, Lily only one. Lily felt cold. She had paid too much attention to Rose's prediction that they would get quite hot skating. Gerard, who, thinking it wrong to be obsessed with clothes, dressed with a casual discernment, was wearing a dark green high-necked cash-mere sweater over a white shirt, a dark blue scarf of very light wool, a long navy jacket of hand-woven tweed and blue-black corduroy trousers. Jenkin wore his usual winter suit with a thick jersey, a heavy overcoat and his stripy woollen cap. Tamar also wore a substantial overcoat above her jumper, and leg warmers over her trousers and had covered her head and most of her face with a beige-coloured scarf. Gulliver had, after much thought and inde-cision, put on pale brown corduroy trousers, his best and longest jersey, blue with the strawberry design, and his short green Loden coat. (p. 250)

A case could be made for this extravaganza, one supposes, as a parody of fashion journalism, or as a mock-epic of futile middle-class discriminations, but coming at the reader in a sudden avalanche just before the mid-point of the novel these cameo descriptions have an air of real desperation about them. One can readily imagine Murdoch checking herself at this moment in order to rehearse some professional home-truths: novels need characters, alas, and characters, especially if they are about to go skating, need clothes; let the clothes do the character-building work; let an accumulation of winter gear prevent this variegated crew of human types from drifting away into inane generality. Novels need to have stuff in them – fabrics, dry goods – if they are to maintain a proper distance from tracts, treatises and moral essays. Let there be tweed, cashmere and corduroy, the narrative voice urges, lest we lose ourselves in an immaterial play of essences.

But if we put too much pressure on explanations and excuses of this kind, and see such writing merely as a self-aware novelist's attempt to do the right or the expected thing, we are likely to miss a much more important element in *The Book and the Brotherhood*, and this is its proud insistence on generality, its determination to be a drama of ideas rather than manners, and of moral conflict rather than sociological description. Cashmere and other stuffs represent a temporary falling away on Murdoch's part from a project that gets its power and its rootedness in human affairs from quite different sources. The best of the work lies precisely in its capacity to outsoar its characters, their gear, and the complacent Oxonian provinciality in which their brotherhood is first established.

By the time she came to write this extraordinary novel, Iris Murdoch was a self-declared Platonist both in her philosophising and in her fiction. In her Romanes lecture of 1976, published in the following year as *The Fire and the Sun*, she had written a long love letter to her supreme predecessor, but one that gave a familiar argument an unusual inflection. Mercifully, Plato himself had been an imperfect Platonist. He had banished artists from his ideal Republic but had been unrepentant in his own artistry:

He fought a long battle against sophistry and magic, yet produced some of the most memorable images in

European philosophy: the Cave, the charioteer, the cunning homeless Eros, the Demiurge cutting the *Anima Mundi* into strips and stretching it out crosswise. He kept emphasizing the imageless remoteness of the Good, yet kept returning in his exposition to the most elaborate uses of art. The dialogue form itself is artful and indirect and abounds in ironical and playful devices. Of course the statements made by art escape into the free ambiguity of human life. Art cheats the religious vocation at the last moment and is inimical to philosophical categories. Yet neither philosophy nor theology can do without it. (p. 87)

The lesson that Murdoch draws from Plato in this and numerous comparable passages is that philosophy needs its novelists, its poetic pluralisers of the human field, its explorers of the human passions, its danger-seekers and risk-takers. Plato was exemplary not only because he devoted himself with visionary fervour to the quest for goodness and truth, but because he brought a lively attention to bear on other movements of the soul, including those that in certain incarnations were perverse and destructive. He confronted his demons, wrote about them, exposed his writing to their energising touch, and in all these respects was an enabling role model. Plato, as Murdoch eloquently describes him, was not so much the proponent of a system as the dramatist of the human imagination seen in the exercise of a formidable transformational power. He separated what needed to be separated, and fused whatever a hidden kinship tended to unite. For him, dialogue was the essential vehicle of creative thinking. He was, in short, rather like Murdoch in her late manner.

The book to which Murdoch's title refers is a work of radical political theory, and its author, David Crimond, the complete intellectual seducer, but the content of the book, like the internal faceting of Crimond's personality, is steadfastly withheld from view. What matters about the man is the intensity and exorbitance of his passion: these are the qualities that persuade his friends to finance his research and writing, and that stir them each in turn to an answering exaltation of feeling. What matters about the book is the cleansing fire that it is expected to light in the academic community and beyond. It is of course curious to be reminded by Crimond's name of the Scottish Psalter and a consoling hymn-tune, just as it is curious to be asked to imagine that a work of supercharged persuasive potency on quite this scale might find its way into the catalogue of Oxford University Press. But far from flinching at such incongruities, Murdoch seizes upon them with glee. Behind any oddity, any contingent coming together of this and that, a grand mental motion may perhaps be glimpsed, and garnering these motions into an extended frieze is the noblest of tasks for the Platonising storyteller.

The range of Murdoch's survey is extraordinary. At the simplest level, this story of a seducer and his victims may seem to err in the direction of excessive unity. Crimond is a powerful figure because other characters so readily succumb to his devilry and make it their own:

> Perhaps it was this small parcel of vanity in his great love that he was paying for now? He loved Jean, he 'forgave' her, but his stricken vanity cried out to be consoled. Would he become, at the last, a demon set free? Oddly he sometimes felt Jean respond to it, this demonic freedom, unconsciously excited by it, as if taught by his new bad self. (p. 524)

This is Duncan recovering from his cuckolding by straining to resemble his wife's former lover: if you cannot beat the devil, become him. But although the centrally placed Crimond temperament is contagious in this way, and creates a network of affinities among the otherwise disparate individuals who crowd Murdoch's cast list, the novel has more power sources than one. Tamar, for example, in the guilt and shame that her abortion prompts, or Father McAlister in the promise of redemption that he holds out to the miserable girl, or Gerard in his declaration of love for Jenkin, are all clearly separated from each other, and from the spell that the kilted Crimond begins to cast in the first sentence of the novel. In the end, all the characters may be seen as different embodiments of a single life-energy, but before the end, in the lengthy interim of fictional composition, each has been given a distinct moral and psychological complexity, and a speech-music of his or her own.

Sometimes the characters speak to each other loudly, as if at a public meeting, but more often their tirades are internal, and stage-managed in that 'indirect free style', that Murdoch had so often employed before in her fiction:

> A sense of the unreality, the sheer artificiality, of individual existence had begun to possess her. What was it after all to be 'a person', able to speak, to remember, to have purposes, to inhibit screams? What was this weird unclean ever-present body, of which she was always seeing parts? Why did not her 'personality' simply cease to be continuous and disintegrate into a cloud of ghosts, blown about by the wind? (p.515)

This is philosophy being done inside the distorting medium of a panic attack, on the verge of a scream, and with divine fury running through it. And in order to write like this Murdoch needs a versatile ventriloquising skill. In *The Fire and the Sun* she spoke now as Plato and now as professional modern commentator on the Dialogues, and a single multiform voice was in charge of the graduated transitions from the one to the other. In *The Book and the Brotherhood* the voice is stretched across a much wider spectrum, and it takes more chances. It collects ecstasies, abjections, jealous rages, suicidal and homicidal exhilarations, and distributes them even-handedly among the members of an underemployed middle class. As philosophical dialogues go it is all rather baggy, and at times rather inconsequential, but its sense of intellectual urgency is complete and unwavering. The Murdoch characters are sentient creatures drawn, each of them, towards the most extreme states of awareness that lie within their reach, thinking as they go, murmuring to themselves their distinctive word-tunes. There is pressure towards philosophical generality in much of what they say to themselves, as if individual existences were always being tempted to turn themselves over to 'existentiality' at large:

> She could perceive the world at last, her eyes were cleared, her perceptions clarified, she had never seen such a vivid, coloured, detailed world, vast and complete as myth, yet full of tiny particular accidental entities placed in her way like divine toys. She had discovered breathing, breathing such as holy men use, the breathing of the planet, of the universe, the movement of being into Being. (p. 168)

But Murdoch has here put into the mouth of Jean Kowitz her own resistance to a smooth-contoured and characterless Being as well as her acquiescent drift towards it. Particularity, the ragged edges of things and the fluctuating pulse of personal experience, must be safeguarded by anyone who wants to call herself a novelist. There are of course many ways of writing novels, and Murdoch's way involves marshalling rather few material objects and correspondingly many upheavals of consciousness. For her, the 'tiny particular accidental entities' that matter most are mental events, and it is by putting these end to end and giving them duration that a novel begins to take shape.

Murdoch's main achievement in *The Book and the Brotherhood* is to have assembled an array of intensities and extremities, and to have drawn clear demarcating lines between them. She remembers with approval Plato's description of the demiurge in the *Timaeus*: he is the cosmological force who 'cuts the world-soul into strips'. She is haunted by the figure of Apollo in Titian's Marsyas painting: he is the young god who, with patient application, strips away another creature's skin. In both cases, this benign believer in the sovereignty of good has been detained by a mesmerising image of violence. What might, in other places, seem no more than simple sadism is, in these special places, sublimated and made salutary. Artists must be prepared to cut, even if this means disturbing the equilibrium of the human soul and thereby incurring the displeasure of Plato in his guise of metaphysical system-builder. Telling the truth about a world that has so much pain, destructiveness and death in it demands of the artist nothing less. 'How nice objects are', Murdoch once wrote to a friend, thanking him for a gift, 'I'm glad we live in a thingy world'. The gift, however, had not been an indifferent representative of the class 'things', but a Tibetan ritual dagger. A writer in the Iris Murdoch manner needs a dagger as well as a pen.

MALCOLM BOWIE, 2003

THE BOOK AND
THE BROTHERHOOD

PART ONE

Midsummer

_____

'David Crimond is here in a *kilt*!'

'Good God, is Crimond here? Where is he?'

'Over in that tent or marquee or whatever you call it. He's with Lily Boyne.'

The first speaker was Gulliver Ashe, the second was Conrad Lomas. Gulliver was a versatile, currently unemployed, young Englishman in his early thirties, pointedly vague about his age. Conrad was a more gorgeously young young American student. He was taller than Gulliver who was rated as tall. Gulliver had never hitherto met Conrad, but he had heard of him and had addressed the remark which caused such excitement to, jointly, Conrad and his partner Tamar Hernshaw. The scene was the so-much-looked-forward-to Commem Ball at Oxford, and the time about eleven p.m. It was midsummer and the night was not yet, and was indeed never entirely to be, dark. Above the various lighted marquees, from which various musics streamed, hung a sky of dusky blue already exhibiting a few splintery yellow stars. The moon, huge, crumbly like a cheese, was still low down among trees beyond the local streamlets of the river Cherwell which bounded the more immediate territory of the college. Tamar and Conrad had just arrived, had not yet danced. Gulliver had confidently addressed them since he knew, though not well, Tamar, and had heard who her escort was to be. The sight of Tamar filled Gulliver, in fact, with irritation, since *his* partner for the momentous night was to have been (only she had cried off at the last moment) Tamar's mother Violet. Gulliver did not particularly like Violet, but had agreed to be paired with her to oblige Gerard Hernshaw, whom he usually obliged, even obeyed. Gerard was Tamar's uncle, or 'uncle', since he was not Violet's brother but her cousin. Gerard was considerably older than Gulliver. Gerard's sister Patricia, who was to have had Jenkin Riderhood as her partner, had also not turned up, but had (unlike Violet, who seemed to have no reason) a good reason, since Gerard's father, long ill, had suddenly become iller. Gulliver, though of course thrilled to be asked, was irritated by being paired by Gerard with Violet, which seemed to relegate Gulliver to the older generation. Gulliver would not have minded partnering Tamar, though he was not especially 'keen' on her. He found her too shy and stiff, she was pale and thin and rather schoolgirlish, she was wispy and waifish and lacked style, she did her short straight hair in a little-girl way with a side parting. He did not like her virginal white dress. Gull, who was not always sure that he liked girls at all, preferred ones who were bolder and able to take charge of him. In any case there was never any question of Tamar, since she was known to be going to the dance with her new acquaintance, this clever young American, whom she had met through her cousin Leonard Fairfax. Gerard, apologetic about Violet's defection, had said vaguely to Gulliver that he could no doubt 'pick up a girl somehow', but so far this did not seem likely to be possible, all the girls being firmly held onto by their chaps. Later on of course as the chaps got drunk the situation might change. He had wandered about in the warm blue twilight for some time hoping to meet someone he knew, but Tamar's had been the first familiar face, and he felt on seeing her annoyance rather than pleasure. He was also annoyed because he had not, after much consideration, put on his frilly lacy blue evening shirt, such as most of the younger generation were now seen to be dressed in, and was wearing the conventional black and white uniform which he knew that Gerard, Jenkin, and Duncan would have on. Gulliver, who thought himself good-looking, was tall and dark and slim, with straight oily dark hair, and a thin slightly hooked nose which he had come to terms with when someone called it aquiline. His eyes, which he had been told were beautiful, were of a very pure unflecked liquid golden brown. He very much wanted to dance and would have felt

2

thoroughly cross with Gerard for messing things up if it had not been that Gerard had paid for Gulliver's (very expensive) ticket without which he would not be there at all. While these thoughts were mingling and colliding in Gulliver's mind, Conrad Lomas, with a murmured apology to Tamar, had shot off like an arrow in the direction of the marquee where David Crimond was said to be. He *ran* upon his unusually long legs across the grass and disappeared, leaving Gulliver and Tamar together. Tamar, surprised by the amazing speed of his departure, had not immediately followed her swain. This should have been Gulliver's opportunity, and he did indeed wonder for a moment whether he should quickly ask Tamar to dance. He hesitated however, knowing that if Tamar refused he would be upset. Nor did he want to find himself, perhaps, later on, 'landed' with her for some long time. He had really, in spite of his cherished grievances, quite enjoyed wandering around by himself and being a *voyeur*. Moreover, the idea had just occurred to him of returning to the room where Gerard and the oldies were still drinking champagne, and asking Rose Curtland to dance. Of course Rose 'belonged' to Gerard, but Gerard wouldn't mind, and the notion of putting his arm, where it had never dreamt of being, round Rose Curtland's waist, was certainly an appealing one. His moment for Tamar passed and she began to move away.

Gull said, 'That was Conrad Lomas, wasn't it? Whatever got into him?'

Tamar said, 'He's doing a thesis about something about Marxism in Britain.'

'So he'll have read all Crimond's stuff.'

'He *idolises* Crimond,' said Tamar, 'he's read everything he's written, but never met him. He wanted me to get someone to introduce him but I felt I couldn't. I didn't know he'd be here tonight.'

'Neither did I,' said Gulliver, and added, 'neither do *they*.'

Tamar, with a vague wave, set off in the direction of the tent into which Conrad had disappeared. Gulliver decided not to go back to the others yet after all. He wanted to wander about a little longer. This was not his college or his university. He

3

had done his degree in London, and although he regarded Oxford and Oxford ways with sardonic detachment he was ready, on this unique evening, to give himself up to the charm of his surroundings, the ancient buildings floodlit, the pale exquisite tower, the intense green of illumined trees, the striped tents as of an exotic army, and the peregrinating crowd of colourful young people of whom, now that he had had a few drinks, he did not after all feel too uncomfortably envious. Perhaps the immediate thing to do was to have some more drink. He made his way toward the cloisters where he could get some whisky. He was tired of Gerard's champagne.

Tamar had not failed to notice Gulliver's indecision about asking her to dance. She would have refused but felt hurt at not being asked. She clutched her embroidered cashmere shawl closely about her, crossing it upon her breast and humping it up high about her neck. The day had been cloudlessly hot, the evening was warm, but there was now a slight breeze and Tamar felt chilly, she tended to feel the cold. Her white evening dress swept the grass upon which she imagined that she could already feel the dew. She reached the marquee where the lights had been turned up, since the pop group were knocking off for refreshments, and the dancers were standing about upon the wooden floor talking. She could not see Conrad anywhere, but soon noticed a closely packed group of young people, like a swarm of bees, in one corner where a high-pitched voice with a slight Scottish accent was holding forth. Tamar did not like Crimond, she was frightened of him, but she had had occasion to meet him very rarely, and, since the row with Gerard and the others, never. It did not occur to her to go over to the group of worshippers and join Conrad. She sat down for a while on one of the seats round the edge of the tent and waited. She noticed Lily Boyne, who had been reported as being with Crimond, sitting alone on the other side. Lily had taken off one of her sandals and was examining it, now smelling it. Tamar, who did not want to talk to Lily, hoped that Lily would not notice her. Of course she knew Lily Boyne, who was a friend, at any rate a sort of friend, of Rose Curtland and Jean Cambus, but Lily made Tamar feel

4

ill at ease, slightly made her shudder. In fact Tamar *disapproved* of Lily and so preferred not to think about her. When the loud music and the flashing lights started up again Tamar moved out into the dark. The deep vibrating beat of the music upset her, she wanted very much to dance.

Tamar was poised ready to fall in love. It is possible to plan to fall in love. Or perhaps what seems like planning is simply the excited anticipation of the moment, delayed so as to be perfected, of the unmistakable mutual gesture, when eyes meet, hands meet, words fail. It was thus, in these terms, in this expectant state of being, that Tamar had allowed herself to look forward to this evening. She had in fact met Conrad, who had been at Cambridge and was soon returning to America, only a few times, and usually in company. On the last occasion, seeing her home, he had kissed her ardently. Her cousin Leonard Fairfax, who was in America studying art history at Cornell, had introduced them by letter. Tamar had let herself like, then more than like, the tall American boy, but had as yet made him no signal. She had dreamt about him. Tamar was twenty, at the end of her second year of studying history at Oxford. She was apparently grown up, but her shyness and her appearance made others, and indeed her herself, think of her as younger, naive, not quite an adult. She had had two love affairs, the first inspired by anxiety, the second by pity, for which she blamed herself severely. She was a puritanical child, and she had never been in love.

Rose Curtland was dancing with Gerard Hernshaw. They were in the tent where 'sweet' old-fashioned music was being played, waltzes, tangos, and slow foxtrots, interspersed with eightsome reels, Gay Gordons, and ambiguous jigs which could be danced to taste. The sound of the famous pop group was now audible in the distance. In yet another tent there was traditional jazz, in another 'country music'. Rose and Gerard, who were good dancers, could cope with all these, but it was an evening for nostalgia. The college orchestra was playing Strauss. Rose inclined her head gently against Gerard's black-clad shoulder. She was tall but he was taller. They were a good-looking couple. Gerard's face, describable as 'rugged',

5

had been better characterised by his brother-in-law the art dealer as 'cubist'. There were a number of strong dominant surfaces, a commanding bone structure, a square even brow, a nose that appeared to end in a blunt plane rather than a point. But what might have seemed a hard set of mathematical surfaces was animated and harmonised by the energy which blazed through it, rendering it into an ironic humorous face, whose smile was frequently a mad and zany grin. Gerard's eyes were a metallic blue, his curly hair was brown, now less than it used to be the colour of an undimmed chestnut, but still copious and ungreying although he was now over fifty. Rose's hair was blond and straight, plentiful and rising up sometimes into a fuzz or aureole. Looking lately into her mirror Rose had wondered if all those lively light brown locks were not, *all together*, changing into a light grey. She had dark blue eyes and a positively pretty slightly *retroussé* nose. She had kept her figure and was wearing a simple very dark green ball dress. Rose had a conspicuous air of calmness which annoyed some people and comforted others. She often wore a faint smile, and was wearing one now, although her mingled layers of thought were by no means entirely happy. Dancing with Gerard was an icon of happiness. If only she could experience that sense of eternity in the present about which Gerard sometimes talked. She ought to be able to be happy now simply because of Gerard's firm arm round her waist, and the so slight but authoritative movements of his body whereby he led her. She had looked forward to this evening ever since Gerard had announced his plans for his friends. It was he who had arranged the presence of Tamar and Conrad. But now that what she had wanted was here she was allowing herself to be wilfully absent. She smiled a little more, then sighed.

'I know what you're thinking about,' said Gerard.

'Yes.'

'About Sinclair.'

'Yes.'

Rose had not just then been thinking about Sinclair, but the thought of him was so profoundly associated with the thought of Gerard that she felt no qualm in assenting. Sinclair was

6

Rose's brother, 'the golden boy', so long dead. Of course she had thought about him earlier that evening when entering the college, remembering that other far off summer day when she had come visiting her undergraduate brother at the end of his first year, and Sinclair had said to her, 'Look, that tall chap over there, that's Gerard Hernshaw.' Rose, a little younger than Sinclair, had been still at school. Sinclair's recent letters had been full of Gerard, who was two years his senior. Rose inferred from the letters that Sinclair was in love with Gerard. It was only on that day in Oxford that she realised that Gerard was equally in love with Sinclair. That was all right. What was not so all right was that Rose had promptly fallen for Gerard herself, and remained, after all these years, hopelessly, permanently, in love. The extraordinary affair which she had had with Gerard less than two years after Sinclair's early death was something they never spoke of afterwards, perhaps, such was their curious discipline, never even in their thoughts turned over, as one turns over memories, reworking, refurbishing, exposing to air and change. It lay rather in their past as a sealed package which they sometimes very gently touched but never, alone or together, envisaged opening. Rose had had other lovers, but they were brief shadows, she had had proposals of marriage, but they did not interest her. Now, feeling the pressure of Gerard's hand upon hers very slightly increase, she wondered if he were now thinking of *that*. She did not look up, removing her head from the place where it had momentarily rested against his shoulder. After Sinclair left Oxford he and Gerard had lived together, Gerard working as a journalist, Sinclair continuing his studies in biology and helping Gerard to found a left-wing magazine. After Sinclair's glider crashed into that hillside in Sussex, and after the very brief dream-interlude with Rose, Gerard gave up left-wing activities and went into the Civil Service. He lived at that time with various men, including Oxford friends, Duncan Cambus, who was then in London, and Robin Topglass, the geneticist, son of the birdman. Robin later married a French Canadian girl and went to Canada, Duncan married Rose's schoolfriend Jean Kowitz and went into the diplomatic service. Marcus

7

Field, probably not one of Gerard's lovers, became a Benedictine monk. Gerard had always had plenty of close men friends, such as Jenkin Riderhood, with whom he had no sexual relations; and in more recent years seemed to have settled down to living alone. Of course Rose never asked. In fact she had stopped worrying about the men. It was the women she was afraid of.

The waltz had ended and they were standing together in the pleasant relaxed rather limp attitude of people who have suddenly stopped dancing. Rose said, 'I'm so glad Tamar has met such a nice boy at last.'

'I hope she'll grab him and hold on.'

'I can't see her doing anything so vigorous. He'll have to do the grabbing.'

'She's so gentle,' said Gerard, 'so simple in the best sense, so pure in heart. I hope that boy realises what a remarkable child she is.'

'You mean he might find her dull? She's not a bright young thing.'

'Oh, he couldn't find her *dull*,' said Gerard, almost indignantly. He added, 'Poor girl, always in search of a father.'

'You mean she might prefer an older man?'

'I don't mean anything so banal!'

'Of course we're impressed by her,' said Rose, 'because we know her background. And I mean rightly impressed.'

'Yes. Out of that mess she's come so extraordinarily intact.'

'The illegitimate child of an illegitimate child.'

'I hate that terminology.'

'Well, I suppose people still think in these terms.'

Tamar's mother Violet, never married, was the child of Gerard's father's deplorable younger brother Benjamin Hernshaw, also never married, who abandoned Violet's mother. Tamar, who, it was said, only survived because Violet could not afford an abortion, was the result of an affair with a passing Scandinavian which was so brief that Violet, who claimed to have forgotten his name, was never sure whether he was Swedish, Danish or Norwegian. Upon Tamar's waifish charm, her mousy hair and big sad grey eyes, no particular theory could be rested. Violet herself had resolutely taken the name Hernshaw and had passed it on to Tamar. Violet's 'messy life', looked so askance at by Patricia, even by Gerard, had continued during Tamar's childhood, but without any comparable accidents.

'Violet was remarkably attractive to men,' said Rose. 'She still is.'

Gerard said nothing to this. He looked at his watch. He was wearing, of course, the black and white rig deplored by Gulliver Ashe, and which suited him so well.

Rose thought, I'm still jealous of any woman who comes near him, even poor little Tamar whom I'm so fond of! Sometimes she thought, I've wasted my life on this man, I've waited though I've known I'm waiting for nothing, he has accepted so much and given so little in return. Then she would think, how ungrateful I am, he has given me his precious love, he loves me and needs me, isn't that enough? Even if he does think of me as a sort of ideal sister. All the same, now he's retired from the Civil Service, he says to write things, he says to start a fresh phase of life, to perfect himself or something, he could suddenly start some mad new thing like loving women – and coming to me for advice! Then she thought, what nonsense! – and after all, haven't I been happy?

'How's your father?' she asked.

'Not well – but not – actually dying. Of course there's no hope, it's just a matter of how long.'

'I'm very sorry. Patricia didn't think it was a crisis?'

'No, he's a bit worse, and we couldn't get hold of the nurse. Pat's very good with him, she's an angel of patience.'

Rose had seen little of Gerard's father in recent years, he had been living in Bristol, in the house in Clifton where Gerard had been born. Only lately, after becoming ill, he had moved to Gerard's house in London. There was a bond between him and Rose which also made them ill at ease together. Gerard's father had so much wanted Gerard to marry Rose. Just as Rose's father had so much wanted Sinclair to marry Jean Kowitz. If Sinclair had survived he would have had the title. As it was it went to the Yorkshire Curtlands (second cousins, the grandfathers had been brothers), who were also to inherit Rose's house when Rose was gone. We are all without issue, thought Rose, all those hopeful family plans frustrated, we shall disappear without trace!

'Surely Patricia and Gideon haven't decided to *settle* in that upstairs flat you made for your father?'

'No, it's just that their lease is up, they're house-hunting.'

'I hope they are! When is Gideon back from New York?' Patricia's husband, Gideon Fairfax, art dealer and financial wizard, now spent much time in that city.

'Next week.'

'You said they were trying to get you out and take over the whole house!'

'Well, Pat keeps saying I don't need all that space!'

The existence of the new 'upstairs flat' had put ideas into Rose's head. Why should not she, and *no one else*, occupy that flat? Rose had for years cherished, perhaps in some dusty abandoned but persisting part of her mind still cherished, the hope that 'in the end', and 'after all', she might marry Gerard. Later this idea became more modestly that of 'sharing a house', of being *with him*, in some sense in which, for all their closeness, and their generally acknowledged closeness, she certainly was not now.

They had moved to the edge of the crowded floor, and Rose knew that in a moment Gerard would suggest that they return to 'the room', that is to the quarters of Professor Levquist, Gerard's old classics tutor, which Levquist had lent to Gerard and his friends to be their base during the dance. (Levquist's family, originally Baltic Jews called Levin, had adopted the Scandinavian suffix as protective coloration.) Rose said, to delay him, 'Have you decided anything about the book?' She was not referring to any book being written by Gerard, there was as yet no such thing, but to another book.

Gerard frowned at the unwelcome question. 'No.'

The waltz music began again. Hearing the fast familiar strain they smiled and moved together. Soon Gerard was whirling Rose round and round, tightening his hold, shifting his grip, moving his left hand up her arm, then embracing her round the waist with both arms and lifting her swift feet from the floor.

A little later Rose and Gerard made their way to Levquist's rooms just off the cloisters. Rose felt, but would not of course admit it, a little tired. They found Jenkin Riderhood in possession. Jenkin, who had clearly been drinking for some time, quickly put down the bottle of champagne. Jenkin, a little younger than Gerard, was an old friend, one of the original 'set' which included Sinclair, Duncan, Marcus, Robin, who had been close friends as undergraduates at the college. Of the survivors Jenkin was, or perhaps just seemed, the least successful. Duncan Cambus had been having a distinguished career, first as a diplomat, then in the Home Civil Service. Gerard had reached greater heights, tipped for the highest office in his department, when he had suddenly, quite lately, many felt unaccountably, taken an early retirement. Robin, now defected to Canada and rarely heard from, was a well-known geneticist. Sinclair had decided to be a marine biologist, and was about to visit the Scripps Oceanography Institute in California when his glider crashed. Rose had intended to go with him, Gerard was to follow, together they were going to discover America. At Oxford Gerard, Duncan and Jenkin had all done 'Greats', Greek and Latin, ancient history and philosophy, and had all got their 'firsts'. Rose, who came of a Yorkshire family, with Anglo-Irish connections on her mother's side, had studied English literature and French at Edinburgh. She had done a variety of things, never achieving anything which could be called a career, taught French at a girls' school, worked for an Animals' Rights organisation, been a 'women's journalist', tried to write novels, returned to part-time journalism and ecology. She did unpaid social work and occasionally went to (Anglican) church. She had a small annuity from a family trust which she felt she might have been better off without; she might have tried harder. Her friend Jean Kowitz, with whom she had attended a Quaker boarding school, had been at

Oxford where, through Rose, she got to know Gerard and the others, including Duncan Cambus whom she later married. Jean was a clever academic who should, Rose felt, have 'done something' instead of just being a wife. Jean and Duncan were childless. Jenkin Riderhood was, and had always been, a schoolmaster. He was now senior history master in a London school. He had never applied for a headship. He was a diffident solitary man, easily pleased by small treats. He knew a number of languages and liked going on package tours. He was known to have had some romances (that seemed to be the word) with girls at Oxford, but his later sex life seemed to be non-existent, was at any rate invisible.

Jenkin said, 'I've just been to look at my old rooms. There was an undergraduate there writing an essay. He called me "sir".'

'I'm glad he had such good manners,' said Rose, 'they don't all.'

'What's it like out there?'

'A forest in Ancient Egypt,' said Gerard. 'I hope the champers is holding out?'

'Bags of it. Piles of sandwiches too.'

Jenkin, who was sweating and flushed with drink, brought forward a plate of cucumber sandwiches and began to mop up with a napkin some of the champagne which was swimming about on the table. He was stout, not tall, and looked fidgety and bulgy in his evening dress which was old and made for a considerably slimmer Jenkin. He had however retained his boyish look and clear soft complexion and could be better described as chubby. His faded strawy blond hair hung down about his head, still concealing a small bald patch. He had streaky blue-grey eyes, a pursed-up thoughtful often-smiling mouth and longish teeth. His face was saved from being cherubic by a rather long substantial nose which gave him an animal look, sometimes touching, sometimes shrewd.

'I'm sorry Pat couldn't come,' said Gerard, pouring some champagne for Rose. Jenkin was to have been, in Gideon's absence, Patricia's partner.

'Oh I'm OK,' said Jenkin, 'loving it. Damn! Sandwiches

should bloody stay together.' His cucumber had leapt out onto the floor.

'Did Violet say why she couldn't come?' said Rose.

'No, but one knows why. She doesn't want to see a lot of happy laughing young people. She doesn't want to see a lot of happy laughing us.'

'Who is to blame her?' murmured Jenkin.

'She was probably glad to be asked,' said Rose. 'She may not have wanted to see Tamar being so happy. Parents can love their children and envy them too.' She added, 'We must do something about Violet.' This was often said.

'I didn't spot Tamar and Conrad, did you?' said Gerard. 'I forgot to tell them to come up here for drinks.'

'They won't want to be with us!' said Rose.

'They look so young, the young, don't they,' said Gerard. 'Ah, *la jeunesse, la jeunesse*! All those clear smooth transparent unspoilt unworked faces!'

'Not like ours,' said Jenkin, 'scrawled over with passion and resentment and drink!'

'You two look like children,' said Rose, 'at least Jenkin does. Gerard looks like –' Wanting to avoid some ridiculous comparison she left the sentence unfinished.

'We were children *then*,' said Gerard.

'You mean we were Marxists,' said Jenkin. 'Or we imagined we were Platonists or something. You still do.'

'We thought that we could live some really civilised alternative society,' said Gerard, 'we had faith, we believed.'

'Jenkin still believes,' said Rose. 'What do you believe in, Jenkin?'

'The New Theology!' said Jenkin promptly.

'Don't be silly!' said Rose.

'Don't you mean the New Marxism,' said Gerard, 'isn't it much the same thing?'

'Well, if it's new enough –'

'New enough to be unrecognisable!'

'I never go to church,' said Jenkin,' 'but I want religion to go on somehow. There's a battle front there, where religion and Marxism touch.'

13

'Not yours,' said Gerard, 'I mean not your battle. You don't want to fight for Marx! That mix-up is totally incoherent anyway.'

'Well, where is my battle? I'd like to be somewhere out at the edge of things. But where is the edge?'

'You've been saying this sort of thing for years,' said Gerard, 'and here you are still.'

'Jenkin is a romantic,' said Rose, 'so am I. I'd like to be a priest. Maybe it will be possible in my lifetime.'

'Rose would make a marvellous priest!'

'I'm against it,' said Gerard. 'Don't eat all the sandwiches.'

'You agree to being called a sort of Platonist?' said Rose to Gerard.

'Oh yes!'

'That's what you're going to write about, now you've retired?'

'You'll write about Plotinus, like you said?' said Jenkin.

'Possibly.' Gerard evidently did not want to talk about this, so the other two dropped the subject.

Rose put down her glass and went to the window. She could see the floodlit tower, the moon risen and now small, a concise circle of silver, lights in the trees by the river. Her heart heaved within her as if it were some huge thing which she had swallowed and wished to regurgitate. She suddenly wanted to sob with joy and fear. The slim pinnacled tower, in the fierce light against the dark blue sky, resembled a picture in a Book of Hours. It also reminded Rose of something, some kind of theatre, some time, perhaps many times, when she had seen illumined buildings at night and heard superhuman voices, such as the one which she now instinctively expected to hear, telling her in slow ringing tones some picturesque piece of history or legend. *Son et lumière* in France, England, Italy, Spain. A memory came of something in French, some un-placed piece of poetry, perhaps not even heard correctly. *Les esprits aiment la nuit, qui sait plus qu'une femme donner une âme à toutes choses*. That can't be right, she thought, what a ridiculous idea anyway. Of course she did, herself, in a way, do just that, endow all sorts of silly senseless things with 'souls', certainly not with any exalted gesture worthy of being announced to the world by a godlike voice beside a magic tower. In her, it was more like superstition, or some sad overflow of wasted love. Breathing deeply she turned round, leaning back against the sill and smiling her faint smile.

The two men looked at her with affection, then at each other. Perhaps Gerard at any rate knew something of what she was feeling, he knew and did not know. Rose understood how little he wanted her, ever, to fail to be her calm self.

Jenkin said, 'What about some more champagne? There's a shocking number of bottles stashed away.'

'Where are Jean and Duncan, I thought they might be here,' said Rose, as the champagne cork hit the ceiling.

'They were earlier,' said Jenkin, 'Jean hauled him off, she couldn't bear not to be dancing.'

'Jean's such an athlete,' said Rose. 'She can still stand on her head. Do you remember how she stood on her head in a punt one day?'

'Duncan wanted to stay and drink, but Jean wouldn't let him.'

'Duncan's drinking too much,' said Rose. 'Jean's wearing that red dress with the black lace that I like so. She has her gipsy look.'

'You look stunning, Rose,' said Jenkin.

'I love you in that dress,' said Gerard, 'it's so *intensely* simple, I like that wonderful dark green, like laurel, like myrtle, like ivy.'

Rose thought, it's time for Jenkin to ask me to dance, he doesn't want to, he doesn't like dancing, but he'll have to. And Gerard will dance with Jean. Then I shall dance with Duncan. That's all right. I feel better. Perhaps I'm a little drunk.

'It's time I went to see Levquist,' said Gerard. 'Would you like to come, Jenkin?'

'I've already been.'

'You've already been?' Gerard's indignant tone was activated from the remote past. An old pang of indestructible timeless jealousy seared his heart with the speed of fire. It burned with an old pain. How they had all coveted that man's praise, far away in that short golden piece of the past. They had coveted his praise and his love. Gerard had carried off the famous prize. But what he really wanted was to be praised and loved the most. It was hard to believe now that Jenkin had been his nearest rival.

Jenkin, who knew exactly what Gerard was thinking, began to laugh. He sat down abruptly spilling his drink.

'Did he ask you to translate something?' said Gerard.

'Yes, the brute. He planted me in front of a piece of Thucydides.'

'How did you manage?'

'I said I couldn't make head or tail of it.'

'What did he say?'

'He laughed and patted my arm.'

'He was always soft on you.'

'He always expected more of you.'

Gerard did not dispute this.

'I'm sorry I didn't say I was going to see Levquist,' said Jenkin, serious now, 'so that we could go together. But I knew that he'd play that old trick on me. I don't mind failing, but I'd rather you weren't there.'

Gerard found this explanation entirely satisfactory.

'How you men do live in the past!' said Rose.

'Well, you were remembering Jean just now,' said Jenkin, 'standing on her head in the punt. It was May Morning.'

'Were you there?' said Rose. 'I'd forgotten. Gerard was there, and Duncan – and – and Sinclair.'

The door flew open and Gulliver Ashe blundered in.

Gerard said at once, 'Gull, have you seen Tamar and Conrad? I quite forgot to tell them about coming up here.'

'I saw them,' said Gulliver. He spoke clearly but with the careful solemnity of the drunk man. 'I *saw* them. And at that very moment Conrad rushed off, leaving her alone.'

'Leaving her *alone*?' said Rose.

'I conversed with her. Then I too left her. That is all that I can report.'

16

'You *left* her?' said Gerard, 'how could you, how perfectly rotten! You left her standing by herself?'

'Her escort not being far off, I presumed,' said Gulliver.

'You'd better go and look for her at once,' said Gerard.

'Give him a drink first,' said Jenkin, hauling himself up from his chair. 'I expect Conrad's turned up again.'

'I'll have a word with him if he hasn't!' said Gerard. 'Fancy leaving her alone even for a moment!'

'I expect it was a call of nature,' said Jenkin, 'he rushed in behind the laurels, the myrtle, the ivy.'

'It was *not* a call of nature,' said Gulliver. He could see from the behaviour of his audience that they did not yet know his great news. 'Do you know? Well, obviously you don't. Crimond is here.'

'Crimond? Here?'

'Yes. *And* he's wearing a *kilt.*'

Gulliver took the glass of champagne offered to him by Jenkin and sat down in the chair Jenkin had vacated.

Their dismay was even greater than Gull had hoped for. They stared at each other appalled, with stiffened faces and indrawn lips. Rose, who rarely showed her emotions, had flushed and put a hand to her face. She was the first to speak. 'How *dare* he come here!'

'It's his old college too,' said Jenkin.

'Yes, but he must have known –'

'That it's our territory?'

'He must have known we'd all be here,' said Rose, 'he must have come on purpose.'

'Not necessarily,' said Gerard. 'There's nothing to be alarmed about. But we'd better go and find Duncan and Jean. They may not know –'

'If they do know they've probably gone home!' said Rose.

'I bloody hope not,' said Jenkin. 'Why should they? They can just keep away from him. God!' he added, 'and I was just looking forward to seeing the old coll and getting quietly plastered with you lot!'

'I'll go and tell them,' said Gulliver. 'I haven't seen them, but I expect I can find them.'

'No,' said Gerard, 'you stay here.'

'Why? Am I under arrest? Aren't I supposed to look for Tamar?'

'Duncan and Jean may come here,' said Rose, 'hadn't someone better be – ?'

'Yes, all right, go and look for Tamar,' said Gerard to Gulliver. 'Just see she's OK and if she's alone dance with her. I expect that boy has come back. Why did he rush off?'

'He went to gape at Crimond. I don't see what all the fuss is, about that man. I know you quarrelled with Crimond about the book and all that, and wasn't he keen on Jean once? Why are you all so fluffed up?'

'It wasn't quite as simple as that,' said Gerard.

Jenkin said to Rose, 'Are you afraid that Duncan will get drunk and attack him?'

'Duncan is probably drunk already,' said Rose, 'we'd better go and –'

'It's more likely that Crimond will attack Duncan,' said Gerard.

'Oh no!'

'People hate their victims. But of course nothing will happen.'

'I wonder who he's with?' Rose asked.

'He's with Lily Boyne,' said Gulliver.

'How extraordinary!' said Gerard.

'Typical,' said Rose.

'I'm sure he's here accidentally,' said Jenkin. 'I wonder if he's got his Red Guards with him?'

Gerard looked at his watch. 'I'm afraid I must go and see Levquist, otherwise he'll have gone to bed. You two go and look for Jean and Duncan. I'll watch out for them too on the way across.'

They departed, leaving Gulliver behind. Gull was at a stage of drunkenness at which the body, dismayed, sends out unmistakable appeals for moderation. He felt very slightly sick and very slightly faint. He had noticed the slowness of his speech. He envisaged the possibility of falling over. He could not easily focus his eyes. The room was moving jerkily, and emitting flashes rather like the pop group effect. (The group was the Waterbirds, the college having failed to secure the Treason of the Clerks.) Gulliver, conscious of a desire to dance, was not sure whether his condition favoured it or precluded it. He knew from experience that if he wished to go on enjoying the evening he must have an interval from alcohol, and if possible something to eat. After that he would look for Tamar. He was anxious to please Gerard, or more exactly afraid of the results of not pleasing him. As he had come in to break his news, a queue had already been forming outside the supper tent. Gulliver, who hated this sort of queueing, and who felt that without a partner he might attract suspicion or, worse still, pity, had eaten well in a pub before arriving at the dance; but that now seemed an infinitely long time ago. Moving cautiously about the room he found a bottle of Perrier and another plate of cucumber sandwiches. He could not find a clean glass. He sat down and began to eat the sandwiches and to drink the water which tasted headily of champagne. His eyes kept closing.

The three friends passed out of the cloister and onto the big lawn where the marquees stood. Here they separated, Rose going to the right, Jenkin to the left, and Gerard straight on toward the eighteenth-century building, also floodlit, where Levquist kept his library. Levquist was retired, but continued to live in college where he had a special large room to house his unique collection of books, left of course to the college in his will. He also kept, in his sanctum, a divan bed so that he could on occasion, as tonight, sleep among his books rather than more domestically in his other rooms. His successor in the professorial chair, one of his pupils, continued in an insecure and subservient relation to the old man. Levquist was indeed not easy to approach. This was an awkward fact, given the strong attraction which he exerted upon many of those who had dealings with him.

Gerard looked about him as he went, glancing into the tents and scanning the supper queue, without seeing any sign of

Jean or Duncan or Tamar or Conrad or Crimond. The noise of music and voices and laughter made a textured canopy, there was a smell of flowers and earth and water. The lawn, between the supper tent and the marquees, was dotted with shifting groups of young people, and a few embracing couples standing alone kissing. There would be more of these as the night wore on. Gerard set his foot on the familiar stairway and experienced the familiar shock of emotion. He knocked upon the dimly lighted door and heard the harsh sound, scarcely verbal, with which Levquist invited entry. He entered.

The long room, barred with jutting bookshelves, was dark except for a lamp at the far end upon Levquist's huge desk where the old man sat with hunched shoulders, his head turned toward the door. Beside the desk the big window facing onto the deer park was wide open. Gerard advanced along the dark well-worn carpet and said, 'Hello, it's me.' With deliberate restraint, he did not now lard all his speeches with the word 'sir', nor could he bring himself, though well aware that he could not be by any means Levquist's only 'old pupil' visitor that evening, to utter his own name.

'Hernshaw,' said Levquist, lowering his cropped grey head and taking off his glasses.

Gerard sat down in the seat opposite to him and stretched out his long legs cautiously under the desk. His heart beat violently. He was still afraid of Levquist.

Levquist did not smile, neither did Gerard. Levquist fiddled with his nearest books and with an open notebook in which he had been writing. He frowned. He left Gerard to open the conversation. Gerard stared at the large beautiful grotesque Jewish head of the great scholar. 'How's the book getting on, sir?' This was just a standard opening move.

This book was Levquist's interminable book on Sophocles. Levquist did not regard this as a genuine question. He replied, 'Slowly.' Then said, 'Are you still in that office?'

'No, I've retired.'

'Rather young to retire, aren't you? Were you at the top?'

'No.'

'Why retire then? You've got the worst of both worlds.

Power, isn't that what it was all about? What you wanted was power, wasn't it?'

'Not just power. I like arranging things.'

'Arranging things! You should have arranged your mind, stayed here and done some real thinking.'

This was an old traditional liturgy. Levquist, who scarcely believed that very clever people could exercise their minds anywhere else, had wanted Gerard to stay on at Oxford, get into All Souls, become an academic. Gerard had been determined to get away. The political idealism which largely prompted his flight soon lost its simplicity and much of its force; and a humbler perhaps more rational desire to serve society by arranging it a little better, had led him later into the Civil Service. Gerard was, as he was intended to be, hurt by Levquist's familiar jibe. Sometimes he did wish that he had stayed on, tracing the Platonic streams down the centuries, becoming a genuinely learned man, a justified ascetic, a scholar. He said mildly, 'I hope to do some thinking now.'

'It's too late. How's your father?'

Levquist always asked after Gerard's father whom he had not met since Gerard was a student, but whom he remembered with some sort of, not fully intelligible to Gerard, respect and approval. Gerard's father, a solicitor, had been, for instance, entirely unable upon the first occasion of their meeting, which Gerard recalled with a shudder, to converse with Levquist about Roman law. Yet this, by contrast, ordinary ignorant man, patently unafraid of his son's formidable teacher, had, perhaps just by this simple directness, made himself memorable. Gerard in fact respected and approved of his father, saw the simplicity and truthfulness of his nature, but was used to finding these qualities invisible to others. His father was not brilliant or erudite or witty or particularly successful, he could seem mediocre and boring, yet Levquist, who despised mediocrity and ruthlessly refused to allow himself to be bored, had at once met Gerard's father upon the ground of the latter's best qualities. Or perhaps he was just startled to meet some 'ordinary person' who was not, in his presence, a little awed.

'He's very ill,' said Gerard in answer to Levquist's question, 'he's –' He suddenly found himself unable to bring out the next word.

'Is he dying?' said Levquist.

'Yes.'

'I'm sorry. Well, it is for all of us a short walk. But one's father – yes –' Levquist's father and his sister had died in a German concentration camp. He looked away for a moment, smoothing over the close-cropped silvery fur which covered the dome of his head.

Gerard, to change the subject, said, 'I hear Jenkin came to see you earlier.'

Levquist chuckled. 'Yes, I saw young Riderhood. He was quite stumped by that piece of Thucydides. A pity –'

'He hasn't got anywhere?'

'A pity he's let his Greek slip so. He knows several modern languages. As for "getting anywhere", ridiculous phrase, he's teaching, isn't he? Riderhood doesn't need to get anywhere, he walks the path, he exists where he is. Whereas you –'

'Whereas I – ?'

'You were always dissolving yourself into righteous discontent, thrilled in your bowels by the idea of some high thing elsewhere. So it has gone on. You see yourself as a lonely climber, of course higher up than the other ones, you think you might leap out of yourself onto the summit, yet you know you can not, and being pleased with yourself both ways you go nowhere. This "thinking" that you are going to do, what will it be? Writing your memoirs?'

'No. I thought I might write something about philosophy.'

'Philosophy! Empty thinking by ignorant conceited men who think they can digest without eating! They fancy their substanceless thought can lead to deep conclusions! Are you so unambitious?' This was an old conflict too. Levquist, teacher of the great classical languages, resented the continual disappearance of his best pupils into the hands of the philosophers.

'It's quite difficult,' said Gerard patiently, 'to write even a short piece of philosophy. And at least it has proved to be rather influential empty thinking! Anyway I shall read –'

'Play around with great books, pull them down to your level and make simplified versions of your own?'

'Possibly,' said Gerard, unprovoked. Levquist, used to roughing up his best pupils, always had to get rid of a certain amount of spleen upon them when they reappeared, as if this was necessary before he could speak gently to them, as perhaps he really wished to do, for there was usually some kind thing which he wanted to say and held in reserve.

'Well, well. Now read me something in Greek, that sort of reading you were always good at.'

'What shall I read, sir?'

'Anything you like. Not Sophocles. Perhaps Homer.'

Gerard got up and went to the shelves, knowing where to look, and as he touched the books he felt some fierce and agonising sense of the past. It's gone, he thought, the past, it is irrevocable and beyond mending and far away, and yet it is here, blowing at one like a wind, I can feel it, I can smell it, and it's so sad, so purely sad. Through the window open on the park came the distant sound of music, which he had not been aware of since he entered the room, and the wet dark odour of the meadows and the river.

Sitting again at the desk Gerard read aloud from the *Iliad*, about how the divine horses of Achilles wept when they heard of the death of Patroclus, bowed their heads while hot tears poured from their eyes onto the ground, as they wept with longing for their charioteer, and their long beautiful manes were darkened with mud, and as they mourned Zeus looked down on them and pitied them, and spoke thus in his heart. Unhappy beasts, why did I give you, ageless and deathless as you are, as a gift to Lord Peleus, a mortal? Was it so that you too should grieve among unhappy men? Indeed there is nothing that breathes and crawls upon the earth more miserable than man.

As Levquist reached across and took the book from him and they avoided each other's eyes, Gerard was, in the swift zigzag of his thought, thinking of how Achilles, mad with grief, had

23

killed the captive Trojan boys like frightened fawns beside the funeral pyre of his friend, then how Telemachus had hanged the handmaids who had slept with the suitors who were even now dead at the hands of his father, and how, hanging in a row upon a line, they jumped about in their death agony. Then he thought of how Patroclus had always been kind to the captive women. Then he thought again about the horses shedding burning tears and drooping their beautiful manes in the mud of the battlefield. All those thoughts occurred in a second, perhaps two seconds. Then he thought of Sinclair Curtland.

Levquist said, for his mind by some other secret thought-way had also reached Sinclair, 'Is the Honourable Rose here?'

'Yes, she came with me.'

'I thought I saw her when I was coming over. How she still resembles that boy.'

'Yes.'

Levquist, who had an amazing memory, reaching back very many years over the generations of his pupils, said, 'I'm glad you've kept your little group together, these friendships formed when you are young men are very precious, you and Riderhood and Topglass and Cambus and Field and – Well, Topglass and Cambus got married, didn't they –' Levquist did not approve of marriage. 'And poor Field is some sort of monk. Friendship, friendship, that's what they don't understand these days, they just don't understand it any more. As for this place – you know we have *women* now?'

'Yes! But you don't have to teach them!'

'No, I thank God. But it spoils the scene – I cannot tell you how much it mars it all.'

'I can imagine,' said Gerard. He would have felt the same.

'No, the young men don't make friends now. They are superficial. They hunt the girls to take them to bed. In the night when they should be talking and arguing with their friends they are in the bed with the girls. It is – shocking.'

Gerard too conjured up the dreadful scene, the degeneration, the collapse of the old values. He wanted to smile at Levquist's indignation, yet he also shared it.

'What do you make of it all, Hernshaw, our poor planet?

Will it survive? I doubt it. What have you become, are you a stoic after all? *Nil admirari*, yes?'

'No,' said Gerard, 'I'm not a stoic. You accused me of being unambitious. I'm too ambitious to be merely stoical.'

'You mean morally ambitious?'

'Well – yes.'

'You are rotted by Christianity,' said Levquist. 'What you take for Platonism is the old soft masochistic Christian illusion. Your Plato has been defiled by Saint Augustine. You have no hard core. Riderhood whom you despise –'

'I don't,' said Gerard.

'Riderhood is tougher than you, he's harder. Your "moral ambition" or whatever you call your selfish optimism, is just the old lie of Christian salvation, that you can shed your old self and become good simply by thinking about it – and as you sit and dream this dream you feel that you are changed already and have no more work to do – and so you are happy in your lie.'

Gerard, who had heard this sort of tirade before, thought, how exact he is, how acute, he knows I have thought all those things too. He answered flippantly, 'Well, at least I am happy, isn't that a good thing?'

Levquist stared at him, pouting his thick lips and drawing down the corners, his face become a sneering mask.

Gerard said, 'All right.'

Levquist went on, 'I am close to death. That is no scandal, old age is a well-known phenomenon. But now the difference is that everyone is close to death.'

Gerard said, 'Yes.' He thought, it consoles him to think so.

'All thought which is not pessimistic is now false.'

'But you would say it has always been?'

'Yes. Only now it is forced upon all thinking people, it is the only possible conception. Courage, endurance, truthfulness, these are the virtues. And to recognise that of all things we are the most miserable that creep between the earth and the sky.'

'But this cheers you up, sir!' said Gerard.

Levquist smiled. His dark blue-brown eyes gleamed out

moistly from between the dry saurian wrinkles and he shook his over-large cropped head and smiled his demon's smile. '*You* are cheered up, you were always the optimist, you think always, at the last moment, they will send a trireme.'

Gerard assented. He liked the image.

'But no. Man is ever mortal, he thinks by fit and start, and when he thinks, he fastens his hand upon his heart.' As he spoke Levquist lifted his big wrinkled hand to the upper pocket of his shabby corduroy jacket. Living his life amid the greatest poetry in the world, he retained a touching affection for A. E. Housman.

Somebody knocked on the door.

'There is another,' said Levquist. 'You must go. Salute your father from me. And salute the Honourable Rose. This was a short talk, come again, not just on such a day, to see the old man.'

Gerard stood up. He felt, as on other occasions, a strong impulse to move round the desk and seize Levquist's hands, perhaps kiss them, perhaps even kneel down. Would the classical suppliant rite of embracing the knees enable him to carry off such a gesture, make it something formal, not to be rejected as a 'soft' rush of graceless emotion? As on other occasions he hesitated, then inhibited the impulse. Did Levquist know of his feelings, of their tenderness and strength? He was not sure. He contented himself with a bow.

Levquist growled permission to enter. Then he uttered a name.

Gerard passed a rosy-cheeked forty-year-old in the doorway. Aching with jealousy, and with remorse at not having managed a more affectionate farewell, he descended the stairs.

Tamar was looking for Conrad, Conrad was looking for Tamar. Rose and Jenkin were looking for Jean and Duncan and Conrad and Tamar. Gull was looking for a girl to dance with.

Tamar had wandered away from the tent, whither Conrad had rushed to see his idol, in a momentary fit of pique which she now bitterly regretted. She had come back almost at once and even approached a group of young worshippers, but could not see Conrad there. Conrad, unable to get near Crimond, had stood a while spellbound on the outside of the circle. Then, realising Tamar had not followed him, he searched the marquee, and, uncertain of the point at which he had entered, had set off on a circular track about what he thought was the place where they parted company. Tamar had then set off on a straight course toward the next marquee, the waltzing one, toward which they had been making their way when they met Gulliver. She stood for a while here staring about, saw Rose waltzing with Gerard and retired quickly. She was very fond of her uncle and of Rose, but shy with them, and anxious now not to be discovered without her partner, whom she blamed herself for having lost. Soon after Tamar had faded back into the darkness Conrad arrived, also saw Rose and Gerard, and with a similar motive made himself scarce. Tamar had meanwhile gone toward the cloisters, where there was a buttery which served sandwiches, and which Conrad had suggested they should locate just before they decided to dance first. Conrad hurried back toward the Waterbirds tent where the famous pop group were rumoured to be about to perform again. Tamar searched through a lot of people who were drinking and laughing beside the buttery and went into the chapel, another point mentioned by Conrad as to be visited later. She passed back through the cloisters and out toward the river just as Conrad entered from the other side.

Time passed, supper was over, and the dance had entered a new phase, the big expanse of grass between the glowing stripy marquees was covered with beautiful people, the handsome boys in their frilly shirts, now somewhat undone at the neck, the girls in their shimmering dresses, sleek and flouncy, now considerably less tidy, where here and there an errant shoulder strap, snapped when dancing the Gay Gordons, was being exploited by a laughing partner, and elaborately woven mounds of hair, so carefully constructed hours ago with innumerable pins, had come undone or been demolished by

27

eager male fingers and streamed down backs and over shoulders. Some couples in darker corners were passionately kissing each other or locked in wordless embraces, the longed-for climax of the longed-for evening. Some dresses carried tell-tale stains of grass. The rival musics continued unabated, the Waterbirds raucously shouting into a maelstrom of flashing lights and electronic din. The dancing in the various tents was slightly less dense but wilder.

Tamar had started to cry, and, attempting to compose herself, had wandered away toward the river and was standing on the bridge. Lights upon the bank strewed the water with streamers or ribbons of brightness which frisked here and there upon the surface before being suddenly darkened and plucked under. As she leaned over she could hear, under the other more distant din, the faint river sound, self-absorbed and permanent. When other people moved onto the bridge she crossed it, but turned back when she saw in the darkness the discreet forms of bowler-hatted security guards, strategically set to keep the envious rabble who had not paid for the expensive tickets from sneaking in to the glittering celebration. She went across the lawn toward the 'New Building'. A little earlier than this Conrad had run into Jenkin. Jenkin, who saw how upset the boy was, did not 'tick him off', but could not conceal his dismay that Conrad had, as he confessed, mislaid Tamar immediately on arrival and before they had even had a dance. After this encounter Conrad was even more upset, realising that his failure (for he entirely blamed himself) would now come to the ears of Gerard, even perhaps of Crimond. Mainly he felt wretched for having so deplorably, perhaps unforgivably, offended Tamar, whom he had so much looked forward to being with, dancing with, kissing, on what was to have been such a wonderful evening to which she too must have looked forward. He had not, like Tamar, framed beforehand the idea of falling in love. But now, running more frantically, randomly, from place to place, senselessly revisiting the same scenes and missing others altogether, charging across the grass and jostling young men with brimming glasses and stepping on girls' dresses, tormented by continual hope and continual disappointment, he felt all the anguish of a frustrated lover. A little later he nerved himself to go up to Levquist's rooms where Jenkin told him (information which Gerard had so unfortunately forgotten to impart to Tamar) that there was a 'base', but when he arrived there was no one there. He stood awhile in the empty room which was scattered with bottles and glasses, too unhappy even to give himself a drink, and then, as waiting was even more painful than searching, ran off again. Tamar, exhausted, was sitting in one of the tents, bowing her head to conceal her tears and trying to make up her face. She had put down her cashmere shawl somewhere, she could not recall where, and was feeling cold. Conrad, looking in hastily, failed to see her.

Meanwhile Rose had run into Lily Boyne. Lily and Rose liked each other, but there was caution and incomprehension on both sides. Lily thought that Rose regarded her as rather uneducated and 'common'. Rose was afraid that Lily thought that Rose regarded her as uneducated (which Rose did think) and 'common' (which Rose did not). In fact Rose did not possess this concept, but vaguely posited something of the sort. She feared Lily might think she was 'snooty', which Lily did not think. Rose found Lily rather 'bouncy' and could not always get the 'tone' of her witticisms or answer them spontaneously. But Lily admired Rose for being calm and sensible and kind and nice, which not all of Lily's acquaintances were, and Rose admired Lily for being tough, and imagined her to be brave and 'worldly' in ways which remained, for Rose, mysterious and obscure. They did not in fact know each other very well. Lily Boyne had come into the ken of Gerard and his friends through Jean Kowitz (Jean Cambus, that is, but her maiden name somehow lingered as some maiden names do), who had met Lily a few years ago in a context of 'women's lib', and come to know her better in a yoga class where they both frequently stood on their heads. This was before Lily became, briefly, famous. Lily had been, as Gulliver once remarked, one of those numerous people who are simply famous for being famous. Lily was now, or rather was credited with being, a rich girl. She had emerged from a poor and chaotic home, started adult life at a polytechnic, played about with pottery and graphic design, imagined herself a painter, then earned her living as a typist. In due course, and in a moment of reckless despair, she married a frail penniless art student called James Farling. How often since had she blessed that pale unhappy boy for having actually persuaded her to *marry* him! She kept her maiden name of course. Soon after the marriage a series of unforeseen demises in the Farling family brought the family fortune, about which Lily had known nothing, to rest upon James. James was an unworldly boy who cared little for money and had in any case been, before the intervention of the fates, remote from inheritance. Rich, he still cared little, and was only just prevented by Lily, who cared much, from handing it all over to his indignant surviving relations. Then, urged by his wife to spend, he bought a motor bike, riding which, on the day he bought it, he was killed. After that the family fell upon Lily to destroy her. Lily fought back. Her case seemed clear, but clever lawyers had already been at work to find flaws in James's claim. It became a *cause célèbre*. In the end the matter was settled out of court, after Lily had surrendered numerous goodies. Lily did not emerge without discredit since, in her rage, she had told some transparent lies. But she was, for a short time, a popular heroine, the 'poor girl', fighting against the avaricious rich, the lone woman fighting a cohort of men. It was in the latter role that she attracted the ardent attention of Jean Kowitz who was at that time very concerned with various women's liberation causes. It was almost as if Jean had fallen in love with her, so angry and excited did she become on Lily's behalf. Rose too was drawn in and saw quite a lot of Lily, who also, through Jean, became acquainted with Gerard and the rest. When the fighting was over and the publicity died down Jean rather 'went off' Lily; she took a high line about Lily's telling lies. But Rose kept up with her, partly feeling sorry for her. For Lily's wealth brought her little happiness, and was in any case being steadily eroded by a stream of plausible men. She had acquired expensive tastes and the idea that she deserved fame. She seemed to have few friends and little notion of how to conduct her life.

'Rose!' screamed Lily, 'what a perfectly scrumptious dress! You always get it right! So simple, so absolutely you!'

They had met near to the Waterbirds marquee and had to raise their voices. The sound of shoes drumming upon the hollow wooden boarding made a continuous ground bass.

'You look lovely,' said Rose, 'rather oriental. I adore those trousers.'

Lily, who was alone, was dressed in baggy orange silk trousers, drawn in at the ankle by spangled bands, and a floppy white silk blouse weighted by gold chains and anchored by a purple sash into which a transparent silvery scarf covering her shoulders was also tucked. This gear had by now begun to come adrift, the trousers escaping from the bands, the blouse from the sash, the silver scarf hanging down behind on one side. Lily was shorter and thinner than Rose, very thin in fact, and had a thin almost gaunt pale face and short dry weightless fair hair and a long neck. It is possible for a girl to have too long a neck, and Lily's could be said to be on the border between the swan-like and the grotesque. She had a way of accentuating it by thrusting her head forward and staring out of her face as through a muslin mask; she experienced this as cat-like, as 'putting on her cat face'. Her lips were exceedingly thin, a continued cause of distress. Her eyes, 'melted sugar eyes' one of the plausible men called them, were a disconcerting pale brown with a dark rim and blue and brown stripes leading in to the pupil, thus resembling some kind of sweetmeat. She was wearing a lot of make-up, also in need of attention, and had generously outlined her lips with silver paint. She spoke with a drawling north London voice which had become deracinated and sometimes sounded American.

'I came with that shit Crimond,' said Lily, 'now he's ditched me, the swine. Have you seen him anywhere?'

'No, sorry,' said Rose. 'I wonder if you've seen Tamar?'

'The little thing, is she here? No, I haven't seen her. Christ, what a din. How are you these days?'

'Fine –'

'Let's meet –'

'Yes, let's be in touch.'

They parted. Tamar, seeing Rose talking to Lily, retreated toward the archway which led through into the deer park.

As Gerard emerged from Levquist's staircase he found Jenkin Riderhood waiting for him at the bottom.

As he came out he was conscious that the night sky, which had never really darkened, had become very faintly lighter, and this touched him with a sad prophetic emotion. In the intense concentration of his encounter with Levquist Gerard had completely forgotten everything else, where he was, why he was there, even the references to his father, Sinclair, Rose, had appeared as part of Levquist's thought rather than of his own. Now he suddenly remembered the news which Gulliver had brought to them. First of all however he said to Jenkin, 'Have you found Tamar?'

'No, but I met Conrad. He'd lost her and was still looking!'

'I hope you gave him a wigging.'

'It wasn't necessary, he was in a terrible state, poor boy.'

'We must – what's the matter, Jenkin?'

'Come with me. I want to show you something.'

Jenkin took hold of Gerard's hand and began to pull him along across the trampled grass through the scattered strolling of bemused dancers, some still enchanted, some happy beyond their wildest dreams, some concealing grief, some simply drunk, the fading magic of the new light showing their faces more intensely. Near the end of the arcade a youth was being sick, his partner standing guard with her back to him.

Jenkin led Gerard to the 'sentimental' tent where he had danced with Rose, and where a wilder strain of music could now be heard. An eightsome reel was in progress; but the floor had emptied, and an audience, standing in a dense ring, was watching eight evidently expert dancers, the men wearing kilts, who were performing in the centre. One of these was Crimond. It was evident who, in the rotatory movement of the dance, his partner was. Jean Cambus had hitched much of her long red dress up over a belt round her waist, revealing her black-stockinged legs, and her flying skirt came little below her knees. Her narrow hawklike face, usually as pale as ivory, was flushed and dewy with sweat and her dark straight heavy shoulder-length hair, whirling about, had plastered some of its strands across her brow. Her fine Jewish head, usually so stately and so cold, had now, her dark eyes huge and staring, a fierce wild oriental look. She did not, in the weaving of the dance, turn her head, her small feet in low-heeled slippers seemed to dart upon the air, only when her gaze met her partner's did her glaring eyes flame up, unsmiling. Her lips were parted, indeed her mouth was slightly open, not breathless but as if with a kind of rapacity. Crimond was not sweating. His face was, as usual in repose, pallid, expressionless, even stern, but his slightly freckled skin, which normally looked sallow so that he could have been called pasty-faced, was now gleaming and hard. His hair, narrowly wavy and longish, once a flaming red now a faded orange, adhered closely to his head, no flying locks. His light blue eyes did not follow his partner, nor did they, when he faced her, change their cold even grim expression. His thin lips, drawn inward, made of his mouth a straight hard line. With his conspicuously long thin nose he reminded Gerard, watching, of one of the tall Greek *kouroi* in the Acropolis museum, only without the mysterious smile. Crimond danced well, not with abandonment, but with a magisterial precision, his torso stiff, his shoulders held well back, as taut as a bow and yet as resilient and weightless as a leaping dog. His picturesque garb had also remained orderly, the elaborate white shirt, the close-fitting black velvet jacket with silver buttons, the sporran swinging at the knee, the silver-handled dirk in place in the sock, the neat buckled shoes. His male companions, all excellent dancers, were dandyish too, but only Crimond had not unbuttoned his shirt. The heavy kilts, their closely pleated backs rippling and

33

swirling, emphasised their owners' indifference to the force of gravity.

Jenkin watched Gerard for a few moments to see that his friend was suitably affected, then turned to watch himself. He murmured, 'I'm glad I saw this. He's like Shiva.'

Gerard said, 'Don't –' The new image, intruding upon his own, was not inappropriate.

The music suddenly ended. The dancers became immobile, hands aloft; then gravely bowed to each other. The audience, released from enchantment, laughed, clapped, stamped their feet. The orchestra immediately began again, with the sugary strain of 'Always', and the floor was at once crowded with couples. Crimond and Jean, who had been standing with hanging arms staring at each other, took each a step forward, then glided away together, lost to sight among the dancers.

'What tartan was that?' said Jenkin to Gerard as they moved away.

'Macpherson.'

'How do you know?'

'He told me once, it was the one he was entitled to.'

'I thought it might be any old one.'

'He's meticulous. Where's Duncan?'

'I don't know. As soon as I saw *that* I ran to wait for you. I didn't want you to miss it.'

'Kind of you to drag yourself away,' said Gerard with a slight edge.

Jenkin ignored the edge. 'Shall we separate and look for Duncan? I can't see him here.'

'It looks as if –'

'As if things have gone too far already.'

'I don't think Duncan would be pleased to see us.'

'You don't think we should sort of shadow him. Keep an eye on him?'

'No.'

Gulliver was suddenly accosted by a woman.

He had, after eating almost all the cucumber sandwiches,

34

begun to feel miraculously better, not really drunk at all, and with that came a frenzied desire to dance. He had wandered about, not looking for Tamar (he had forgotten about her) but for some girl whose man had perhaps felicitously passed out and lay somewhere under a bush in drunken slumber. However the girls, though looking themselves rather the worse for wear, or even positively sozzled, seemed still to have their man in tow. It was impossible now to deny that the dawn was breaking, that the light which had never really gone away all night, was declaring itself to be day. Some terrible birds had begun to sing and from the woods beyond the meadows came the intermittent chant of the cuckoo. Hastily seeking some continuation of night time, Gull had been drawn to the pop tent where, in spite of the lightening canvas, darkness still seemed to reign amid the dazzling flashes and the noise. The pop group had gone and their music, continuing, was now machine-made. Here the capering was at its wildest, resembling acrobatics rather than dance, a kind of desperation overcoming the young people as they scented the morning air. The men had abandoned coats, occasionally shirts too, the girls had hitched up dresses and undone fasteners. The effect, after earlier formality, was oddly like fancy dress. Staring at each other, wild-eyed and open-mouthed, the couples leapt, squatted, rotated, grimaced, waved their arms, waved their legs, expressive, thought Gulliver, of a scene out of Dante's *Inferno* rather than of the vernal joy of careless youth.

'Hi, Gull, dance with me! I've been dancing by myself for at least an hour!' It was Lily Boyne.

Her frail arms were instantly about him, seizing him at the waist, and they whirled or rather whizzed out into the centre of the deafening maelstrom.

Of course Gulliver knew Lily through 'the others' but he had never felt any interest in her, except briefly on one occasion when he heard someone refer to her as a 'cocotte'. She had seemed to him a pathetic figure whose importunate pretensions were merely embarrassing. Lily now looked like a rather small crazy pirate, perhaps a cabin boy on a pirate ship in a pantomime. Her orange trousers were rolled up revealing

thin bare legs, her white blouse was unbuttoned, sash, silver
scarf, golden chains had all vanished, dumped with her
evening bag Lily could not remember where. Her face, red
with exertion and earlier potation, was covered in a multi-
coloured grease of smudged cosmetic, making her resemble a
melting wax image. Her silver lips were grotesquely enlarged
into a clownish mouth. But as they danced, not touching each
other, now near, now far, jumping violently about, cannoning
into other dancers of whom they were entirely unconscious,
grinning, glaring, panting, bound together by their crazed
eyes, Gulliver felt that he had discovered a perfect partner.
Lily, as she swayed away, pirouetted, leapt, circled him about,
waving her arms hieratically like an ecstatic priestess,
appeared to be saying something, at least her mouth was
opening as if in speech, but he could not, because of the din,
hear a word. He nodded his head madly, uttering into the
storm of marvellous noise a stream of senseless exclamations
inaudible even to himself.

Tamar had not found Conrad but she had found Duncan.
Duncan had lost track of Jean earlier on, lingering to drink
while she set off into the fray. He was soon informed, by a
helpful well-wisher, of Crimond's presence. Perhaps the same
man had already alerted Jean; or perhaps Jean had known all
along, he conjectured later? After some searching he witnessed, unseen, the end of the eightsome reel also witnessed by
Gerard and Jenkin, and saw Jean and Crimond disappear
together before the next dance. After that he took himself off to
one of the bars to get as drunk as possible, and to nurse, almost
as a consolation, his pain and anger, and his fear that everything would turn out for the very worst. He did not, at this
stage, want to find his wife; and when, later still, in the
'old-fashioned' tent, he saw Jean come in with Crimond and
join the dancers, he sat hunched up in the comparative
obscurity at the back, deriving an agonised satisfaction from
being invisible while he feasted his eyes.

Tamar, still seeking Conrad, but now very tired and cold,

36

and additionally miserable because she could not find her cashmere shawl, entered the tent and at once saw Jean dancing with Crimond. Tamar knew that there had been some sort of 'thing' about Jean and Crimond a good many years ago, but she had never reflected on it, and regarded it as ancient history. What she saw now made her feel surprise, shock, and then a kind of fear and jealous pain. Jean had long been a very important person in Tamar's life; she might even have been said to have a 'crush' on Jean, to whom she had, in adolescence, brought problems which she could not discuss with her mother, or even with Rose or Pat. She was fond of Duncan too, and was regularly invited to tea, later to drinks. After a moment or two Tamar, glancing round the marquee, saw Duncan sitting with his arm on the chair in front of him, leaning his chin on his arm, and intently watching the dancers. A number of people passed between them, a dance ended and another started, and Tamar, alarmed at what she was seeing, decided to withdraw. Duncan had seen her however and waved to her, beckoning her to join him. Tamar now felt she could not depart and threaded her way past sitting and standing people, overturned chairs, and tables loaded with empty bottles, reached Duncan and sat down beside him. As she sat down, glancing back at the dance floor, she saw Jean and Crimond leaving the tent on the other side.

Duncan was a huge man, said to be 'bear-like', or sometimes 'leonine', stout and tall with a large head and a mass of very dark thick crisply wavy hair which grew well down onto his neck. His big shoulders, habitually rather hunched, gave a look of retained, sometimes menacing, power. He seemed not only clever but formidable. He had a long wavering expressive mouth, dark eyes, and a strange gaze since one of his eyes was almost entirely black, as if the pupil had flowed out over the iris. He wore dark-rimmed glasses, had an ironical stare and a giggling laugh.

'Hello, Tamar, having a lovely time?'

'Yes, thank you. You haven't seen Conrad have you, you know, Conrad Lomas? Oh – perhaps you haven't met him.'

'Yes, I met him at Gerard's, he's a friend of Leonard's, isn't he? No, I haven't seen him. Is he your swain? Where's he got to?'

'I don't know. It's my fault. I left him for a moment.' Feeling she might be going to cry, she closed her eyes hard against the tears.

'I'm sorry, little Tamar,' said Duncan. 'Look, let's go and get ourselves a drink, eh? It'll do us both good.' However he did not get up yet, just replanted his feet and leaned a little more upon the chair in front of him. He was suddenly not sure that he would be able to rise. He gazed at Tamar, thinking how pathetically thin she was, almost anorexic, and how with her hair done like that, cut in a straight bob and parted at the side, she looked like a girl of fourteen. The white ball dress did nothing for her; it looked like a sloppy petticoat. She looked better in her usual rig, a neat blouse and skirt.

Tamar looked anxiously at Duncan. She had taken in the scene and could now receive some vibrations of his suffering, which made her feel embarrassed rather than sympathetic. Also, it was clear that Duncan was very drunk, he was red-faced and breathing heavily. Tamar was afraid that at any moment he would fall flat on the ground and she would have to do something about it.

At that moment Duncan heaved himself to his feet. He stood for a moment swaying slightly, then put his hand onto Tamar's thin bare arm to steady himself. 'Let's go and find that drink, shall we?'

They began to make their way toward one of the exits, passing as they did so near to the dance floor. The band was playing 'Night and Day'.

Duncan said, 'Night and day. Yes. Let's dance. You'll dance with me, won't you?'

He swept her onto the dance floor and, suddenly surrendered to the music, found that his legs had lost their stupidity and like well-trained beasts were able to perform the familiar routine. He danced well. Tamar let herself be led, letting the sulky sad rhythm enter her body, she was dancing, it was her first dance that evening. Some tears did now come into her eyes and she wiped them away on Duncan's black coat.

In the jazz tent Rose was dancing with Jenkin. Jenkin had accompanied Gerard back to Levquist's rooms off the cloister where it occurred to them that Duncan might have taken refuge. 'He won't want to see us,' said Gerard. 'If he's there it proves he does,' said Jenkin. But there was no one in the room. Gerard elected to stay there just in case, while Jenkin, still full of his idea of becoming Duncan's invisible bodyguard, had set off again. Soon after that he met Rose and felt obliged to ask her to dance. They went to the jazz sound, which was nearest, and Jenkin was dutifully propelling her round the circuit, through the increasingly dense and unbuttoned crowd who, aware of the dawn, had reinvaded the floors. Dancing with Jenkin was a simple and predictable matter since he danced in the same way whatever the music. He had of course told her what he and Gerard had seen. He had even suggested that they should go and have a look in case the performance was being repeated. But Rose had evidently felt this to be bad form, and Jenkin, dashed, had recognised it to be such.

Rose, feeling perhaps that she had expressed too much emotion upon the subject earlier in the evening, was now trying to play it down. 'I expect Crimond has sheered off and Jean and Duncan have been together for ages. There's nothing to it. Only you'd better not say you saw her with *him*!'

'Of course I won't, and of course you're right. But, my God, what *cheek*!'

'What are you going to do about the book?' said Rose, changing the subject, as Jenkin stepped on her foot.

'We, Rose. You're on the committee too.'

'Yes, but I don't count. You and Gerard must decide.'

'We can't do anything,' said Jenkin. He was worrying about Duncan wandering around like a miserable dangerous bear.

Conrad Lomas appeared from nowhere, making his way across the dance floor, thrusting the insensate couples aside.

'Where's Tamar? Have you seen her?'
'We should be asking you that!' said Rose.

Gerard, alone in Levquist's rooms, where the curtains were still pulled against the light, looked gloomily at the chaotic scene, used glasses and empty bottles perched everywhere, on the mantelpiece, on the chairs, on the tables, on the bookcases, on the floor. How can we have used so many glasses, he thought. Of course one loses one's glass oftener and oftener as the evening goes on! And damn it, there are no sandwiches left, or only one and it hasn't got any cucumber in it. He ate the limp piece of bread, then poured himself out some champagne. He was tired of the stuff, but there was nothing else to drink. Jenkin had claimed to have hidden a bottle of whisky in Levquist's bedroom 'for later', only Gerard did not feel strong enough to search for it.

He fervently hoped that Levquist's scout would be able to clear up the mess before Levquist returned after breakfast. He must remember to tip the man. Then he recalled with anguish that he had, in the electric storm of his visit to Levquist, forgotten to thank him for the loan of the room, a notable privilege since other distinguished old pupils were certainly also in the field. He began to plan a gracefully apologetic letter. Levquist would of course have observed the omission and probably derived malicious pleasure from it. He then reflected upon the interesting fact that ever since 'that business', now so far in the past, Levquist had never, in meetings with Gerard or Jenkin, mentioned Crimond's name, although he usually referred to the others, and Crimond too had been his pupil and one of the group. Someone must have told him. Gerard then wondered, not for the first time, whether Crimond kept up any sort of friendship with Levquist. Perhaps he had been to see him *this very evening*! How horrible, how somehow poisonous it was, Crimond being here. Gerard shared Rose's reaction of: how dare he! To which Jenkin had rationally replied: why not? But dancing with Jean . . . Gerard had noticed with displeasure how the whole episode, in so far as it could be called that, seemed to have excited Jenkin. Gerard found it shocking, sickening, thoroughly ill-omened and bad. He wondered if he were drunk, then, how drunk he was. The telephone rang. He lifted the receiver. 'Hello.'

'Could I speak to Mr Hernshaw, if he's there?'

'Pat –'

'Oh Gerard – Gerard – he's gone –'

Gerard reassembled his thoughts. His father was dead.

'Gerard, are you still there?'

'Yes.'

'He's died. We didn't expect it, did we, the doctor didn't say – it just happened – so – suddenly – he – and he was dead –'

'Are you alone?'

'Yes, of course! It's five o'clock in the morning! Who do you think I could get to be with me?'

'When did he die?'

'Oh – an hour ago – I don't know –'

Gerard thought, what was I doing then? 'And were you with him –?'

'Yes! I was asleep with the doors open – about one or so I heard him moaning and I went in and he was sitting up and – and mumbling in a ghastly high voice, and he kept jerking his arms and staring all round the room, and he wouldn't look at me – and he was white, as white as the wall, and his lips were white – and I tried to give him a pill but – I tried to make him lie back, I wanted him to sleep again, I thought if he can only rest, if he can only sleep – and then his breathing – became so awful –'

'Oh God,' said Gerard.

'All right, you don't want to know – I've been trying to get hold of you for ages, ever since, the porter kept telephoning various rooms, I just got a lot of drunks. Are you drunk? You sound as if you are.'

'Possibly.' He thought, of course Levquist has no telephone over there – but that was earlier anyway – what was I doing? Watching Crimond dance? Poor Patricia. He said, 'Bear up, Pat.'

'You are drunk. Of course I'm bearing up. What else can I do. I'm just half mad with grief and misery and shock and I'm all by myself –'

'You'd better go to bed.'

'I *can't*. How long will it take you to get here, an hour?'

'I can do it in an hour,' said Gerard, 'or less, but I can't leave immediately.'

'Why ever not?'

'I've got a lot of people here, I can't just leave them, I can't go without telling them and God knows where they all are at the moment.' He thought, I can't go without seeing Duncan.

'Your father's dead and you want to stay on dancing with your drunken friends.'

'I'll come soon,' said Gerard, 'I just can't come at once, I'm sorry.'

Patricia put down the receiver.

Gerard sat with closed eyes in the silence that followed. Then he started saying, 'Oh my God, oh my God, oh my God', and hid his face in his hands and panted and moaned. Of course he had known it was coming, he had calmly mentioned it to Levquist, but *this* was unlike anything which cowardly imagination could have schooled him with beforehand. He had known what he did not will to imagine, the *fact*, the irrevocable *fact*. Love, old love, sensibilities and dimensions and powers of love which he had forgotten or never recognised, came speeding in from all the far-spread regions of his being, hot with pain, crying and wailing with the agony of that severance. Never to speak to his father again, to see his smiling welcoming face, to be happy in his happiness, to experience the absolute comfort of his love. He felt remorse, not because he had been a bad son, he had not, but because he was no longer a son, and there was still so much to say. A *place* wherein he himself *was* as in no other place had been struck out of the world. Oh my father, oh my father, oh my dear father.

He heard steps upon the stairs and hastily rose to his feet and rubbed his face although there were no tears on it. He turned a calm gaze to the door. It was Jenkin.

Gerard decided instantly not to tell Jenkin about his father.

He would tell him later when they were driving back together to London. He did not want to start to tell and then be interrupted by one of the others. Better to say nothing. Jenkin would understand.

Jenkin, who constantly read Gerard's mind, had been aware that Gerard disapproved of what he might have thought of as Jenkin's excitement, even glee, at the little bit of drama promised by the evening. He also felt that Gerard had thought poorly of Jenkin's appreciation of Crimond's flying kilt. Jenkin was bothered too by his *gaucherie* with Rose, his inability to dance well, and his abrupt dismissal of her question. He too was not at all sure how drunk he was. When Rose declined the next dance saying she was tired, Jenkin made a quick circuit looking for Duncan but did not find him. He pursued a white-clad figure who looked like Tamar, but who vanished on his approach. Tamar had by this time finished her dance with Duncan and been sent away by him with a vague, 'Well, off you go, and enjoy yourself.' She did not feel any urge or duty to stay with him, he was clearly very drunk and either did not want her to continue seeing him in this condition or had quite forgotten that she had no partner. She started to walk about aimlessly in conspicuous spaces hoping that someone she knew would see her. About the cashmere shawl, she had given up hope, perhaps someone had stolen it.

Gerard, who constantly read Jenkin's mind, was aware of the little cloud that hung over his friend and hastened to dispel it. 'My dear fellow, do you think you could find the whisky you alleged you hid? I'm fed up with this stuff.'

They went into Levquist's neat student-like bedroom with its narrow iron bedstead and washstand with basin, water jug, and soap dish, and Jenkin began foraging in Levquist's bed-clothes. The bottle of whisky was found, and a carafe of water on the bedside table, handy because there was of course no bathroom or running water. Gerard tidied the bed. They took these trophies back into the main room and dosed two champagne glasses with whisky.

'It's day out there, can't we pull the curtains?'

'I suppose it is,' said Gerard, 'how ghastly!' He pulled back the curtains and let in the dreadful cold sunlight.

'I couldn't see Duncan anywhere, but I gather a lot of people are in the deer park.'

'They're not supposed to be.'

'Well, they are.'

Heavy uncertain footsteps were heard on the stairs. 'That must be Duncan,' said Jenkin, and opened the door.

Duncan blundered in and made straight for an armchair and fell into it with a crash. He stared up blankly for a moment. Then passed his hand over his face as Gerard had done earlier, frowned, and gathered himself. With an effort he sat up a little.

'Good heavens, you're soaking wet!' said Jenkin.

It was so. Duncan's trousers and part of his jacket were drenched with water, muddy too, and muddy water was dripping darkly onto the carpet.

Duncan noticed this and said, 'Christ, what will Levquist say!'

'I'll deal,' said Gerard. He fetched two towels from the bedroom, gave one to Duncan, and with the other began to mop up the pool on the carpet, while Duncan dabbed at his clothes.

'I'm sloshed,' said Duncan. Then he explained. 'I fell in the river. Crazy!'

'I'm sloshed too,' said Jenkin sympathetically.

'Is that whisky? Can I have some?'

Jenkin poured out a small whisky and filled the glass up with water. Duncan took it with an unsteady hand.

More footsteps were heard on the stairs. It was Rose. She came in and saw Duncan at once. 'Duncan, dear, there you are, I'm so glad!' She could not think what to say to him next, so exclaimed, 'So you're all onto whisky, are you, no I won't have any! What's that mess on the floor?'

'I fell in the Cher,' said Duncan. 'Idiotic old drunk!'

'Poor darling! Gerard, put the electric fire on. And stop doing that, you're only making things worse. Give me the towel. See if there's any water in the jug in the bedroom.'

There was. Rose, tucking up her green dress, on her knees, began an artful operation with little doses of water and careful use of the towel, blending the muddy stain into the fortunately fairly dark and ancient carpet. 'I'm afraid we're messing up Levquist's towels, but the scout will replace them. Don't forget to tip him, Gerard.'

Someone was running up the stairs, stumbling in his haste, and now bursting open the door. It was Gulliver Ashe. Not immediately noticing Duncan he cried out his news. 'There's been such a to-do down there, they say that Crimond has thrown a man into the Cherwell!' Then he caught sight of Duncan and the water scene and put his hand over his mouth.

'Go away, Gull, would you,' said Gerard.

Gull reeled away down the stairs.

Gulliver had lost Lily Boyne; he was sorry about this, he had enjoyed dancing with her, yet he was not absolutely sorry since he had come to realise that although he had drunk nothing recently except a glass of champagne which he had discovered on the grass, he was once more feeling very drunk, and a little sick, and also extremely tired. Lily, who had in the course of dancing divested herself of her white blouse, which she had rolled up and thrown away among the dancers (where it was caught and appropriated by a young man) revealing a just decently extensive and lacy petticoat beneath, had also at last declared herself 'flaked' and gone to sit down. Gull had gone out to attend to a natural need and coming back had found her gone. It was after this that he had heard some people talking about Crimond. Expelled from Levquist's rooms he now began to wander, first round the cloister where he managed to acquire, although he didn't really want it, a glass of beer, and then out onto the main lawns between the tents.

It was now full daylight, the terrible inquisitional finalising daylight had come, sending away the enchanted forest and all the magic of the night and revealing a scene, more resembling a battlefield, of trampled grass, empty bottles, broken glasses, upturned chairs, errant garments, and every sort of unattractive human debris. Even the tents, in the relentless sunshine, looked dirty and bedraggled. The blackbirds, thrushes, tits, swallows, wrens, robins, starlings and innumerable other birds were singing loudly, the doves were cooing and the rooks were cawing, and, nearer now, in the big trees of the deer park, came the hollow repetitive cry of the cuckoo. Dance music continued unabated however, sounding in the more open space of the high cloudless blue sky and surrounded by all that bird song, diminished and unreal. A queue was forming for breakfast, but a considerable number of people seemed unable to stop dancing, possessed by ecstasy or by a frenzied desire to maintain the enchantment, and to postpone the misery to come: remorse, regret, the tarnished hope, the shattered dream, and all the awful troubles of ordinary life. Gull would have liked some breakfast, the idea of bacon and eggs was suddenly extremely attractive, but he did not fancy waiting in the queue by himself, and he felt a more urgent and immediate need to sit down, preferably to lie down. He decided to rest for a short time and to come for the grub later when the crush was less. The desecrated littered grass was also scattered here and there with prostrate human figures, mostly male, some fast asleep. Making his way between these Gulliver even passed, though of course did not recognise, Tamar's cashmere shawl, now a stained screwed-up bundle, which had been used by someone to deal with a disaster to a bottle of red wine. A faint mist was hanging over the Cherwell. He found his way through the archway and out into the deer park. The park had been declared, for ecological and security reasons, out of bounds to the dancers. Now however, presumably since the dance was nearly over, the bowler-hatted guardians had melted away and couples were strolling here and there in the groves of trees. In the distance, in misty green glades, deer wandered and rabbits ran impetuously to and fro. Gulliver staggered on a little way, breathing the delicious fresh rivery early morning air and appreciating the untrodden grass. Then he sat down under a tree and fell asleep.

Tamar had at last found Conrad. For a while she had sat on a chair in one of the tents and actually slept for a short time. When she came out the sky was light and the sun had risen. The light was terrible. The skirt of her white dress had become mysteriously covered with grey smudges. She felt terrible, like an ugly ghost. She decided to comb her hair with her little comb, then accidentally dropped the comb and did not turn to pick it up. She walked slowly, for something to do and because she might attract more attention if she stood still. Everything about her looked unreal and appalling, the laughter and the music came to her in gusts like little blows, making her blink and frown. Her head drooped, her mouth drooped. She came to the pop tent where recorded music was still being played, was about to pass it, then looked in. In a second the world changed. There he was, Conrad, her tall fellow, leaping, smiling, twirling round and round by himself. Tamar was about to cry out and rush to him. Then she saw that he was dancing with Lily Boyne.

Tamar turned quickly away, raising her hand to shield her face, and began to run away across the grass. She raced, lifting her skirt, through the cloisters and on to the main gate and out into the High Street. The curving High was empty, beautiful, solemn, in the quiet early sunshine. Tamar made her way, desperately, like a fugitive, hurrying now not running. During her run the strap of one of her sandals had snapped, and she hurried on, skipping a little, limping a little, past the silent magisterial buildings which were glowing in the clear cool sunlight against the radiant blue sky. She felt cold, but the coat which, anticipating this chill daybreak, she had brought with her was locked up in Conrad's car. Fortunately, during the whole nightmare of the dark hours, although she had lost her shawl, she had not mislaid her little evening bag, with cosmetics, money, keys, which she had carried unconsciously looped onto her wrist. She rushed along, holding her dirtied skirt high, her dress crumpled, her hair uncombed, her face unpowdered, in the direction of the bus station. The few early passers-by saw her streaming tears and turned to look after her. As she reached the bus station and boarded

a bus for London all the bells of Oxford were tolling six
o'clock.

After Gulliver's departure, the four in the room did not look
at each other. Rose brought the electric fire near to Duncan's
soaked trousers, asked if it was too hot, and commented with a
laugh at the steam which immediately began to rise. Duncan
replied suitably, said really he was almost dry, not to trouble
and so on. Jenkin and Duncan went on drinking whisky. It
was agreed to be unfortunate that there was now nothing to
eat, Gulliver was blamed for having eaten up all the sandwiches. Jenkin wished he had brought some chocolate, said he
had intended to. Gerard and Jenkin discussed whether one of
them should sally out to the breakfast scene and bring back
some sausages and bread. They wondered if they could now
do this without having to queue. No decision was reached.
They were all silently wondering if Jean would turn up and
what on earth they were going to do if she did not.

After about half an hour Jean Kowitz-Cambus did appear.
She clopped audibly, neatly, up the stairs and entered the
room already wearing her coat over the famous red dress with
black lace which Rose admired so much. Jean had evidently
planned her appearance and her entrance carefully. She was
already dressed for a quick departure and had attended to her
make-up and arranged her hair. Her very dark hair, sleek and
glowing like the feathers of an exotic bird, so orderly in its even
lines that it might have been enamelled, flowed evenly back
from her delicate hawk-face. Her rather stern, though calm,
expression relaxed suitably to Rose's greeting.

'Darling Jean, you've come, oh *good*!'

Rose put her arms round Jean, Jean patted Rose's shoulder
and said how lovely it was to hear the birds singing. Gerard
and Jenkin stood back. Then Jean approached Duncan who
remained slumped in his chair. She said, 'How's the old man?
Sozzled as usual? Can someone help him up?'

Duncan stretched out his hands, and Jenkin took one hand and Gerard the other and they hauled him to his feet.

Jean and Duncan then had a conversation. Jean said where was his coat, and he said he thought he had left it in the car, but where was the car? Jean told him where it was, not in the car park, but in a road nearby. They both said it was a good thing it was not in the car park, Jenkin agreed, you could get boxed in, young people were so thoughtless. Rose said lightly that she hoped that Jean was driving, and Jean said she certainly was. Jean kissed Gerard and Jenkin and Rose. Duncan kissed Rose and tried to argue with Gerard about contributing to the tip for the scout. Rose hugged Jean and kissed her and stroked her hair. Then she put her arms round Duncan in a special embrace. Jean told Duncan to come along and took his arm. Amid various valedictory remarks and waves of the hand they took their leave. Their footsteps receded down the stairs.

After a suitable interval of silence, Jenkin stifled a little snort of laughter, then went to look out of the window and compose his face. Rose looked at Gerard who frowned slightly and looked away.

Gerard, expected by the other two to make a statement, said, 'Well, I daresay it's all all right, and we won't have to think about it any more, I certainly hope so.'

'You may be able not to think about it,' said Jenkin, returning from the window with a composed face, 'but I doubt if I will.'

'Gerard's good at not thinking about things when he doesn't feel he ought to,' said Rose.

'Or feels he oughtn't to,' said Jenkin.

Gerard said briskly, 'Time to be off. I'll leave an envelope for Levquist's chap.'

Rose wished she was going to drive back to London with Gerard, but she had brought her own car, partly because Gerard had said he was driving Jenkin down, and partly because she wanted to be able to leave earlier than the others if she felt very tired. She fetched her coat which she had left in Levquist's bedroom. They all did a little elementary tidying up, but their heart was not in it. They went down the stairs and through the cloister and faced the warm sunlight and the deafening chorus of birds and the loud cries of the cuckoo.

Gulliver was having a marvellous dream. A beautiful girl with big liquid dark eyes and long thick eyelashes and a moist sensuous mouth was leaning over towards him. He felt her warm sweet breath, her soft lips touched his cheek, and then his mouth. He woke up. A face was close to his, and big dark beautiful eyes were gazing into his eyes. One of the deer, finding this black bundle curled up under a familiar tree, had thrust a dark wet muzzle down towards it. Gulliver jolted up. The deer sprang back, gazed for another moment, then trotted with dignity away. Gulliver wiped his face, wet with the creature's gentle touch. He got to his feet. He felt terrible, he looked terrible. He began to walk back. He felt giddy, bright lights danced around him and little black hieroglyphs kept appearing at the side of his vision.

As he emerged, rubbing his eyes, from the archway of the New Building onto the main lawn, he stopped dead. A dreadful and extraordinary sight which he could not interpret met his gaze. Somewhere, how far away he could not at first estimate, for the phenomenon was so odd, a long line of people, two long lines of people, one above the other, were drawn up directly opposite to him and staring straight at him. He felt helpless panic as at some shattering of a natural law. He rubbed his eyes. They were still there, standing rigidly at attention and looking at him in silence. Then he realised what it was. It was the dance photograph. Nearer, with his back to him, the photographer was marshalling his camera which was mounted on a tripod, looking through it at the posed silent ranks which were looking at him. The dancers were immobile, mostly solemn, many of them looking as terrible as Gull, their clothes disordered, their faces bleary with exhaustion, exposed, graceless and haggard, in the cruel light of day. Under the song of the birds the silence of the music made itself felt. Frowning and focusing his eyes Gulliver scanned the large staring assembly for any familiar faces. He could not see Gerard or Rose or Tamar or Jean or Duncan or Crimond. He spotted Lily however. She was standing beside Conrad Lomas with her arm around his waist. Gulliver began to slink along the front of the building in the direction of the car park. He wondered if his car would be boxed in. It was.

Gerard turned the key in the door and entered the silent house. In the car driving to London he had told Jenkin of his father's death. Jenkin had been shocked and distressed, and the spontaneity of his grief for Gerard's father, whom he had known for many years, was touching. But after the first few exclamatory exchanges Jenkin had begun to think, to worry about how much Gerard would suffer, to wonder whether Gerard felt guilty because he had not left the dance at once. Jenkin did not say any of this, but Gerard intuited it behind some clumsy expressions of sympathy and was irritated. He was driving into the sun. He told Jenkin to go to sleep and Jenkin obediently did so, tilting the seat back, settling his head, and going to sleep instantly. The presence of his sleeping friend was soothing, at the moment Jenkin asleep was preferable to Jenkin awake. Coming into London they hit the early rush hour, and as the car crawled slowly past Uxbridge and Ruislip and Acton Jenkin continued to sleep, his hands clasped upon his stomach, his shirt rumpled, his legs stretched out, his trousers undone at the waist, his plump face expressing trustful calm. The sleeping presence, surrendering itself to his protection, calmed Gerard's painful thoughts, held them off a little, catching their sharpness as in a soft bandage. When they reached the little terrace house in Shepherd's Bush where Jenkin lived Gerard woke his friend up, came around and opened the car door and pulled him out, not forgetting the little suitcase into which Jenkin had put, so he said, a woollen cardigan to put on if it was cold, and slippers in case his feet became swollen with dancing. The chocolate had been left behind. Gerard refused the suggestion, less than wholehearted perhaps, that he should come in for a cup of tea. They both felt it was time to part, and the door closed before Gerard had even started the car. He had no doubt that Jenkin would go upstairs, undress, put on pyjamas, pull the curtains, get into bed, and fall asleep again at once. Something about the orderliness of his friend's arrangements irritated Gerard sometimes.

Now he was in his own house in Notting Hill, standing in the hall and listening. He did not call out. He hoped Patricia was asleep. The house, a fairly large detached brick-built villa, had belonged to Robin Topglass's father, the bird man, then to Robin. For some time Robin and Gerard had lived in it together. Then when Robin got married and went to Canada he sold the house to Gerard. He stood in the familiar smell and familiar silence of the house, seeing and feeling the presence of the familiar quiet things, the paintings of birds by John Gould which had belonged to Robin's father, the carved Victorian hallstand which they had bought at an auction, the red and brown Kazakh rug which Gerard had brought from Bristol. The house seemed to be waiting for Gerard, expecting something of him, that he would bring comfort, restore order, take charge. Yet also the house was a spectator, it was not all that involved, it was not a very old house, it was built in 1890, but it had already seen many things. It had seen much, it would see more. Perhaps it was just watching with curiosity to see what Gerard would do. Gerard hung up his coat, which he had brought in from the car, upon the hall stand. He took off his black evening jacket and his black tie. He undid his shirt at the neck and rolled up his sleeves. His heart, quiet earlier, began to race. He took off his shoes and began, holding them in his hand, to mount the stairs, stepping long-legged over the stair that creaked.

On the landing, he saw that the door of Patricia's bedroom was closed. He did not hesitate but walked on and opened the door of his father's room. The curtains were pulled against the sunshine but there was a bright twilight in the room. The long thin figure on the bed was entirely covered by a sheet. It was somehow startling that the face had been covered up. The bedclothes had been removed. So had all the paraphernalia of illness, pills, bottles, tumblers, even his father's glasses had gone, even the book he had been reading, *Sense and Sensibility*. Gerard put down his shoes and crossed the room and pulled the curtains well back. Their movement made a familiar running metallic sound which, in the particular silence of the room, made Gerard shudder, perhaps at some unconscious memory from a time, much earlier, when he had slept in the room himself. He looked out at the harsh sunlight which revealed the back garden surrounded by an old brick wall dark with grime, the damp mossy rockery, the gaudy rose bushes (Robin's choice) in full flower, the walnut tree, the many trees in other gardens. He turned and quickly, gently, not touching what lay beneath, drew back the sheet from his father's face. The eyes were closed. He had wondered about that in the car. He drew a chair up beside the bed and sat down. So lately dead, so only just, but so absolutely, gone. He thought, I shall lie so one day, neatly upon my back with my eyes closed and look just so thin and so long; unless I drown and am never found, or smash to pieces like Sinclair. The face was not exactly calm, but withdrawn, absorbed, expressing perhaps a quiet thoughtful puzzlement, the good kind face, abstracted, already alien, already waxen and very pale above the faint beard, already shrinking, like his father's face yet unlike, like a work of art, as if someone had made quite a good but rather stolid simulacrum. One could see that the soul was gone, no one looked out, the puzzled look was something left behind, like a farewell letter. He lifted the sheet at the side to look at one of the hands, but quickly replaced it. The hand looked uncanny, more alive, its familiar thin spotty claws relaxed. The neck was darker in colour, sunken, the muscles and tendons prominent, the skin stretched not wrinkled. The wrinkles of the face looked like artificial lines scored in pale thick wax. His father's face, so long youthful, had lately become very wrinkled, the eyes deep in skinny folds, the lower lids curiously fractured in the centre, forming runnels for a perpetual discharge of moisture from the eyes. These were now dry, the face was dry, the hidden eyes were tearless. Death dries the tears of the dead. The dead dry face looked older, the ageing process, after the great change, being gently metamorphosed. Faster it would go on soon, and faster. His father looked gaunt, a gauntness disguised before by the glow of stoical humour which made every further misery of terminal illness into a self-depreciating joke. Without the transparent-rimmed glasses and the false teeth the mask looked ancient now, the nose thinner, the chin sunk, the helpless affronted mouth a little open. So he had eased himself into death as into a garment which now, perfectly, fitted him.

Gerard's imagination engaged with the fact that Patricia had seen him die. Gerard had seen people dead but he had never seen anyone die. He thought, when it comes it is, isn't it, so fast. Well, that must be true by definition, 'fast' doesn't really apply. There just has to be a last moment. What we call a slow death is a slow dying. We may still picture the end as if it were a leap over a stream, but there is no stream and no one to leap. Just a last moment. Could one know, think 'it will come in *this* minute'? A condemned criminal could know. At that stage many of us are condemned criminals. It was such a very little time since yesterday when his father had wished him a happy goodbye as he left for the dance. 'Tell me all about it tomorrow.' Gerard had not slept since he had seen his father living. That seemed important too. For Patricia, the sudden going must have been perceptible, one moment the struggle to communicate, to help, the talking, the soothing, the saying, 'rest, you'll feel better soon', then at some next moment the utter solitude, the job over, nothing to do, alone. Oh God. How is it done, thought Gerard. It can't be difficult, anyone can do it. It could be more like a little movement, a sort of quick turning away. I shall make that movement one day. How shall I know how? When the time comes I shall know, my body will tell me, will teach me, urge me, push me at last over the edge. It is an achievement, or is it like falling asleep which happens but you don't know when? Perhaps at the very last moment it is easy, the point where all deaths are alike. But that must be true by definition too. Here, with a habitual movement, Gerard forbade his thoughts to wonder how long before it happened Sinclair knew that he was to die. That had been too much worked on, once. Thoughts must not go there. He shuddered now looking at the dead flesh, so recently alive, so frightful, so abhorrent to the living. He covered the face and rose and stepped back, trying to see the long still form on which the white sheet made sculptured folds as something general, a sort of monument.

He went to the window and looked at the pale oblong leaves of the walnut tree, tugged at by the breeze, transparent in the sun, looking like messages, a tree of messages, like paper prayers that had been tied to the branches. He felt such a painful aching pity for his father. It seemed absurd to pity someone for being dead, yet so natural too. The helplessness of the dead can seem, at that first realisation, so agonisingly touching, pathetic rather than tragic, the powerlessness, the defencelessness, of those 'strengthless heads'. Poor poor dead thing, oh poor thing, oh my poor dear dear dead father. Now love released runs wild when it is too late. I should have seen him more, he thought, oh if only I could see him now, even for a minute and hug him and kiss him and tell him how much I love him. How much I loved him. He pictured his father's face, his loving eyes, as he had seen them yesterday, that sleepless yesterday which had become today. There was so much to say, so much he ought to have said. He ought to have spoken to him about the parrot, only the moment had never seemed to come, so he had put it off, and then towards the end it had seemed too dangerous a matter, too difficult and painful to inflict upon a dying man – yet also perhaps that reference, that speech, was just what the dying man was longing for, was waiting for, but could make no sign. Sometimes when Gerard had felt it 'coming over him' that he should say some good thing about it, he had told himself that it no longer mattered, it had long ago been *forgotten*. Why drag it up now – better leave it alone, the years had mended it. But more often he felt sure that the years had not mended it and it was not forgotten. He had not forgotten, how could his father have? The parrot had come into the family when Gerard was eleven and Patricia was thirteen. It had arrived when its owners, clients of Gerard's father, had left England in a hurry, leaving behind a confusion in their affairs which Gerard's father was to sort out, and the bird, who was to be found a home or handed over to a pet shop. Gerard loved the bird instantly, passionately. Its sudden presence in the house, its exalted winged bird presence, was a miracle to which he awakened with daily joy. Gerard's passion triumphed, not without some opposition, the bird stayed. It, or rather he, was a male, who had been given by its previous owner a whimsical condescending name which Gerard consigned to oblivion. The bird was a grey parrot and Gerard, divining his true name, called him 'Grey', a gentle simple name, a calm quiet colour, an open lucid sound which its owner was soon able to reproduce. Gerard's mother and his sister usually called the parrot 'Polly', but Grey scorned this and it never became a proper name. Gerard, helped by his father, looked after Grey, who was said to be a young bird. Grey glowed with health and beauty and grace. His clever eyes, surrounded by an ellipse of delicate white skin, were pale yellow, his immaculate feathers of the palest purest grey, and in his tail and wing-tips, the softest most radiant scarlet. About his neck and shoulders he wore, as Gerard saw it like a mobile coat of chain mail, a collar of small closely packed 'fishscale' feathers which slithered about upon his athletic frame most expressively according to his moods. The furry leggings above his claws were of almost white down, and under his wings was an intimate softness as of fluffy wool. He could whistle more purely than any flute and dance as he whistled. His musical repertoire when he first arrived included 'Pop Goes the Weasel' and part of the 'Londonderry Air' and 'Jesu Joy of Man's Desiring'. Gerard soon taught him 'Three Blind Mice' and 'Greensleeves'. He could imitate a blackbird and an owl. His human vocabulary had progressed more slowly. He could say 'Hello' and (impatiently) 'Yes, yes', and (excitedly) 'Yippee!' He could also say, often with amusing appropriateness, 'Shut up!' What most touched, and also disturbed Gerard among those utterances from Grey's past was the way he would sometimes say in a tender slightly drawling woman's voice, 'Oh – pretty – one.' Perhaps there had been a woman who loved Grey and missed him; but that was the past, and Gerard did not often think of it, Grey was *his* parrot now. Under Gerard's regime, Grey was a wayward learner however. He quickly picked up the sound of Gerard's mother's voice saying in quiet exasperation, 'Oh *dear*, oh *dear*!', but he resisted Gerard's 'pieces of eight', turning his intelligent attentive head firmly away, blinking his eyes as if bored, refusing the nebulously sibilant sounds. He was soon able however not only to say his own name, but to utter something recognisably like the interesting sentence, 'Grey is grey.'

Grey was for a time a novelty which sufficiently amused all the family, but later, since Gerard and his father cleaned the cage, fed the bird, examined him for ticks and mites, treated his little ailments, took him to be checked up by the vet, he became more 'their' parrot and of less interest to Patricia and Gerard's mother who soon stopped talking to him and often ignored him. His cage was moved from the drawing room to Gerard's father's study. The intelligence and presence of Grey was for Gerard a continual source of trembling joy, a feeling he described to himself as 'touchment'. The parrot was a world in which the child was graciously allowed to live, he was a vehicle which connected Gerard with the whole sentient creation, he was an avatar, an incarnation of love. Gerard knew, he could not doubt, that Grey understood how much Gerard loved him, and returned his love. The clever inquisitive white-rimmed yellow eyes expressed, so soon, fearless faith and love. The gentle firm clasp of the small dry claws, the lightness of the entrusted body, the sudden scarlet of the spread tail, expressed love, even the hard dense stuff of the curving black beak seemed mysteriously endowed with tenderness. Of course Grey was soon out of his cage, flying about the room or perched on Gerard's hand or on his shoulder, leaning his soft feathered head caressingly against his cheek, clambering round the back of his neck and peering to look into his face. Eye to eye they often were as Grey, back in the cage to which he returned willingly, swung or jolted and danced to and fro upon his perch, or climbed around the bars, sometimes upside down, pausing to gaze or to listen or to demand attention. The sense of an attentive responding intelligence was indubitable. Grey parrots are not in general very big. Gerard would often take the bird, gently gathering the folded wings, to nestle the small head and light fragile body against his chest, or hold him

58

inside his shirt against his beating heart. He stroked the soft feathers, cradling the frail hollow bones, while the delicate claws grasped his fingers with perfect trust.

The parrot, accepted for a while as Gerard's pet, began later to divide the family. Gerard's mother (her name was Annette) was mildly and reasonably annoyed by bird droppings on the carpet. She and Patricia came to resent the proprietary attitude of Gerard and to a lesser extent his father (whose name was Matthew) about the bird, and were irritated by Gerard's continual chatter about Grey's exploits. Possibly, he thought later, they were both jealous. They had in any case never spent the time and care necessary to become really friendly with Grey. In approaching a wild thing it is necessary to move quietly and predictably, to speak gently and softly, adopt regular routines, behave respectfully, be patient, reliable and truthful. All this Gerard knew by instinct. Patricia, perhaps out of jealousy and envy, took to teasing the bird, poking at him jerkily, offering food then whisking it away. Gerard of course was angry. Patricia said she was just playing with Polly, who after all belonged to her too. Gerard explained to his sister, frequently and at length, how to treat the bird with whom they were privileged to live. (He never used the word 'pet'.) Patricia continued the persecution in his absence until one day Grey seized hold of an intrusive finger and bit it. There were screams and tears. After that Patricia kept well away from the parrot and the furore died down. The time came for Gerard to go to boarding school. Gerard told Grey not to worry, he would be back before long, he took an emotional farewell pressing his face against the bars as his father was calling him to the car. All his letters babbled of Grey, sending his love. At the longed-for half-term, ferried home in a friend's parent's car, he rushed joyfully into the house and into the study. Grey was not there. He ran to the drawing room, to the kitchen. He *screamed*.

The explanations followed. No, Polly was not dead, it had not escaped, it had just gone away, it belonged to someone else now. It had gone to the very best pet shop in the city centre, and had been bought by some people, some very nice people the shop man said when he telephoned, no, he didn't know who they were, they were passing through, they had taken Polly away in their car. 'You'll never see it again!' Patricia cried. Gerard's father, averting his face, said nothing. The explanations gabbled on. It was just too difficult to look after it with Gerard away, they could not take the responsibility, it had become wild and vicious, it had tried to bite Annette, they had read in a book, it was kinder to the bird, and so on and so on.

Gerard was hysterical for ten minutes. Then he fell silent. He did not speak to any member of his family for two days. Annette wanted to take him to a psychiatrist. After that, quite suddenly, he resumed polite ordinary apparently cheerful relations with them all. Nothing more was said about the parrot. 'Thank God that's over!' said Annette. Gerard's father knew better. He knew how terribly, how unforgivably, he had failed his son. He had given in, he had allowed the women to bully him, to outwit him, he had, for a quiet life, surrendered to their noisy arguments, to their jealousy and their malice. He had believed their (Gerard had no doubt) lies. He knew it as the years went by, reading that lack of forgiveness sometimes in his son's thoughtful looks, in the very faintly cool quality of some acts of politeness and consideration. Even undoubted kindness, even love, retained that indelible icy line. They never spoke of the matter again.

Could it be true, thought Gerard, could it actually have any meaning, to say that he had 'never forgiven' his father? About 'the women' he minded less. He expected less of them. His love for them, for he did love them, was something less formal, less a question of absolutes, of honour, of responsibility, of truth. He even came later on to see their attitude as not totally unreasonable. His father's failure, his weakness, his *duplicity* (for it seemed that the infamous crime had been committed soon after Gerard's departure) wounded Gerard deeply. Some perfect thing, some absolute safety, some ground of being, was, with his belief in his father's perfect goodness, gone out of the world forever. Equally deep, equally enduring was Gerard's mourning for his irreplaceable bird-friend. Through all his childhood, indeed through all his life, he continued to miss Grey. Ideas of searching for him, going to the pet shop, asking for clues and so on, had been instantly dismissed as useless, productive only of worse pain. Later when Gerard was an adult he sometimes thought, and it was such a very sad and moving thought, how Grey was probably still alive somewhere. If he passed a pet shop he would occasionally stop and look to see if there were a grey parrot, and if it were Grey. He felt sure that he would recognise Grey, and Grey would recognise him. But he felt frightened too, a reunion might somehow, for some reason, be too awfully distressing. In fact he was certain that Grey was alive. He never spoke again about the parrot to his parents or his sister, and never mentioned his existence to his later friends; never to Sinclair or to Duncan, to whom he had been so close after Sinclair died, never to Robin or Marcus, or Jenkin or Rose, or to any of his friends did he breathe a word about him. Only once, in St Mark's Square in Venice, with Duncan long ago, when a pigeon alighted on his hand and he exclaimed with grief, did he come near to telling, and confessed to 'a most unhappy memory'. Oh – pretty – one. In conversation, if parrots were mentioned, he changed the subject; and he never again had any relation with any beast, no cat, no dog, no bird, entered his life. A re-enactment was impossible, and it would have been too painful a reminder. How frail these gentle creatures are who deign to share our lives, how dependent on us, how vulnerable to our ignorance, our neglect, our mistakes, and to the wordless mystery of their own mortal being.

He thought, I ought to have said something about Grey to my father, brought the subject up somehow. Yet what could I have said, in what form of words and to what good effect? I couldn't just say, 'I forgive you', or 'I have long ago forgiven you'. Would that be true anyway, and if a lie would it not be instantly seen as such? In any case this terminology would be too solemn, like an imputation of guilt. It was not a burden to put upon a dying man, a prolonged discussion would have been unthinkable. Yet, when there was so little time left, was not that exactly the moment to say those things? Or were such ventures only tolerable in a formal context, best left to priests? Perhaps his father had ceased to feel guilty, had long ago dismissed the whole matter. That was unlikely. Gerard had, he thought, or imagined, at many moments through his life, understood the particular look of those gentle penitent eyes. On the other hand, it was also possible that, as he nursed the wound, to himself, to his son, over the years, his father might have felt resentment against Gerard, not only for his withdrawal, but for having somehow occasioned the whole business in the first place by his fanatical attachment to that wretched bird. As for the withdrawal, that must surely have become imperceptible by the time Gerard was at Oxford, the 'iciness' had been internalised. The 'forgiveness' was, had to be, something enacted over a long period, and perhaps had effectively been so enacted, since Gerard's affection for his father had been, and must have been seen to be, so wholehearted, in spite of the secret pain which no longer prompted any accusation. Was the fact that they had never spoken about it, that Gerard had never spoken, since it was for him to make the first move, really so important, so awful? Yes. Yet as the years went by it became harder to raise the subject without some sort of unpredictable shock, without the danger of making matters worse. It could not be casually touched upon or easily woven into ordinary reminiscence. At the end it was too late to make any gesture, as much too late yesterday, he thought, as it is today. And he thought, I'm sure Grey has outlived my father, parrots live longer than we do, he could outlive me too, I hope he will, I hope he is happy. How odd it still is, not knowing where he is, and how odd that when I have forgotten so much I have not forgotten this and can call up *the same* emotions? And that I feel just this now when my father has died. He stared out of the window at the tree of prayers, frail ephemeral supplications to remote and cruel gods. Turning back towards the long still figure on the bed, he felt tears come to his eyes at last.

Patricia Fairfax opened the door. 'Why are you here?' she asked. Then, seeing the question was ridiculous, said, 'Have you been here long? I was asleep.'

'Not long,' said Gerard, mopping his eyes with the back of his hand.

'Come downstairs. Why have you no shoes on? There are your shoes. Put them on. Have you looked at him?'

'Yes.'

Patricia stared at the shrouded figure, then turned and hurried down the stairs. Gerard followed, closing the door.

'Would you like some coffee, something to eat?'

'Yes, please.'

'I suppose you've been up all night.'

'Yes.'

They went into the kitchen, Gerard sat at the scrubbed wooden table, Patricia turned on the electric stove. Gerard had felt, he still felt, irritated at the calm way she had taken over his kitchen. He had felt bound to invite Pat and Gideon for what was to have been a short interval after the lease of their flat was unexpectedly terminated, now they behaved as if they owned the place. He felt extremely tired. 'Pat, dear, don't worry about eggs or anything, just give me some bread.'

'Don't you want toast?'

'Toast. Yes, no, it doesn't matter. Have you eaten anything?'

'I can't eat.'

Gerard felt ashamed that he could. 'Tell me what happened.'

'He was all right last night.'

'He was all right in the afternoon when I left him, he seemed better.'

'I settled him down and went to bed. Then about one o'clock I heard him moaning and moving, making those little noises, you know, you said like a restless bird – and I got up and went to him and he was awake, but – he wasn't making much sense –'

'Rambling a bit?'

'Yes, that happened before – but really, now – he was *different* –'

'Different – how – do you think he *knew*?'

'He was – he was – frightened.'

'Oh God –' Oh the pity of it, he thought, how terrible, how I pity him, oh the pity, oh the grief. 'Pat, I'm sorry I wasn't there.'

'You would have been if you hadn't regarded that dance as so absolutely important.'

'Was he in pain?'

'I don't think so. I'd given him the usual stuff. But he had such a – a terrible *urgent* look in his eyes, and he couldn't keep still, as if all his body were wrong and intolerable.'

'An urgent look. Did he say anything clear?'

'He said several times, "Help me."'

'Oh – dear – Did he ask for me?'

'No. He talked about Uncle Ben.' Benjamin Hernshaw had been Matthew Hernshaw's 'disreputable' younger brother, Violet's father, Tamar's grandfather.

'He always loved Ben. Have you telephoned Violet?'

'No, of course not.'

'Why of course?'

'I wasn't going to ring her in the middle of the night, was I? She never liked Dad, she isn't interested, she knows there's nothing for her in the will.'

'How does she know?'

'I told her.'

'Was that necessary?'

'She asked me.'

'We must give her something.'

'Oh for God's sake don't start on that, we've got enough to worry about.'

'Dad didn't mention her because he assumed we'd look after her.'

'Just you try, she'd bite your hand off, she hates everybody!'

'She did accept money from Dad, I know – we must tell her he talked about Ben. What did he say about him?'

'I don't know, he was mumbling – remember Ben, or remember Ben's something or other –'

'Well, there you are –'

'Look, Gerry, we must decide –'

'Pat, *wait* – Did you know he was going to – to die?'

'Only just before the end – then suddenly it was – so clear – as if he'd explained it –'

'Ah – and you saw him go?'

'Yes. He was lying there and twisting and turning and talking about Ben. Then suddenly he sat up straight and looked at me – with that awful puzzled frightened look – and he looked all about the room – and he said – he said –'

'What?'

'He said slowly, and quite clearly, "I'm – so – sorry." Then he leaned back onto the pillow, not falling, but slowly, as if he were going to sleep again – he made a little tiny odd sound, like – like a – *mew* – and I saw it was over.'

Gerard wanted to ask, what did you see, how did you know, he felt, later on I won't be able to, everything must be said now, but he did not ask. He would have time later to think about that dreadful pitiful 'I'm sorry'. He thought, he was looking for me at that moment.

Patricia was dry-eyed and controlled, her emotion evident in her hesitations and in the hard clipped exasperated tone in which she answered Gerard's questions. She now made coffee. She opened a drawer, chose a clean red and green check table cloth and spread it on the table, then set out plate, cup, saucer, knife, spoons, butter, marmalade, sugar, milk in a blue jug, sliced bread aligned in a bowl. She set the coffee pot on a tile.

'Do you want hot milk?'

'No, thanks. Aren't you having coffee?'

'No.'

She gave him a paper napkin. The paper napkins represented her regime, used in preference to Gerard's linen ones. She sat down opposite to him and closed her eyes.

The house felt terrible, disjointed, gutted. Sitting quietly in it at last, Gerard felt his body aching with grief and fear, with grief which was fear, an exhausted denatured sensation, a loss of being. He concentrated on Patricia. It was possible, he knew, to esteem and admire people and enjoy their company and dislike them heartily. It was also possible to be irritated, maddened and bored by people whom one loves. He had thus loved his mother and Pat. Through time and custom, simply by enduring, this love had grown stronger. This was no doubt a proof that 'family' meant something to him, or perhaps that he had got used to putting up with them for his father's sake; though for his father's sake too he had resented their separatism, their little league against 'the men', critical, mocking, secretive. He had never liked their laughter, had been enraged as a child by his mother's jesting at his father's expense, had resented his father's humble surrender of his authority and his dignity. Yet they had had a harmonious time on the whole and, apart from that one terrible episode and its reverberations, he could not claim an unhappy childhood. His father had been too old for the second war, Gerard too young. He had continued to love them all, and much later to see, with sympathy, his mother and sister as strong frustrated women. Patricia had wilfully thrown away her education and was now irked with excesses of energy for which she could find no use. She was a loving and business-like mother and wife but yearned for some indefinable larger scene, more status, more power. He looked at her now, her face relaxed in tiredness, perhaps in sleep, her lips parted, her mouth, as in a tragic mask, drooping heavily into long harsh lines. She was a striking woman, inheriting her mother's long smooth face, her stern and noble look and perpetual frown, a brave powerful face whose owner would no doubt be a valuable companion on a desert island. The idea of 'putting a brave face on it' suited Patricia, she had 'nerve', and had been a tomboyish child. Her shortish fair hair, a little streaked with grey, well cut at intervals, usually tousled, often patted into shape by its owner, looked youthful, was still shaggy and boyish. In recent years she had put on weight. Even now in repose her shoulders were back, her prominent chin well tucked in, her bust set forward under a flowery apron which Gerard was noticing for the first time. It was only lately that Gerard had realised that his sister had begun to envy her younger cousin's trim figure and enduring good looks. Patricia, once handsome, could never have been called beautiful; but Violet Hernshaw's face had that enduring structure which can command esteem at any age. Of course Pat was established as 'successful', her husband wealthy, her son 'brilliant', whereas Violet, as Pat now often sympathetically observed, had made a complete mess of her life, and her charms had brought her only bad luck. Ben had abandoned his mistress and his little daughter, he had been a crazy fellow who took to drugs and died young. Matthew, had tried to 'save' him, had been deeply grieved by his failure; perhaps he felt guilty as well. Matthew had been sober, conscientious, gentle. Now he was gone too. Gerard was aware of laying his head down on the table. He recalled, then saw with the eyes of dream, how his staid father, who rarely touched alcohol, used sometimes to startle them all by singing slightly *risqué* music-hall songs, his grave face transformed by a lunatic jollity. They found his occasional crazy merriment childish, touching, and embarrassing.

'You'd better go to bed,' said Pat's voice.

Gerard lifted his head. He had been dreaming about Sinclair and Rose. He had been young in the dream. It took him a second or two to remember that he was no longer young and Sinclair was dead. 'How long have I been asleep?'

'Some time.'

'You go to bed. I'll fix things. We must ring up the undertaker –'

'I've done that,' said Patricia, 'and I've rung the doctor about the death certificate.'

'I'll ring Violet.'

'I've done that too. Look, Gerard, we were talking the other day about the house in Bristol, why don't you go and live there? You said you loved that house. You don't have to live in London now.'

Gerard became wide awake. Typical Pat. 'Don't be silly, why should I live in Bristol, I live here!'

'This house is far too big for you, it doesn't suit you, you're only here by accident. I've just been talking to Gideon on the telephone. We'll buy it off you. You'll like Bristol, you need a change.'

'Oh shut up, Pat,' said Gerard, 'you're crazy. I'm going to bed.'

'And another thing, now Dad's gone I want to be on that committee.'

'What committee?'

'The book committee. He was on it, to represent the family. Now I should be.'

'It's nothing to do with you,' said Gerard.

'It's our money you're spending.'

'No, it isn't.'

'That's how Dad saw it.'

Gerard went upstairs into his bedroom. The sun was blazing in. He pulled the curtains and dragged the bedclothes aside and began to undress. As he lay down he began to remember the strange events of the night which were now confused, ugly and sinister, with his sister's words into a cloud of fantasy which seemed to be hanging above the heavy weight of that dead body which lay so still and so close, its face blinded. Oh my poor dead father, he thought, and it was as if his father were in terrible pain, the pain of death itself. He turned on his face and groaned and shed some tears of misery into the pillow.

'Well, what do you propose to do?' said Duncan Cambus.

'I'm going,' said Jean.

'You're going back to him.'

'Yes. I'm sorry.'

'Did you arrange to meet him?'

'No!'

'So you decided this with him last night?'

'Last night – it is last night, isn't it – or this morning. We didn't say anything to each other last night. *We didn't exchange a single word.*' Jean Cambus's eyes widened and glowed as she said this.

'You think he'll expect you?'

'I don't think anything – I'm going. I've got to. I'm very sorry. Now.'

'I'm going to bed,' said Duncan, 'and I advise you to do the same. I advise you, I *ask* you, not to go. Stay, wait, please.'

'I must go now,' said Jean, 'I can't wait. To wait would be – impossible – all wrong.'

'An error of taste, a lapse of style?'

These were the first words exchanged by Duncan and his wife since their departure from Levquist's rooms. The walk to the car, the drive to London, during most of which Duncan had slept, had been accomplished in silence. Now they were home, back in the sitting room of their flat in Kensington. On arrival there both of them had felt it imperative to step out of their crumpled evening clothes, and had, in different rooms, hastily, as if arming for battle, put on more sober gear. Duncan, seated, had taken off his damp and muddy evening trousers and put on some old corduroys, with a voluminous blue shirt, not buttoned, not tucked in. Jean, standing before him, had covered her black petticoat and black stockings with a yellow and white kimono, pulled in fiercely at the waist. Duncan was no longer flushed with alcohol, but his tired face looked disintegrated, wrecked, a senseless massive face, pale

69

and flabby, covered in soft pencilled-in lines. He sat very still, staring at his wife, leaning forward a little, his big hands pendant from the arms of the chair. He had washed his face and his hands and cleaned his teeth. Jean had washed off her elaborate make-up and brushed her thick dark straight hair, which stayed where it was put, back over the crown of her head. She had been a striking beauty when, in another era, in that now so remote, so dream-like past, she had flirted with Sinclair Curtland. Jean had known Sinclair, through Rose, when they were all children. He and she had been 'close' before Sinclair went up to Oxford, they had somehow, inconclusively, remained so, after, always, in spite of Gerard. Had they ever seriously considered that match which everyone seemed so anxious to bring about? Jean's older face was beautiful too, a little sulkier, still delicately china-pale, wilful and keen, often now recalling that of her Jewish father, so obsessively devout, so obsessively successful. Her mother, also Jewish, had been a talented pianist. They had observed the festivals. Jean had cared for none of these things, not synagogue or music, or the romance of business in which her father had tried to interest her, his only child. She had been obsessively intellectual. Some wondered why she married Duncan, others why she married at all. Her parents had loved her, though they had wanted a boy. Her mother was dead, her father flourishing in New York. He had dreamed of a Jewish son-in-law, but Sinclair was special.

Duncan rubbed his eyes, he found himself swaying slightly, a desire to sleep could be imperative even now. 'When will you come back?' he said. He had taken in the situation, he did not mean tomorrow or next week. He added, 'You pulled it off last time, coming back I mean.'

'You wouldn't stand it a second time,' said Jean. 'And yet – who knows what you might stand. I love you, but this is different.'

'Evidently.'

'I love you forever – but this is – Anyway *they* won't be able to stand it, and that will affect you.'

'Who's "they"?', as if he didn't know.

'Gerard, Jenkin, Rose. Married people shouldn't have best friends. Maybe we'd always have been better off if we hadn't always been continually watched, oh how closely they watch. And they'll stick with you, like they did last time. It's you they care about, not me.'

Duncan did not dispute this. 'They're not against you, they won't be, Rose won't be, you have an eternal pact with Rose.'

'You think women too have life-long friendships sealed in blood. It isn't so.' Yet it was true that she had an eternal pact with Rose. 'The two princesses' Sinclair had called them. 'Why the hell did you let Crimond throw you into the Cher, why did you *tolerate* it!'

'I didn't have much choice.'

'Don't play the fool now!'

'Jean —!'

'All right, all right. What happened?'

'I can't remember very clearly,' said Duncan. 'I wasn't after him. I mean I wasn't looking for him. We met suddenly in the dark. I don't think I said anything. I think I hit him, or tried to. We were just beside the water. He pushed me in.'

'God. It was just like — it was just like the other time. Why are you so *weak*, why can't you get things *right*?'

'You mean kill him?' said Duncan.

'It's as if you enjoyed it — of course I know you don't, you just bungle everything. Did you hit him with your fist or with your open hand?'

'I can't remember,' said Duncan. In fact he could remember very well; and reflected how often, how interminably, he would relive that scene, just as he did the other one, the *Urszene*. Retiring to relieve himself, he had come face to face with Crimond in the dark. It only now occurred to him that Crimond must have been watching him, trailing him, and had engineered the sudden meeting. It was the kind of unexpected encounter where one would be shocked into doing something, clasping an extended hand, offering an impromptu kiss or a blow. Duncan had moved his right hand, *deciding*, he remembered, not to close it into a fist. He had intended to slap Crimond on the side of the head, but had again, evidently, decided not to, but had hit him on the shoulder, quite hard it seemed since Crimond had jolted back a pace. Then Crimond had seized him, holding him by his clothes, and swung him round toward the edge of the river. Duncan lost his balance and fell down the bank. Yes, he remembered it all. He wondered whether, if it had been the other way round and he had pushed Crimond into the Cherwell, Jean would now be leaving.

'So all you can say is that you've got to go?'

'You'll be on the telephone to them.'

'Don't be contemptible as well as cruel.'

'Of course they are my friends too. I'm gambling the whole issue.'

'I don't like the gambling image either. To imply you just crave excitement does you less than justice. I suggest you get dressed and have some coffee and calm down.'

'I'll take a suitcase,' said Jean, 'and come back for the rest some time when you're at the office. You can go to bed and to sleep, you're reeling with sleep. When you wake up I'll be gone and you can curse me.'

'I shall never curse you. I just think you're a bloody traitor.'

'I don't know what to say. I don't know what the future holds, whether I'll be alive even.'

'What the hell does that mean?'

'To go near Crimond is to go near death, somehow. I don't mean anything in particular by that – just, it's danger. He doesn't fear death, he's a Kamikaze type, in a war he'd get a VC.'

'He keeps guns and has a very nasty fantasy life, that's all.'

'Well, you used to keep guns when you belonged to that club, you fancied yourself as a marksman. You and Crimond were always messing with guns at Oxford. No, but if he ever stopped working he might be very desperate.'

'And kill himself or you? You said he once proposed a suicide pact!'

'Not really, he just likes taking risks. He's brave, he doesn't evade things, he tells the truth, he's the most truthful person I've ever met.'

'You mean brutal. You can't be truthful without other virtues.'

'He has other virtues! He's dedicated, he's an idealist, he cares about poor people and –'

'He just wants to be admired by the young! You know what I think about Crimond's "caring"!'

'He's a strong person. You and I connect through our weaknesses. Crimond and I connect through our strength.'

'I don't think that means anything, it's vulgar rhetoric. Jean, on the day we got married you said, this is for *happiness*.'

'Happiness. That's one of our weaknesses.'

'You certainly won't find it there. But don't think it will be death or glory this time. You are choosing a dull and dreary servitude with a mean cheap little tyrant.'

'Ah – if I could only tell you how little I value my life –'

'You are telling me, and it doesn't mean anything except that you want to insult our marriage.'

'I don't,' said Jean frowning. She was leaning back against the closed door and had kicked off the dusty slippers in which she had danced all night. 'That's not right. You mentioned happiness – I'm just trying to convey to you how little it matters to me –'

Duncan pulled himself up a little in his armchair. He said to himself, I'm trying to make her argue, I'm trying to keep her just a little longer, like asking the executioner for two minutes. He thought, so I have despaired already? Yes. Now it is as if I expected it. But, oh, the happiness, the happiness, which she now sees as nothing. He said, 'Look, this love of yours for Crimond seems to me without substance, almost something stupid, it's not to do with real life at all. You're like two mad people who crave to be together but can't communicate –'

'Mad, yes,' said Jean, 'but – we communicate.' Her eyes widened again and she sighed hugely, touching her breast and rolling her head.

'My dear – when you chucked it last time it was for good reasons.'

'I can't remember the reasons, except that loving you must have been one, and I still love you – but, well, here we are –'

'If only we'd had children, that would have anchored you in reality. I've never managed to make all this real for you. You've been like some kind of visitor.'

'Don't keep saying that about children.'

'I haven't said it for years.'

'All right, we've never played the husband and wife game which you call real. That hasn't stopped us from loving each other absolutely –'

'"Absolutely"?!'

'I'm sorry, everything I say now must seem gross and stupid, it's part of how things have totally changed that I can't speak to you properly. But you understand –'

'You expect me to understand you so perfectly and love you so much that I won't mind your going to another man, and for the second time!'

'I'm sorry, my darling, I'm so so sorry. I know this wound won't heal. But this has to be. And – this doesn't make it any better for you – it isn't, for me, really anything to do with the future – the future doesn't in that sense exist one way or the other.'

'You leave the future to me, now that you've utterly desolated and defiled it. But you will have to live your own foul enslaved future day by day and minute by minute – quite apart from anything else, your stupidity amazes me.' Duncan, with some difficulty, hauled himself up out of his armchair. 'Everything about this infatuation, everything that I imagine about you and Crimond being together, fills me with *loathing* and *horror* and *disgust*.'

'I'm sorry. It's terrible. It's carnage, it's the slaughterhouse. I'm sorry.' She opened the door. 'Look – do stop drinking – don't take to drink now, cut it down a bit.'

Duncan said nothing, he moved away towards the window, turning his back on her. Jean watched him for a moment, looking at his broad back and hunched shoulders and pendant shirt. Then she left the room and closed the door. She ran to her bedroom and began cramming things into a suitcase in desperate haste. She slipped out of the kimono and stepped into a skirt. She made up her face carefully, simply. Her face with Duncan had been stern and calm, the face of what *had to be*. Now in the mirror she saw a mad scattered convulsed face. All the time, as she packed and dressed and dealt with her face, she was shuddering and trembling, her lower jaw moving compulsively, a faint growling in her throat. She put on her coat, found her handbag, stood still for a moment controlling her breath. Then walked out to the front door and out of the flat.

Duncan, who had been looking down through the leafy branches of the tall plane trees at the garden in the square, heard the soft click of the closing door and turned round. He saw on the carpet the dusty discarded slippers and picked them up. He did not want to be moved by them either to anger or to tears, and he dropped them into a waste paper basket and went through into his bedroom. He and Jean occupied separate rooms now. Not that that had any great significance in the huge peculiar apparatus of their marriage, their unity, their love, which had lasted so long and survived so much and was now perhaps finally over. Something cosmic and crucial had occurred, his whole body knew it and he panted for breath. It had happened again, the impossible, the unbeliev-able had occurred, it had happened *again*. Why had he not wept, screamed, fallen to his knees, beseeched, raged, seized Jean by the throat? He had coldly despaired. Hope would have been death by torture. He had never for a moment conjectured that Jean might be mistaken, never conceived of saying: 'It's all in your mind, if you turn up he'll be dismayed and embarrassed.' He entirely believed that in all that long night they had not exchanged a word. That bore the unmis-takable mark of Crimond's style. Duncan *knew* that Crimond now expected her to come with the same certainty that she had in coming.

It was in the despair and the finality that he sought refuge. He could not have endured speculation. The suddenness of the thing made it now seem so like death. Jean's abrupt vanishing, the unspeakable reappearance of Crimond, the dreadful fall into the river. It was all one absolute cosmic universal smash. How wrong Jean had been to imagine that he would now telephone the others. He felt at that moment that in losing her he had forfeited all his relation to the world, and had no desire left for any human contact. He supposed that later he would be discredited in front of his friends, humiliated and disgraced, ashamed of this second defeat, of the fatal 'bungling' of which his wife had accused him. Now his misery made no account of shame. Of course, he would 'take her back' if she came, but she would not come, would not want to return to what was left of him after this laceration. She would have to assume that he hated her. If Crimond ditched her, whether this happened tomorrow or years from now, she would go right away into an aloneness and a freedom which she had perhaps yearned for during all the time when she had put so much energy into keeping faith with Duncan and with her idea of their mutual love. She would go away and work and think, take counsel with her powerful father in America, discover some world to conquer, go to India or Africa, run some large enterprise, use up elsewhere all that restless clever power which, as his wife, she had wasted on happiness. Yes, they had done it for happiness, and Jean might be right to see this as weakness.

Of course she had, as Jean Cambus, done all kinds of things, but not the one great thing of which Jean Kowitz had dreamed. She had been a secretary to an MP, edited a magazine, served on numerous committees, written a book on feminism. As a diplomatic wife she had run a house and servants and a whole busy social world which was also a valuable information service. She would have been an excellent diplomat herself, and no doubt imagined how she might, had things been otherwise, have been by now an ambassador, a minister, the editor of *The Times*. How could she not *now*, he thought, whatever happened about Crimond, be ready to bolt for freedom? Perhaps Crimond would prove to be a stepping-stone? Would it comfort him to think so? He groaned, feeling, smelling, as it came bubbling to the surface, all that old murderous jealousy and hate which had been packed away, a dangerous atomic capsule, submerged for so long in the darkest sea caverns of his mind. It had been easy *then*, in the *interim*, which had now, declared as such, begun already to be part of history, to reflect in a lofty way upon the unworthiness of jealousy, its senselessness and lack of substance. Within the last twelve hours an era had ended and could already be seen, alien and complete. Jealousy now was his teacher and in its light he saw the truth, that Jean really loved Crimond with an extreme love, a love as absolute at death, and in comparison with which her freedom was as nothing. She would, if he would have her, indeed be Crimond's slave; and in this context, in this picture, she had not exaggerated in speaking of the approach to him as something mortally dangerous. What a futile mess it had all been, all the striving of his life, everything he had done and hoped for. Now she was being given, and by Crimond himself, a second chance. For Duncan did not doubt for a moment that Crimond had come to the dance in order to appropriate her.

It had all started a long time ago. Jean denied (but how could he be sure, how could she be sure?) that she had loved Crimond then, when they were all young together, when Sinclair Curtland had been the one who had taken her to dances, when they had all been so hopeful and so free. Of course Crimond impressed her, he impressed them all, he perhaps even more than Gerard was the one of whom everything was expected. How little they had done, all of them, any of them, compared with the marvels which they had *then* hoped and intended! Crimond had failed too, at any rate had not yet succeeded. They had, at a certain period, all talked too much about Crimond, partly because he was the only one of their group who retained the extreme left-wing idealism which they had once shared. Something happened to them all when Sinclair was killed. He was the golden boy, the youngest, the pet, the jester, loved by Gerard who was (since Crimond somehow clearly was not) the 'leader'; only of course there was no leader since they were all such remarkable individuals and thought so well of themselves! After Sinclair died they seemed for a while to scatter, their opinions changed, they were busy with new careers, with travel, with searches for partners. Duncan and Robin lingered in Oxford for a while, but then came to London, Robin to University College Hospital, Duncan to the Foreign Office. Time passed, and Duncan married Jean and spoke to her of happiness, being so entirely happy himself at possessing this beautiful admired woman whom he had quietly adored during years when she was so much in the company of others. Crimond was becoming a well-known figure in left-wing politics, a respected, or notorious, theorist, a writer of 'controversial' books, a candidate for parliament. He was, and had since remained, the most famous member of their original set. Crimond came of, and boasted of, modest origins, born in a village in Galloway, son of a postman. He made sure that he was not to be regarded as a pampered cloistered intellectual. Jean, whose opinions were now perceptibly to the left of Duncan's, was for a time a declared supporter of Crimond and even became one of his research assistants. She wrote a pamphlet for him on the position of women in the Trade Unions. When he contested a parliamentary seat (unsuccessfully) she was secretary to his agent. Something must have started then, at that time when Crimond was so important, so well known, a star, the darling of the young. Later on, after the debacle, when she came back, she told Duncan that at that early period she had fought against her feelings, finally ran away from his proximity. She had said (but was this true?) that she was never then his mistress. Again times changed. Duncan had given up the academic world and was now in the diplomatic service, Robin (who later returned to London) was in America at Johns Hopkins University, Gerard was in the Treasury, Marcus Field (after his shocking conversion) was in a seminary, Jenkin was a school teacher in Wales, Rose was a journalist in York, living with her northern relations. Less was heard of Crimond, he was said to be 'calming down', becoming more reflective and less extreme, even considering an academic post.

Duncan had never entirely liked Crimond in those young days, he thought him conceited, and was irritated by his prestige with the others. He suppressed his dislike because he was a friend of his friends, and because Duncan was, even then, intuitively nervous of him. They were both Scottish, but Duncan's Highland ancestors had long ago taken the road to London. When Jean took to admiring Crimond and even working for him Duncan began to be quietly a little jealous, but without any undue alarm. He was glad when Crimond disappeared from London and was said to be in America, then in Australia. Time passed. Duncan was posted to Madrid, then to Geneva. After this he was sent, on a temporary posting, to Dublin, before proceeding (as he was promised) to a coveted and lofty position in eastern Europe. Jean was disappointed at being despatched to Ireland, which she regarded as a backwater, but she soon found Dublin quite amusing enough; in fact both Duncan and Jean rather fell in love with the country, and went as far as to buy a tower in County Wicklow. Property was still at that time remarkably inexpensive in Ireland, and the tower (brought to their attention by a writer friend called Dominic Moranty) was an 'impulse buy' of Jean's who discovered it, loved it, and thought she might as well buy it as it was so cheap. Duncan chided her, then when he saw what they had acquired, praised her. The tower, described in the prospectus as 'probably very old', made of old stones culled from some ruin or ruins, was, as various architectural features suggested, no doubt set up in the late nineteenth century. It had been at some point, perhaps in its original construction, attached by a rough stone and brick arched passage to a closely adjacent, indefinitely ancient, stone-built cottage or cabin. The wooden floors and cast-iron spiral staircase in the tower were sound, and both buildings had been sufficiently 'modernised'. There was no electricity (which delighted Jean), but there was good 'soak-away' sewage with a septic tank. A pump, easily repaired, brought water up from the old well in the cottage. The previous occupant, now deceased, said to have been a 'painter man', had used the tower at intervals until fairly recently and the interior, though primitive and now unfurnished, was in reasonable shape. There were fireplaces, turf for sale at an accessible village, and plenty of wood lying around for free. Jean envisaged a lamp-lit fire-lit life of elegant romantic simplicity, and set about looking for suitably rural furniture. The tower had a fine view of the two sugarloaf mountains and, from its upper room, the bedroom, a glimpse of the sea. Its living accommodation consisted of only two floors, but above those a round hollow crown rose to a suitably imposing height. Duncan was delighted with the place, and glad too that Jean should have this plaything to distract her attention from a proposed campaign in favour of contraception and abortion which had seemed likely to conflict with the niceties of their diplomatic position.

It was summertime, a dry warm Irish summer for once, and they took to spending their weekends at the tower, tinkering with its arrangements, sometimes travelling to buy furniture at local auctions. It was a happy time. The tower standing in its own miniature valley, now also their property, was surrounded by sheep-nibbled grass. There was a small stream and a grove of poplar trees, and a scattering of wild fuchsia and veronica. They had of course already done a good deal of pleasant rambling round the small beautiful country which they had hardly ever visited before, and Jean had already decided that they must write their own guide book to Ireland, all available guides being declared 'hopeless'. They had visited Joyce's tower and Yeats's tower. Now they too had a tower which Jean said should be called Duncan's tower. They were not however destined to enjoy Duncan's tower for long. At a dinner party, Crimond's name was suddenly mentioned. He was jocularly said to be 'coming over to solve the Irish question'. He was going to write some long piece about Ireland and was proposing to take up residence in Dublin for the rest of the summer. Duncan never forgot how, on receiving this news, his wife's face became positively contorted with pleasure.

Duncan was amazed at how miserable he was at once made by the idea of Crimond's presence in Dublin. He felt almost childishly that all his pleasures had been suddenly stolen and there were no treats any more. When, shortly afterwards, Crimond arrived, and settled himself in a flat in Upper Gardiner Street, Duncan put on a gallant, almost excessive, show of being delighted to see this old college pal. He introduced Crimond to all his favourite Irish people (including Moranty) and saw him warmly welcomed and instantly privileged as the dearest friend of already popular Duncan and Jean. Duncan had been finding his diplomatic post a difficult and taxing one. The ambassador was in hospital. He was virtually in charge. Relations between Dublin and London, never peaceful, were going through a particularly 'delicate' phase. The two prime ministers, plotting something (or planning an 'initiative' as these usually futile plots were euphemistically called), were under attack not only by opposition parties but by elements in their own parties. Duncan had to make visits to London. He was extremely busy and ought to have been thinking hard about what he was doing instead of having to think all the time about Crimond. Crimond had meanwhile moved to a flat in Dun Laoghaire, with a view of Dublin Bay, and had given a party to which he invited Jean and Duncan, and to which, Duncan being engaged, Jean went alone. He had already become an object of interest and seemed to be getting on very well with the Irish. His political views, in so far as those concerned Ireland, were declared to be 'sound'; and the smallness and gossipy closeness of intellectual Dublin made it impossible for Duncan not to hear his name frequently mentioned.

Duncan, playing his 'friendly' part, had of course invited Crimond to a small summer evening gathering at the tower. Crimond was delighted with the place, enthusiastic, full of a spontaneous boyish pleasure which Duncan could see being appreciated by the other guests. Jean was explaining about the furniture, about altering the kitchen, about planting things, not a 'garden' of course, that would be out of place, but a few shrubs perhaps, and laying down a bit of pavement. Crimond was full of ideas. Duncan overheard one of the guests inviting Crimond and Jean to visit a garden centre near his country cottage where you could get old paving stones, and statues – surely they needed statues, a statue anyway, to catch the eye and look mysterious among the poplar trees? Crimond held forth about statues. People became very drunk and laughed a lot. It seemed to Duncan that Crimond, who scarcely drank and was not very convivial by nature, was acting a part. The next day Duncan had to go to London. When he came back Jean told him that she and Crimond had visited the garden centre and ordered some paving-stones and bought some shrub roses and a lawn-mower. After that, during his absences, and sometimes not during his absences, Jean joined Crimond, in Crimond's hired car, for occasional jaunts to famous places. Once they went to Clonmacnoise, which Duncan had not yet seen, and came back rather late. Sometimes other people were (Jean said) with them, sometimes not. Jean and Crimond took over the idea of the guide book to Ireland. During this period Jean was in a state of great excitement and high spirits. Duncan observed her face continually, studying it with an almost morbid intentness, seeing in it the joy brought to her by another man, and also her attempt to conceal this joy.

Of course for the newcomer or tourist, Ireland is simply charming. But it is also an island, divided, angry, full of old demons and old hate. Duncan felt this burden every day in his work and increasingly as his sympathy and his knowledge grew. It soon emerged, and this too upset Duncan who was ready to be maddened by anything which Crimond did or was, that Crimond, although he had hardly ever been to Ireland, knew a great deal more about the island than Duncan did. Anyone who engages deeply with Ireland must engage deeply with its history. Crimond turned out to be crammed full of Irish history. Duncan found himself forced to listen to Crimond airing his views, to a gratified audience, about Parnell, Wolfe Tone, even Cuchulain. Nor did Duncan care to hear Crimond's republican political opinions ever more boldly on display, and his sneers at the British government, uttered in Duncan's company with what seemed a deliberately provocative lack of tact. Duncan declined to be provoked, he watched, he studied his wife's face; and listened quietly to her propounding Crimond's theories about Ireland.

Duncan, crippled by suspicion and hatred, made miserable by fear and by his detestation of his own abject and contemptible state of mind, was impelled to action by an accident, the sort of accident which often occurs in such situations. He had of course wondered what else Jean and Crimond did together besides jaunting around in the car and visiting ruined castles and garden centres. One Sunday morning when Duncan and Jean were spending the weekend at the tower, Jean had gone out early to pursue a plan she had evolved to dam the stream and make a pool or pond. Duncan was to come and help her after the breakfast which she would soon return to make. The sun was shining. Duncan stood at the window of their bedroom, the upper room of the tower, and looked out between the silky green flanks of the mountains at the glittering triangle of blue sea. The sky was cloudless, a lark was singing, a swallow was singing, the stream was murmuring. They still constantly said to each other when they were in bed: listen to the stream. He could see his wife below, her trousers rolled up, standing barefoot in the stream, bending down, then straightening up, then waving to him. There was all the paraphernalia of complete happiness, that happiness of which he so well knew himself to be capable: only he was in hell. He waved back. He turned into the room, blinking from the sunshine and the dazzle of the sea, and looked at the disordered bed where they had slept together. They had long ago stopped hoping for a child. They had been to doctors who had offered different useless explanations. Then he saw something at the side of the curving room, on the floor, a little thing or shadowy quasi-thing lying there upon the boards against the wall of dark slightly uneven stones. He went over to it and picked it up. It was light and pale and insubstantial. He closed it in his hand and his heart beat very fast and he sat down heavily on the low divan bed. He could feel the hot blood rush to his face and up to his brow. He opened his hand and held the little thing in his palm and examined it. It was a ball of what might have been dusty fluff, but was, he saw, human hair, reddish hair such as a person, a man, might draw off the teeth of a comb, after he had combed his hair, and idly let fall upon the floor. No one came to the tower to clean or dust or deliver goods or mend, no one had a key to the tower except him and Jean. This was not his or Jean's dark hair which he held in his hand, it was Crimond's red hair.

Jean called from below that breakfast was ready. Duncan put the hair ball into his pocket and went downstairs and listened smilingly to Jean's ideas about her pond. He ate a boiled egg and went out and helped her to move some stones and dig a hole and watched her delight as it filled with water. Later that morning he announced that he had to be in London for two days later that week. When the time came Jean drove him to the airport as usual. When she had left him he bought some sandwiches and hired a car and drove it by a roundabout route toward a place upon a hillside which he had already, studying the landscape, determined upon where there was a thicket of gorse and a fallen tree covered with ivy just upon the crest, and a clear view of the tower in the valley below. He parked the car and climbed the hill to his viewpoint and crept in behind the tree where the tall growth of ivy had woven a screen, and peered through the ivy leaves and through a hazy flowery gorse, shifting about until he could sit, leaning against the tree trunk, and see the tower and the bumpy track which led to it. He took his field glasses from their case and hung them round his neck and waited. He felt a hideous tormenting excitement. Nothing happened, no one came. The ivy was in flower and very many bees were walking and flying over the yellowish flowers with their spotty stamens. The dark powdery smell of the ivy mingled with the coconut smell of the gorse. By now it was afternoon. The sun shone, he took off his jacket, he sweated. His body was heavy and gross, he was short of breath and panting. Soon what he was doing became so loathsome to him that he had to get up and go away.

He drove the hired car south along the coast road as far as Wicklow and booked into a small hotel. The hotel had no bar or restaurant so he went into the pub next door and began drinking whiskey. He found the sandwiches which he had bought so long ago at the airport and ate one and drank some more whiskey. He took Crimond's hair out of his pocket and looked at it. Of course he had thought it possible that something serious was going on; vague speculation is life, positive proof is death. Well, he thought, postponing his certainty, I haven't *got* proof. Jean and Crimond could have gone up to that room just to look at the view of the sea. But Jean had never said she went to the tower with Crimond. He could not make up his mind whether or not to repeat his horrible vigil the next day. It might be better to go back to Dublin to their flat in Parnell Square. He did not imagine anything would be happening there. If those two were together it would surely be at Crimond's flat; except that his flat, at the top of a terrace house on the sea front, was far too public. No, if it was anywhere it must be at the tower. But why *bother*, he thought, as the evening grew darker and the bar fuller, why go trying to find trouble? We'll soon be somewhere else, it's just an episode, it happens to everyone. But he felt, I simply want to be *sure*, if they're doing that I *must* know – and then I can give up, let it slide, shut my eyes. Why should I let those two cripple me with grief? I won't say anything to Jean now. I'll just ignore it.

He began to feel self-consciously miserable and ill-used in a way which for a time brought consolation. He saw himself there, hunched up, a big dark man with a mat of dark crinkly hair and a big red glowering face, getting stupefyingly drunk among a lot of Irishmen (of course there were no women in the bar) who were all getting stupefyingly drunk too. He thought, *their* wives deceive them, there can be no doubt, and they are deceiving their wives, so what am I moaning about, we are all a lot of vile rotten stinking sinners, black as hell, liars and traitors and probably murderers too, who deserve to be exterminated like rats or burnt alive. And yet here we are, drinking together – what does it all matter – I've never deceived Jean, but haven't I sometimes wanted to? And perhaps now I will too, we'll each go our own way as they say. And as he heard the lilting coaxing Irish voices all round him he felt the soft flowing sounds getting inside his head and he began to think in Irish idioms and talk to himself in an Irish brogue. So why should I mind now if my darling wife is a bloody whore, why should I worry what that fellow does to her, or want to kill him for it, sure he's doing what we all do, vile beasts as we are, isn't it better to be sitting quiet and drinking, and isn't whiskey itself better than God? Men were sitting near him, beside him, jogging his arm and talking to him, and he talked to them too, and became distant and thoughtful at last and lurched back to the hotel and went to bed.

The next morning he woke up very early feeling like a sick dying animal. He had a pain in the stomach and a pain in the head and a dry shrivelled mouth and his whole body was heavy and aching and smelly and fat. Through the flimsy torn curtains cold daylight filled the window. He lay for a while almost whimpering with self-pity with his head under the bedclothes. Then he suddenly sat up and stood up, dressed without washing, paid his bill, found his car, and set off back northward. There was a cold white light at the sea horizon pressed down by a low ceiling of thick grey cloud. Curtains of rain could be seen descending ahead, yet from somewhere the sun managed occasionally to shine illuminating the grey wall of cloud and the vivid green hillsides and brightly coloured trees. Upon the farther mountains on his left segments of rainbow came and went. He drove very fast. He had a violent headache and a dark iron pain in his diaphragm, boiling particles and flashing lights skidded above the focus of his eyes as he frowned intently upon the flying road. His reflections of last night, his not sure, his why bother, his ignore it, his merciful cameraderie with other sinners, all that was gone. He felt himself, sitting upright in the car and dominating his body's wretchedness, as a black machine of will, a vindictive machine black with misery and rage, powered by one intention, to find and destroy. He no longer entertained any temperate delaying sense of uncertainty, no haze of doubt now gentled his mind. Uncertainty had been a restless torment, but certainty, clarity, was a hell fire from which, in which, one ran screaming. All this he thought and felt as he drove so urgently fast along the wet shining road with the frenzied windscreen wipers hurling aside the now persistent and increasing rain.

When he turned off the main road into the lanes which led toward the tower he began to feel faint and had to stop the car and lean his head upon the wheel. He thought he might be sick. He wondered if he would be able to go on. The rain was lighter now, more like a driving mist, the clouds were higher, the still invisible sun was making an intense greyish light in which the grass at the little field beside him shone violently green. He got out of the car and stood in the rainy air with his head bowed forward, breathing open-mouthed. He thought, I am mad, I have become temporarily insane and must somehow stop myself. He felt as if his hate, without ceasing to be hate, had been changed into pure fear. Too much could happen, terrible things could happen which could change his whole life, he could destroy the world, he had that power now, to destroy the world. He thought this, knowing that he could not now check the engine which was driving him on. He stood upright and saw nearby a stone wall, and a horse and a cow looking at him. The rain had stopped. The horse had come over to the wall. He thought he might eat a sandwich, he still had some left, he might go over and stroke the horse, that would be a sensible sort of delay, would it not, to stay quietly there with the horse and the cow. He got into the car and drove on. He said to himself, there will be no one there and I can drive on into Dublin and go to the flat and *rest*, and things will be ordinary and I shall be able to think quietly and without the pain. He tried to wonder whether to drive straight to the tower, but found himself driving along the lane which ran behind his hillcrest viewpoint. He stopped the car and got out and looked at his watch. It was just before nine o'clock. He began, panting and gasping with the effort, to climb up the steep wet grass slope toward the summit, leaning forward and grasping grass tufts and little bushes to haul himself upward. When he reached the top he did not attempt to hide, but stood there upright looking down into the valley. Crimond's car was on the track.

Duncan walked, slowly now and seeming to glide dreamlike

87

over the ground, down the hill toward the tower. It took him about ten minutes to reach it. He heard the birds singing and noticed some very small flowers growing in the grass. Everything was very wet and now shining in the sunlight. At the bottom of the slope some black-faced sheep stared at him with amazement and hurried away. He crossed the stream just above Jean's pool. As he moved he had a sudden clear vision or hallucination of Crimond naked, tall, pale, thin as a lance, slim as an Athenian boy, long-nosed and brilliant-eyed. The doors of the cottage and the tower were both open. There was no one in the kitchen. Duncan entered the tower and began to climb the spiral staircase. He climbed firmly, not in haste, not trying to mute his steps. The staircase led to a small landing, not directly into the bedroom. Duncan opened the bedroom door.

There was a flurry going on inside. Crimond was standing, not completely naked as Duncan had pictured him, but pulling a shirt over his head. Jean was on the bed, sitting on the far side of it, and had pulled the quilt up round her, looking back over her shoulder towards the door. Duncan remembered later that he had actually reflected for a second or two whether he should now stand and look at them and say something. During that second or two Crimond succeeded in getting his ·shirt on. The next moment Duncan launched himself forward, attacking like a large wild animal which propels its whole weight onto its victim to crush it. He hit Crimond with his whole body, knocking him backward and seizing him, clasping him in savage bear-like arms, feeling the thin crushable bones inside his clasp, dragging at the shirt, feeling the smoothness of Crimond's skin and the terrible warmth of his flesh. As he held on he kicked violently with his booted foot against the slim bare leg. Jean screamed. They reeled a moment, then Duncan felt a jabbing pain in his side where Crimond had freed one arm. For a moment he relaxed his grip, received Crimond's knee in his stomach, and staggered back into the open doorway, and they separated. Jean screamed again, 'Stop! Stop!' There was a second's interval. Then Duncan, now uttering whimpering cries of rage, launched himself again with clawing hands outstretched. Crimond stepped to meet him and with a long straight arm punched Duncan as hard as he could between the eyes. Duncan fell back and tumbled all the way down the spiral staircase into the room below.

This was the fight which had such long and dreadful consequences; and Duncan knew at once that the terrible thing that was to happen had happened to him. How he managed to fall, to roll his big thick body, all the way down those iron stairs he could not afterwards imagine. His head, his shoulders, his back, his legs, crashed against the rails, against the hard sharp edges of the treads, he struck the floor below with a violent echoing impact and lay for a moment stunned. But even as he lay there, even it seemed later as he was falling, he knew that whatever else might have been damaged, something frightful had happened to his eyes. The pain was extreme, but worse than the pain was the sense that both were injured, and one of the precious orbs actually crushed. He got up slowly, wondering if he had also broken a limb. The centre of his field of vision seemed to have disappeared and the periphery was full of grey bubbling atoms. He hobbled slowly, carefully, out of the door and across the level grass toward the hillside. He did not pause to wonder why no one followed him down to see if he was badly hurt. Jean told him later that Crimond had to keep her in the room by force. The door had slammed after him, perhaps no one heard him fall. Now he was anxious only to get away and reach a hospital as soon as possible. He crossed the stream walking through the water, he crawled up the hill clutching the wet grass. Then with intense concentration he drove himself back to Dublin.

He went first to the Rotunda Hospital, who sent him on to an eye clinic. Once there, and sitting down on a chair, he became for a short period almost completely blind. He was led about by porters, by nurses, answered questions, lay flat while drops were put into the eyes, bright lights shone upon them, machines lowered over them. He was told that normal vision would probably return to one eye, the other would need an operation. Meanwhile, since he was certainly suffering from concussion, he had better go home and rest. Pushed out of the door clutching a card telling him when to return, Duncan found he could see enough to walk back to his flat in Parnell Square. Before he reached it he had come to an important conclusion. *Nobody must know what had happened.* He had of course told the doctors simply about a fall. Now it was essential to conceal, if possible, both his mutilated condition, and the shame of his defeat. That meant, and at once, leaving Dublin where everybody found out everything. He passionately did not want to see Jean and was relieved that there was no sign of her. He was wondering whether he would ever be able to read again, to work again. His world had changed indeed; he had changed it himself, by force. He telephoned the embassy to arrange his absence, he summoned a taxi and went to the airport. He wore dark glasses to conceal his bruises. He remembered that the hired car was still parked in a road near the Rotunda. He posted the keys to his secretary, Miss Paget, asking her to return the car. He caught a plane to London and a taxi to Moorfields Eye Hospital. It had been a long day.

Their house in London, then in Putney, was let, so Duncan stayed at a hotel. He sent a note to Jean simply giving the address of his club. He was busy with his physical condition, attending University College Hospital for head tests. He tried not to think about Jean's reply. An irritating evasive one arrived saying, 'Why have you run away?' A little later, after his second eye operation, she sent another note saying that she was living with Crimond. This news was confirmed by a letter from Dominic Moranty which said it was 'all over Dublin'. Moranty expressed a sympathy which Duncan could have done without, and indignation that 'everyone' was blaming Duncan for having brought it about by his insane jealousy. Duncan was not surprised that gossip sided with the lovers; and was relieved that Moranty's tactless missive omitted the point which would surely have been of the greatest interest if known. A little after this Duncan sent his official letter of resignation to the Foreign Office. He wrote telling Jean that he had resigned and was staying in London. He added, without complaints or endearments, 'I suggest you return to me.' After a little while Jean wrote that she was sorry he had resigned, that she was staying in Dublin, and would follow his instructions about the flat, the car and 'the property' (she did not say 'the tower'). A PS said, *I am very sorry*. Duncan asked his solicitor to acknowledge the letter.

As Duncan saw it later, he was enabled to go coldly on with this hideous business because he had another engrossing mortal anxiety, another job to do, 'going to work' at Moorfields. He wondered, later, if he should have screamed, accused and begged, at any rate by letter; he could not, in his present state, have presented himself in person. Later he bitterly regretted not having tried, somehow, intelligently, passionately, to get his wife back. Vindictive hatred of Crimond, Crimond whom he regarded practically as a murderer, had made him icy cold to Jean. Had he been able to think simply, whole-heartedly, about her he could have written tear-stained pages. As it was, in his imagination and in his dreams, Crimond stood between them, as thin as a lance, as tall as a *kouros*, pale and glimmering. Meanwhile however his 'work' had been going unexpectedly well, all was by no means lost. His right eye gradually regained normal vision, and his left eye, though oddly 'stained', regained enough sight to help its colleague. He had worn glasses before, and now with perceptibly thicker lenses was able to envisage, and then attain, a return to an ordinary life of walking and reading. The situation was even likely to improve further, and he might expect to be able to drive a car again. 'You don't just see with your eyes, you see with your brain,' his cheerful doctor told him, 'and it's amazing what ingenious adjustments *it* can make!' The same doctor assured him that his 'funny eye', certainly noticeable, looked 'fascinating', even 'positively attractive'.

During this ordeal Duncan had become mortally tired. He had enacted being blind, experienced being unable to read. He had felt the cold shadow of death, being determined if he did not regain the power to read, to kill himself. Now as he gradually recovered from one horror he was seized by the other. His spirit regained, with its strength, its capacity for a different suffering. He re-enacted again and again his walk to the tower, the bedroom scene, Crimond with his shirt, Jean looking over her shoulder, the blow, the fall. He dreamt about Crimond. He did not dream about Jean, except perhaps as a black muddy lump or black ball which figured in many dreams. Day and night he desired her, longed for her presence, fancied her return, reconciliation, happiness. Remorse tormented him and he imagined innumerable ways in which it all need not have happened. He ought to have spoken frankly to Jean instead of spying on her, he ought to have admonished her and warned her, he ought to have protected and looked after his wife instead of becoming her enemy. He ought not to have resigned his job, he ought to have stayed in Dublin and faced it all out there, eyes and all. She had accused him of running away. He had shirked an ordeal which might have won her sympathy, he had too hastily embraced defeat instead of standing out for victory. Now it was too late – or was it? He was paralysed by hatred of Crimond – or was it fear?

Duncan had taken care not to announce his return to any of his friends. At that time Gerard, Jenkin and Rose were all in London, Gerard in the Civil Service, Jenkin teaching in a polytechnic, Rose working for a magazine. The news of course got round quickly enough that Duncan had resigned from the service, then that his marriage was in trouble, then that the third party was David Crimond. Gerard, the first to hear from a friend in the Foreign Office, rang up Jenkin, then Rose, neither of whom knew anything. Rose said she had thought it odd that she had not had a reply to a letter she had written to Jean, for they kept up a frequent correspondence. Gerard, who kept up more intermittent communication with Duncan, also now noted that he had not heard. Jenkin hardly ever wrote to anyone. Gerard took it on himself to check the now more numerous sources of information and concluded that what was rumoured was true. It was obviously not a situation for telephone calls. They were in any case not used to chatting by telephone. Gerard said they must do something, make some gesture. After writing it out carefully in several different drafts he despatched an immensely tactful letter to Duncan in Dublin where he thought (not having imagined so prompt a departure) that his friend still was. Rose wrote a letter, also tactful, but very brief and quite unlike Gerard's to Jean. Both letters 'said nothing', only indicated they had heard something and were feeling upset and sympathetic. Jenkin sent a postcard to Duncan saying: *Be well. Love, Jenkin.* He chose the card with care (it was a peaceful landscape by Samuel Palmer) and enclosed it in an envelope. These missives in due course found their way back to Duncan's London club where he regularly picked up mail, wondering when he would hear again from Jean. Rose, Gerard and Jenkin were meanwhile constantly in touch, and met to discuss the situation at Gerard's house in Notting Hill. (By this period, Robin Topglass was married and gone to Canada.) They were unanimous in being inclined to blame Crimond. They then started to compare notes about him, repeating that they must not be influenced by their distaste for his politics. They concluded that his extremist militant socialism must show something about his personality, that he was a 'fey', unpredictable person. They agreed that though they had liked and esteemed him at Oxford, they had never really got to know him. They were genuinely worried about Jean and Duncan, but speculation was inevitably interesting. These conversations (during which they constantly said, 'Of course we don't know the facts!') were inconclusive, but from them dated Rose's positive dislike of Crimond which became important later on. Meanwhile no one seemed to know where Duncan was.

Later, after the welcome verdict from Moorfields, when Duncan, who had heard nothing more from Jean and had not written to her either, was more positively attempting to put his life in order, he found himself bitterly regretting that he was now left without a job. At this point, not because of this regret but because he felt that the time had come, he at last wrote a note to Gerard, simply giving his address and asking him round for a drink. By now Duncan had given up hotels and had rented a small flat in Chelsea where he had been leading a crazy solitary incognito existence. What passed at this meeting was never later on divulged by either of them. In a way, little passed, but the meeting itself was momentous. Duncan gave Gerard a brief general account of what had happened, omitting the drama at the tower. According to this account, Duncan, having gradually realised that Jean was in love with Crimond and that they were probably lovers, had come into possession of evidence (he did not say what evidence and Gerard did not ask) that they actually were lovers, and had soon after been told by Jean that she proposed to leave him. Since then, apart from a letter confirming that she was living with Crimond and had no intention of coming back, he had heard nothing. Gerard naturally wanted to know a good deal more, but naturally did not press for it. The occasion was also important for Duncan because he was able to 'try out' his damaged eye upon an important witness. In fact Gerard failed to notice the odd eye, and had to have his attention drawn to it by Duncan's reference to 'some eye trouble'. They got a bit drunk together and remembered, though they did not mention, the time when they had been lovers after Sinclair died. Gerard, without audibly bemoaning Duncan's hasty resignation, which he could not see to be necessary, raised the question of a job. Teaching? No. Politics? Certainly not. Why not the Home Civil Service? Duncan, after indicating that he was 'done for', 'fit for the dole queue' and so on, agreed that this was not a bad idea, transfers from the diplomatic field to Whitehall did occur, and although he had so abruptly 'cut the painter' a sympathetic view might be taken. A short time after this he entered the Civil Service, not in the department which he would have chosen, but in a quite sufficiently promising and interesting post.

The fight in the tower had taken place in June. After Duncan had acquired his new job he had sent a letter to Jean saying that he loved her and hoped she would return. This was in August. He received no answer. He was still getting occasional letters from Dominic Moranty confirming that Jean and Crimond were together and becoming accepted as an established couple. Duncan now had even more time and energy to be miserable. He was still attending the eye hospital but the original terrible fears for his eyesight were over, and he had also stopped imagining that he was 'done for'. He had dissuaded Rose and Gerard from, admittedly vague, plans for 'doing something about it' (going to Dublin, remonstrating with Jean, denouncing Crimond and so on). He settled down to despair. For the time, friends and acquaintances thronged round him, a deceived and abandoned man is always popular, satisfying to contemplate. He was grateful to Gerard and Rose and Jenkin, who genuinely cared. But he wanted, so much more than the diversions which they invented for him, to sit alone with his own misery, his grief, his loss, even his jealousy, his obsessional images of Crimond, his remorse and regret, his sick yearning for his dear wife. He wanted to make terms with his unhappiness, to go over and over the terrible past, running through every 'if only . . .', until he had exhausted all these things and been exhausted by them.

Then suddenly, in November, Jean came back. It was a cold evening, a little snow was falling. Duncan was sitting as usual, with a whisky bottle and book, beside the gas fire in his little flat. The bell rang. It was late, he did not expect visitors. He went down some stairs, turned on a light, opened the front door. It was Jean. Duncan turned at once and began to go back up the stairs to the open door of his flat. He could still remember, later, the feeling of the banisters as he hauled himself up. He had put on weight, he was tired, he was a little drunk. He heard the front door close and Jean's steps behind him. She followed him into the flat and into the sitting room closing the doors. She was wearing a black raincoat and dark green mackintosh hat, both lightly spotted with snow. She took off the hat, looked at it, brushed off the snowflakes and dropped it. Then she let the coat slide off backwards onto the floor. She uttered a little whimpering sigh, looked quickly at Duncan, then turned her head sideways and plucked at the neck of her dress. Duncan, who had retreated to the fireside, stood with his hands in his pockets gazing at her with a calm faintly inquisitive look which did not at all express his feelings. He had felt of course, as soon as he saw her, certain that she was really and truly coming back to him. This was no conference under a flag of truce, it was surrender. A golden light shone before his eyes and an explosive dilation of his heart stretched his breast to bursting. He was ready to cry with tenderness, to faint with joy; but what steadied him and dictated the charade, upon which he later looked back with satisfaction, was a sense of *triumph*. It was a delectable and well-earned reward. He felt too a release of anger as if *now* he could shake her, beat her. Just for these sustained seconds she was at his mercy. This was the unworthy thought which made him able to seem so calm and unmoved. Jean too, before his eyes, went through some steadying hardening transition. Perhaps she had hoped for an instant welcome and to allow her tears to flow. There had been some beseeching in her first glance. Now she frowned, smoothed down her hair, turned to him again and said, 'I expect you want me to make a statement.'

Duncan said nothing.

'Well, briefly, I've left Crimond, that's over, and I'd like to come back to you, if you'd like that. If not I'll go away, now, and we can arrange a divorce or anything that suits you.'

Jean's face was still red from the cold and the sudden warmth of the room, and her chin was wet where the snowflakes had got at it under her hat. She looked down at her raincoat on the floor, and evidently realising that it had been a mistake to take it off since she might be leaving directly, picked it up and began putting it on again.

Duncan had by now controlled himself for so long that he found it positively awkward to set about expressing his feelings, and felt silenced by realising that he had a choice of words. Then, watching her, he said spontaneously, 'What are you doing with that coat? Put it down.'

Jean dropped the coat and Duncan stepped forward and took her in his arms.

Thus ended the first episode of Jean and Crimond and thus began the renewed marital happiness of Jean and Duncan which lasted over many years until the occasion of the summer dance which has been described.

The problem about the book was really a quite separate matter which can be more briefly explained. It was separate, and yet it somehow increasingly wove itself into the fates of the friends, in and out as the years went by, and became, at least emotionally, connected with Crimond's behaviour to Jean and Duncan. It all started long ago, when Sinclair was alive, and it was, as they all later recognised, deeply affected by, as it were, Sinclair's hand protectively outstretched above the contentious volume.

When they were all still young, in their twenties, when Gerard and Sinclair were living together and founding and editing their short-lived left-wing magazine, they saw a good deal of Crimond. Crimond, not at that time well known, was splashing about in politics and had just been expelled from the Communist Party for left-wing deviation. He was living in Bermondsey in what he called 'a rooming house' and being conspicuously penniless and crammed with revolutionary virtues. They were all to varying degrees left-wing. Robin was, though not for long, also in the Communist Party, Sinclair declared himself a Trotskyist, Duncan and Jenkin were radical Labour supporters, Gerard was what Sinclair described as a 'William Morris Merry England Socialist'. Rose (then a pacifist), and Jean, had just left the university. Long exciting sometimes acrimonious political arguments went on at Crimond's place or at Gerard and Sinclair's flat, or at 'reading parties' at the Curtland parents' house in the country. Sinclair was very fond of Crimond, though not in any degree or way which could cause Gerard any jealousy. They were all free and generous and unjealous in their affections, in the style approved of by Levquist, and they noticed this too and felt pleased with themselves. They were all fond of Crimond, though he was even then the person least closely involved in the group. They also, and this was important, admired and respected him because he was more politically active, more dedicated, and more ascetic than they were. He was also more politically educated, and apt to assemble his ideas into theories. (He had been a very able philosophy student.) He began to write the pamphlets for which he was later renowned.

He lived very frugally upon occasional journalism and savings made from his student grant at Oxford, he had not, and did not seek, a job. He travelled little except for regular visits to Dumfries to see his father. He was known to be good at 'living on nothing', he did not drink, and had worn the same clothes ever since his friends could remember. He liked living with very poor people.

About this time, during the exciting political arguments, Crimond spoke of a long quasi-philosophical book which he intended to write, and whose agenda he sometimes, at their insistence, enlarged upon to Gerard and the company. By now Crimond's savings were beginning to run out and (as he told Gerard when closely questioned) he was proposing to take a part-time job; any job, he said, so long as it was unskilled. Clearly it was no good trying to persuade Crimond to 'join the establishment' by becoming an academic or an administrator. Gerard had a poorly paid job with the Fabian Society, but Rose and Sinclair had 'money of their own', and Jean, whose father was a banker, was rich. Crimond's situation was discussed, and it was deemed a pity that he should have to spend time on other work when he ought to be thinking and writing. 'He ought to write that book!' Sinclair said, and added only half in jest, 'I feel it is the book which the age requires!' It was also Sinclair who suggested that they should all join together and contribute on a regular basis to enable Crimond to devote himself to full-time intellectual work. 'After all,' said Sinclair, 'writers have often been supported by their friends, what about Rilke living in those castles, and the *Musilgesellschaft* which supported Musil?' It seemed probable that some such project was then actually communicated to Crimond and contemptuously rejected, at any rate nothing happened. The idea persisted however of what Sinclair referred to as the *Crimondgesellschaft*, later known among them simply as the *Gesellschaft*.

Time passed. Sinclair was dead. Crimond had joined the Labour Party. He was becoming a popular figure on the far left, and was respectfully agreed to be an important intellectual. He became a parliamentary candidate. Duncan was in

London (after Geneva and before Madrid) and Jean was working (unpaid of course) as Crimond's research assistant. Gerard and Rose had not forgotten Sinclair's imagined *Gesellschaft* and, as it later appeared, Rose preserved the notion that this enabling of Crimond would constitute a sort of memorial to Sinclair who had so much admired him. The fact that Crimond had remained on the extreme left, while the others now held more moderate opinions, was not of course taken to matter. In a way, as Gerard and Jenkin agreed, they all felt a bit guilty before Crimond, that is before his ascetism and his absolute commitment. After the election (it was a hopeless seat, he did not expect to be elected) Gerard, prompted by Rose, questioned Crimond again about the book which he once said he would write. Jean and Duncan were by now in Madrid. Crimond, who had moved into larger no less shabby quarters in Camberwell, said he was about to start writing it. He also mentioned (in answer to questions) that he had taken a part-time job as an assistant in a left-wing bookshop. Gerard consulted the others, Rose, Jenkin, Duncan and Jean. He also consulted his father, and Jean consulted hers. A sort of informal document, not of course a legal instrument, was drawn up describing the proposed *Gesellschaft* as a group of supporters who would contribute appropriate sums of money annually in order to give Crimond enough free time to write his book. Matthew, Gerard's father, joined in because he had been an ardent socialist when young and felt ashamed of being bored by politics now. Jean's father, Joel Kowitz, who was to make the largest contribution, joined because he adored Jean and did everything that she asked. The next question was, would Crimond accept the money; there was disagreement, even bets, about the likelihood of this. Gerard, in some anxiety, invited Crimond round, explained the plan and presented the document. Crimond immediately said no, then said that he would think about it. More time passed. Finally Crimond, pressed by Gerard and then by Jenkin, agreed.

So the *Crimondgesellschaft* came into being. Of course no time-limit was mentioned. The committee, consisting of these members (only Joel never turned up), was to decide whether contributions should be increased (in pace with inflation) or adjusted (in relation to contributors' circumstances). A kind of silence then ensued. The benefactors did not like to ask questions about the book in case they might seem to be anxious about their investment, and Crimond, after suitable initial gratitude, provided no reports or acknowledgements. In fact, as they ruefully noticed, he promptly and almost completely broke off relations with his 'supporters', and was only by hearsay known to be travelling in America. (It's only to be expected,' said Jenkin understandingly.) There followed in due course, and not very long after, the drama in Ireland and its sequel, which has been recounted, which caused them all, especially Rose, a good deal of distress, and even anger against Crimond. After this, and after Jean's return to Duncan, friendship, even communication, with the offender seemed for a time no longer possible, although of course the monies in aid of the book, maintained at a generous level, continued to be paid as promised. Rose uttered feelings which the others hesitated to express in saying that Crimond ought not now to accept their help. But of course, as they all more soberly agreed, it was necessary to separate their ruffled feelings from their promise, and from the particular interest which had prompted it, an interest which referred back to Sinclair's original idea, and even further to Sinclair's affection for Crimond.

Loyalty to Jean and Duncan seemed for some while to preclude any communication with Crimond, but as time went on it seemed to Gerard absurd to make such a point of ignoring him. Gerard was incapable of 'cutting' someone he knew, had in this instance known so long; as one grows older the *fact* of having known someone 'all one's life' becomes more important. In any case he was interested in Crimond and reluctant to lose touch with so unusual a man. So it was that Gerard did infrequently see the miscreant, ostensibly to ask about the book, though this subject was rarely raised and never pursued. Jenkin too, said disapprovingly by Rose to be 'soft' in this respect, saw Crimond now and then, coming across him in a more natural and ordinary way in political contexts, Jenkin, unlike Gerard and Duncan, having remained a member of the Labour Party. Crimond was still a member too, though threatened with expulsion and eventually expelled. This second expulsion, which caused a stir and even a serious row in the party, was said to have pleased Crimond very much, even completed some sort of proof of the soundness of his ideas. He declared, in a speech unintelligible to his young audience who had never read Kipling, that now, like Mowgli, he would 'hunt alone in the forest'. If he expected cries of 'And we will hunt with thee', they did not come; there were however numerous gratifying expressions of sympathy in many quarters. Crimond continued to be politically active and audible, speaking at meetings, writing articles and publishing *ad hoc* pamphlets. He was increasingly said, however, to have 'missed the bus'. He would never, with his extreme views, get into parliament, he was not regarded as an academic, he had no coherent intellectual position, and was also criticised for lacking any effective day-to-day connection with the *praxis* of the working-class movement. He had (it was said) no status except as a phenomenon, and his following of disaffected young people was not large enough to be dangerous. He appeared, indeed, as a lonely revolutionary hunter: a view which, on later estimates, did him less than justice.

Years passed during which Crimond continued to receive a salary which set him free to indulge in political activity which his 'supporters' increasingly disapproved of, and to write, or pretend to write, a book which, if it ever appeared, must exert a dangerous and pernicious influence. It became more difficult to feel that this was simply a matter of keeping a promise, and began to be thought of as a ridiculous, irrational, intolerable situation about which *something must be done*. This was the state of indecision which Crimond's second abduction of Jean Cambus seemed likely to bring to a head.

At about the time when Gerard was asleep at the kitchen table at the house in Notting Hill, and Duncan, in Kensington, was dropping Jean's slippers into a wastepaper basket, Tamar Hernshaw, in Acton, was sitting in a state of appalled misery facing her mother Violet. The flat was small and extremely dirty. Violet's bedroom, where the bed was never made, was full of the plastic bags which she compulsively collected. They were sitting in the kitchen. The floor was littered with newspapers, the table was covered with used plates, milk bottles, sauce bottles, pots of mustard, pots of jam, crusts of bread, bits of old cheese, a squeeze of butter in a greasy paper, a pot of tea, now cold, made for Tamar, who had not touched it. The discussion, which had been going on now for some time, had begun to repeat itself.

'I can't get a job,' said Violet, 'you *know* I can't get a job!'

'Couldn't you –?'

'Couldn't I what? I can't do anything! Even if I could get a part-time job as a waitress – we need big money, not scraps of what I could earn by killing myself slaving! You keep telling me I'm not young –'

'I don't, I just said –'

'*Everything's* gone up! You live in a dream world where you don't think about money. All right, it's my fault, I wanted you to have a good education –'

'I know, I *know*, I'm grateful –'

'Well now's the time to show it. Everything's gone up, rates, taxes, food, clothes, the mortgage – God, the *mortgage*, you don't even know what that is! We can't afford the telephone, I'm having it disconnected. And feeding you as a vegetarian costs the earth. You drift along as if everything will always be ordered to suit *you*! But I'm in debt, I'm seriously in debt, if we don't do something drastic we'll lose the flat.'

'I've got a grant,' said Tamar, restraining tears, for she was beginning to see that the situation was hopeless. 'And you know I can live on practically nothing – I don't need any clothes and –'

'You'll get anorexia again if you aren't careful, it isn't fair to you –'

'I can judge what's fair to me!'

'No, you can't. You've had good years at the university enjoying yourself –'

'Can't we borrow from Gerard – or from Pat and Gideon –'

'I'm not going to go crawling to them, and I'll never forgive you if you do! Haven't you any pride, any respect for *me*? And what's the use of getting even more into debt?'

'Or I could borrow from Jean –'

'From *her*? Never! I detest that woman – Oh I know she's your idol, you wish she was your mother!'

'Look,' said Tamar, though she knew this was even more out of the question, 'they're *rich*, Gideon is anyway, and Jean is, they'd *give* us the money.'

'Tamar, don't make me sick! You don't imagine I like telling you all this – I hoped I wouldn't have to. Please try to face *reality*, and help me to face it!'

'I *can't* give up Oxford now, I *must* do my final exams or the whole thing's thrown away – it's now or never –'

'You've got a funny idea of education if all you care about is a bit of paper to say you've passed an exam! You must have learnt something in two years, surely that'll do you, anyway it'll have to!'

'But I want to go on – if I get a first I can get another grant to stay on and do a doctorate – I want to *really* study, I want to be a scholar, I want to write, I want to teach – I *must* keep going now – later on is no good.'

'So you want to be Doctor Hernshaw, that's it, is it?'

'I won't cost you anything –'

'You're costing me something all the time by not earning! That money Uncle Matthew gave us has all gone –'

'I thought it was invested.'

'Invested! We can't afford investments! I've had to spend it – to buy your expensive books and that ball dress – *and* now you've lost your coat and that grand shawl someone gave you –'

'Gerard gave it to me –'

'And you lost your partner, can't you get anything right? At least now you can sell all those books – Don't look like that, and don't say I'm trying to ruin your life because I ruined my own, I know you're thinking that. I know *they've* said it to you –'

'No –!'

'Well, they will now.'

'It's only a year to wait, can't we wait? I must do my exams –'

'You can pick it up later, you could go on studying at evening classes, lots of people do that. They say it's better to be a mature student anyway.'

'Oxford doesn't work like that, you can't just drop in and out, you have to keep straight on, it's *very* difficult to be there at all and the exams are *very* difficult, you have to keep on studying ever so hard, I *can't* leave now, it would spoil *everything*, I'm *ready* now, I've been working very hard, *I've got it all in me* – my tutor told me –'

'You mean you'll forget all those facts? You can mug them up again. You'll do better after you've been out in the real world, you'll probably see it's a waste of time anyway. You're just infatuated with Oxford, you think it's all so impressive and grand – but what has university education done for that lot, Gerard and his precious friends, except make them into prigs and snobs and cut them off from ordinary life and real people? Don't you realise that *you* are becoming a snob?'

'If I go on and get that degree I'll be able to get a better paid job and earn more money –'

'Tamar, you haven't understood, you haven't been *listening*. I can't afford to keep you any more. I can't afford to keep anything any more. I *owe money*, if I don't pay it I'll be in a law court. I can't earn it. You must. It's as simple as that.'

They sat silently looking at each other across the table. Tamar had hastily taken off her ball dress and was now barefoot in a shirt and jeans. The two women, for Tamar though she seemed so childish was indeed a woman, presented a marked contrast. They were so unlike that it might have been imagined that Tamar sprang, like Athena, out of her father's head without female assistance: her vanished unknown father who did not know that she existed, and about whom, especially when she lay awake at night, she so often and so ardently thought. She was exceedingly thin and had suffered from anorexia nervosa when she was sixteen. The thinness of her face enhanced her eyes which were large and mournful and wild like those of a savage child, both fierce and frightened, and were of the greenish-brownish colour known as hazel. Her thin silky hair which was straight and cut to the earlobe and parted at the side was of a matching brown colour, not exactly mousy, a sort of dulled yet lively woody brown with intimations of green, the colour of trunks of trees, of ash trees or cherry trees or old birch trees. Her legs were long and thin and being shapely could be called slender. Her neck was thin, her nose was short, her hands and feet were small. Of her youthful breasts, small and exceedingly round, she thought little, though a few discerning persons had thought much. Her complexion was pale and clear, her cheeks flushing faintly, her eye lids delicate as if transparent, as was her neck.

Violet was in more obvious ways handsome and was, as Rose Curtland had remarked, still an attractive woman, which was not very surprising as she was not much over forty. She was taller than her daughter with a fuller finer figure, she wore her chestnut hair (now discreetly tinted) in a fringe, her eyes were markedly blue. She was short-sighted, and when she put on (as rarely as possible) her big round spectacles she could look clever and slightly stern, like a shrewd bossy office woman. Her beautifully shaped mouth, which could also look stern, a stern rose-bud, had lately begun to droop a little. The expression which in Tamar's face was sad, was in her mother's more positively resentful, even bellicose. As they now tensely stared at each other the similarity between them was, in their fierce concentrated expressions which mingled guilt and fear and old familiar misery, at its most evident. Violet had plenty to be bellicose about. She had been dealt a rotten hand by fate, or, to use an even more painful image, had stupidly thrown away such good cards as she had. As an illegitimate child with a feckless drug-addicted rarely visible father, she certainly had a bad start. Her mother had resented her existence. Violet, well aware of the baleful repetition, resented Tamar's existence. An important difference was that whereas Violet and her mother had quarrelled endlessly and bitterly, Tamar and Violet did not quarrel much. This was, Violet knew, no credit to her but was largely because Tamar was, to her mother, a 'bit of an angel'. This angelicness was at times a consolation, but more often a source of guilt which increased Violet's sense of being ill done by.

She had left school at sixteen to get away from her mother. She lost touch with her mother and was pleased to learn later that she was dead. After her father's death his family made serious attempts to help her, but she kept aloof from them. She worked as a maid in a hotel, saved up and did a typing course, worked as a typist. When she was twenty she was beautiful and had various unsatisfactory lovers. At this stage she made some serious mistakes. She rejected someone whom she should have seen as a promising suitor. Perhaps, she thought later, she was simply not in love, and was still too young to realise that a solitary penniless girl cannot afford the luxury of marriage for love. Her most lasting mistake was of course Tamar and the wandering Scand. As Violet had frequently explained to Tamar, she would have been promptly 'got rid of' if her mother had had, at the crucial time, enough money to arrange it. This was in the old days when such abortions were illegal, secret and expensive, and there was no respected 'right to choose'. Violet was not able to choose and Tamar was unchosen and often made to feel so. The story ran that Violet, not even willing to think of a name for the unwelcome brat, let her be christened at the registry office by the registrar, a lay preacher who suggested 'Tamar' and his secretary, who offered her own name, 'Marjorie'. Tamar received a decent school education at the expense of the state and proved to be clever and very industrious. Violet was pleased when she went to Oxford, but was envious, and jealous too when Tamar began to know some men and could be presumed to have lovers. Violet was also able to value her daughter's docility, her desire to please, her quiet acceptance of a very limited way of life. Several sums of money had been, secretly, accepted from Uncle Matthew, but money offered by Gerard and Patricia was rejected with scorn. Tamar was allowed to accept Christmas presents however, and the cashmere shawl, from Gerard, was one of these.

'I could get a job in the long vacation,' said Tamar.

'Sorting letters in a post office? No! You must work properly, you must get us out of debt, you must *keep* us out of debt, you must *settle down* to being the breadwinner from now on!'

'Can't we just *wait* —'

'No, we can't! *I've done enough for you!*' said Violet, voicing the thought at which Tamar was arriving. They looked at each other for a second with faces made similar by misery and anger.

Tamar smoothed her face. She knew it was no use trying to explain to her mother the difference between a university education and being a mature student going to evening classes. It was *now* that the precious gift must be seized. She had already learnt so much, more than she had ever dreamt herself capable of, and that was just the beginning of the *metamorphosis* which was now to be so brutally cut off. She saw that the loss was terrible, no less than the loss of her whole life, the instant substitution of some sort of tenth-rate life for the one to which she had looked forward, to which she felt she had a *right*. Restraining her tears she tried to take in that there was no alternative to surrender. She knew how little money there was, and she believed what Violet said.

The telephone rang. Violet left the room. From where she sat Tamar began spiritlessly piling the dirty plates together on the stained cloth and assembling the jars and pots which never left the awful table into an orderly group. She entertained for a second only the traditional thought, which lived between them like a folk idea, that her mother had ruined her own life and was intent on ruining her daughter's. Tamar had early understood the huge dark mass of her mother's bitterness, she had seen how it was possible to expend all one's spirit, all one's life-energy, in resentment, remorse, anger and hatred. She could picture (for she heard enough about it) her mother's relation with her mother, and felt even as a child, not only the automatic force of her mother's desire to 'get her own back', but also in her own heart a dark atom of that responding bitter anger. She had seen how a life can be ruined and had *decided* that she would not ruin her own in such a game of repetition. It might be said that, recognising a choice between becoming a demon and becoming a saint she had chosen the latter. She saw that her safety lay, not in calculated hostility or intelligent self-regarding warfare, but in some genuine surrender of self. This was her 'angelic' gamble, which so irritated Violet who thought she 'saw through' it, and which led Gerard to regard Tamar as a virgin priestess. A habit of docility and never answering back had not been too hard to acquire. Only now did poor Tamar begin to see how agonisingly painful and (it must be seen) irreparably damaging surrender of self could be.

Violet returned to the kitchen. 'Uncle Matthew has passed away.'

'Oh – I'm so sorry,' said Tamar, 'Oh *dear* – I wish I'd gone to see him – I wanted to – only you wouldn't let me –' She began to cry, not the storm of tears which must soon begin, but sad unhappy guilty special tears for Uncle Matthew who had so shyly and so kindly wanted to be her friend, and whom she had so rarely visited because her mother did not want her to be beholden to Ben's family.

'And if you're wondering,' said Violet, 'whether he's left us anything in his will, let me tell you he hasn't.'

Matthew Hernshaw had failed to carry out his intention to 'do something' for Violet and Tamar because of an indecision which was characteristic of him. He could not make up his mind how much to leave them, knowing that if he did not leave them enough Gerard would disapprove and if he left them too much Patricia would be annoyed. What he did firmly intend to do was to leave a letter, addressed to both his children, asking them to look after Ben's granddaughter. He several times began to draft his letter but could not decide exactly what he wanted to say. This unformulated request was what he attempted unsuccessfully to communicate to Patricia when he was dying. Oh if only he had spoken sooner! That was Matthew's last thought.

Tamar, who had not been wondering about Uncle Matthew's will, replied, 'He'll expect Gerard and Pat to help us.'

'Pat will decide,' said Violet. 'She'll send us a cheque for fifty pounds. We don't want their mean charity! What Gerard might be able to manage is to find you a job – that's it, he'll fix you up, that's the least he can do! So that's settled! It is – settled – isn't it?'

Violet was gazing at Tamar with a tense beseeching stare, ready to dissolve into joy or into anger. Tamar, looking at the jam jars and mustard pots, could picture her mother's face. She bowed her head and the storm of tears began. Violet, beginning to cry too, came round the table, moved a chair up beside her child, and hugged her with gratitude and relief.

At about the time when Violet and Tamar were crying in each other's arms, and Gerard, who had stopped crying, was lying on his bed and thinking about his father and about Grey, and Duncan was lying on *his* bed and trying to cry and not succeeding, Jean Kowitz, faint with an inextricable pain of joy and fear, had reached the house south of the river where Crimond lived. His address was in the telephone book. Jean had not needed to consult this volume however. She had regularly checked his whereabouts, without any intention of going to see him, to know where he was as a place to avoid – and perhaps simply to know where he was.

The address materialised as a shabby three-storey semi-detached house with a basement. It was faced with grimy crumbling stucco dotted with holes showing the bricks, also damaged, beneath. The window frames were cracking and almost bare of paint, and an upstairs window appeared to be broken. The house, though dirty and neglected, its scars searched out by the brilliant sunshine, was somehow solid and more imposing than the rat-hole in which Jean had imagined Crimond to be living. It and its neighbours were evidently divided into rooms and flats. Many of the houses had a row of names beside their doors. Crimond's house had only two, his own and above it some sort of Slavonic name.

The big squarish front door, scrawled over with fissures and reached by four steps up, was ajar. Jean pushed it a little and peered into a dark hallway containing a bicycle. There was a bell beside the door, but by itself, not related to the names. Jean pushed the bell but there was no sound. She stepped into the hall. It was hot and stuffy and the dusty air entered from outside with no hint of refreshment. The uncovered unpainted floorboards creaked and echoed. Some stairs led upward. The door of the front room was wide open and Jean looked in. The first thing she saw, spread out on a chair, was the kilt which Crimond had been wearing at the dance. The walls were entirely covered with bookshelves. There was a television set. She backed out and investigated the two rooms at the back, one book-filled, with a narrow divan bed and door to the garden, the other a kitchen. The garden was small, tended, Crimond liked plants. Jean put both her hands onto the handlebar of the bicycle to stop them from trembling. The metal, greyishly shiny, was cold and sickeningly real. She removed her hands and warmed them against the hideous beating of her heart. She noticed on the floor near the bicycle her suitcase and her handbag which she must have put down when she came in. Suppose Crimond were not there. Suppose he simply told her to go away. Suppose she had *entirely misinterpreted* the wordless time they had spent dancing together.

She was incapable of calling out. A glass door, locked, closed off the stairs to the first floor. She was trembling and shuddering, her hands compulsively fluttering, her jaw jerking. She saw under the stairs an open door which must lead to the basement. She began slowly to descend, her feet cautiously testing the hollow treads. A closed door faced her at the bottom. She touched, but did not knock, then opened it.

The basement room was huge, occupying the whole floor space of the house. It was rather dark, with one window opening onto the sunless area below the front of the house. The wooden floor was bare except where in a corner a rug lay beside a large square divan bed. The walls were bare except for a target which hung at the far end opposite the window. There was a large cupboard against one wall and beside it two long tables covered with books. Near to the target was a large desk with a lighted lamp upon it where Crimond, wearing his narrow rimless spectacles, was sitting and had been writing. He lifted his head, saw Jean, took off his spectacles and rubbed his eyes.

Jean began to cross the long stretch of the floor towards him. She felt as if she would fall before she reached him. She picked up a chair which was standing nearby and dragged it to the desk and sat down facing Crimond. Then she uttered a little bird-like cry.

'What's the matter?' said Crimond.

Jean did not look at Crimond, was indeed incapable of looking at anything in particular, since the room, the dull pale window, the lamp, the door, the bed with an old wrinkled rug beside it, the target, the white paper on which Crimond had been writing, Crimond's face, Crimond's hand, Crimond's glasses, a tumbler of water, the kilt which had somehow made its way downstairs, were all composed into a sort of vividly illuminated wheel which was slowly turning in front of her.

Crimond said nothing more, he waited, watching her while she gasped, shook her head to and fro and opened and closed her eyes.

'What do you mean, "What's the matter"?' said Jean. Then after a few more deep breaths, 'Have you had any sleep?'

'Yes. Have you?'

'No.'

'Then hadn't you better? There's a divan in the back room upstairs. It's not made up, I'm afraid.'

'So you weren't expecting me.'

'Pure carelessness.'

'*Were* you expecting me?'

'Of course.'

'What would you have done if I hadn't come?'

'Nothing.'

There was a pause. Crimond regarded her shrewdly, a little wearily. Jean looked down at Crimond's feet, in brown slippers, under the desk.

'So you possess a kilt.'

'I hired it. One can hire kilts.'

'I see you still have your target.'

'It's a symbol.'

'And the guns. You'll say they are symbols too.'

'Yes.'

'Did you plan this long before?'

'No.'

'How did you get a ticket for the dance, they were all sold out.'

'I asked Levquist.'

'Levquist? I thought you quarrelled with him years ago?'

'I wrote and asked him. He sent the ticket by return with a sarcastic note in Latin.'

'What would you have done if he hadn't sent it?'

'Nothing.'

'You mean, oh never mind what you mean. How did you know I'd be at the dance?'

'Lily Boyne told me.'

'Did you think that was a message from me?'

'No.'

'It wasn't.'

'I know that.'

'What about Lily Boyne?'

'What about her?'

'You came with her.'

'It is customary to arrive with a woman.'

'Was it to save face in case I ignored you?'

'No.'

'You knew I would not ignore you?'

'Yes.'

'Oh, Crimond, why – why – why *now*?'

'Well, it's worked, hasn't it?'

'But look, about Lily –'

'Let's stick to essentials,' said Crimond. 'Lily Boyne is nothing, she tried to make my acquaintance and I noticed her because she knew you. I like her.'

'Why?'

'Because she is nothing. She values herself at nil.'

'You find her despair amusing?'

'No.'

'All right, forget her, I see why you used her. What were you writing when I arrived?'

'A book I have been working on for some time.'

'You mean the book?'

'A book, the book if you like.'

'It is nearly finished?'

'No.'

'What will you do when it is finished?'

'Learn Arabic.'

'Can I help you with the book, do research like I used to?'

'That stage has passed. Anyway you should do work of your own.'

'So you used to tell me. Are you glad to see me?'

'Yes.'

'Let's stop messing about in this conversation. I've left Duncan. I'm here. I'm yours, I'm yours for good if you want me. After last night I assume you do.'

Crimond looked at her thoughtfully. His thin lips were drawn into a straight line. His longish very fine pale red hair had been carefully combed. His light eyes which so often gleamed and glittered with thought or sarcasm, were cold and stilled, hard as two opaque blue stones. 'You left me.'

'I don't know what happened,' said Jean.

'Neither do I.'

'It shouldn't have happened.'

113

'But it showed something.'

'That doesn't matter now. It *can't* matter. If it mattered you wouldn't have come to the dance.'

'Oh that. It was on impulse.'

'Oh that! Crimond, understand, I have left a husband whom I esteem and love, and friends who will never forgive me, in order to give myself to you entirely and forever. I hereby give myself. I love you. You are the only being whom I can love absolutely with my complete self, with all my flesh and mind and heart. You are my mate, my perfect partner, and I am yours. You must *feel* this now, as I do, as we did last night and *trembled* because we did. It was a marvel that we ever met. It is some kind of divine luck that we are together now. We must never never part again. We are, here, in this, *necessary* beings, like gods. As we look at each other we verify, we *know*, the perfection of our love, we *recognise* each other. *Here* is my life, here if need be is my death. It's life and death, as if they were to destroy Israel – if I forget thee, O Jerusalem –'

Crimond, who had been frowning during this declaration, said, shifting in his chair and picked up his spectacles, 'I don't care for these Jewish oaths – and we are not gods. We'll just have to see what happens.'

'All right, if it doesn't work we can always kill each other, as you said then! Crimond, you've produced a miracle, we're together – aren't you pleased? Say you love me.'

'I love you, Jean Kowitz. But we must also recall that we have managed without each other for many years – a long time during which neither of us made any signal.'

'Yes. I don't know why that was. Perhaps it was a punishment for our failure to stay together. We had to go through an ordeal, a sort of purgatory, to believe we could deserve each other again. Now the appointed time has come. We are *ready*. I have left Duncan –'

'Yes, yes – I'm sorry about Duncan. You also mention your friends who will never forgive you, or me.'

'They hate you. They'd like to thrash you. They'd like to humiliate you. They felt like that before – and now . . .'

'You sound pleased.'

'It doesn't matter about them, compared with us they don't exist. Can we go and live in France? I'd like that.'

'No. My work is here. If you come to me you must do what I want.'

'I'll always do that,' said Jean. 'I thought about you every day. If at any time you'd made the least gesture – but I imagined –'

'Enough of that. Never mind what you imagined, here you are. Now I must get on with my work. I suggest you go upstairs and lie down. Have you eaten, would you like anything to eat?'

'No. I feel I shall never eat again.'

'I'll fetch you later. Then we can both sleep down here where there's room for two. Then we'll discuss what we'll do.'

'What do you mean by that?'

'How we'll live together. How what must be will be.'

'Yes. It *must* be. All right. I'll go and rest. This is real. Isn't it?'

'Yes. Go now.'

'I want you.'

'Go now, my little hawk.'

Jean rose promptly and went upstairs. She thought, we haven't touched each other. That's as it should be. That's his way. We haven't touched each other yet, but all that we are has sprung together into one substance. It's like some great atomic charge, we *are* each other. Oh thank God. She went into the back room and pulled the curtains and kicked her shoes off then crawled onto the divan drawing the blankets up over her head. In an instant she was asleep, tumbling slowly over and over through a deep darkening air of pure joy.

PART TWO

Midwinter

———————

'I think there's some beer somewhere,' said Jenkin.
'Don't worry, I've brought some drink,' said Gerard.
'Sorry.'
'This has happened before.'
'I believe so.'
'God, it's cold!'
'I'll turn on the fire.'

Gerard was, after an impromptu telephone call, visiting Jenkin at Jenkin's little terrace house off the Goldhawk Road near the Arches. Jenkin had lived in this house for many years, ever since the polytechnic days before he returned to school-mastering. Jenkin's road was still very much as it had been, full of what Jenkin called 'ordinary blokes'. Neighbouring areas were however becoming 'gentrified', to Jenkin's disgust. Gerard often came to this house. Today he came without warning, not because anything particular was, but because an awful lot of things were, on his mind.

The momentous Commem Ball was now months away in the past. It was a foggy evening in late October. Jenkin's house, which had no central heating, was indeed cold, a house which let all weather come inside. Jenkin in fact welcomed the weather at all times of year, the sight of a closed window made him uneasy. Whatever the temperature he slept in an un-heated bedroom with a breeze blowing. He allowed himself a hot water bottle in winter however. He hastily now, to please his friend, closed several windows and turned on the gas fire in the little sitting room. Jenkin lived mainly in the kitchen and did not occupy this 'front room' or 'parlour', which he kept for 'best'. The room was, like everything in Jenkin's house, very neat and clean, and rather sparse and bare. It was not without some pretty objects, mostly donated by Gerard, but the spirit of the room resisted these, it failed to merge them into the calm homogeneous harmony which Gerard thought every room should possess, it remained raw and accidental. The faded wallpaper, light green with shadowy reddish flowers, was varied here and there by patches of yellow distempered wall beneath, where Jenkin had carefully removed areas of paper which had become torn. The effect was not unpleasant. The very clean carpet was faded too, its blue and red flowers merged into a soft brown. The green tiles in front of the fire were shiny from regular washing. The wooden-armed chairs, ranged against the wall until company arrived, had beige folk-weave upholstery. The mantelpiece above the fire was adorned by a row of china cups, some of them gifts of Gerard's, and a stone, a grey sea pebble with a purple stripe, a present from Rose. To these Jenkin had just added, brought in from the kitchen together with two wine glasses, a green tumbler containing a few red-leaved twigs. The gas fire was purring. The thick dark velveteen curtains were pulled against the foggy dusk. A lamp, a long-ago present from Gerard, was alight in a corner. Gerard rearranged the cups, turned off the centre light, and handed over the bottle of Beaujolais Nouveau to be opened by his host. Jenkin, when nervous, which he often was, had a habit of making little unconscious sounds. Now as, watched by Gerard, he manipulated the corkscrew, he uttered a series of throaty grunts, then as he poured the wine into the glasses and set the bottle down on the tiles, began to hum.

Jenkin, though so old a friend, remained for Gerard a source of fascinated, sometimes exasperated, puzzlement. Jenkin's house was excessively orderly, minimally and randomly furnished, and often felt to Gerard cheerless and somehow empty. The only real colour and multiplicity in the house was provided by Jenkin's books, which occupied two upstairs rooms, completely covering the walls and most of the floor. Yet Jenkin always knew where each book was. Gerard had always recognised his friend as being, in some radical even metaphysical sense, more solid than himself, more dense, more real, more contingently existent, more full of being. This 'being' was what Levquist had referred to when he said of Jenkin, 'Where he is, he *is*.' It was also paradoxical (or was it not?) that Jenkin seemed to lack any strong sense of individuality and was generally unable to 'give an account of himself'. Whereas Gerard, who was so much more intellectually collected and coherent, felt sparse, extended, abstract by contrast. This contrast sometimes made Gerard feel cleverer and more refined, sometimes simply weaker and lacking in weight. At Oxford Jenkin had, as Levquist approvingly remarked, 'cut out' philosophy, and followed linguistic and literary studies throughout his degree. As a schoolmaster he had at first taught Greek and Latin, later French and Spanish. At the polytechnic, and at school, he also taught history. He was learned, but without the will and ambitions of a scholar. He came from Birmingham and Birmingham Grammar School. His father, recently dead, had been a clerk in a factory and a Methodist lay preacher. His mother, also a Methodist, had died earlier. Gerard had used to accuse Jenkin of believing in God, which Jenkin denied. Nevertheless, something remained from that childhood which Jenkin believed in and which made Gerard anxious. Jenkin was a serious man, possibly the most deeply serious man whom Gerard knew; but it was not at all easy to predict what forms that seriousness might take.

'Gerard, do sit down,' said Jenkin, 'stop walking round the room and rearranging things.'

'I like walking.'

'It's your form of meditation, but it should be done in the open air, you're not in prison *yet*. Besides, I'm here and you're bothering me.'

'Sorry. Don't cook the wine, how many times must I tell you.'

Gerard removed the wine bottle from the tiles and sat down opposite to his friend beside the fire in one of the upright meagrely upholstered wooden-armed chairs, rumpling with his feet a small Chinese rug which he had given Jenkin several Christmases ago. Jenkin leaned down and straightened the rug.

'Have you decided what you're going to write?'

'No,' said Gerard frowning. 'Nothing perhaps.'

'Plato, Plotinus?'

'I don't know.'

'You once said you wanted to write on Dante.'

'No. Why don't you write on Dante?'

'You translated yards of Horace once. You could translate the whole of Horace into English verse.'

'Are you serious?'

'I love your translations. You don't want to write about your childhood?'

'Good God no!'

'Or about us at Oxford?'

'Don't be silly, dear boy!'

'It could be a piece of social or political history. What about art? I remember that monograph you wrote on Wilson Steer. You could write about pictures.'

'Only frivolously.'

'A novel then, an intellectual philosophical novel!'

'Novels are over, they're finished.'

'Why not just relax and enjoy life? Live in the present. Be happy. That's a good occupation.'

'Oh do shut up –'

'Seriously, happiness matters.'

'I'm not a hedonist. Neither are you.'

'I sometimes wonder – Well, it looks as if you'll have to write a philosophy book.'

'Let's leave this subject, shall we?'

Jenkin did not want, just now, to have an intense conversation with Gerard. There were just certain moves to be gone through, without, he hoped, raising certain subjects. Although he had known Gerard so well for so long he still attempted to manage or construct the conversations which he had with his awkward and sometimes sharp-tongued and touchy friend. Although he was, as they all were, very interested in 'what Gerard will do', he felt enough, for a sort of politeness, had been said. If he went on Gerard would become depressed or annoyed. It was obviously a painful topic. Jenkin mostly wanted to tell Gerard about his plan for going on a package tour to Spain for Christmas. Of course Gerard would not want to come because he loved English Christmases. And Jenkin liked travelling alone. He began, 'I'm thinking of –'

'Have you seen Crimond lately?'

Jenkin flushed. This was one of the subjects he wanted to keep off. Jenkin had no absolute objection to telling lies, but never told any to Gerard. He said truthfully, 'No, I haven't seen him again, not since –' But he felt guilty. He looked at Gerard, so sleek and collected in his bottle-green jacket, his sculptured face shadowed by the lamp, his eyes narrowed as he looked down into the gas fire. Gerard was smoothing his thick dark curly hair, tucking it back behind his ears. He was uttering an almost inaudible sigh. What is he thinking? Jenkin wondered.

I hate it that Jenkin sees Crimond, Gerard was thinking. It weakens our position. Though heaven knows what exactly our position is. A position should be a strong point to move from. But what move can we make? God, it's all got so horribly mixed up and messy.

'Of course we'll have Guy Fawkes as usual,' said Jenkin.

'Guy Fawkes. Of course. Gideon will want to send up all the rockets.'

'And then it'll be time for the reading party and then we'll be in sight of Christmas.' It's like talking to a child, thought Jenkin. The, once or twice yearly, reading parties at Rose's house in the country had been going on, with a number of longish intervals, ever since they were students. Rose and Gerard had recently revived the custom which had lapsed for a while.

'Oh yes – the reading party –'

'Will you invite Gulliver?'

'Yes.' Gerard frowned and Jenkin looked away. Gerard felt guilty before Jenkin about Gulliver Ashe. Jenkin had actually *said*, 'Don't lead him up the garden.' Gerard had, probably, undoubtedly 'encouraged' Gulliver, vaguely, not with any-thing in view, not for any good reason, not for any reason really except that he had looked rather beautiful when Gerard was feeling lonely. Of course nothing happened except that Gerard seemed to be 'taking him up' and making him a bit of a favourite. Gerard's interest had proved ephemeral; what remained were Gulliver's accusing glances, a resentful air of having rights, a faint impertinence.

'Gull still hasn't got a job,' said Jenkin.

'I know!'

The summer and the autumn had changed many things. Jenkin had been to a summer school and to Sweden on a package tour. Rose had stayed with her father's relations in Yorkshire and her mother's relations in Ireland. Gerard had been to Paris, then to Athens to see an archaeological friend, Peter Manson, who was working at the British School. Tamar had unexpectedly given up the university and taken a job in a publishing firm which Gerard had found for her. Of course Gerard had offered Violet financial help, he had offered it in his father's name, and Violet had rudely refused it. Gerard felt guilty about Tamar, he now felt he ought to have made more effort to discover what was going on. Violet said Tamar was fed up with Oxford, Tamar confirmed this, Gerard, annoyed with Violet, failed to pursue the matter. He had been unhappy and preoccupied at the time, grieving about his father, dismantling and selling the house in Bristol, so full of childhood relics, feuding with Pat and Gideon, worrying about Crimond, worrying about Duncan. Duncan had ostentatiously taken no leave and worked throughout the summer. News of Jean and Crimond was sparse. They were said to be still living in Crimond's house in Camberwell. They were rumoured to have been to a conference in Amsterdam.

'I hope Duncan will come to the reading party,' said Gerard. 'Christ, I wish I knew what to do about him.'

'There's nothing to do,' said Jenkin. Just let determined things to destiny hold unbewailed their way.'

'That's craven.'

'At the moment, I mean. Duncan obviously isn't going to make any move. And if we interfere we could just make trouble.'

'You mean get hurt? Are you afraid?'

'Of *him*? Of course not. I just mean we could mess up further a situation we don't understand.'

'What don't we understand? I understand. I just don't know what to do. If you're saying that in this modern age adultery doesn't matter –'

'I'm not.'

'Jean will have to come back to Duncan – I suppose. There's no life she can lead with that man, he works like a demon all day, he's crazy really – and she's a moral sort of person after all –'

'She loves the fellow!'

'That's nonsense, it's psychological slavery, it's an illusion. The sooner she returns the less damage will be done.'

'You think, after a certain time, Duncan might reject her?'

'He could generally detach himself out of self-defence, go cold on her. Why should he suffer so? He'll drink himself to death.'

'You feel we should help him positively, aggressively if necessary?'

'If we could think how.'

'Gang up on Crimond and beat the hell out of him? He'd like it, he'd play the victim and then take a terrible revenge.'

'Of course I don't mean that sort of stuff! He wouldn't like it and we couldn't do it.'

'I wasn't serious.'

'Well, *be* serious.'

'We can hardly go and fetch Jean away by force. You were saying something about Tamar last night, but I didn't get the hang because Rose came in.'

'Rose is terribly upset about Jean.'

'Is she seeing Jean?'

'No, of course not!'

'I don't see why she shouldn't – *we* have to defend Duncan –'

'She'll do what we do.'

'But about Tamar – you seemed to think that *she* could somehow bring Jean and Duncan together again?'

'It's an intuition. Tamar is a remarkable person.'

123

'Couldn't Rose do it?'

'She's too connected. She hates Crimond. And she and Jean are so close, or were. Jean would hate above all things to be proved wrong by Rose.'

'I see what you mean. Tamar used to see a lot of Jean and Duncan. I remember you said they ought to adopt her! But I don't fancy involving Tamar, she's so young.'

'That's her passport, they couldn't see her as a judge. She's got a special integrity. Out of that unspeakable background –'

'Or because of it.'

'She has seen the abyss and stepped away from it, stepped firmly in the other direction – oh how firmly she steps!'

'She's in search of a father. If you see yourself in that role –'

'Absolutely not. I just thought I'd suggest –'

'Don't burden her too much. She has a very high regard for you. She'd worry terribly if she wasn't able to do exactly what you wanted. I expect she's got enough worries.'

'I think something like this might be just what she needs, a task, a mission, to be a messenger of the gods.'

'You see her as a sort of virgin priestess.'

'Yes. Are you joking?'

'Never in the world – I see her like that too. But look – supposing someone were to say that surely in these days women often leave their husbands for other men and by-standers don't think this is something intolerable they've got to stop at all costs. Why is this case different? Is it because Duncan is like our brother, or because Crimond is exceptionally awful, or –?' Jenkin here gave Gerard a wide-eyed look which meant that he was putting something out simply for clarification; they had been arguing since they were eighteen.

'Storms gather round that man. Someone could get hurt.'

'You think Duncan might try to kill Crimond? Duncan can bide his time, but he's violent and fey too.'

'No, but he might have a sudden irresistible urge simply to see Crimond, to argue with him even –'

'And Crimond might kill him, out of fear, or hate –?'

'Men in the wrong hate their victims.'

'Or by accident? You think it'll end in single combat? Or

Crimond might kill Jean, or they'd jump off a cliff together, or –?'

'He likes guns, you remember at Oxford, and Duncan said he was in some rifle club in Ireland, it's hard luck on him he missed the war, he'd have been dead or a hero, that would have been his *aim* –'

'I think you're too obsessed with Crimond's awfulness. He's a romantic.'

'We forgive romantics.'

'An *âme damnée* then.'

'We forgive them too. Don't make excuses for him, Jenkin!'

'You want your Crimond to be as bad as possible!'

'He likes dramas and ordeals and tests of courage, he doesn't care if he destroys people because he doesn't care if he destroys himself –'

'He's a utopian thinker.'

'Precisely. Unrealistic and ruthless.'

'Oh come – He's courageous and hard-working and indifferent to material goods and he really cares about deprived people –'

'He's a charlatan.'

'What is a charlatan? I've never understood that concept.'

'He doesn't care about deprived people or social justice, he doesn't go anywhere near the real working-class struggle, he's a self-obsessed theorist, he makes all these things into ideas, into some passionate abstract web he's weaving –'

'Passion, yes. That's what attracts Jean.'

'She's attracted by the danger – by the carnage.'

'A Helen of Troy complex?'

'She likes cities to fall and men to die because of her.'

'You are too unkind,' said Jenkin. 'Crimond is a fanatic, an ascetic. That's attractive enough –'

'For you perhaps. I think you see him as some kind of mystic.'

'Remember how we all once saw him as the modern man, the hero of our time, we admired him for being so dedicated, we felt he was more real than we were –'

'I never felt that. What I do remember was, when someone

said he was an extremist, he said, "One must have the support of the young." That's unforgivable.'

'Yes,' said Jenkin, and sighed. 'Still, I'll never forget seeing him dance that evening last summer.'

'Like Shiva!'

'Weaving his passionate web!'

'Precisely. Crimond's stuff is just a fashionable amalgam, senseless but dangerous – a kind of Taoism with a dash of Heraclitus and modern physics, then labelled Marxism. The philosopher as physicist, as cosmologist, as theologian. Plato did a good job when he threw out the preSocratics.'

'Yes, but they're back! I know what you mean and I don't like it either. But aren't we now mixing up two separate problems?'

'You mean his private morals and his book. But they aren't separate. Crimond is a terrorist.'

'That's how Rose sees him. All the same, he knows an awful lot and he can think. The book may be a great deal better than the slapdash provocative opinions he sometimes utters.'

'Has he shown it to you?'

'No, of course not!'

'Do you plan to meet him?'

'I don't plan, I just don't run a mile! We've got to see him sometime to ask him about the book.'

'Yes, yes, I'm going to call the committee, we'll have to see him –'

'We must get the style right.'

'I think "tone" is the word. You say "ask about the book" – but there's nothing we can do except curse privately that we're all spending our money year after year to propagate ideas we detest!'

'It's a dotty situation. Jean could support him, but of course he wouldn't – and it doesn't alter our obligation.'

'I'm certain he doesn't touch a penny of Jean's money.'

'Has the book changed or have we? The brotherhood of western intellectuals versus the book of history.'

'You're talking his language. There is no book of history, there is no history in that sense, it's all just determinism and *amor fati*. Or if there is a book of history it's called the *Phenomenology of Mind* and it's out of date! Or do you think we've really given up? Come, come, Jenkin!'

'"What by nature and by training we loved, has little strength remaining, though we would gladly give the Oxford Colleges, Big Ben, and all the birds in Wicken Fen, it has no wish to live".'

'Don't quote that at me, dear boy. You don't think it or feel it.'

'Perhaps it is not only our fate but our truth to be weak and uncertain.'

'You think we are in Alexandria in the last days of Athens!'

'I certainly don't think we have the right to give away the birds in Wicken Fen, they don't belong to us. May I have another glass of wine?'

'It's your wine, dolt, I gave it to you!'

Gerard stood up as if to go, and Jenkin rose too, looking up at his tall friend and rumpling his wispy strawy hair.

Gerard said, 'Why the hell does Duncan have to *lose* all the time, why is *he* the one that falls in the river! I wonder what really happened in Ireland –'

'I think we shouldn't wonder so much,' said Jenkin, 'sometimes we try to think in too much detail about other people's lives. Other people's consciousness can be so unlike our own. One learns that.'

Gerard sighed, recognising the truth of this, feeling the inaccessibility to him of Jenkin's consciousness. 'What were you up to at that summer school, Jenkin, you're not going over to God, are you?'

'Sit down.' They sat down again and Jenkin filled the two glasses. 'I just like to know what's happening.'

'In Liberation Theology? In South America?'

'On the planet.'

They were silent for a moment, Jenkin hunched up, pulling in his short legs, becoming almost egg-shaped, Gerard elongated, his legs outstretched, his arms hanging, his tie undone, his dark hair every way.

'I hate God,' said Gerard.

' "He who alone is wise wants and does not want to be called Zeus." Heraclitus wasn't altogether a disaster, you know.'

Gerard laughed. He reflected how much, in the many years that had passed, he had defined himself by his difference from his friends, differences felt in that degree of detail which is obtained by continuous careful talking. In a way, their lives together had been quite like their childish hopes. Yet also he was increasingly conscious now of that loneliness of human beings to which Jenkin had referred.

'If he does or doesn't want something it implies he exists.'

'You ought to write about Plotinus and St Augustine and what happened to Platonism.'

'What indeed. Levquist said I was rotted by Christianity!'

'You think you're on a ladder going up, and you *do* go up.'

'You think you're on a road going on, and you *do* go on.'

'We all do that, there's no merit in it.'

'You live in the present. I can never find the present.'

'Sometimes I wish I could give up metaphors and just think.'

'Think what?'

'What a rogue and peasant slave I am.'

'That's a metaphor. I hate all that Christian praise and blame. And yet –'

'You're a puritan, Gerard. You blame yourself for the lack of some ideal terrible discipline!'

'I remember *you* said that we're all sunk in the illusions of egoism like in a big sticky cream cake!'

'Yes, but I don't mind too much. Why destroy the healthy ego? It does a job. You're making me feel hungry. Will you stay for supper? Please do.'

'No. I think there's a human task. You think there are human fates. Maybe that way you learn more.'

'Oh I don't know. While you were talking I was picturing the Berlin Wall. It's white.'

'I know it's white.'

'It's like what I think of evil. One must think of it. Perhaps all the time. In oneself too. Start from where one is.'

'You always mix things up,' said Gerard. 'The Berlin Wall

is not where *you* are. It's true that we can't imagine virtue much above our own level except as pure loss. But one must try to think about being good, not just shedding contrite tears and rogue and peasant slave stuff. That's just self-gratification!'

'You can't by-pass where you are by an imaginary leap into the ideal!'

'All right, but it's better to *have* an ideal, rather than just trudging on and thinking how different we all are!'

'You're so self-reliant,' said Jenkin. He said this casually because he was tired of this abstract talk which Gerard liked so, and because he wanted Gerard to stay to supper but was not sure there was anything in the larder above the macaroni cheese and fish cake level. One of the supermarkets might still be open. He'd have to go out and buy more wine anyway. Then he realised how much Gerard would resent being called self-reliant.

'Self-reliant!' Gerard rose again and picked up his overcoat off a chair.

Resigned, Jenkin also rose. 'You won't stay to supper?'

'No, thanks. I'll try to fix that committee meeting.'

'What about Pat and Gideon?'

'I won't have them on the committee, I've told them it won't do. They want to contribute anyway, I've told them they can't. I've told Gull he mustn't pay either now he's un-employed. I suppose all this ought to be discussed. Oh hell.'

'Pat and Gideon can't be pro-Crimond.'

'They aren't. They just want a finger in the pie. Gideon finds it all amusing.'

'He's in London?'

'Yes. He's trying to buy a Klimt.'

'I imagine you don't want a taxi?'

'No, I'll walk. I love this fog. Goodbye.'

As the front door closed behind Gerard, Jenkin returned into the aloneness which he valued so much. He leaned against the door with a positive thrill of solitude. He had wanted Gerard to stay. He was now also glad that he had gone. Jenkin had once said, a remark which Gerard remembered, that he would never marry because that would prevent him from being alone at night. Now there was supper to think of, and what was on the radio (he had no television) and Gerard to think of, always an interesting subject. Then supper to be (quickly) prepared and (slowly) eaten. Jenkin believed one should attend carefully to food while eating it. There was the wine to be finished too. A radio talk (if short), some music (if classical and familiar). Then he might read some Spanish poetry and look at the map and think about his jaunt at Christmas.

He turned off the gas fire in the sitting room and carried the wine bottle and two glasses to the kitchen, returned for the green tumbler and the maple leaves and turned out the light. He put the green tumbler upon the tiled shelf above the sink which he kept clear for such purposes. As he put it down he said, 'There you are!' Jenkin felt happy; but there was a flaw in his happiness. He felt, he intuited, that his life was about to change in some way he could not yet determine. The thought of this veiled change was alarming, also exciting. Perhaps it was just, though this was much, a feeling that it was time to stop schoolmastering. Would he then be, like Gerard, wondering what to do with his thoughts? No, he could never be like Gerard or have, in that sense, thoughts. He was certainly not going over to God as Gerard had professed to fear. It was as if some large white blankness were opening before him, not a dead soiled white like the Berlin Wall, but a radiant live space like a white cloud, moist and warm. What would he be doing this time next year, he wondered. So it was as close as that, his new and different future? He had said nothing to anybody, not even to Gerard.

Jenkin spread some clean newspaper upon the wooden table and set out a plate, a knife and fork. He poured the remainder of the Beaujolais into his glass and sat down and sipped it. He thought about Gerard walking home alone through the foggy lamplit streets. Then he imagined himself walking alone. He too was a walker. Only while Gerard walked wrapped in the great dark cloak of his thoughts, Jenkin walked through a great collection or exhibition of little events or encounters. Trees, for instance, an immense variety of dogs whose gentle soft friendly eyes met his with intelligence, rubbish tips containing the amazing variety of things which people threw away, some of which Jenkin would take home and cherish, shop windows, cars, things in gutters, people's clothes, people with sad or happy faces, houses with sad or happy faces, windows at dusk where through undrawn curtains one could watch people watching television. Sometimes, sitting at home, Jenkin imagined individual other people, people he had never met, these were always lonely people, a girl in a bed-sitter with her cat and her potted plant, an elderly man washing his shirt, a man in a turban walking along a dusty road, a man lost in the snow. Sometimes he dreamed about such people or was one himself. Once he thought so intensely about a tramp at a railway terminus that he actually set off late in the evening and walked to Paddington to see if the tramp was there. The tramp was not there, but a variety of other solitary persons were there, waiting for Jenkin.

Jenkin never imagined stories attached to these people. They were pictures of individuals whose fates were sketched in their faces, their clothes, their momentary ambience, and were in this respect like the real people he met in the street. His grasp of his few friends was in the same way intense and limited. He was intensely aware of the reality of Gerard, of Duncan, of Rose, of Graham Willward (a master at his school), of Marchment (a social worker, formerly an M P, who also knew Crimond); but he did not like to speculate about them beyond the formulation of hypotheses necessary for ordinary life. They were mysterious pictures which he often looked at, mysteries upon which he sometimes meditated. He had little social curiosity and was devoid of gossip, so some people found him dull. He was an only child who had loved his parents and believed in their religion and in their goodness. Later he painlessly shed his Christianity. He could not believe in a supernatural elsewhere or imagine the risen Lord except in anguish. He found equally alien the (as he saw it) quasi-mystical, pseudo-mystical, Platonic perfectionism which was Gerard's substitute for religious belief. Yet he retained, perhaps after all from the examples so dear to him in childhood, a kind of absolutism, not about any special human task or pilgrimage, but just about jobs to be done among strangers. The simplicity of his life which seemed to some spectators an asceticism, to others naive and childish, or a pose, was for him part of his absolute; but was also, as he was well aware, a programme for happiness. Jenkin disliked muddles, cupidity, lying, exercises of power, the masses of ordinary sinning, because they involved states of mind which he found uncomfortable, such as envy, resentment, remorse or hate. 'He's so *healthy*,' someone had said of Jenkin half scornfully, and Jenkin would have understood the element of criticism involved. He had become too much at ease, too much at home in his life. Gerard was not at home, made continually restless by a glimpsed ideal far far above him; yet at the same time the glimpse, as the clouds swirled about the summit, consoled him, even deceived him, as with a swoop of intellectual love he seemed to be beside it, up there in those pure and radiant regions, high above the thing he really was. This Jenkin saw in Gerard as the old religious illusion. Gerard was always talking about destroying his ego. Jenkin quite liked his, he needed it, he never worried too much, he hoped to do better, trusting to his general way of life to keep him 'out of trouble'. I'm a slug, he sometimes thought. I move altogether if I move at all, I only stretch myself out a little, a very little.

It was not that Jenkin felt in general that he should set forth somewhere to serve the human race. He knew that by teaching languages and a bit of history to all sorts of boys he was performing an important service and probably doing what he was best at. Was it not simply self-indulgent romanticism, this idea of carrying his 'simplicity' a little further? He wanted a change. He was having a change, a sabbatical term. He was supposed to be studying something, writing something. Instead he was cherishing this restlessness. He wanted to get away. He wanted to get away to be with the people he often thought about. How far away, as far as Paddington, as far as a bed-sitting room in Kilburn? Farther than that. As far as Limehouse or Stepney or Walworth? Farther than that. Yet was not even that far a matter of romanticism, escapism, delusion, dereliction of duty, a dream of feeding on others' misery and making of it a full self? He wanted, did he, to be right out on the frontiers of human suffering, out on the edge of things, to *live* there, for *that* to be his home? The heroes of our time are dissidents, protesters, people alone in cells, anonymous helpers, unknown truth-tellers. He knew he would not be one of these, but he wanted to be somehow near them. Nothing mattered much except easing pain, except individuals and their histories. But what did that mean for *him*, with his new secret dreams of setting off for South America or India? Even his Liberation Theology was romantic, consisting merely of a popular picture of Christ as the Saviour of the poor, of the left-behinds, of the disappeareds. Though sometimes he also thought, could not just that *be* theology after all, not the learned tinkering of demythologising bishops, but theology broken, smashed by the sudden realisable and realised horror of the world? This could be so even if his own thoughts of departure amounted to no more than the perusal of a holiday brochure, the merest fact that, somehow, he wanted to get away. He wanted, for instance, to get away from Gerard.

Needless to say there were no ordinary or obvious reasons why he should want to get away from Gerard. He had loved Gerard all his adult life. They had never been lovers. Jenkin's sexual aspirations, usually unsuccessful and now in eclipse, were toward the other sex. But a great love involves the whole person and Jenkin's attachment was perhaps in the true sense Platonic. Gerard was like a perfect older brother, a protector and a guide, an exemplar, a completely reliable, completely loving, resource, he had been, and had uniquely been, for Jenkin, pure gold. Perhaps these were precisely the reasons why he wanted to get up and run? To test himself in a Gerardless world. Reverently to remove something so perfect just because it was perfect. He was too cosy and settled in his little house with his little friendly things. It was required of him to be elsewhere, with other people, not friends, there could be no more friends, and no more things either. Of course going away, going *right* away, wouldn't mean quarrelling with Gerard, but it would mean abandoning him, being so alien and far off that Gerard, if he figured at all, would become a mere tourist in his life. That break, that breaking, was somehow essential; and on quiet evenings when Jenkin was alone in his house, listening to the radio and going to bed early, what he intended could seem to him not only absurd but terrible, a kind of death, a pure loss: what Gerard said virtue looked like when you saw it from below. Well, it wasn't virtue he was after either. His wish was something far more wilful.

When Gerard left Jenkin and began to walk from Shepherd's Bush to Notting Hill through the fog, wrapped in the great dark cloak of his thoughts, he found himself remembering a story someone had told him about the method of fishing on some island in the South Seas. What the natives did was this. They let out from the beach an enormous round net stretching forward deep into the sea. At the appropriate time – Gerard could not recall how long the process took – the huge net was, with efforts demanding the co-operation of the whole village, winched in toward the shore. As the enormous bundle slowly approached the land and began to be visible above the surface, the net was found to contain a mass of huge fish and what the narrator (who immediately gave up swimming) called 'sea monsters'. The creatures, as they found themselves confined and being removed from their element, began a ferocious and fantastic threshing about, a maelstrom of terror and force, a flailing of great tails, a flashing of great eyes and jaws. They also began to attack each other, making the sea red with their blood. When Gerard told the story later to Jenkin he spontaneously used it as an image of the unconscious mind. Later he wondered why the comparison had seemed apt. Surely *his* unconscious was full of quiet peaceful fish? Jenkin was more concerned about the poor dying creatures and reiterated his frequent notion, never acted upon, that he ought to become a vegetarian. Gerard was not sure why he remembered this now. Talk with Jenkin always sent waves of force through Gerard's mind, usually beneficent and pleasant ones. Today however the vibrations had made him uneasy as if, though everything seemed as usual, the wavelength had changed. He thought, something's wrong with Jenkin, or perhaps something's wrong with me. He could not make out, reflecting, whether the uneasiness was really about Jenkin or about Crimond. Perhaps the flailing monsters were monsters of jealousy. Gerard was much given to jealousy, a sin with which he struggled and which he meticulously concealed.

'The rainy Pleiads wester, Orion plunges prone, the stroke of midnight ceases, and I lie down alone. The rainy Pleiads wester, and seek beyond the sea, the head that I shall dream of, and 'twill not dream of me.' This poem of A. E. Housman, a rendering of some Greek thing, was often, during these days, repeated to himself by Gulliver Ashe as a kind of liturgy, not exactly a prayer. It brought him some comfort. Not that it had, for him, any precise meaning or application. He was not, at that time, dreaming of any particular head, beyond the sea or not. He was certainly lying down alone, but he had been doing this for some time and was used to it. The little desolation of the poem had for him some larger and more cosmic ring. Gulliver was unemployed. It had taken him some time to realise this as a *condition*, and one likely to endure.

Gerard, who had got Tamar a job, had also got one for Gulliver, but Gulliver had almost immediately lost it. Gerard had been 'very nice about it', and had twice asked Gulliver to come and see him, but Gull now avoided Gerard. Being, sort of, ashamed was, he was beginning to see, one of the signs of the condition. Gulliver's job, which lasted four weeks, was with some grand printers and designers who specialised in art books, where Gulliver was to be a 'research assistant'. Later he suspected this job had simply been invented to oblige Gerard. Gull was virtually the office boy, then was required to muck in for an absent porter and carry books. The porter did not return, Gulliver, fed up with carrying books, demanded some research. Someone was rude to him and he walked out.

Gulliver had 'done' English at a London college and emerged with a good degree and a lot of embryonic talents. He had been a successful student actor and considered a stage career. He also wanted to be a writer, to edit a left-wing periodical, to go into left-wing politics. He got himself into an acting school where he decided he would really like to be a director or stage designer. He left because someone offered him some book reviewing, and he wanted to start a novel. The book reviews went well, he finished the novel, but could not find a publisher. He applied for and gained a job in the BBC as a trainee producer in radio. He wanted to transfer to television but was not able to. His second novel had also failed to be published. Gulliver attributed its failure to lack of time, and left the BBC to live on his savings and devote himself to writing. He published some short stories, one of which was made into a television play. He tried to get back into the BBC and failed, but got a job in a theatre workshop. He did a little acting and a little stage managing and even acquired an Equity card, but nothing lasted. He became a drama critic on a literary periodical. In this way years passed and Gulliver was now over thirty. So far he had enjoyed his adventures, sure he could always 'turn his hand to something'. Now things began quietly to get worse. He failed to gain a coveted editorship, the periodical could no longer afford him, the theatre workshop had ceased to exist. There was less money around, there were economies everywhere. He wrote a few more stories but no one published them. He had not the spirit to try another novel. At the time of the midsummer dance he had been unemployed for several months.

Gulliver had been supported through the later years of an

unhappy childhood, and through his happy student days and after, by an idea of himself as rather beautiful and raffish. As a student actor and in his early post-graduate years he had been markedly good-looking and attractive to both sexes. He found himself at home with both, but, with high expectations, failed to find the desired wonderful partner. In his raffish persona he at one time frequented various, reportedly *louche*, gay bars. He wore black leather and studded belts and chains and sinister boots. He could never decide whether this was mere play-acting or whether it was a brave and ingenious search for reality. There was always a lot of talk about 'identity'. But when he went to the gay bars he couldn't tell pretence from real. Later he wondered why he hadn't been murdered. He never told Gerard about that period. Another thing which he never told Gerard was that it was in a rather special gay bar that he had first heard Gerard's name mentioned. Of course Gerard never came near these places, but people talked about him. He had first got to know Gerard through a rescue operation for a little *avant-garde* theatre in Fulham; Gerard made a financial contribution and turned up once or twice. The theatre did not survive long however. Gulliver's heart still beat a little fast for Gerard, but he had never expected to be *that sort* of favourite, it being generally known that Gerard did not now have them. Gull was sufficiently flattered to have become friendly with Gerard's friends, and to have been (at a moment when Gerard was feeling guilty about him) co-opted onto the book committee. In fact, such was Gerard's habitual reticence that the 'encouragement' which he imagined he had given Gulliver existed largely in Gerard's mind, and had scarcely appeared perceptibly in the external world.

Gulliver had applied for job after job, gradually reducing his expectations and humbling his pride. He applied to the BBC, the British Council, the Labour Party, the local Town Hall, the University of London. He tried and failed to get a grant to continue his education. Of course he looked for acting jobs but soon realised this was hopeless when good and experienced actors were out of work. He applied wildly for jobs at an increasing variety of institutions and offered himself as numerous kinds of school teacher or social worker. He discovered he had many unsuspected talents and enthusiasms: he was very good with children, with old people, with lunatics, with animals, he was very young, very mature, very experienced, very versatile, very ready to learn. He had no success, aware that every job attracted hundreds of applicants. He had not yet applied to be a porter, waiter, unskilled factory hand, assuming he would be rejected, and regarding this anyway as a desperate perhaps fatal move. He had savings, he kept on hoping; but by now he had clearly envisaged the possibility that, although he was young and talented and had a university degree, *he might never be employed again.*

Gulliver had gone through the routines of pitying the unemployed and blaming the government. Now he was experiencing the thing itself. Often did he think resentfully, it's not fair, I'm not the *kind of person* who is unemployed! Waking in the morning the misery of his situation quickly blackened his consciousness. He had not realised how solitary he was, or had now become. He had been lonely as a child, but when he was a student imagined himself established, received into society, destined to be forever surrounded by friends. Now he was realising that if you are unemployed and have no money you can cease to be a person. He realised how 'subjective' this was, influenced even by the current language of do-gooders who were so ready to deplore and describe what they were not experiencing. It was absurd to feel so ashamed, so bedraggled, so useless. He just knew that he was being destroyed by an alien force, sinking into an abyss out of which he would never climb. He pictured himself in a few years, a shambling figure, begging from old friends. The bloom had departed, only for a brief moment is the flesh perfect, now he was becoming creased and stained. He hated the sight of younger men, a terrible symptom. Soon he would be unable to keep up appearances, which to get a job you must do. He had no family to turn to, he had hardly known his father, had suffered a hostile step-father and step-siblings, he was the outsider, the misfit, his mother turned against him. He had taken pleasure later in demonstrating his contempt for them all, communication dwindled. There was nowhere to go. He would soon have to leave the modest flat which he rented. He sold his car, gave up his telephone and shunned his literary friends with their expensive luncheons. He could not accept Gerard's help a second time, nor present himself in this abject state. Jenkin sent three postcards, but Gull had never been able to see the point of Jenkin. He felt a tiny bit romantic about Rose, who had rung up and, after his 'phone was disconnected, written asking him for a drink. He refused of course. He had sent her, anonymously, some flowers. That cheered him up a little.

'And there was a funny little thing that rolled about in her room, like a little ball. She said I must never touch it. Of course I tried to, I wanted to pick it up, but it always rolled away somehow, underneath something. I was never sure whether it was alive or not.'

'But look, your grandmother wasn't a *real* witch, I mean there *aren't* real witches, just poor mad creatures, or cheats who pretend to be –'

'I think she was a mid-wife, or had been, perhaps not an official one, but she knew all about herbs, she used to collect them when the moon was full. If you wanted to hurt somebody you picked the herbs when the moon was getting smaller –'

'She must have been mad –'

'She wasn't, nor a cheat either – you don't understand, witchcraft is an old religion, far older than Christianity, it's about power. I think she hated her parents, they belonged to some awful strict Christian sect, she *hated* Christianity.'

'Well, there's a psychological explanation.'

'When you say explain you mean explain away! Sometimes she said she was a gipsy, sometimes she said she was Jewish. People were afraid of her, but they asked her for help too, she could do all sorts of things. She was a dowser, and she could get rid of poltergeists, and she could make it rain by urinating – and she did abortions, of course –'

'Of course!'

'She had the evil eye, she had one strange eye, and –'

'Like Duncan! I don't imagine *he's* got the evil eye – he must wish he had, poor chap!'

'She had a lot of books, I think she thought she'd discover something amazing.'

'Mad people do.'

'All right, we're all a bit mad then. Why do you think they planted yew trees in churchyards? And it's like socialism.'

'Like *socialism*?'

'Yes, it's an anti-society society, it's a form of protest, it's like what Crimond does, and –'

'Oh Lily,' said Gull, 'do stop mixing everything up together, first it's your awful grandmother and now we've got onto Crimond again!'

'Well, he wants power too, he's writing a magic book.'

'You know him, don't you?'

'I used to know him,' said Lily in a cautious tone. 'We haven't seen much of each other lately.'

It had just occurred to Lily that it would be rather nice if Gulliver were to believe that she had been Crimond's mistress. She had never dared to hint this to anyone. Even now she felt afraid that Gulliver might see what she was hinting and not believe her; or worse still believe her, and say something about it to Crimond. What exactly had she said? She had already forgotten. That was the wine.

They were having a picnic lunch at Lily's flat. Lily's flat, near Sloane Square, was well provided with big windows with window seats and broad Edwardian doors made of teak. The bow window of her drawing room, where they were picnicking at an oval table, looked out onto a street where the wind was removing large yellow leaves from the tall plane trees and laying them carefully upon the pavements. A fire was burning in the grate. The room was multi-coloured, cluttered, almost garish; sensual and oriental, as Gulliver thought of it, possibly something to do with the awful grandmother. Perhaps he was the ideal spectator of that room. Gulliver liked Lily's crazy mixed-up taste, the almost-black wallpaper, the modern green and ivory chequered carpet with *trompe-l'oeil* recessions, which was like a pavement in an exotic courtyard, the sofas on which Lily lolled, covered with tapestries and embroideries, the polished surfaces crowded with boxes and figurines, expensive little things which Lily had bought impulsively at expensive shops. He liked the way it smelt of new things, even the old things seemed new here.

Yes, they were friends. Gull had never had a woman friend before. This was the only thing that had happened lately that was not ill-omened and awful, and even over this some ambiguous cloud was hanging. He could not believe in anything which would not soon be spoilt. It had not been Gull's idea, it had been Lily's. This fact had already been discussed. In the late summer when Gerard was in Greece and Rose in Yorkshire, and Gulliver was just beginning to despair, he received a card from Lily asking him to lunch at a restaurant in Covent Garden. He decided to refuse, then went. They met again a few times, at restaurants, at Lily's expense. Gulliver had not expected to get on with this rather ridiculous person, but he did. He had first met her some time ago at a party of Rose's and had scarcely given her a thought. Was he now attracted by her money? This was the first time they had, at Gull's suggestion, lunched at her flat. He was tired of seeing her pay and feared this might be noticed. Gull felt at ease with Lily because he did not fear her judgment or indeed care much what she thought. There was a grain of some relaxing superiority which he had probably imbibed from the people with whom he had first met her. At the same time he felt bound to keep up appearances with her, and that was good for him. With Lily he played the penniless writer, the garret genius, implied he was not really interested in getting a job, that he had always wanted to be alone and live simply and write. He told her that drop-outs were the saints of the modern world. Lily admired his asceticism. Of course there was nothing romantic involved. Lily talked a bit about the plausible men, Gull a bit about the gay bars. It was all remarkably easy and casual.

Lily was pleased to have acquired Gulliver. She regarded him as a minor extension of Gerard and a link with 'that world'. She believed his 'penniless writer', 'drop-out saint' story, and was unaware that he no longer saw Rose and her friends. She considered Gulliver a social asset or stepping stone, but she also enjoyed his company and found it nice to have just this kind of friend. They were, they both agreed, misfits, eccentrics, unusual people. She had enjoyed hearing about his rotten family, and telling him about her rotten family; how her father had vanished before she was born, how her mother, who had been converted to Catholicism, had handed her over to the paranormal grandmother, of whom Lily (though now proud of her) was terrified. From school she escaped to the 'crummy polytechnic' where she learnt to type and messed about with painting and pots. The Catholic mother died of drink, the grandmother, who planned to live to be a hundred and twenty, died suddenly under mysterious circumstances, murdered (she claimed) by the spells of a rival witch. Lily had lost touch with both of them. 'I never loved them,' said Lily. 'They never loved me. It was all a dead loss. Ah well.'

They had been eating ham and tongue and salami and peperonata and artichoke hearts and lima beans. Both Gull and Lily liked eating but not cooking. They had drunk a lot of cheap white wine. (Lily was not fussy about wine.) Cheese was to follow, and chocolate gâteau with cream, then Spanish brandy which Lily preferred to French. The flat was dusty, because Lily, very suspicious and fearful of thieves, would employ no char, and did not like dusting, it was also untidy, but Lily was in other ways systematic, even ritualistic. The 'picnic' was slow and orderly, the pretty plates and glasses carefully arranged upon a tablecloth made of an Indian bedspread; Lily had never really learnt to paint at her polytechnic, but the instinct that took her there expressed, perhaps, an artistic temperament. She was also, Gulliver learnt by observation, exceedingly superstitious, worrying about ladders, bird omens, crossed knives, inauspicious dates, numbers, phases of the moon. She was afraid of black dogs and spiders. She believed in astrology, and had had her horoscope cast several times, undismayed by finding that the prognoses did not agree. She also had a number of mixed-up ideas about Yoga and Zen. Another of Lily's little mysteries was that she could look remarkably old or remarkably young. When old, a pinched mask of anxiety descended on her face, stained wrinkled skin obscured her light brown eyes, her long neck looked starved and stringy, and her skin sallow and pitted, as if drawn toward her mouth in a querulous pout. At other times her face was smooth and youthful and alert, its pallor glowing, her sweetmeat eyes shining with intelligence, her slim figure taut with energy. With this would go a fey liveliness sometimes suggestive of desperation. Lily's clothes also varied between a zany smartness and messy uncaring dowdiness. Today, smartish, youngish, she was wearing tight black corduroy trousers, bare feet, a high-necked blue silk shirt and an amber necklace. Gulliver, who always dressed for Lily, was wearing his oatmeal jersey with red spots over a white shirt, his best jeans and boots, and his gorgeously brown soft leather (reindeer) jacket, which he had had to take off because Lily's flat was so warm.

Gulliver did not pick up, indeed had not noticed, Lily's hint about her relationship with Crimond. He had just bitten his tongue. He often did this now. Was it a sign of something, loss of physical coordination perhaps, a symptom of some fell disease? How on earth, when he came to think of it, did his tongue manage anyway, leading such a dangerous life between those powerful clashing monsters? He said, 'Have you seen Jean Cambus?'

'No, not lately.' Lily did not want to admit that her friendship with Jean belonged to the past.

'What a business,' said Gulliver. They had frequently discussed it of course. Gulliver could not help feeling pleased that other people were in a mess too; fancing being cuckolded twice by the same man! 'If I were Duncan I'd be so sick with rage and shame and hate, I'd shoot myself!'

'Why ever should he?' said Lily. 'He ought to go and *get* Crimond, with a gang. My women's lib friends would *kill* someone like Crimond, like I once saw in a judo demo, a woman was showing what to do if a man attacks you, was she tough! She had that man down, he was a great big chap too, right on his face, and she was twisting his arm, and all the women in the audience were screaming "Kill him! Kill him!" It was great.'

Gulliver shuddered. 'I don't see Gerard and that lot doing anything violent. They tend to sit and think.'

'That circle of cultured gents!' said Lily. 'They sit apart like little gods with no troubles. Even when their dear friend has trouble they do nothing.'

'There's nothing they can do,' said Gulliver. 'Gerard cares a lot really, he looks after people.'

'He's too bloody dignified,' said Lily.

Gulliver laughed sympathetically. He was in a mood to demote Gerard a little. He felt he had been too impressed. He had copied out some of his poems for Gerard early last year. Gerard had been nice about them, but Gull noticed them in a wastepaper basket later.

'And Jenkin Riderhood's a wet,' Lily went on, 'he's a teddy bear man.'

'He's a complacent little chap,' said Gulliver, 'but he's harmless.' He instantly blamed himself for this horrible utterance. He found himself gossiping in this loose spiteful way with Lily and saying things which he didn't mean, which she seemed somehow to elicit. I'm degenerating, he thought, it's because I'm demoralised. 'You side with the women.'

'Rose Curtland is nice,' Lily admitted. 'She can't help being a bit posh. She's *timid* though, and that exasperates me, I can't stand timid women. The best of the bunch is little Tamar.'

'Tamar?' said Gulliver surprised. He had not heard Lily mention Tamar before.

'Yes,' said Lily. She added, 'She was kind to me once.' Tamar had once made a point of talking to Lily and staying with her at a party, at the Cambuses house in the old days, where Lily was getting left out. Lily never forgot this.

Gull was touched. 'She's a good kid, but not exactly precocious, she's a modest violet.'

'Thank heavens for a girl who can be like that these days! She's pure, she's innocent, she's sweet, she's unspoilt, she's fresh, she's everything that I'm not. I'm shop-soiled, I guess I was born shop-soiled. I adore that child.'

Gulliver was surprised by this little outburst. Perhaps he had underestimated Tamar, perhaps he ought to notice her more? But of course Lily's emotion was really concerned with herself and not with young Tamar.

'She'll be someone,' said Lily, 'the others are soft, they live in the past, in a sort of Oxford dream world. Tamar was right to get out of that, she's brave, she's a survivor type. You've got to be hard to understand what's happening today, let alone *do* anything about it.'

'Jean's hard,' said Gulliver, 'she's very fond of Tamar too, and Tamar had quite a crush on her.'

'Really?' Lily wondered for a moment whether she could somehow get Jean back, perhaps with Tamar's help. But it was no good. 'I'm out of it,' she said. 'I can't get on with men, and I can't get on with women either.'

'You get on with me.'

'Oh, *you* –!'

'What do you mean, oh me?'

'Actually the idea that men and women are different is put about by men and by slave women. That Freud thing, penis-envy, means nothing but Freud feels superior. We used-up liberated women are best placed to see and know all. I don't know why I say "we". I'm the only one who sees and knows all.'

'That's because you're a witch,' said Gull. 'I know you met Jean at that yoga class where you stood on your head, but where did you meet Crimond?'

'Crimond, Crimond, he's a bore, why do we have to talk about him all the time?'

'How was it you came to that dance with him?' Gull had been wanting to ask this question for some time, but only now felt bold enough.

'Oh pure accident, some other girl dropped out at the last moment, that was nothing. I don't know him all that well really – but then who does.'

Lily was secretive about Crimond, not because anything

had 'happened', there was nothing thrilling to hide, and, though she did not mind if people suspected otherwise, it was true that she did not know him at all well. What was precious to her, and to be concealed, was simply the uneventful, but to her deeply significant, history of her thoughts and feelings about this man. Lily first heard of Crimond in the days when he was a famous extremist and idol of the young, an influential friend of well-known left-wing MP's, addressing crowded meetings and appearing on television. Then, at a time soon after Jean's return to Duncan and just before Lily's marriage she got to know Jean at the yoga class. Of course Jean never mentioned Crimond, but the Women's Lib group which Lily then frequented talked a lot about the affair, and though they did not esteem the institution of marriage voted Crimond a swine, a bully, a male chauvinist pig, and not at all politically sound on the liberation of women. When Crimond was speaking at a meeting near where Lily then lived in Camden Town she went along to look at him. She was captivated. It was not exactly being in love, Lily did not presume thus to entitle her obsession with Crimond. It was more like being *enslaved* in a situation where this was just something that happened to people and they took it for granted as a matter of fate and made the best of it. Some such picture, for Lily did not reflect upon the details, expressed the sort of hopeless unfrenzied fatalism of her condition. She pondered for a while about what to do. She went to another meeting, and another, travelling once across London, once to Cambridge. She managed on the second occasion, pushing her way through a bevy of excited students, his 'Red Guards' as someone called them, actually to talk to him. She pretended to be a representative of the local branch of the Socialist Women's Workshop, a body she had heard of, and asked if she could come and see him. Looking at his watch he said she could write to him care of his publisher, and vanished. Lily gave herself up to a long interval in which to gloat over the idea of writing to him. But as the interval lengthened she realised that she could not write, she could not compose a clever enough letter. He would not answer and she would be in hell. She found out where he lived and went round one morning, faint with fear, found Crimond alone, and offered her services as his messenger, his secretary, his house-maid, anything in his life. He told her to go round to the local Labour Party where they would give her some work to do. Departing almost in tears Lily was suddenly inspired to mention (which was then not too untrue) that she was a friend of Jean Kowitz. She also had the wit to use Jean's maiden name. Crimond now really looked at her. Then he said, 'Off you go.' Lily was disappointed, yet she also knew that henceforth she existed for him.

Now she wrote a business-like letter saying (which was untrue) that she did a lot of typing for writers and scholars and would be glad to type anything for him. This received no answer. But when, after a judicious interval, Lily arrived early and sat in the front row of one of Crimond's meetings, he recognised her and smiled. She then wrote again simply offering 'typing service' and sending good wishes. An imper-sonal communication from a secretarial agency asked her to do a rush job for Mr Crimond. Lily, taking leave from her office, worked demonically, then took the perfected typescript round in person. Someone took it from her and paid her, Crimond, glimpsed through a door, shouted thanks. Mean-while, in real life, Lily was submitting to the embraces of sweet anaemic James Farling, whom, still Crimond's slave and valuing herself at nothing, so it didn't matter, she married. There followed the almost instant widowhood which left her with fame and fortune, at any rate with money (she could never get clear how much) and the tattered fame of some, not always friendly, references in the press. Presuming upon the degree of real being conferred by these assets she began to send Crimond occasional postcards with little messages of good wishes and references to her 'typing bureau'. Time passed during which she went on through euphoria into depression. She began to feel that everyone was 'after her money', de-clared she was 'through with men' and would become a 'recluse'. She renewed a friendship with a painter called Angela Parke whom she had known as a student, but quar-relled with her because of some imagined 'slight'. She began to believe that 'people' now thought of her as a stupid, vulgar, pushing woman who thought that money would 'get her in anywhere'. She did a lot of solitary drinking. She worried ineffectually about her money which seemed to be disappearing. She felt continually snubbed, she had no friends and no world.

Lily was however, during this period, perceptibly supported by her curious one-sided relationship with Crimond. This was the one thing which remained intact and pure. Crimond played for her, during this time, the role of God. Here was one relation which required of her only the best and which could not be degraded. It was also of course a source of fear, since the power of this remote being over her was terrifying. Her postcards were of course never answered, but some more typing turned up, and she managed actually to see Crimond a few times and have brief conversations with him. On one happy day he called her 'Lily'. She took in that she need fear no rebuff. Crimond, of whom so many robust people were afraid, could afford to be casually kind to the weak. Gradually she was able to frame more sensible plans for her immediate existence. She made spasmodic attempts to 'improve her mind', read a few high-brow novels and watched the 'better' programmes on television. She even attended (though briefly) evening classes in French. She felt she was actually changing a little. Earlier she would not have been capable of conceiving and achieving the odd little friendship she now had with Gulliver Ashe. Meanwhile her relation with Jean's 'set', of which she had hoped much, remained disappointingly undeveloped. Jean had virtually dropped her, only Rose Curtland kept hold of her, inviting her to occasional gatherings of which nothing further came.

The gods, who in their bored way arrange such things in the destinies of mortal men, brought it about that as soon as Lily had, after prolonged and risky trying, established a very small real relationship with Crimond, her period of enslavement came to an end. Of course she still loved and valued Crimond more than anything in the world, but she was no longer the helpless slave of his consciousness. She could even begin to see that he was not perfect, was able to criticise him to other people, even to enquire boldly about his sex life, of which however little was known. A lot of fear disappeared from her existence and she felt generally better. In the innumerable hours of reflection which Lily had of course devoted to the matter, she had turned over the idea that she 'meant something' to Crimond because of a presumed connection with Jean. She did not know what to make of this hypothesis, even whether or not she liked it. She told herself sensibly that really she meant nothing to Crimond, who casually tolerated her as he did innumerable other insignificant hangers-on. But still, half in secret from herself, she developed the idea that Crimond was somehow *keeping her on*, not for herself of course, but as a tool, a possible line of communication. It began to please Lily to think of herself in this respect as a 'sleeper', somebody stored away for possible future use. It was again a paradox that when the moment came for Lily to play indeed a crucial part in Crimond's life she failed to recognise her role and very nearly did not play it. Lily had learnt from Rose, quite a long time beforehand, about the dance in Oxford, and who was going, even about Tamar and the American boy. As it happened, very shortly beforehand, she had one of her brief infrequent meetings, now much less emotionally terrifying, with Crimond for whom she had done some emergency typing. The typing was always of hastily written political stuff, not of the *book* of whose existence of course she knew, but which she had never seen. Crimond was by now living a much more solitary life in Camberwell, no longer supported by secretaries, helpers, admirers, Red Guards. Lily, coming by appointment, always found Crimond alone and was permitted a short chat, for which she always attempted to prepare something interesting to say. She had never, since that moment at the very start, dared to utter Jean's name, but she occasionally mentioned having seen Rose or Gerard. She thought this might increase her standing in Crimond's eyes, although she knew that relations between him and 'the set' were now extremely cool. Crimond never picked up these references, but did not seem annoyed by them either. In her little babble about Rose, Lily came out with the news of the dance, which was now only a week away, saying 'they're all going' and listing Mr and Mrs Cambus among the others. Crimond *immediately* said (the speed of this response later amazed her), 'I think I'll go too. Will you come with me?' Lily nearly fainted with surprise and joy.

Her joy was less as, on reflection, she saw at once that the purpose of the expedition must be exactly what it turned out to be, and that she was being used at last, as she had long wanted to be, only now it did not feel so consoling, as a tool lying to hand. She even wondered whether Crimond imagined that Lily was actually *bringing a message* from Jean. She could not help however entertaining the wildest hopes of what might happen on that magic evening. She did not see him in the interim; she travelled to Oxford by bus as Crimond, not offering to convey her, had simply said he would meet her at the College Lodge. They went in together and moved toward the nearest tent where Crimond stood with Lily beside him, and started looking about. It was at that moment that Gulliver Ashe saw him. As it happened, Crimond was at once recognised by a group of left-wing graduate students, one of whom knew him personally, and was surrounded. Lily sat down by herself for a while and was at that time sighted by Tamar. As another dance began, the group round Crimond dissolved and Crimond himself disappeared. When Lily saw him again some time later he was dancing with Jean.

During the days and weeks after the dance Lily remained in a state of shock. She soon learnt, from Rose whom she made a point of seeing, that Jean had again left her husband and was with Crimond. Thinking endlessly about this, she began to realise that she had lost him. Some creatures have a mode of defence which when used brings about their death. Lily had achieved her supreme moment of being actually of use, indeed of crucial use, to Crimond, but had thereby ended their relationship. It was impossible, *entirely* impossible, for her to go near him now. No more typing, no postcards, no visits, no little chats, nothing. As soon as she realised that this was so, all Lily's old silly love for him came flooding back, tinted now with all those vain illusions and the bitter memory of how happy and proud she had felt walking with Crimond across the grass toward the dancing. She thought she would die of the chagrin, the shame and the loss. Then, as she heard Rose and other people saying that it wouldn't last, Crimond was impossible, Jean was bound to leave him, Lily began to console herself with new pictures of being, one day, his old and dear friend, the one who, when all others proved faithless, had not left him. Of course she never revealed to anyone that she had told Crimond about the dance; and she could even feel a weird thrill to think that *she* had brought it all about. She almost felt sometimes, as she waited and waited and made no sign, as if she had a kind of secret power over him.

'There's no need for you to say anything special to Jean,' said Gerard to Tamar. 'Just go to see her. You yourself are the message.'

Gerard had invited Tamar and Violet for a drink assuming that Violet, who was annoyed if not asked, would as usual not come. However both had turned up. Patricia had then dropped in and had, felicitously for Gerard, taken Violet away to show her the new decorations initiated by Gideon in the upstairs flat. Gerard had Tamar briefly to himself.

They were in the drawing room of Gerard's house in Notting Hill. The room, as someone said, looked like Gerard, sombre and serious, but quietly stylish and smart, in greens and browns and hints of dark blue and wisps of dark red, nothing too much. It was a big room with a door to the garden. The green sofa had blue cushions, the blue easy chairs had green cushions. Upon the dark brown carpet beside the wide fireplace, where a modest fire was burning, was a brown and red geometrical rug. The walls, papered a light speckled brown, bore English watercolours. There were a few tables with shaded lamps and a few significant things on the mantel-piece. Gerard, who disliked being looked in at by hypothetical entities in the garden, had pulled the dark brown velvet curtains as soon as it was dark.

They stood together by the fire. Tamar, fingering a little sherry, was dressed as usual in her 'uniform', a skirt and blouse and jacket. She chose colours which were like her own colouring of tree-trunk brown and green and greenish grey. Her skirt and buttoned shoes were a subdued brown, her stockings were grey, her jacket was dark green, not unlike the colour of Gerard's jacket. Her blouse was white, worn with a light green scarf. Her mouse-brown tree-brown hair was neatly combed. Her large green-brown eyes looked up with trustful doubt at Gerard. He was not exactly a father-figure. Tamar kept the place of her unknown father piously empty. She often thought of him but never spoke of him. It was odd to think that he did not know she existed. Gerard, not classified as an uncle either, was a long-beloved figure of authority. Because of her mother's antipathy to 'them' (which of course included Pat and Gideon) Tamar had, especially of late, kept the tiniest bit aloof from Gerard. She hoped he understood.

'You think it would be all right to see her? It wouldn't look as if I were sort of prying – like a messenger from the enemy –?'

'No. Look at it naturally. You've always been very fond of Jean and she of you, you've seen a lot of each other. If you *don't* go she may feel you condemn her.'

'I wouldn't like her to feel that.'

'Exactly.'

'But she'll know I'm seeing Duncan too. I mean, I won't say so unless she asks, and she won't ask. She won't mention Duncan. But she'll know.'

'That's natural too. She won't expect you to have dropped Duncan! They've always been like parents to you.'

'Don't say that, I have parents.'

'Sorry, I know what you mean, I hope you know what I mean. Jean won't think you come as a spy, and she certainly won't think that Duncan sent you.'

'But you're sending me.'

'Well, in a way – but of course I haven't discussed this with Duncan. I just want to encourage you to do what I think you want to do only you feel too shy. Tamar, I'm not asking you to do anything at all except *be* with those two occasionally, be with them separately, without any other end in view.'

'But *you* have an end in view.'

How absolute the child is, thought Gerard. 'I'm not hiding anything,' he said. 'You know I want Jean and Duncan to be together again, we all want that, and the sooner it happens the less damage will have been done. Anything that hastens that process is good. *You* will be good for both of them, in any case.'

'I'm not sure,' said Tamar, 'I might just irritate them by being so absolutely out of their mess.'

She's being too clever about it, thought Gerard. 'Have you seen Duncan lately?'

'No. I saw him about a month ago, he asked me to tea, he told me to come again, just to ring up.'

'But you haven't been.'

'I don't think he meant it. It was just politeness like asking me to tea was. I think I'm not right. I'm a picture he doesn't want to look at.'

'He'd feel you were patronising him? The young can patronise their elders!'

'No, how could he think that! It's just that if you intrude on someone's grief, you're like a spectator, perhaps one has no right.'

'If we all thought that no one would console anyone. It's better to err on the other side. We fail much oftener by not trying to help than by rushing in. Of course I've said nothing to him –'

'You're all good at saying nothing to each other but being understood all the same!'

'Oh stop fussing, Tamar, just go, see Duncan, just show your face! He can get rid of you if he wants to, he's known you ever since you were born. Go to both of them.'

'All right. But –'

'But what?'

'I'm afraid of Crimond.'

Gerard thought, we mustn't get going on that, if we discuss it she'll work up a phobia. He said, 'Crimond's got his head in a cloud of theories, he won't even notice you. Anyway he'll be working, you can see Jean alone.'

Tamar smiled faintly and made a little gesture of submission, peculiar to her and which Gerard had observed since her childhood, raising and opening a hand palm upward.

'Good child,' he said. 'Now are you eating enough? You're awfully thin.'

'I eat. I'm always thin.'

'Have you heard anything from Conrad?'

'No. Not since just after the dance.' Conrad Lomas had written to her an apologetic letter to say he was just off to the States and would write from there. He said he'd spent the whole evening looking for her (he seemed to blame her really) and that he'd left her coat with the Fairfaxes. She had not heard from him again.

Gerard thought he had better leave the subject of Conrad. 'How's the job, are you still enjoying it?'

'Yes, it's very interesting, they gave me a manuscript to read.' Tamar had of course not told Gerard of the screw that had been put upon her to give up Oxford. She vaguely, not explicitly, feigned assent to Violet's account that she had 'cleared out' because 'fed up'. Wanting to be spared the agony of being questioned, she had quickly made friends with resignation and despair. She did not want to betray her mother to *their* meddling good intentions, and to have *them* fighting uselessly with Violet would merely prolong the pain.

'It's a good firm,' said Gerard, staring at her. He thought, I ought to have asked questions and made a fuss. I've been so obsessed with Crimond and that *other business*. I must look after Tamar and not just send her on errands. I keep thinking she's sixteen. Yet she's such a strong little person. She's quite capable of judging me. He dropped his gaze.

Tamar, looking up, keeping her lucid eyes fixed upon Gerard, reached out and grasped the mantelpiece with one hand, her small fingernails aligned beside a black soapstone seal who lived there. Gerard, whose tastes though quiet were eclectic, had collected a few pieces of Eskimo sculpture. She looked at the seal, which she was fond of, but did not touch it. It was slouched in such an elegant way, its plump shoulder turning, its doggy head raised. So far from judging Gerard, Tamar was feeling pure love for him, the quiet gentle free peaceful flow of communication which may be had with an old wise friend in whom one knows there is no malice, only thoughtful good will, and with whom one may stand in silence.

'I want to give you something,' said Gerard, and for an instant he thought of giving her the black Eskimo seal. But he knew he would regret the gift. He liked the seal too much himself.

Tamar, looking happy at last, said, 'Gerard, look, don't think I'm dotty – I'd like, I'd *really* like – something to *wear* – something of yours – something old you might be throwing out – a glove or a scarf or – something you've worn, you know – like a favour, or –'

'To carry on your lance?'

'Yes, yes –'

'That's brilliant, I know exactly!' Gerard went out into the hall and returned at once with his college scarf. 'Here, my old college scarf – you'll be wearing my colours!' He draped the scarf round her neck.

'Oh – can you spare it?'

'Of course, I can always get another! You can see how ancient this one is.'

'Oh, I'm *delighted* – now I won't be afraid – thank you so much!'

She drew the ends of the scarf down over her breasts to her waist, pulling at them and laughing. Gerard, laughing too, thought how quaint of her to see herself as a young knight going into battle wearing my favour! How touching. She is an odd child.

The door opened and Patricia and Violet came in.

As soon as her mother entered the room Tamar went out, as a light goes out. She was extinguished. The sparkling mischievous look, a rare look for her, vanished in a second, her face closed up, and the quiet free connection with Gerard was instantly cut off. Tamar now, wearing, Gerard thought, a mask which was so habitual that it could scarcely be so called, looked aloof, composed, withdrawn. Not betraying anxiety, she looked solemnly and attentively at her mother.

The cousins, seen together, had some slight resemblance. Gerard's father and Gerard's uncle Ben, especially as they appeared in some old photos which Gerard had discovered in the house in Bristol when he was clearing it out before it was sold, had looked alike when young. Patricia and Violet, it now seemed to him, carried the ghost or aura of this resemblance in a certain intentness of stare, the firm neat assertive mouth and the resolute 'brave' look. Only in Gerard's father and in Ben this alert look had been humorous and ironical, whereas in their offspring it was more opinionated and stern, in Violet's case aggressive. Pat was taller and stouter, with a plump face and a large chin, Violet altogether leaner and more shapely. Both wore above the nose the vertical lines of a permanent frown. They were now looking accusingly at Gerard and Tamar, whom they suspected of plotting something. Gerard, looking at them, felt his face twitch with pain. Among the old photos he had found some which he had taken of Grey. Of course he had destroyed them at once. Sad that one hastens to destroy, for fear of suffering, the mementoes of love. It had also occurred to Gerard as he looked at the photos of Ben, as a boy, as a youth, that his father had probably felt guilty about his younger brother, about not having tried to rescue him, sought him out and helped him more, about having accepted too easily and too soon the idea of him as a 'hopeless crazy fellow' with which Gerard had grown up. Perhaps that too was something which he ought to have talked over with his father. Now however Gerard was thinking about Grey and how he used to spread out one long wing in a kind of salute, flirting his scarlet tail, and gazing so consciously and so solemnly into Gerard's eyes.

Gerard, sensing Tamar's slight movement beside him, knew that now she just wanted to get away. She did not like hearing her mother talk to other people, especially not to Pat and Gerard.

Violet, peering myopically under her long fringe and holding her large round blue-rimmed spectacles in her hand, said to Tamar, 'What's that old thing you've got round your neck, is it a scarf?'

'Yes, it's Gerard's college scarf, he's just given it to me.'

'You can't wear a man's scarf.'

'Yes, I can! All college scarves are like this anyway.'

'But you weren't at Gerard's college. It looks as if it needs a good wash.'

Tamar's face expressed dismay at the idea of this sacrilegious deGeraldisation of her trophy. Gerard thought, God knows what that scarf smells of by now, it's never been washed in its life!

'I don't think college scarves ever get washed,' said Gerard, 'it would destroy the patina. I don't think that scarf would *like* to be washed.' I sound just like Jenkin, he thought. The image of Jenkin, suddenly superimposed on that of Grey, cheered him up.

'This college piety makes me shudder,' said Pat.

'Did you like the new decorations?' Gerard asked Violet.

'Must have cost a packet.'

'It was Gideon's idea,' said Pat. 'He's so good with colours. There's lots of space up there, when we bring in our furniture and some of the Bristol stuff it'll be quite civilised – and if we reorganise the whole house we can get everything in.'

'I don't want everything in,' said Gerard. 'And I wish Gideon would leave the rockery alone.'

Tamar was still fidgeting. Patricia and Violet were patting their hair into shape and smoothing down their clothes with identical gestures.

'Pat says you're going to move up there and let them have the rest of the house,' said Violet.

'That's news to me!'

'I think it would be very sensible. This place is far too big for one person. My flat would just about fit into this room. And I think you should sell the Bristol furniture, some of it's very valuable. Stop looking at your watch, Tamar, it's rude.'

'I think we should give some of the Bristol furniture to Violet,' said Gerard to his sister, after his guests had departed. Violet had refused to let him pay for a taxi.

'She dropped a hint about that upstairs! There's no room in her rabbit hutch, she'd spoil those nice things, they'd be covered with old newspapers and teapot rings and plastic bags. We might give her some of the kitchen stuff. But she wouldn't take it anyway. She just plays the poor relation for all it's worth. She wants to make us feel guilty.'

'She succeeds. I wish we could do something for Tamar.'

'So you keep saying, but it's no good, Tamar's got a death wish. She can't even get around to cleaning the flat! Violet never got over that swinging adolescence, she still dreams she's twenty and it's all before her and Tamar never happened. Tamar has never seemed to her entirely real, just a nasty hurtful ghost. She's made Tamar feel like a ghost. Tamar's fading away, one day she'll be as thin as a needle, the next day she'll be gone.'

'No –!'

Gideon Fairfax came in, bland, calm, curly-haired, red-lipped, with his clever pretty exquisitely shaven rosy youthful face. His shirt tonight, with his dark suit, was a glowing blueish green. He dyed his shirts himself. Gerard could never make out why his polite pleasant cultivated brother-in-law irritated him so much.

'Has she gone? I've been lurking.'

'She's gone,' said Pat. 'All the same I'd like to have her figure.'

'Gideon, I wish you'd leave the rockery alone!' said Gerard.

'My dear Gerard, the thing about a rockery is that it cannot be left alone, left alone it becomes all messy and earthy and Victorian and eventually vanishes, it's a perpetual challenge. I only weeded it and removed some stones and put in some plants, it'll be a picture next year.'

'Gideon is an artist,' said Pat.

'And I see you destroyed all those ash saplings.'

'My dear, they get everywhere.'

'I like them everywhere.'

Gideon was of course not an artist, not even an art historian, he was simply someone who could not help making money. His tastes did not always coincide with Gerard's, but Gerard had to admit that Gideon, beside understanding the market, did really like pictures.

'How's Leonard getting on at Cornell?' Leonard Fairfax was studying art history in America. Patricia and Gideon had long been worried in case Leonard were to fall in love with Tamar. There had been no sign of this however.

'I saw him in New York. He's started to play baseball!'

'Good God!'

'A pity that Lomas boy fell through for Tamar,' said Patricia. 'She doesn't seem to be interested in sex at all. Or she could be homosexual. I didn't at all like her passion for Jean Cambus. Thank heaven she won't be seeing *her* again!'

'Did you get the Klimt?' Gerard asked Gideon.

'Alas, no!'

'Did Gerard send you?' said Jean.

Tamar hesitated.

'Come, deal justly with me!'

Tamar smiled. She said, 'Well, he encouraged me. I wanted to come anyway – only I was afraid to.'

'Why?'

'I thought you mightn't want to see me.'

'Why shouldn't I?'

'Because you might want to cut off all contact with us.'

'I like your "us" – so you count as one of the gang!'

'No, not really – but I thought it might upset you –'

'Embarrass me, accuse me?'

'No, no –' Tamar blushed because something like that had

been in her mind. 'Jean, don't be so strict! You're not cross with me for coming, are you?'

'No, my dear child, of course not, I'm just curious. So you're not the bearer of a message from anybody?'

'Certainly not.'

'Why did Gerard want you to come?'

'Nothing special, just to keep contact.'

'So you're to report back to Gerard?'

'He never said that!' It was true that he had never said it, but of course he would want a report. Tamar realised she should have expected just these questions – and now she was close to telling lies.

Their meeting had been awkward. Tamar, after reflecting carefully about how to proceed, had rung up from a telephone box in Camberwell about four o'clock on a Saturday, saying she was near and could she come. Jean said yes. When Tamar came through the front door there had not been the usual kiss, just a quick handshake. Jean had led the way to the back room which was full of bookshelves with a divan up against the books and a door to the garden. Jean was wearing a dressing gown. The divan was covered with an old faded cotton counterpane on top of which were two handsome dresses. Tamar took off her coat, keeping Gerard's scarf about her neck. The sky had become darker since her arrival and now it was raining. Outside the little lawn was strewn with leaves, the yellow chrysanthemums, fading to brown, drooping against their windblown sticks. The room was cold and felt derelict and unlived in, the floor echoed, the house felt dusty and damp. Tamar thought, it's a *senseless* house, and her heart sank.

'Well, I'll let you off,' said Jean. 'I know you're a good girl. I'm glad to see you.' She added, 'In case you're wondering, he's not here.'

There was a slight pause. There were so many things which could not be uttered, it was necessary to reflect. Jean said, 'God, how dark it's got, I'll put the light on.' She switched on a dim centre light which seemed to make the room darker. They were sitting opposite to each other on upright chairs, as in an interview between a social worker and a client. Tamar looked down at the nails in the unpainted wooden boards.

'How's Oxford?'

Tamar startled, said, 'I'm not at Oxford, I'm working for a publisher.' It seemed amazing that Jean was so out of touch, so far away.

'But why –?'

'My mother was in debt.'

'Why didn't you ask me?'

'My mother wouldn't accept money.'

'I'm not offering it to her, I'm offering it to you! Are you stupid, can't you *grow up*? She wants to isolate you, she wants to ruin you.'

'Not really – she loves me.' Tamar could see what it was like for her mother in whose wounded heart there was indeed hatred, hatred for Tamar, but somehow love too.

'I'll go and see her.'

'No, no, she's against you anyway, she's jealous because I'm fond of you.'

'God, how wicked human beings can be. I'll think of something.'

Tamar could not help wishing that some quick magic could mend it all. Why couldn't money solve everything? Money here seemed to glow with rationality, sense, justice, almost virtue. But it was impossible. Tamar could not either leave her mother or save her. It was like something awful in a fairy tale. The money to pay the debts could only come from Tamar's work. No other money would do. There was no place here for common sense or reasonable compromise. Tamar's ordeal would not make Violet happy or grateful. Yet anything else was unthinkable.

'My father will think of something,' said Jean. 'You'll just have to tell a few lies. Tamar, don't look like that, I'll smack you!'

'What pretty dresses,' said Tamar, pointing to the bed.

'All right, change the subject, but I won't tolerate this repulsive sacrifice. I've just bought these, I was just going to try them on.' Jean jumped up, threw off her dressing gown,

161

revealing herself in a short white petticoat and black suspenders and black stockings. In this attire she might conventionally have resembled an adornment of an old-fashioned nightclub, but to Tamar's eyes she looked more like a pirate, a soldier, like a Greek soldier, someone striding forth, her stockings become boots, the lace of her petticoat the permitted embellishment of a crack regiment. Her face too, so pale, almost white, with its thin sharply contoured aquiline nose, looked like that of a young commander, perhaps a sultan, portrayed in profile by an Indian miniaturist. Her bare shoulders, her arms, her glimpsed thigh, were white too, delicate transparent skin faintly marbled here and there with little blue veins. Her dark hair, curving with her head, glowed bluish. Tamar had never seen her look so splendid, so young and strong, so, in spite of her pallor, glittering with health. Tamar sighed.

Hands rising into sleeves, Jean swiftly slid into one of the dresses, then adjusted it for display. It was a straight grey feathery-light silk dress with a high oriental collar and a design of gentian-blue leaves. The exquisite dress, caressing Jean's slimness, also looked to Tamar like some sort of angelic uniform. She exclaimed.

'Yes, it's lovely, isn't it. But Tamar, you must learn to dress! I should have taken you in hand long ago. It's time you gave up those insipid girlie blouses and skirts and those little low-heeled shoes that look like slippers. Get a decent *dress* that says something, with a *shape* and a definite *colour*, not those muddy browns and pale greens. You're pretty, and if you dress smartly you'll *look* pretty. Do try this one on and see how nice it looks on you, please do, you can just slip off your jacket.'

Jean had pulled off her silk dress and Tamar was taking off her jacket when Crimond came in. The first thing Jean said to him was, 'You're back early.'

Crimond looked startled, even dismayed, at seeing Tamar. Tamar, blushing, resumed her jacket and made a dive for her coat and her bag. Jean put on her dressing gown.

Tamar said, 'I must go.'

Jean said, 'Don't go, stay and have some tea.'

'No, no, I must be off, I hadn't realised how late it was.' She made for the door which Crimond, with a slight inclination of his head, held open for her.

Jean went with her to the front door. 'Thank you for coming, child, come again. We'll fix that other matter up somehow.' Tamar was still putting on her coat. The door closed promptly behind her.

Jean went back to the room where Crimond was sitting on the divan. He said, 'That girl was wearing the scarf of my college.'

'I suppose it's Gerard's,' said Jean, looking warily at Crimond. Sometimes she was afraid of him.

'Or your husband's. Did *he* send her?'

'No, of course not! It was her own idea.'

'I don't believe that. Or did you arrange it? You didn't say she was coming.'

'I didn't know! She rang up after you'd gone, she said she was nearby and could she call.'

'You were upset that I'd come back early.'

'No –'

'If I hadn't seen her would you have told me she'd been with you?'

'Well –'

'Tell me the truth, Jean.'

'Yes, I'd have told you. But I knew you'd hate it and imagine it was a plot! It wasn't a plot! She's a poor harmless little girl, she's not part of *their* thing. Why are you so suspicious, why are you so insecure?'

'Insecure! You ask a dangerous question. You told her to come again, and there was something you'd fix up. What was it?'

'I want to give her money so that she can stay on at Oxford.'

'You can send her a cheque. I don't want you to see her. Your husband sent her as a little ambassador of bourgeois morality. She came as a spy. Did you take her downstairs?'

'No.'

'Did you kiss her?'

'No.'

'Don't you usually?'

'Just in a social way –'

'Why not today?'

'Because we both felt awkward –'

'You were embarrassed, you blushed in front of that inquisitive little person, you felt yourself in the wrong before her, that's why they sent her. She's in love with you, isn't she?'

'She had a sort of crush on me when she was seventeen –'

'I come in and find you undressed and her undressing.'

'Don't be crazy! I wanted her to try on one of my dresses!'

'You would let her contaminate your dress with her baby milky body! Can't you understand that I find all this disgusting, repulsive?'

'Oh stop it, *stop* it!'

'I won't have spectators. You sent Lily Boyne here to tell me about the dance. You talked to her about me. You invited that girl, you probably talked to her too.'

'I *told you* I didn't send Lily! And *of course* I didn't talk about you to Tamar! Crimond, we must believe each other. Come back to reality! I believe every word you say. I don't start imagining things! If I couldn't believe you I'd go mad – if we can't believe each other we'll both go mad.'

'If you lie to me I'll kill you.'

'I won't see Tamar again. I'll tell my father to send her a cheque. Just calm down! I can't *bear* it when we lose contact with each other like this, it's like dying if I lose that contact for a second. I live you, I breathe you –'

Crimond looked down at the floor, then looked up. His cold angry face that gleamed like metal, his deadly pain-giving face, was gone. His thin lips were parted, his mouth drooped a little, he had a tired almost wistful air. He looked at her, then looked away and breathed deeply. Jean knew it was over. She had been standing before him. Now she came and sat beside him on the divan and he put an arm round her shoulder, a quiet tired comforting arm.

'I live and breathe you,' he said. 'I believe what you say. It was unpleasant seeing that girl here. I don't like little girls.'

'I'm glad you've come back for supper. You decided to skip the meeting?'

'It was cancelled. I bought some necessary books. I didn't waste time.'

'Will you marry me?' Jean sometimes asked this question. She wanted the marriage bond, Crimond did not.

'Why are *you* so insecure? You don't need a guarantee.'

'I know. But I'd *like* us to be married.'

'I can't see why. If you want a divorce go ahead.'

'You said you didn't want me to divorce.'

'I don't want you to see that man.'

'I needn't. My father's lawyer in London would do it all.'

'Do what you like.'

'*Then* would you marry me?'

'Jeanie, don't *bother* me about this!'

'I want us to live in France.'

'My work is here.'

'You have all those people you go to see in Paris. Couldn't we have a flat in Paris?'

'No. We couldn't afford it.'

'Perhaps when your book's finished we could travel together, all round Europe, you could give lectures, you'll be famous then – Oh I do want us to go away together, to be away together.'

'One day we'll go away together – perhaps into death.'

'And I wish you'd spend my money. I wish you'd let me spend our money.'

'Don't let's have that argument again. You've bought two pretty dresses. Falcon, falcon, don't fret, little falcon. You must work, you must study, you are wasting your mind. You must find something to do.'

'I want to help you.'

'You must find something of your own to do, sokolnitza. Come now, let's go downstairs.'

When Jean had come to Crimond on the morning after the dance she had come without any clear idea except that she must be in his presence, and if possible stay there forever. A little later she proposed that she should help him in his work, co-operate with him as she had done before. Crimond replied that he needed no help, she would not understand, he would simply waste time trying to explain to her what he wanted her to do. Crimond did not type and wrote his thoughts down in longhand with a fountain pen. (He could not conceive of any other method of serious thinking.) Jean suggested that she might helpfully learn to type, or even to use a word processor. Crimond said that he used an impersonal efficient typing agency, could not have stood the sound of a typewriter in the house, and found the idea of a word processor revolting. He lectured her on how she must find some employment, chided her for not using her talents. The idea was mooted, by Jean who thought it would please Crimond, that she might do some social work; she made a few investigations and decided she would not be suited to social work, and Crimond agreed it would be a waste of her time. He was more anxious that she should use her academic skills, do a degree, take a course, study a language. Crimond himself was a good linguist and could read (though he could not speak) French, German, Italian, Spanish and Russian. He also retained his Latin and Greek and often opened books of classical poetry. Jean, wishing to be useful to him, wondered if she should learn Chinese, but it was agreed that this would be unlikely to yield dividends in the near future. It was debated whether she should learn Greek, but Crimond turned out to be hostile to this idea. Jean's only effective foreign language was French. She bought a German grammar but could not interest Crimond in her progress. Her Oxford degree in history was now remote and she felt no inclination to try to make herself into a historian or a school teacher. She would have liked to do a degree in English, but did not like to suggest this as it might seem frivolous. She suggested a short course in computer science, but Crimond did not like computers. He was also very firmly against her trying to learn any philosophy. Another difficulty was that he did not really want her to be away from the house.

Jean was not without occupation however. She was finding herself, now that she was with Crimond, simply more and more in love. She was *living* upon love. When she was alone, she would for long times shudder and tremble with it. She had never experienced *presence* so vividly before, the total connection with another being, the interpenetration of bodies and souls, the intuitive absolute of mutual self-giving, the love of two gods. The obliteration of self, the dazzling blindness of the love-act which was both part and all of their lives, constituted a mystery or ritual with which she lived in a continuous present of anticipation and remembrance. The silences together, the sleep together, made her weep with joy or sob inwardly with tenderness. Part of her security was Crimond's absolute sovereignty in all matters. It was he who decreed the times and details of their going to bed. Though intensely passionate, Crimond was also in many ways extremely puritanical. He did not speak about sex, used no coarse words, scarcely any words at all. He never let Jean see him undress; she also undressed quickly and discreetly, being seen as far as possible either totally dressed or totally undressed. (The scene with Tamar annoyed him, Jean knew, partly because of a breach of this rule.) Their relationship, or mode of being, was now, they were agreed, quite different from what it had been in Ireland. There, their furtive love-making, which had seemed so wonderful, had been shadowed by fear, not only of Duncan's discovery, but also of the anticipated end of something which seemed accidental and too good to last. In Ireland they were homeless, and that had involved a kind of restless freedom which had really flawed their love. They had, as it seemed, looking back, been searching for happiness, at least Jean had been. Now they were living in an ecstasy to which happiness was irrelevant. Once when she had told Crimond that she was happy he had seemed surprised as if he was to note this as one thing among others. She thought, he has the concept of ecstasy but not of happiness. Happiness was not what *this* was for. When Jean, waking while he slept beside her, or waiting for his return home, felt, breathing slowly and deeply, the quietness, the cosmic reality of this joy which now had no term, she thought that surely it was occupation enough to fill the days and hours of her whole life. She had been re-created, given new being, new pure flesh, new lucid spirit. She could perceive the world at last, her eyes were cleared, her perceptions clarified, she had never seen such a vivid, col-oured, detailed world, vast and complete as myth, yet full of tiny particular accidental entities placed in her way like divine toys. She had discovered breathing, breathing such as holy men use, the breathing of the planet, of the universe, the movement of being into Being.

About all *that* there was no doubt at all. It may be wondered whether and how Jean also, at times, remembered her hus-band and his grief, and her friends who regarded her as a traitor and whom she could now never see. Rose never wrote; Jean did not expect her to. It was better so. Such thoughts did appear, swift as black passing swallows in the clear bright air of her love. She did not either question or suppress these reproachful blurs and streaks, she let them pass, consigning her sin, if such it was, to some objective record, some spirit perhaps, whereby it could be contained in the totality of her new world, not dissolved or hidden but placed. Her duty, as her passion, was now Crimond's. Her surprise at Tamar's appearance (she had almost forgotten who Tamar was) was the shock of realising that the two regions which she had so resolutely separated could actually communicate. Someone could come from over there. Gerard, in reckoning upon some such (as he hoped salutary) jolt, had been thus far prescient. The 'virgin priestess act', in which he had also had faith, was not entirely without efficacy; Jean, seeing Tamar, did feel, at least for seconds, that she had left a mess behind. This impression soon passed however, and Jean's dismay at Crimond's arrival was her instant preview of what he was likely to say and did say. Of course she did not imagine that Crimond really regarded Tamar as involved with Jean in any plot or special relation; but she knew how much he must detest any sense of being judged or spied on by *them*. *They* must be deemed to be non-existent. The fact remained (and Jean reflected upon this paradox also) that *they* paid Crimond's salary. Crimond refused absolutely to touch Jean's money. This was in spite not only of Jean's constant urging, but of an extraordinary letter which Jean's father had lately written to Crimond. Jean's father, who had had an orthodox Jewish childhood in Manchester and now lived in New York, was a moralist, a liberal Jew, an observer of festivals, who had sent his daughter to a Quaker school. He could tolerate mixed marriages but disapproved of broken marriages. On the other hand, he rather liked Crimond whom he had met in Dublin in the earlier part of the Irish episode. He knew of Crimond's political activities from the days of his early fame, and after meeting him read some of his articles and pamphlets. Joel Kowitz, capitalist and maverick radical with a taste for the picturesque, had found Duncan Cambus rather a tame match for his marvellous daughter and only child. He had hoped that Jean would marry Sinclair Curtland, and was not indifferent to the title. He did not mind Sinclair's evident homosexuality which he thought of as a natural, even perhaps necessary, phase in the development of upper-class Englishmen. Now, although he disapproved of fugitive wives, he could not help liking Jean's new choice, of which she informed him immediately after her flight. Joel saw in Crimond a man of power and spirit, a fascinating eccentric, not unlike himself. After some reflection, and convinced after a passage of time that Jean was not having second thoughts, he wrote a very careful letter to Crimond, implying acceptance of the situation, and expressing hopes for Jean's welfare and happiness, towards which, in her new circumstances, her financial resources could materially assist. He hoped in short, though he did not put in quite so bluntly, that Crimond would spend Jean's money. Jean had not of course suggested that Crimond might be unwilling to do this, but Joel had rightly judged Crimond's character. Crimond showed Jean the letter, asked her to thank her father for it, and without further comment continued to refuse to touch her money. Jean, reading between the lines of her father's touching and unusual letter, could see something else, more important and more tragic. Joel Kowitz, banker and believer in miracles, had always wanted a grandson. He assumed that Duncan was, in this respect, the one who had failed, and he hoped that, with another mate, Jean might yet be capable of some last-minute success. He could not help regarding her as eternally young. Jean, who did not discuss other changes in her life with her father, knew that a miracle would indeed now be required. She reflected, and this was another dark blur or pain-point in her new life, that if she had stayed with Crimond in Ireland she might have borne his child. Crimond had said then very positively that he did not want children. But a *fait accompli* might have changed his mind. It would also have made it impossible for Jean to go back to Duncan.

The fact certainly remained that, apart from a little discreet use by Jean of her funds upon her own clothes and little household extras, the spending money of the *ménage* came mainly from the *Crimondgesellschaft*. Crimond still earned a little from journalism, but he shunned lecturing or talking on television, and refused lucrative invitations to America. They lived frugally. Crimond occasionally travelled, briefly and alone, to conferences, seminars, meetings, in Paris, Frankfurt, Bologna. He also went to Scotland to see his father. Jean would have liked to meet his father, but Crimond would not allow this. He gave money to his father, and also to the old half-blind Polish lady who occupied the upstairs flat. He gave Jean a housekeeping allowance. There was no 'entertaining' except at the level of cans of beer which Jean was instructed to bring in when, not often, some 'associates' were coming. Crimond himself did not drink, and Jean had managed, helped by love and by the reproaches of her lover, to give up alcohol. Jean did not meet the 'associates' who argued with Crimond in the Playroom (as he called his workroom). Crimond seem to have a variety of connections but no friends. Once a gang of gaily dressed young people turned up and asked if one of them could take a photograph of Crimond out on the steps, surrounded by the others. Crimond agreed to this affably and seemed even to be gratified; this touched Jean, and also made her sad. He was lonely now, who had once been such a folk hero. The major expense was travelling, which

Crimond seemed to have no difficulty in meeting; in fact there seemed to be, in his way of life, no place for the lavish expenditure of Jean's money, and Jean had to comfort herself by the thought that she and her father were, there was no doubt, the major donors to the *Gesellschaft*. Only Gerard actually knew how much everyone gave. But it was certainly not comfortable to think that the 'delinquents' were being supported by people, including her husband, who now had double reasons for disapproval. There was, as Jean knew from earlier discussions, no likelihood of the stipend being withdrawn. The 'Friends of Crimond' had agreed to finance the book until its completion. They might however, as Jean also knew from these discussions, become restive, ask for reports and predictions, even ask to see the text and somehow call Crimond to account. Jean shuddered when she imagined what this might be like.

Jean did not question Crimond about the book, and of his long hours in the playroom asked only, 'How did it go?' She looked at, but did not open, the piles of notebooks. Once or twice she inspected a current page left open on the desk, but found the subject matter obscure and Crimond's tiny inky writing hard to read. She shopped, she cooked, she looked after the house but did not venture to prettify it. She gave up drink, but did not entirely give up buying clothes which was a natural function. She was used to wearing new dresses. At first she 'dressed' on occasional solitary visits to central London, to art galleries and matinées. But she feared to meet someone she knew, and these jaunts soon began to seem pointless and out of place. She wore her pretty clothes on some evenings for Crimond who, though disapproving of extravagance, humoured this diversion. Perhaps he felt she must be allowed to retain some small symbol of her former splendour; perhaps that image of the splendour enriched his sense of possession. Crimond had a car, a Fiat, which he occasionally used to go to meetings in the Midlands. He never drove into central London. Jean, soon after her arrival, had fetched her own car, a Rover, to Camberwell, but had hardly ever driven it since. Her Rover and Crimond's Fiat lived outside on the street, sometimes close, sometimes apart, according to the Fiat's wanderings. Crimond no longer used his bicycle, which remained in the hall. Jean had suggested that she might get a bicycle too and they might go riding, but this had not proved a fruitful idea. She did not mind having no jaunts and no society, and after a while the idea of 'social life' began to seem impossible and abhorrent. Sometimes, encouraged by Crimond, she went to tea with Mrs Lebowitz, the old Polish lady upstairs, who reminisced about the Warsaw Rising. Crimond rose early and worked all day on the book, taking a cup of tea (he never drank coffee) for breakfast and sandwiches for lunch. About six or seven he stopped and they had high tea in the kitchen. Then they watched television in the front room, the news and political debates in which Crimond vociferously joined, often amusingly, sometimes furiously. They talked easily and continuously at such times, about politics, about books, about pictures, about their childhoods, about places they had been to, especially about cities (Crimond hated 'the country', he had had enough of that when he was a boy), about Ireland, about the history of their love. They did not talk about people they knew. They drank chocolate and ate creamy and sugary cakes (which Crimond liked) at eleven, then went to bed on the big divan in the playroom. On some days, though not often, Crimond knocked off at three and they spent the afternoon making love.

Crimond did not like music, but he enjoyed literature and painting, about which he knew a great deal. He was particularly fond of poetry. All his old college books were on the shelves in the television room, which he called the library, and sometimes he read Greek and Latin poems to Jean and translated them, sometimes he treated her to Dante and to Pushkin. Jean, whose Latin was rusty and her Italian poor, and who knew no Greek or Russian, did not attempt to follow these performances, but watched his animation with intense pleasure. He avidly perused book catalogues, was excited when they arrived, and did not only purchase 'work' books. He had been athletic at Oxford, he cared about fitness, he did exercises before his breakfast tea. His only visible 'hobby' was guns, which he collected, and could use, as she had seen in

Ireland, but in which he did not attempt to interest Jean. Her worries about whether he would be irked by her continual proximity soon vanished. He said, 'I work so much better now you're in the house.' On one or two evenings he asked her to sit in the Playroom, not near him but at the far end where he could see her, and read or sew. She had learnt that he liked to see her sew. When he was tired he sometimes cried out, 'I can't *rest*, I can't *rest*!' He would call Jean to him and she would stroke his head, back from the brow and down onto his neck, or 'draw' his sallow freckled face, smoothing his cheeks and his closed eyes and passing her fingers down his long nose. Then he would begin to work again. His industry was terrifying. 'We're crazy people,' he would sometimes say, 'it's like Kafka.'

'It's like happy Kafka,' said Jean.

Or he would say, 'Our love is entirely necessary and entirely impossible.' To which she was to reply, 'It's necessary, because we have proved it is not impossible.' To which he would answer, 'Good. So it exists necessarily like God.' She was touched, surprised, deeply moved, even terrified by his dependence upon her. 'You are the only woman I have ever wanted or ever will or could want.'

Downstairs, they sat on the big double divan, low, hard, almost square, covered with a very old quilt of faded green covered with geometrical designs which Crimond said had been woven in the Hebrides and had once covered his parents' bed.

'I wish you didn't have these guns in your life. Have you got a licence?'

'Ssssh!'

'Why do you like them? All right, I know that men like guns, but why do you?'

'I've always played with guns. Country people have them. They were around when I was a child. My grandfather was a gillie.'

'You never told me that.'

'Well, he was a part-time gillie, so was my father when he was young. They loaded the guns for the gentry and piled up the dead birds. You've probably never witnessed those horrible scenes. You're romantic about firearms because they've never been part of your life.'

'*You're* romantic!' Jean decided not to tell Crimond that Sinclair had more than once taken her to a 'shoot'. How odd memory was. She saw Sinclair suddenly so clearly with his blond mane and his short straight nose and his luminous intimate dark blue eyes which were so like Rose's, and his jaunty roguish teasing air of a spoilt boy which was so unlike Rose's gentle patient withdrawn look. He was holding a shotgun as, in Jean's memory picture, he turned towards her. His knee-breeches were covered with flecks of golden bracken. Jean had hated it, hated seeing the birds fall. Rose hated it too. 'Do you imagine you'll have to defend yourself one day?'

'I don't think so,' said Crimond, taking her question seriously. 'It's just a matter of precision, I like precision.'

'Oh, I know you're good at it, I remember at Oxford, and in Ireland. You said the target was a symbol, you haven't shot at it since I've been here.'

'I know you don't like it. I'm going to get rid of most of the guns soon anyway.'

'But not all?'

'I want to be able to kill myself if necessary.'

'Not sleeping pills? Of course you'd prefer a more stylish exit.'

'And more certain.'

'I feel sometimes you'd like a war.'

'I don't think so, it would interrupt my work.'

'Really you'd like the Bomb to fall and get rid of all that messy clutter of the past and all that kitsch and false morality you hate so much!'

'We are fat with false morality and inwardness and authenticity and decayed Christianity –'

'Yes, but there must *be* morality! After all you're a puritan, you detest pornography and promiscuity and –'

'It's the final orgy, the last stand of the so-called incarnate

174

individual, who has withered into a little knot of egoism, even the concept stinks. It's the end of a civilisation which gloats over personal adventures.'

'Crimond! You're a person and an adventurer! You enjoy being an incarnate individual! Or do you let yourself off because you're a philosopher and can *see* it all – or because you can't help being a product of a corrupt era? And you say 'final', but what next? *We've* got to clear it up, we can't rely on bombs or God! Sometimes I think you even want to hate sex, only you can't, you mixed-up son of a Galloway postman!'

Crimond, who had been holding her hand, released it. Their knees were not touching. Crimond out of bed was not a kisser or cuddler. He did not waste the electricity of passion by continual contact. Sometimes he seemed to treat Jean almost formally. Only occasionally, out of bed, did he signal her to come near, to hold his hand or gently caress his hair or face.

Crimond, ignoring Jean's unusual outburst, took a cue from her last words. 'I meant to tell you, I must go to Scotland next week.'

'How is he?'

'He's as usual. But I must go.'

Jean knew that Crimond worried continually about his father, now becoming bed-ridden and losing his wits. Crimond did not want to talk to her about this. She was becoming light-headed, almost weary, with her desire for him and with the incarnate joy of the nearness of satisfaction. She did not try to recover his hand.

Crimond then said, returning to their conversation: 'Perhaps. The individual cannot overcome egoism, only society can aspire to do that. I have always, except in one miraculous instance, felt degraded by sex.'

'When you said it was necessary but impossible did you mean because it's a miracle?'

'No – just because – Let's stop talking.'

'I wish you'd talk to me more about your ideas.'

'My ideas only live in written words. Come, Jeanie, my queen, my falcon, my sweet goddess, my only love, come to me, come to bed, oh my sweetness, my food, my breath, my life, my dear love, my last home –'

Any suffering which Gerard, at times, imagined Duncan to be enduring was less than the reality thereof. Duncan's ability to keep up appearances, to put on a brave face and a cool manner, did in fact a little deceive his friends, though they were, they thought, believing the worst. Duncan went to the office, performed his duties creditably as before, smiled at his colleagues, joked and chatted, while all the time a black machine was working frenziedly inside his head. Blackness, that was what he experienced, a feeling of blackness over everything, a black veil over the lamp, black dust upon the furniture, black stains upon his hands, and a black cancerous lump in his stomach. He was not sure whether it was better to suffer the blackness as a great totality of deadly misery, or to analyse it into connected portions which could be separately rehearsed. He did not deliberately banish hope; there was just, on any view, nothing to hope for. He thought often about suicide and this sometimes very slightly eased the pain. It was possible to end this tortured consciousness.

His friends brought him, and he felt they were well aware of this, no relief, indeed made things, if this were possible, worse, by their assiduous attention and concern, their avoidance of painful topics, together with their implied indignation on his behalf. They wanted him to fight; or rather they wanted to *do something*, for which they required his support or imprimatur. The polite indifferent silence of his office colleagues irritated him less. Gerard and Rose continued to invite him to lunch, to dinner, to drinks, to the theatre, although he consistently and formally refused. Rose rang at carefully timed intervals and asked if she could drop in. Sometimes, not to be too boorish, he said yes, and she came with flowers, stayed for a drink, talked to him about indifferent matters (the news, a film, a book, her new dress) and looked at him with her gentle persuasive loving blue eyes in a way which made him want to scream. She had also lately reminded him of two forthcoming events at which his presence was traditional, the Guy Fawkes night party at Gerard's, and the Reading Party at Rose's country house, Boyars. Duncan to stop her talking about these festivals, which he had for so long attended with Jean, said he would come. Gerard, who evidently felt it his duty to force his company on his suffering friend, turned up more often, suggesting or announcing his arrival on various evenings just after Duncan's return from the office, staying for an hour, never for supper, to which Duncan never invited him. Gerard too talked of indifferent matters, the news, government policy, office life, but also at intervals made openings, ignored by Duncan, for discussion of 'the situation'. Jenkin did not come. He sent one letter in which he sent his love and said that, as Duncan knew, he would be *very* glad to see Duncan, if Duncan ever wished, either at his house or at Duncan's. After that he sent a few picture postcards, selected at the British Museum, mostly with classical Greek subjects, vaguely mentioning a possible meeting sometime. Duncan did not reply, but he kept the postcards.

Most evenings, therefore, since he tolerated no other visitors, Duncan was alone and spent the time drinking whisky. He had cashiered the cleaning woman and allowed the flat to descend into a disorder which he occasionally ameliorated for Rose's benefit and lest she should insist on dealing with it herself. He had endeavoured to strip the flat of any traces of Jean's presence. Soon after her defection Jean had returned during the day and removed her jewellery, a lot of her clothes and cosmetics, some books, some objects from her childhood home; but much of her had remained. Duncan gave away her remaining clothes to a charity shop, smashed or burnt a number of other things, and put away some books and pictures into his little study and locked the door. The places where these things had been remained however but too visible. He also gave away the china which she had bought and they had used, and brought out instead some Edwardian china which had belonged to his mother and which Jean had condemned as 'pretty-pretty'. He ate lunch in the office canteen and made himself a snack supper at home, drinking and watching television. He searched the programmes looking for disasters, earthquakes, nuclear accidents, floods, famines, murders, kidnappings, torture. He watched thrillers, especially violent ones. He shunned anything romantic or about animals. He had used to enjoy concerts and opera, but now hated to hear serious music, even a few bars of it would make him curse and reach for the switch. Bedtime was terrible. He took sleeping pills of course and not always with success. We are told to go to our grave as to a bed. Duncan went to his bed as to a grave, but one in which he lay active, struggling, suffocating, weeping.

There are states of obsession where it is, it seems, possible to think of one thing *all the time*. Duncan's obsessive subject was of course large and allowed him the activity of turning round its different facets. He enacted the whole story of Jean's relation with Crimond, starting with trying to remember (which he could not) when and how at Oxford they had first met. Had Jean met Crimond before she met Duncan? It was his impression (but was he right?) that Jean and Crimond had paid no particular attention to each other at Oxford. Jean had been busy flirting with Sinclair who was in love with Gerard; while Duncan, already in love with Jean, was trying to kill his painful hopes by seeing her as Sinclair's wife. But must she not have noticed the clever and good-looking Crimond? Something certainly started later on when Crimond was famous and Jean was his research assistant. Was Jean, then, already Crimond's mistress? This was poisonous food for much thought. Then they were abroad and Crimond was in eclipse. Duncan recalled the evening when, at the news that Crimond was coming to Dublin, Jean could not conceal her joy. Then there was on a later evening, again in company, that intense look, that *stare*, exchanged between them. Then waving them off together, departing in Crimond's car to explore Ireland. When did he *know*? Oh the certainty, the *certainty*, so often weakly thrust away, always renewed and increasing. Then, the hideous vividness of that memory picture, the ball of hair and Jean calling from below, a memory renewed daily with a ghastly particularity when Duncan combed his own hair which was now copiously falling out, drew the fluff of hair from the comb and dropped it in the wastepaper basket. Oh Christ, Crimond complacently combing his hair after tumbling Jean! The fake departure and the *last kiss*, the Judas kiss he gave to Jean before he left her at the airport. The sojourn with the sinners in hell in the Wicklow bar. The horse and the cow and the black-faced sheep and the little flowers. The ascent, the descent, the fight – The fight came in slow motion, and though he thought constantly about the blow, as in a dream he could not evoke the physical pain, the agony of the event was humiliation and shame. Duncan had once been a skilled fighter – a wrestler – but he had simply blundered at the fellow. Would it have been better if he had hurt Crimond seriously? Ought he to have exposed Crimond at once and branded him as a leper? Ought he, then, or later, to have made Jean tell him every detail, every bedding, everything, rather than letting it all be passed over, 'taken into consideration', forgiven? He had let Crimond off because he was worried about his eyesight and did not want the public rumpus of declaring himself a cuckold, he had let Jean off because he was so glad to have her back, because he was *grateful*. He should have destroyed Crimond and punished her. He had been weak and soft, he had got what he deserved, it was all his own doing. These were thoughts which, detached from any manageable reality, led away towards madness.

Duncan was becoming more and more out of sympathy with his body, he hated the bulky graceless mound which he had to move laboriously about. He was even now still putting on weight. He had once been a big thick-set muscular man, a formidable figure with his broad shoulders and his great commanding head, a bear, a bull, a lion. Now he was simply a fat man with a puffy face like a gross baby, his nose was thicker, his nostrils enlarged and sprouting hair, he had been handsome, he had become ugly, the ugly old cheated husband, a traditional figure of fun. He envied Gerard his taut physique and his undimmed idealism, he envied Jenkin his simple uncluttered uncomplicated innocent life. He pictured again and again and saw in his dreams Crimond's slim tall form, pale as marble, his fierce face, his long nose and gleaming eyes. How could that graceful powerful figure not be preferred to his gross trunk? In his self-hatred Duncan found only one thing to pity, his damaged eye, his poor eye with its curious stain of black. His softened sadness for the creature, as if it were a little sentient thing that had come into his life and had to be looked after, sometimes seemed like a momentary comfort, as he stared at his big head in the mirror, put on his dark-rimmed spectacles, and tried to recapture the quizzical humorous lovable face he had once had.

Sex with Jean had never been perfect, but it had been live, continuous, necessary. They had lived together like two good animals, their physical contacts instinctive, always touching, soothing, caressing. The absence of this *dimidium animae* left him with a hideous paining wound which oozed blood and festered. Sometimes he wished that his love for Jean could just be eaten up by hate and shame, crushed and ground into pieces. In the extreme of this agony it was not Crimond but Jean that he wished to be dead, not as a revenge, but just, like an injection of morphia, as an instant cure. But of course there was no such cure, the Jean who tortured him would exist forever; and however ruthlessly and systematically he tried to sever all the little links which bound his person to hers, he continued to suffer so that he could gasp and bellow like a wounded bull.

This late Sunday afternoon in October as he was shaving (he needed to shave twice a day) and studying his cheeks, reddened with drink and covered with little breaking veins, he was thinking about Tamar Hernshaw who had invited herself for a drink that evening. Duncan did not want to see Tamar, but had been unable deftly enough to handle her telephone call which took him by surprise at the office, and had found himself asserting that he would be delighted. Contrary to what was believed by Gerard and the others, Jean and Duncan had never looked on Tamar as some sort of daughter. Such a relationship would have been, for both of them, too painful, mocking them with a semblance of the real child that had never come. They were both very fond of Tamar however, they cared about her and pitied her. Jean had been touched by Tamar's 'crush' and even moved by it toward a physical warmth which was almost maternal. In earlier days Tamar used to come to tea with Jean and stay until Duncan came home. Duncan was embarrassed by children and had solved the problem by treating Tamar, even when she was quite a small child, as an adult and conversing with her solemnly as with an equal intellect. For this procedure, which had worked remarkably well, Tamar was silently and deeply grateful.

'This is Jean, as she was when I first met her.'

'But she's just the same now,' said Tamar, 'she's so beautiful!'

It had not been Tamar's idea to look at all those old photos. Duncan, already a bit drunk when she arrived, had brought out the photograph albums and was having an orgy of reminiscence, sitting beside her on the sofa. She was afraid he would burst into tears at any moment. They sat in front of the electric fire which Duncan had put in front of the fireplace where Jean used to burn wood. The room was dark except for one lamp. This saved Duncan the trouble of tidying it up.

'There's Sinclair looking roguish, he was pleased with himself that boy. There's Gerard looking dignified.'

Tamar looked solemnly at Sinclair who had died young, only a little older than she was.

'The dark burly chap who looks like a rugger blue is me.'

'Were you a rugger blue?'

'No.'

'Who's the girl?'

'That's Rose, she's changed, she's got a timid girlie look in that picture. There's Robin Topglass playing the fool. The weird creature watching him who looks like a dwarf is Jenkin. That's Marcus Field who became a monk. The Jewish fellow with the flowing hair is Professor Levquist. I'd forgotten how young he still was in those days.'

'Who's the man who looks like a comedian?'

'That's Jean's father. He never liked me. Of course you've met him, haven't you. He doesn't look like that now. There's cricket at Boyars.'

'Rose is batting!'

'Yes, she was quite good. They played cricket at their school. Jean treated it as a joke. You can just see Jean in the distance at long-stop. Gerard was jolly good at cricket, damn near got his blue. Sinclair could have too only he never took anything seriously. He was a very stylish player. That's Boyars again, a lot of us with three maids and two gardeners, standing on the steps.'

'That's the past! Rose does it all now with that old woman who lives there.'

'That pretty girl in the front is that old woman. The dog is Sinclair's dog. He was called Regent. I haven't thought about that dog since . . .'

This was one of the points at which Tamar was afraid Duncan would start to cry. She wished the reminiscing would stop. At every turn of the page she was afraid that the face of Crimond would appear. She need not have worried. Duncan had long ago removed every trace of Crimond from the album: Crimond with a squash racket, Crimond with a tennis racket, Crimond with a rifle, Crimond with his arm round Jenkin, Crimond in a punt, Crimond in white flannels, in evening dress, in doublet and hose (in a Shakespeare play), holding one end of a banner saying *Hands off the Soviet Union* (Robin was holding the other end), Crimond smiling, laughing, joking, arguing, orating, looking zany, whimsical, noble, thoughtful, solemn. The fellow was everywhere, as this indubitable evidence showed, had been mixed and mingled into all their doings, all their thoughts, and projects, all the gaiety and all the idealism of their youth.

'How pretty all the girls look,' said Tamar, 'and so well dressed.'

'That was at a garden party. Yes, the girls were pretty in those days. That's Marcus Field's sister. That's a girl called Tessa something, she was a friend of Jean's, she died in a fire. *Jeunes filles en fleurs.* As you are now,' he added politely.

Tamar could not connect herself with those tall elegant young women. She felt sorry for Tessa something who had died in a fire. She felt, these people really existed at Oxford. I only half existed. Tamar had engraved upon her mind, as a text to be meditated upon, Violet's claim (repeated to everybody) that if she had had enough money for an abortion Tamar would never have happened. This half-nothingness which Tamar might have stored to feed resentment, she treasured rather as proof of some kind of separated dedicated oddity; she was fatherless, motherless, unnaturally conceived, a waif from a land unknown. This was what Gerard saw (and Tamar knew what he saw) as a stainless virgin quality, something good, as if like Cordelia her truth was nothing. Tamar was not sure whether it was good, but she ardently wished never to disappoint that opinion.

'Did you enjoy yourself at Oxford?' said Duncan as, to Tamar's relief, he closed the albums. He evidently felt that he ought to pay more personal attention to his guest.

'Oh yes, I loved the work. I didn't seem to get to know many people though, I didn't have a lot of friends like you and –'

'Well – everyone experiences a different Oxford. Did you have any lovers?'

Tamar blushed scarlet and moved slightly away from Duncan, pulling down her skirt over her slender legs. She had been aware when she arrived of the smell of whisky on his breath, and she felt repelled by his bulk at close quarters. She was surprised by his question which she felt he would not, in any ordinary state of mind, have asked. She answered it readily enough however. 'Yes, I had two – well, rather brief – relationships. I liked both the boys, they were very nice, but I think we weren't in love – we were just anxious to have had the experience.'

'To get it over! What a way to see it! Then why do it more than once?'

'I don't know, it just happened – I wanted to see, to be sure – and they were very kind, it was really good – but they didn't stay around and I didn't really want them to.'

'It sounds rather a quiet scene! What was it you wanted to be sure of?'

Tamar was suddenly uncertain, at least uncertain how to put it. She had known, and clearly known, that she did not want to remain a virgin, literal virginity would have been an irrelevant burden to her, an unnecessary source of anxiety and tension. Better, indeed, to get it over in circumstances where, as she rightly foresaw, no one would get hurt. The two, not thrilling but not unpleasurable, experiences with the nice boys had revealed to her, which was what she wanted to know, 'what it was like', leaving her free, until something really serious turned up if it ever did, to forget about it! So far she had not found anything really serious, though she had got as far as imagining that Conrad Lomas might be. Condensing and editing these reflections she said to Duncan, 'I wanted to have the thing with someone I liked and respected without being committed. I didn't want intensity.'

'You're a cool one, little Tamar.'

It was the day after Tamar's visit to Jean. Of course Tamar had no intention of talking to Duncan about Jean, that was out of the question, and he had not lingered over her photos in the albums. Gerard had said there was no need to say anything in particular but simply to be there. Tamar did not think that her being there had been any use to Jean, and did not expect it to do anything for Duncan either. She was merely concerned here to obey Gerard, and looked forward to making her meagre report to him, which she felt she could not do until she had seen both of them. Jean had told her to come again, but Tamar wondered if another visit would be either wise or welcome. There had been no doubt about Crimond's displeasure, even disgust. Tamar had cried in the train going back to Acton. She had felt too, like a scorching electrical ray passing through her body, the emotional tension between Jean and

Crimond. She had cried in the train with shock and fear, but also with excitement. About *that* experience she would not tell Gerard.

'I think I'd better go home,' said Tamar, 'my mother will be –'

'Oh don't go yet,' said Duncan, who, though usually alone in the evening, could not now bear the loss of a drinking companion, 'have another drink. Why, you haven't finished that one.'

'I feel quite tipsy already. Oh dear!'

Tamar had put her glass on the floor and now, reaching for it, had moved her foot and tilted it over. The sweet sherry which she had preferred, had extended a long tongue of dark liquid across the pale rug. 'Oh,' cried Tamar, 'look what I've done, how dreadful. I'm so sorry, I'll get a cloth from the kitchen –'

'Oh don't bother, for heaven's sake, I'll –' Duncan heaved himself up to follow her. He did not want her to see the kitchen.

Tamar got there first, and turned on the light. The sight was indeed horrendous. Unwashed dishes, mildewed saucepans were piled in crazy mounds not only in the sink but on the floor. Empty whisky bottles and wine bottles, some upright, some not, had been there long enough to collect layers of greasy dust. The floor was slippery with egg shells, rotting vegetables, mouldy bread. The rubbish bin overflowed with empty tins and slimy packaging. Tamar thought at once, I'll clear all this up before I go! Something to do with her relationship with her mother made it impossible for Tamar to clean or tidy the flat at Acton. But here she felt an instant power to do magic, to make all beautiful, all in order, to do at least this thing for Duncan for whom she was feeling such intense pity. But first she would deal with the awful sherry stain. The cupboard where she knew that cloths and mops were kept was beyond a shelf upon which a variety of oddments were huddled together. To reach the handle of the cupboard door she quickly moved a dirty glass jug, then a packet of instant soup, then an old half empty tin of beans, then a tea-cosy . . . It was already too late, as she seized the tea-cosy, to do anything about the fact that there was a teapot inside it. The teapot was already in the air. Tamar screamed and grasped at it. But it smashed at her feet, distributing fragments of coloured china and brown tea and spatterings of wet tea leaves about among the empty bottles. Tamar burst into wild tears.

Duncan heard the crash, he reached the door to find his mother's pretty teapot in smithereens and Tamar wailing. The teapot was an old friend.

The violence, the *achievement* of breaking the teapot, seemed for a moment like a blow aimed at himself. The shattered thing was terrible, like the murdered corpse of a loved animal. Then the next instant, it became something horrible which he had done, his own disgusting black misery externalised as if his tortured body had sicked it up. He looked down at it and saw hell. He even heard himself say 'Hell'. He experienced, as in a mystical vision, the infinite wretchedness of the whole of creation, its cruelty and its pain, the pointlessness of life, the pointlessness of his life, his shame, his defeat, his condemnation, his death by torture.

Tamar seeing his dismay and hearing the word which he had uttered redoubled her wails. She too felt a shock wave of desolation and terror, but this for her was tempered and redeemed by a clearer and more precise feeling of sorrow for the poor teapot, and pity and love for Duncan.

'Stop it, Tamar, it *doesn't matter*, come out of here.'

Shaking her head and weeping Tamar now managed to open the cupboard and got out a cloth which she soaked under the tap, and ran back to the drawing room where Duncan turned on another light. She knelt to mop up the spilt sherry, dropping her tears onto the rug, trying to blend the edges of the stain into the patterned rug, wringing out the cloth to soak the area in water. Then, passing Duncan at the door, she ran back into the kitchen and began hastily picking up the pieces of the broken teapot, scraping up the tea-leaves with her fingers, and mopping up the tea. After that she began, staring down through a haze of tears, running hot water into the sink and dabbing the dirty plates with a mop.

'I said *stop!*' Duncan turned off the tap, took the mop away, took hold of Tamar's hand and led her back to the drawing room. They sat down again on the sofa. Duncan offered Tamar a large white handkerchief. Her tears abated. The clouded horrors faded. They looked at each other.

Tamar saw, as before, his stout bulk, his flushed plump wrinkled face, but she saw in the same look his big animal head with its flowing mane, his huge nostrils like a horse, his sad melancholy of a beast who has been a prince, and now that he had taken off his heavy glasses the apologetic but intent and humorous gaze of his dark eyes.

She said, 'I do like your strange inky eye, it's beautiful, have you always had it?'

'Yes. The rug looks all right already. But your stockings are all stained with tea.'

Tamar laughed and adjusted her skirt. With the centre light on she could now see the desolation of the room. The pictures had been removed from the walls, the bookcase was empty, the mantelpiece was bare, the armchairs, pushed back against the wall, were covered with newspapers and random clothes. Everything was dusty. Tamar recognised the scenery of unhappiness as it existed too in her own house.

Duncan, seeing her glance around, said, 'You'd better go now, Tamar, this is no place for a white woman.'

'But I want to wash up and clean the kitchen.'

'No. Thank you for coming. Are you coming to Guy Fawkes at Gerard's? Perhaps I'll see you there. Please don't worry about the teapot.'

Once again Tamar cried on the way home, but with different tears.

'Who was Guy Fawkes anyway?' said Lily Boyne.

It was the evening of the Guy Fawkes day party at Gerard's

house, and everyone, with the exception of Gideon, seemed to be feeling nervous or out of temper.

'He tried to blow up the Houses of Parliament,' said Gulliver.

'I know that, silly, but who was he and why did he want to blow up the Houses of Parliament?'

Gulliver, already irritable because he had arrived five minutes ago and had not yet been offered a drink, and now irritated at being asked a tiresome question to which he only vaguely knew the answer, replied, 'He was a Catholic.'

'So, what's wrong with that?'

'There weren't supposed to be any Catholics, at least they had to keep their heads down.'

'Why?'

'Oh Lily – don't you know any history! England was Protestant since Henry the Eighth. Fawkes and his pals objected. So they tried to blow up James the First when he was opening Parliament.'

'He sounds like a brave man defending his ideals, a sort of freedom fighter.'

'He was some sort of shady thug, he may have been a double agent or an *agent provocateur*. People think now there never really was a plot, it was all organised by the government to discredit the Catholics.'

'Oh. You mean there was no gunpowder?'

'I don't know! I suppose they had to pretend to discover something! Then they hanged a lot of Catholics, and Guy Fawkes too.'

'I thought they burnt him.'

'We burn him. They hanged him.'

'But why, if it was him who arranged it all for their benefit?'

'I suppose he knew too much. Someone promised to get him off, but then didn't or couldn't.'

'I feel very sorry for him,' said Lily, 'he was a protester.'

'He was a terrorist. You can't approve of blowing up parliament.'

'It wasn't democratically elected in those days,' said Lily, 'it was just a lot of boss types. I've never understood whether

Guy Fawkes day is to hate Guy Fawkes or to love him. He's a sort of folk hero really.'

'I suppose people like explosions.'

'You mean we're all terrorists at heart? I expect this will dawn on someone one day and Guy Fawkes will be banned, he'll have to go underground.'

They had arrived, separately, rather early and were now standing, in the awkward lonely attentive attitudes of too-early guests, beside the open fire in Gerard's drawing room which was lit only by candles. It was the tradition that, except in the kitchen, only candlelight should be allowed on Guy Fawkes night. Gulliver was annoyed, and annoyed with himself for being annoyed, that Lily had been invited. Gulliver had attended now for several consecutive years. Lily had never been invited before. Last year it had been very select. Gull was now, observing Lily more closely in the candlelight, annoyed by her bizarre appearance. He was troubled by the possibility that Gerard had invited Lily because he thought Gulliver liked her. On the other hand, if she had to be there, he wanted her to make a creditable show. Mistaking the tone of the party, and envisaging it as some kind of carnival, Lily had spent some time earlier in the evening painting her face with red and yellow stripes. Just before departure however her courage had failed and she had hastily washed the stripes off, leaving a number of streaks and blotches which were now showing through the powder which she had hastily dabbed on. Gulliver himself, trusting to profit by the candlelight, had ventured to put on some discreet make-up.

Lily was remembering an occasion in her childhood when she had seen a large realistic guy burnt on a bonfire. The children laughed as the guy jumped about in the heat and even raised his stumpy hands up in the air. Lily had felt horror and terror and devastating pity and a kind of rage which, as she could not intelligibly direct it against anyone else, she turned upon herself. She bit her hands and tore her hair. She felt that old emotion for a moment now and raised one hand to her hair, the other to her heart.

Rose came in carrying a tray of glasses and a jug which she

put down with a bump and a tinkle on the table. She turned on a lamp. She too was irritated with Gerard for asking Lily. She felt this ridiculous unworthy irritation even though she liked Lily and invited her to her own parties. Rose was feeling tired. She had spent a lot of the day making sandwiches and smoked salmon canapés and shopping for cheese and the kind of little cakes which Gerard was partial to. It was not exactly a buffet, more a bunfight as Jenkin once put it. The main thing, Jenkin said, was to get a little drunk. He was the one who bought and organised the fireworks, which Gerard paid for. Jenkin was now in the garden with Gerard and Gideon fixing posts for the catherine wheels and digging in the bottles to take the sticks of the rockets. Thank heavens it was not raining. Rose was also exasperated with Patricia who had welcomed Gulliver and Lily as if it were her house. Rose, who had left her coat upstairs on Gerard's bed as she usually did, had found it removed by Pat to a downstairs cloakroom where guests were being told to leave their things. Then when Rose carried her carefully packed food into the kitchen she found Patricia in control expressing amazement that Rose had brought all that stuff when she, Patricia, had already made a terrine, a steak and kidney pie, a vegetable curry, a ratatouille, various salads, and a sherry trifle. Rose did not say that surely Patricia knew by now that Gerard, who hated standing about with a plate and a knife and fork, or perching on a chair with a plate on his knee, spared his guests this indignity, and at such a party, only tolerated food which could be held in the hand. She did not even protest when she saw Patricia putting away her sandwiches at the back of the fridge. Perhaps Rose should have consulted Patricia beforehand about the food. But Patricia and Gideon, though always asked to this party, did not often come, and Rose was not yet used to the idea that they now lived in Gerard's house and were all ready to be the life and soul of the evening. Violet was always invited too, and sometimes actually came, this was another hazard. Rose was also in a state of anxiety about whether Duncan would turn up and whether if he did he would get impossibly drunk. The general view was that Duncan would not come. Rose identified very much with Duncan's suffering and probably understood it even better than Gerard did. She also grieved and worried about Jean and very much wanted to write to her, but felt she could not do so without telling Gerard beforehand, which she was not prepared to do. Gerard had told Rose portentously that Tamar had seen both Jean and Duncan and had reported back to him, though he did not say what she had said. Rose did not share Gerard's view of Tamar as all-wise and all-holy, and she thought poorly of his idea not least because Tamar might get seriously hurt or upset. If Tamar had been upset she certainly would not tell Gerard. Rose resolved to talk to her herself later on.

Rose was wearing a markedly simple dress, a sort of oatmeal shift with a brown leather belt, suited, she felt, to this occasion at which, she now also realised, she and Jean had often been the only women. Patricia had put on a swishy black evening skirt with a striped blouse. Lily was clad in a bulky voluminous much pleated robe of light blue crepe, hitched up in Grecian fashion over a low invisible girdle, revealing dark red suede boots. Rose, now noticing the curiously mottled, indeed marbled, appearance of Lily's face, turned off the lamp which she had turned on. She poured out two glasses of the mixture in the jug. These were gratefully accepted. 'It's fruit cup.'

'Dangerous stuff,' said Lily, 'always stronger than you imagine!'

'People always say that about fruitcup,' said Rose, then felt she had been rude. She tried to think of something to ameliorate the impression, could not, and felt annoyed with herself and Lily.

The bell rang and Rose could hear Patricia at the door welcoming Tamar. Rose poured herself a glass of the fruit cup, which was indeed stronger than it seemed, and drank it quickly. She was afraid that Gerard would want her to invite Gulliver and Lily to the Boyars reading party and she would have to do so. Gulliver, though invited to Guy Fawkes, had never yet been invited to Boyars.

Lily said thank heavens it was not raining.

Tamar came in. She was not wearing her usual coat and

skirt uniform, and had ventured into a brown woollen dress with an embroidered collar. A near candle revealed her pale transparent milky cheek, flushed a little with the cold, and her cleanly parted silky fair hair, with its evenly cut ends, held in a round slide. Holding Rose's warm hand in her little cold one for a moment, she kissed Rose. Then after a moment's hesitation she kissed Lily. Lily liked Tamar but was never sure that Tamar liked her. Tamar smiled at Gulliver, and they made vague gestures. She declined the fruit cup, said she would get herself a soft drink in the kitchen, and went off.

Meanwhile Gerard and Gideon had come in from the garden, leaving Jenkin, the enthusiast, to complete the arrangements, which included the removal of all extraneous obstacles from the lawn. They came in, not by the doors into the drawing room which were still closed and curtained, but by a corridor which passed the kitchen and led to the dining room and hall. In the dining room the long table, which had been pushed back against the wall and covered with a green baize cloth, then by a sturdy white damask cloth, was already occupied by plates, cutlery, wine glasses, open wine bottles, salad bowls, Rose's smoked salmon canapés which had been allowed out, bread, butter, biscuits, the terrine and the ratatouille, also a display of ham and tongue which Patricia had felt inspired to add at the last moment. The steak and kidney pie, the curry and the potatoes would come in hot. The trifle was still in the fridge. Rose's sandwiches were not to appear. The fate of the little cakes was still uncertain. Gerard, who had learnt, but too late, of Patricia's plans, viewed this elaborate spread with dismay. The usual arrangement was that sandwich-style food would be available throughout the evening for people to come and grab informally by hand whenever they felt like it. These pretentious dishes suggested a dinner hour, a queue, guests standing or sitting awkwardly with heaped plates, a scene which he *detested*. Patricia arrived with a bowl of mayonnaise which she had made in the afternoon.

The dining room was rather dark, looking out on the bushy front garden, with its pair of ash trees, and the street. The heavy bottle-green curtains were pulled, the walls, striped dark brown, and dark ochre, liberally (by Gerard's standards, for he did not like clutter) covered by nineteenth-century Japanese paintings, shadowy exquisite things with sparse smudgy lines and dashes of colour, representing birds, dogs, insects, trees, frogs, tortoises, monkeys, frail girls, casual men, mountains, rivers, the moon. Gideon respected these, though they were not his cup of tea. He regarded most of Gerard's mediocre collection with contempt. Looking now at a drawing of a dragonfly on a bulrush he said, 'Yes, that's quite cute. But why don't you try to collect some good pictures? I could advise you.'

'I don't want to develop expensive tastes and be like people who can only drink the best wine! I like grand art in galleries. I don't want it in my house.'

'I'm not talking about grand art, but you might aim a little higher! I confess I don't share your passion for English watercolours. Wouldn't you like a Wilson Steer? You were keen on him once. I could look out for one – of course it wouldn't be cheap. Or a Vuillard. Vuillard is the chap to buy now, he's still underpriced.'

'Far too grand for me.'

'Chagall, Morisot?'

'No thanks.'

'The wallpaper is good. Our Longhis would look nice on it, and the little Watteau.'

'Look, Gideon,' said Gerard, 'this is my house, I don't want to divide it up. You find a place of your own to live in. You aren't poverty-stricken. You've been here long enough.'

'Plain speaking. All right, Gerard, we don't want you to divide the house, we want the house.'

Patricia came in again, carrying a jug of fruit cup, hearing Gideon's words. 'Yes, Gerry, you owe it to the family.'

'I have no family,' said Gerard.

Patricia ignored this bad joke. 'Leonard will be married soon, I don't mean he has anyone in view, but he intends to marry. This house is unique, it's most unusual in this part of London. We've always wanted to live in Notting Hill. It has

193

this big garden with trees, and there are those good rooms at the top, *and* attics, it's a family house. Doesn't it strike you as unjust to occupy all this space?'

'No.'

'By the way, Tamar says she doesn't want Perrier, she wants orange squash, I wonder if there's any in the sideboard?'

'I regard you two as my lodgers, except that I pay the bills.'

'I can give you a cheque, old man.'

'Don't be silly.'

Tamar appeared at the door. 'Look, *please* don't bother, Perrier is perfectly all right, I don't want orange squash – Hello Gerard, hello Gideon.'

'Tamar!' said Gideon. He went over and kissed her.

Patricia said, 'He quite fancies her, don't you, dear?'

Gerard, who did not care for jokes of this kind by married people, concentrated on Tamar. He thought, she is like fresh air, fresh water, good bread. He said nothing but he smiled and she smiled back.

'Well, here is the orangeade, so you'd better have it,' said Patricia who had been peering into the sideboard. 'I suppose Duncan will want to drink whisky all the evening. I'll leave the whisky and gin out in case anyone wants it, but don't encourage them.'

Jenkin was taking the opportunity to linger in the garden. The frost was on the grass and he could feel the pleasant crunching of it underfoot. Feeling warm inside his overcoat, woollen cap and gloves, he enjoyed the cold air, nosed it, caressed it with his face. The two heavy cast-iron seats with the swan heads and feet had been moved, with the help of Gerard and Gideon, to the end of the garden beyond the walnut tree, the large flowerpots had been removed from the centre of the terrace, the bottles for the rockets were in place, the posts for the catherine wheels had been hammered in, the fireworks sorted out and set in order in the kitchen corridor, with the sparklers and the electric torches. Jenkin puffed out his steamy breath and watched it in the dim light which came along the side of the house from the street lamps, and also from

Gerard's bedroom where the light was on and the curtains had not been pulled. Breath, soul, life, our breaths are numbered. He breathed deeply, feeling the cold penetrate down into the warm channels and recesses of his body, and felt that never dimmed and never disappointing satisfaction of, after being with other people, being alone. He lifted his head like an animal who might, upon some empty hillside, let out some lonely inarticulate cry, not a sad cry, though not without a sad tone or echo, but just a deep irrepressible cry of being. So in silence he let out his noiseless bellow to the chill night air and the stars.

It was still early but had been dark for some time and in London gardens all about the fireworks had begun to go off. The warm glow of bonfires could be seen here and there, the occasional long leaping flame, and sudden golden lights revealed the brick façades of houses, and the branches, some leafless, some evergreen, of distant trees. There were abrupt whirring and whizzing and popping sounds, small sharp explosions, and the special sizzling noise of ascending rockets and their sighing or crackling burst high in the air and brief glory of scattering or slowly falling stars. Jenkin loved rockets. Gerard always, as a matter of form, invited his next-door neighbours to the Guy Fawkes party, but they never came. The neighbours on one side found firework merriment embarrassing, and those on the other, who had children, set up their own celebration rather earlier than Gerard's. This party was now nearing its close, the rockets had been seen off with ritual cries of 'aaah!' and there was a murmur of talk from the other side of the wall. Jenkin became aware that he was being watched. A row of faces, children's faces, had appeared at the top of the wall. Jenkin looked at the small heads and said, 'Hello.' The children looked at him in silence. Then suddenly, all together, they disappeared, and there was a little muffled burst of laughter from the other side. Jenkin had never really got used to children. That was perhaps one of the secrets (and it was a secret) of his success as a schoolmaster. He understood the awful private miseries of children, their horrors. In school, he enjoyed that easy, enviable, almost absolute authority which seems like a gift of nature, persuasive, magical, very rarely coercive. But he was not romantic or sentimental or maty, he was aware of children as another race, chauvinistic, hostile, often unintelligible. His pupils were a set of individuals to whom his relation was scrupulously professional. A perceptive person (his friend Marchment) once said to him, 'Jenkin, you don't really like children!' He did like children, but not in the general and conventional sense. That row of heads, made by some trick of the light to look red, as if of some island tribe or painted natives, unnerved him, making him aware of the instability and vulnerability of his present state of mind. He felt he had suffered a defeat. Perhaps this was his last Guy Fawkes party?

'Why, Violet, you're looking really smart tonight!' said Gideon. 'Isn't she?'

Violet actually blushed and wriggled like a coy maiden, as Patricia said later. She had certainly made an effort. She had put away the blue spectacles; it emerged later that she had treated herself to contact lenses. She had also, with the help of a hairdresser, made her hair look more attractively tousled, the fringe less dominant, less straight and less severe. She was wearing a fairly simple well-cut light-blue cocktail dress with some glittering decoration round the neck.

'You look almost sophisticated,' said Patricia, 'but those spangles at the top won't do, I expect you could get them off. I do wish you'd come over and help us like you used to, and Gideon needs a secretary, don't you, darling? Everyone needs to be needed –'

'We didn't expect you,' said Gideon, smiling benevolently.

'I expected her,' said Gerard, 'come and get a drink, I'll mix you a special.'

Violet followed Gerard into the dining room and Gerard quickly closed the door. He said, 'Violet, we do so want you to think again about the money.'

'Who's "we"?' said Violet, deepening the frown lines above her nose and the tragedy lines below her mouth.

'Pat and me and Rose.'

'How does Rose come in?'

'She just agrees with us.'

'It's none of Rose's business.'

'All right, but look, Violet, be rational, be *kind* to us. Father said in his will that he trusted us to look after you. You must let us execute his wishes – it's like being forced not to keep a promise.'

'He said no such thing in his will, he didn't mention me in his will.'

'What makes you think that?'

'Pat told me. Not only no money, but no mention.'

Damn, thought Gerard. What do I say now? 'Violet, my father wished us to help you, he assumed we would.'

'If he had wanted me to be "helped" after his death he could have arranged it! Anyway I don't want "help"!' Violet's face, now that of a demonic cat, also expressed a kind of spiteful glee. 'Pat wants me to be her housemaid, you heard her just now, she wrote me a patronising letter, and you tell me lies about Uncle Matthew's will. I may be poor and a relation but I'm not going to play the part of poor relation to gratify you and Pat!'

'Well, we are determined to help Tamar. She must go back to Oxford.'

'Oh, I know it's all a plot to help her, not me! Nobody really cares about me! Tamar's perfectly all right, she's got a good job. Later on she might not get a job, it gets worse each year, she realises she's *lucky*.'

'We shall help Tamar.'

'You know perfectly well she won't accept it, you're just humouring your conscience! It would be psychologically disastrous for her. Can't you leave her alone? You think she's some sort of sturdy virtuous peasant girl. She isn't, she's a precarious unstable neurotic. She couldn't stand the pace at Oxford, she'd have had a breakdown. Why do you think your precious Oxford is such a wonderful place for a girl to be? You know Tamar never enjoyed it, she just made herself ill with work! Tamar needs a quiet orderly life and a steady job. She's not an intellectual, thank heavens!'

Gulliver put his head round the door, took a look at Gerard and Violet, said 'Sorry!' and disappeared.

'Why can't you be happy?' said Gerard. 'You seem not to want to be.'

'That's my business. Oh, you understand *nothing*!'

Gerard poured out a glass of the fruit cup and gave it to Violet. 'I'm sorry. You mustn't be cross with Pat, she means well. We'll talk again later.'

'You said you'd mix me a special!'

Gerard took a bottle of gin from the sideboard and poured a generous quantity into Violet's glass.

'Do you expect me to drink *that*?' She kept the glass however and went off smiling.

Rose had rescued her sandwiches from the fridge and brought them into the drawing room, where Gulliver had declared he was hungry. The sandwiches were now cold and damp, Gulliver and Lily were eating them however. Rose then fetched her canapés from the dining room, just vacated by Gerard and Violet. The form had always been that people ate and drank all the evening and wandered about as they would. Now Patricia wanted to make a drama of herding everyone to collect their plateful. This also raised the question of when exactly the fireworks were to begin.

'What's the matter with Tamar?' said Patricia, coming in and looking disapprovingly at the rapid unauthorised consumption of food which was going on. 'She can't keep still, she won't sit down, she keeps sliding about the place like a cat. I suppose she wants a tête-à-tête with Gerard.'

'She's just shy,' said Rose, 'she's so self-effacing.'

'I don't think she's effacing herself, she keeps jumping around like a performing flea! I expect it's mummy's presence.'

'Violet looks lovely. She can still do it when she tries.'

'She usually prefers the hag act. Tonight it's "I care for nobody, no not I." She can turn herself into anything, she's better adapted to life really, she doesn't suffer like we do. I've never seen so many fireworks, the side passage is full of them. They're just like schoolboys, aren't they, our men.'

Rose did not care for 'our men'.

Jenkin came in from the garden, entering through the glass doors and pushing his way between the curtains. 'Has Duncan come?'

'No, but Violet has.'

'Duncan won't come,' said Rose.

But just at that moment the door bell rang.

Patricia's knife and fork and plate policy worked out much as Rose had anticipated. The regulars, trained by Gerard, resented the innovation and ignored the pie and curry and trifle arrangement, eating up the sandwiches and canapés, and thereafter, scorning the plates and utensils, making their own impromptu sandwiches by tearing open rolls and jamming in lettuce leaves and bits of ham and tomato which then fell out onto the carpet. Gerard's little cakes, discovered in the larder, were popular too, so was the cheese which Rose had provided. One or two guests out of politeness (Jenkin) or because they were genuinely interested in the steak and kidney pie (Gulliver) or because the whole thing had been their own idea (Patricia) fussily found a place to sit and some piece of furniture to sit at and uncomfortably, while the others strolled about, sat down to a pretence of ordinary dinner. Gideon, to Patricia's annoyance and chagrin, defected to the strollers. Claret was now provided, and the fruit cup was still available. The gin and whisky were not in demand at the early stages, even by Duncan who was the last to arrive and startled his friends by asking for Perrier, then drinking the cup, then only at a later stage the whisky. By then Gulliver and Lily were also on whisky. Lily, who had earlier discovered the gin-laced glass abandoned by Violet and drunk it up, was by now distinctly tipsy. Tamar caused distress by eating nothing; at last she accepted a plate of the trifle which was discovered next morning, untouched, upon a window ledge behind a curtain. She also, for a while, disappeared, and was found by Rose upstairs in Gerard's bedroom in the dark, sitting at the window and, she said, watching the children next door who had been capering round the garden in their night clothes. By the time coffee was served it was getting very late and the evening was in danger of being wrecked by what Gerard subsequently called 'that simulacrum of a dinner party'. It appeared that no one was in charge. Gerard had pointedly given up the responsibilities of a host, Rose who would normally have kept an eye on the time had withdrawn into the position of a spectator. Jenkin was in some kind of a dream, almost seeming gloomy, perhaps getting steadily drunk on the powerful claret. Gideon, impishly enjoying himself as usual, was everywhere about with a smile on his face, waiting to see what would happen. Violet too was smiling, drinking very little, picking up pieces of kidney in her fingers out of the pie, and spooning trifle into her mouth and replacing the spoon in the bowl. Patricia was already in the kitchen washing up.

'What about the fireworks?' said Jenkin, suddenly awaking from his reverie.

'It's too late for fireworks,' said Gerard, 'we would disturb the children next door.'

'According to Tamar, they're all out in the garden in their nighties,' said Rose.

'Well, we could send up a rocket or two, there isn't time for the whole lot, everybody wants to go home!'

Gulliver, realising that he might soon be dangerously drunk, had already proposed that he should leave, forgetting that the letting off of fireworks was the purpose of the evening.

'Where's Tamar?' said Jenkin.

'In the kitchen helping Pat wash up!' said Rose.

'Where's Duncan?' said Gerard.

'Drinking whisky in your study.'

'I rather hoped Tamar would take charge of him tonight,' said Gerard, 'but she's so withdrawn.'

'She probably wants another heart-to-heart with you!' said Rose.

'At any rate Duncan started on Perrier. Do you think that was Tamar's influence?'

'Look, we *must* have our fireworks,' said Jenkin, 'I'll start, you just herd them out. Don't forget the torches and sparklers.'

Jenkin, anxious not to have his programme curtailed by Gerard, had already set off the Golden Rains and several Roman Candles and a Peacock Fountain before the whole company, wearing their overcoats, had ambled or stumbled out into the garden. Everyone was given a torch, a bunch of sparklers and a box of matches. The sparklers, little metal sticks to be held in the hand while the ignited end spitted brilliant sparks, were to provide audience participation and, during intervals between the 'pieces', extra light. However some of the guests dropped their sparklers on the grass (Gull and Lily) or absently put them in their pocket (Duncan) or were too haughty (Pat and Violet) or too shy (Tamar) to ignite them. Rose and Gerard dutifully, and Gideon with a great deal of facetious to-do, set light to theirs at intervals and waved them about, revealing the rather dazed faces of their fellow guests in the very bright very white light of the sizzling sparks. Fireworks were, to keep them all in countenance, still to be seen glowing and ascending here and there from distant gardens where children were late to bed or adults still at play. Looking up in a moment of darkness Rose saw, in the upper windows of the house next door, the faces of children looking out. She lit another sparkler, held it up to reveal herself, and waved to the children. Dazzled by the glare, she could not see whether they waved back. Gerard had never made friends with these children, and they were strangers to Rose.

Jenkin had now reached the penultimate stage, which was the catherine wheels. The rockets came last. He had nailed three large wheels onto three posts set back near (but not too near) the walnut tree, the highest post in the centre. As he went round with his torch checking the three contraptions the others, who had provided murmurs, even cries, of admiration for the earlier events, fell silent, and it was for a moment dark in the garden. One or two torches, momently switched on, illumined feet, some sensibly, some foolishly clad, and patches of wet trampled frosty grass. The air was becoming very cold, noses felt frozen, and those without gloves buried their hands deep in their pockets. Gulliver, badly wanting another drink, was supporting himself by a hand on Lily's shoulder.

Suddenly, almost simultaneously, the big catherine wheels became alive, turning for a moment or two quite slowly, then accelerating into huge dazzling circles of fire which uttered a terrifying burning noise as of an inferno. Everybody gasped suitably, and indeed the sight and the sound were not only impressive but frightening. No one fidgeted, all stood still, staring open-mouthed and tense at the three great fiery circles.

Lily, who had been silent for some time in a self-concentrated state of quiet drunkenness, suddenly said, close to Gulliver's ear, 'Why are they called catherine wheels?'

Gulliver, startled out of his own intoxicated meditation, replied, 'Saint Catherine was martyred on a wheel.'

'What?'

'Saint Catherine was martyred on a wheel, tortured, killed.'

'How on a wheel, what did it do to her?'

'I don't know,' said Gulliver, annoyed by this irrelevant and somehow improper disturbance, 'I believe it was turned over a lot of spikes or something.'

Lily pondered for a moment. Then she turned and went back toward the house. Gulliver, deprived of her support, sat down abruptly upon the grass.

The catherine wheels began at last, saddeningly to their spellbound watchers, to slow down, then one after the other gradually to go out, spurting a few last bursts of fiery angry sparks, then for a few moments continuing to turn, glowing dimly, then burnt out and blackened, upon their posts. There was a general sigh.

Showman Jenkin, determined not to lose his audience, immediately set off the first of the rockets.

Gerard, who had seen Lily slip off and not return, decided it was time to go and see if she was all right. He moved quietly away as the others were gazing up at a drifting constellation of different coloured stars.

Lily, after she left the scene, had blundered in through the drawing room doors, finding herself behind the heavy curtains which threatened to suffocate her. She struggled in panic, in darkness, losing her sense of direction, trying to find either the middle or the ends of the heavy clinging curtains. At last she blundered out into the candle-lit room and hurried through it so as to get further away from the garden. She went to the lavatory, and turning on the light, saw her mottled face in the mirror for the first time. She took refuge in the dining room and sat down beside the little low rickety table upon which she and Gulliver had perched their plates when having dinner or supper or whatever it was. Alcohol can open the dark gates of the unconscious and through this orifice there flooded upon Lily, in the name of Saint Catherine, a phantom host of memories of her Catholic mother, who had been much given to imploring the aid of various helpful saints. Lily often thought about her grandmother, but very rarely about her mother. Now, with the accusing memories, came awful guilt and remorse. Her mother had believed in hell. Why had Lily rejected and abandoned her poor mother who had died drunk and alone in terror of eternal flames? Why was her mother not alive now so that Lily could run to comfort her? Mixed with these thoughts about her mother's suffering came pious images, horrible to Lily as a child, of Saint Sebastian shot full of arrows, Saint Lawrence roasted on a grid. And of course Jesus, slowly tortured to death by crucifixion. Then it occurred to Lily that the three posts of the catherine wheels were like the three crosses of Calvary. She burst into tears. Gerard came in.

The rockets were now going up in quick succession, rushing up so suddenly, so violently, so dangerously, with a hissing tearing whistling sound, tearing the dark air, up and up so high, and then the achieved efflorescence which came with a wonderful sense of relief, of a kind of peaceful or happy or glorious death, an explosion of golden bullets or a fountain of jagged stars, like the self-giving benediction of an amorous god. Other rockets in other gardens were flying up too, quick, quick, as if the mad licensed festival were nearing its end and, under pain of some doom, all must now be done quickly. The air was full of explosions. Rose thought, war sounds like this. To rest her dazzled eyes she stopped looking up and saw for a moment in the light of a match Jenkin's entranced delighted face, his lips parted, his eyes round with excitement. What is he celebrating, she wondered, what god, what vision, what golden secret desire? A shower of particularly long-lasting starlets showed her the other upturned faces, Gideon's laughing with rapture, Pat's calmly pleased, Gulliver's childishly gleeful. Duncan looked melancholy but quiet, his big head tilted back, his dark mane sweeping his coat collar. Violet's face startled Rose, it was radiant with some intense emotion, determination or despair or hate. Tamar, standing just behind her, was not visible. Rose then noticed that Gerard and Lily were missing.

'I wish I was dead,' said Lily. 'I'm good for nothing. I'm rotten, I'm wicked.'

Gerard, sitting next to her at the table, said, 'Stop it, Lily, I won't have you saying such untrue things in this house!'

'My accountant says my money's running out.'

'I'm sure it isn't, it must be invested.'

'I don't know, I don't know what invested is. Oh I'm so unhappy, and I *can't* be happy.'

'Of course you can, I *know* you can. You can help other people.'

'I hate other people, I hate myself, I can't trust anyone, nobody cares about me –'

'Oh stop it! Of course people care, I care for example. If you're worried about your money or anything you can always come to me.'

'Can I?' said Lily in amazement. She dried her tears on the soft billowy sleeve of her dress, the front of which was stained with red wine. She turned to Gerard a drunken ravaged face crazy with relief and said suddenly, 'I've always wanted to look at these pictures, I've never been able to, they look so nice.'

'We can look at them now,' said Gerard. They got up and he lifted a candle. 'There's a butterfly, there's a snail, there's a beetle flying, there's a frog, the Japanese like frogs, there's a girl washing her hair . . .'

The noise outside was becoming louder and louder. Gideon was exclaiming with pleasure, Violet's eyes were shining, her mouth was open, Patricia's hands were at her face. Why do they like those awful terrifying sounds, thought Rose. Do I like them? Perhaps I do. Oh where is Gerard? She saw Gulliver turning away and gliding in long strides towards the house.

Gulliver opened the dining room door and saw Gerard holding a candle up beside one of the pictures which Lily was looking at. Gulliver felt an uncomfortable pain in his diaphragm. It was a feeling he had not had for some time. He recognised it as jealousy. But why, for whom, of whom, about what? He closed the door again.

A great flight of rockets suddenly flew upward. Then from quite nearby came a long series of deafening explosions, much louder than anything which they had heard yet. They covered their ears. Patricia cried out, 'That's not fireworks, it *can't* be, it must be bombs, it's *terrorists*!'

'No!' cried Jenkin in ecstasy, 'it's the party at the French Embassy!'

Rose had gone into the house. She went to the dining room and turned the light on.

As the light of the rockets went out and the echo of the explosions ceased, Duncan moved over to where Tamar was standing, and extended his hand quietly sideways towards her, and for a moment her small hand clasped his.

'Jenkin didn't send those flowers,' said Rose, 'I asked him – and I'm sure Duncan didn't.'

'I'm glad Duncan came, that was Tamar's doing. She thought her visit to him wasn't a success, but evidently it was!'

The guests had gone, Patricia and Gideon had retired, Rose and Gerard were sitting in the drawing room beside the glowing remains of the open fire, holding glasses of whisky and soda. The candles, carefully secured in their candlesticks by Rose, had burnt down in an orderly manner and were extinguished. Electric lamps now made the room bright and calm.

'Did you talk to Duncan?' asked Rose.

'Scarcely. He told me one thing. He said Tamar had broken a teapot!'

'You mean when she visited him? Hot? Full of tea?'

'I don't think so, it was when she was trying to tidy up his kitchen, she knocked it off a shelf. Duncan didn't seem to mind, he thought it was a *joke*, he became helpless with laughter when he was telling me!'

'Hysteria, drink. It can't have been a joke for poor Tamar who was trying to help. I can picture Duncan's kitchen, rather like Violet's! I assume he didn't say anything about Jean and Crimond.'

'No. I think he'll talk to me, but not yet.'

'What are we going to do about Crimond, I mean about the book?'

'Oh, I don't know!' said Gerard impatiently. He felt that 'the others' were steadily pushing him toward some sort of confrontation with Crimond, some sort of showdown. He hated showdowns. On the other hand, he didn't want anyone else messing round with Crimond, if anyone dealt with Crimond it had to be him. But he disliked the prospect extremely.

Rose, reading his mind, said, 'It needn't be a fight! We can reasonably ask for a progress report! All this time he's had our money and not even sent a postcard to say thanks, book getting on! Anyway it's time we called a meeting of the committee.'

'Yes, yes. I'll call it. You know, Gulliver *still* hasn't found a job.'

'I think Gulliver was wearing make-up.'

'Rose, I'm tired, you're tired. Off you go.'

Rose felt a little drunk and very disinclined to go home. She had frightened herself this evening, had been deeply disturbed by her ridiculous and unworthy feelings of jealousy about Lily and Tamar. Am I to grieve if he even looks at another woman, do I, *I*, then feel so insecure? Yes. After all these years I am absolutely without defence, I can be broken in an instant. Nothing whatever binds him to the relation that we have now, he is scarcely aware of it as a state of affairs that can change, or indeed as a state of affairs at all! I suppose it's good that he takes me so much for granted, she thought, but just that also means that I have no rights. *Rights?* So now she was thinking about rights! She could imagine Gerard's reaction to any language of that sort! But I must talk to him, she thought, I must tell him, I must, oh it sounds so weak and spiritless, ask him to reassure me. But how can I put it, and what can he say? I must be open and sincere. But what do I want? What I want now is not to go home but to go to Gerard's bed and lie with him until the world ends. Can I tell him *that*? Does he know?

'Don't ring for a taxi,' she said, 'I'll get one easily if I just walk to the end of the road. Don't bother to come.'

'Of course I'll come! Where the hell did Pat put my coat?'

Out in the street when the taxi stopped and its door was open, Gerard kissed Rose on the lips as he often did and she put her arms round his neck as she often did.

Tamar left the office early that evening. She had got used to the office, although the head of the firm called her 'Totsy', and one of her female colleagues had lectured her on her clothes. The unattached young men liked her and teased her but made no advances. She was going to see Duncan. A note from him had suggested she should come again, and she had rung up and arranged to come.

In the situation into which Gerard had prompted her to enter, Tamar had felt herself in the role of a slave-girl who, without any special relation with either, was to bring the hero and the heroine together. She was, in this, to be unnoticed and unrewarded, a mere tool. Looking back later she realised that she had never believed that she could in any way assist that reconciliation, but had simply believed in Gerard's belief and felt pleased (so there was some pleasure in it) to be chosen. Something however had happened now to complicate her task. She was not sure when exactly it had happened: perhaps when Duncan had cried 'Stop!' and led her by the hand back to the sofa, or just after that when they were sitting on the sofa looking at each other, or possibly later on that night when she was at home in her bedroom thinking about Duncan and his huge head and mane and his gentle quizzical clever look. She certainly could not put it that she had fallen in love with him, that was, because of the difference in their ages and his status in her life, entirely impossible. But her feelings of sympathy, her desire to help and heal, were intensified, she thought about him more and could recognise stirrings of a sexual nature. Tamar was not dismayed. No one knew of this, mild and harmless after all, condition and no one would ever know. She had had similar vague feelings when she was younger in equally unviable situations, for a master at school, for Leonard Fairfax, for Jean, even for Gerard, and knew that these things were innocent, could be concealed and suppressed, and would pass. She had felt some acute anxiety at the Guy Fawkes party, wondering if he would come, then when he came feeling both pleasure and a sort of fear which prompted her to avoid him, 'sliding round the house like a cat', as Patricia had put it. When in the dark, at the end, he took hold of her hand and squeezed it Tamar had felt a warm impulse of joy. They exchanged no words and left separately soon after. Reflecting later upon this incident she was touched by his, as she saw it, desire to reassure her. She had decided not to go to see him unless positively invited. When the invitation came she was pleased, but wondered whether it were not prompted by some sort of now necessary politeness.

Something else had happened to Tamar in the interim; she had received a large cheque from Joel Kowitz in New York, coming, he said, although he had signed it himself, from a Jewish Educational Foundation. Tamar knew that the cheque was prompted by Jean and did not believe in the Educational Foundation. She opened the envelope at breakfast watched, as was usual when she was opening her letters, by her mother. Violet snatched the cheque and would have torn it up, only Tamar snatched it back, promising that she would return it to Joel, which she would have done in any case. After she had posted it back to him with a suitably grateful letter she found herself wondering why she had not paid the cheque into her bank and snapped her fingers at her mother. But of course she could not do that. She reflected on the reasons, wondering if they were good ones. When Tamar had decided that she must give up Oxford she had set herself to it as to a dedicated task, a *duty*, something absolutely inevitable. To think it didn't *have* to be so would have been agonising. Violet had set out and Tamar had studied the details of the financial position. It was very serious. Violet could not get work, Uncle Matthew was dead, Tamar's job was urgently necessary to reassure the bank manager. Tamar *understood* why her mother would not accept help. Nor did she forget Violet's cry of 'I've done enough for you!' It was a matter of honour.

Duncan's flat, on this occasion, looked different. Three lamps were on in the drawing room and a fire was burning in the grate. The room, though still dusty, was tidy, and some of the stacked-up books had found their way back onto shelves. The kitchen, which Duncan had shown to Tamar as soon as she arrived, was a bit cleaner and more orderly, though Duncan had not been able to dominate a by now inherent chaos.

Tamar had handed back, washed and ironed, the big white handkerchief which she had carried away with her on the last occasion, and had resisted a temptation to keep. They were now sitting on the sofa which had been drawn up near to the fire, Tamar was sitting with her feet tucked under her, one thin ankle and a buckled shoe visible from under her dress, and Duncan had given her to read a letter from a solicitor, acting for Jean, who requested Duncan's cooperation in the arrangement of a divorce.

On the previous night Tamar had had a curiously vivid dream. She dreamt that she was lost in an enormous circular hotel, 'as tall as the Tower of Babel', and could not find her room or even remember which floor it was on. In a desperate and distressed state of hurry, she kept rushing up and down staircases and round circular corridors, staring at numbers and trying locked doors. At last she found a door which seemed like the right one and opened it. It opened into a small bathroom. Lying in the bath, which was dry, was a woman in a long red dress with a black network mask over her face. Sitting beside the bath and staring at Tamar with intense silent hostility was a woman with brown hair and glasses, dressed as a nurse. Tamar understood at once that the woman in the bath, who was unconscious or possibly dead, was the victim of some terrible infectious plague, the existence of which was being hushed up by the hotel authorities. Starting back from the door in horror she became aware of a tall thin figure standing behind her, a man with blond almost white hair and very light blue eyes. Tamar thought, he's a doctor, then *he's my father* and he's an *Icelander*! The next moment the tall figure moved away and with a ritualistic deliberation laid the palm of his hand against the wall of the corridor. The wall slid aside, revealing what Tamar recognised as the interior of a very big steel safe. Her father walked into the safe, the wall slid back into place, and Tamar beat upon it with her hands in vain. Trying to interpret the dream, Tamar decided that the nurse was, of course, Violet, and the woman in the bath, dressed as she had been at the dance, in red and black, was Jean. These two were sinister, heavy with the horrid unreality and (as Tamar felt it) unclean ambiguity of dream images. Her father was different; he very rarely appeared in Tamar's dreams, and when he did his apparition carried with it a kind of clarity and certainty, a kind of innocence, as if it were indeed no mere delusive ectoplasm from the unconscious, but a periodical visit from another plane. He was always tall (though never hitherto Icelandic), and always a benevolent though elusive figure. The memory of this dream suddenly, and with an extra vividness, recurred to Tamar as she sat on the sofa beside Duncan and read the momentous letter. She thought, perhaps he *is* an Icelander, an idea which had not occurred to her before. He had appeared as a doctor beside a dying, perhaps dead, patient. Tamar then thought, *perhaps he is dead.* In the dream he had entered into a steel box and the door had closed. She had entertained the possibility, but never before thought as a deep emotional thought, that he might be dead. She had so much needed and wanted to believe that he was still living and still somewhere. Perhaps he had come to her to say goodbye. That strange gesture of laying his palm upon the wall had some sort of mysterious finality. Now she thought, *he is dead*, and her hand holding the letter trembled, and with her other hand she touched Duncan's sleeve, and she turned her troubled face towards him.

Duncan took the letter from her and put it on the floor. He had received it that morning. He had of course known that among the variety of Jean's possible moves this was one, but he had not really expected it. He had found himself unable to face the office and had spent the day at home engaged in, as he put it to himself, remaking his mind. He kept repeating, as he had done earlier, I've got to survive, I won't let those two kill me. But now the image of Crimond, which had somehow protected him from the utterness of loss, giving him the occupation of anger, faded; and he saw only Jean, Jean gone, Jean, his dear Jean, coldly effecting the legal and absolute end of her connection with him. At the same time some little air of warmth which knew nothing of the death of love seemed wafted from her towards him, waking all sorts of little innocent expectations and memories, the way she ran to him when he returned in the evening and put her arms around his waist, how they told each other their day. *They had been happy.* He kept trying to 'face it', to 'realise it at last', to see it as 'true'. How was this to be done? He measured now how much, when he had thought all hope was gone, he had still hoped. He would have to answer the lawyer's letter, to make hideous assertions, to assent to hideous arrangements, in order to *help* Jean never to have to see him or think of him again. He thought, I'll do it for her and then I'll kill myself. About Crimond he ceased thinking. The fact of irretrievable loss, now before him like a black cliff, annihilated Crimond as it would soon annihilate Duncan.

Duncan had taken hold of Tamar's hand at the Guy Fawkes party out of a sense of gratitude and because he wanted to reassure her about the teapot. The feel of her warm hand in his cold hand (neither was wearing gloves, but Tamar's hand had been in her pocket) gave him an unexpected shock and reminded him of how they had sat together on the sofa and looked at each other after the teapot disaster. He had written to invite her again because he had now resolved to ask her if she had seen Jean. He also invited her because she was harmless and he could bear her sympathy and because her visit was an incentive to tidy the flat. After the arrival of the letter he forgot Tamar and only remembered her just before she came.

Tamar, still dazed by the sudden recall of her dream, tried to concentrate upon what she had read in the letter. 'Do you think she means it, do you think it will happen? Perhaps –'

'Yes,' said Duncan, 'it will happen. Tamar, I'm a mad man, I'm mad, I'm dangerous, don't torment me.'

'Oh if you only knew how much I want to help you, I'd do *anything* if I could only make all well –'

'You can't. All well would be Jean back again as she once was, and that can never be, never, never – this is the end.'

'It's not the end, you'll go on living, people love you –'

'That's a fiction,' said Duncan, swallowing some more of the whisky. Tamar was sipping her second glass of sherry. 'I can see a lot of things now in this awful light. I doubt if Jean ever really loved me, I doubt if anybody has ever really loved me. What's certain is that nobody can come near me now. Oh, a lot of people are interested, a few are kind, but nobody *loves* me. Don't mock me with those empty conventional clichés.'

'Don't say such bad untrue things! People's love may not

help you, but it's there. You say they can't come near. All right, but I'm here, I'm near, and *I* love you!'

'Don't, Tamar, please –'

'I *love* you!' As she said this Tamar turned towards him and stretched out her arms, slipping her hands round Duncan's thick bull neck and thrusting them under the heavy cool mass of his dark hair. Taken by surprise Duncan put his arm round her shoulder, Tamar knelt and drew herself towards him, then twisting, still holding on by her hands now locked under his hair, found herself sitting on his knee. They both gasped. Tamar stayed awkwardly in position, her head against the rough tweed of his jacket collar. Then something in their attitude horrified them both, the sense perhaps, never clarified, of her as a child and him as a father, and she sprang back, propelling herself like a startled animal into the farther corner of the sofa, where she gazed at Duncan with her cheeks flaming and one hand containing her beating heart.

She said, 'I'm so sorry. I just felt – I do love you, and so do other people, and I wanted to tell you so.'

'Tamar, come back,' said Duncan, 'come here.' He had taken off his glasses.

The note of command was new and Tamar felt its novelty and understood its sense even though it was only later that she reflected upon the seemingly inevitable stages of their movements, plotted as in a strange game. She rose to her knees, then sat again beside him, tucking in her legs as she had before, holding one of her thin ankles in one hand. She turned her head against his nearer shoulder, stretching out one arm along the sofa behind him. He now put both arms around her, gentling her into an easier position, capturing the awkward stretching arm, supporting her as she now was, half kneeling, with her face in his hair and mouth against his hot neck. They stayed thus for a moment with two accelerated hearts beating violently against each other. Then with closed eyes they found each other's lips and kissed carefully twice. After that Duncan pulled her along so that she was leaning against the end of the sofa and drew his legs up so that they, again awkwardly, were half reclining side by side and face to face.

'I love you, Duncan,' said Tamar. 'I love you. I'm sorry. Don't be angry with me.'

'I'm not angry with you, how could I be. Oh Tamar, if you only knew what an absolute hell I'm in.'

'I so much want to help you, but I can't, I *know* I can't, and I shouldn't have come but I did want to say that I love you. Oh, don't be in hell –'

'Get that woollen thing off, I want to put my arms round you properly.'

Tamar slithered out of her cardigan which fell on the floor and Duncan's arms came round her and the buttons of his jacket pressed into her breasts. A moment later he too had slipped his jacket off and gathered her against his stout chest which was bursting out of his shirt, while one hand undid the buttons on her high-necked blouse. A great heat came out of Duncan's body, so that Tamar, pressed against it, felt almost scorched. Her love and her pity for him merged into a swift dizzy physical joy of self-giving as she felt herself strongly enclosed by his arms, his faintly rough cheek scraping hers and his large hot hand laid upon her throat.

After a few moments of this Duncan sat up, pulling her with him. 'This is absurd, there isn't room for us on this sofa, would you mind if we went and lay on my bed? I just want to hold you and be comforted by you. It's for me to say, don't be angry!'

Tamar's hands were clasped round his neck and she hung from his neck as, not waiting for an answer, he rose, then stooped and lifted her up in his arms. Tamar had never been carried by a man before. He said, 'How light you are, you weigh nothing.' He carried her into the guest room, which Duncan had occupied since Jean left, and laid her down on the bed. He unlaced her shoes and removed them, holding her warm feet for a moment in his hands, then removed his own shoes, and undid the buttons of his shirt. He lay down beside her, occupying himself with undoing the remaining buttons of her blouse. Tamar lay on her back. Duncan lay against her with his big heavy dark head between her breasts. He said, his moist breath muffled against her, 'Forgive me.'

'I love you,' said Tamar, 'I love you absolutely. I've loved you ever since – ever since teapot –' She was going to say 'ever since the dance', for it came to her that even then she had been ready to give to Duncan all that great store of love which she had put in readiness for someone else. But not wishing to remind him of the dance, she said, 'Ever since forever.'

Duncan, kissing her breasts, murmured with his wet mouth against her smooth skin, 'Good old teapot.' Then he said, 'Do you mind if we undress a bit more?' They undressed a bit more, quickly, but not completely, flinging garments away and clinging desperately together, warm flesh seeking warm flesh.

'You're not angry with me? No, I know you're not. You're an angel. You're the only thing in the world that isn't made of evil and darkness and hell. You're *saving* me, it's a miracle, I couldn't have believed it, you've made me come alive again, I'm back in the world, I can imagine not dying of grief, I can imagine wanting to live. I feel something again, love, gratitude, surprise. Do you understand?'

'Yes, but it's only for a moment,' she said. 'I mean, with us, it's only for a moment. I'm so glad and so grateful – I'd do anything for you, anything, so that you could live and be happy. This moment will pass. But you must go on living and feeling things and knowing that it's not all hell and you won't die of grief.'

Duncan was silent. Then he said, 'I love you, kid, I'm so grateful to you – I didn't expect this –'

'You're grateful and I'm glad, I'm so glad. This will pass. Jean will come back, I *know* she'll come back. That's what I want for you more than anything, that's why I came, that's what I'm for –'

Duncan's hand that was holding one of hers squeezed it with violent force. Then he took her hand to his face and kissed it and laid it on his cheek. A little later he said, 'Do you mind? Just roll over for a moment, I'm going to pull off the counterpane and the blankets. I want us to be more completely together. Don't worry, I can't make children, I probably can't make anything with you now, I just want to hold you entirely in my arms. Oh pardon me, Tamar, help me, help me, help me –'

Gerard had found a parrot. It was in a pet shop in the Gloucester Road. It was very like Grey, but was certainly not Grey. Gerard, who had been passing, was outside the shop, the parrot was in its cage in the window. They gazed at each other. The parrot was shy, then coy, then grave, very conscious of being closely observed. It stood attentive, head on one side, one foot raised. Gerard did not smile. He looked at the parrot with a tender melancholy stare, a reverent humble stare, as if the parrot were some sort of small god, yet at the same time he wanted to say, 'I'm sorry, oh I'm so sorry,' as if to a pitiable innocent victim. He even murmured half aloud, 'I'm sorry,' meaning, he supposed, that he was sorry that the parrot was a captive, in a cage in London, and not flying about in the tall trees of the rain forests in central Africa where grey parrots come from.

It was a very cold afternoon and a little snow was falling in small frail flakes between Gerard and the parrot. The snow fell slowly like a visible silence as if it were part of the ritual making a private place wherein Gerard and the bird were alone together. Gerard's reflections and feelings expanded about him into a stilled thought-chamber wherein he ceased to hear the traffic or be aware of the passers-by. He thought of his father lying dead with his waxen alienated face, his high thinned nose and sunken chin, and pathetic open mouth, his poor defeated dead father, whose image was now and forever connected with the ghost of the grey parrot. Perhaps, indeed it was very likely, that Grey was alive while his father was dead. Gerard wanted to tell this, felt he was somehow telling it, to the parrot in the shop. The cage was hung quite high up, so that the parrot and Gerard were eye to eye. There were no other creatures in the window. The pity and love which Gerard felt for the parrot, the tender sad guilt, were very like the feelings which he had when he thought about his father, about the things which ought to have been said and the affection which ought to have been more openly expressed. Do the dead know how much we loved them, *did* they know, for they know nothing now? As Gerard was thinking these thoughts, he found that he had instinctively moved his hands, beginning to lift them towards the cage. He recognised the movement as the shadow-start of one he had so often performed of opening the door of Grey's cage and putting in his hand and watching the bird climb onto his fingers, feeling the cool scaly clutch of the feet, then lifting the little oh so light almost weightless living being out of the cage to cradle it against him while he stroked the soft feathers. At this remembrance tears came into Gerard's eyes.

And it was as if the parrot now before him understood, and felt sympathy and sorrow, while remaining, like a close but calm friend, detached, surveying but not swept into the dark pool of grief. The bird was now moving to and fro, rhythmically from one foot to the other, exactly as Grey used to do; then arresting its dance it spread its wings revealing the sudden ordered fan of grey and scarlet feathers. The movement could not but seem to be a cordial gesture. Then the wings closed and were fussily adjusted and settled. The parrot was staring intently at Gerard with its wise yellow eyes framed in ellipses of white dry skin. It stared at him firmly, purposively, as if to keep his attention and preserve their telepathic communion. Then it bent forward, seizing the bars of the cage in its strong black beak, turned upside down and began a slow clambering circumnavigation of the cage, all the time turning its head so as to continue to gaze at Gerard. This was just what Grey used to do. When he saw the parrot upside down engaged in its laborious climb Gerard, in spite of the memory, smiled, then became grave and sad again.

He entertained, then banished, the awful tempting idea of

going into the shop, buying the parrot, carrying the heavy cage away carefully, returning home in a taxi, putting the cage upon a firm table in the drawing room and opening the cage door, for after all he and the parrot were friends already . . . It was impossible. It was only later that he remembered that his sister was in the house to which he was bringing back a dream parrot. He put his hand against the glass near to the parrot's upside-down head and pressed the glass hard to convey, in the form of a frustrated caress, a sort of blessing. Then he looked quickly away and set off down the street where the snow was just beginning to be seen upon the pavements.

Gerard was going to the much-discussed and frequently put off committee meeting of the *Gesellschaft* at which they were to decide 'what was to be done' about Crimond and the book.' The meeting was to take place, unusually, at Rose's flat in Kensington. It was normally held at Gerard's house, but the presence of Patricia and Gideon made this now impossible. Gerard had refused to pursue with his sister the question of her and Gideon joining the group to replace Matthew. He said he would raise the matter at the next meeting. He was reluctant, not perhaps for very clear or good reasons, to let those two join in, though of course their financial contribution would be welcome. Gerard was feeling generally nervous and irritable about the meeting. He had had the awkward task of ringing up Duncan to make sure that he did not want to attend. Duncan certainly did not want to attend, but said that of course he would continue to subscribe. There had been an awkward moment of silence, after which Gerard said he hoped to see Duncan at the Reading Party, and Duncan said 'maybe' and rang off, leaving Gerard feeling he had been inadequate and unkind. He often of course invited Duncan to his own house, but Duncan never came, perhaps because of Pat and Gideon, whom he did not like, perhaps because he now found Gerard's company painful.

The committee diminished by the absence of Duncan and Jean, and (as Gerard now reflected) fundamentally altered by the disappearance of Gerard's father, would on this occasion consist of Gerard, Jenkin, Rose and Gulliver Ashe. Matthew's presence had prevented outbursts of emotion, for instance from Rose and Gulliver, who indulged their indignation more informally elsewhere, and had contributed to the policy of calm indecisive *laisser-faire* favoured by Gerard. Matthew represented tradition, live-and-let-live, altogether a more casual scrutiny of what was supposed to be going on. He refused to see any point in making a fuss or anything much to make it about. Although Gerard was in charge, and he *was* in charge, his father, politely deferred to by all, had largely determined the atmosphere. Now, he thought, it'll be gloves off. Both Rose and Gull, for different reasons, wanted blood, they wanted a skirmish, a clarification, a show-down. How obsessed they had all become about that book! When it eventually appeared it would probably be a small matter, a damp squib. A possible tactic, and this had occurred to Gerard more than once, would be to send Jenkin as the ambassador. Jenkin, occasionally, actually met Crimond at meetings and discussions. Jenkin always (and as Gerard knew, conscientiously) reported these 'sightings' to him, and Gerard, with equal delicacy, did not ask for details. He knew that the connection was slight, though this did not prevent him from being annoyed by it; and he did not want to send Jenkin now, formally, to see Crimond in case such a meeting might make or strengthen a bond between them. He wanted to keep *this* matter in his own hands. Rose would wish this too; yes, Rose positively wanted him to confront Crimond. Was he then to see himself as riding into battle carrying Rose's favour upon his lance? The image reminded him of Tamar. That at least was something he had done well. Duncan had come to the fireworks party and would, he believed, come to the Reading Party. That was Tamar's doing, good for Duncan and good for Tamar too. Duncan, who felt too ashamed and defeated to talk frankly to Gerard, might find relief in talking, not necessarily about his 'problem' but about anything, to Tamar whom he would not regard as a judge; and Tamar, who was certainly unhappy, would be cheered by a sense of being trusted. The prospect of his own sortie pleased Gerard not at all. What he feared most was a flaming row, after which, if he had behaved intemperately or irrationally, he would feel ashamed and discredited and *connected* with Crimond by bonds of remorse and indecision and sheer intense annoyance. If there *was* a row Gerard would feel, such was his nature, compelled to attempt to make peace: negotiations which would probably land him in yet messier and more remorseful situations. Gerard hated muddles and any consciousness that he had behaved badly. Also, he did not want to have to think so much about Crimond. He had a quite different problem of his own which he wanted to think quietly about, involving a new course of action upon which he would soon have to decide.

'I'm sorry to keep repeating myself,' said Gulliver, 'but I don't see why we should keep paying out money every year to support a book that we passionately disagree with, which we aren't allowed to look at, which he may have abandoned ages ago, which perhaps never existed at all!'

'Oh come,' said Jenkin, 'of course it exists, Crimond isn't a cheat, Gerard saw some of it once –'

'A hundred years ago!' said Rose.

'The point is,' said Gerard, 'that we can't ditch Crimond. We said we'd support him and there it is, we made a promise.'

'The point is,' said Rose, 'that it's not the book we said we'd support. I think it never was. Crimond misled us. Crimond is not the man we thought he was. He believes in violence and he believes in lies. He says in one of those pamphlets that truth may have to appear as a lie – and that we are sick with morality, that morality is a disease to be got over!'

'Rose, he meant bourgeois morality!' said Gerard.

'He said morality. And he admires T. E. Lawrence.'

'So do I,' said Gerard.

'He supports terrorists.'

'It's hard to define terrorists,' said Jenkin, 'we agreed earlier that violence is sometimes justified –'

'We've been into all that!' said Gulliver.

'Don't defend him,' said Rose, 'I'm not going to help to

finance a book that excuses terrorism. We'd all be blamed later for that, people would think he represented our views.'

'I don't think Crimond meant –' said Jenkin.

'How do we know what he meant?' said Gulliver, 'he wraps it up so. Rose is right, he can't distinguish truth and falsehood.'

'Those are old things,' said Gerard, pointing to some pamphlets which Gulliver had discovered and brought with him as 'evidence'.

'It was a phase he went through –' said Jenkin.

'How do we know that?' said Gulliver to Jenkin. 'What he thinks now may be even crazier. And why don't we know what he thinks now? Because he only lets his stuff out to the initiated! You seem to believe he's some sort of dedicated hermit! *Of course* he belongs to a highly organised underground movement!'

'It's true that he writes things which are circulated privately,' said Jenkin. 'He doesn't publish in the ordinary way any more. Someone showed me a recent thing, quite short –'

'And was it as pernicious as these ones?' asked Rose.

'I don't know whether pernicious is the word, it certainly wasn't less extreme – but it expressed some deep ideas. Rose, he's a *thinker*, the activists attack him for not caring about the working class!'

'All right, it's his ideas we don't like!' said Gulliver. 'Ideas do things too, as you know perfectly well! Of course he's not a Stalinist, he belongs to some sort of mad Trotskyist-anarchist group, smash the nearest thing is their creed, any sort of chaos is a form of revolution!'

They had been arguing now for nearly an hour. Everything about the argument upset Gerard. Rose and Gulliver were both surprisingly venomous, they seemed to be consumed by personal hatred for Crimond. Gulliver detested Crimond because (and Gull had told Gerard this) Crimond had once snubbed him savagely at a public meeting. But he also hated what he took to be Crimond's theories, and was speaking from the heart in defence of ardently held political convictions.

Gulliver, riffling his dark oily hair back with his hand and opening his golden brown eyes defiantly wide and expanding the nostrils of his aquiline nose, looked spirited, distinctly younger and more interesting. At one point Gerard smiled at him and received a signal of gratitude from the brown eyes. Gerard then felt guilty and thought, I must *help* that boy, does he blame me, I hope not. Rose's emotion (she was quite flushed with indignation) Gerard attributed not only to strong political principles, especially concerning secret societies and terrorism, but also to her belief, of which he had often been made aware but on which he had never commented, that Crimond was Gerard's enemy and might some day do him harm. Also involved were Rose's deep feelings about Jean, Rose felt anger with, and fear for, her life-long friend and blamed Crimond for both of these distressing sensations. Gerard had not discussed this matter with her either. Is Crimond my enemy? Gerard wondered. It was an unpleasant idea. Gerard had also been upset, during the argument, by Jenkin's quiet determination to excuse Crimond. It was some time since Gerard had had a really detailed discussion of politics with Jenkin. He had always assumed that their views on this matter more or less coincided. Supposing he were now to discover, and feel obliged to pursue, some really serious and disturbing difference of opinion? This possibility of a damaging breach was instantly transformed in his mind into the image of Jenkin somehow *defecting* to Crimond. But this was, *must* be, unthinkable. Gerard was more immediately annoyed by the aggressive atmosphere in which he was being driven to go and 'have it out' with the rascal.

They were sitting at the round rosewood table in Rose's flat which overlooked a little square garden enclosed by railings. Between bare branches of trees, before Rose had pulled the curtains, the lighted windows of houses opposite made a pattern of golden rectangles. Snow was still slowly falling. It was now after five o'clock and the lamps were on in Rose's sitting room. It was warm in the flat and their overcoats and umbrellas, now dry and unfrozen, were piled upon the Jacobean chest in the hall. Rose's flat was comfortable, a bit shabby, full of a miscellany of things which had come from her maternal grandfather's house in Ireland. The 'fine' stuff, the Waterford glass, the Georgian silver, the pictures by Lavery and Orpen, Rose had given to her cousins in Yorkshire after Sinclair's death, at a time when she felt dead herself and wanted to throw away all the things that might have lived in her brother's house and belonged to his children, to strip herself of all those insidious small reminders, the terrible details, leaving but one great comprehensive pain. That had been before she had found herself, so miraculously, in bed with Gerard. We were suffering from shock, she thought, we were broken and not put together, we were half made of wood like puppets not quite changed into real people. It was something not quite real and for him, she felt, forgettable like a dream. *Did* he remember, she even wondered? If only it, *that*, could have happened earlier – but it couldn't – or later – but it didn't. It was several years before Rose really wanted to acquire anything, even clothes, for herself. Her remaining pieces of furniture, mainly from Ireland where she now had no close relations, were handsome enough but un-looked-after, imperfect, damaged, scuffed, stained, even broken. The mahogany sideboard was scratched, the Davenport lacked a foot, the rosewood table had wine-glass rings, the Jacobean chest in the hall upon which the thawing coats were enjoying the warmth of the central heating had lost a side panel which had been replaced by plywood. Rose had once meant to have the bathroom carpeted and the curtains cleaned. She had meant to have the furniture 'seen to', but she kept putting it off because her life always seemed so provisional, a waiting life, not settled like other people's. Now it was probably too late to bother. Neville and Gillian, the children of her cousins, the heirs, sometimes chided her for not having the table properly French polished and the chest restored. The young people cared about these things. They would be theirs one day.

'I wonder if he's actually mad,' said Rose.

'Of course not,' said Jenkin, 'if we get obsessed with his *Schrecklichkeit* and simply call him crazy we won't *think* about what he says –'

'He's on the side of the evil in the world,' said Rose. 'He's a bully, and I hate bullies. He's dangerous, he'll kill someone.'

'Rose, calm down. We were all Marxists once –'

'So what, Gerard – and I wasn't! He's a conspirator. I don't believe he's a solitary thinker, or that he belongs to some dotty little group – I think he's a dedicated underground communist.'

'I'm not just blindly defending him,' said Jenkin, 'I don't know exactly what he thinks, if I did I'd probably hate it, but we must find out. He's gone on *thinking* about it all and we haven't, we must give him that –'

'That's a damn silly argument –!'

'Shut up, Gull, let me talk. Crimond has worked, he's tried to put something together. He believes, or he believed, that he could make some sort of synthesis –'

'The book that the age requires!'

'And we didn't just laugh at him in those days.'

'There can be no such book,' said Gulliver.

'All right, if we think that now, we should ask ourselves why! We've lost a lot of confidence since then. Our heroes, dissidents who fight tyrannies and die in prisons, are enabled by history to be soldiers for truth. We are not – I mean quite apart from not being brave enough, we aren't martyred for our opinions in this country. The least we can do is try to think about our society and what's going to happen to it.'

Gerard murmured, 'Yes, but –'

'Crimond says it's the end of our society,' said Rose. 'He said he wanted to destroy "that world", meaning *our* world.'

'I don't see what stops us from being heroes too,' said Gull, 'except bloody cowardice of course.'

'I think Crimond *is* a lone wolf,' Jenkin went on, 'I think he's really a romantic, an idealist.'

'Utopian Marxism leads straight to the most revolting kinds of repression!' said Gull. 'The most important fact of our age is the wickedness of Hitler and Stalin. We mustn't tolerate any stuff which suggests that communism is really fine if only it can be done properly!'

'Don't be cross with me,' said Jenkin. 'I was going on to say that at least Crimond's sort of Marxism is utilitarian, he *cares* about suffering and poverty and injustice. It's like the Catholic church in South America. Suddenly people begin to feel that nothing matters except human misery.'

'He wants to destroy our democracy and have one-party government,' said Rose, 'that's scarcely the way to fight injustice!'

'Rose is right,' said Gulliver. 'Democracy means you accept disagreement and imperfection and bloody-minded individualism. Crimond hates the idea of the individual, he hates the idea of being incarnate, he's a puritan, he's not a bit romantic, he's something new and awful. He praises horror films because they show that behind cosy bourgeois society there's something violent and disgusting and terrible which is *more real!*'

'I think it's time to adjourn this meeting,' said Gerard. 'We've talked enough, everyone's said what he thinks several times over –' Jenkin was looking upset, Rose as if she might burst into tears.

'We ought to have it out with him,' said Gulliver, 'at least someone should. Bags I not.'

'And not me,' said Jenkin.

'Gerard must go, of course,' said Rose.

'All right, I'll see him,' said Gerard, 'at least we've decided something.'

'Who'll have a glass of sherry?' said Rose.

They all got up. Jenkin said he must go at once. He looked at Gerard and a telepathic message passed between them to the effect their neither was cross with the other. Gulliver, who was less telepathic and was feeling excited and pleased with himself, hung around and accepted a second glass of sherry.

'Perhaps we could pay Crimond to go and live in Australia!'

'Poor old Australians!' said Rose.

'I wish it was as easy as that,' said Gerard.

'By the way,' said Gull, 'Lily Boyne said she'd like to join our little *cosa nostra*. She's not a fool, you know, and she has the right sort of views. I meant to say earlier but I forgot.'

'I should have thought the right sort of views would make her keep away!' said Rose.

'Well, you know what I mean. Anyway, since she said it I pass it on.'

'Hang it,' said Gerard, 'I forgot to mention about Pat and Gideon wanting to muck in.'

'It's not a moment for new recruits,' said Rose, 'not till we know where we are.' She looked at her watch and Gulliver soon said he must go. 'Gulliver, Gerard says you'll be able to come to the Reading Party, I'm so glad, and I've asked Lily too. Let us know your train and we'll pick you up at the station. Oh, and bring your skates.'

'*Skates?*'

'Yes, with luck the water meadow will be frozen.'

After Gulliver had gone they sat down on either side of the electric fire which occupied the fireplace.

'How odd about Lily wanting to join,' said Gerard.

'She wants to be part of the family,' said Rose.

'Are we a family? Well, we must look after her too.'

'Gull got quite excited. He's a nice boy.'

'Yes, and good-looking.'

'Gerard. When you see Crimond. Be careful.'

'Of course I will. However cool I am, I bet he'll be cooler! Why, Rose, you're crying!'

Gerard got up, drew his chair near to hers, and put an arm round her shoulder. Her face was flushed and her wet cheek when he touched it was hot. As he drew her head down to this shoulder and felt her cool hair against his chin he remembered the grey parrot which would now be asleep in its cage.

'Did you sleep well?'

'Yes, did you?'

'Yes, very well.'

Duncan said, 'Why do people always ask other people whether they slept well, meaning simply did they sleep? One may sleep continuously and have a terrible night. There is good and bad sleep.'

'You mean dreams?' said Rose, who was standing at the door.

'I mean sleep.'

No one felt inclined to pursue the matter or to enquire which kind Duncan had had.

The first two speakers were Gull and Lily, and the time was breakfast time on Saturday, the guests' first breakfast at the Boyars Reading Party, and for Lily and Gull, who were new to the house, their first Boyars breakfast ever, and their first real view of the scene, inside and out, since, like the others, they had arrived for dinner, in the dark, on the previous evening.

Rose had of course arrived earlier in the day, not really to supervise anything, since her elderly servant Annushka, the 'young girl' in the photograph which Duncan had showed to Tamar, had made all the usual immaculate preparations. This servant, the daughter of a gardener, originally 'Annie', had been given the affectionate diminutive by Sinclair when, as a child, he had emulated his great-great-grandfather by going through a Russian phase. It was this same ancestor who had invented the name 'Boyars', for no very clear reason. Why not 'Czars', Sinclair had complained. Rose thought the name derived from Tolstoy via *Où sont les Boyars?*. Rose came early just to breathe the air, to look about, to put on her Boyars persona, and to wonder, as she always did, why she did not come here oftener.

Gull and Lily had arrived together by train, Tamar by another train, all met at the station by Rose. Duncan had arrived by himself by car, Gerard had driven Jenkin down as usual. Patricia and Gideon who seemed to think they had an open invitation had, to general relief, announced that it was their time for being in Venice. In fact for reasons nobody bothered to penetrate they hardly ever visited Rose's house.

Gulliver had come down first to breakfast and had eaten a boiled egg. Duncan had eaten fried eggs and bacon collecting them from the hot-plate on the sideboard. Gulliver now blamed himself for having bothered Annushka to get him a boiled egg. He would have liked eggs and bacon better, he now decided. However he was wearing his dark-blue double-breasted Finnish yachting jacket and felt good. Gerard had eaten a piece of bacon with fried bread. Jenkin was at the sideboard helping himself to eggs, bacon, sausage, fried bread and grilled tomatoes. In the old days there had used to be kidneys too, and kedgeree. Lily had eaten some toast with homemade gooseberry jam. Tamar had toyed with a piece of toast and rapidly vanished. Everyone had had coffee except for Lily who asked for tea. Rose, who got up very early and never ate breakfast, had had her early tea with Annushka, and, flitting about, had not sat down with her guests. She had explained to the newcomers the layout of the house and the various 'walks' that were available. There were plenty of places to sit and (since this was the title of the gathering) read. There was the drawing room, and the dining room which had a pleasant window seat, the billiard room (sorry no billiards, the moths had got at the cloth), where you could play records, the library of course (do take out any book) and the study (Rose would not be occupying it). As for walks, it was best to keep to roads and paths, there was a framed map in the study. There was the walk to the river, the walk to the church, the walk to the wood, though the way through it was rather overgrown, the walk to the Roman Road and along it, and of course the walk to the village which was called Foxpath. Yes, there was, Gull had asked the question, a village pub, it was called the Pike. The name referred to the fish of course, not the weapon; an eccentric publican who put up a sign to celebrate the Peasants' Revolt was soon disciplined by public opinion.

Naturally the guests had brought books though not everyone was ready to declare or discuss his choice. Duncan had brought two fat Government publications, Gulliver had brought the poems of Lowell and Berryman and had vowed to write some poetry during his stay, Lily had brought a travel book on Thailand, Gerard had brought Horace's *Odes* and a volume of Plotinus in the Loeb edition, Rose had brought *Daniel Deronda*, Jenkin had brought the *Oxford Book of Spanish Verse*, a Portuguese grammar, and a book by a Jesuit called *Socialism and the New Theology*. (He kept these latter works well out of Gerard's sight.) Tamar had apparently brought no book but had retired to the library to find one. The 'regulars' felt but did not mention the absence of Jean whose comical taunts and restless badinage had always stirred up what might otherwise have proved *too* quiet a scene. Rose anticipated that Gull and Lily would be bored.

Since they had got up it had begun to snow, at first with tiny indecisive flakes, now with larger ones. The countryside, already streaked by a previous fall, was now entirely white. Rose had warned the newcomers to bring boots and also warm jerseys to wear if necessary inside the house as well as outside. There *was* central heating, and wood fires all day in the 'public rooms' and at evening in the bedrooms, but Boyars was (as Rose complacently said) not a warm house.

'Is the water meadow frozen?' asked Gerard.

'I think so,' said Rose, 'it must be. I'll go over and look this morning.'

Gerard and Rose, who could skate well, kept their skates at Boyars. They disliked the weird and garish atmosphere of indoor skating rinks. Jenkin could not skate but liked watching the others. Duncan could not skate and did not like watching the others who were always, he claimed, and that included Jean who was a good skater, showing off. Tamar could skate but had forgotten to bring her skates. Rose thought an old pair of Annushka's might fit her. (Annushka, a beautiful skater, had given up.) Lily said she had skated a bit once and was game to try. Gulliver admitted to being able to skate. He did not however reveal, even to Lily, that he had just, for the occasion, bought a pair of skates, the first he had ever possessed. He had spent some time the previous morning rubbing mud over the shining boots to dim their newness. It had been a foolish and expensive purchase. He had still not managed to find a job.

'I say, Rose,' said Jenkin, 'there's a ladybird walking on the sideboard. What shall we do, put her on those plants? Shall I catch her?'

'I will,' said Rose. 'I'll put her in the stables. They creep into crannies in the wood, then they fly out in the spring. It's amazing how sturdy insects are.'

'They'll survive the Bomb,' said Jenkin, 'I suppose there's some comfort in that.'

Rose took a wineglass from the cupboard, captured the ladybird and took charge of it.

A white cat with greyish tabby blotches entered with tail erect and was captured by Lily. 'Rose, what's the name of your pussycat?'

'Mousebrook,' said Rose. In fact the cat's full name was Mousebrook the Mauve Cat, but Rose did not feel matey enough with Lily yet to tell her that.

'What a funny name!'

'Skating this afternoon, don't you think?' said Gerard.

'Yes,' said Rose. 'This morning you boys must work. Look at that snow! It's real brass monkey weather.'

What on earth does that mean, Lily wondered, as she struggled with recalcitrant Mousebrook.

After breakfast, while the others were still arguing about their 'day', Duncan hurried upstairs to his bedroom. He had already made his bed. Annushka did not make beds, as Rose always reminded them. The room had seemed cosy last night in the firelight. Now the fire was out and the room was cold and filled with a relentless greyness by the moving curtain of snow. Duncan was not in the room which he had always occupied with Jean. Rose had moved him, with tactful intent, to a smaller room at the back of the house where, as she said, the view was better. The view was at least different, but Duncan was cross at being given a small room with no contiguous bathroom. He gazed out at the view through the irritating little diamond-shaped lattice panes of the pointed Strawberry Hill Gothic window characteristic of this part of the house. He sympathised with Rose's great-grandfather who had altered (or 'vandalised') the front of the house by altering the pseudo-Gothic to sturdy Edwardian and adding a grace-less but useful extension. He opened the window so as to see better, then closed it abruptly against a massive entry of bitterly cold air and a snowflake or two. His room looked out over the back lawn and garden, the conifers and extensive shrubbery, the rosy walls of the vegetable garden, a segment of woodland, the gentle mild hills of the English countryside, a distant farm, and the Roman Road, a dead straight miles-long section of a famous Roman highway which here ribboned over the hills and dales, constituting a sort of landmark. The Roman Road was not now a main road. The main road, not a motorway but a substantial artery, lay a considerable distance off in front of the house on the other side of the river.

Duncan, distracted for a short while by company, now returned to his wound. He had eaten too much breakfast and felt sick. His whole being felt sick, sick, sick. He had announced on the previous evening that he must go very early on Sunday to prepare for a meeting. He had intended earlier not to come at all, but had decided he ought to appear so as not to seem to be avoiding Tamar. Now that seemed a ridiculous reason. Why should anybody think he was avoiding Tamar, what motive could they imagine he might have for doing so? This calculation was a measure of the guilt he felt about what had, so briefly, so quickly, happened that evening. He could scarcely now picture what state of mind, what sudden desper-ate need for consolation, had led him to take that little girl, that *child*, into his arms. It didn't, now, seem like lust, it was simply an irresistible craving for love, for a woman's love, for being held close in a woman's arms and hearing her say, as *she* had said, 'I love you, I'll always love you.' It was as if Tamar had murmured, 'I'll protect you, I'll shield you, I'll take your

231

hurt away, I'll carry you out of the world, I'll make you invisible and perfectly safe for ever and ever.' Perhaps she had said something like that. I was very drunk that evening, Duncan said to himself. I must have been dreadfully drunk to act in that way. Was I disgusting, brutish, awful? She didn't seem to think so *then*, I could have been anything and be loved. But what did she feel later? Duncan did not like to believe that she now saw him as a drunken brute. But then neither did he want to believe that she *really* loved him. What would that mean, what could it bring about? What words could he use, what words could he ever use, to tell Tamar that he was grateful, but it was indeed something momentary and he could not return her love? Was that what he felt now about Tamar, little innocent Tamar with her schoolgirl hair and slender legs? He thought, she'll assume, she'll *know* that it was an aberration. I was in a state of shock, I'd just had the solicitor's letter, I hope she took *that* in. Oh God, why did I act so stupidly, why do I have to have *this* as well! I can't go on living with myself much longer. Of course it was her doing, she started it, I'd never have made a move, I'd never have wanted to! What a minx, what a temptress, what terrible ill luck, what an accursed doomed creature I am.

Duncan had not exactly recovered from the solicitor's letter, but had adjusted his mind so that the letter was not a death sentence, not a total extinction of hope. This was partly the result of a talk with Gerard which had taken place the day after Tamar's visit. Duncan showed Gerard the letter and they discussed it. It was a relief to talk, for once (for Duncan had not lately been eager to see his friends) to Gerard, though Gerard's lively pleasure in the talk annoyed him. Gerard loved listing pros and cons. He still thought of himself as the leader, the healer, the one who was never in trouble, the one who had remained young; while Duncan had become heavy, cumbersome, wrinkled and old. Even his hair, though it was thick and dark and crinkly, was like a heavy wig upon his head, while Gerard's hair curled and shone like a boy's. These were ludicrous thoughts of course, as ludicrous as a new feeling of jealousy about Jenkin, as if Jenkin, always around the place, made it increasingly difficult for Duncan to talk freely to Gerard as he had once done. The fact that they had *once* been so close however remained as an eternal guarantee. Gerard had suggested, or rather elicited from Duncan, the idea that the solicitor's letter did not mean anything final. It could even be some sort of try-on or something which Crimond had ordered Jean to do as a matter of routine. Duncan must not be seen to take it seriously. Thus inspired Duncan had replied to the solicitor that he was surprised to receive the letter, he did not want a divorce, he loved his wife and desired and expected her to return to him before long. Since then nothing more had been heard. Gerard said that was a good sign.

But what was the use of signs and hopes when all being was corrupt and bad, when one had been metamorphosed into something so defeated and contemptible and base? How can an absolutely humiliated person be reinstated, accorded the *respect* which love implies, even be *forgiven* for having let himself fall so low? It was no use appealing to justice here. How *could* Jean want to come back? If Crimond ditched her she would run to Joel, indeed she might do anything. Jean was brave, she was unlike Duncan, she would run against the guns baring her breast, she would never come crawling back, she would find some new amazing thing to do. She was still young. Crimond too, he was young. Duncan dreamed at night, and later more and more in long obsessive fantasies by day, about that farther past in which the *myth* of his defeat, his *fall*, had been, once and for ever, established, about the blow, the stairs, and Jean's voice calling from below, so affectionate, so false, as he stood holding in his hand that little tangle of Crimond's hair: Crimond, tall, thin, white, naked, pale-eyed, brilliant-eyed, walking about as he pleased in Duncan's sleeping and waking fantasy. He was as obsessed with Crimond as he was with Jean, and as awfully bound to him.

He had not communicated with Tamar, or heard from her, in the now lengthy interim. He had considered sending a very vague letter, but letters are dangerous. Better to say nothing. They would both say nothing, do nothing, that was how it would be, so that the act itself would be gradually un-done, dissolved by time. Thank God he could rely on Tamar's silence. The idea of Gerard finding *that* out . . . Duncan would never speak to anyone about it. He had never spoken to anyone about his eye. Only about Tamar, he would forget.

He had paraded, as his 'reading', a Government White Paper and another Stationery Office publication, about tax, but he had no intention of looking at these. Really to read, he had secretly brought two thrillers, which of course he would not take downstairs. He consumed more and more thrillers in these days. He sat down on his bed and opened one, got up and put on his overcoat, then sat down again. Longing for his wife pervaded him, *shook* him, in the form of misery and rage. He would soon resign from the Service, become a recluse, disappear, perhaps kill himself. He would do something terrible. He would kill Crimond. He would have to.

Rose Curtland was standing at her window watching the snow falling slowly, thickly, steadily, in plump flakes, in straight lines, since the wind had dropped, like a curtain, like a grille, outside her window, fascinating, dazing, beginning to conceal the landscape. Rose had put on a woollen shawl round her shoulders. The house was cold and uneasy with a new and special unease. Perhaps it was the end of an era. Perhaps they would never again be, all of them, together in that house as they had so often been in the past. Everyone seemed to be uneasy, touchy, nervous; everyone that is except Gerard who always was, or always appeared to be, calm, in charge of himself and others. Duncan was, of course, poor Duncan, unhappy and anti-social, a bit aggressive. Tamar seemed to be ill, had eaten practically nothing at dinner and at breakfast, had admitted that she had a headache. Jenkin, always a problem because of his tendency to disappear, had been excessively invisible, running off at once after dinner when everyone was supposed to sit round the drawing room fire and drink whisky. Annushka, arthritic and not allowed by Rose to carry wood, was cross because Rose had chided her for asking Gulliver to carry wood instead of telling Rose who would have carried it herself. Even Mousebrook the Mauve Cat, deserting his usual winter place, elongated upon the tiles at the back of the big cast iron stove, was irritable and out of sorts and had jumped suddenly away and run off when Rose tried to pick him up. Mousebrook was described as mauve because his tabby grey looked mauvish, and had looked so to Rose on the night, eight years ago, when Annushka had brought him as a stray kitten in out of the rain. The name Mousebrook, appearing out of the air, was clearly his own.

Rose occupied the big corner bedroom beside the turret in the 'Gothic' part of the house. She loved this side with its glittering high-pointed windows, facing toward the garden, and the turret with its little French-style leaded dome, and deplored the philistinism of her great-grandfather who had, after *his* father had sold 'the big house', so insensitively altered and enlarged the pretty place, whose complete elegant beauty survived only in photographs. Sinclair had talked about restoring it. From her two main windows Rose enjoyed the same view as Duncan's, over the garden toward the Roman Road. The turret room, which opened directly out of her bedroom, and which she used both as bathroom and dressing room, looked three ways, toward the back, toward the side and toward the front. At the side beyond the stable block and the orchard, visible between curving fields, was a segment of the village of Foxpath, while nearer to the river, and about half a mile from the village, was the church, its light grey tower rising above the snowy trees. A small congregation still trudged out there on Sundays, Rose always turned up too when she was in the country, and some of her guests usually came out of politeness or curiosity. The view toward the front, best from the big front bedrooms of the Edwardian façade, showed the front lawn, the fancy iron gates, a brick wall along the lane, fields, water meadows, and the twisting of the river marked by big pollarded willows. The view on the farther side of the house which was encrusted with useful Edwardian 'horrors', was toward the woods, also showing, as a straight line drawn over the curve of a distant hill, the continuation of the Roman Road. There was one good bedroom on that side which Rose had given to Gulliver. The two best bedrooms in front were occupied, as always, by Gerard and Jenkin, Lily was in the room on the village side usually occupied by Duncan and Jean. Rose felt that Duncan would be especially unhappy there alone, and besides, Lily, as a new guest and a woman, must be given a fine room. A small bedroom between Rose's and Duncan's remained unoccupied. Tamar was in the upper turret room, above Rose's dressing room, which she had always occupied since childhood on her visits to Boyars. Annushka had a self-contained flat on the ground floor beyond the kitchen.

The Reading Parties, two or three in a year, which had originally lasted a week, and now usually lasted three days, were designed originally to fit into university vacations while avoiding summertime travels, and Christmas when other obligations might divide the group. Rose always spent Christmas in Yorkshire at the house of her cousins, Reeve and Laura Curtland, the parents of Neville and Gillian. She felt bound to observe this custom, it was the only time when she regularly saw what remained of her family, though she made occasional visits at other times. Rose did not get on too well with Laura Curtland, a rather peevish *malade imaginaire*; and since Reeve had become more of a recluse and Laura more of a (as Rose saw her) self-pitying invalid, they rarely came to London. Rose, who had always assumed that her cousins regarded her as 'odd', now felt that they saw her, and pitied her, as an eccentric ageing spinster; but when it came to it she quite enjoyed these Christmases and was fond of her relations who certainly knew how to leave her alone. Neville and Gillian, grown up now and at the university, Gillian at Leeds and Neville at St Andrews, were talking about a London flat; so, they would be more frequent in her life, expecting to be invited to Boyars, even perhaps to be allowed to borrow the house, and generally patronising her with the naive insolence of the young. Rose was alarmed at how much this prospect depressed her; she was not used to thinking of herself as cut off from young people, and she liked the vivacious pair in question. Gerard had always spent Christmas with his father and his sister and Gideon, and till lately Leonard, at the house in Bristol, and it had never been suggested that Rose should join that family party. Jean and Duncan, fleeing English festivities, had usually disappeared to France. Violet and Tamar, refusing all invitations, had a Christmas by themselves, always described by them as 'quiet', and assumed by others to be abysmally dull. Plans for this year were still vague, but with Matthew gone and as Pat and Gideon showed no signs of being elsewhere, Gerard assumed that the trio, with Leonard if he condescended to turn up, would celebrate the feast at Notting Hill. He would, no doubt, for Christmas Day at least, invite Duncan and of course Jenkin. Jenkin's Christmases were mysterious. Rose believed that he went to 'help out' at some charitable 'settlement' in the East End, and then got drunk with his schoolmaster friends. He never told anyone, not even Gerard, exactly what he did. Rose wished that she too could be in London, but could not, without prior notice and without a signal from Gerard, 'disappoint', if that was the word, her worthy cousins.

Rose turned back from the window and the dazed slow falling of the snow to her pretty bedroom, so coolly and clearly revealed in the snow-light, which had scarcely changed since her parents had slept in it, and Rose had slept in the upper turret room. Rose came less often now to Boyars; the house was slipping from her. Annushka felt it, the cat felt it. She had begun recently, for the first time, to feel afraid at night, frightened not by the silence of the countryside, but by the silence of the house itself. She had begun to think about *later on*. If only she had someone really of her own to leave Boyars to. If she left it to Gerard he would leave it, or give it, back to her family, if she left it to Jenkin – well, what would Jenkin do, sell it to help the poor probably. It was no use leaving it to poor Duncan, or to Jean who was as rich as Croesus and had no children – or to Tamar who would certainly make a disastrous marriage. Well, why not to Tamar? How cross Neville and Gillian would be! Tamar would have guilt feelings and hand it over, it would burden her, she would have no luck. How dreadfully childless they all were. Now supposing Tamar were

237

to have a son . . . What foolish, even pathetic thoughts, caged thoughts, mean thoughts, so remote from those happy, free, as it seemed *virtuous* days, when Sinclair was at Oxford and Gerard and Jenkin and Duncan and Robin and Marcus, whom she now so dimly remembered, had come to this house and really *worked* and *argued*. That was before Jean's marriage, and Rose had been the only girl. It had all depended on Sinclair, if he had only lived . . . But these were bad dreams, a constant rat-run of her mind, where she always pictured Sinclair as so happy, so lucky. He too could have made a disastrous marriage, given up his studies, squandered what was left of the family fortune and taken to drink. He might have caused her endless grief instead of endless joy; but what could that matter, so long as he was there? Strange, she thought, they all died in accidents, my Irish grandfather was killed out hunting, my Yorkshire grandfather fell from a mountain, my father died in a car crash soon after Sinclair's death, if I had married Gerard and had a son he would probably have scarred my heart with fear and anguish before he too got burnt or drowned.

'When are you going to see Crimond?' asked Jenkin.
'Next Thursday.'
'Oh. So you've actually fixed it, you rang him up?'
'Yes.'
'Have you told the others?'
'No.'
'Where?'
'My place.'
'Play on home ground?'
'I can't invite myself to his place!'
'A pity. I'd like to know what it's like.'
'So you haven't been there?'
'No. Look, Gerard, I'm not in Crimond's pocket! We just run into each other at meetings!'

'All right,' said Gerard irritably, 'you don't have to tell me!'

'I do have to tell you, evidently!'

It was a little later in the morning and the snow had abated. They were in Jenkin's room, preparing to go for a walk. Gerard was ready. Jenkin was putting on his boots. Gerard was anxious to get out quickly so as to avoid being seen by Gull, who might want to come too. He intended to slink out by a side door through the 'offices', but feared that Jenkin might oppose this as being 'underhand'. Though Gulliver's bedroom was on that side, Gulliver had recently been seen curled up beside the drawing room fire. These were base calculations but Gerard wanted very much to talk to Jenkin alone.

'What time of day,' said Jenkin, 'I'd like to imagine it.'

'Morning, ten o'clock. Do hurry up. We'll go out by the side toward the woods.'

'I thought we were going to the village, I want a drink at the Pike.'

'Oh do you! I can't understand your passion for pubs.'

'They are universal places, like churches, hallowed meeting places of all mankind, and each one is different. Besides, they'll have the Christmas decorations up. Where's my cap? All right, I'm ready now.'

Jenkin followed Gerard down the stairs and out of the hall toward, but not into, the kitchen, past the gun room (no guns) and the brushing room (ancient boots) and the washing room (modern technology) and out onto the untrodden snow of a little courtyard. Gerard closed the door quietly and strode on, Jenkin hurrying after him. The very cold clean air made them gasp. They passed low derelict outbuildings, like a deserted village, hung with icicles silently pointed out by Jenkin, and began to walk along the outside of the tall brown-leaved beech hedge which skirted the back lawn. To the left, upon an eminence a mile away, were the woods, ahead of them a view, beyond the garden trees, of open empty snow-covered hillsides. There was no wind. Everything was very silent. Silence possessed them and they did not speak.

The sky, uniformly clouded, and lying closely over the land, was yellowish, shedding a sombre yellow light. The snow close by, upon the leaves of the hedge and upon the conifers and red-berried holly bushes, showed sparkling white in contrast to the dark greens and browns, but farther away upon the curves of the hills it looked sleek and tawny. The cold air was unstirring, the garden immobile except for the crunch of their boots breaking the crisp frozen surface of the new-fallen snow, which was already patterned here and there by the straight or curving tracks of foxes and by the wandering hieroglyphs of various birds. They passed on, veering now behind the house, along the line of the herbaceous border where plants which were not snugly underground appeared as snowy mounds, and into the shrubbery. Here the thick ilexes and conifers made a roof of snow and the earth was suddenly brown, covered in pine needles, soft and seemingly warm underfoot, and the silence even more intense. Beyond this was a path leading toward the stable block, through the orchard and thus over a stile to a footpath which meandered between fields in the general direction of the village.

Meanwhile Rose had left her bedroom. She had 'pulled herself together', reminded Annushka to make her special fudge which Jenkin liked, put on her boots and her coat and her fur hat, and made her way to the stables carrying a basket containing the captive ladybird in its glass. As she walked she murmured 'Ranter and Ringwood, Bellman and True,' an old charm of Sinclair's guaranteed to calm the nerves and alleviate the 'blues'. She climbed the worm-eaten wooden stairs to the big loft, released the ladybird who crawled sagaciously into a cranny, and unlatched the square loft door which opened onto countryside in the direction of the Roman Road.

She knelt in the opening, surveying the yellow air and the motionless white scene which contained no sign of human habitation, nothing, beyond the orchard trees, except fields and hills, and more distant hills. In the early spring Rose would leave the door open for the swallows whose shadowy dartings would continue throughout the summer. She had come for apples. Upon the floor of the loft, avoiding here and there the holes between rotting boards, lay a sea of Cox's Orange Pippins. The reddish greenish apples, recently harvested by Sheppey the plumber and his sturdy son, placed carefully so that no one touched another one, gave out a faint crisp fragrance. These English apples, much cherished by Rose's forebears, had always seemed to Rose to be good apples, innocent apples, mythological apples, apples of virtue, full of the sweet nourishment of goodness. They would keep till April, even till May, turning gradually to a faintly wrinkled gold, and becoming smaller and sweeter. Rose liked their later incarnation best, but her father had preferred to eat them straightaway.

At the far end of the loft was a store of a different kind, a large pile of stones: smooth sea pebbles of different sizes and colours covered with lines and scrawls of natural abstract art, swirls, crosses, lattices, blotches, stains, white upon black, blue upon brown, red upon purple, pure white, pure black, mostly ovoid but some almost spherical, all collected by Sinclair, who had known each individual stone personally and given some of them names. When he was no longer there the stones had been placed, carefully but without intelligible order, in the little bedroom next to Rose's room; and from there removed to the stables by Neville and Gillian, then aged fifteen and sixteen, in order to clear the room for a school friend, when their parents had borrowed Boyars for a 'house party' in Rose's absence. Rose never again lent Boyars to the Yorkshire Curtlands, or indeed invited them to the house except in terms of an 'open invitation' of which they rarely availed themselves. She contained her rage; but she never brought the stones back to the house. She visited them occasionally, and, more rarely, selected one to take back to London. Sometimes she gave one to Gerard. Once she had given one to Jenkin.

She heard a faint sound and two figures, dark against the snow, walked into her motionless picture, Gerard and Jenkin: Gerard moving with his rhythmical yard-long stride, Jenkin hurrying beside him. They were not talking. Rose, kneeling, a tense watching animal, saw through the cloudy exhalations of her breath, the pair pass out of the orchard, climb over a stile, and set off along the footpath. She did not watch them out of sight.

'What will you talk about?' said Jenkin, breaking the spell of the snow silence at last.

They had abandoned the footpath, which would, as Gerard had wordlessly decided, bring them to the village too soon, and were walking along the Roman Road. They walked in the middle of the road, along which no car had passed since the snow fell. Far in front of them and far behind the road stretched on empty and white.

'We won't talk,' said Gerard.

'How do you mean?'

'I shall just ask him to say something about the book.'

'Describe it, say when it'll be finished?'

'If he wants to. I certainly won't press him.'

'If you don't engage him in conversation he won't say anything!'

'That's up to him. I won't have a long discussion with the blighter.'

'That's not what the others want,' said Jenkin.

'What's not what the others want?'

'Rose and Gulliver, they want something definite, something we can act on, they want a scrap.'

'And you?'

'I want – communication.'

'Between me and Crimond?'

'Between us and Crimond.'

They walked on, more harmoniously in the rhythm of talk, Gerard a little more slowly, Jenkin lengthening his stride, breathing the pure bitterly cold windless air, warm inside their big overcoats. Jenkin's big winter cap came down over his ears. Gerard was bare-headed. The snowy fields were quiet and desolate round about them, enchantedly still, and the snow-light was yellower and denser, dark, as if the day were already darkening to nightfall.

242

'There's nothing to act on,' said Gerard.

'So you're just going through the motions to please them.'

'Yes.'

'But they won't be pleased.'

'Damn it,' said Gerard, 'what do you all want me to do? We don't like Crimond or his book but we're stuck with both. Better just forget it and get on with other things.'

'Pay up and don't think.'

'Yes. Don't you agree?'

Jenkin was silent for a bit. He said, 'He does *work*, you know. He's read and read and thought and thought.'

'He's read and thought himself into a blind alley. He used to have a few rational followers, now his stuff just inflames the crazies and a few adolescents. Jenkin, you know what Crimond believes, and that it's absolutely opposed to what we believe. You don't want me to encourage him, do you?'

Jenkin did not answer this. He said, 'One might be interested all the same, even if it's only in the phenomenon. There's so little respect for learning these days –'

'You mean miners don't read Marx any more!'

'Learned people, intellectuals, have lost their confidence, their kind of protest is being esoteric. And at the other end it's smashing things. There's a gap where the theories ought to be, where the *thinking* ought to be.'

'I'm not sure,' said Gerard, 'all right, maybe we need another philosophical genius – but meanwhile we may be better off without theories, particularly that kind. Any nonentity who wants to feel himself remarkable and licensed to kick what he can't understand is "against the bourgeoisie". There are times when only pragmatism is honest. What they call opportunism. Crimond's *material* is no good, his whole background is rotten. He read *State and Revolution* at an impressionable age and then fell for the Frankfurt School. It's for thrills. All that is old hat, all those people are living in the nineteen thirties, it's not *new*, it's just the old emotions rigged out as thinking. They've seen Soviet socialism, but they can't get rid of the idea that there's something wonderful hidden away in the old package.'

243

'All the same,' said Jenkin, 'Marxism hasn't gone away. And you must admit there were good things in the package which we've simply helped ourselves to.'

'Marx changed our view of history, but only as one way of looking among others. Jenkin, wake up, you're *dreaming* about this stuff! Marxism claims to be a *science*, even Marx thought so in the end, all those pathetic simplifications expressed in that revolting jargon are taken to be the fundamental principles of reality! All right, the top cadres see through it, but that just proves that Marxists are either naive fools or cynical liars!'

'Well, yes, but – if it could only liberate itself into being moral philosophy!'

'That's been tried, and either it's the same old rubbish, or a refutation of Marxism!'

'All right, all right. I can't picture Crimond's book, I must say I'm curious. At least he's trying to put it all together. I see him as a sort of religious figure, someone right out on the edge of things, expecting some sort of general change of being.'

'I'm sorry to hear you romanticising this rotten magic!'

'Hope is something, perhaps even a virtue. I suppose every age thinks it's on the edge of an abyss – one has to think outward, onward, into the dark.'

'Only as far as one can *see*. After that it's fantasy. We can't imagine the future. Marxism is attractive because it pretends it can.'

'So we decide the future must look after itself, we've given enough, we'll just be kind to our friends and enjoy ourselves.'

'Jenkin, you make me sick! You were the one who said that it's not only our destiny but our duty to be powerless!'

'That's not quite what I said, but never mind. You may be right – but one can feel restless.'

'And is your restlessness soothed by thinking that *someone* still believes in a system and has all the old illusions?'

'Perhaps misguided moral passion is better than confused indifference.'

'That's the trap all liberals fall into. Are you really such a tame helpless pessimist?'

'So much of our thought is going to be smashed, it's *got* to be smashed, God for instance –'

'As if that mattered!'

'I think it matters what happens to religion, I don't mean supernatural beliefs of course. We must keep some sort of idea of deep moral structure.'

'Which Marxism denies!'

'People have talked about "demythologisation", but South American and African Christianity will put all that stuff through the shredder.'

'So long as Plato and Shakespeare don't go into the shredder too!'

'Oh, they will. Or they'll have to go to the catacombs together with God and the Holy Grail! Maybe that doesn't matter. Maybe nothing matters except feeding hungry people.'

'Well, that's certainly not what Crimond thinks, he's given up political action, he's only interested in his own thoughts, he's not concerned with real human miseries.'

'Yes, but –'

'You are beginning to exasperate me.'

'Sorry, I'm just thinking about your meeting him. The thing about that man is that he's a puritan, he's a fanatic, his ancestors were Scottish Calvinists, so he's got a huge sense of sin and death-wish, he believes in hell but he's a perfectionist, a utopian, he believes in instant salvation, he thinks the good society is very close, very possible, if only all the atoms could shift, all the molecules change, just very slightly – maybe this could happen, maybe it won't, everything is changing, deeply, terribly, like never before, and maybe it's *hell* ahead, but he thinks it is his job to say it's possible to accept it all and sacrifice almost everything and somehow make the new thing into a good thing, and that's –'

'Jenkin, stop this,' said Gerard. 'Just stop it.'

They walked on in silence, now, as the words ceased, noticing their surroundings, the hedges thickly encased in snow, the brown fuzz of old man's beard appearing here and there, the straight road like a white river, streaking onward, dipping from view and rising further on, the snow surface brittle and frozen now, the snow soft and woolly beneath as they achieved their footprints. The light was changing becoming whiter, lighter, almost misty. The sky was a uniform white-grey, not hinting sun, but with an intense soft glare, as if snow particles, almost invisible, were crowding suspended in space. Then far away ahead of them upon the road a black thing appeared, a motor car. They looked at it with amazement. It dipped down out of view, then reappeared closer to them, moving very slowly, until they could hear the soft sibilant sizzling sound of its black wheels in the snow. They stood aside. As it passed them the people in the car waved and they waved back.

The village of Foxpath, not visible from the road, was reached by a lane bordered by huge yew trees, from some of whose more slender branches the piled snow had fallen, revealing dark glossy pointed foliage and pale red waxen berries.

'The Pike will be open now,' said Jenkin at last.

'Yes.'

'Don't be cross, Gerard.'

'I'm not, my dear creature, I'm just thinking how differently we see the world.'

'Honestly, I don't think I understand politics any more, I just want a few decent simplifications. Utilitarianism is the only philosophy that lasts.'

'There aren't any decent simplifications. All this stuff about feeding the poor is *religion*. OK, doing it is good. But as an idea it's just a bit of romantic Christian myth. You think this idea takes you all the way.'

Jenkin's long nose was red with cold and his eyes were watering. He had pulled his wollen cap down over his ears and was hunched up ape-like inside his overcoat.

'Don't walk so fast, Gerard. I'm just a practical chap, it's *you* who are religious. Yes, as we keep telling each other, we do see life differently. I see it as a journey along a dark foggy road with a lot of other chaps. You see it as a solitary climb up a mountain, you don't believe you'll get to the top, but you feel

246

that because you can *think* of it you've done it. That's the idea
that takes *you* all the way!'

Gerard with a sidelong glance at his friend acknowledged
both the attack and the disarming tone of its delivery. 'I don't
think one can *see* much above where one is, *up there* it just looks
like death.'

'That's what *I'd* call a romantic myth.'

'I believe in goodness, you believe in justice. But we don't
either of us believe in an ideal society.'

'No – but I feel I *live* in society, you don't – I think you don't
notice it.'

By this time their lane had joined a road which led into the
village, the snow was trodden, cars had passed, there was a
sound of dogs barking, echoing in the snow spaces, and the
high cries of children tobogganing on a hillside half a mile
away. The church, beyond the village, upon a small eminence,
was here in view, not shielded by trees. Soon they were
walking on trampled pavements between cottages, their roofs
of slate and thatch heavy with thick snow and fringed with
icicles, their walls, of pale powdery rectangular stones, sparkling with frost. 'Good mornings' were exchanged, and 'cold,
isn't it!' There was an air of excitement and comradeship in
the dry windless cold and the brightening white light. Gerard
had never really got to know Rose's acquaintances in Foxpath.
There was for instance an elderly Miss Margoly whom Rose
used to speak of, the tall box hedge of whose garden they were
just passing, and a Scropton family whose pretty square house
was set back from the road. Then there was the house of
Tallcott, the doctor, who was 'good but brusque', then the
village shop where one could get 'almost everything', the new
house of the local builder, the cottage of Mr Sheppey the
plumber, the dressmaker's cottage, the cottage where
Annushka was born and her nieces still lived. The big pond
was frozen, two people were skating, others cautiously and
triumphantly walking on the ice, together with puzzled ducks
and geese. A few flakes of snow now wavered in the air,
scarcely resolved to fall. At last the Pike, the sign of the savage
toothy fish, picturesquely rising among bulrushes, hanging

247

immobile in the cold quiet air. *Real Ale.* Unbuttoning their coats and removing their gloves, they went into the hot crowded bar.

The room, dark after the dazzling white scene outside, smelt of warm wet wool, wet clothes, wet carpet. Yes, thought Gerard, amid the deafening chatter, as he looked around in vain for somewhere to sit while Jenkin was exchanging pleasantries at the counter, this is what *he* likes and *I* don't! How long do we have to stay here? He's ordering pints. We shall be late for lunch.

Suddenly feeling tired he pulled off his overcoat and rubbed the frost off his eyelashes and shook the snowflakes out of his curly hair. He rubbed his cold nose, thawed by the heat into a dripping wetness. He pulled down his smooth jersey and adjusted his just-visible collar and tie.

He doesn't have to worry about virtue, thought Gerard, he lives a simple life devoid of temptation and remorse, he lives in decent simplifications, all he sees is a mass of particular sufferers – and of course he's right about the mountain and how one cheats by a leap into the ideal. We've talked about this before, but it's never had such a deep cutting edge, it goes right down to the bone. Thank God he's stopped asking me what I'm going to write. Perhaps I'll write about Plotinus, he thought, a quiet rambling book about Augustine and Plotinus with some observations about today, their time was just like ours really. How sublime it all seems when one looks back, that moment when Plato's Good was married to the God of the psalms. But what an awful perilous mess it was too, philosophy versus magic, just like now. Only we haven't got a genius to teach us a new way to think about goodness and the soul.

Jenkin turned and looked at Gerard and smiled. Then he pointed upward. Gerard looked up. The Christmas decorations were in place, the glittering red and silver chains crisscrossing the ceiling, the sparkling tinsel stars, the little pendant figures of angels. He looked again at Jenkin and his pointing finger. Perhaps I'll write that book, thought Gerard; but first of all there's something about Jenkin Riderhood which has got to be decided, it's got to be found out and sorted out and done something about. Oh God, it's such a terrible risk – it's as if his life were at stake, or mine.

The flooded water-meadow, a huge space adjoining the river, was superbly frozen. The land, which belonged to Rose and was let to an amiable farmer, had once been common land and was still discreetly so regarded by the village. Rose ignored her fishing rights, to the disgust of Reeve and Neville. The wilful English winters did not often produce reliable enduring expanses of ice, and so the Foxpathers were not much given to skating and on the whole preferred to show off on the village pond. A few however were dotted here and there on the flat snow-covered ice-sea of the meadow as Rose and her party approached.

It was after lunch. Lunch, though announced as 'light and simple', had been fairly substantial, consisting of cold meats, hot potatoes, salads, then tipsy cake, then cheese, and accompanied by claret, which everyone said they must 'go easy' on, but mostly did not. It had been generally agreed that skating, if it was to take place, must do so at once, otherwise everyone would retire and fall asleep, and anyway it would be dark by four thirty. Duncan, who had drunk most claret, had announced his intention of sleeping it off forthwith, so the little group consisted of Rose, Gerard, Jenkin, Tamar, Gulliver and Lily. Tamar and Jenkin, non-skaters, had come for the show. Rose was glad that Tamar, who had refused even to try on the proffered boots, had come along. She was afraid that the child, who had eaten very little at lunch, would elect to spend the afternoon alone. She had already 'taken possession' of the library where the others tended to leave her in peace, and had been seen reading or (it was Rose's impression) affecting to read *The Tale of Genji*, which Rose had recommended to her some time ago. Rose had intended to have, but had not yet had, a 'good talk' with Tamar who looked more than usually reserved and wan.

A little more snow had fallen, covering the earlier tracks of man and beast, and had now ceased. The air remained windless and breathlessly quiet, suspended in a kind of magical pause which made people lower their voices. The afternoon light was already changing, the white sky darkening into a reddish glow. The expanse of meadow showed mainly white, but, seen close to, where skaters' curving tracks had passed, the gleaming ice beneath the snow was iron-grey. The Boyars party made quite a colourful set. Rose and Lily had taken some trouble with their appearance. They were both wearing fur hats, Rose's brown, Lily's black. Rose wore a long dark green jacket of heavy tweed, a thick high-necked brown jersey with a green silk scarf at the neck, knee-breeches and thick socks. Lily wore a white polo-necked skin-tight jersey, with a V-necked red jersey over it, a loose fluffy belted black cardigan of angora wool, and black woollen trousers tucked into red socks. Noting Rose's well-worn knee-breeches, she had remarked that tucking one's trousers into one's socks looked just as good and was easier. (She at once regretted this observation.) Both women, as they announced, had on their thickest woollen vests, Rose two, Lily only one. Lily felt cold. She had paid too much attention to Rose's prediction that they would get quite hot skating. Gerard, who, thinking it wrong to be obsessed with clothes, dressed with a casual discernment, was wearing a dark green high-necked cashmere sweater over a white shirt, a dark blue scarf of very light wool, a long navy jacket of hand-woven tweed and blue-black corduroy trousers. Jenkin wore his usual winter suit with a thick jersey, a heavy overcoat and his stripy woollen cap. Tamar also wore a substantial overcoat above her jumper, and legwarmers over her trousers and had covered her head and most of her face with a beige-coloured scarf. Gulliver had, after much thought and indecision, put on pale brown corduroy trousers, his best and longest jersey, blue with the strawberry design, and his short green Loden coat. He already felt both bulky and cold. He and Gerard were bare-headed. Gulliver, who had felt it *infra dig* to wear headgear, now intensely envied Jenkin his silly woolly cap. Gerard and Rose and Lily wore smart high leather boots. Tamar and Jenkin wore heavy walking shoes. Gulliver wore trim wellingtons.

Gull was in a state of intense anxiety. He had bitten his tongue badly at lunchtime and it was still hurting. He had, to begin with, and quite erroneously as it happened, imagined that he was being invited to Boyars as part of some sort of test. He was being looked over with a view to something or other. He was to be 'shown off' to somebody or other, introduced to some grand personage, a theatre director or impresario or minister of the arts, whom he was intended to impress and who would then offer him a job. Or perhaps Rose's cousins would be there, the titled ones, and he would get on famously with and eventually marry Rose's niece Gillian whom he had heard Rose describe as a handsome clever girl. He felt all ready to meet some entirely new person, male or female, either would do, who would entirely change his life. Or perhaps, this was another kind of thought, Gerard had some grave personal problem, some dreadful secret even, divulged to no one else, and had decided that Gull was the only person in whom he really wanted to confide; and he imagined how, late at night, Gerard would come wild-eyed to his room, tell all, and implore Gulliver to set out on some dangerous and essential mission. 'I shall leave tonight!' Gulliver would instantly say in this scenario. When he discovered that Lily had been invited too he had a sense of disappointment, as if her inclusion must somehow devalue the whole affair. When, later still, he found that no strangers were to be present at all, only the usual little coterie, he felt even more let down, though consoled by reflecting that it was a compliment to be thus treated as 'one of the family'. Lily's presence too, after the first mean pang of resentment, was a relief and a pleasure, as they immediately paired off, supporting each other, comparing notes, and giggling in corners. '*We* are the children here,' said Lily, 'and *they* are the grown-ups! I think it's rather fun!'

Gulliver was no stranger to country house weekends, in his successful theatre days he had been invited here and there and counted himself a sophisticated young fellow who did not in general suffer from social shyness. He was, after having got over old expectations and old resentments and recent fantasies, hoping at least to come closer to Gerard, to be established as a genuine permanent friend. He wanted to please Gerard and not to make a fool of himself. The possibility here of not coming up to scratch worried him seriously. He was still a bit afraid of Rose but revered her and found her attractive, and was glad that she seemed to like him. He remembered the evening of the dance when he had so much wanted to dance with her but had not had the courage to ask. Duncan he regarded with awe, with a fear of Duncan's animal persona, his bull-like bear-like presence, his totemistic strength, his ability to kill with one blow of the paw. He would have liked to be friends with this minotaur, but Duncan though polite was remote, and Gulliver found a spiteful compensation in reflecting that after all poor old Duncan was a cuckold who had been pushed into the Cherwell by David Crimond. He made nothing of Jenkin, conscious of being a little jealous in that quarter. Jenkin was very kind to him, but it was like being obliged by an elf. He felt sorry for Tamar, whose troubles he had heard discussed, but she was cold to him and he did not try to approach her.

And now, with this accursed skating party, he had placed himself in a perfectly disastrous position. Why on earth had he said that he could skate, when in truth he could only skate badly? Why had he purchased those hideously expensive skates and skating boots (when he could have bought some proper boots like Gerard's for half the sum) which he was awkwardly carrying in a plastic bag which was visibly tearing under their weight, and coming closer and closer to that appalling sheet of slippery ice as to a place of judgment? He need not have admitted to having ever skated in his life, he could have come along without shame as a spectator, as Tamar and Jenkin had done. He had simply not wanted to be left out, he had childishly cried 'me too', he had drunk too much claret and eaten too much tipsy cake, he had not imagined what a poor figure he was bound to cut. Skating is a ruthless sport. One can get away with being a mediocre tennis player or a moderate cricketer, but skating is like ballet, unless one is fairly good one is contemptible. Gerard and Rose were, he guessed, good. Lily it was true said she had done it 'a bit' and 'not for ages', but she did not seem to mind being a novice. The trouble was she had somehow, on the basis of vague things Gulliver had said, come to believe that he was really an adept being modest! She imagined he would support her, help her to get the hang. He faced, in her eyes too, inevitable disgrace. That morning, when his imagination had caught up with his situation, he had contemplated staging a sprained ankle. But he had not the will-power to do it, and now it was too late. The sprained ankle would arrive on the ice!

Rose led the way from the path, where the frozen earth on each side was frilled up into little stiff waves, over crisp frozen grass which appeared beneath their footsteps, round the edge of the 'rink' to where, a little above the level of the ice, a lopped tree trunk, perhaps put there long ago for that purpose, served as a seat. She was carrying, with her skates, a cassette player, in case, as she put it, anyone wanted to dance. (Dance!! thought Gulliver.) The skaters sat down and began to take off their walking footwear and put on their skating boots, while Jenkin and Tamar wandered on, upon the higher ground, in the direction of the river. Gulliver felt, and felt that they all felt, a kind of trembling excitement, a shudder of anticipation almost like sexual desire, as they thus transformed themselves, as in some physical change of being, from slow walking animals into fast sliding ones. It was three o'clock, the sun would set soon after four, and the sky, its dome contracting, was becoming red and glowing darkly. The snow was pink, the figures of the few skaters upon the ice, black. Voices sounded oddly, subdued, ringing yet enclosed.

'Who's the old lady in black skating over there?' asked Lily, who seemed in no hurry for the metamorphosis. 'She must be crazy to skate in that long skirt.'

'That's no lady, that's the parson!' said Gerard, in whom the cold and the light and the prospect of speed had inspired an unusual jollity.

'That's our local vicar,' said Rose, 'Angus McAlister, or Father McAlister as he likes to be called. He's fairly new here. He always wears his cassock! Remember last year, Gerard?'

'He's showing off!' said Gerard. 'Look how gracefully he controls his skirt! And now he's put his hands behind his back like in that picture by Raeburn!'

'He's a bit dotty,' said Rose. 'He uses the old prayer book and wants to be "Father", he even hears confessions! – but he's very evangelical too. If you come to church tomorrow you'll hear him preach.'

'That'll be nice,' said Lily dubiously, struggling at her laces with clumsy cold gloved hands.

Rose was first upon the ice. She skipped down the little slope and sped off gracefully and very fast, tracing swift arcs in the snowy surface, circled for a bit, then came back calling to Gerard and holding out her hand. Gerard, more awkwardly, descended the slope, then leapt onto the ice and raced towards her. They held hands for a moment, whirling each other round, then shot apart in different directions, Gerard flying off toward the far end of the meadow, Rose to talk to the skirted priest who, increasing his pace, skated easily beside her.

It's just as I feared, thought Gulliver, they're blooming experts! If I can stay upright I'll be lucky. The best plan is for Lily and me to mess about at this end for a short time, just for appearances, while they're flashing around in the distance, and then quickly get this gear off and go and look for Jenkin and Tamar at the river. I can save my face if I can be just *seen* to be *skating*! They're so pleased with themselves actually they won't bother to watch my performance. Or will they? When it gets darker I'll be invisible anyway. If only dear old Lily doesn't pull me over!

The afternoon was darkening but the reddish light was more intense, making the scene for the moment more vivid. The dark figures of the skaters were *working*, it seemed, upon the hidden ice, making it, by their quick weavings, more visible, instinctively cutting the still unmarked snow with their sharp feet. Most of the villagers, who had a longer walk home, had gone now, the whizzing priest had disappeared. Gull was trying to get his cramped foot into one of his skating boots. His foot, immobilised with cold and locked into an impossible position, dabbed miserably at the space, which was blocked now by the tongue of the boot. He had taken off his gloves and his hands were frozen.

'Gerard and I walked to the village this morning,' said Jenkin to Tamar, 'and the village pond was frozen – well, of course it was frozen – and the ducks and geese were walking about on the ice. They looked so touching, so awkward and puzzled and indignant! You could see how heavy those geese were, planting their feet so carefully, they were quite aggressive too, they wouldn't get out of the way, the skaters had to avoid them. They must have felt it was the last straw, their pond gone solid and humans rushing about! We went to the Pike. They've got the Christmas decorations up. I always love this time before Christmas, don't you, when people start setting up Christmas trees and hanging holly wreaths on their doors. When do you put up your decorations?'

'We don't put up decorations.'

'Well, neither do I much – just a few old baubles. The Pike is nice and friendly, don't you think?'

'I don't like pubs.'

'You should give them a try. You needn't be nervous.'

'I'm not nervous.'

'See how red the sky has become, and everything's so motionless and so quiet, like an enchantment. Now we've left the others we might be in Siberia! Do you know, we haven't seen a single bird since we left the house? I suppose they're all hiding in the thickest bushes with their feathers fluffed up. I can't think how they survive in this weather.'

'They don't, lots of them die.'

They had been tramping across the grass whose longer blades appeared here and there above the snow, outstretched like little green ribbons hatched over with crosses made by the frost.

Jenkin had been busily making conversation, trying to stir Tamar's attention, pointing things out to her, the tracks of animals, the perfect shape of a leafless oak, a small holly bush covered with red berries in the hedge that bordered the meadow. Now they had reached the river and looked down in silence at the stiff frozen shapes of broken water plants which rose out of the quite thick fringe of ice which bordered either bank. In the centre the river rushed, fierce, silent, fast, fed by other snows, and black, black in between its edges of ice and snow.

Tamar looked down, lowering her head and fumbling at the knot of her scarf, then pulling the scarf more closely forward over her brow.

Jenkin had been watching Tamar since their arrival at Boyars. He shared the common knowledge of her troubles, he so acutely felt, now, her sadness, her unapproachable remoteness, he wished he could 'do something' for her. He had known her all her life, but never well, had never figured as 'jolly uncle Jenkin', or as someone in whom she might confide or trust. Jenkin, for all his schoolmasterly talents, had never achieved with Tamar, as child or adult, the easy and authoritative relationship which Gerard enjoyed with her.

While Jenkin was wondering what topic of conversation to try next, Tamar suddenly said, 'Do you think Jean will come back to Duncan?'

He said at once, 'Yes, of course. Don't let *that* make you sad!'

'Has he heard from her just lately?'

'Well – he had a solicitor's letter, but he wrote saying he loved her and expected her back, and there's been nothing since, which must be a good sign. That other thing *can't* last – it didn't before and it won't now. She'll be back!' Jenkin was not sure whether he really felt this confidence, but he wanted to reassure Tamar.

'It's such a pity they never had children,' she said, still looking down at the river, 'but perhaps they never wanted any, not everyone does.'

'Duncan certainly did, he was longing for a child. I'm not sure about Jean.'

'Oh look – isn't that a dead cat?'

Something humpy and streaky and dark was tumbled by in the fierce rush of the river. It was a dead cat. 'No, no,' said Jenkin, 'it's a bundle of reeds. Come on, let's go back. Why, I think it's starting to snow again.'

Lily had finished lacing her boots, but was sitting paralysed, watching the distant gyrations of Rose and Gerard. 'Come on,' said Gulliver, 'or are you funking it? Never mind, I'll have a try. Pray for me.'

He rose to his feet, balanced upon the ridiculously thin edges of the skates, which at once sunk into the snowy grass. Stretching both arms out to balance himself and lifting up each foot carefully he made his way down the slope. Unfortunately there was nothing to hold onto, no friendly tree extending a sturdy branch. Near to the brink, he thrust one foot forward onto the ice. The foot rejected the hard slippery alien surface, declining to plant itself firmly as a foot ought to, but moving uneasily, slipping away, turning feebly over on its side. Gulliver withdrew the foot. If only he could *stand* on the ice for a moment or two he might manage to move cautiously forward in some reasonably skaterly manner. After all, he *could* skate, that is he had proceeded on skates in an upright position for short distances on ice rinks of his youth. He edged carefully forward a little so that both his skates were embedded at the verge of the ice, which was not at all clean-cut, but a messy area where humpy earth and grass were covered with a brittle mix of ice and snow. Here he again got one foot forward onto the smoother ice. But the other foot, taking his weight for a moment, had sunk a centimetre or two deeper into the earthy perimeter. The problem of removing it while balancing on the forward foot seemed insoluble. In calm despair, with arms outstretched, Gulliver gazed ahead of him into the red dusk. He thought, I can't go forward, I can't get back, I shall have to sit down. Thank God Rose and Gerard are somewhere else, I can't even see them. At that moment a hand appeared and took hold of his outstretched hand. Lily had evidently ventured down to the edge behind him.

257

Gulliver gripped the supportive hand and by some miraculous manoeuvre managed to get his other foot onto the ice, while resting quite a lot of weight upon Lily's hand, and now upon her arm which had also appeared beside him. He was standing! He let go of Lily and began to walk upon the ice, not sliding but walking, balancing as on stilts. Now, how did one get going? His legs resisted the desire of his ankles to turn quietly over, his expensive boots bore him stiffly up, his stomach, his diaphragm, his shoulders, his pendant arms, sought intently for a certain rhythmical movement, a leaning and a swaying, a distribution of the weight, so that the feet, used after all to taking turns on *terra firma*, could in this weird and artificial predicament, proceed to a harmonious cooperation. Gulliver inclined himself forward, advancing one skate, then as it slid a little and took his weight, with an instinctively remembered motion bringing on its fellow. He was still upright! He could do it! He was skating!

At that moment somebody appeared beside him and said, 'Well done!' It was Lily. She moved past him. She was skating too. What was more, and Gulliver somehow took this in instantly, not only could she skate, but she could skate *very well indeed*. Lily was now in front of him, moving backwards. He saw in the crimson twilight her face under her black fur hat, with reddened cheeks and nose, bright with triumphant joy. She made a little circle, then a larger one, then with a wave set off across the ice at an astonishing speed. Gulliver sat down abruptly.

Rose and Gerard, who had been skating together holding hands at the farther end of the meadow where a few villagers, mainly young boys, still lingered, were returning toward the centre when they met Lily. They heard her before they saw her, since Lily as she was released into an element which suited her perfectly, uttered, as her speed increased, a loud cry, like a savage bird's cry, or the aggressive scream uttered by Japanese masters of the martial arts. Lily, with a group from her school, had learnt to skate as a child at the rink at

Queensway. The others gave up, she stayed, she had, a teacher told her, a natural talent, she learnt to dance, she learnt to leap, she won a competition. For a short time skating seemed a means of dominating the world; but somehow she never really believed in it, the glamorous enclosure of the ice rink was a dream palace which she always left with a sense of doom, a secret artificial place which made the squalor of her real place more awful by contrast. It brought her no social life, and she lacked the will and confidence to take up the challenge of becoming even better. So the pursuit lost its charm amid the miseries and muddles of her student life, and when the money came and she had so many gratifications and so little sense of the value of anything it did not occur to her to return to what now seemed like a phase of her girlhood. Her paralysis in the scene at the water meadow arose from a sudden painful memory, as her hands touched the laces of the boots, of her younger unspoilt self; also, like Gull, she was not at all sure she would be able to do it. Of course she would still be able to skate, but would she still be able to skate *very well*? The wild scream expressed her instant discovery that her talent had not abandoned her.

Just before Lily appeared, swift as an arrow or an announcing angel in the middle of the ice, Rose had suggested to Gerard that they might now, since almost everyone had gone, put on some waltz music on their side of the meadow and dance, as they always did, had done for years and years in winters when the ice was hard. The both danced well, but were tactfully anxious not to impose their display upon other enjoyers of the ice. Now when they had the meadow almost to themselves they might evoke the sudden magic of the music in the winter picture. Gerard and Rose had also, with tact, kept well away from Gull and Lily so as not to risk being witnesses of their perhaps more modest performance. Now, suddenly, here was Lily Boyne, flashing past them, returning from a distance at express speed, waving one leg while spinning on one foot, leaping high into the air and landing on the tips of her skates, seeming to move not on the surface of the ice but above it. Gerard cried out, 'Lily, Lily, you're a *star!*'

Rose watched the acrobatics, then decided quickly. She said to Gerard, 'You dance with Lily.' Then she sped away at her own fastest pace in the direction of the base camp. A few moments later the music of Strauss transformed the scene.

Gulliver had not arisen after his sudden descent, he had no wish now to explore his recovered ability any further. Shameless and unwitnessed he crawled on the ice back to his starting point, crawled up the slope and hoisted himself onto the log. With relief he undid his boots and released his crushed feet and his aching ankles. His front was covered with mud and snow, and his pale brown corduroy trousers stained and soaking wet. He found he had lost one of his gloves. It had probably come off when Lily grabbed his hand. He thought he could see it lying a little distance away on the ice. He sat watching Lily's distant gyrations. Then Rose suddenly materialised, sprang up the bank on her skates like a goat, and turned on the cassette. At that same moment Jenkin and Tamar appeared out of the dusk.

Gerard and Lily, nearer now, who had been circling round each other and talking, their voices coming as thin but clear indecipherable sounds through the increasingly cold air, as the music started came magnetically together. An irresistible impulse of joy joined them, Gerard's arm was round Lily's waist, her hand gripped his shoulder with an unexpected strength. Lily was a better dancer than Gerard, but as when a mediocre tennis player can suddenly improve when matched with a good player, Gerard inspired, and with subtle pressures of her hands and body *led*, by Lily, danced better than he had ever danced before.

The four upon the bank, Gull sitting, the others standing, watched the dancing in intent silence. Tamar's scarf had fallen back onto her shoulders and Jenkin, observing her out of the corner of his eye without moving his head, saw, after a moment or two, a tear moving down her cheek. Gulliver, dazed by what was so rapidly happening, watched the astonishing performance as it approached nearer and nearer to them. He became conscious of a strange feeling in his midriff, an electrical disturbance, a pain, a sense of mingled elation and anguish. The gracious powerful bitter-sweet music collected together the darkening sky, the fading glow of the twilight, the intense cold, the pallor of the snow, and the great quiet empty countryside all around, so soon to be entirely dark.

The dance did not last long. Amid plaudits and laughter Gerard and Lily ascended the bank. Lily tossed Gull his glove which she had gracefully retrieved as she glided in. Rose distributed electric torches to everybody, and chattering away they all set out along the footpath back to the house. It had begun to snow again, the white wandering flakes visible in the light of the torches.

'You put poor old Rose's nose out of joint all right,' said Gulliver to Lily.

'You're *coarse*,' said Lily, 'that's your trouble, *coarseness*.'

It was after dinner. The skating party had descended upon the house tired, cold and excited, to find that it was tea-time in front of the blazing drawing room fire, sandwiches and scones, plum cake and home-made jam and clotted cream, and two big teapots and milk and sugar all standing ready, as Annushka had seen the light of the returning torches from afar. They had been away longer than expected, and not everyone felt like tea. Some were for hot baths, some for drinks. Out of politeness to Annushka everyone drank tea and, when confronted with the goodies, and amid advice about not spoiling one's appetite for dinner, most of the skaters fumbled with the scones which with blackcurrant jam and cream were delicious. Duncan appeared, looking sleepy and hot, enquired after their adventures, and ate most of the sandwiches. Gerard and Jenkin lingered a while over the scones. Gulliver took a piece of the plum cake away to eat later. After baths and rest and drinks, dinner, served late, was no anti-climax, consisting of lentil soup, roast beef and Yorkshire pudding, and gooseberry tart and cream. Everyone, except Tamar, ate hugely. After that they all, except Tamar, who said she was tired, sat in the drawing room drinking coffee and cherry brandy and eating some of the heavenly fudge (agreed to be remarkable) which Annushka had made for Jenkin. Rose retired soon, first to visit Tamar, then to her own room. Gull and Lily, yawning hugely, declared themselves for bed and foregathered *chez* Lily. Duncan and Jenkin and Gerard stayed on in the drawing room with the whisky bottle.

Gulliver regretted his remark, indeed was amazed at it. He was drunk, that was the trouble. The coldness, the exertion, the experiences, the emotions, the hot bath, all that food, all that drink, had produced a condition of unstable excitement which made continued drinking absolutely essential. It turned out that both he and Lily had brought a flask of whisky along 'just in case' so there was nothing to stop both of them continuing to indulge, and Lily was rather drunk too. The horrid remark, rightly criticised by Lily, had been, somehow, the outcome of Gulliver's attempt to make sense of his mixed up state of mind, produced by Lily's exploits, what might be described as Lily's triumph. He had not at all minded the first bit when he was so hopeless and she was so brilliant, he had felt no resentment at her flying about like a winged goddess while he was crawling up the bank ruining his trousers. He had easily identified with her glory in a manner expressed by: one up for our side! The dancing was another matter. The pang which it occasioned was easily identified as jealousy, the self-same pain which he had felt on Guy Fawkes night when he had opened the dining room door. But now, as then, he wondered, *which* am I feeling so possessive about? Or was it just a general sense of being excluded, obliterated, dropped, forgotten and made of no account? His remark about Rose had leapt out as an attempt, he now saw, to lessen his own discomfort by attributing it to someone else.

'Yes,' said Gulliver humbly, helping himself to another glass of Lily's whisky.

They were sitting, in Lily's bedroom, in armchairs which they had drawn up in front of the blazing fire, onto which Gulliver had just tossed some extra bits of wood from the basket at the side. Sparks which leapt out onto the rug had been hastily stamped upon. Several lamps were lit in the room which was dominated by the huge double bed with its old carved dark oak headboard. The wallpaper, blue with a lattice design, had faded into powdery obscurity, and the furniture, over-awed by the bed, was diffident and shabby. An oak chest under a hanging mirror served as a dressing table, a sideboard without its doors made a bookcase, a small octagonal table near the window supported more books, novels by Lawrence and Virginia Woolf chosen by Rose for Lily, and Lily's book on Thailand not yet opened. A little green sofa upholstered in much worn green velvet in flower and leaf patterns occupied the space between the windows. There were several water-colours representing the Yorkshire property and the 'old big house' which had been sold by Rose's great-great-grandfather. Over the fireplace there was a large modern red and orange and black abstract painting, which Gerard had bought from Gideon for Rose when Rose, prompted by Jean, had admired it at an exhibition. It later became a favourite of Jean and Duncan and was hung in their room and called 'their' painting.

'Are you going to church tomorrow?' said Lily. 'Do we have to?'

'I'm not sure,' said Gulliver, 'I hope not.'

'You've been here before, haven't you?'

'No.'

'I got the impression you had been. You were telling me all about it.'

'I was putting on an act. I'm not only coarse, I'm disingenuous.'

'Let's not go to church. We could go to the pub. There's one in the village, Jenkin said.'

'It won't be open till twelve.'

'Oh. Sunday.'

'I suppose we could go for a walk.'

'If we aren't snowed in. Wouldn't it be fun to be marooned here like people in a detective story!'

'I don't think so.'

'I wonder if it's still snowing, let's look.'

They went to one of the windows and dragged back the heavy velvet curtains and thrust up the sash. No diamond-paned Gothic on this façade. A wall of icy air advanced into the room. 'Turn out the lights,' said Lily.

They stood in the darkness leaning out of the window. The snow had ceased. A single distant light, a faint yellow spot, showed the outskirts of the village. The white landscape was invisible. But up above, the curtain of cloud had, over a part of the heavens, been rolled back and they could actually see stars, one star in particular very bright, and round about and beyond a hazy mass of other stars, a thick golden fuzz of superimposed stars, almost, at the zenith, completely covering the black dome of the sky; and as they looked in the midst of the gold dust, a star fell quickly and vanished, then another star fell. 'Good Lord,' said Lily, in a low voice. 'I've never seen a falling star before, and now I've seen two.'

After a few moments they stepped back, closed the window and drew the curtain. Gull put the lights on again and they looked at each other.

Gulliver, fortunately informed beforehand by Gerard that he need not bring evening dress, was wearing his best dark suit, white shirt, and soberly spotted bow tie. He had not been too drunk to comb down his sleek oily dark hair surreptitiously as he came up the stairs. This sleekness gave him a slightly sinister look (which pleased him) but also (he did not realise) made him look older. He looked thin, thin-faced, sallow, hungry and tired, like a minor character playing an unsuccessful lawyer or ill-intentioned priest. Only his pure brown eyes (like a pond of obscure but fragrant water, someone in a gay bar once told him) retained a childish boyish expression of uncertainty and fear. Lily, who had been wearing at dinner a long close-fitting dress covered with green sequins, which everyone politely said made her look like a mermaid, had now changed (not caring that Gull saw her momentarily in her petticoat) into a magnificent dark blue and white dressing gown. Lily looked tired too and a little petulant. A fold of stained lizardish skin descended over one of her pale brown dark-rimmed eyes. She moistened her thin silver lips and fluffed up her scanty pale dry hair. (Gull's hair would have looked better if he had fluffed it up occasionally instead of combing it down.) They returned to their chairs by the fire.

'Do you believe in flying saucers,' said Lily, 'do you think people from other galaxies are coming here to observe us?'

'No.'

'I do. It's immensely probable. There are millions of planets like ours. Of course they don't want us to see them. They're writing books about us.'

'All right, maybe they're here and we can't see them, maybe they're in this room. The point is they make no difference.'

'How do you know? How do you know how different things would be if they weren't there?'

'They might be better. They couldn't be worse. So they can't care much. When they've finished their books they'll wipe us out, and a good thing too.'

'Of course the whole universe will end one day. So what's the point, if it's all ending, what's the use of anything? I wonder if this house is haunted, I must ask Rose. It's near to a ley line.'

'What makes you think so?'

'I feel it. Roman roads run along ley lines. What do you think about ley lines?'

'I think they're things that don't make any difference, like saucers.'

'They're physical, you know, you can find them by dowsing, where two underground streams meet. And they're concentrations of thought-energy too, where human beings have been, all those legions marching along, all those emotions!'

'If the legions made the energy no wonder the ley line runs along the road.'

'Oh, but it's cosmic energy too, like in stone circles. A ley line runs through Stonehenge. Are there any Stones about here? They all connect, you see.'

'I believe there's a stone of some sort in the wood.'

'I'll go and look at it, if it's charged with energy I'll know. My grandmother used to say –'

'Lily, this is all nonsense, it's irrational!'

'*You're* irrational, you won't look at evidence, you just know! I say, do you think I ought to go and see Tamar? She's eating practically nothing and she's as pale as a fish.'

'She's always pale and eats nothing, and she'll be asleep now. Let's have some more whisky.'

'Poor Tamar, oh poor poor little Tamar –'

'Lily –'

'Rose has such a calm smooth face, and she's so much older than me. My face looks bombed. You know, they've got it in for Crimond, they're going to smash him.'

'Who are?'

'They, the little earthly gods, the smarties, the know-alls. I heard them talking after dinner. God, I think I'm drunk, I'm seeing double or perhaps it's Saucer people.'

'Lily, dear, stop raving will you?'

'I'm on Crimond's side, I know you hate him, but I don't –'

'Lily, just stand up for a moment, please.'

They stood together before the fire and Gulliver put his arms round her waist, drawing her up against him. He felt her thin hard fragile brittle body against his, then suddenly her heartbeat.

'Now let's sit down, over here.'

They moved to the little green sofa and Lily sat on Gulliver's knee and buried her face in the shoulder of his best suit covering it with make-up.

'You know, I'd better tell you, I'm running out of money, the accountant told me, God knows where it's all gone to, people only care about my money, I'm nothing, I'm just a shell, I'm like a squashed snail –'

'Lily, stop it! Look, can I stay here tonight?'

'You don't know how awful it is to be me –'

'Can I stay –?'

'Oh if you want to, there's plenty of room, I don't care, but it won't be any good.' She started to cry.

Tamar was being closely observed now by Rose who was sitting on her bed. Rose had brought Tamar up a chocolate drink, specially made by Annushka, which Rose knew that Tamar liked, and Tamar had drunk a little of it. Rose had also brought aspirins and sleeping pills which had been refused. Tamar had politely insisted that she was quite well, nothing was the matter, she had eaten quite a lot really, she never had much appetite, she had slept perfectly well last night and would sleep perfectly well tonight. She was enjoying the *Tale of Genji*, there it was on her bedside table, and she was looking forward to reading a little before she went to sleep. Then she had suddenly started to cry. The tears were brief, like the automatic opening and closing of a sluice gate, large tears, they rolled down copiously for half a minute, then ceased. Rose tried to hold her hand, the hand with which she had been wiping away the tears, but she hid it in the bedclothes. Sitting up in bed in the little round room, with her striped pyjamas and thin tear-stained face, she looked like a small boy. Rose thought, she's ill, she may be in for a depression, I must speak to Violet, but what's the use of speaking to Violet, oh God, if I could only *get hold* of this child, kidnap her, take her away, and *keep her*! Perhaps I should have done just that years ago. But Violet is such a savage creature, she has so much will.

'Tamar, you're ill. I want you to see Doctor Tallcott, the doctor here in the village.'

'Doctor – no!' Tamar looked quite alarmed.

'Your mother needn't know – Well, see your own doctor then. Of course Violet says he's no good –'

'I'm *not* ill, I'm perfectly all right, I just want to be left alone, please, Rose dear, don't be cross with me –'

'Darling, I'm not!' Rose knelt down beside Tamar's bed

and captured the little thin hand which had strayed out again, and kissed it. 'Will you really sleep now, can I do anything, bring you anything?'

'No, no, I'm *all right*, I'll sleep now I think, I won't read *Genji*, I feel you've done me good, don't worry about me, it's *nothing*, I promise you, *nothing*.'

Rose had to be content with that. She left the room and stood for a moment outside. Tamar's light went out.

Rose went downstairs to her own bedroom. This room always reminded her of her mother who had been so pretty, so anxious to please everyone, so lost after her son and her husband had both so quickly, so incredibly, so suddenly, disappeared; so much under her husband's thumb, under Sinclair's, later under Rose's, even Reeve's. Rose still missed her mother, and looked about for her. She remembered being outraged when someone, a friend of Reeve's, had called her 'idle'. Her mother was not idle, she was always busy, though not always with tasks which people would think had much point. The flowers were so beautifully done in her day. Rose and Annushka lacked that talent. The room, not intentionally altered by Rose, had gradually disintegrated and faded while remaining generally the same: the old-fashioned dressing table with the glass top, which used to be dusted over with her mother's face powder, the big 'gentlemen's wardrobe', dating from the days when she and Rose's father had occupied the double bed – how far away that seemed now, as if in another century – the shabby armchairs not suitable for guest rooms, the Axminster carpet covered with shadowy flowers, the pink and white striped wallpaper, the pink nearly invisible, the paper peeling, the ghostly rectangles of vanished pictures. The tapestry renderings of Biblical scenes had belonged to her mother's mother, herself an expert embroiderer.

Rose sat in one of the chairs and thought a bit about Tamar. Then she thought about Jean. All these thoughts were painful, fearful, remorseful. She considered going downstairs again and joining the others, but Gerard and Jenkin and Duncan would probably be locked in some theoretical argument, and she did not feel like entertaining Lily and Gull who had been in the process of going to bed anyway. She had better go to bed and seek the silent innocence of sleep and the silly anxiety of dreams. Dear sleep, like death. She noticed *Daniel Deronda* lying on the bedside table under the pink-fringed shade of the lamp. She couldn't read it. She thought, perhaps I have come to the end of reading. *J'ai lu tous les livres*. She knew all her favourites by heart. No novel pleased her now with that glad feeling of escape and refuge. She did not want to read biographies, or the well-informed political books which Gerard sometimes recommended. No one reads books of imagination now, one of Reeve's friends had told her (Tony Reckitt, a farmer, the man who had called her mother 'idle'), they want facts. Rose could not do with facts, but the other things had gone too. Was she becoming, like the century, illiterate?

Outside in the snowy darkness a fox barked. For a moment Rose took the sound to be a dog's bark before she recognised the crazy sound of the fox. In any case, no village dog would be so near, unless it was lost. A barking dog in the country always made her remember Sinclair's dog, Regent. He had disappeared soon after Sinclair died. For a long time Rose had expected him to return, scratching at the door, down at Boyars, or in London. Even now she expected him, a ghost dog, coming back to look for his master. Listening to the fox bark again, wildly, crazily, sadly, desperately, she shuddered. Then she actually began to feel afraid.

She thought, am I growing old at last? I must take a grip upon myself, upon my life. It's all about Gerard, this pointless feeling, this fear. Rose had suffered anguish, *terror*, as she watched Gerard and Lily dancing upon the ice. That utterly unexpected intrusion, that *theft*, had made her want to weep and scream. She would never forget those moments and the entirely new and special and intense feelings of jealousy, even of rage, even of hatred, with which she had witnessed Lily Boyne's triumph. She had congratulated Lily afterwards, put her arm round her shoulder, laughed and smiled with Gerard as he exclaimed joyfully. It had been a terrible portent, a warning arrow. Yet what was she afraid of, did she think

Gerard would fall in love with Lily? It's the same old trouble, she thought, it's the same old endless illness. There were dear good men that I might have married, that I loved, but I wasn't in love, my heart was a captive with a life sentence. I am a fool, it's *wicked* to be so stupid.

As if to allay the fear, the loneliness which the fox's cry had carried to her out of the dark, she began to feel and welcome the love-pain, the hideous *desire*, the longing for Gerard which came to her sometimes, which she had felt so intensely when she stood at the window of Levquist's room at the dance and saw the tower bathed in light. Sometimes it seemed to her that Gerard had *become* her brother, taking Sinclair's place. Did he feel this, had he uttered that dread word once, and then seeing her wince never repeated it? Perhaps it was a sense of her as a sibling which made him so calmly content with their deep intimate yet somehow passionless, even hygienic, relation. God, how I want to smash it all sometimes, she thought, and rush at him screaming. How displeased he would be by such a 'tantrum', as she could hear him call it, and how kindly he would forgive her! Her position was hopeless, however ingenious she was there was no move she could make. It was too late now to have his children. Rose averted her thoughts from these too conceivable beings. But why was she thinking of that? Marriage with Gerard had never been a possibility, she could not even accuse him of having 'led her on'. That strange episode after Sinclair's death was more like a kind of sacred rite, something with no consequences, to be wrapped in a religious silence. She recalled something she had heard Jenkin say about Gerard. 'The thing to remember about him is that he is basically dotty!' She had been annoyed at the time; later it had even brought her comfort.

But I must do something, thought Rose, who had risen now and was walking up and down, to still the pain. I must see him now, *tonight*, I must *see* him. I'll go down soon, and if he's in his room, even if he's gone to bed, I'll knock on his door, I'll talk to him properly, now I feel so extreme, I'll have the courage. I'll be frank and honest, there's a way of saying it which won't appal him. What it comes to is that there must be a pact between us, I must be *certain* of him. Am I to spend the rest of my life watching Gerard in a state of terrified anxiety? Yet how, really, could she put it? Just be mine only and don't go away. Live with me, live near me, let me see you every day, let me be closest, let me be dearest. Promise never to marry, unless you marry me. Surely these were ludicrous, even immoral, demands. I just want an *assurance* from him, she thought, something to live on, to take away pains like these. I *must* go to him now, when I see him I'll find some words.

Rose went to the dressing table mirror and looked at her calm untroubled face and her wide open eyes which Marcus Field had called her 'fearless eyes'. She scrubbed a little powder onto her nose and combed her hair, her blond hair which was now turning to a pallid, gilded grey. She shook out the skirt of her long dress. Then she left the room and went swiftly and silently down the stairs. Lights were on. She listened in the hall. Silence. She went into the drawing room. All the lamps were on but the room was empty, the furniture all askew, glasses and coffee cups everywhere, the fire burning brilliantly, an empty whisky bottle in the grate. Rose put the guard in front of the fire, put the bottle in a wastepaper basket, left the cups and glasses as they were, turned out the lights in the drawing room and the hall, glided up the stairs again and along the landing. She could see the light under Gerard's door. She paused, she crept and listened. No sound. She tapped on the door and heard Gerard say 'Come in', and she opened the door.

Jenkin and Duncan were sitting on Gerard's bed, while Gerard, on one knee, was rummaging in his suitcase. They all leapt up. 'Rose darling,' cried Gerard, 'an angel to the rescue! I thought I'd brought some whisky but I can't find it! Be a sweet dear and bring us a bottle from somewhere, would you?'

Gulliver's Housman poem about 'the head that I shall dream of, and 'twill not dream of me' would have been suitable that night, for utterance by Rose, since Gerard, now alone, was certainly not thinking about her, he was thinking about Jenkin.

Jenkin and Duncan had gone and Gerard was sitting on his bed. He was feeling rather, unusually, drunk. Duncan had been even drunker, but he was used to it and had been drinking hard all day. He had maintained, during an excited argument, a perfect clarity of speech, but had been unable to walk straight and had departed with one arm round Jenkin's neck. Jenkin, who had apparently drunk at least as much as Gerard, remained agile, fresh, his boyish tints unimpaired by the flush which reddened Duncan's face and to a less extent Gerard's. They had been arguing, not of course about personal matters, but about the reasons for the astonishing success of Christianity in the fourth century AD. I hope we didn't make too much row, Gerard thought, touching his flushed cheek with a little shame.

Last night Gerard had dreamt of his father. His father, seated at a desk before which Gerard was standing, was wearing on his right hand a large black leather glove such as falconers use for the hawk to perch upon. The word 'jesses' came into Gerard's mind and he thought, where are the jesses? Staring portentously at him, his father thrust his hand into the drawer of the desk and brought out something wrapped up in newspaper which he handed to Gerard with the words, 'It's dead.' Gerard, horrified, thought, that means *the bird* is dead. He began to fumble with the newspaper and managed to undo it. Inside was not a dead bird but a small live rabbit. He put the rabbit inside his coat where it nestled, making him warm. When he looked up he saw that his father had extended his gloved hand meaningfully toward him. Gerard drew off the glove – and saw with horror that his father's hand was bleeding copiously, it was in fact a *flayed* hand. At that moment Gerard also realised, I was mistaken about the rabbit, it's not alive, it's dead. He woke up in a state of great distress. He thought about Grey opening his wings and looking at him with his wise gentle witty eyes, and all his childish imaginings of 'where is he now' came back with a timeless ache. He recalled his father shortly before he died with a sad pathetic frightened look which he occasionally wore for a second and then wiped away. His father was afraid of death. Gerard had enacted death when he was eleven years old. Now he felt something like death reaching out and touching him with a dark gloved finger. There were partings, there were endings, there were precious things which went away forever.

He had looked forward to feeling happy at Boyars. This 'looking forward' as to a 'treat' had made him realise how much lately he had *not* been happy. Was he then *accustomed* to being happy, had he taken it for granted as being his usual state, even his *right*? Of course he was still in mourning for his father. There was a direction in which he constantly turned, to be confronted by an absence. He missed something in the world, his father's absolute love. His father was present to him now as blank pain, and he could not help attributing this pain too to the absent one. As Gerard lay in the dark morning (it was nearly seven but still pitch black) he began to think about Crimond as if Crimond too had been part of the dream. He could not remember having dreamt about Crimond and hoped he was not starting to do so now. He was certainly nervous about seeing him. He was afraid, though he did not admit this to the others, that Crimond might somehow 'turn nasty'. The prospect of the meeting made him realise how little, now, he really knew Crimond, it would be meeting a stranger. For years they had simply avoided each other, like the two polar bears. (This was a story of Sinclair's, which had become legendary, about someone in the Arctic who saw two polar bears walking slowly towards each other from either side of some enormous empty plain of ice. As they came near they turned, without haste, one to one side, one to the other, ignoring each other, and padded on their way.) However Gerard did not think there would be anything he could not handle, and he would see to it that the meeting was suitably short and inconclusive.

Sitting now alone upon his bed after the drunken evening, Gerard at first entertained an uncomfortable feeling about Duncan. He had perceived, at Boyars, at close quarters,

Duncan's terrible state of mind, he had smelt the chaos and the grief. But he had not, since the limited and business-like discussion of the divorce letter, initiated or invited an intimate talk. Was Duncan, though showing no sign, waiting for him to do so? Most onlookers, including some of Duncan's colleagues and Gerard's ex-colleagues who knew the interesting story, seemed to expect Jean to return penitent and make Duncan happy again. Gerard, who was not given to gossiping, even with himself, had not indulged in detailed imaginings, either ghoulish or rosy, about the future of his unfortunate friend. He certainly did not take it for granted either that Jean would return or that Duncan would be better off if she did. Had Duncan ever been happy since the Irish business? I can't possibly advise him, thought Gerard, but perhaps it's time to talk again. I must make a point of it. Only now, damn it, he's leaving early tomorrow morning. I'll see him in London. In fact, looking back more soberly upon the evening it occurred to Gerard that perhaps Duncan had resented Jenkin's presence and tried to make it telepathically clear that he wanted to be alone with Gerard, while Jenkin, intercepting this message, had at once declared himself tired and ready to go, but had been prevented by Gerard who wanted Duncan to go so that he could talk to Jenkin.

Gerard's thoughts about Jenkin, tending for some time in a certain direction, were now approaching crisis point. The reasons for this state of feeling were obscure. It might be to do with his father's death, with a sudden shortage of people who loved him *absolutely*, a premonition of loneliness, when there would be no more places where everyone danced with joy when he arrived. A more rational prompting was Gerard's fear that Jenkin was planning to *go away*. At dinner Jenkin had announced with a casualness which Gerard saw to be assumed, that he planned to be out of England at Christmas. Did he not realise that, for the first time for many years, Gerard would be spending Christmas in London? Gerard intuited, had for some time felt, a certain preoccupied restlessness in his friend, as if Jenkin were looking over Gerard's shoulder at something much farther off. Of course Jenkin had said nothing to Gerard about any general departure plans and Gerard, afraid, had not asked. But Gerard had not failed to notice the interest in 'new theology', the stuff about 'the poor', the Portuguese grammar. He thought in flashes things like: Jenkin will leave us, he'll go away, he'll go to South America or Africa, and he'll be *murdered*. Only he *mustn't* go away, thought Gerard, if he goes, I'll go with him. *I can't do without Jenkin*. This was his state. What was such a state called?

What's the matter with me, thought Gerard, I'm hot and cold, I'm shivering, my hands are trembling. I never really *told* my father how much I loved him. If Jenkin were to die I'd wish I'd told *him*. Perhaps it's all very simple. I've known Jenkin well for more than thirty years, why this sudden overflow of feeling now? I love this man, but is there anything special, anything new, which I'm supposed to do about it? I am realising that Jenkin could cause me the most terrible pain, if we quarrelled, if he went right away, if he died. Such is the power he has over me. The idea crossed Gerard's mind, am I actually falling in love with my old friend, do such things happen? Perhaps after a death love runs wild, perhaps it will all pass. But I must *secure* him, I must keep him *safe*, I must keep him *here*, I must not let him go away. How am I to be *sure* he will not go away? I must simply tell him that I *need* him, I must make a *pact* with him, he must be made to promise to stay with me. I must be able to see him more, much more, now that I have this feeling about him, or realise that I've always had it, only now it's urgent. Is this growing old, is it knowing at last that time and death are real? I don't feel old, this strange emotion makes me feel young. Good heavens, thought Gerard, am I really in love?

I must be drunk, he thought, I am drunk. I don't think I'll feel different in the morning, but I'll have a bit more sense. Really, how can I say all this to dear old Jenkin? He'd think I'm daft, he'd be embarrassed, he might be disgusted. If he was he'd keep it to himself but I'd know all the same, I'd see he was upset or annoyed. It might harm our friendship, at least it might cast a shadow, and then I'd imagine he was avoiding me and I'd be in hell. Supposing he were cold to me. The risk is terrible. I've lived alone now for years and years – and he has lived alone, perhaps always. The amazing thing is that I don't really know him all that well, we've never been *that* intimate, I just don't know how he'd react. Perhaps it's better to say nothing.

Everyone was going to church except for Gulliver and Lily and Duncan. Duncan in fact had already departed, he left after breakfasting very early. No one saw him go except Rose. At Sunday breakfast Rose had told her friends, as she always did, that of course there was no need for anyone to go to church. She would go with Annushka, because this was part of her country life, but no one else need come. Gerard and Jenkin said, as they always did, that they would come with her, and Tamar said that she would come. Gull and Lily said they would walk to the wood, and then to the village along the Roman Road to investigate the Pike. It was agreed that they would all meet later at the pub.

Gull and Lily were in rather a giggly mood. The previous night had not at all been what Gull had hoped and expected. No sooner were the two of them in bed, and after the most inconclusive of preliminaries, they had both fallen into a deep drunken slumber, awakening only in time not to be too late for breakfast. Lily had found this extremely funny. Gulliver, after feeling rather disconcerted and discredited, decided to find it funny too. He felt, at least, that he had done something decisive, and, as Lily was so relaxed, even casual, about the whole thing, that gave him time to discover what exactly it was that he had done.

Today the sun was shining, the sky was blue, almost cloudless. The rooms were filled with light. Everyone looked out of the windows and exclaimed with surprise, pointing out to each other the glittering snow crystals and the melting icicles. There was talk of building a snowman. The lawns were criss-crossed now with human tracks and Gulliver and Jenkin had been out just after breakfast to walk round the garden and throw snowballs at each other. Rose had already taken a conducted tour to the kitchen window where a mob of red-wings could be seen, fat round birds bigger than thrushes, with red breasts and striped necks and little demonic faces and sharp probing beaks, frantically devouring the berries of the cotoneaster.

Everyone seemed to be in a vague wandering-about sort of mood. Tamar, wearing a dark brown velveteen dress for Sunday, was sitting on the window seat in the library, holding *Genji* on her knee, contemplating her slender legs in brown stockings, and getting up at intervals to stare at the rows of books. Gerard had wandered off to the billiard room, where the moth-eaten billiard table was hidden by a canvas cover, and had put on Mahler's first symphony on the record player. He liked the melancholy bereaved sound of the second move-ment. This sound, though he turned it down, penetrated faintly to the drawing room where Lily was sitting on the sofa with her shoes off playing patience. Gulliver, who had got his feet wet in the garden, had gone up to his room to change his shoes and socks and look at himself in the mirror. He was wearing his loose cable-stitch dark grey cardigan and grey and dark blue striped shirt with the high collar and a dark mauve tie and grey and black very small-check trousers. The mauve tie was inconspicuously patterned in pink. He decided that, since he was not going to church, it was all right. He sleeked down his hair and put on his saturnine look. Jenkin, dressed for church in his best suit, had gone to sit in the library near Tamar in case she wanted to talk to him, which she did not. He opened his *Oxford Book of Spanish Verse* and read a sonnet addressed '*to Christ Crucified*' which he liked. He watched Tamar who was irritably aware of his gaze. When she closed her book sharply, he made haste to retire. After that he went upstairs and put on his overcoat and boots. He very much wanted to walk in the snow by himself and had decided to slink off. Gerard was now listening to some Haydn. Jenkin told Rose, preoccupied with Annushka in the kitchen making treacle tart, that he was going for a walk and would see them at church. He left by the front door. Gerard emerged and was annoyed to find that Jenkin was gone. Rose told him that they would be leaving for church in three-quarters of an hour. Gull was in the drawing room reminding Lily that she wanted to go to the wood and look for Stones, but she said she had changed her mind and wanted to stay by the fire. Gerard went to look for Tamar, and took her to look at the redwings, which she had missed, but they had eaten all the berries and moved on.

'We praise thee, O God, we acknowledge thee to be the Lord, all the earth doth worship thee, the Father everlasting, to thee all angels cry aloud, the heavens and all the powers therein, to thee Cherubim and Seraphim continually do cry, Holy, Holy, Holy . . .'

Rose and her party, on country Sundays, usually occupied the second pew which was left vacant by the villagers if it was known that Rose 'had company'. Today they were installed in the following order: Gerard, then Rose, then Annushka, then Tamar, then Jenkin, who had arrived first. The church was, for a country church situated outside the village, reasonably attended; that is, there were, including Rose's contingent, some twenty people present. For evensong in the summer, when it made a pleasant walk, there were usually more. A wavery harmonium accompanied the hymns. There was no choir. The church, thirteenth-century, not distinguished for anything in particular, was comparatively unspoilt, except by the removal of the clerestory and of some unspecified 'monuments' some hundred years ago. The big 'decorated' east window, through which the snow-and-sun light was now streaming, had plain glass, the other windows had leaded panes with green and pink glass, the crenellated tower, windowless, containing the six bells, occupied the west end. The interior, without transepts, porches, pillars or side chapels, resembled a big high decrepit untidy whitewashed room. It was also now, although there were three big paraffin heaters, very cold. There were some exceedingly pretty eighteenth-century memorial tablets, a plain sturdy Norman font, and a low-standing stone pulpit, meanly narrowed and crushed against the wall as if some devil had half succeeded in wafting it out of the church altogether. The front pews were seventeenth century, with handsome 'poppy-heads' carved into various kinds of foliage. These pews also possessed, which the Edwardian pews behind, now rarely occupied, lacked, delightful kneelers, embroidered by village ladies of the older generation. Rose wondered why these very nice objects were not stolen, since the church, in accordance with Father McAlister's ideas, were never locked. Perhaps people depraved enough to steal from a church lacked a relevant sense of beauty. Two stone angels appeared from the wall in the chancel, perhaps part of a rescue party sent to prevent the devil from removing the pulpit. These had been, originally, painted, and had been repainted in controversial colours by Father McAlister's predecessor. There had been a wall-painting in the nave, but only the vaguest shadow remained, perhaps a resurrection with people climbing out of tombs. Beside this, more clearly traced though equally ancient, was the message: *Ask, and it shall be given you; seek, and ye shall find; knock and it shall be opened unto you.* Matthew 7.7. This too had been smartened up by the presumptuous paint of the previous parson, to the indignation of the locals including Rose who thought that these things should be allowed to moulder in peace.

Father McAlister had climbed the two steps into the little pulpit, and standing with his back against the wall, had turned toward his small congregation who had politely turned toward him, shuffling their frozen feet and depositing lumps of snow upon the stone floor. Father McAlister was tall, but was now, because of the cold, hunched up inside his robes, his hands invisible, his head descending between his shoulders. It was quite a striking head, large, with wiry grey-brown hair which stood up in a commanding wave from his broad brow, a fiercely curving mouth and dark authoritative eyes which were fixed now upon the group in Rose's pew. Gerard, who had been thinking about Jenkin and not listening, began, as Father McAlister's emphatic tones battered his ears, to pay attention. 'Him that hath a high look and a proud heart will I not suffer! So speaks the Lord our God. And what also does God say? Oh listen. He says that He is nigh unto them that are of broken heart, and saveth such as be of contrite spirit, the sacrifices of God are a broken spirit – a broken and contrite heart, O God, wilt Thou not despise. Blessed are they that mourn for they shall be comforted, blessed are the meek for they shall inherit the earth. The grace of God, O my friends, is poured forth upon the humble ones, upon the afflicted and ashamed, but upon the proud God's curse falls and shall bring them low. God hateth pride and curseth it – the pride of this age of cruel power, the power of machines, the power of material possessions, the power of the oppressors who are everywhere with us – the pride of those who possess riches, the pride of those who think that education and intellect have set them up on a high hill. How woefully deluded are they and how great shall be their fall! The Lord is not with them, the Lord is with the poor, the broken ones whose contrite tears acknowledge that they are nothing. Oh yes, sin demands punishment, sin itself is punishment, but in our fear and our shame is the very working of grace. Before the countenance of God our souls shrivel like moths in a flame, but the fear of the Lord is the beginning of wisdom, and the consciousness of sin, and that alone, O my dear friends, can open our blinded eyes and make clean our blackened hearts. Sin befouleth the fair image of God, so that the sinner may feel that he knows not God, even that there is no God. But stay with your sin, bide steadfastly beside it in knowledge and in truth and in faith, and call upon the Spirit, crying "Come Lord, Come Lord!" Surely He will come. And now to God the Father, God the Son, and God the Holy Ghost, we ascribe as is most justly due all might, majesty, dominion and power, now and forever more. Amen.'

'Do you think he was getting at us?' Rose said afterwards, outside.

'Yes!' said Jenkin.

'His assumptions, even if correct, were impertinent,' said Gerard.

'Is he unpopular?' Jenkin asked.

'No, rather popular! Last summer people walked over from the next parish just to hear him!'

'Masochism has always been one of the charms of Christianity,' said Gerard.

'He doesn't seem to be a learned man,' said Rose, 'but he's very eloquent and sincere. I thought at first he was just a ranter. He's certainly a change from Mr Amhurst!'

'I enjoyed it!' said Jenkin. 'Did you, Tamar?'

They had sung 'For those in peril on the sea' which always brought tears to Rose's eyes, and afterwards Rose had talked to Miss Margoly, and Julia Scropton who played the harmonium, and Annushka's niece Mavis who was engaged to be married, and Mr Sheppey who was to come up on Monday and look at a drain. The parson had not reappeared.

The exterior of the church was as unpretentious as its interior, adorned only by some corbels carved as grotesque heads, but the situation was attractive, upon a small eminence with fine beech trees, and with a graveyard of handsomely lettered gravestones, dating from the seventeenth to the nineteenth centuries with little change in style. The vicarage had been pulled down and Father McAlister lived in a little modern house in the village.

It had been agreed that the churchgoers, who had come directly to the church by a footpath, should return the longer way via the village so as to join Gull and Lily at the Pike and even have some drinks there as lunch was to be cold and as late as they pleased. The congregation, all known to Rose, were straggling along toward the village, but Rose's party lingered a moment to enjoy the view of the older village houses, a section of the Roman Road, the roofs of Boyars visible over garden trees, and further off and higher up the wood decked with snow. Coats, prudently removed in church, had been hastily put on again, together with gloves and scarves and (except for Gerard) headgear. Tamar had put on a little close-fitting felt hat. She did not answer Jenkin's question, perhaps had not heard it. The sun was still shining and their footsteps, crunching through the frozen surface of the snow, made a pleasant brittle sound as they now walked along, Rose first arm in arm with Annushka, Gerard and Jenkin behind with Tamar between them.

They had walked only a little way when there was a sound of someone running behind them. It was Father McAlister. They all stopped.

The priest had doffed his vestments and put on an overcoat. As he ran towards them he held his cassock gathered up into one hand. He had a black beret on his head, perched above his ears. He looked younger, red with cold, somewhat unshaven. When he reached them he stopped and stretched out his bare hands on either side in a gesture which might have expressed apology, or some kind of availability as in a blessing. He addressed Rose in a firm authoritative voice, with a very slight Scottish accent. 'Miss Curtland, forgive me – but could you introduce me to this young lady?' Without turning to her he indicated Tamar.

Rose, surprised, said, 'Yes, of course. Miss Hernshaw. Tamar, Father McAlister.'

The priest went on, still not looking at Tamar. 'Would you mind if I talked to Miss Hernshaw for a few minutes – if she is willing, that is?'

Rose, ruffled by this sudden intrusion, and wanting to protect Tamar, said, 'Well, just now we're going to join some friends –'

Tamar said at once, 'I'll go with him. I'll be back for lunch, don't wait – I won't be long.' She turned and began to walk back towards the church. The priest followed her.

'Really!' said Rose. 'What's all that about? I think it's cheek! What can he want?'

'He saw her face,' said Jenkin. 'He thinks she's afflicted.'

'It's not his business! He'll upset her!' Rose felt indignant and distressed. She had understood that Tamar was ill, she had tried to help her. Now this interfering priest had taken her away.

'I'll wait here,' said Rose.

'Better let her come back by herself,' suggested Jenkin.

After some hesitation they walked on toward the village. As they came near they saw Lily and Gulliver coming out to meet them, sliding on the trodden snow.

Tamar went first into the church and sat down where she had sat during the service, and Father McAlister came and sat beside her, looking at her. He pulled off his beret and his overcoat.

'Won't you take off your coat?'

Tamar did not take off her coat, but she unbuttoned it and took off her little blue felt hat with the narrow brim and looked at Father McAlister with her wild green-brown eyes. She rolled up her hat and thrust it into her pocket. Then she ran both hands through her straight short silky hair, straining it back from her face. 'What is it?'

'There is no one here,' said the priest. 'We are alone here. Except for the Divine Presence.'

'What did you want to say?'

'You are in grief. You look as if you are in mourning. Have you lost a loved one?'

'No.'

'Then what is the matter?'

'Why on earth should I tell you?'

'I am a minister of God. In talking to me you talk to God.'

'I don't believe in God,' said Tamar.

'Let us not worry about words,' said Father McAlister. 'We are in the presence of what is holy, of Christ crucified and Christ risen. Christ saves – that is the reality in our lives. Did you know Jesus when you were a child?'

'No. Only – well – at school – but, no –'

'Were you baptised, confirmed?'

'No, my mother didn't like those things, she didn't approve of them. I can't think why you –'

'Don't be proud with me, child, I am nothing, a servant, an instrument, a slave. And yet something, a vehicle of love. You need love. Belief does not matter. It is need that matters. Tell me your first name, I didn't catch it when Miss Curtland spoke it.'

'Tamar.'

'Ah, a name from the Bible.'

'I was named after the river.' This was an idea put into Tamar's head by one of her earliest school teachers.

'I want you, whatever your trouble may be, to turn to Jesus, to the living Christ, who is more real to us than God, closer to us than God, closer to us than ourselves –'

'Thank you,' said Tamar, 'I know you mean well and I thank you for your kindness. I hear what you say. Now I must go.'

She made to rise but Father McAlister had suddenly taken her wrist in a strong grip and held her where she was. 'I want you to know that you have a Saviour to whom *nothing is impossible*. You need love. Perhaps you need forgiveness. You need healing. Turn to the boundless perfect love which heals and pardons. Kneel, Tamar.'

Tamar slipped down onto her knees, onto one of the soft beautiful embroidered kneelers which Rose liked so much. As soon as she had felt the priest's hand holding her ever so firmly tears had gathered in her eyes. Now they began to pour down her cheeks and she sobbed.

Father McAlister released his hold and falling on his knees beside her began to pray, looking up into the white light. 'O Lord Jesus Christ, master and king, merciful judge, giver of that peace which the world cannot give, who healeth the hidden heart and taketh away the sin of those who with true repentance turn unto Thee, falling wearied and broken at Thy blessed feet –' He stopped abruptly, and there was silence except for Tamar's sobs. She hid her face in her hands and the tears ran through her fingers and down over her thin wrists and onto her coat. He said to her, in a conspiratorial whisper, 'Come on – tell me all about it!'

Still crying and drooping her head, she began to tell him. One of the things which Tamar told the priest in the sun-lit snow-lit church was that she was pregnant.

'How is your father?' said Crimond.

'He's dead,' said Gerard.

'Oh, I'm very sorry to hear that.'

'He died last June. He'd had cancer for some time. How is your father?'

'Soldiering on. He's older than yours if I remember. He has a heart condition.'

'I'm sorry –'

'I remember your father, we met at Oxford, and later again in London. He was very kind to me.'

Gerard could not remember Crimond meeting his father, but it had evidently happened.

Crimond had followed Gerard into the dining room. It was Thursday at ten o'clock and Crimond had arrived punctually to be asked to give his 'explanation'. It was a dark day and the snow had disappeared from London.

After some reflection Gerard had decided to have the meeting in the dining room, sitting at the table. It seemed more business-like, less relaxed, the room was darker and more enclosed. He had thought of putting out paper and pens as for a committee, but this had seemed ridiculous. The highly polished dining table had nothing on it. Two chairs were placed, not far apart, at one end, the other chairs were against the wall.

Gerard had been annoyed the previous evening, when he returned from the London Library, to find that Gideon and Patricia, just back from Venice, had begun to put up Christmas decorations and had started with the dining room. The two lamps which he had put on filled the room with reflected points of light on elaborate glittering red chains and on the shiny scarlet and green holly branches which had been liberally stuffed in behind the Japanese paintings. Patricia had asked him to bring some holly from Boyars, but he had forgotten, so she had bought some at Harrods. He had mentioned casually, so as to avoid fuss if they found out later, that Crimond was coming to see him on business and they were to be left alone. Of course Pat and Gideon were extremely interested, but had expressed no sinister intent of joining in. Rose of course had been absurdly nervous about the meeting, and had ended by making Gerard nervous. He had told her that he would give Crimond about an hour, that their business, which would be simple enough, should be finished within less than that time, and yes, all right, she could ring him if she wanted to after eleven. Gerard had decided to make things as perfunctory as possible. Crimond would get the message. Gerard didn't want a showdown, he simply wanted to ask a few polite questions and would be satisfied with vague answers. He would be, as Jenkin had put it, 'going through the motions'.

Crimond's arrival had disturbed him more than he expected. They had stood in the hall and exchanged remarks about the weather while Crimond had taken off his scarf and overcoat. They had stood by the dining table talking about the difficulty of parking one's car. Then after a moment's silence Crimond had asked about Gerard's father.

It was a considerable time since they had met face to face. Gerard had shaved carefully and put on his bottle-green jacket and combed his hair and wondered if he looked older, and decided he did not. Crimond, he thought, did look a bit older. The brilliant dancing figure of the midsummer ball which Jenkin had compared with Shiva now seemed like something else, something seen in a vision, a manifestation of the essence of Crimond. The person who stood before Gerard in the rather dim light of the dining room looked tired, was shabby, had been out in the cold. The glow, perhaps the freckles, had gone from the pallid countenance. Yet he was still very slim and straight, his longish hair retaining its red colour and its springy wave, his face smooth except for the wrinkles round the eyes. The eyes, in spite of the polite remarks, were hard and wary. He was neat and well-shaved and wearing a tie, but his jacket and his shirt were well worn, the shirt frayed, the jacket, and not recently, patched at the elbows.

'Do sit down,' said Gerard, indicating a chair. He had

decided beforehand where each of them should sit. They sat.

'I remember those pictures from your flat in Chelsea,' said Crimond. This was the flat which Gerard had shared with Sinclair. He added, 'And I think at the other flat –'

'Yes. I had some. I've collected a few more.'

Crimond brought a notebook and a pen out of his pocket and arranged them side by side on the table. Then he stared expectantly at Gerard. This might have been a moment for a smile, but neither of them smiled. Crimond's long nose wrinkled slightly. Gerard felt awkward and uneasy. He said, 'It's kind of you to come here.'

'It's kind of you to ask me.'

'As I said in my letter, it's just about the book.'

'Yes.'

'How's it getting on?'

'Fine.'

'Is it finished?'

'No.'

'You're still writing it?'

'Of course.'

'It's just that – well, we felt, some of us felt, that we would like some sort of progress report on how the book was developing, what it's turning out to be about –'

Crimond raised his eyebrows. 'It's about politics. It's the same book.'

'Yes, but – what sort of politics? I mean, you used to be rather extreme, and – especially since the book *is* so long – we wondered if – we thought it might be rather more reflective and less – less inflammatory –'

'Oh yes,' said Crimond flatly, as if Gerard had answered his own question.

'It's not a revolutionary book?'

'Yes, of course.'

'I mean advocating violence and –?'

'Look,' said Crimond, 'who's "we"? You say "we felt" and "we thought".'

'I mean the committee.'

288

'Who is the committee now?'

'Well, just me and Jenkin and Rose and Gulliver Ashe. My father's gone, of course.'

'Why Gulliver Ashe?'

'We co-opted him.'

'You didn't tell me.'

'I'm sorry,' said Gerard. 'Perhaps we should have told you, it just didn't seem necessary –'

'I see. Look, Hernshaw, is this about money? Is it that you don't want to pay up any more?'

'No,' said Gerard, 'it's not about money!'

'Perhaps you all feel that *now* I don't need to be supported by *you*?'

Gerard took a moment to understand what Crimond meant so far had it been from his thoughts. 'No, we don't think that!'

'I am not using anyone else's money, except yours, that is.' Crimond's pale face flushed for a moment, and he put his hand up to his cheek.

Gerard did not like to mention Jean's name, but he wanted to assure Crimond that none of them had calculated that Crimond would now be rich! 'Of course. We never for a moment – *that's* not what we –'

'So it's about your own money, why shouldn't it be – you feel you can't afford me any more?'

'No, we can, we will –'

'What's it all about then?'

'Crimond, just *think* – you've been writing this book for years and years and we don't know what's in it! In a sense we've been responsible for it, we'll be regarded as having sort of commissioned it, and as agreeing with it!'

'You did not *commission* it.'

'All right, but you see –'

'Perhaps you should have thought of all this earlier.'

'Well, we're thinking of it now.'

'I can't see what this interrogation is supposed to achieve,' said Crimond in a thoughtful tone. 'You agreed to finance the book – all right, it's taking a long time. You say this is not about money. I don't see that you can have anything else to say about the book, except that you disagree with it, or you think it's rotten. Do you imagine I'm going to alter it to please you and Rose and Jenkin?'

'No –!'

'You say you want to know what's in it, but there's no point in my trying to tell you now, there's a great deal in it.'

God, thought Gerard, I'm simply being defeated by this man. Of course the idea of seeing him like this is a perfectly silly one, as he is pointing out. I must find some way of ending this ridiculous meeting with some kind of dignity.

'We don't want to interfere, Crimond.'

'I'm glad to hear it.'

'We just want to be –'

'Reassured?'

'We assume – and I'd like to be able to tell the others – we assume this is – well, it must be – to put it bluntly – a sort of serious philosophical book and not a call to arms! I mean it's not like that famous pamphlet about perpetual conflict?'

Crimond looked thoughtfully, frowning, staring at Gerard with his cold eyes. 'That was a short statement.'

'The pamphlet was, yes – but I imagine the message of the book is different – I mean your political views in those days were rather extreme and simple – we were all extreme and simple once – perhaps we changed sooner than you did – but now –'

'But now you think my politics must be about the same as yours and Jenkin's and Rose's?'

'I don't mean exactly! I mean on essential points.'

'Mention an essential point.'

'Well, do you believe in parliamentary democracy?'

'No.'

'What do you think about terrorism?'

Crimond continued to stare. Then he said, 'My dear Hernshaw, if we are to have a discussion it can't go on like this.'

'Perhaps it need not go on any further,' said Gerard. 'You say you don't believe in democracy and don't answer about terrorism. That's enough to make clear –'

'That you can not be reassured.'

'Look, I'm sorry I asked you to come like this. Of course there's nothing to be argued about. We said we'd support you and we will, and you are quite right to point out that we can hardly complain now! I won't keep you. I'm very sorry.'

Gerard made a movement as to rise, but as Crimond did not move he sat back in his chair. Crimond said, 'You want to know what the book's about. I'm prepared to say something about it, why not. We could have some discussion.'

Gerard hesitated. He had composed a reasonably peaceful face-saving end to this uncomfortable scene. Did he really want to talk to Crimond? 'Yes, all right.'

Crimond settled back. 'Well, you start then, ask questions, to get things going.'

'You said you didn't believe in parliamentary democracy. Why not?'

Crimond had opened his notebook and was leaning forward. He said after a moment, 'That's not the right question. I can't answer that now, later perhaps. It needs more background. Try again.'

'Do you belong to any political party?'

'No.'

'To any section, pressure group, secret society, militant movement, that kind of thing?'

'If it was secret I would be unlikely to tell you – but no, I don't belong to any group of that sort.'

'You're a lone wolf?'

'Yes – now.'

'You did belong –? Why did you leave?'

'Because of the book. I didn't want to waste time arguing with people who understood *nothing*.'

Gerard was beginning to relax. He thought, it's all right after all, it *is* a philosophical book, it's a harmless theoretical work. We've been making a fuss about nothing. 'So it's a theoretical book?'

'Of course.'

'Would you still call yourself a Marxist?'

'Yes. But that doesn't give much information these days.'

'You're a revisionist?'

'I'm not a Stalinist if that's what that question means. I'm not a Leninist either. I don't like the term revisionist. I'm in the Marxist stream.'

'Whom do you follow?'

'*Follow?*'

'Well, whose views do you discuss in the book, whom do you endorse?'

'No one.'

'You mean it's detached, it's a sort of history of ideas? I'm glad to hear that –'

'Any book about politics mentions past ideas, Hegel, Marx and Lenin mention past ideas.'

'You'd call it a political book?'

'Yes, of course!'

'But whose politics?'

'My politics!'

'You mean it's an original book of political philosophy?'

'It's an original book,' said Crimond in an exasperated tone. 'Do you imagine I'd work like a demon for years and years just to mull over somebody else's thoughts? These are my thoughts, my analyses, my prophecies, my programme!'

'So it's not a philosophy book?'

'How weird your categories are! It's philosophy, if you like – but what does that mean – it's *thinking*, and it's a programme of *action*. That's its *point*.'

'So it's like a very long pamphlet?'

'No. It's not a long simplification. It's about everything.'

'Everything?'

'Everything except Aristotle. I regard him as an unfortunate interlude, now happily over.'

'We can agree on that.' Gerard ventured a faint smile, but Crimond was glaring at the surface of the table which he was beginning to scratch intently with his finger nail. Gerard decided not to stop him. 'But, Crimond, if, as you say, you've cut yourself off from ordinary practical politics and become a lone wolf, how can you talk about a programme of action? You claim to be a Marxist, so you know that politics is very fine work, you've got to be inside it all the time, pushing and pulling, to get anything done at all. Or do you imagine that you can institute a revolution by propounding a theory?'

Crimond stopped scratching the table and stared at Gerard with his blue eyes wide open and his thin mouth thrust forward. His long nose, his whole face, pointed fiercely at Gerard. Perhaps he's really a bit mad, Gerard wondered, I never seriously thought that before. As Crimond did not answer his question Gerard went on, speaking quietly and patiently. 'A reflective book can be very valuable and can do more good. So if what you call your "programme" is all wrapped up in ideas, so much the better.'

'Hernshaw,' said Crimond, 'I am not, as you seem to imagine, mad, I am not a megalomaniac –'

'All right!'

'I just happen to believe that I am writing a *very important book*.'

The door of the dining room opened abruptly and Patricia put her head in, then entered. 'Hello, you two, would you like some coffee?'

'No, thanks,' said Gerard, then to Crimond, 'would you? No? Pat, you remember Crimond, you met ages ago I think. My sister Patricia.'

Crimond, who had risen, and clearly did not remember her, bowed slightly.

'Or tea, or some sherry? Or biscuits?'

'No. Pat dear, do leave us alone!'

The door closed. Crimond sat down. Gerard was wondering what thread to pick up when Crimond, who had returned to inspecting the table, threw back his head and ruffled up his reddish hair and said, 'I gather you've retired, what are you going to do?'

'Write,' said Gerard, irritated by Crimond's brusque tone.

'What about?'

'Plotinus.'

'Why? You're not a historian, and you can hardly call yourself a philosopher. You probably stopped thinking long ago. What you did in the civil service wasn't thinking, you could do that job in your sleep. Thinking is agony. Your book on Plotinus will turn out to be an article on Porphyry.'

'We'll see,' said Gerard, determined to keep his temper. Was there going to be a row after all?

'Do you believe in God?'

'Of course not!' said Gerard.

'You do, you know. You've felt superior all your life. You think you're saved by the Idea of the Good just because you know about it. The planet goes down in flames but you and your friends feel secure. You attach too much importance to friendship.'

'If this is to become a slanging match it had better end here. I wanted to get an impression of you and your book, and I've got it.'

'You've never really cared for anything except your parrot.'

Gerard was astounded. 'How on earth did you know –?'

'His name was Grey. You told me about him on the very first occasion when we met, when we walked back from a lecture and we went into the Botanical Garden and into the greenhouse. Do you remember?'

Gerard did not remember. 'No.' He was amazed and upset. 'I never told anybody. I certainly don't recall telling you.'

'Well, you did. I'm sorry, don't get angry. And what I said just now was nonsense, just spite. I do want to talk to you though. Our second innings, perhaps, to use Raffles's terminology.'

'I see no parallel,' said Gerard, recovering. 'We never had a first innings. But go on.'

'You've forgotten that too. A second innings is always played differently. Never mind. Another of your troubles is that you're afraid of technology.'

'Perhaps you don't mind the idea of a world without books?'

'It's inevitable, so it must be understood, it must be embraced, even loved.'

'So after all you turn out to be a historical materialist! What about *your* book?'

'It will perish with the rest. Plato, Shakespeare, Hegel, they'll all burn, and I shall burn too. But before that my book will have had a *certain influence*, that's its point, that's what I've been striving for all these years, that little bit of influence. *That's* what's worth doing, and it's the *only thing* that's worth doing now, to *look* at the future and make some sense of it and *touch* it. Look, Gerard, I don't think I'm God, I don't think I'm Hegel, I don't even think I'm Feuerbach –'

'All right, all right.'

'I just belong to *now*, I'm doing what has to be done *now*, I'm *living* the history of our time, which you and your friends seem to be entirely unaware of –'

'All right, what *about* what has to be done now? What about poverty and hunger and injustice? What about practical politics and social work?'

'Don't misunderstand me –'

'And please don't scrape the table with your finger nails.'

'Sorry. Of course we have to deal with poverty and injustice. People like you donate money to charities and then forget it all. As for social work you've never been near it in your life, it's something which other inferior people do. One has to think *radically* about these problems –'

'You believe in revolution, in violent revolution?'

'All revolutions are violent, with or without barricades. There will *be* revolution so we must *think* revolution.'

'Perhaps we've reached the stage where you can tell me why you don't believe in parliamentary democracy?'

'It's obvious. As a form of authority it can't survive. The world in the next century is going to look more like Africa than like Europe. We've got to have the courage to try to understand the whole of history and make genuine predictions. That's why Marxism is the only philosophy in the world today.'

'But there's no such thing as history! Your theory is based on a mistake. All it comes to is wreck the nearest thing and imagine something good will automatically come about! You combine irrational pessimism with irrational optimism! You foresee terrible things, but you also think that you can understand the future and control it and love it! Marxism has always "saved" its extremely improbable hypotheses by faith in a Utopian conclusion. And you accuse me of believing in God!'

'Yes. Absolute pessimism and absolute optimism, both are necessary.'

'Is that what's called dialectical thinking?'

'You've always been too frightened of talking nonsense, that's why you could never really do philosophy. I am not a utopian, I don't imagine that the state will wither away or the division of labour will cease or alienation will disappear. Nor do I think that we shall have full employment or a classless society or a world without hunger in any future that we can conceive of now. It's the wasteland next. Of course I think this society, our so-called free society, is rotten to the core – it's oppressive and corrupt and unjust, it's materialistic and ruthless and immoral, and soft, rotted with pornography and kitsch. You think this too. But you imagine that in some way all the nice things will be preserved and all the nasty things will become less nasty. It can't be like that, we have to go through the fire, in an oppressive society only violence is honest. Men are half alive now, in the future they'll be puppets. Even if we don't blow ourselves up the future will be, by your nice standards, terrible. There will be a crisis of authority, of sovereignty, technology will rule because it will have to rule. History has passed you by, everything happens fast now, we have to run to stay in the same place, let alone get a step ahead to see where we are. We've got to rethink everything –'

'Wait a minute,' said Gerard. He felt his heart beating faster, he felt hot and took off his jacket. 'You say men will be puppets and technology will rule, but surely, whether you call yourself a Marxist or not, you must be working *against* such a society, not for it! All right, the present is imperfect and the future looks grim, but we must just hold onto what's good, hold onto our values and try to weather the storm. You say rethink everything, but in the light of what? We must be pragmatic and hopeful, not in love with despair! We can't know the future, Marx couldn't predict the future, and he was looking into one a good deal steadier than ours. We must defend the individual –'

'What individual?'

'Come off it,' said Gerard.

'The bourgeois individual won't survive this tornado, he has already disintegrated, he has withered, he knows he's a fiction. I am not in love with despair, I am in love if you like with a good society which doesn't yet exist. But one cannot even glimpse that society unless one *understands* the collapse of this one.'

'I suppose you see yourself as a commissar in a world state of puppets who can't read or write! The elite would have the books, the rest would be watching television!'

'*We* won't be there, we are trash, we deserve nothing not even whipping, of course we are in pain, we are living through our own dissolution, all *we* can do –'

The telephone began ringing in the hall. Patricia opened the door. 'It's Rose, wanting you.'

'Oh *hell*,' said Gerard, and went out closing the door behind him.

Rose's voice was anxious and apologetic. 'Oh, my dear – are you all right?'

'Of course I'm all right!'

'I'm terribly sorry I didn't ring sooner, I'm away from the flat – I've had a rather odd morning, I'll tell you later. I would have rung sooner only I couldn't find a telephone box. How did it go?'

'How did what go?'

'Your talk with Crimond!'

'It's still going on.'

'Can't you get rid of him? Is it –?'

'Rose, could you ring later on sometime? Sorry, I must go now.' He put down the telephone and hurried back into the dining room.

Crimond had got up and was studying one of the pictures representing a geisha in a boat.

'Don't go, David. Do sit down.'

Crimond was looking more relaxed. Enlivened by the

argument he looked younger and less tired. 'Did Rose think I'd done you a mischief?'

'She was anxious!'

'I hope I've dealt an intellectual wound.'

'Not yet!'

'I have to go soon —'

'Sit down.'

They sat down. There was a moment's silence.

'You were saying all *we* can do —'

'Yes,' said Crimond, 'we've got to understand suffering, express suffering, see it, breathe it —'

'"The whole creation groaneth and travaileth in pain together — *until now*."'

'Yes —'

'You don't imagine you can abolish suffering!'

'You should reflect upon the assumptions which underlie that remark!'

'All right — not all, but most?'

'Most, much — we've got to think about the whole of history, about all the people who went under and were trodden on, and think of it as part of what's happening now wherever people are crushed or frightened or hungry —'

'This is self-indulgent rhetoric,' said Gerard. 'And as for Marxism, it may not make them hungry, but it certainly makes them frightened!'

'That's a cheap point. We have to try to see further and hope more. Right thinking is difficult in a wrong world. We have to think in terms of an entirely new person, a new consciousness, a new capacity for *happiness*, a kind of happiness the human race hasn't yet dreamt of. The individual you rate so highly, best personified of course in yourself, is just a cripple, half a person, well, he was half once, now he's just a whining sliver — and he's one of the lucky ones. There are immense sources of spiritual energy which are completely untapped —'

'Your theory is schizophrenic, you talk about a crisis of authority and men being puppets and going through the fire, and the next moment it's spiritual energy and new people with new happiness — But what happens in between? Your ideas lead straight into tyranny – and you imagine you can see the ideal society just beyond it! You said you weren't a utopian –'

'The utopian impulse is essential, one must keep faith with the idea that a good society is possible –'

'There is no good society,' said Gerard, 'not like you think, society can't be perfected, the best we can hope for is a decent society, the best we can achieve is what we've achieved now, human rights, individual rights, and trying to use technology to feed people. Of course things can improve, there can be less hunger and more justice, but any *radical* change will be for the worse – and your dreams will only make us lose what we have –'

'Do you seriously mean,' said Crimond, 'that you cannot conceive of any social system which is better than western parliamentary democracy?'

'No. I cannot. Of course there can be –'

'Yes, yes, little improvements, as you say.'

'Large improvements. And of course tyrannies can keep people alive who would starve under freedom, but that's a different point. A free society –'

'I don't think you know what freedom means. You imagine it's just economic tinkering plus individual human rights. But you can't have freedom when all social relations are wrong, unjust, irrational – when the body of your society is diseased, deformed – we must clear the ground –'

'A democracy can change itself –'

'Can you see this bourgeois democracy changing itself? Come! We've got to see it all, Gerard, we've got to live it all, we've got to suffer it all, we've got to see how *disjointed* it all is. You think of yourself as an open-minded pluralist – but you've got a simple compact little philosophy of life, all unified, all tied up comfortably together, a few soothing ideas which let you off thinking! But we must think – and that's what's such hell, philosophy is hell, it's contrary to nature, it hurts so, one must make a shot at the whole thing and that means failing too, not really being able to connect, and not pretending that things fit when they don't – and keeping hold of the things that don't fit, keeping them whole and clear in their almost-fittingness – oh God, it's so hard –'

'You mean your book –' said Gerard. He had been on the point of becoming angry and was restraining himself. The return to the book was an escape route.

'Oh – the book –' said Crimond. He stood up and began to rub his eyes. 'Yes, it's hell – one needs that last bit of bloody courage which takes you on past your best possible formulation into – oh –'

'I look forward to reading it,' said Gerard, rising too. He was feeling exhausted. 'One thing does puzzle me though, why you want to call all this rigmarole Marxism. Of course I know that Marx's early utopian ideas are all the fashion now – But why put yourself inside that conceptual cage?'

'The cage – yes – the cage – but it's not that cage – it's not like you think. Well – well – I'd like to persuade you, I'd like to persuade *you*. I could teach you a lot of things. I haven't many people to talk to now. Of course you're not ideal because you know so little. But I find it easy to talk to you – perhaps for historical reasons.'

'I wonder if you'd like to talk to the committee?' This idea has just occurred to Gerard.

'Would they listen? No – it's not a good idea. I don't mind talking to you, but –'

'Think it over. Thank you for coming.'

They went out into the hall and Crimond put on his coat and scarf. He drew a rolled-up cap out of his coat pocket and held it. There was an awkwardness, as if they were about to shake hands. Gerard opened the door, upon which, during their discussion, Patricia had hung a holly wreath. Crimond set off quickly and did not look back. Gerard closed the door and leaned against it.

The 'rather odd morning' which Rose had mentioned on the telephone to Gerard had been spent with Jean. In becoming more and more anxious about her friend, Rose's feelings had been painfully mixed up. She did not write to Jean because Crimond might read the letter and somehow blame Jean. She could not just 'call in', risking an encounter with Crimond; nor did it make any sense to telephone for even if Jean answered, she could hardly talk to Rose with Crimond nearby, and if she was alone she might still not wish to talk, might be abrupt, even putting the telephone down, thereby upsetting Rose very much indeed. Rose did not want to force Jean suddenly to choose between rudeness to Rose and disloyalty to Crimond. Perhaps this precluded any approach at all. Quite apart from these more mechanical problems Rose was troubled about her own purposes and motives. Any communication with Jean might make difficulties at that end. Crimond was certainly suspicious, possessive, possibly violent. Rose would be taken to be an emissary of Gerard, perhaps of Duncan. It was such a delicate matter. Ought not Rose to be resigned to not seeing Jean and to knowing nothing? But Rose did not like knowing nothing. Was this because of concern for Jean's welfare, or out of curiosity? Rose very much wanted to talk to Jean to find out *what was going on*. She wanted to *see* Jean, to look at the woman who now belonged to Crimond. She wanted inside information to pass on to Gerard. She wanted to assess the likelihood of Jean's return to Duncan, and also to find out if there was any way in which she could *help* Jean. With Gerard she had imagined many possible situations, by herself probably every possible situation. Jean might need outside help to escape, or at least to be resolute enough to envisage escaping. She needed, surely, a signal from her friends, evidence of continued love, perhaps simply to be told that Duncan longed for her to come back. If the opposite were the case and she needed no such support and assistance, that was important too. Rose and Gerard would have to decide what, if anything, to say to Duncan. Also of course Rose wanted information because she wanted information, the whole thing was so *interesting*. What decided her at last to make a move was however simply her desire to be with Jean again, to take her in her arms and kiss her.

The occasion was presented as soon as Rose knew that on a certain day at a certain time Crimond was to be with Gerard. Rose's plan was to drive to South London early, find a telephone box near to Crimond's house, and when she was sure Crimond must have left, to telephone Jean and say she was very near and could she drop in for a minute. The plan worked. Jean said curtly 'Yes', and a few minutes later Rose was in the house.

Now they were downstairs in what Crimond called the Playroom, Rose sitting on her coat, which she had slipped off, on the divan, and Jean, facing her, on a chair drawn over from the desk. Their meeting at the door had been emotional but not effusive. They gripped each other's arms, turning quickly away without an embrace.

The Playroom was darkish except for two shaded lamps, one on the desk, the other perched on a pile of books on one of the tables. The room was cold and smelt of paraffin. Jean looked thinner, looked tired, seemed to be wearing no make-up, was dressed in a dark blue woollen dress and a brown cardigan and had just taken off an apron. She looked well however and beautiful, her dark hair more shaggy, longer, less neat, her dark eyes fierce. She had what Rose had once called her Jewish heroine look. Rose now felt, confronting her, almost afraid, at a loss, ready to cry, afraid too that Jean might suddenly weep angry ferocious savage tears. It had proved so far difficult to make conversation.

'I was at Boyars in the snowy weather. The meadow was frozen.'

'Did you skate?'

'Yes. Lily Boyne was there. She skates very well. I was surprised.'

'I don't see why you should be surprised.'

'No – I suppose not – I just didn't expect it.'

'How's Tamar?'

'Not well. She's eating very little and looks unhappy.'

'Can't you do anything?'

'I try. She came to see you, I believe.'

'I assume you arranged it.'

'Well – would you like to see her again?'

'No.'

'She's very fond of you. Doesn't he like you having visitors?'

'Why did you come?' said Jean.

'To see you. And to see if there was anything in the world I could do for you.'

'There is nothing.'

After a moment's silence Rose said, 'Will he come straight back after he leaves?'

'Will who come straight back after he leaves where?'

'Will Crimond come straight back here when he leaves Gerard?'

'Is he with Gerard?'

'Yes! Didn't you know?'

'He doesn't always say where he's going,' said Jean, 'I don't ask. I don't know whether he'll come straight back.'

'You don't seem to know much about him.'

'I don't know everything about him.'

Jean, her hands on her knees, sat staring at Rose, waiting for the next question, as in an interrogation.

'Does Crimond shoot at that target?'

'He used to.'

'I remember he was a marksman, he won some prize. I hope he's not preparing for a revolution.'

'I think he's amusing himself.'

'What do you do?'

'What do you mean?'

'I mean both of you, what do you do all day, do you stay here, do you travel, do you entertain, do you visit people, do you go to concerts, are you happy?'

'We're mostly here,' said Jean, 'we don't "entertain", people sometimes come.'

'Do you discuss his work?'

'We discuss all sorts of things, but if you mean the book, no, not that.'

'The book really exists?'

'Of course. It's over there. You can look at it if you like.'

Rose looked toward the desk, where the lamp showed a pile of different-coloured notebooks, one open. She felt a superstitious aversion to looking at the book. 'No, thank you –'

'You imagine I'm unhappy, perhaps you hope I'm unhappy.'

'No,' said Rose, 'I just thought you might be bored.' She had begun to feel they were talking in their sleep, not communicating at all, wasting precious time. Now Jean frowned and the atmosphere became tenser and more alert. Rose went on, in the new tension and sense of closeness, to say something which she had resolved to say, felt she must say, even rehearsed. 'Duncan loves you. He wants you back. We all love you, we miss you. I wish you'd come back.'

Jean seemed to reflect on these words but replied only, 'I'm sorry to disappoint you all, I'm not bored and I'm not unhappy. I have never been more *completely* happy in my life. If you want a message to carry back, there it is.'

'You left Crimond last time, there must have been reasons.'

'I have a kind of happiness which I think you've never known or dreamt of.'

'Have you *forgotten* your love for Duncan? You did love him, surely you do love him?'

'Last time was different. I wasn't then able to conceive of a *complete* removal of my being, a *complete* change. I've *grown* into that ability in the time between. It's a meeting with an absolute. When you can see what is perfect, what is imperfect falls away, it withers. Now, it's face to face, not in a glass darkly. One cannot dispute, one cannot resist.'

'And apparently one cannot explain.'

'One cannot explain.'

'Forgive me,' said Rose, 'I wanted so much to talk to you, and there's so little time, I'm saying a lot of things very badly. I must go before Crimond comes back. Gerard said he'd give him an hour –'

'*Give* him an hour!'

'I don't know how long it will take him to get back, if he comes back at once – you see I'm trying to say what matters, what matters to me, God knows when I'll see you again. You know that I love you, we've been friends forever, I must say things. I think you're living inside an illusion. It's all so one-sided, so unfair. You don't know where he goes and what he does, you've given him over your whole life, you've given up your friends and your world, and you don't meet his friends or inhabit his world. He has not shared his things with you. You don't even share in the book. As far as I can see, you have no relationship now except with him, a sexual relation which is part of his life and all of yours! I'm sorry – if I'm saying crude emotional things it's because I'm angry on your behalf –'

'Oh don't be, don't be,' said Jean, who had listened to this tirade with a weary air of absent indifference. She sighed and got up again and went behind her chair and tilted it a little towards her. 'Would you like some coffee? I'm afraid there's no alcohol in the house.'

'Of course I wouldn't like some coffee!' said Rose, exasperated. 'Oh Jean –'

'I don't deny our love,' said Jean, '*our* love, I mean, between you and me, I have no doubt that it will survive forever, even if we were never to see each other again, which of course we will, it is something unique and uniquely durable. But you must take it that we inhabit two absolutely different worlds. You rely on continuity, you live by a certain quiet seamless order in your life, it suits you, you've lived and thrived on it, whereas it has gradually suffocated me.' She let the chair fall back with a jolt.

'Oh well, if it's just desire for change – If you've chosen discontinuity that implies that you don't entirely believe in Crimond's love, you can't see your future together, you are insecure.'

'I am the only woman he has ever loved or could love. I believe in his love and our future is together whatever happens. But of course, unlike you, we can't foresee what will happen. There is insecurity, not in our love, but in the world. Crimond is brave and he has made me brave. You live in the old dreamy continuum where everyone is nice and dependable and good and every year has the same pattern. I have left that place, with him I am outside, in the dangerous contingent real world, love is dangerous, absolute and dangerous, one lives with death – and to live so is really to *live*. You don't understand what being deeply in love and being deeply loved is like, how it brims over one's whole existence and sanctifies and glorifies everything one does or thinks or touches, how it makes the world immense, as huge as the universe and full of light – you don't really know anything about sex and the way one can live and breathe it, when it's a total occupation, something which is everywhere, in everything, and makes you into a god! When that happens one doesn't worry about rights or shares or the little mean petty calculations which belong in the old small anxious selfish life. Self is obliterated. You've never had that experience, you've never been deified by love, you're a quiet girl, you're a puritan really, in the depths of your heart you feel that sex is wrong. Why didn't you get married? Why did you attach yourself to a hopeless proposition like Gerard? Why didn't you marry one of the others? Marcus Field, for instance, he was madly in love with you –'

'Was he? He never said so.'

'He thought Gerard owned you, he thought Gerard would marry you. You could have had children –'

'Oh stop it!' said Rose. 'You're just – just hopelessly *romantic*! Did you ever seriously think of marrying Sinclair?'

'Yes. But – I don't know that I would have done – even if he'd wanted it –'

'If you'd married him he'd be still alive.'

'Because I'd have stopped him gliding?'

'Because the causal chains would have been different.'

'Anything could have made the causal chains different.'

'I know.'

Rose, realising that she would soon be in tears, looked away down the room toward the far end where the target in the dim light looked like a mandala. She felt very cold and pulled her coat on. Leaning back a little she felt the rough prickly material of the old quilt under her hands. She thought, after I go Jean will smooth out the quilt. I wonder if she will tell

Crimond that I was here? I must go, I *must* go now before he comes back. I've lost Jean, we've lost each other, I've said all the wrong things. I'll regret it all so much, so much.

'I must go, darling.'

'Yes. I'll see you out. Wouldn't you like to see the book? Come.'

Rose fumbled with her scarf and gloves and followed Jean, her booted feet striking an echo on the bare floor, Jean's slippered feet soundless.

The book lay open underneath the lamp, the right-hand page written in Crimond's small neat scarcely legible writing, the left-hand page blank except for a sentence or two and a question mark. Jean turned the leaves back, showing other pages, the text varied here and there by capital letters and things written in red, then set the book back as it had been, when Crimond had finished writing that morning. It was like being shown a holy manuscript or rare work of art, something to be marvelled at, not, by the uninitiated, actually studied. Jean then indicated piles of similar notebooks beside the desk containing the massive completed parts of the work so far. Rose, who had not wanted to see the thing, did not feel any instant hostility to it, as if she might wish to tear it up. What struck her, with a kind of surprise, was its inert separateness, its authoritative thereness, its magnitude. Feeling she ought to say something, she said, 'What a long task.'

'Yes.'

'When will it end?'

'I don't know.'

They went upstairs to the hall, and stood and looked at each other by the unopened door. Rose's tears spilled over and they embraced, closing their eyes.

'Why didn't you tell me you were going to see Gerard?' said Jean.

They were sitting on the divan in the Playroom. Jean had

smoothed it out where Rose had been sitting. Crimond was still wearing his overcoat.

'I would have told you if you had asked me where I was going. I would have told you now anyway. That's not important. I was irritated about it beforehand, I didn't want to talk about it.'

'Was it all right?'

'Not very.'

'If he was rude I hope you told him to go to hell.'

'Oh he wasn't rude. I was foolish. I haven't talked to anyone about all that for a long time. I said too much and I was incoherent.'

'Rose said he'd decided to give you an hour!'

'I had decided to give him half an hour. But when I saw him –'

'When you saw him –?'

'Well, I've known him even longer than I've known you. It wasn't a proper argument, I'm afraid he'll have rather a poor impression –'

'He'll see, one day!'

'Oh – one day – And you, my queen and empress, my little hawkling, tell me, why did Lady Rose Curtland come to see you?'

'Curiosity,' said Jean, 'and to tell me Duncan still loves me.'

'And so, are you going back to him?'

'Crimond, don't hurt me.'

'Rose has upset you.'

'Oh all right, and Gerard has upset you! Actually she annoyed me, that's all. You don't feel she's unsettled me?'

'I feel precisely that.'

'You go on and on tormenting me. Why do you do it? You can't believe –'

'Oh I don't believe – we are talking of feelings. If one had the most precious diamond in the world in your pocket wouldn't you be afraid of losing it, wouldn't you keep putting your hand in to be sure it was still there?'

'Yes. I feel like that too. But I don't keep persecuting you with my terrible fear.'

'I tell you of my fear so that you can instantly reassure me. Jeanie, my life rests upon your love, you must take my fear away at ever second, my consciousness depends on yours, I breathe with your breath –'

'Oh my love – pride, rose, prince, hero of me, high priest.'

'Tell me something that Rose Curtland said to you, something about us, she must have said something about us, something to persuade you to go back.'

'Oh, just idiotic things.'

'Like what?'

'She said she thought I might be bored!'

'And are you?'

'She said I didn't seem to know much about you.'

'What made her say that?'

'The fact that I didn't know you'd gone to see Gerard.'

'You told her that I hadn't told you.'

'It came out. I'm sorry. And when she asked if you'd mind her having come, I said I didn't know. I suppose I shouldn't have said that.'

'It doesn't matter. You don't have to conceal anything. I should be angry if I thought you'd lied to her. Whatever you say, she will think we are unhappy, and hope we are doomed. But are you bored?'

'Crimond, don't go on like that! What about our lunch? I've got that vegetable soup that you like, and I'm making a stew for this evening.'

'You're making a stew for this evening. That sounds like real life. Sometimes I think we're playing at it.'

'At what?'

'Real life.'

'Crimond,' said Jean, 'my sweet dear love, sometimes a devil gets into you that wants to undermine us. You say such destructive things, and almost as if you wanted to bring it all down. You negate our reality, and you do it wantonly.'

'Oh Jeanie, I'm so tired, I'm so tired, I can't rest, I can't rest –'

Jean put her arms round him, round the bundle of his shoulders and his overcoat, and drew his head down to her shoulder and stroked his hair over the crown of his head and down onto his neck under the coat collar, and looked away over his head across the chill room to the open door. His head was cold. 'You work too hard,' she said, 'I know you have to. I wish I could make you rest. I so often want to. You must teach me how. I know we rest in bed. But you don't rest any other way – and neither do I.'

Crimond lifted his head and put his cold lips gently to her cheek. 'What do people do who can rest, my angel of peace?'

'I wish I were an angel of peace.'

'You are, you are my peace, I have no other.'

'People who can rest read books and go for walks and arrange flowers and weed their gardens and wash their cars and listen to music and rearrange their possessions and have their friends to informal suppers and have lots of general conversation.'

'At least we read books.'

'You read work books, and poetry. I can't read at present. It'll come back.'

'Perhaps your friend Rose is right. She wants us to fail. She isn't really your friend. She's spiteful, as women are.'

'And irrational, I suppose! You want to liberate the world but you still think in your heart that women are inferior, you think they aren't quite real.'

'All men think that,' said Crimond, raising his head from where it had been resting, and thrusting her away a little. 'And most women too. Why deny it, women are different, their brains are different, they're weaker, women cry and men don't, that symbolises it.'

'Have you never cried?'

'Not that I know of.'

'Perhaps you will one day.'

'Perhaps, when the world ends.'

'You're certainly not very sound on the liberation of women. Maybe after all Islam will rule the world.'

'It is a possibility I have considered.'

'So you think *me* irrational and inferior and unreal?'

'Not you, little one. You are not a woman. You are an errant spirit. We are both from elsewhere, we are visitors here, aliens, and by a happy chance we have met each other.'

'No wonder we think everyone else we know is half alive.'

'You must find something to do, something to *study*, you are wasting your talents.'

'I will find something, I will, don't *worry* about that!'

'I believe you are bored sometimes, you must be, Rose is right. You've given up so much, all your friends, your social life –'

'What I've given up is worthless to me. You've given up your solitude. I wonder if you sometimes regret it?'

'No, no, my heart and my soul – it was fated. You won't leave me, will you, little falcon?'

'How could I leave you, I am you, I cannot tear myself out from the sheath of my limbs.'

'You see, we do read, we do. Perhaps one day we shall go for a walk. Yes, yes, if we are to be dismembered we shall be dismembered together.'

'If only you could be more quiet with me. You said I was your peace. But you are always starting away as if you'd had an electric shock.'

'Then I shall never be at peace with you,' said Crimond, 'if peace is quietness. I meant something else.' He pulled off his coat and sat, apart from her, leaning forward with his head in his hands. 'You are my weakness, my weak point, that is part of our impossibility.'

Jean sat stiffly, frightened, as she often was. After a moment she said softly, slowly, 'When the book is finished perhaps we could travel a little. I'd so much like to be with you in France and Italy. You go on about the importance of Europe. You could visit people and talk to them.'

'When I finish the book I shall cease to be, and so will you.'

'Sometimes you talk nonsense, deliberate tiresome non-sense.'

'Perhaps the book will never be finished.'

'Of course it will, and then you'll write another.'

'My darling, can you see us growing old together?'

'You won't grow old,' she said. Could he, her Crimond,

grow old? Then she said, 'I love you – whatever is to be we'll be together. Oh Crimond, don't torment me with this talk –'

'I shall be bald, your lovely live hair will be limp and grey, we shall be weak and crippled. We shall look at each other in fear as we diminish more. I don't want ever to get used to you, Jeanie dear, why should we, *we* carry the long mortal burden of age and decline, we who are living gods in this place? I cannot leave you behind, any more than you can leave me behind. Better to consummate our love in death.' As he spoke he was rubbing his hands over his face and his eyes and through his hair. 'Oh I am so tired, so tired – my *mind* is so tired –'

Jean felt afraid. He had talked like this before. 'Yes, yes, of course, you are tired, you should stop working, rest, *rest*, just for a *day*.'

'I can't rest, you don't understand, you betray me, you don't listen to my *words*. I'm sorry. Sometimes I feel I am a knife poised at your heart.'

'I do listen, I do understand, you are wondering what you will do when you have finished the book, you imagine you'll become dull and ordinary, the book has kept you in a state of excitement for so many years, I've seen you trembling with emotion as you write –'

'You imagine that explains something, you imagine it explains something *away*. No, no, there is no away, it's deeper than that, it's you and me, we are crushed by our impossibility –'

'Crimond, we *make* our possibility, we make it day by day –'

'Day by day is an illusion, it's all *now* –'

'Do you want to kill me?'

'Only when I kill myself. Jeanie, I love you, you love me, that's what it's about. The perfection of our love is now, *now* we are absolutists, we are *gods*, later is only less.'

'Crimond, my darling, you know that I will do whatever you want, *whatever* you want, I am yours, I am you, I will go with you wherever you go. Here is my life, here is my death. But –'

'But you think we should have lunch!'

'But the book is not finished, and after it is finished there will be another book – Besides –'

'Besides?'

'I want to dance with you again.'

'Perhaps we shall dance together again, sometime, at the end of the world.'

'And you will learn to weep then, at the end of the world. Please don't frighten me by saying these mad things. I know you want eternity, but we can make eternity in time. That's what love is, after all. Come –'

'No, I can't eat, I can't work –'

'Come to bed.'

'Oh my Jeanie, my queen, if only there were only that –'

'That child is going to die,' said Violet Hernshaw to Gideon Fairfax. 'She is determined to die. She will die of a wasting sickness, of a mysterious virus, of tuberculosis, depression, starvation –'

'Well, can't we stop her?' said Gideon, leaning back in his chair.

'Who's we?'

'You and me. Let's team up. Eh?'

'No.'

'You don't want to stop her, you don't mind if she dies, you want her to die?'

'What you say means nothing, it's a vulgar psychological cliché, you don't know anything about real misery and living with death. You don't know death exists.'

'That may be true,' Gideon conceded, 'though objectively, if I may use that familiar adverb, it looks as if you don't want Tamar to succeed, even as if you would prefer her not to exist. Would you really not care if she committed suicide? However, as you say, it's a cliché.'

'She won't commit suicide. She's a survivor. You all think she's a pure maid and a frail flower. But she's a tough little atom. Why didn't you let me know you were coming?'

'You no longer have a telephone.'

'I can't afford one. You did it on purpose. You could have written.'

'I couldn't plan that far ahead. A picture drama is in progress.'

'You thought a letter would be evidence.'

'Evidence of what? My interest in Tamar, my interest in you?'

'You came about her.'

'And about you, you as part of her, you as yourself.'

'You are sorry for me, you pity me, you despise me –'

'How you do leap from one idea to another! We used to see

314

quite a lot of Tamar, now she refuses our invitations, I think that's because of you. Do you mind if I have a serious talk with her quite soon?'

'I would mind very much.'

'I'm very fond of that child, so is Pat, so is Leonard –'

'Pat was always dead scared Leonard would want to marry Tamar. Don't worry! My family isn't going to come anywhere near yours, ever!'

'Actually I came to say that Patricia and I would like to adopt Tamar.'

'You mean legally?'

'If possible. *De facto* anyway.'

'You want power over her. That's Pat's idea, to keep her off Leonard.'

'You always had a suspicious mind, but this is paranoia. That's one point, about adoption, I'm just putting it on the map. More immediately, we want to put up the money to get Tamar back to Oxford. I know you've said 'no' to Rose and Gerard, but I want to persuade you that we're a special case, that I am anyway.'

'Tamar is the only thing I've got, and you want to take it away.'

'You had no education so you don't want Tamar to have hers.'

'I don't take money from other people.'

'You prefer to live on Tamar's earnings.'

'I've worked for years and years to support that girl! Why should I go on forever? She's young, she's got a good job, it's right that she should earn. You sneer at me for being uneducated. I'd earn too if I could get a job.'

'I am about to offer you one.'

'To "help out" as Patricia's "house-keeper". No, thanks!'

'You could help me in the office. I think Pat said something about this to you at Guy Fawkes. Seriously, Violet, just look at this flat, look at yourself, look at the situation. You and Tamar are like two sick animals in a filthy box, one looks every day to see if they're still alive. I don't want to stand by and watch you destroy yourself with envy and grief and chronic unhappiness and lack of love. You're intelligent, you're good-looking, if you'd comb your hair, you could do with some make-up too, you're still young. My business is expanding, I'm going to have a gallery in Cork Street, and a glossy office with rubber plants and a lot of smart machines, and I want someone there that I can trust. You could learn the business, one side of it anyway, it's not all that arcane. It's the sort of thing Patricia couldn't possibly do and she'd hate it anyway. But *you'd* be capital at it, and it would interest you, instead of crouching here and dying of dullness and boredom. Don't you want to use your mind, use all that *cleverness* you're wasting now on endlessly documenting your resentment? You and Tamar could live with us too, make an extended family, for a while any rate, you could have the flat we're in now. This place is beyond help.'

'What do you propose doing with Gerard?'

'Oh we're going to get him out. I want that house. If we can't we'll buy another house, a larger one.'

'I thought Patricia wanted me to clean and cook like before.'

'That was just for an emergency. What I'm suggesting now is something entirely new. I want to transform Tamar and transform *you*. I want to shake you both and clean you up and dust you down and dress you in smart beautiful clothes and bright colours. You're *dowdy*, you've got no sense of *colour*. I might even go into the dress designing business myself, printing fabrics anyway. Violet, I'm serious.'

'No, you're not,' said Violet.

Gideon had appeared unexpectedly at about eleven in the morning, entering through the unlocked door, and found Violet sitting in her tiny kitchen over breakfast reading the newspaper. A pile of dishes tottered in the sink. The dresser was heaped with tins, bottles, string, mouldering bread, saucepans containing messes, unopened envelopes containing bills. Gideon, observing this conglomeration from the corner of his eye, thought it resembled an abstract expressionist picture which he had just bought. Violet had taken her glasses off when he came in. Taken unawares, she looked terrible. Her brown hair, unwashed and in need of trimming, hung in rats' tails, her face was greasy, her old floppy cardigan was inside out, her jersey was too tight and too short, and her skirt lop-sided and not properly done up. She was wearing bedsocks. She sat crouching and glaring, deepening the two lines above her nose, her eyes wet slits between dry wrinkles. The expensive contact lenses had proved a failure. She evidently felt that since she was taken unawares looking terrible she would make a feature of it.

Gideon, scented with aftershave, sat perched on a chair opposite to her upon which he had hastily placed a clean-looking plastic bag from the dresser. He tried to rock the chair a little. It came reluctantly away from the gluey deposit on the floor with a slight sucking noise. Gideon was wearing a dark suit with a reddish pink shirt and a pale yellow tie with blue shapes on it. His curly hair, darker and more closely curled than Gerard's, shone with health, his chubby red lips were moist, his plump cheeks glowed, they had enjoyed the cold air.

'You think Tamar's so perfect,' said Violet, 'everybody does. Why are you fussing about her now?'

'She's too perfect. I can't help feeling she's in danger. Someone at her publisher's told someone who told me that she looked really ill. You yourself said that she was dying.'

'She's been impossible lately. She won't eat and she looks a little misery and says nothing, she won't speak to me, it's like having a ghost in the house.'

'Does she have any social life, any sign of boy friends?'

'No. She wouldn't say anyway. She goes out in the evening. I think she just walks round and round the roads. Anything to get away from me and the television!'

'Seriously, Violet, won't you let me help? You accepted Matthew's money.'

'How did you know that? That was something else, it was money he owed to his brother, it wasn't much in any case.'

'All right, and you won't deal with Rose and Gerard, but I'm different, they're muffs, I'm a doer. I can give *effective* help, I can take charge. Besides – I'm different because I'm me.'

'I've forgotten who you are.'

'Don't you remember "Hello, swinger"?'

'No.'

'We've known each other a long time.'

Probably Violet's most terrible secret was that she had known Gideon when they were young, barely twenty, before he met Patricia, in fact Violet introduced them. Gideon, then a shy thin Jewish boy studying history at a London college, had made little impression. Gideon's father (a refugee who had adopted the name of Fairfax out of a Gilbert and Sullivan opera) had a junk shop in the New King's Road. Violet had been in love with a music student who was starting a pop group. By the time she was prepared to take an interest in Gideon Patricia had already appropriated him. The notion that Gideon had been a bit 'keen' on her, and proving unwelcome had transferred his attentions to her cousin, travelled with Violet, a dark cancerous nugget, which, as she grew older, became blacker and larger. For years she wondered if Gideon had ever said anything to Pat about that shadowy non-event, later she assumed he had not. She and Gideon never spoke of it, but, as Gideon progressed from poor student to tycoon, their mutual consciousness of this 'something' seemed to become, without ever really amounting to 'anything', more substantial.

'You don't want to help us,' said Violet, 'it's just an exercise of your perpetual euphoria, you are in every way successful, your success shines brighter here by contrast. It's a way of triumphing over us. We're to join the line behind your chariot. You want to make us look up at the sky and sing, but we can't. Some people have streams of happiness laid on, others have the black river. We belong to another race.'

'The world of the happy is not the world of the unhappy, as Gerard often says, quoting some philosopher. But what that philosopher did not realise was that the happy can sometimes kidnap the unhappy and carry them kicking and screaming into the world of happiness. That is what *money* can do, Violet, that is what money is *for*.'

'You love money, you love power, that's all. You are an utterly selfish person.'

'Yes, all right, but can't you attribute any benevolent motive to me? You know how fond I am of Tamar.'

'Oh Tamar, Tamar. I expect you're in love with her, you find her physically attractive, you want to be her favourite uncle, and God knows what else —'

'Oh shut up. Come on, Violet, just lift your head up, yes, look at the sky and the sunshine for a change. I hate that picture of you trudging behind the chariot. I want you and Tamar *in* the chariot. Where will you be at Christmas?'

'Here, as usual, of course.'

'I won't try to imagine how ghastly that must be. Look — we don't have to spend Christmas at Bristol any more, now that poor old Matthew's gone, we can be anywhere. Why don't you and Tamar come with us? We could rent a house in Italy. Tamar's never been to Italy. We'd have some fun. Why not, please?'

'That's your idea, not Pat's, and it's a silly impertinent idea. We don't want to be patronised by you and Pat, we don't want to play the humble grateful poor relations! Tamar wouldn't want to come anyway, she never wants to go anywhere now.'

'It's Pat's idea too, as it happens, I wouldn't float it on my own!'

'You want to share your happiness with the poor. Well, the poor don't want it. Pat's kindness humiliates me. Like last time, I was treated like a servant. It upsets Tamar very much. Pat just wants me there as a visible proof of how happy and lucky *she* is! When one is really afflicted sympathy is the last thing one wants. I can live with my miseries if only people would *leave me alone!*'

'Your miseries are self-inflicted,' said Gideon, 'and you are very unjust. You were not treated like a servant. You make any sort of generosity or kindness impossible, and you do this on behalf of Tamar, as if she were as mean and suspicious and full of spiteful hatred as you are.'

'You despise me,' said Violet, 'you treat me like dust, and you seem to think you have a right to, you wouldn't speak in this outrageous way to anyone else.'

'No, I wouldn't, and maybe I have a right to.'

'You come here as a tourist to see how hideous this place is and how hideous I am so that you can go back and tell Pat!'

At that moment Tamar appeared at the kitchen door. Tamar did indeed look like a ghost, not a transparent wraith, but rather the substantial stick-like kind, which might be a broom handle or a signpost but clearly and terrifyingly is not. She was wearing a long brown overcoat, and a large brown beret which was pulled down over her ears and made her look like a weird pale-faced animal, faintly pathetic, faintly unpleasant. Only her large animal-like eyes, staring with hostility into the kitchen, conveyed, as animal eyes can do, a kind of spirit. Gideon, who had not seen her for some time, was instantly shocked, as by the sight of some unnatural mental-physical degeneration, even metamorphosis.

He immediately said, 'Oh Tamar, what a bit of luck, here you are! I was just saying to your mother how nice it would be if you were to spend Christmas with us in Italy, we're renting a house –'

Violet said, 'What are you doing here at this time, have you got the sack?'

'I've taken the afternoon off,' said Tamar.

'Tamar, what about Christmas, Italy?' cried Gideon, jumping up, as Tamar seemed to be turning to go.

'No thanks.' Tamar disappeared, banging the kitchen door behind her.

'You see?' said Violet.

As he walked away through the cold dark foggy London morning toward his car Gideon pondered upon the mystery of Violet and Tamar. How could people *not want* to be happy? It was utterly contrary to nature. In Gideon's view, human beings do, and certainly ought to, reach out instinctively and ingeniously toward the fruit of happiness, seeking through all the branches and shaking the tree if necessary. He pondered, but did not want to ponder too deeply. He would try again of course. He had exaggerated slightly in saying that the Italian idea had been Pat's too. He had (as Violet had later assumed) never talked to Pat, or to anyone, about the moment (but had there ever really been such a moment?) when he had found twenty-year-old Violet attractive. He did not want to add anything to that little oddity, but neither did he dismiss it. It did not trouble him, it sometimes amused him. He loved his wife, and had found with her the happy life whose possibility he had intuited when he first met her; those two were closer than many outsiders liked to think. Pat certainly also wanted to help that miserable pair, though her motives were perhaps slightly different from his. About this too he did not ponder for long. Gideon could see Tamar's image as a perfect angel, certainly as a 'strong good girl', and he instinctively understood how this appearance, partly a reality, arose from her determination not to be ruined by her mother. Violet had called her a survivor, a tough little atom. Only as Tamar's impulse so patently lacked joy Gideon could not really believe in it, he saw her, as Gerard did not, as but too likely to 'break down'. Perhaps the process was now visibly beginning. He did in fact find her physically attractive, and wanted, but in no sinister or improper manner, to kidnap her and transform her, clothe her, take her to Paris, Rome, Athens, buy her a car and a rich successful handsome virtuous young husband. He also wanted to kidnap Violet and shake her into life, but that was a more complex wish, and probably a fruitless, even imprudent or senseless one. He recalled the days when she was 'swinger' and he was (a silly nickname which he refused to remember) without any deep emotion but with a kind of loyalty, he was touched by the memory and by her as a continuing element in his life; and he pitied her, though this was a feeling he did not care for, and continually altered into something else, perhaps into the euphoria and the selfishness and the power of which she accused him. As he walked along he banished the problem, he would have another idea about it later. He thought instead about his father whom he loved but with whom, in some profound way, he had never really *got on* (as he, for instance, got on with Pat). Of course his father was glad that his son was rich, and glad (must be glad) to be now surrounded with what money would buy. But he had wanted his son and only child to be a doctor and still spoke nostalgically of the old hard days in the New King's Road. Mutual love (for it was mutual) does not ensure mutual understanding. Thank heavens Leonard got on so well with his grandfather, as he had, as a child, with his grandmother, now long dead. She had been a contrary person too. Of course both of them had had terrible childhoods. Easily releasing his ancestors and their childhoods Gideon began to think about some Beckmann drawings which he thought he could obtain for a reasonable price. Then, as he approached his beautiful car, he thought, far more deeply and vaguely, about himself, and began to smile.

Tamar had taken the half-day off in order to visit Lily Boyne. In her lonely agony, Lily seemed to be the only person who could organise the practical assistance which Tamar now urgently needed at least to consider.

When, after her visit to the chemist's shop, Tamar, alone in her little bedroom, had established without doubt that she was carrying Duncan's child, she thought that she would go mad, she thought she would have to kill herself, the idea of doing so was indeed the only barrier against madness. In her few timid *amours* Tamar had always had a dread of pregnancy, this dread had been a chief reason for her avoidance of, almost repugnance for, physical love. She had witnessed the sordid miserable dilemmas of her fellow students; and some instinctive puritanism, a part of her severance from her mother, made her fastidious about anything at all approaching promiscuity, and gave her a deep and not just prudential horror of the idea of children out of wedlock. She had been happier without 'involvements', and was sure she had never been really in love. About the occasions when she had been got to bed she felt guilt and remorse. She had not in any way anticipated her sudden intense feelings about Duncan, protected against any such development by the fact that he was so

322

much older. She was used to him as an elderly friend, an avuncular figure, remoter than Gerard and subsidiary to him. When Tamar found herself beginning to fall in love with Duncan she was surprised, unnerved as by something weird and uncanny, then pleased, even exalted. *It*, or something very like it, had happened at last, but (and was this not, for *her*, the point?) in the most confined and fruitless way. Falling in love: to be so utterly in the *power* of someone else, all one's freedom, all one's *reality*, stolen away into another place and controlled by another person. And precisely because it was a totally blocked path (Tamar saw this later) she, immured, enchanted, gave herself up to the new sensation as to a delightful purifying painful fate. This was what she felt, briefly enough, but with a careless intensity, before the love-making. He would, of course, *never know*. She would serve and help him, would somehow (she knew not how, but perhaps this too was fated) reunite him with his wife; then retire with her secret pain which would in time be transformed into a source of untainted pleasure.

After the love-making Tamar's state of mind, which had been clear and single, even a kind of peace of mind, became a dark battlefield of incompatible emotions. To have actually taken her big animal-beloved into bed, to have hugged him in her arms and consoled him *thus*, could not but produce a mad elation which fed and fed upon an *increase* in her love. But this terrible love was now doomed and wicked. At the same time she found herself trying to continue her dream of somehow 'making it all good', for *them*, and for her. Was there not still a way, was there not always a way, to be innocent and unselfish? Apparently not, since by her *wilful* act she had done some irreparable spiritual damage, some huge damage which would have consequences for herself and others. She had lost that original and blameless Duncan whom she had held so tenderly within her reticent and silent power, giving him up forever, in return for the momentary pleasure of telling her love. And yet again, how could she have resisted, how denied him then when he begged her to love him? She would have seemed to him selfish and cowardly and cold, turning her very love into a lie, he would have felt himself rejected, he would never have forgiven her and she would never have forgiven herself. Sometimes she thought, or was tempted to think, since she regarded the idea as a consolation, that the vast 'damage' with its awful consequences was something which applied only to herself, not touching Duncan or Jean at all. Was it not the damage to her self-esteem, was it not the result of *that*, the marring of her role, that so terrified her? Whatever those larger 'consequences' might turn out to be, there were immediate baneful and hateful ones which demanded her attention. She would have to imagine Duncan's feelings and behave accordingly. She guessed that he would now be regretting the episode, would be anxious to 'cool' it, to put an end to any absurd ideas which she might harbour about it. After all he had other troubles and could persuade himself not to take her 'childish' avowals too seriously. He would rely upon her 'common sense'. Later on the matter could seem trivial. There would be no portentous sequel, his feelings would remain kindly, even affectionate, even grateful; for the present, he would distance himself. One day, when Jean was home again, he would tell her and they would smile over it. Or would he tell Jean? Tamar *hated* wondering about this, and tried to stop herself from doing so. She fully intended to assist the painful distancing process. So it was after the act, and before the terrible discovery. Tamar had trusted Duncan entirely when he said he could not have children, there had been no question of 'precautions'. Not believing the evidence of nature, she had given herself a pregnancy test chiefly as an exercise of superstition.

Now the implications of her position unfolded around her. The child was an impossibility, an abhorrence; yet it was a *child*, a real creature with, if it lived, an infinitely extended *future*: Duncan Cambus's child, *her* child. She had often heard it said that 'they' had wanted children. She had also heard it said that Jean would certainly come home. She had seen the death-misery in Duncan's face. She had imagined his joy when his wife returned. Duncan had wanted a child. Well, now he had a child.

The terrible aliveness of the child absorbed her to a degree which almost swallowed thought, as if the child were already an authoritative presence, a prince (for Tamar felt sure it was male) claiming his territory and asserting his rights. This absorption, this sense of a miraculous other being, such a source of joy to a true mother, was here torture. How could Tamar let it be known that she had Duncan's child, a revelation which would almost certainly prevent Jean's return, and would, even if Jean did return, darken that marriage ever after? Yet how could Tamar bring herself to destroy the child, the miracle-child of Duncan Cambus and Tamar Hernshaw, *her* child? Did not the sheer existence of this being make everything else trivial by comparison? Was she doomed to curse her child, to hate it, because of Duncan, because of Jean, because she lacked the special *courage* that her situation demanded? Would it be possible to conceal the child, pretend he was someone else's, have him adopted? She knew that if he lived she could never bring herself to let him go. If only she could treat it simply as a matter of *Duncan's* rights, and run to him saying, 'Here is your son.' Would he be delighted, appalled? He may once have wanted a child, but not now, and not *this* one. She thought, I've done what my mother did, *I've ruined my life*, I've got me a child by an impossible man. Oh if only I could disappear, taking the child with me, become someone else and never be heard of again! I can't gamble with the future like that, I can't *think* about it, I need more *time*, but the clock is ticking.

Would it all have to come out anyway, and if so why not confess it now? She had already told one person, the priest, Father McAlister, who had told her to keep the child and trust in God. Tamar was sure that Father McAlister would not tell anybody. But the fact that she had told him showed that she *could* tell, and might again. Of course she had not told him any details and had, in the essence of the matter, misled him, so that his advice could have little meaning for her. She had said that she did not know what was the *right* thing to do, but had not set out the problem. She had refused to discuss the father, just saying he was a student. The priest had realised, and had said as much, that she was concealing something essential, but had added that whatever the situation was, his advice was right. He wanted to see her again, and was ready to come to London, but Tamar, in a state of horror of herself, declined and fled. The unburdening did her no good, it was another thing to regret and to fear.

And now she had committed another folly, she had told Lily Boyne. She already regretted this too. She understood why she had done it, she had done it to gain time, or rather to *cheat* time. She had felt that, while she was deciding what to do, she might at least establish the details of some of the possibilities. She wanted to find out where and how one could have an absolutely private abortion and how much it would cost. Of course abortion was legal, she could have one on the Health Service, there were numerous agencies who could advise her, but these open moves would almost certainly lead to discovery. The tale she told to Lily, not without detail, was circumstantially false (she was learning how to lie), about a friend from Oxford who had suddenly turned up for one imprudent night. Tamar was not wrong in assuming that Lily 'knew all about it'. Lily had had an abortion herself, she told Tamar, and knew how the poor girl felt. She knew just the place, she even offered to pay for it, an offer which Tamar refused. She swore that she would never tell a soul, cross her heart. When Tamar went away, saying that she would think it over, she felt that by talking about abortion with Lily she had in effect made her decision. Was this what she wanted to feel, that the die was already cast? Did she really, after all that she had said to herself, *hate* her child? Today she was going back to talk to Lily again, as if this had become a significant and fruitful way of passing the time.

Lily was reclining on her sofa which she had made up as a 'day bed' with a red- and black-striped sheet and matching cushions from Liberty's. She was wearing a green light-woollen shift-dress over a white silk shirt. She had put some newly advertised oil on her hair, and her face, with little make-up, was serene. It was very warm in the flat. The curtains were pulled against the fog and all the lamps were on, although it was only three o'clock in the afternoon. Tamar had left her mother's flat soon after her arrival there, she had only come back to fetch an extra jersey and was anxious not to be detained by Gideon. She spent the interim before the time of her appointment walking round the streets, as her mother rightly guessed she did in the evenings. She ordered a sandwich in a café but was unable to eat it. She and the child walked and walked. She and the child went up in the lift to Lily's flat.

Tamar had drawn a chair up close to Lily and was sitting with her hands on her knees staring at the ground. She felt so foul, so guilty, so wretched, so torn apart by the decision which she appeared to be making, so agonisingly conscious of that piece of extra being within her, she felt she might be unable to speak. She did speak however, in a dead voice, a corpse voice, asking questions and saying the things that were necessary.

Lily, looking at Tamar, could see that she was very miserable, and was very sorry for her. At the same time, Lily could not help feeling a little cock-a-hoop, it was a feather in her cap, she felt an access of power. She thought, out of all that precious collection of bloody sages, Tamar has turned to little me! Of course, in such cases a woman runs to a woman, and Lily had a warm feeling about this act of female solidarity. She also felt a little, how could she not: how are the mighty fallen! The fact that grand perfect Tamar was in such a mess made Lily feel a bit more philosophical about her own messes. She felt important too at being trusted with such a secret, and she was happy to feel trustworthy, even wise. She thought, Tamar might have gone to Rose, but Rose would have been shocked, Rose certainly wouldn't have known where to send her, and would probably have told her to keep the wretched tot! In any case she could hardly expect Rose not to tell Gerard, and that's just where she wants to keep her image clean! Poor child!

The place which Lily recommended was a private clinic in Birmingham. (Angela Parke had been there in similar circumstances.) Tamar seemed to imagine that anything happening in London would automatically be known to *them*.

'It doesn't hurt, you know, and it's very quick. You've been sensible and acted early. You won't feel a thing. They like to keep you to rest for a day or two. Then you'll be as free as air. I can see you're feeling awful now, you're taking it hard. This is the worst time, I can tell you. You'll feel quite different when it's all over, you'll feel such *relief*, you'll be dancing and singing! See it as an illness which is going to be cured, see it as a growth you've got to get rid of. Abortion is *nothing*, it's a method of birth control. Don't be too solemn about it. It happens to all of us – well, almost all.'

'Will I have to give my name?'

'Well, some girls give false names, but that's a risk and the doctors don't like it. You'd better give your name – have you got any other name besides that funny one?'

'Yes, Marjorie.'

'Marjorie, how quaint, that's not a bit like you! I love your name, actually. You can be Marjorie Hernshaw, that sounds quite ordinary. I wonder if you might pretend to be married, say you wanted to keep it from your husband, that would put people off the track! No, better not. Anyway there'll be no track. *Don't worry!* Of course I won't breathe a single word. The whole thing will disappear into the past, it'll blow away like smoke, you'll feel clean and whole and free again.'

'Didn't you feel –' said Tamar. She could not go on. She must not think about babies thrown away with the surgical refuse, dying like fishes snatched out of their water, dying like little fishes on a white slab. Angrily she rubbed the tears from her eyes, she had no right to tears here. She stared down at the green and ivory squares on the carpet as they danced to and fro. She felt faint.

'No, I didn't!' said Lily firmly. She was not going to let Tamar's tears affect her, or make her recall her own episode as anything other than a felicitous solution of a problem. 'Nor will you, after it's done! Shall I ring up for you?'

'No!'

328

'They may not be able to do it at once, you know, and time does matter.'

'No. Lily, look, you very kindly said last time that you'd pay –'

'I will, I will –'

'I don't want that, but if it turns out to be necessary I'd be glad to borrow a little –'

Tamar, reflecting afterwards, had been dismayed at the magnitude of the sum required, which she could not see how to squeeze out of her savings. She gave most of her salary to her mother.

'Yes, of course! I suppose *he* doesn't object? Not that it matters if he does, it's your affair anyway.'

'No, he doesn't object.'

'Why can't he pay?'

'He hasn't any money.'

'Says he hasn't!'

'He's gone now, anyway.'

'Bloody men, do anything to get you, take no precautions, then when there's trouble, vanish. I bet you didn't even tell him. You must get on the pill, you know. Well, when shall we start? After all, you've made up your mind, haven't you?'

'No – not yet –'

'Tamar, darling, don't be a *fool*, don't be *sentimental*, just *think*. No man wants a girl with an illegitimate child, they regard it as a slur on their manhood to take on a girl with someone else's child. If you're trailing a kiddie it's hell to get married, it's even hell to have a lover. The chaps don't like the idea that some little darling will suddenly open the door! Anyway, what about your career, what about your job, what about your *mother*? Are you going to ask Violet to look after the little beast while you're at work? Or are you going to give up work and live at home on national assistance? Think what it'll be like year after year! The wretched infant will be miserable, it's a right recipe for misery for two. It'll hate its school, it'll hate the other kids, it'll be victimised, *you'll* be victimised. It's still like that, you know, in the, ha ha, permissive society! And if by any chance you do marry and have other children, *that* child will be an outsider. *Picture* it all, for heaven's sake! And don't imagine it's a good idea to put it off and have the child and see how you feel then, or think it's easy to have it adopted! When it's *there*, the dear little bundle, it'll all be a hundred times more agonising, besides the fact that pregnancy can be ghastly. Do you want to be carrying it around signing forms with tears streaming down your face? Then you'd have the worst of both worlds, because everyone would know! Now no one need know! For God's sake have the guts to have it done now. Do I make myself clear?'

'Yes.'

'Well then, silly, shall I ring up?'

'No.'

The bell rang from below and Lily with an exasperated grunt slithered off the sofa and went to the answer-phone. 'Who's there?' She covered the speaker. 'It's Gulliver. Shall I tell him to go to hell?'

'No, no, I'm just going anyway, I must go.'

'O K, come up,' she shouted into the 'phone, then turned to Tamar. 'Now look, child, you must come back and see me tomorrow, and tell me it's all right to go ahead. You will, won't you?'

'All right,' said Tamar.

'Come at eleven tomorrow morning.'

'Yes. Thank you.'

'Wait and say a word to Gull, he likes you, he won't think anything, if he does I'll tell him a cock and bull story, I'm good at that.' She went to open the door for Gulliver. 'Gull, Tamar's here, she's just going.'

Tamar had her coat on and had pulled her brown beret well down over her brow. 'Hello, Gull, I must run. Thanks, Lily.'

'See you tomorrow, dear.'

Tamar fled.

'What's the matter with her?' said Gulliver. 'She's been crying. What have you been doing to her?'

'Just helping her.'

'What's up?'

'Just boyfriend trouble. I've been giving sage advice.'

'How you girls do stick together,' said Gulliver affectionately. 'Are you glad to see me?'

'Yes. I've been thinking about you. You smell of cold and fog, it's a nice smell.'

'It's as black as night out there.'

'Well, it almost *is* night. I love London in winter when there's hardly any daylight at all. Where are those side-whiskers you said you'd grow?'

'I can't grow side-whiskers in two days!'

Gull, who had thrown his overcoat on the floor, was wearing a light grey suit with a dark green cardigan, and a white shirt with an orange yellow tie. He rubbed his cheek where the promised appendages were yet the merest stubble. He looked at Lily, who had picked up his coat, looking her up and down from her curiously sleek hair down to her small short-toed feet. He could see the 'old doll' look, but often now she looked to him younger. Her weak voice and tinkling laugh which had once irritated him now sounded sexy. Her sagging socks and leg-warmers looked sexy too. Dear Lily was so non-ideal, but she was there, and no one else was; and he got on so well with her, and it had occurred to him that he had rarely ever got on with anyone. His view of her had of course been considerably glorified by the skating scene, which he frequently rehearsed in waking and sleeping dreams. Last night he had dreamt that he was dancing with Lily in a palace in Japan. Well, they had danced together, in reality, at that midsummer dance, but he must have been extremely drunk and could scarcely remember.

'Let's go dancing one day,' said Lily, throwing his coat over a chair.

'You're a thought-reader. If only I could get a job.'

'You can't postpone everything till after that. I need a man in my life.'

'Well, I'm in your life –'

'Don't go away, will you.'

'But I'm no good at *anything*.'

'Let's go and stay in a hotel. I adore hotels. It might be better in a hotel, it would be more dramatic.'

'If alcohol won't do it, I'm sure drama won't. What have you done to your hair?'

'What does sex matter anyway, it's a mere technicality. Love is what matters.'

Gulliver advanced on Lily and picked her up in his arms. He had never done this before. He was gratified by his success in managing it. She was very light. He held her for a moment, then let her down slowly and held her in front of him. Surprised by his swoop, she was flushed and her pale brown eyes blinked with laughter.

'Suppose we were to get married,' said Gull, 'after I get a job?'

'Don't be *silly*!'

The next moment she said, 'Oh Gull, sometimes I feel so unhappy, there are such *awful* things in the world!' And she began to cry, weeping tears for the sorrows of the world, for Tamar and for the lost children, and for her own inability to love and be loved.

Gerard, Rose, Jenkin and Gulliver were sitting round one end of the table in the dining room at Gerard's house. Crimond had just taken his place at the other end. It was eleven o'clock in the morning. Rain had ceased, but the sky remained pale and overcast and an east wind was blowing. The room was a little chilly, Gerard's ideas of central heating being (by Fairfax standards that is) rather Spartan. To Gerard's surprise, Crimond had rung up soon after their talk to suggest that it might be a good idea after all if he were to see the *Gesellschaft* committee and explain some of his ideas, since he felt they might be under some misapprehension about the book. Gerard was agreeably surprised by this reasonableness, and looked forward to hearing some more temperate account, now that Crimond had had time to think the matter over. The others were surprised too, Rose a little nervous, all of them curious.

Gerard said, 'I am sure we are all most grateful to Crimond for coming here to tell us about his book.' After this introduction, he turned to Crimond with a gesture of invitation.

There was an uncomfortable silence. Crimond continued to stare at Gerard. Rose and Gulliver looked at the table. Jenkin looked anxiously at Gerard. Gerard looked at Crimond with an expectant look which gradually faded.

Gerard at last said, 'Well –'

At the same moment Crimond said, 'I haven't anything particular to say. I gathered that the Committee had questions to ask me. But if there are no questions –'

'I'm sorry,' said Gerard, 'of course if you'd rather answer questions we'll do it that way. Would anyone like to set the ball rolling?'

He looked round at his companions. Rose and Gulliver continued to gaze at the table. Jenkin, biting his lip, had turned toward Crimond. Silence continued, and Crimond ostentatiously closed the notebook which he had opened in front of him, and shifted his chair a little.

At last Jenkin said, 'I wonder if you could tell us your views about trade union reform?'

'You mean how to give more power to the unions?'

'I mean making them more democratic and –'

'*Democratic?*' said Crimond, staring at Jenkin, as if he had uttered some amazing foreign word.

'Of course the right to strike is fundamental –'

'I am not concerned,' said Crimond, 'with mundane details about methods of negotiation. The trade unions are naturally one of the most potent forces in the revolutionary struggle –'

'What is this "revolutionary struggle"?' said Rose, who had been blushing as she prepared to speak.

'The struggle for the revolution,' said Crimond impatiently.

'What revolution?' said Rose.

'Revolution,' said Crimond, 'is a Marxist concept –'

'We know that!' said Gulliver.

'Which envisages a total alteration of our social structure, initially involving a shift of power from one class to another –'

'You queried the word "democratic",' said Rose, 'could you tell us why?' Rose had had a haircut, and her shaggy mane, distinctly blond in the lamp light, had been thinned and reduced, revealing her brow, giving her a sterner more soldierly look. She darted, as she spoke, a glance of her dark blue eyes at Crimond, then resumed her scrutiny of the surface of the table, discovering there the faint scratches caused by Crimond's finger nails on his previous visit.

'It's an old tired concept,' said Crimond, 'and at this stage a thoroughly misleading and mystifying one –'

'So you don't believe in parliamentary democracy?' said Gulliver.

Crimond ignored Gull, continuing to look at Rose, and went on, 'What you call democracy is a rigid, inefficient, unjust and patently outmoded form of life, supported by an established pattern of violence which you appear to find invisible –'

'You would prefer an efficient one-party state, under a regime imposed by a single revolutionary group?' said Rose.

'The phrasing of your question betrays certain assumptions,' said Crimond, allowing himself, perhaps out of politeness, the faintest possible smile. 'Our present regime is "imposed", our old liberal notion of "consent" has faded away, we *know* that the gross injustice and the cowardly muddle which we see everywhere in this society *cannot be remedied*. The democratic state cannot govern, the people are in the streets – cannot you see the future in the streets of our cities? The conception of democratic parliamentary party government is now a barrier to thought which must be got rid of. The process of change itself is bringing into being new social structures which will in time embody a more positive and effective form of government by consent. Whether or not you call this one-party government is a question which will be obsolete when the transformation has taken place. And mean-

334

while – we shall be better prepared for the future if we see how terrible, how *doomed*, the present is, how much men suffer and hate, and how awful and how complete a revenge is already in preparation –'

'So you approve of terrorism?' said Gulliver.

'I don't like that emotive word,' said Crimond frowning. 'Our way of life rests upon violence, and invites it. Cases must be judged on their merits. Those who disapprove are usually those who don't care.'

'Well, I don't like your not liking the word,' said Gulliver, 'you are simply shirking the issue, and you insult us by implying that we don't care!'

'Oh, I think you are all awfully nice people,' said Crimond, looking not at Gull but at Gerard, 'who imagine that the nice weather will last your life-time. I think you are wrong.'

Gerard, adopting a calm reflective tone designed to cool the rising temperature, intervened. 'But your kind of "transformation" has already been tried, it leads to tyranny, to arrangements which are *far more* rigid and unjust and inefficient! We are imperfect, but we are a free open tolerant society governed by democratic process and law, we don't have to destroy ourselves to make changes, we are changing all the time, and mostly for the better, if you compare fifty years ago! Are we to throw all this away in return for some chimerical hypothetical utopia set up by a few activists after a violent revolution? You told me you weren't in touch with the working-class movement, you spoke just now of "mundane details" which didn't concern you, I think you're a solitary theorist, having interesting ideas, but nothing to do with real problems of power, or how societies really alter –'

'I don't believe he's out of touch,' said Gulliver, 'and I don't believe he's solitary either. He wants to smash this society. That's the only thing his lot can do, and that's real enough.'

'Your whole picture of western civilisation is a "theory",' said Crimond to Gerard. 'Your whole way of life supports poverty and injustice, behind your civilised relationships there's a hell of misery and violence. What do dissidents do when they come to the west? They grieve, they fade, they find it all utterly hateful, they can *see* it. There's something called history, I don't just mean a concept invented by Hegel or Marx or perhaps Herodotus, I mean a deep strong relentless process of social change. *That* is what you simply refuse to notice. You think reality is ultimately good, and as you think you're good too you feel safe. You value yourselves because you're English. You live on books and conversation and mutual admiration and drink – you're all alcoholics – and sentimental ideas of virtue. You have no energy, you are lazy people. The real heroes of our time are those who are brave enough to let go of the old dreamy self-centred self-satisfied morality and the old imperialistic moral person who was monarch of all he surveyed! For instance, we have to learn to live with machines, to *think* about how to live with machines, with computers, with information theory, with physics – the old complacent liberal individual is already lost, he's a fake, he's finished, he cannot constitute a value –'

'Oh stop!' said Rose. She was trembling with anger. 'You've sold your soul to –'

'Yes, I've sold it,' said Crimond, 'and I'm proud to have sold it, what's the use of a soul, that gilded idol of selfishness! I've sold it, and I'm going to *do something* with the power which I've got in exchange. That is the essence of the new world and its new being. You all idolise your souls, that is yourselves. Ask whom you identify with, that will tell you your place and your class. The people of this planet are not like you, *they* must be served, *they* must be saved, the hungry sheep look up and are not fed –'

'You're poisoning them!' said Gulliver.

'Your "people" are abstractions,' said Rose, 'they're just a vague idea that feeds your sense of power, your sort of Marxism is old and done for, that's what's finished! You're not a new sort of person, you're just an old-fashioned insolent power maniac who thinks he's superman! You say the individual doesn't exist – what about people who are starving in Africa –?'

'Your morality is sentiment,' said Crimond, 'I don't say it's worthless, but it's mainly a matter of cherishing your conscience. You're awfully keen on ecology and helping animals, you deplore famine and you send a cheque, you deplore violence, then you can forget it for a while, you don't want to look at the real causes of what's wrong with the world. Why can't we feed the planet, why are almost all human beings mere shreds of what they might be? There's a huge human potential, a higher finer stronger human consciousness, a whole adventure of our species which hasn't even started yet! And of course there are problems to be solved, which you don't ever conceive of, let alone think about!'

'This is too much,' said Rose, 'now you're saying things simply to offend us!'

'You're not very polite to me, if it comes to that. You asked me to come here. You can't think of any way of answering me, you can't even engage in intelligent conversation about my ideas, so you get angry!'

'You say we value being English,' said Gull. 'You've evidently got an inferiority complex about being Scottish, and not even a Highlander! I hate your ideas.'

'Well, I hate yours,' said Crimond, 'and you seem to hate everything since you lost your boyish charm.'

'Crimond –!' said Gerard.

Rose said, 'I hate bullies, and you're one!'

Crimond said, 'You all envy me because I can think, I can work, I can concentrate, I can write. All you can do is puff with indignation.'

Jenkin, who had for some time been looking down at a piece of paper which Gull had passed him which read *Vile hateful* CHARLATAN, said, 'Look, David, it won't do.'

Crimond said, 'What won't do? Exchanging insults? I entirely agree. I'm just going.'

'No, I mean your whole position. There's a large lie in it somewhere.'

'Oh I daresay. But there are no hard surfaces in your world. To shift things you have to exaggerate a bit!'

'You've evidently decided not to finish your book, because

you know it's no bloody good and you're afraid to show it!' said Gulliver.

'The only one of you who's worth tuppence ha'penny is Jenkin,' said Crimond, getting up, 'and he's a fool. By the way, I had better tell you that I've just finished the book, so you needn't pay me any more money, if that's what you're worrying about.'

Crimond had gone. Rose was in tears. Gerard had brought in some sherry, to which Gulliver was helping himself. Jenkin was standing at the window looking out at the yellowish haze outside.

'Talk about home truths!' said Gull, who was feeling ashamed of having lost his temper and angry that he had let' Crimond taunt him. The sherry was making him less ashamed and more angry.

Gerard who had been walking up and down was now sitting beside Rose who had buried her mouth and nose in a handkerchief. Rose was angry with Gerard. Emerging, she chided him. 'Why did you let that happen, why did you let them shout at each other?'

'You shouted too,' said Gulliver.

'Crimond didn't shout,' said Gerard, 'he let us do that! Of course it won't do, but he won the match.'

'I don't think he won the match,' said Gulliver, 'I wish I'd kicked him down the road. But fancy the book being finished! I wonder if it really is?'

'Of course it is, if he says so. I must ring up and tell Duncan.'

'Why did he come here then?' said Rose. 'He must have come simply to attack us. What extraordinary spite! Not a word of gratitude.'

'I believe he really came to try to explain the book. We should have been less aggressive at the start. You're right, Rose, it's my fault, I should have taken charge, I should have thought out what to say, we ought to have discussed it beforehand.'

'Why the hell should we –' said Gull.

'But, Gerard, you had that talk with him, you knew what kind of thing he was likely to say. Why did you get us all here so that he could throw mud at us?'

'What he said today was a caricature of what he said to me. The whole thing is funny in a way.'

'It's a joke I can't see.'

'He was putting on an act, he wanted to chill our blood, he wanted to frighten us.'

'Well, he didn't frighten me, he just annoyed me very much,' said Rose, blowing her nose, 'And our side didn't exactly distinguish itself. I think he was in deadly earnest. I wonder if he's actually mad? There's something awfully creepy about him.'

'He's certainly a fanatic,' said Gerard. 'His ancestors were Calvinists. He believes in magic.'

'So Calvinists believe in magic?' said Gull.

'Yes. Instant salvation.'

'He's got some sort of awful death wish,' said Rose. 'I think he's murderous, he's callous, he doesn't think people are real.'

'He said to me that people are puppets or will be.'

'There you are.'

'What do you think, Jenkin?' said Gerard to Jenkin's back.

Jenkin returned from the window and sat down beside Rose. 'Rose, dear, don't be distressed. Of course he's in earnest, but Gerard's right, he was play-acting to startle us!'

'Well, what *do* you think?' said Rose crossly.

'I'm *longing* to see the book.'

'But if it's all tosh like that –'

'Oh, it won't be tosh, it'll be deep – but I wish I could have explained.'

'Why didn't you then?' said Gerard. 'If you'd only condescended to enter the conversation a bit earlier –!'

'I couldn't think how to put it, and you were all being so talkative – I wish I could – see *exactly* how – all his stuff – is based on a mistake . . .'

'You said a lie,' said Gerard.

'Yes – well – a lie – that's what one hates – still he may be right in a way that –'

'That what?'

'That one has to exaggerate.'

They left one by one, Jenkin first though Gerard tried to detain him, then Gulliver who was (only of course he didn't say so) going to have lunch with Lily and tell her everything that had happened, then Rose who wanted Gerard to have lunch with her, only he declined. When he had given them a suitable start Gerard left the house himself. Patricia and Gideon were in Paris at the Signorelli exhibition, so Gerard did not have to flee them, but he wanted to be outside and walk, sit in a pub and have a sandwich, think it all over.

He walked for some time in the chilly haze, panting out his moist breath, letting the cold air take him by the throat. He felt displeased with himself for not having controlled the meeting, but he felt too a curious exhilaration. So the book was finished; he longed to read it, but he dreaded it too. What did he fear – that it would be very bad, or that it would be very good? He found himself feeling sorry that the book was finished, as if it were the end of an era, the relaxing of a tension which had had some life-giving resonance. What nonsense. And, today, what a lot of rhetoric and demagoguery, and, when one reflected, rather childish panache! Yet what a curious being, was it after all so surprising that Jean Kowitz was this man's slave? It flashed on Gerard's mind that Crimond was a changeling, a mischievous destructive airy spirit, who visited the earth like Halley's comet every so many years, perhaps every hundred, perhaps every thousand, not a great spirit, no doubt a small one, one of many, but a daemon, who seized ruthlessly upon a woman suitable to be his mate, and (so Gerard's fantasy went on) upon his departure killed her, or by the withdrawal of his power simply brought about her death, then vanishing in a puff of smoke or a revolver shot. A daemon who could, who knows, actually mediate with other, higher, stronger powers.

Some children were singing Christmas carols in a doorway.

The haze was merging into a heavier thicker yellow light which would now persist until dark. Gerard felt full of energy. Was it possible he had actually enjoyed being denounced by Crimond?

Violet searched the flat several times before she rang Gerard's number to say that her daughter had gone mad, and had now disappeared. The sequence of events was as follows. Violet had of course, as she told Gideon, been noticing for some time that Tamar was not eating, was in a state of anxiety, was perhaps heading for a depression. Her feelings about this state of affairs, though not by any means as callous as those she had expressed to Gideon, were certainly mixed. Part of her was actually pleased to see her daughter unhappy, the same part which would have been affronted to see her happy. There was, to this way of thinking, a sort of justice in a miserable Tamar, and of injustice in a joyful Tamar. Nor was Violet, in another part, indifferent to Gideon's suggestion that she might be blamed for letting Tamar descend into depression, even perhaps into suicide. She did not want to be so blamed. She wanted to be the victim, not the killer. That Violet did not believe Tamar's sufferings to be all that serious was perhaps due to yet another part of Violet's mind which cared for Tamar as her possession, her product, indeed her daughter. Someone who maintained (as Gideon did for instance) that in spite of all appearances Violet really loved Tamar would have been telling a partial truth. Violet did have an affection for her daughter, and this helped her to believe that no serious trouble was involved, that Tamar was just going through a phase, or putting on an act.

Tamar's apparent affliction came to a sort of crisis when she announced to Violet that she was going away for several days. Where? She couldn't say. Why? Her employers wanted her to have some field experience with the travellers who visited the bookshops. She would, with others who made the arrangements, be staying at hotels, she did not know where. No, she would not have to pay for the hotels. After that she was absent for several days. Violet did not believe this story, which she tested, after Tamar's departure, by an anonymous telephone call to the publishers, who told her that Miss Hernshaw was unwell and at home. Violet, musing on this, decided that Tamar had gone off with a young man. This idea made Violet exceedingly uneasy, in fact she hardly dared to entertain it, and comforted herself by feeling sure that Tamar would soon return, as glum and as passively docile as ever. It was the time after Tamar's reappearance that convinced Violet that her daughter had gone mad, and not quietly mad but raving mad.

Tamar, arriving in the afternoon, did not speak to her mother or answer her questions or even look at her. She went straight to her bedroom, took off her coat and her shoes, and lay on the bed, ceaselessly weeping and moaning and mumbling to herself, and tossing to and fro, and uttering little hysterical screams. When Violet brought her some coffee and a sandwich she rejected them with such violence that everything fell on the floor. She tore at the sheets and stuffed them in her mouth. She lay thus crying and moaning from daylight into night, and was still wailing when Violet (who managed to sleep a little from exhaustion) woke in the morning. The sheer strength and energy of Tamar's grief made it seem mad, surely a creature must be insane to utter such terrible sounds so continuously; there is something called insane strength and, as it seemed to Violet, this was it. She went out to telephone the doctor. When she came back Tamar had vanished.

Gerard's number did not answer. Gerard had gone to the British Museum, Gideon was at his new gallery, Patricia was out buying Egyptian cotton sheets at Harrods' sale. Violet then rang Rose. Rose was in, and was suitably impressed and alarmed. No, Tamar was not with her and she had no notion where she might be. As Violet was in a telephone box, Rose said she would continue the search by telephone, Violet should go home and wait and not worry, Tamar would probably come back soon. Rose rang Jenkin who was duly upset too, but did not know where the vanished child might be. No, he did not think they should start informing the police just yet. Rose said she would ring him back if she got any news. Then she rang Duncan who sounded agitated and surprised, but could not help. He asked Rose to be sure to let him know when Tamar turned up, he thought Violet was probably being neurotic and irrational as usual. After that Rose rang Gerard's number again, in vain, and Gulliver's number, but Gull was out applying for a job. After that she rang Lily.

Lily answered, asked Rose to hang on for a moment, then murmured into the telephone that yes, Tamar was with her, she was perfectly all right, but *please* do *not* let anyone come round. Lily then rang off abruptly. Rose rang Jenkin and Duncan. Jenkin said he would take a taxi to Violet to tell her Tamar was all right. Rose said she was going round to Lily.

As Lily's she rang the bell and announced her name. After an interval Lily came down to the front door, opened it a crack, and said 'Yes?' in a hostile manner. In answer to Rose's anxious questions she replied that Tamar was *all right*, was *not ill*, was resting, and please could they be left alone, sorry. The door closed and Rose went home puzzled and anxious, and telephoned Gerard who was still out.

Tamar was of course not at all 'all right' and could almost be described as mad. The operation was over, the inconvenient embryo was gone. But the sense of relief and liberation prophesied by Lily had not come about. Tamar went into the clinic as one in a dream, walking like an automaton with glazed eyes. She came out all aware, all raw anguished tormented consciousness. She saw now, *now* when it was so dreadfully absolutely just too late, that she had committed a terrible crime, against Duncan, against herself, against the helpless fully-formed entirely-present human being whom she had wantonly destroyed. She had condemned herself to a lifetime of bitter remorse and lying. She was sentenced to think of that lost child every day and every hour for the rest of time, the child, *that* child, that unique precious murdered child would be part of every picture she could ever frame of the world, and she would have to keep this appalling secret forever, until she was old, except that she would never be old, she would die of grief. Why had she done it, why had she *hastened* into such an act, longing for it to be over, longing for

344

the relief, as if there could be such relief, not foreseeing the horror of it, now that the child was dead, as dead and senseless and swept away as the drowned cat she had seen in the river at Boyars as an omen of death? At the clinic, weeping not yet screaming, she had been given sleeping pills and had slept and dreamed of the child, who would now be in every dream, a sinister revengeful accuser turning all rest into nightmare. Now sleep seemed impossible except as some awful brief interlude of haunted fantasy. Awake at night she fancied that she could hear a child crying. She had to suffer consciously, turning and twisting like one impaled. The priest had said she was in mourning – yes, she had been in mourning for the creature that she was going to kill.

The sight of her mother filled her with loathing. Her mother had wanted to kill her, lack of money not lack of will had brought Tamar into the world. If only Lily had not been there, Lily with her money and her worldly wisdom and her false enticing consolations. Tamar could have had longer to think about the deed which had now slipped with such terrible ease out of the future into the past. Tamar detested Lily, she detested Gerard, who had sent her to Duncan like a lamb to the slaughterhouse, sent her thoughtlessly, using her, sacrificing her, for his own purpose, to salve his own conscience, to exhibit his own power, casting her into deadly peril. She detested Rose and Jenkin and the whole sickening conspiracy of complacent 'well-wishers', who saw and understood nothing, smiling painlessly through life, breathing the perfumed air of their own self-satisfaction. She detested Duncan who had wantonly, carelessly, for the sake of an instant of weak comfort, for a little easy bit of sex, given her the deadly virus which would make her life a living death. Her youth was not only blackened and blasted, it was *over*. Now her face would wrinkle, her limbs would ache and stiffen, she would hobble, she would hunch, she would become old, so dreadful was the illness with which he had infected her. And yet – and this was a further twist of anguish – Tamar could not detest Duncan, she loved Duncan, and recalled with awful clarity that exalted feeling of pure virtuous suffering which she had experienced so little a while ago when she had felt herself so easily, so sweetly, falling in love with Duncan, when she had felt a pure selfless love which was to be a secret forever. Oh if only she could get back to *that* pain, *that* suffering, *that* secret, for such pain was joy and such a secret heaven. Now she had a secret which would consume her, gut her, over which she would bend wailing as over a black burden. Well, she would have to die soon, no being could continue in this pain, she would starve to death, or form in her emptied womb a cancer to destroy her.

Tamar knew well enough too that in choosing her adviser she had chosen her path. She had *wanted* to be told what Lily told her, and to hear it uttered in exactly Lily's tone, that tone of easy worldly cheerfulness which made little of the act as if it were a casual obvious matter, just another form of contraception, something which 'happened to everyone'. Dulled, drugged, by a false promise, and because she had been unable to face the dreadful pain of her dilemma, the pain of indecision, she had not had the courage required to *wait* and to *think*, she had killed Duncan's child, his only child, the child he had wanted and yearned for all his life. She had done it, as it had seemed, for Duncan's sake, for Jean's sake, for the sake of a rotten doomed marriage, and so as not to be disgraced in the eyes of people such as Gerard and Rose who now meant nothing to her, she had done it for *nothing*. Infinitely more important, more precious, more life-giving and life-saving, it seemed now, was the being of that miracle child, a blessing, a God-sent gift, to Duncan, to herself, perhaps even to Jean. Only Jean did not matter, she hated Jean too. How easily, she thought, she could have weathered that storm, she and the child in a boat together, as she saw them so clearly, riding brave-eyed over the waves. She and the child setting out upon their happy free *good* life together. And in the end everyone would have helped them, everyone would have been so kind. But the child was dead, or even worse, changed into a wicked deadly demon, black with resentment and anger, living on as a horrible filthy ghost, dedicated to punishing its murderous mother, lethal to any other child who might, from that accursed womb, succeed it and live. Tamar's sense of the reality of *that* hate, *that* curse, was one of the most dreadful parts of the future existence which she saw stretching away before her. She had killed the good child, the true child, and created a venomous wicked thing, formed out of her own wickedness, an envious jealous killer, living upon the darkness of her own blood. The thought that this evil child would kill her future children, would not let them live, or more cruelly would cripple them with foul sickness, with deformity, with insanity, coexisted for Tamar with the sense that she herself would not now live long, was beyond the reach of reason and love, was as darkened and solitary as if she had been immured in a bricked-up cell and left to a certain imminent yet torturingly slow death.

Tamar, who was lying on the sofa, quiet for a while with her face hidden, while Lily was playing, or trying to play, patience at the table, began again to moan quietly, saying 'Oh, oh, oh,' over and over again. Then in a convulsion she wailed and turned onto her face, tearing at the cushions and thrusting them into her mouth. Lily was appalled and terrified by Tamar's condition, she had never witnessed such grief and did not know what to do. She heartily wished she had never received that wretched confidence or got so blithely and thoughtlessly involved in this drama which was turning into a nightmare. She saw *now* that she ought not to have hustled Tamar into a decision whose consequences, as she ought to have realised, were so uncertain. She had said what she thought Tamar wanted to hear, and done what she thought Tamar wanted done. Now it was as if she too were implicated in some awful, perhaps disastrous guilt. Of course *no one must know*, she had said again and again since Tamar's arrival that she would never breathe a word, never utter a hint, Tamar's secret was safe with her, and so on. But Tamar herself, her condition of near insanity, of frightful perhaps deathly illness, *that* could not be concealed. Tamar showed no signs of recovery and Lily had elicited screams from her guest at the suggestion that a doctor should be sent for. It was equally, indeed even more, impossible to ask for help from *them*. There was no one for Lily to turn to or whose advice or help she could ask. Even Gull, who had discovered from Jenkin that Tamar was with Lily and had rung up, had to be put off with a vague story. Lily had felt unable to lie to Rose, though she now wished she had put a calmer face on the matter. Besides, Violet had to be told that Tamar was 'all right'. And now they were all tactfully keeping away! Oh God. I'll *have* to get a doctor, thought Lily, I *must* have some help, I can't be responsible for all this by myself. Oh I do blame myself so much, I was just pleased when she came to me, I felt superior because I could help, I was glad because she had confided in me and not in them. Oh why ever did I get myself involved in this ghastly business and how will it end!

Lily's burden of remorse was meanwhile intensified by the vindictiveness of the reproaches which, in intervals of moaning and wailing, Tamar was now heaping upon her.

'Why did you send me off to that place, why didn't you let me wait, you kept saying how I had to hurry, you made it all seem so easy, you said how wonderful it would be afterwards, if only I'd waited, even a day or two, I'd have felt differently, I'd have thought about what it meant, but you hustled me on, you said it had to be, and now I've ruined my life, I've destroyed everything, and it's all your fault –'

'I can't sleep, I can't *sleep*,' said Crimond. Jean was at her wits' end. She was weeping tears, death tears, weeping for her life, for the happiness which she now felt that she would never have.

Crimond paid no attention to her tears, he seemed by now to be talking to himself.

Earlier he had been reading poetry to her, some poetry in Greek which he seemed unaware that she could not understand. He had sometimes read her Greek before, but only a little at a time and had translated it. Now the reading was different, going on and on more like a liturgy or an exorcism. That in itself had been a relief.

Jean had not expected the book to be finished, she had assumed that the book was to be lived with for a long time, perhaps for many years yet. She was used to it, used to willing it and loving it as a part of Crimond's mystery. When he suddenly said, 'It is finished', she was taken completely by surprise. She now remembered Crimond's baleful remarks which she had not taken too seriously at the time. She was afraid; how would Crimond live without the book, what would he do, how would he be, was it some *complete* change? Of course, she supposed, he would have after-thoughts, think of addenda, there would probably be a long period of transition. His state of euphoria reassured her for a while. He told her, making it into a joke, how he had dumbfounded Gerard and his friends by his sudden announcement. He had indeed told *them* before, though only just before, he told *her*. She did not mind that. As, for a day or two, his cheerfulness continued, there was a quiet new 'sense of being on holiday', and Jean allowed all sorts of ordinary happy thoughts, which she had carefully and dutifully inhibited, to come out of their seclusion and throng gaily in her head. She thought, she even *said*, and he did not contradict her, 'We'll go away now, shall we, we'll have a break, we'll go to Rome or Venice, we'll see some lovely places together, won't we, my darling, we'll escape together and be so happy, that's what we'll do!'

Crimond did not say no, he said nothing, but it later seemed to her that he had simply not heard, not listened, was wrapped up entirely inside himself, first into that vague, stunned rather uncanny cheerfulness, and now into a restless desperation.

The book was gone. Crimond's big jersey, his pen and ink, his glasses, the shawl which he put over his knees when working, were all neatly in their places on his desk and chair. But the lamp was switched off, the piles of coloured notebooks had gone, carried off to Crimond's typing agency who would now photocopy, then type, the entire work. Crimond took some care over these arrangements, but betrayed no anxiety when the numerous boxes were carried away up the stairs and put in a van. Since then he had not sat at the desk, but at a table in the front room upstairs, reading, or dealing with correspondence. He had also cleared out the cupboards in the playroom, destroyed a lot of manuscript, and also brought out and cleaned three of his guns, two revolvers and a pistol. He told Jean that he had sold the rest of his collection, and was now going to sell these. At least this, if he meant it, was a good sign, and Jean counted it, at first, as marking the beginning of their 'new world'. She watched him anxiously during the first days, glad when he was quietly reading, quietly talking. She questioned him about the book, had he expected to end it, would the typescript need a lot of revision? He gave vague smiling replies. Sometimes he craved her company and even walked with her to some shops. She suggested that she should drive him somewhere, anywhere, in her car which needed exercise and he said, yes, perhaps, why not. Then the mood of despair came upon him and he began to talk about death.

At night, sleepless, and preventing her from sleeping, he held her, without love-making, exceedingly close as if his whole body were feeding upon hers. Jean was exhausted, frightened, worn out by an intensity of love, his love, her love, which sometimes seemed something so *final* that she found herself thinking, somehow or other we are done for. How will it end? Their condition seemed to be crowding on toward some disaster. Yet at other times, when Crimond seemed to be gripped by a kind of elation, she felt that the despair was just an understandable phase which was even now passing. Last night, clasped together, they had slept a little.

'You *did* sleep, didn't you?'

'Oh yes –'

The morning sun was shining into the little kitchen where they took their meals. Its neatness, its cleanness, about which Jean cared very much, made her feel that ordinary life was possible. If she could only stop Crimond from saying the extraordinary things with which he was wearing down her sanity.

'Won't you have some toast?'

'No, just coffee.'

'You are eating less and less.'

Crimond said nothing now but stared at her for a while, his face composed but his blue eyes extremely wide and rounded.

'My darling, I'm sure you'll sleep even better tonight, we *must* sleep, you're suffering from lack of it, I'll hold you, I'll look after you, I'll give you my life –'

'There is no logic in fearing death,' said Crimond, 'I just don't want to make a terrible mistake.'

'Please stop this sort of talk.'

'It's not all that easy to shoot oneself, one could find oneself living on blinded or witless. It's a terrible risk. I could be sure of killing you, but not so sure of killing myself. The hand can tremble, the bullet can find some freakish path, leaving one paralysed, still alive. Oh the horror of that –' He spoke quite calmly, reflectively.

'Fortunately you don't have to shoot either yourself or me! Here's your coffee.'

'I don't want to see you dead, my Jeanie, we must go together.'

'Let us go to France together, let us go anywhere away from here. Let me take you away for a while. You'll get over it all, this state of mind will pass.'

'I don't see how it can,' said Crimond, in a reasonable tone as if some quite ordinary project were being discussed.

'What about your father –'

'He's dead.'

'You didn't tell me.'

'He died at the end of October. I'm glad he's gone. He was no longer himself. His being was anguish to me. Now he is at peace.'

'I'm sorry.'

'Don't be sorry.'

'Oh my dear – you'll write another book.'

'I think my life's work is over.'

'Don't you want to see this one published, to hear people discussing it?'

'No. It will be misunderstood.'

'Then shouldn't you be there to explain it?'

'*Explain* it? The idea is loathsome.'

'*Please* try to get out of this awful mood. We must just *go on*, we'll go on together, we love each other, just be *brave* enough – I'll do everything you want. I'll make your happiness, I'll *invent* it, I'll go out shopping now and buy you a honeycomb, I know how much you like that –'

'Oh my sweet being! You'll get me a honeycomb! Ah, if it was only as simple as that –!'

'But, Crimond, it *is*.' Jean, leaning across the table, tried to take his hand, but he drew it back, still staring at her with his calm face.

'Jean, do you want to go back to your husband, back to Duncan, you love him, don't you?'

'Oh my God – you think I'll go back to Duncan one day and you want to kill me before it happens! Don't be crazy and drive me crazy! You *know* I don't love him, I love *you*. Look at me, I'm sane, I'm steady as a rock, I love you and I'll *look after* you forever.'

'You could go back to him and live.'

'And leave you to shoot yourself. Just stop *romancing*, you're just doing it to torment me, to say it's all my fault. If I wasn't here would you be talking about death?'

'No, but that's your gift to me – you are the motive, the blessing, the gift from heaven, the best the gods ever sent me. You make death possible.'

'I don't understand you. You are being perfectly hateful today.'

'You are my weakness. Now that the book is gone there is nothing left but our love, our vulnerability to each other, if we go on we shall destroy each other in some small unworthy way – I want it to be something glorious, worthy of our love, that is courage, that is eternal life.'

'This is sickening romantic nonsense,' she said, 'and you don't believe a word of it! If you just want to get rid of me, say so! Is it a sort of trial, if I pass the test I die, if I fail you leave me? Surely there are simpler solutions!'

'Why be the slaves of time? Jeanie, it's a short walk, this life. Why do people value it so? We have our great love, it is something timeless, let us die in our love, inside it, together, as if we were going to bed –'

'Stop, my darling,' said Jean, who felt the tears coming to her eyes. 'You are tiring me out. I've been trying – so hard – to be sane and strong for you –'

'It's best to choose one's exit.'

'I'm not in a fit state to decide to die, and neither are you!'

'Jeanie, I want us to die together.'

'Oh, fine – but how –?'

'On the Roman Road.'

'*What?*'

'You know, down at Boyars. Oh Jeanie, my love, don't fail me –'

'What do you mean?'

'It's a long straight road – at a high speed – two cars could meet . . .'

Gerard, leaving the British Museum at lunch time, rang up Jenkin and learnt from him that Tamar was upset about something and was at present at Lily's place and said to be 'all right'. Jenkin, just back from his visit to Violet, saw no point, since the situation seemed so obscure, in alarming Gerard. Gerard, with other things on his mind, was not alarmed. He arranged to come round to Jenkin's place about eight thirty that evening for a drink. He had lunch in a pub, and then went into St James's Park and sat down on a seat near the lake to think. He felt very strange, excited, frightened. He found himself trembling. He was not sure whether or not he liked this state of mind, or whether or not he approved of it. The two scenes with Crimond, his own private confrontation and Crimond's counter-attack on the *Gesellschaft*, had not yet exhausted their shock waves, and he found himself dwelling on remembered details in both scenes which inspired a disturbing mixture of emotions. Sitting bolt upright on the seat in the park he smiled, then frowned, then bit his lip, then shook his head, then shuddered. An acquaintance, Peter Manson's sister, passed by and recognised him but did not greet him because (as she explained when her brother rang up from Athens) 'he looked so peculiar'. The sun was shining. There had been a heavy frost and many of the more shaded places still carried a thick sugary crystalline sprinkling upon leaves and grass. The seat was wet and Gerard was sitting on his copy of *The Times*. The air was very cold. The sun was already declining and lights had come on in the pinnacled and turreted offices in Whitehall which looked in the glowing light like fairy palaces. The excitements, pleasant, unpleasant, interesting, stirred up in Gerard's mind by Crimond's antics, were curiously mixing with his thoughts, or more evidently his feelings, about Jenkin. He had confronted Crimond and certainly not come off best. Now, in a very different way, he was proposing to confront Jenkin. He would clarify things, he would ask awkward questions, he would have it all out at last; and again the rather unnerving idea occurred to him that although he had known Jenkin long and knew him well, he did not really know him very well.

As Gerard sat so upright looking out across the water some children were feeding the ducks. Some big Canada geese had come along too, lumbering out of the water and raising their great powerful beaks for bits of bread. The feet of the children and the feet of the birds left tracks in the thin frost which still coated the asphalt pathway. The forecast was rain but the weather was very quiet and relentlessly cold as if it could never change. Gerard felt frightened. He was afraid, when he saw Jenkin, of talking too much. In such a situation a few ill-chosen words, words which could never be recalled, could be remembered for a long time. I must be cool and clear-headed, thought Gerard, I must try to concentrate upon some central point which is incapable of being misunderstood. The idea of a sort of reassurance. Just not to go away. But really – what could be more ambiguous and indeed ridiculous? Jenkin would be surprised and embarrassed, as he would be by anything resembling an affirmation of love; and then perhaps, later on, feel annoyed, disgusted, alienated. It might all seem to him weird, even creepy, certainly uncalled-for. Then Gerard would be biting his hands off with remorse, while Jenkin gallantly tried to pretend that 'nothing had happened'. The risks were terrible – but they were terrible either way. How dreadfully he might accuse himself later of having done nothing. Over a long time love-and-friendship love can be so taken for granted that it becomes almost invisible. Its substance thins and needs to be renewed, it must at intervals be reasserted. Suppose Jenkin were to go away (and, awful thought, find *someone else*, a woman, or a man) partly because he had never really understood how highly Gerard valued him? I wish I'd said something earlier, thought Gerard, something spontaneous and intuitive. Now it's all become so damned abstract and formal and solemn – I'll scare him stiff while I'm fumbling to begin.

It was nine o'clock. The promised rain had come. Gerard, taken unawares, had got his hair wet, which annoyed him. He had arrived punctually. Jenkin had put the gas fire on earlier and closed the window in the sitting room and pulled the curtains and turned on the lamp and remembered to turn off the centre light. He had brought in from the kitchen window sill a brown mug with a single twig of viburnum fragrans which Mrs Marchment had given him out of her front garden when he had been to see Marchment about a letter to the *Guardian* and to gossip about Crimond. He had put a plate of arrowroot biscuits upon the small table on which Gerard had now set down his glass. Jenkin was drinking tea. He was, he told Gerard (which much disturbed the latter) 'cutting down on drink'. Gerard was drinking the wine which he had brought

355

along himself as usual. They had been talking about Crimond's book.

'It's being typed now, Marchment says. He's still on speaking terms with Crimond. Hardly anyone else is.'

'You haven't seen Crimond?'

'No. Do sit down, Gerard.'

'I wonder who will publish it.'

'I don't know. We might get hold of a proof copy. I'm *dying* with curiosity.'

'What's that plant? It smells so.'

'Viburnum something.'

'It's got no business being in flower at this time of year.'

'It always is, I'm told. Shall I take it away?'

'No. Where did you get this stone?'

'I told you, Rose gave it to me.'

'I remember.' Gerard replaced the stone, which he had been holding in his hand, upon the mantelpiece. The stone was curiously cold. He sat down. He said to Jenkin, 'I've been thinking about you.'

'Oh – jolly good –'

'Are you going away?'

'Yes, I'm going to Spain for Christmas, on a package tour, I told you at Boyars.'

'I thought you'd be with us. Now it's possible for the first time, with my father gone.'

'I'm sorry –'

'But I mean – are you really going away, far away, for a long time? You've seemed so restless, not yourself.' Gerard thought, what am I saying, it's I who am restless and not myself. He added, 'Not that I've any reason to think – after all why should you –'

'Oh, I'm *thinking* of it,' said Jenkin, as if this was obvious.

'Where to?'

'I don't know, really – Africa, South America – I sort of think – after all – I want to get out of England and do something else, something different.'

'What you sort of think sounds to me like running away,'

356

said Gerard. 'It's sentimental, it's romantic. You're just feeling a bit fed up with schoolmastering. It's too late for you to take on the African mess or the South American mess, it's a lifetime job. You can't be serious!'

'I'm not thinking of being an expert or a leader or anything –'

'Of course not, you see yourself as a servant, the lowest of the low! But an untrained servant not in his first youth is not likely to be much use. You just enjoy picturing yourself in some scene of awful suffering! Aren't I right?'

'Why are you being so nasty?' said Jenkin amiably. 'I can dream, can't I? But I am serious about it – somehow – not because I think I'd be terribly good at it –'

'Then why?'

'Just because I want to. Of course there's something in your idea of the "picture", but that's peripheral, I can't be bothered with motives.'

'I know, you want to be out on the edge of things, you want to live outside Europe in some sort of hell.'

'Yes.'

'And you think that isn't romantic nonsense?'

'Precisely. I mean, I think it isn't romantic nonsense!'

'I ask you not to go.'

'Why? I just said I was thinking about it!'

'We need you. I need you.'

'Oh, well – you can all rub along without me, I should think – anyway it's an idea I've got – it's time for a change – I can always come back I suppose. I think I'll have a drink after all.' Jenkin disappeared to the kitchen, humming nervously to himself.

Gerard, seeing his back, the set of his shoulders, the particular way that the tail of his jacket was always so hopelessly crumpled, felt a wave of emotion which almost made him exclaim. He thought, this is no good, I'm not getting anywhere. I've bothered him already, and I hate that. He'll refuse to be serious now about anything I suggest, he'll just shuffle it off.

Jenkin returned with a glass and a can of beer. Gerard said,

'Let's go on holiday together, just you and me, it's ages since we did that.' And why is it ages, he wondered, I could have asked him anytime, I could have insisted.

'You mean a walking tour in the Lake District, sharing a tent in the rain?'

'No. I was rather thinking of a good hotel in Florence.' But the tent idea was not unattractive.

'OK, if I'm still around in the spring. But I somehow think I won't be. I've got that now-or-never feeling.'

'We could travel together. Go to Australia. Go to Africa if you like, or Brazil. I noticed that Portuguese grammar at Boyars. If you're determined to go I might come too.'

'Very kind of you, but you'd hate it, you know! I mean if we went where *I* want. Anyway, I have to go alone, that's part of the deal.'

'What deal, who with?'

'Oh, not with anyone – with myself – with fate if you like – or God, only he doesn't exist.'

'So it's a pilgrimage. That's pure sentimentality, it's play-acting.'

'You're making me say silly things. I just don't want to be too blunt!'

'Oh, be as blunt as you like!'

What is happening, thought Gerard, are we going to *quarrel*, or have I been imagining how fond he was of me, have I been quite mistaken? I can't say the things I meant to say now, they've been spoiled, ruined. He'll think ill of me now, and I can't bear that, in a moment I shall be pathetic! Or in order not to be pathetic, I shall seem resentful. Which is worse?

'I don't think you lot need me all that much,' said Jenkin in a tentative tone. 'I've always felt like the odd man out.' He had never said anything like that before.

'What perfect nonsense!' said Gerard, regaining a little confidence. 'You're central, you're essential, even Crimond saw this. He said you were the best!'

'Oh – Crimond –' They both laughed, though a little nervously.

'It's not true that I'm essential,' said Jenkin, 'Duncan has

358

never altogether liked me, Robin was always impatient with me, so is Gull, Rose laughs at me, Crimond thinks I'm a fool. Don't interrupt me, Gerard. Of course this is a stupid way to talk, but you're forcing me into it. This stuff about being needed is part of an illusion we've kept up all these years. I know I'm talking nonsense and making you angry, because of course there is something close, something unique, and perhaps such things are always partly illusion, partly real. It's just that I've felt the illusion bit more lately, that's part of wanting to go away. I haven't been *alone* enough, and that's because I've had to play – that game – which of course wasn't a game, but – You see, I *must* be alone in the way one can be in what you called hell.'

'You're wrong about the others, they treasure you.'

'Like a mascot.'

'Rose adores you – but let's not argue about that – I don't even care about it – and maybe you're right that such things are hopelessly mixed up between illusion and reality, perhaps all things are –'

'What don't you care about?'

'Them, the others – well, I do care, yes, I do – and I deny what you said about being odd man out – but I could do without them.'

'You know, Gerard,' said Jenkin, staring at him at last, 'I don't think you could! You've been supported by them all your life. You've *liked* being chief among us, why not, the cleverest, the handsomest, the most successful, the most loved – and it's true you have been these things, you still are – but you do depend on it or something like it, and I don't. Please don't misunderstand me, I'm not thinking of going away because I've discovered that nobody loves me! I'm just chucking out your argument about I mustn't go because I'm needed. I'm not needed. It's you they all look to, it's you they all depend on, and so –'

'They –?'

'Well, we, I've depended on you too, as you know. That's another thing I've got to get away from. Sorry, I didn't mean to say that. Everything I'm saying now can be misunderstood,

I wish you hadn't started this conversation, I *hate* this sort of conversation.'

'You've got to get away from me?'

'Yes, but it's nothing personal, Gerard! It's just part of wanting to be properly by myself. I've begun to feel I was kidnapped in my cradle, kidnapped by a group of the dearest best people in the world, but –'

'I'm sorry it's nothing personal! It isn't – excuse this, but since we're being so frank – it isn't that you're jealous of the others, or imagine that I'm closer to them than to you, because if that's it you've got it very wrong –'

'*No*, that's not it! Really, Gerard!'

'Sorry. I seem to be making rather a mess of some things I wanted to say to you.'

'Well, I think you've said them and no harm's done, so let's leave it there.'

'I *haven't* said them, I've given the wrong impression –'

'Let's change the subject.'

'Do you want me to go?'

'No, not unless you want to. Please yourself.'

'Jenkin!'

'I don't understand what all this is supposed to be about, and I suggest that we leave it! There are plenty of other things we can talk about, serious things and nice things – I didn't mean to be short with you – I'm sorry –'

'I'm sorry. May I start again?'

'Oh Lord – if you must!'

'I don't want you to go away and I beg you not to go away. I need you, *you*, and not anybody else. I love you, I need you –'

'Well, I love you too, old man, if it comes to that, but –'

'Look, Jenkin, this is serious, it's the most serious thing in the world, in my world. I want to get to know you better, much better, I want to come closer to you, I want us to share a house, I want us to live together, to travel together, to *be* together, I want to be able to see you all the time, to be with you – I want you to *come home* – you've never had a home – I want you to come home to *me*. I'm not saying this is possible, I'm telling you what I want, and very very much want – and if you consider what I say and understand it you'll see why it is I don't want you to go away.'

There was a moment's silence. Jenkin stared at Gerard, not exactly with amazement, but with a bright, even radiant, open-mouthed open-eyed attention. 'Gerard – is this a proposal of marriage?'

'It's a declaration of love,' said Gerard in a testy irritated tone, 'and well, yes, if you like it's a proposal of marriage. I expect you find it all a bit quaint, but since you use the phrase –'

Jenkin began to laugh. He rocked. He put his glass down on the tiles of the fireplace and leaned forward, one hand on his ribs, the other pulling at the neck of his shirt, he wailed with laughter until his mouth and eyes were wet, several times he tried to check himself and say something, but the words were overtaken by another paroxysm of mirth.

Gerard watched him sternly, dismayed, but glad that he had managed at last to make something like the clear coherent speech which he had intended to utter. As soon as he had spoken he felt an immediate freedom, an open space, a connection with Jenkin which had been lacking before. That utterance gave him, in his increasing disarray as he watched the effect of his words, a feeling of warmth.

Jenkin at last became calmer, mopping his eyes, his lips, his brow with a large torn handkerchief liberally stained with ink. 'Oh dear – oh dear –' he kept saying, and then, 'Oh Gerard – I'm so sorry – will you ever forgive me – I'm a monster – how can I have laughed like that – it's disgraceful –'

'Did you actually hear what I said?'

'Yes – every word – I took it all in – "come live with me and be my love" – and I'm so *grateful*, I'm so *touched* – I feel really – humble, privileged – you quite overwhelm me!'

'Cut that out.'

'A proposal – and sex too? Oh Lord!' He began to laugh helplessly again.

'Why not,' said Gerard, now cold and frowning, 'but that's not the point. It doesn't matter. I've said what I mean. I don't know you very well, Jenkin, I want to know you better, I want our friendship to become closer –'

'To blossom like an old dry thorn tree?'

'But since you find it so overpoweringly funny I'd better take that as an answer and take myself off. I'm sorry if I've disturbed you, and I shall be very sorry if later on, when you think about it, you find what I've said offensive. I daresay you'll find it ridiculous enough. I hope this curious little episode will not in any way affect the friendship which we have enjoyed so long and which you just now described as an old dry thorn tree.' As he said this Gerard got up and reached for his damp overcoat which he had draped over a chair.

Jenkin leapt to his feet. 'Oh but I won't, I don't, I can't find it offensive or ridiculous or – or – *anything* like that – of course I'm so *flattered* –'

'I daresay you are,' said Gerard putting on his coat.

'But – and – you know – of course our friendship is affected, it's deeply affected, it can never be the same again.'

'I'm sorry to hear that.'

'Don't be sorry, please understand, if you wanted us to become nearer together, well, we've come, don't you see? Shock tactics do things, they break barriers, they open vistas – I'm very sorry I laughed –'

'I liked your laughing,' said Gerard, 'but I don't know what it meant and I doubt if it's a good omen for me!'

'Don't go,' said Jenkin, standing where he was by his chair, with his radiant attentive face on which the wrinkles and tears of laughter could still be seen. 'Oh dear – how can I say it – something here is absolutely *all right* – Why is one so shy of using the word "love"?'

'I'm not. Perhaps you won't go away – leave us – leave me?'

'I don't know. But don't worry. I'm very glad that you said all that. You won't regret it, will you?'

'I hope not. I expect we'll talk again about all sorts of things, those serious and nice things you mentioned earlier.'

'Oh yes – but about these things too – and please – don't be – don't feel – Look, Gerard, stay here for a bit, will you? Let's just sit quietly and look at each other and calm down and have another drink and listen to the rain. My God, I think I need some whisky after this!'

At that moment, as they stood gazing at each other, there was an extraordinary banging sound. Someone, not finding the bell in the darkness, was pounding on the door with a fist, producing a loud echoing noise. Jenkin sprang across the room and out into the hall. Gerard followed him, instinctively turning on the centre light. He saw, beyond Jenkin, in the now open doorway, a strange figure, which he remembered afterwards as like a tall thin utterly bedraggled blackbird.

It was Tamar, bare-headed, her hair, darkened by the rain and disordered by the wind, covering her brow and cheeks with a dark network, her long black mackintosh shining with water, her arms hanging empty-handed by her sides like broken wings. As she stepped or staggered in Jenkin gripped her and held her. Gerard moved past him to shut the door against the downpour.

Tamar, released by Jenkin, slipped off her coat which fell to the floor. She began slowly, as if every movement were exhausting her, to draw back her dripping wet hair from her face. Jenkin picked up her coat, then materialised with a towel. Tamar began mechanically to dry her face and hair.

Gerard said, 'Tamar, Tamar! What is it? Were you looking for me?'

Tamar, not looking at either of them, said, 'No, I want to talk to Jenkin.'

Tamar's skirt, stained with water, was clinging to her legs. She turned toward Jenkin and seemed about to fall stiffly into his arms. He supported her, then began to propel her into the sitting room.

Gerard said, 'I'd better go.' He waited another moment.

Jenkin, at the sitting room door, said, 'Goodnight then, my dear, we'll talk again, just don't worry —'

Gerard went out into the rain, closing the door behind him. He had no umbrella and no hat. He was ridiculously annoyed at having uttered his silly assumption that Tamar must have been looking for him. He walked along with the rain soaking his hair and running down his neck. He was extremely disturbed by his talk with Jenkin and very sorry that he had not been able to stay longer and, as Jenkin had so wisely suggested, simply sit quietly together. He could not make out what had happened between him and Jenkin and whether it was a good move or a disaster. He felt a separate and sharp pain simply at having had to leave Jenkin's presence. This was new. He felt a new kind of dread. He tried, as he walked along the pavements where the light of the lamps was reflected in streams of water, to drive away his sudden forebodings and hold onto Jenkin's laughter as onto something good.

Tamar was sitting beside the little gas fire and gazing at it. She had wrung water out of her wet skirt. She had refused food, tea, coffee, but had accepted a glass of whisky and water, which she had held onto without drinking and now put down on the floor. Jenkin, in distress, was asking, 'Tamar, dear child, what is it, tell me, please tell me?'

She lifted her head at last, not looking at Jenkin but sightlessly across the room, and said, 'Yes, yes, I'll tell you. I became pregnant with Duncan's child, and now I have killed it.'

Jenkin, who had been standing, retained his shock, stepping back as if some great object had been propelled against his body. His face flushed and he gasped. He sat down opposite to her, pulling his chair near and leaning forward. 'Tamar, dear, take it easy. Just tell me exactly what you mean.'

Tamar gave a very long deep shuddering sign and went on in a dead listless voice, 'Oh I don't mean I had the child and drowned it or anything like that. It was never born. I had an abortion.'

'What a terrible experience,' said Jenkin, stupid with pity and anguish. 'But – but – you say it was – Duncan's child?'

'Yes, I went to bed with Duncan once – I mean on one occasion. I felt I loved him, I wanted to comfort him. He said he couldn't have children. So perhaps it was a sort of miracle. Only I killed the child.'

'Are you sure it was Duncan's?'

'Yes. Yes. Yes.'

'Does he know?'

'No, of course not. It must be a secret. You said he wanted a child, and there was a child, only now it isn't alive any more.'

'Why didn't you – you didn't think of telling him, or –?'

'No!' Tamar wailed the word, but her face was rigid, looking past Jenkin into the corner of the room. 'How *could* I? You said Jean was coming back to him. I wasn't going to stop that from happening by standing there and saying that I had his child. I thought the best thing to do was to get rid of it. Only I didn't know what I was doing. I didn't know what would happen to me afterwards, that I'd be in hell for it with nothing to do but to die.'

'Tamar, don't look like that, I won't let you be in hell.'

'It's murder, it's the irrevocable crime for which one suffers death. I shall never have another child, that one would kill any other child. It wanted to live, it wanted to live, and I wouldn't let it! I can't tell anybody – but keeping it secret eats my inside away –'

'But you've told me, and I'll help you.'

'You can't help me. I only came here to say it was all your fault –'

'Why –?'

'That day down by the river you said Jean would come back and they'd be happy again, and you advised me –'

'Tamar, I didn't advise you –'

'You couldn't have known whether Jean would come back or not, she hasn't come back, perhaps she won't and I'll have done it for nothing. When the child was alive I wanted to tell Duncan, I wanted to run to him and tell him and say I loved him, but now I hate him and I can never see him again because I killed his miracle child in a fit of madness. And only a few days ago it was alive, and it was *mine* –' Tamar began to cry at last, still rigid, her mouth open now, her eyes pouring tears which fell from her chin onto her lap.

Jenkin had tried to take hold of her hand but she had pulled it away, jerking herself back. He was appalled by what he heard. In the few minutes she had been with him Jenkin had seen into the hell she spoke of, and although he spoke of helping her he did not see any way in which it would be possible. He wished he could take away her consciousness so that all this pain would cease. 'Tamar, try to hold onto yourself, I'm going to help you, just *hold on*. Have you told anybody else about this?'

'I told Lily I was pregnant, she gave me the money, I didn't say who it was, she said it happens to everyone. And I told that parson in the country, I just said I was pregnant and he said keep it. I wish I'd come to you, even last week, you'd have said keep it and I'd have kept it, I wish I'd told you then on that day by the river, if only you'd asked what was the matter, I'd have told you and everything would be all right, only you didn't ask me, you went on and on about Jean and Duncan and how *they*'d be all right, it was all about *them*, and I wanted to tell you about *me* – And now I hate you too, I hate everybody, and when one hates everybody one dies. I hate myself with such a hatred, I could kill myself by torture, I wish I could die tonight, I wish you could kill me and burn me.'

'Stop, Tamar, you're distraught, drink some of the whisky. Stop wailing, be quiet, here, drink some of this.'

Tamar drank a little, her hand trembling, slopping it onto her dress. She stopped crying.

'Let's sort this out, I can see it's something terrible, awful for you, but you're mixing it all up and blaming yourself for everything – we've got to be able to *think* about it, I'll help you, you don't hate me, you came to me, you must stay with me and trust me, you need people, you need love –' Jenkin found himself babbling, just to keep the conversation going, hardly knowing what he was saying, uttering random words to try to soothe the massive wound which had so suddenly been uncovered to him.

'Nobody loves me,' said Tamar, now in a dull matter-of-fact tone, 'nobody *can* love me. It's impossible. I'm a person *outside* love, and I have *always been*.'

'That's not true. But, look, I'm going to ask you questions. I'm sorry if it hurts, but I *must* try to understand, you know I won't tell anyone. This thing, this one occasion, with Duncan, was there anything before it or after it, had you realised he was in love with you?'

'No, he wasn't, and there was nothing. I went to see him twice because – because Gerard asked me to.'

'Gerard asked you?'

'He thought I might be good for Duncan because I was so innocent and harmless. On the second time he'd just had a letter about divorce from the solicitor, and I felt so sorry for him, I said I loved him, and I did love him.'

'Do you still love him?'

'No. Then he put his arms round me and we went to bed.'

'And after?'

'After, nothing. He may have decided Jean would come back after all, or that I was a nuisance, a nasty incident, something he wished hadn't happened. He ignored me at Boyars. I understood.'

'And that weekend you knew you were pregnant?'

'Yes. But I didn't come to see him, I just came to get over being with him and knowing he didn't love me and it was all over.'

'You didn't think it might go on?'

'No. I saw it couldn't – and I'd ruined all the things that Gerard thought – and all *that* was over forever. I knew it even before I realised I was pregnant. The things I asked you down at the river, I really knew how it was, though I hadn't thought about Duncan so terribly wanting a child.'

'I was just talking,' said Jenkin. 'I don't know whether Duncan wants a child. He said once that he did –'

'Anyway he wouldn't have wanted this one. But *I* wanted it.' The tears began to flow again. She said, 'Oh, I'm so tired – I want to sleep.'

'You must live with this as people do live with terrible losses. It is possible, you will discover how.' He thought, there's so much here that can't be mended, or only miraculously. I wish I could share this burden with someone else, but I don't see how I can. 'Is there anyone else you'd like to talk to? What about that parson, Father McAlister? You told him –'

'He forced me to tell him. He talked about Jesus and how

367

pure love made you penitent and your guilt was washed away and so on. But he didn't know what it was all about, I can't go back to him.

'Look, who knows you're here, beside Gerard? Does Lily?'

'No, I ran out while she was shopping, then I walked about in the rain.'

'Then I must ring Lily, and your mother must be told too –'

'No!'

'People must simply know where you are. I won't tell them anything else. I think I'll ring Gerard, and he'll tell them. Tamar, won't you please eat something? No? Then you must go to bed when I've fixed the room. We can talk again tomorrow.'

Jenkin had made up the bed in the spare room and put in a hot water bottle and laid out a pair of his pyjamas. She crawled into bed in a state of complete exhaustion. Jenkin was about to take her hand and kiss her, but she had already fallen asleep. He watched her for a while, and then made a signal over her, a private signal of his own, for her protection.

As he went to the telephone to ring Gerard he suddenly recalled, which he had quite forgotten, the odd little scene with his friend which Tamar had interrupted. He paused with his hand upon the telephone. He could not remember exactly what he had said, he had the impression that he had been rather rude to Gerard in the earlier part of the conversation, and then he had laughed at what Gerard had said later. Well, there was nothing *there* that would need a miracle to mend. All the same he would have to think – He lifted the 'phone quickly and dialled Gerard's number.

'Hello.'

'Gerard.'

'I was hoping you'd ring. What's the matter with Tamar?'

'She's all right. She's asleep, I mustn't wake her. I just thought, would you mind ringing Lily to say she's here? And if Lily's alarmed Violet –'

'Yes, yes, I'll sort all that out.'

There was a moment's silence.'
'Gerard –'
'Don't worry.'
'I won't.'

Jenkin sat down by the fireplace and poured himself out some more whisky. He felt upset, racked with pity, frightened, also excited. Inside a mix of disturbing sensations there was a cherishing gladness that there was in his house, safe and resting, a wounded creature who had run to him for protection. It was odd to feel he was not alone in the house.

He tried to be calm and quiet. His laughter had been partly shock-laughter, a protection from any more immediate response. Yet it had been funny too, absurdly funny. *Come home.* Was he tempted? Yes, he was. Throughout the years Jenkin had been conscious, more conscious than Gerard, of, with their closeness, the distance between them. He had reflected upon this distance, this steady secure space, as if it were perhaps asking for a hand to be stretched across it. His hand? As he thought this, sitting by the fire and remembering he made an embryonic gesture. He had inhibited the possible gesture out of a kind of timidity or chaste shame, a sense, life-long it seemed now, of Gerard's superiority. Had he feared the, kindest possible of course, barely perceptible perhaps, rebuff? Nor had he ventured to imagine what that step closer would be like, what it would entail, what his life would be like *without* that clear void (he pictured it as a kind of trough of sky, pale blue and full of light) across which he looked at Gerard. Sometimes it seemed ridiculous, something too solemn, a conceptualising of the unconceptualisable, to think about his relation with Gerard in this way. If they were destined to come closer, to be more intimate, to meet oftener, or however one described it, would not this happen spontaneously, and if it did not happen was that not because there were good reasons, invisible perhaps but good, why it should not happen? Why all the fuss? Well, there was no fuss, only this awareness, some-times manifested as jealousy, of which Jenkin, who concealed this carefully from Gerard, was certainly capable. And now, and unexpectedly, that so important structural space had suddenly been annihilated. The king had come to him, cap in hand – and Jenkin had laughed at him. Come home? I don't think I can come home, thought Jenkin, it's not in my nature to come home or have that sort of home. Even this home, this house, is a shell that must be broken. All right, so this is romanticism, it is sentimentality. But I must go away soon, sooner than I had planned, if I am not to run to Gerard.

There was another piece of the puzzle, old and faded but still there, which had been jolted by Gerard's surprising declaration. That was the question of Rose. Jenkin was so used to being just the tiniest bit in love with Rose that it was scarcely to be called that any more, nor did he use such terminology to himself. Jenkin had loved women and had had, though not at all lately, more adventures than his friends imagined, or others who thought of him as hopelessly sexless. But Rose was a special case. He had never spoken of his odd not too uncomfortable feeling to anyone except once to a close Oxford friend, Marcus Field, who also loved Rose. Jenkin, sage even then, had kept his feelings on a lead. Rose's love for Gerard went far back into the shades of history, almost as far back as Gerard's love for Sinclair. Gerard had let her love him, what else could he do? Yet (Jenkin very occasionally allowed himself to think) was he not a trifle complacent about it, ought he not perhaps to have told her to go away and find someone else? However that might be, an element, not exactly a motive, in Jenkin's decision to escape was his desire to get away, not only from Gerard, but from Rose.

Yet – how much of that delicately balanced picture of motive and decision, which he had been so long constructing and had now been completed, had been shifted, even seriously damaged, by Gerard's extraordinary move? Jenkin had never had a homosexual relation or dreamt of considering his close friendship with Gerard in that light – nor did he now allow himself to wonder what exactly it was which now existed and previously had not. What he felt was a sudden increase of being. Gerard had *called* to him, and the echoing call stirred things in deep places. Come live with me and be my love. Perhaps, after all, this changed everything?

Gerard had telephoned Lily, and Rose, whom Lily had alarmed, and driven round to Violet's to tell her Tamar was with Jenkin. He stayed a while with Violet. She told him, and seemed glad to be able to do so, about Tamar's weeping and screaming fits which had preceded her flight. Violet did not know why Tamar was in such a state. Violet was certainly unnerved, upset, frightened, perhaps even shocked into genuine loving concern for her daughter. Gerard took the opportunity of saying to Violet with an air of authority that really she *must* allow Tamar to continue her education. Probably Tamar's grief on this subject lay behind her breakdown. Some young people *passionately* wanted to go on learning and studying, and the really difficult things, which would be possessions forever, had to be learnt when still young. If Tamar were frustrated now (so Gerard painted the picture) she might fall into depression and lose her job, whereas if she could return to Oxford she would get a much better-paid job later on. Gerard would be very glad meanwhile to help financially, and so on and so on. Violet, quickly recovering from her softened mood, soon put on an expression, familiar to Gerard, of quiet amused cynicism. He left hoping that he might nevertheless have made an impression.

When he got back to his house the telephone was ringing. It was Rose. He told her about his visit to Violet. Rose was interested in this, but had rung up for another purpose. She just wanted to hear his voice, and to hear him say, as he duly said, 'Good night, darling, sleep well.'

Gerard, in pyjamas and dressing gown, sat on his bed, upright as when he had seen and not seen the children feeding the ducks. Long after Rose was in bed and asleep he sat there motionless reviewing the events of the evening. He waited, allowing the stormy waves of his disturbed feelings to calm down. He breathed. He wished very much that he had been able to accept Jenkin's invitation to stay and sit quietly and have another drink and listen to the rain. And they could have looked at each other and, without speech, composed a new understanding. Well, there would be other times; and perhaps Tamar's coming, though it made impossible that quiet different continuation of their talk, had been a sort of sign. They had been thinking about themselves and each other, when suddenly the urgent needs of someone, whom they were both concerned to cherish, had intruded upon them. This also was a bond, and would enable a natural and immediate continuation of their business together. With this thought, Gerard could even enjoy, transforming it into a wry humility, his annoyance that Tamar had preferred Jenkin to himself as the one to run to!

Gerard thought, gentling himself into calmness, at least I made my little speech, it did express exactly what I meant, it said enough and said it simply – and whatever happens, and I must be prepared for nothing to happen, I shall be glad I told him what I felt. Surely after *this* he won't go away – he won't want to, and he'll see he can't.

But later on, after Gerard had lain himself down to sleep and had slept and wakened in the dark, he felt such a strangeness because he had, for the first time ever, been with Jenkin and been the weaker man. He had come to him as a beggar, standing before him without authority. He had exchanged his power for an infinite vulnerability, and *forced* Jenkin to be his executioner. And as he now thought of Jenkin and of the necessity of Jenkin all sorts of hitherto unimaginable pictures rose up in his mind, and he thought, I must not begin to want what I cannot have. Why did I see it before as something simple? I was so set on saying my little piece, as if that in itself could secure some morsel of my heart's desire, so that something at least would be safe. I thought I might make a fool of myself – but now, what have I done to his imagination and to mine? I never dreamed that things could go badly wrong and that between his good will and mine we might be put in hell. Perhaps I have brought about something terrible, for him, and for me.

'Let me see you turn the headlights up,' said Crimond.

Jean turned them up.

'Now dip them and turn them full up again several times.'

She did so. She was sitting in her car with the door open, Crimond was standing beside her in the dark. His car, with its lights on, was just in front of hers. It was three o'clock in the morning and they were on the Roman Road.

The rain had gone away, the colder stiller weather had returned, the moon had risen, the stars were visible. Jean was trembling violently.

'You *can* drive?' said Crimond.

'Yes, of course.'

They were on the crest of a hill from which a long view of the road, undulating straight onward, was visible by daylight. There was, from the point at which they had stopped, a dip, then a rise, then a mild descent followed by a steady gentle rise to another crest nearly two miles ahead.

'When I get there I'll signal by putting my headlights up slowly three times, and you reply in the same way. If there's any snag, I can't think what snag there could be, we haven't seen another car since we left the main road, but if there is anything I'll flick the lights quickly a number of times to mean wait. And of course you do the same. Then after the first signals, meaning that I'm there and you've seen me, a pause, then the same thing again, both of us together, slowly head-lights up three times. You remember all this, we've repeated it over and over.

'Of course I remember.'

'After the second lot of slow threes, set off at once. Drive with dipped headlights of course, we don't want to dazzle each other. All you have to do is keep on the left, the road isn't very broad so I don't think anything can go wrong. Leave the rest to me. Don't forget to fasten your seat belt, freakish things can happen, you must be *in* the car. Don't muff it, well you won't, we don't want to end up in a couple of wheelchairs, there mustn't be any accidents here. Remember we'll lose sight of each other when you're in the dip, after you come over the hump it's just a little down, then the long rise. If I'd thought, we might have done it the other way round, but it doesn't matter now, and your car is more powerful than mine – it'll be simple, it'll be easy, only for heaven's sake put your foot down, we want to be doing at least eighty when we meet. You won't lose control of the car?'

'No, of course not.'

'Don't risk that – but you won't, you're a perfect driver – get up a great pace, you needn't look at the speedometer, you can entrust the velocity to me, just get up a pace and keep going and *stay on the left*. That's all I think. Now, I'll get in my car. We agreed we'd said our goodbyes – only they're not goodbyes, we'll be together now, always.'

As he turned quickly to go Jean got out of the car and followed him a step or two, putting her hand on his shoulder. She felt him shudder and start away and as he stepped back their hands touched. She stood still, watched him get into his car and close the door, heard him start the engine, then watched the rear lights of the car and the flying headlights rush down into the dip, surmount the rise, become invisible for a moment, then appear again on the long rise toward the distant crest. She got back into the car and closed the door and fastened her seat belt.

Jean's car was a Rover, the more powerful of the two, Crimond's was a Fiat. Jean found herself thinking about the cars. She liked her car, and now she was going to crash it, to smash it to pieces. She thought of Duncan for a moment, as if she were asking herself whether he would mind about the car. Then she thought, leaning back in her seat and feeling almost sleepy, am I dreaming? Is this a dream? It must be. I've *thought* about this all the time since Crimond started talking about it, now I'm dreaming it. Her head jerked and it was like waking up. It was not a dream, she had come to the place they had talked of, at the time they had talked of, the time had come and *Crimond was gone*. The sense of her solitude struck her first.

Then she thought about what was going to happen and she felt cold and black with terror. She began to tremble again and her jaw was shaking. She felt very sick, ready to vomit but unable to do so. Automatically she started the engine. As she did so she thought, there's time yet. I could run into the wood and be sick, I could go mad and wander away among the trees and sit down somewhere. Why need this concern me any more? Did we not do it just by talking about it? Why do I have to *do* anything more, is it not *already over*? She had not noticed the cold air. Now she wound up the window and thought, it's warmer in the car. She was wearing a short coat. Her handbag lay on the seat beside her. Why had she brought that with her? The intense sick feeling appeared as a sense of time. The condensed mass of all her recent thoughts and feelings was exploding inside her head. She was beyond logic and contradictory things could be true.

She had tried, over the last days, to fathom her lover, to try, as she always tried, to *find out what he wanted* and to be *as he wanted*. She had believed, for some of the time, indeed, and perhaps now, that it was a test of courage. It was the sort of thing Crimond did, it was Russian roulette again, the gun which he pretended was loaded when it was not. He had, he said, wanted to *see* her courage. She said, to see my love? Yes, your love, it's the same. This was it again now, he needed like a drug the regular *evidence*, to *see* she was his; and she *was* his, she had come to the Roman Road, to this horrible charade, this scene of *torture*, because she could not gainsay him, she had to obey. She had *not to fail* – either then – or now. If she failed he would leave her. But – if she passed she would die? She thought, he'll save us at the last moment, that will be like him. I'll stay on the left and he will simply pass me by, or he'll come at me and then swerve away. He said, *leave the rest to me*. Well, that is all I can do, that is all of my life now. We'll meet again after and embrace and shed tears and dance. That is how it will be; and then our love will be reinforced, increased a thousand fold, deified. This is the experience of death after which one becomes immortal. But, she thought, supposing it is death, supposing it is really death he wants, and that we shall mingle with each other in death and become a legend? Well, if he chooses that, as the final consummation of our love, that too is what I will; she gave a little cry like a bird and a kind of ecstasy of fear so possessed her body that it was as if it were emitting light. I have surrendered my life to him and if he takes it, well, and if he spares it, well. This is the climax that my life was for, the time which is worth all the rest, which redeems the rest of time. I can no other, and in that I must be at peace. Yet still she thought, it is *impossible* that we shall not meet again, it is *impossible* that we shall not be together again and talk of this. If the gods are to reward us we must be there to be rewarded – unless this is now our reward to live the last moments of our lives in this way.

She was trembling with excitement and terror. Her head felt huge and full of points of electricity, little shocks of intense pain. And all the time she was sitting perfectly still with the engine running, watching the road ahead which seemed to be shuddering and heaving and boiling up in atoms of dark. She was aware of the moon, even of the stars, of the frosty moonlit tarmac just in front of hers, and of the lights of Crimond's car, the pale glow of headlights, the rear lights, briefly lost to view, now well up upon the further slope, slowly climbing up on the waves of the dark. She saw the lights diminish, seem to vanish, the red lights disappearing, there seemed to be an interval, a gulf into which she could fall; then the headlights came slowly out of the dark, first dim then rising to a full flash, three times repeated. Her mouth open now, gasping, finding her hand ready on the switch, she flashed her own lights in reply. The distant signal was repeated, and almost simultaneously she repeated her answer. The far off lights were dipped and she dipped her own. She put the car into gear and released the clutch. The car began to move down the hill and in a few moments the headlights upon the opposite hill disappeared from view. As she began to accelerate Jean felt a sudden surge of energy, something very intense, perhaps fear, perhaps joy, perhaps, in the depths of her body, a prolonged sexual thrill. She pressed her foot down. Faster, faster. At the same time she found herself thinking, after this we'll drive across France. I'll do the driving, he doesn't really like driving. She had so often imagined that going away with Crimond, which would come after the book was finished. When the book was finished they would drive about, as they had done in Ireland, and be perfectly happy. But the book was finished, and were they not already perfectly happy, was not this, what she was doing now as an instrument of Crimond's will, perfect happiness?

When she reached the crest of the dip she saw the headlights of Crimond's car again, much nearer. The road descended a little, then began the long very gradual ascent. Jean kept her gaze fixed upon the pale glowing eyes ahead of her, the eyes which seemed so quickly to be becoming larger and brighter. The Rover sped on beautifully, effortlessly, bird-like. Jean flickered her glance to look at the speedometer, but for some reason could not see it. The pale increasing eyes seemed to have blinded her to all other things in the world. In the world. Will it be quick? she thought. The faster the quicker. Oddly enough, in all the long terrifying, thrilling and somehow unreal discussions which they had had about the Roman Road, Jean had never tried to imagine any of the detail. There had been so much metaphor, so much myth, so much sheer sexual excitement, like a prolonged orgasm, in that extraordinary period, so brief, so crammed and crowded with their united being, after she had realised that Crimond really meant it, that they would actually come to it. That time now seemed in memory like a sunlit battlefield, a joust, with pennants flying and naked deadly lances, not yet stained with blood. From that engagement Jean had been able to escape into endless oscillating speculation about what Crimond really intended. Her imagination had rested intermittently upon perfunctory pictures: the two cars would become one car, there would be nothing on the road except a compact box of metal. But inside the box? She would be there, with Crimond, inside the box, joined together in an eternal blackness. There would be blood, a mingling of blood, a mingling of flesh, but *they* would have vanished, united forever in a clap of thunder. She began to gasp and moan, not yet to scream, though she could already hear the scream she was about to utter.

Is he on the left side of the road or the right side, she wondered. It was still hard to tell. He had told her to stay on the left and leave the rest to him. In your will is my tranquillity. Only now she was alone. But she must not think that. Faster, faster, nearer, nearer. Jean's eyes flickered again, this time toward the near side of the road. There was a long low stone wall, a dry stone wall the pattern of whose golden-yellow stones was hypnotically, very swiftly, unravelling in the headlights of the Rover. A wall. The other side of the road seemed to be invisible, as if covered by a black patch. Then there were those wheelchairs. Crimond had only just mentioned the wheelchairs, but Jean's mind had already set up a picture, as if she had been brooding upon it for years, of herself and Crimond slowly moving about in a large room, passing each other like mindless insects as they laboriously propelled their chairs by turning the wheels with their hands. Old age, was it an image of old age? We don't want to grow old, we don't want to be cripples either, I mustn't muff it. Crimond's car, now perhaps a mile away, or less, was certainly upon the right side of the road, his right, her left, they were joined by a straight line, it would be nose to nose. Her foot was pressing the accelerator into the floor of the car, there was a roaring in her ears, the sound of the engine of which she had been unaware, the wheel seemed fixed in her hands, locked into position. She had never driven so fast in her life, yet she felt in perfect control of the car. If I were to cross his path at the last moment, she thought, he would hit the side of the car, there would be an *accident*. The stone wall was still with her. The pale brilliant eyes ahead which had for a time seemed to grow larger without moving, were now perceptibly coming nearer, rushing nearer, nearer, fast, very fast. Jean began to pray, Crimond, oh Crimond, Crimond. How could she kill her lover? If she could only die and he became a god. He had said, keep on the left and leave the rest to me. The bright eyes were near, hypnotic, glaring dazzling, filling her vision, directly ahead of her, rushing, charging towards her. She thought, he's not going to swerve, it isn't a test, it's the real thing, it's the end. Jean began to scream, she screamed into the roaring of the engine. She could see now, not just the eyes, but the car, illumined now by her own headlights, a black car, with a figure in it, coming, coming. *The box, the box, the box.* Oh my love.

The stone wall suddenly ceased and Jean's gaze, still fixed ahead upon what was about to happen, took in a five-barred gate. She turned the wheel. She missed the gate, but the car crashed through a thick hedge and turned over on its side upon grass. The lights went out. There was a distant screech, then silence, an amazing silence. Darkness and silence.

Jean breathed for a while. She could breathe. She thought about her body and moved parts of it about a little. The car was lying on its left side. Her seat belt was still holding her suspended. She could not, in the black dark, make out what space she was in. She fumbled for the clasp of the seat belt. It seemed to snap and she jolted against the side of the passenger seat which had been propelled forward. Drawing up her knees she rested, holding the steering wheel with one hand. Her head was hurting, and her right foot was hurting, perhaps, even as she hurtled through the hedge, she had been pressing down the accelerator. Her whole body felt battered. She concentrated on breathing.

A light appeared, a wandering light. The door of the car above her, beyond the wheel, began to rattle. Someone was trying to open it. It opened. It's like a box after all, she thought, and someone has opened the lid. The light of the torch shone into the car revealing her knees, the displaced seat, the shattered windscreen, a kind of snow everywhere which she realised was broken glass. Looking at her knees she noticed her stockings, dark brown stockings which she had selected, had *chosen* to wear, when she rose at midnight. Earlier, Crimond had told her to sleep and she had actually slept, though that had seemed impossible. She remembered now that she had forgotten to ask Crimond whether he had slept. She made a guttural sound to discover if she could still speak, then said in a strange voice, 'I'm all right – I think.'

'Get yourself out,' another voice said.

Can I? she wondered. Her body felt so weak, so beaten, and somehow entangled into the interior of the car limply like a dead snake. Bracing one foot against the dashboard and pulling at the steering wheel she began to arch herself upward. She crawled upward, now holding the wheel with one hand and placing the other on the side of the open door. But her arms were strengthless and she was unable to pull herself up. Her head, her head which felt so hurt and strange, she must aim it at the opening and not think about the pain in her foot. Getting past the steering wheel would be the difficulty. At one moment she felt she was kneeling, then, finding a foothold somewhere, perhaps in the passenger seat, she managed to extend her left leg and moved upward displacing the driver's seat which suddenly gave way and fell back. Her head and then her arms emerged through the battered hole of the open door, which the torch light was now revealing to her. Her arms took her weight for a second while her left foot found another quick perch, probably on the steering wheel, and she achieved a sitting position on the edge of the opening and very slowly, using her hands to lift them, pulled first one leg and then the other out of the car.

Crimond, not helping her, was standing a little distance away shining the torch upon her. He said, 'Can you walk?'

Jean half fell to the ground, steadied herself against the car, her hand questing over the twisted red metal so brightly revealed by the light. She thought, I *must* walk. She took one or two paces. Her right foot was hurting but it was serviceable. The pain in her head, absent while she was scrambling out, had returned. She said, 'Yes.'

'Walk then.' The beam of the torch turned away towards the road and Crimond's figure receded.

Jean, who had been absorbed in nursing herself back to life, cried out, 'Oh wait, wait for me, please help me!' She hobbled after him. She could now see, in the ray of the torch, the brown thorny leafless hedge, the gap torn in the hedge, the tarmac beyond, and, as she took another step or two, the lights of

Crimond's car revealing the five-barred gate and the end of the stone wall. He had turned his car to come back.

Crimond had leapt through the gap and was standing on the road. He said, 'I am going now. You may do as you please. I shall not see you again.'

Jean screamed. She cried, 'No, no – Crimond, don't leave me – take me with you, forgive me – I couldn't kill you, I love you, I'd die for you, but I couldn't kill you – oh take me home, take me home, you can't go away without me –'

'I mean what I say. You are nothing to me now. Go away, go to hell, it's finished.'

'You didn't mean us to die, you can't have done. I know you didn't, it was just a test, I did what I thought you wanted!'

Crimond began to walk towards his car, visible now in its headlights.

Jean got to the hedge but could not manage to get through it. She limped to the gate, but was unable to open it.

Crimond was opening the door of his car.

'Wait for me, oh my darling, wait, wait, don't leave me!'

'You have left me. I have no more use for you. Don't come crawling after me and force me to kick you. It's finished, it's over. Can't you understand that I mean what I say?'

'Crimond, I love you, you love me, we said our love was forever!'

'It would have been forever. Now it cannot be. Am I not suffering too? You have taken from me the only thing which I desired and which only you could have given me. This failure ends our pact.'

'I'll come with you, I'll come to you tomorrow, there's nothing in the world for me, only you!'

'Don't come near me again, now or tomorrow or in any future time. You are nothing to me now, nothing. Go away, take your freedom, *take your chance*. We have already said goodbye, don't you remember? It is finished, you have chosen your way of finishing it. We could have killed each other but you have just succeeded in killing our love. That's what has died. Now go away from me, go anywhere you please, only don't come near me ever again. We are strangers forever, I never want to see you again.'

Crimond got into the car and switched on the engine.

Crying 'No! No!' Jean struggled with the gate.

The car shot off back up the hill, then braked and began to turn. Jean, wailing, was fumbling with a ring and a chain.

The car returned down the hill gathering speed and disappeared into the dip. She saw its rear lights again on the hill crest, then nothing. The darkness and the silence resumed, and the moon and the stars reappeared.

Jean had opened the gate and stood upon the road. She stood a while, opening her mouth wide, throwing back her head, screaming and crying, tearing at her clothes and her hair and uttering sounds like a wild animal. Then she began to walk. She must get to London, a car would pick her up, Crimond would come back. She became aware of bodily pain and intense cold. Walking was difficult, was more difficult. She wept now, drooping her head, ready at every moment to fall on her knees. She stopped, still sobbing, to stand and look about her. The countryside was dark. No, it was not entirely dark, there was a light, the window of a house, a little way from the road. There was a path. She began to limp along the path. Only when she was quite close to it did she realise that the house was Boyars.

Rose Curtland was asleep. She was dreaming that she and Sinclair were at the Vatican playing three-handed bridge with the Pope. The Pope was uneasy because a fourth person who was expected had failed to come. At last a bell began to ring and they all ran toward the door, only there was a very heavy tapestry covering it which they had to get past. They struggled, almost suffocating, with the tapestry, and then crawled underneath it. They found themselves in a long completely white hall, at the far end of which, in a white robe and wearing a white wig like a judge, Jenkin Riderhood was sitting on a throne. As she and Sinclair walked slowly and solemnly towards him Rose felt very frightened.

The ringing went on. Rose woke up and realised that the telephone was ringing. She remembered the dream and her fear and felt a new fear now because of the telephone. She switched on her lamp. It was nearly six o'clock. She got out of bed and ran to the telephone in the hallway, picking it up in the dark.

'Hello.'

'Miss Rose – it's Annushka – Mrs Cambus is here.'

'*What?*'

'I'm very sorry to disturb you. Mrs Cambus is here and she wants to speak to you.'

'What's happened?'

After a moment Rose could hear Jean speaking, or rather she could hear Jean sobbing and trying to speak.

'Jean, my darling, dear, dear Jean, what is it – oh don't grieve so – what is it, my dear heart – what's happened?'

Jean said at last, 'I want you to go – to see if Crimond – is all right –'

'Of course I will. But you – are *you* all right? Dear, dear Jean, don't cry so, I can't bear it.'

Jean said, trying to control her voice. 'I'm all right. I'm here – Annushka has been so kind – and the doctor –'

'The *doctor*?'

'I'm perfectly all right – but I'm afraid – that Crimond may have killed himself –'

'You've left him,' said Rose.

'He's left me. But he could kill himself. He could shoot himself. Could you go round –'

'Yes, of course I will, at once. I'm sure he hasn't killed himself, he's not the sort – but I'll go, and then I'll telephone you. But, Jean, you're hurt, the doctor –?'

'I've hurt my foot, it's nothing.'

'You *stay there*, don't move, Annushka will look after you, and when I've seen Crimond I'll drive down straightaway. You just stay there and *rest*, I'll be with you as soon as I can.'

'Yes – if you don't mind – I think I'll stay here – for the moment –'

'Could I talk to –'

Annushka was already on the line. Annushka spoke slowly and calmly, as she always did. Mrs Cambus had had a car accident. Yes, quite nearby, she had been driving to Boyars. She wasn't hurt except for a badly sprained ankle, and some concussion. She saw the landing light, which Annushka always kept on when she was alone, and she walked all the way with her bad ankle. Yes, Dr Tallcott had been there, he came at once. Yes, he said concussion and she was just to rest, he strapped up her ankle and gave her some pills. He said he'd come back. She was on the sofa in the drawing room because she couldn't get up the stairs. They didn't ring Rose at once because –

'Just *keep* her there,' said Rose, 'don't whatever you do let her go away, I'll be ringing up again and I'll drive down very soon.'

Frantically, turning on all the lights, she dressed, fumbling with her clothes, unable to find her handbag and the car keys, forgetting her overcoat. At last she had found everything, even gloves, and had put on her heaviest coat and a woollen cap and scarf. Leaving the lights on she ran downstairs into the very cold empty lamp-lit street. It was six o'clock. There was no sign of dawn.

In the car she let her fear loose. Terrible things were happening and would happen. She could not yet let herself feel glad that Jean had left Crimond. All this, whatever it was, might be part of one huge catastrophe. Suppose she arrived and found Crimond lying in a pool of blood with his head blown off? She had lied to Jean, of course she thought that Crimond was a person who might commit suicide – in fact, if they had really parted, it was very possible. He had finished the book, he had finished with Jean too. Except that perhaps he hadn't, perhaps they would be back together again tomorrow. Oh, let him not be dead, Rose prayed. Almost, she was wanting that Jean should be back with him tomorrow, everything else was so terribly *dangerous*. Jean would go mad,

Duncan would go mad, people would die, it would all end in dreadful chaos, the end of all order, the end of the world.

The streets were almost empty of traffic, the street lights lit up empty lonely pavements. As she crossed the Thames she could see lights reflected in the quivering water. The tide was in. Whatever happened *she must not get lost*. Everything in the dark looked so different, so awful. She could not remember the way and kept looking for landmarks. She began to wail with vexation and fear.

At last she was there, and had run the car up onto the pavement outside Crimond's house. The door was open and there was a light in the hall. Getting out of the car Rose felt her legs weak with fear. The sudden coldness seared her face. She put on her scarf, which she had taken off in the car. She took off her gloves and put her ungloved hand upon the iron railing beside the steps. The railing was frosty and deadly cold and her hand stuck to the metal. She stumbled up into the hall.

The rooms here were dark, she went into each one turning on the light, no one was there. She ran to the stairs leading down to the basement. The stairs were lit and there was another lighted open door down below. She ran down, leaning on the banisters, and hurried into the big basement room.

Crimond was standing at the other end of the room. A centre light was on and a lamp upon the desk at the far end. He was standing so still that Rose, her hand upon the door, had the sudden illusion that actually he was dead, but standing up. He had evidently not noticed her, though she must have made some noise descending the stairs. Then he moved his head slightly, looking towards her with evident surprise, his hand rising to his throat. Rose thought, he thinks I'm Jean. She pulled off her cap and her scarf and undid her coat.

'Rose!'

His utterance of her name gave her an unpleasant shock. She came down the room. She felt an intense desire to sit down. A chair beside the desk was draped with a woollen shawl. She took off the shawl and dropped it on the floor and sat down. Crimond moved away, facing her across the desk.

'So you're all right –'

'You've seen Jean?'

'I've talked to her. She thought you might have shot yourself.'

'As you see I have not.'

'And you aren't going to?'

'Not in the foreseeable future. Probably not at all.'

'You've really – really parted?' said Rose. The room was very cold and her speech puffed steaming out of her mouth.

'Yes.'

'You will leave her alone now, won't you, you won't come after her ever again?'

Crimond said nothing. He just stared at Rose. He was wearing a black jacket and a black pullover with a white high-necked shirt emerging, and with his pale thin face and thin lips he looked like a priest, a cruel censorious dangerous priest.

Rose got up and replaced the shawl on the chair. She felt there was something very important she ought to do and which could only be done now, in this minute, there was some information, or some promise, which she must extract from Crimond, or something which she must tell him. She said, 'I so much hope – I want Jean to be all right. You mustn't trouble her any more. Now that you've managed to separate, you mustn't come near her again ever, let it be absolutely over.'

Crimond continued to stare at her and said nothing.

Rose turned and went back up the stairs. She put on her scarf and her cap and buttoned up her coat and went out in the bitterly cold street and the grey light of dawn. She got into the car and drove away. She stopped at a telephone box near Vauxhall Bridge and rang Annushka telling her to tell Jean that Crimond was all right. Then she set off for Boyars. As she drove along she began to cry.

'But why were you down here, why were you driving along that road, were you coming to Boyars?'

'Yes, I told you –'

'Why didn't you take the road through the village?'

'I lost my way!'

'Why did you think I was here, I'm usually not.'

'I thought you might be, I wanted to get right out of London, I wanted to *drive fast*, right away, somewhere, anywhere, I was driving crazily, too fast, then I shot through the hedge –'

'You said a fox ran across the road and you swerved.'

'Yes, yes, the fox –'

'You'd had this row with Crimond –'

'It wasn't a row! We were both icy cold. We agreed to part.'

'You said he'd left you.'

'We left each other. It's finished. We *agreed*.'

'All the same, you thought he'd kill himself.'

'I was in a state of shock, I'm sorry I bothered you with that. Of course he won't kill himself. He's a cold fish.'

'You didn't tell him you were coming here?'

'Of course not.'

'Is he after someone else?'

'No!'

'Then why – Oh Jean, forgive me for asking you things, I'm so glad that you're here and that you've left that man! But it's so odd, like too good to be true! He took so much trouble to get you away, I imagined he'd hold onto you forever! Are you sure it was mutual, wasn't it you who wanted to escape?'

'That's what you want to believe!' said Jean.

'What I want to believe is that we shall never see him again!'

It was the afternoon. Jean, dosed by Dr Tallcott, had slept till noon. She was in bed in the huge old carved oak bedstead in the bedroom which Jean and Duncan had usually occupied at Boyars. The police had been. Rose had deemed it prudent to ring the local police, whom she knew. Jean's car had already been noticed. The police talked to Jean after she awoke. They brought her her handbag. There was nothing mysterious about the accident. Miss Curtland's friend had swerved to avoid a fox. The police gave her a lecture on not avoiding foxes. Dr Tallcott had come again. He wanted her to go to

387

hospital for checks, but Jean said she was about to go to London to her own doctor. Doctor Tallcott was a man filled with curiosity, a student of human nature, who had intended to be a psychiatrist. Rose had difficulty in preventing him from prolonging an interrogation of his patient. Had she been drinking? Did she take drugs? What, not even tranquillisers? Had she been under stress? Wasn't there anything which she would like to tell to a sympathetic medical man? Rose directed his attention to Jean's ankle, and asked about the concussion, happily so slight. Privately, Dr Tallcott told Rose that he thought Mrs Cambus was in a thoroughly disturbed mental state. Was she living with her husband? He wondered about her sex life. Rose let him wonder. He ventured to doubt the truth of her account of what had happened. Rose doubted it too. For instance, Jean had introduced the fox after twice telling the story without it, and could she possibly have 'lost her way' on a clear night on a road she had travelled hundreds of times?

Jean was sitting up in the big bed wearing one of Rose's prettiest nightdresses. She looked changed, alienated, almost frightening, like a large demonic bird with big eyes and a fierce beak. Her transparent nervous hands looked like claws. She seemed even thinner than when Rose had last seen her, the skin of her face, a yellowish ivory white, stretched over her bones. She was sitting upright against a pile of pillows and cushions; she refused to look at Rose, but kept looking intently and quickly round and round the room. Her lips were parted and she panted slightly.

It was late afternoon, the sun had set into bubbling masses of pink cloud, the lights were on in the bedroom, the curtains not yet drawn. A wood fire was sizzling in the grate. The room already had, for Rose, the quiet, idle, static feeling of an invalid's room, as if the terrible tumult of Jean's life, its past, its future, had for the moment withdrawn. Oh if I could only *keep* her here, Rose thought.

'Shall I draw the curtains?'

'Yes, please.'

She drew the curtains, old brown velvet curtains whose

linings tore a little every time they were drawn. Looking out into red twilight she saw the lights of the last village houses visible between two sloping fields, and nearer at hand Mousebrook hurrying along with what looked like a bird in his mouth.

'Darling, wouldn't you like something to eat? Some soup perhaps, anything you want?'

'No, not yet, don't go away.'

'Or would you like a drink, whisky, brandy?'

'No, no. That picture bothers me, it keeps moving.'

'I'll take it down.'

Rose removed from the mantelpiece a pair of china cats which had been there certainly for fifty years, probably more, climbed on a chair, her legs toasted by the fire, carefully unhooked the big red and orange and black abstract, and stepped down with it. She propped the picture, face inwards, against the wall, removed the chair and replaced the cats. The removal of the picture revealed a square of more conspicuously blue and white latticed wallpaper above the fireplace.

'That design keeps jumping about too.'

'The wallpaper? Would you like another room? You can have any room.'

'No. Don't go away.'

'I won't go away, my darling, I'll never go away!' Rose sat on the bed and touched but did not hold one of the thin translucent bird-hands. 'I want you to stay here for a long long time. I'll look after you. You can rest.'

'Just you.'

'Yes, just me. No one shall bother you.'

'I shall be dead soon. I think I'm dead already.'

'No you aren't, you're very very tired, you've been in a shipwreck, but now you're safe on land, you're warm and safe and looked after, what you need is to rest and sleep and gain strength and live yourself into a new world.'

'A nice idea, but nothing to do with me. Oh Rose – you can't conceive – what I am now –'

'You *will* stay here?'

'What else can I do? If there's some convenient spot you

might immure me. I'd like to hear the bricks climbing up and see the light vanishing.'

'Jean!'

It was later on. Jean had taken some soup and bread. She was dozing, perhaps asleep. She had asked Rose to leave her for a while, and Rose, exhausted and quite ready to withdraw for a little, was sitting by the fire in the drawing room with Mousebrook purring on her lap. Rose, in her own state of shock, was suffering an extraordinary mixture of emotions. A kind of fierce pleasure predominated. She felt she would now be perfectly happy to live on for months at Boyars, simply looking after Jean, she even imagined how they would pass their days, walking and reading and talking. It would be an ideal recapture of old days. However, there must come (how soon?) the moment when Rose must ask Jean if she wished to communicate with Duncan. The question of at least telling Duncan must arise, before he learnt from some other source that Jean had left Crimond and disappeared. Rose herself wanted to bring him the news of Jean's escape, her willing escape of course she would tell him. Jean had set herself free and was ready to come back: could that be the message? Here the picture, looked at close to, became darker. Suppose Jean did not want to go back to Duncan? Suppose she wanted to run to her father in America, or to flee to some unknown place and vanish forever? That awful image of being immured came back to Rose. How could she imagine what Jean's despair and misery might demand? Suppose, on the other hand, that Jean wanted to go back to Duncan, but Duncan would not forgive her? Would there be diplomacy, would Rose be the diplomat? Rose felt so possessive about Jean that she was reluctant to let anyone else come near her! The thought of 'the next moves' made her feel very afraid. Of course nothing must happen until Jean was ready. All the same Rose could not go on keeping her friend's presence a dark secret.

Later on still, after Jean had wakened, accepted a sleeping pill, and gone to sleep again, Rose telephoned Gerard. She had decided that she must and ought to share the problem, and telling Gerard didn't mean telling the world after all. It was nearly midnight, but she knew that Gerard would be up and reading.

'Hello.'

'Hello, Rose darling. What's up?'

'Look. I'm at Boyars. Jean is here.'

'What?'

'She's left Crimond, she's here.'

After a moment Gerard said, 'Has she *really* left him?'

'Yes.'

'Who left whom?'

'They agreed to part.'

'Oh. She won't run back, he won't come and take her?'

'I don't think so.'

'That's wonderful news. But what happened – she turned up in London and you took her to Boyars? Not a bad idea.'

'It's a long story, I'll tell you later. She's just been with me today. Don't tell anyone just yet.'

'Not Duncan?'

'No – not for a day or two – Jean's in such a state.'

'I can imagine. She'll have to be sure she isn't going to change her mind. But the news may get round. Crimond might send it around. Does he know where she is?'

'No. It may be better if no one knows where she is. I mean, she may not want to see Duncan, and if he finds out he may come rushing down. We don't know what either of them wants. She may decide to go to New York, or –'

'Yes, I know. Do you mind if I tell this to Jenkin? He's a wise bird, and –'

'Yes, all right, but no one else.'

'We'll think what to do. You stay with Jean, we'll handle Duncan. Look, darling, it's late, you've probably had quite a day, you can tell me the whole thing later – you go to bed now and so will I, and we'll talk again tomorrow morning. All right?'

'All right – good night then.'

'Goodnight, Rose, and don't worry, we'll think out what's best to do.'

Rose replaced the receiver. She had lost the initiative. She would not after all be the one, as she so much wished, to tell Duncan the news! Well, it was inevitable, she had to tell Gerard, and his suggested distribution of labour was rational and just. But supposing – supposing in that awful Crimond interlude Jean had learned to hate Duncan, or Duncan had learned to hate Jean?

'Nice of you two to invite yourselves,' said Duncan. 'Have a drink, sherry, whisky, gin? I don't see many people now, I keep company with these bottles.'

'Sherry, thanks,' said Gerard.

'Nothing yet,' said Jenkin, 'I'll shout.'

'Do that. You know, I'm thinking of resigning from the dear old office. All right, you, Gerard, will expect me to write a book, my memoirs or how to run the country, or something.'

'I wouldn't know what to expect,' said Gerard, 'a versatile chap like you might do anything.'

'Perhaps I'll take up oil painting. Or drink myself to death, that's always a worthy pastime. But what's the matter with you? Are you my friends, or are you a delegation?'

Gerard and Jenkin, sitting on the sofa while Duncan stood by the bottles, looked at each other.

'Come on, own up – none of those Rosencrantz and Guildenstern glances.'

'We are a sort of delegation,' said Gerard.

'Representing ourselves and Rose,' said Jenkin.

'Well, what is it, you're making me nervous.'

'Jean has left Crimond,' said Gerard.

Duncan handed Gerard the glass of sherry he had been holding. He poured himself out a neat whisky and said, 'Oh.'

'She's at Boyars with Rose.'

Duncan drank some of the whisky, and sat down in a chair opposite. His big sullen wrinkled face, his black-furred bull head, was turned toward Gerard, but his eyelids drooped.

'We felt,' said Gerard, 'that we should come and tell you, simply tell you, in case you heard some story or rumour – and we wanted you to know where Jean was and that she was all right.'

'What is "simply tell me"? You mean you don't propose to offer advice?'

'Of course we don't,' said Jenkin, 'we realise –'

'Did he ditch her?'

'I think Jean left him,' said Gerard, 'anyway she decided to leave, she wasn't forced to.'

There was a moment's silence.

'Well,' said Duncan, rising to his feet again, 'I thank the delegation and ask it to depart.'

Gerard put down his glass. He and Jenkin rose. Jenkin said, 'All this has only just happened. Before you decide what to do –'

'I'm not going to do a damn thing,' said Duncan. 'Why should I? I'm not even interested in your kind news. Goodnight.'

'I'm sorry, I was tactless,' said Jenkin to Gerard as they walked away down the road.

'He made tact impossible,' said Gerard. 'We did what had to be done.'

'It's my fault, I shouldn't have butted in. I've always felt Duncan didn't really like me.'

'Don't be silly. Of course he didn't mean what he said. But I don't know what he did mean. Come back to my place and we'll ring Rose.'

Left to himself, for a while Duncan sat and sipped his whisky. He sat still and breathed deeply, sipping the whisky as if it were a medicine which might relieve some immediate threat of suffocation. Then suddenly he stood up and hurled his tumbler into the fireplace. He strode to the bookshelves and began pulling the books out, sending them crashing in all

393

directions, he ran into the kitchen and swept a pile of plates onto the floor. He moaned, and beat upon the steel draining board with his fists, making a thunderous metallic drumming. He pounded the metal, lowering his head and wailing.

Rose opened the door. She had heard the sound, for which she had been waiting, of Duncan's car arriving upon the gravel drive. Duncan stepped out of the car and without hurry locked it up. He came to the door and through it, wiping his feet carefully upon the mat. It was raining. Rose closed the door and held out her hand. Duncan took her hand and kissed it, something he had never done before. No word was exchanged. Rose led the way into the drawing room.

'How is she?' said Duncan.

'All right. She looks like a ghost –'

'She's expecting me?'

'Yes. I didn't say a time.'

'She still wants to see me?'

'Yes, yes. You want to see her – you're not just coming out of –?'

'Out of what?'

'Sense of duty, thinking it might do her good –'

'I feel it is my duty and I think it might do her good. On the other hand it might not. I am being guided by you.'

'Oh *Duncan*,' said Rose, 'you know what I mean!' She was feeling exhausted and ready to cry.

'Yes. I do want to see her,' said Duncan.

'And you hope –'

'I hope, but I am prepared for the worst.'

'What would that be?'

'Oh anything – her wanting to go back to him and only wanting to see me to explain it, her finding she hates the sight of me, my finding I hate the sight of her. As we said on the telephone, it's a gamble.'

'You said it was.'

'But as I think we agreed, it was better not to put it off.'

'You mean *he* might turn up?'

'Not particularly that. *He* might turn up at any time, whatever happens, between now and the end of the world.'

Rose shuddered. 'Would you like some coffee, or a drink?'

'No, thank you.'

'Well, if you're ready, I'll go up and tell her you're here.'

She went upstairs and into the bedroom. Jean, who had now been at Boyars for several days, was up and dressed and sitting on the green sofa which had been drawn up near the fire. She was wearing a tweed dress which belonged to Rose. The dress was too large for her, but pulled in at the waist by a belt. Her ankle was tightly strapped in an elasticated bandage. She stood up when Rose appeared.

She looked now to Rose like a stranger, a strange bony sharp-featured elderly woman in an ill-fitting dress. Her dark hair which Rose had, after insistence, helped her to wash, was fuzzy and untidy. Her thin hands were always restless, one now repeatedly smoothing her dress, the other picking at her throat. She had cried a great deal in the days at Boyars and her eyelids were red and swollen, conspicuous in her white face. She was tearless now however. As Rose approached her she lifted her hand from her dress and made a curious gesture in the air as if setting aside some invisible web or curtain. Rose could not help wishing that Jean could have been as beautiful as she used to be to receive Duncan.

'I heard the car.'

'Yes, he's here,' said Rose. 'Would you like to see him? There's no need to now if later would be better.'

'He wants to see me?'

'Yes, of course, that's why he's come!'

Gerard, who had made the arrangement with Rose by telephone, had misgivings which he had not expressed. He had simply not been able to make Duncan out. Gerard had expected, as Rose too had expected, some kind of gratifying scene in which Duncan would express relief, his love for his wife, his satisfaction that she had left 'that man', a touching gratitude to those who had stood by him and supported his faith and his hope. Gerard imagined that, after the first understandable shock, Duncan would unburden himself as never before, rehearsing now the fears and hopes with which he had lived during this awful interim, and expressing at least a sober confidence in a future where 'all would be mended'. Duncan had declined any further meeting with Gerard, but they had talked on the telephone. Gerard had emphasised two things, that Jean had *decided* to leave Crimond, the parting was her initiative and her wish, and that Crimond had accepted her decision, so that they in fact parted *by agreement*. He added of course that Jean now very much wanted to see Duncan. He mentioned, vaguely, a car accident and a sprained ankle. Duncan listened to all this without comment, and eventually rang Rose to say that if Jean wished it, he would come. Rose, who had carefully composed what Gerard was to say to Duncan, was in fact not at all sure that she had understood Jean's state of mind. She had been unable, talking to Jean, to make up any coherent picture of what had happened. Jean had been frantic with grief: grief, Rose could only assume, at having lost Crimond. For Rose recalled Jean's first cry of 'He's left me!' and did not believe in the 'cold mutual agreement' which Jean spoke of later. It was Gerard who had been so anxious to hurry on the meeting with Duncan. Rose felt it was premature. But Jean had actually said, in answer, it is true, to Rose's repeated questions, that she wanted to see Duncan, and Rose had passed this on without qualification to Gerard. Gerard was certainly far from clear about Duncan's state of mind, even after he had realised how absurd his earlier expectations were. Duncan's laconic coldness on the telephone had expressed a continuation of his attitude of 'what is it to me?', though he had, evidently after reflection, told Rose (not Gerard) that he would see Jean. But did he wish to see her perhaps simply to revile her? Might he even attack her? Duncan was Gerard's old friend, but he was also a fey creature, a big unpredictable bad-tempered wild animal. Of course, as Gerard later told himself, Duncan must feel the gravest doubts about the story of Jean deciding to leave and Crimond agreeing, and had excellent reasons for believing that Crimond would *never* let Jean go.

'Bring him up then,' said Jean.

The door closed behind Rose. Jean moved toward the centre of the room. She stroked down her untidy hair with her fingers and looked up at the darker blue latticed square where the picture had been and where the colours were still 'jumping about', sometimes the blue foremost, sometimes the white. Her pale face was now flushed, her cheeks red as if brushed with rouge. She moved a few steps back, turning to face the door.

The door opened and Duncan came in alone. He turned and shut the door quietly, then turned back toward Jean. He was smartly dressed in a dark suit, one of his best, with a blue and white striped shirt and a dark tie. He had shaved carefully and combed down his wavy crown of dark, now rather longish, locks. He looked huge in the room, fatter perhaps, bulky, broad. They stared at each other. Jean, trembling, clawed at her throat again. As Duncan moved towards her she felt fear but did not move. She could not have spoken.

She saw a strange frightening look upon his face. Then he said, 'Suppose we sit down? Suppose we sit down *there*?' He pointed to the green sofa.

Jean backed awkwardly, then sat. The sofa groaned under Duncan's weight as he sat down beside her. He turned his big head towards her. Shrinking a little away, she looked at him.

'Do you want to be with me again, Jean?'

'Yes.'

'Are you sure?'

'Yes, yes –'

'Then that's settled.'

He put his arms round her, enveloping her, and they both closed their eyes. The strange look had been his attempt to control an agonising tenderness and pity which he now allowed to distort his face as he looked away over her shoulder.

Rose, now back in London, was surprised a few days later to receive the following letter.

My dear Rose,

I wonder if I could call on you to discuss a matter of importance? I suggest Tuesday of next week at ten. Could you let me know by letter if that is suitable, and if not suggest other possible times? Do not try to ring up, as I have had my telephone disconnected.

With kind regards,
 Yours
  David Crimond.

The letter upset Rose, frightened her, made altogether a disagreeable impression. She assumed that the 'important' matter must be Jean, and that Crimond wanted her to intercede or interfere or mediate on his behalf. What impertinence! Rose at once started to write a reply saying that Jean was happily reunited with her husband, and Rose could see no useful purpose to be served by a meeting. While writing this she reflected that perhaps after all Jean had given a truthful account when she said that the parting had been mutual, and in that sense willed by Jean. After Duncan's reappearance the idea that Jean had left Crimond was of course emphasised by her, and also by Rose. Crimond's appeal, if that was what it was, was at least valuable as evidence for this view of the matter. After further reflection, and before she had completed her indignant letter, Rose began to wonder if there were not possibly something else which Crimond wanted to say to her. Crimond's motive in thus coming, a motive anyway, might even be his wish to display his indifference to Jean's departure. Rose wondered uneasily if this something else might concern Gerard. Perhaps it was in this quarter that her mediation was being asked for? Perhaps Gerard had for some reason refused to see Crimond, and Crimond wanted Rose to remove a misunderstanding? It might be something to do with the book; and the wild idea even occurred to Rose that Crimond wanted her to persuade Gerard to provide a preface! Anything which connected Crimond with Gerard made Rose feel very uneasy. On reflection she thought it was more likely to be something about Jean and Duncan, though not necessarily what she had assumed at first. Perhaps Crimond simply wanted confirmation that Jean and Duncan were now reunited. Rose felt very disinclined to talk to Crimond about her friends, such talk, however careful, might be misleading and seem disloyal. However, she could be brief and it was an opportunity to set the whole matter completely beyond doubt. Last of all it occurred to her, and seemed quite likely, that Crimond was coming formally to thank Rose, and through her the *Gesellschaft*, for their financial support all these years! He had, in this, preferred her to Gerard, since Gerard would want to ask questions about the book. She decided to see Crimond. Her instinct was to tell Gerard at once, but she thought better of it. The meeting was best kept to herself until afterwards, until she knew what it was about and could compose a suitably calm and rational account for general consumption. If she told Gerard now he would fuss and speculate and make her even more apprehensive. So Rose wrote a reply saying simply that she would await him at her flat at the time suggested.

Duncan and Jean were still at Boyars, being looked after by Annushka. Rose and the others were, after so much anxious speculation, overjoyed at what at least appeared to have happened. On that rainy morning, after Duncan had gone upstairs, Rose had sat in the drawing room with the door open unable to do anything except wait and listen and tremble. Annushka brought her some coffee. Should she take coffee to Mr and Mrs Cambus? No! Annushka was just as anxious as Rose, but they exchanged no words on the subject, not even looks. Time passed. Rose walked up and down the drawing room, wandered into the dining room, into the library, into the study, into the turret room, into the billiard room, stood on the front steps and looked at the rain, listening for any sound from up above. What did she fear? Cries, screams, the sound of weeping? Nothing could be heard at all. Then, at a moment when she was back in the drawing room, Duncan came down the stairs. He looked stolid and enigmatic. He said nothing at once but marched across to the fireplace, followed by Rose who had run to meet him.

Duncan replied, gravely, 'I think it is all right.' But by now something in his face, a sort of composed complacency, had told Rose that things were not bad, were perhaps good.

'You mean,' said Rose, anxious for clarification which could be clumsily obtained now and might be more difficult later on, 'You mean you'll be together again, really and truly together?' She avoided asking: have you forgiven her? That might not be the way to put it at all.

'We hope so.' (Rose was glad of that 'we'.) 'It appears that we don't, in spite of recent events, hate the sight of each other. Rather the contrary.'

These few words were, characteristically, the extent of Duncan's report.

'Oh I'm so glad!' said Rose, 'I'm so glad!' and kissed him.

Then, with his permission, she ran upstairs to Jean. Jean cried, Rose cried. Jean had scarcely more to say, except for murmuring that she was relieved and happy and felt she had come out of a nightmare into the real world.

Then Jean came downstairs, Rose ran to tell Annushka, who already knew of course and came into the drawing room to be kissed by Jean and Duncan. Rose opened a bottle of champagne, she and Jean cried some more, they had lunch.

After lunch Jean rested, Duncan sat in the library reading Gibbon, Rose telephoned Gerard. Then Rose rested. She fell into a marvellous sleep and dreamt about an exceedingly beautiful garden in which Rose and Jean and Tamar were dancing with some children. After that they all had tea and talked ordinary talk. Rose suggested and they agreed that Rose should return to London and leave them to themselves for a while at Boyars, so that Jean's ankle could get better: the sprained ankle had assumed a special importance, symbol perhaps of deeper and more painful dislocations. Rose stayed that night and then departed. Of course she and Gerard agreed in the discussions which at once ensued that there was so much to mend, so much to be said, so many gestures to be made and accepted, it would be a long time before those two could be at peace together. Rejoicing was premature, what had really happened remained to be seen. They did rejoice however, and were glad to think of Jean and Duncan together at Boyars, and to have an interval before the anxieties attendant on their return to London, and reintegration into something like their former life. It was agreed that nothing could ever be the same, after the honeymoon at Boyars the recriminations were bound to begin, there was so much resentment and so much pain to be somehow worked through and worked off, it would be a long time before their reunion could be established as secure. Besides, what had really happened between Jean and Crimond, and how would what had happened affect Jean and Duncan? Might Crimond suddenly reappear in the role of Demon King? Along these lines Rose and Gerard and Jenkin went on speculating for some time, and Gulliver and Lily and Patricia and Gideon and everyone in Duncan's office and large numbers of other people less closely concerned had the pleasures of similar, and often less charitable, speculation.

Rose would have been happy in these days, for she believed, having seen them together, that Jean and Duncan would be 'all right', had it not been for her anxiety about Tamar. Jenkin had of course not divulged to anyone what Tamar had told him. Gerard, after a cautious enquiry, sheered off the subject which was evidently secret, and he said nothing to Rose about Tamar's extraordinary arrival at Jenkin's house. Rose knew that Tamar had been 'in a state', had run away from home to stay with Lily, and was now back with Violet. Rose had written to Tamar asking her to lunch, but had had no reply. Gerard and Jenkin seemed to have nothing to say on the subject of Tamar's troubles. Neither had Lily, whom Rose had rung up. Violet's flat was not on the telephone. Rose had been making up her mind to write to Violet, or else to appear unexpectedly at her flat one evening, when the drama of Jean's accident took her to Boyars. On her return to London there was still no letter from Tamar. Rose had written to Violet but had had no reply.

Now it was Tuesday, and the bell at Rose's flat had rung punctually at ten. Crimond had come up the stairs and was in Rose's sitting room.

Rose's first surprise was the extraordinary effect upon her of Crimond's presence in the room. It seemed like some fault of nature. How could *he* be *here*? Of course she had seen him not long ago at Gerard's and had, even more lately, been alone with him in his house. But to find him standing there in her own room, waiting for her to ask him to sit down, was positively weird. She felt the electric field round about him and it made her twitch.

He had left his overcoat in the hall, the door was shut, the electric fire was on. Outside the sun was shining on the white stucco fronts of the houses opposite. Crimond was wearing a black jacket, perhaps the one in which she had last seen him, and a clean white shirt and a tie. The jacket was visibly frayed and worn, but he looked, for him, quite presentable. On the last occasion he had resembled a priest. This time he looked more like a penurious young writer, tired, rootless, clever, frail. He gazed at her with a sad look, then looked around at her room. He said, his first words, 'I've never been here before.'

Rose said 'Yes' to this evident truth. She noticed, now more particularly, his accent, which sounded rather affected, Scots overlaid with Oxford. She felt awkward, had not planned where they were to sit, had somehow imagined that their brief colloquy could take place standing up. She decided it would be more business-like, less like a social scene, to sit at the table in the window. She motioned him to a chair and they both sat down.

Rose said quickly and abruptly, 'What do you want? Is it about Jean?'

Crimond had undone his jacket and put his forearms on the table, stretching out his long hands which were covered with fine red hairs. His nails were carefully cut but imperfectly clean, and the cuffs of his shirt were unbuttoned. He considered Rose's words and said, as if replying to some theoretical or academic question, 'The answer is no.'

'What is it then?'

Crimond made his thin mouth even thinner, looking first at the table and then at Rose. 'That will take a little time to explain.'

'I haven't got much time,' said Rose. This was not true. As Crimond continued to be silent, frowning, his pale blue eyes gleaming at her, she said, 'I think I must tell you that Jean has returned to her husband.'

Crimond nodded, then looked away and took a long controlled breath, not quite emerging as a sigh.

Does he want me to *sympathise* with him! thought Rose. She said, 'Is it about Gerard?'

'Is what about Gerard?'

'Your visit! You wrote saying you wanted to discuss an important matter! I'm waiting to hear what it is!'

'No, it's not about Gerard.' He added, looking at her again and smiling faintly, 'Don't be impatient with me!'

I must be *polite*, thought Rose, it may be a 'thank you' visit after all. She said in a more conciliatory tone, 'So the book is finished.'

'Yes. I'm sorry I didn't say earlier that it was nearly finished. I didn't intend to mislead you all. It was just psychologically difficult to say so. Perhaps I was superstitious, yes, I was superstitious, about the book. I thought I might never live to finish it.'

'It has certainly taken a long time, you must feel quite lost without it.' Rose and Gerard had of course discussed how, and whether, the break with Jean connected with the completion of the book, but had reached no conclusion. Perhaps the ending of his long task had disturbed Crimond's reason. His appearance and his manner struck Rose as extremely odd, and she wondered again if he were actually mad.

'Yes, it's like death.' He spoke solemnly, gazing at her intently. 'It is – a bereavement.'

Rose looked away, looked at her watch. 'Perhaps you will take a holiday now?'

'I'm afraid I am incapable of taking a holiday.' There was a sligh. pause, during which Rose tried to think of some suitable commonplace. He went on, 'I like your dress, it's the same green as you wore at the dance.'

Rose, annoyed by his remark, said, 'I didn't see you at the dance.'

'I saw you.'

That sounds like ill luck, she thought, if the wolf sees you first! Perhaps he really does want to talk about Jean? I certainly don't propose to sit here making polite conversation! 'You said you wanted to talk about something particular. Perhaps you could now say what it is?'

Crimond, who had been staring at her, looked away and again drew a long deep controlled breath. He looked about the room and seemed for a moment at a loss. 'It's something personal.'

'About you –'

'About me. Also about you.'

'I don't see how it can be about me,' said Rose coldly. She felt a tremor of fear, and all sorts of horrible crazy possibilities suddenly made their appearance. She thought, he's going to blackmail me – yet how can he – to get Jean back – or else it's something against Gerard – or – she hoped she was not displaying her emotion. 'Does it concern Gerard too?'

'No,' said Crimond, in a sharp peevish tone, 'it does not concern Gerard, Why do you keep dragging him in?'

'I'm not "dragging him in"!' said Rose, beginning to get annoyed. 'You've been so mysterious and sort of menacing. Perhaps I'm wrong, but I think you are full of ill-will towards us.'

'You are very wrong,' said Crimond, looking intently at her. He seemed now collected and very tense.

'You ought to be grateful to us.'

'I am grateful. But –'

'But what?'

'That's what I came about.'

'Well, then, what is it?'

'I want to know you better.'

Rose was amazed. 'You want all of us to be your friends again, after everything that's happened, after –?'

'No, not all. Just you.'

'Why just me?'

'Perhaps I had better be more frank.'

'Perhaps you had.'

'I came here to ask if you would consider marrying me.'

Rose flushed scarlet, and pushed her chair back. She felt almost faint with a mixture of anger and amazement. She could hardly believe that she had heard rightly. She said, 'Could you say that again?'

'Rose, I want you to marry me. Of course this must seem to you premature –'

'*Premature –!*'

'It would have been possible for me to proceed more indirectly, asking you out to lunch and so on, but such – gambits – would have been in the nature of subterfuges. I thought it better to announce my – my wish – at once, and let the other things follow from that.'

Rose clutched the collar of her dress and shrank back in her chair. She felt very frightened. 'Mr Crimond, I think you are mad.'

'Please, if you will, don't call me "Mr Crimond". I would like you to call me "David", but if at the moment you cannot, I would rather you just called me "Crimond", as other people do. I know that I am sometimes thought to be mad, but you must surely, and surely *now*, see that I am not.'

'This must be some sort of awful joke,' said Rose, 'or else a wicked premeditated *insult*.' She felt angry, she felt cornered. The electrical field, perceptible when he had first entered the room, increased in intensity, surrounded her and made her tremble, almost shake.

Crimond, now a little more relaxed, said in an explanatory tone, 'You know that I am not joking or trying to insult you. A proposal of marriage is not usually regarded as an insult.'

'But – you must be totally out of touch with reality! I can't understand how you can suddenly say this! It can't be anything to do with *me*! You must be doing it as a sort of crazy revenge, against Gerard, or against Jean, to hurt them – except you can't – it's something horrible –'

'Rose,' said Crimond, 'it's not horrible, and it's not any of the things you say –'

'You can't imagine that I could take such a "proposal" seriously! Are you so impertinent – or so naive? I don't know you, I don't like you. You have wantonly damaged the life and destroyed the happiness of my best friend, whom you appeared to be so madly in love with! And now you come to me with this insulting nonsense!'

'I can imagine,' said Crimond, 'that you may resent the proximity of my relations with your friend –'

'I don't "resent the proximity" – really, you are outrageous! I cannot interpret you except as false and wicked – there isn't any – any *context* – which could make what you say otherwise!'

'You argue well –'

'I'm not *arguing*!'

'What you say, and what you imply, deserves an answer. And this is just what I want to offer you. Of course I was in love with Jean. But my relation with her was an impossibility – we twice tried to live it, and proved it twice impossible.'

'Because she was married –'

'No, that was nothing. Because of the peculiar, the particular, intensity of our relationship. I could explain this at more length –'

'Please do not!'

'We attained an apex – after that we were bound to destroy each other. We both realised it. I was devouring her being and making her less. And after a time, she would have hated me. It was better to leave it behind as something perfect, and finished with. It was doomed.'

'So you parted by agreement – it was not just that you left her?' Rose could not help asking that question. In the midst of her fear and anger she could not help feeling a stirring of curiosity. It was all so extremely unexpected.

Crimond said thoughtfully after a moment, 'Essentially it was mutual. I thought there was a certain solution. I expect she has told you.'

'She has told me nothing.'

'I will tell you perhaps later on.'

'Mr Crimond,' said Rose, 'there is no later on. I want you to go away and I won't see you again.'

Crimond ignored this. 'My feeling, my love for Jean has nothing to do with what I want to discuss with you. Of course this shock tactic – I admit it is a shock tactic – needs to be talked over, to be understood –'

'I do not know what to think about you,' said Rose. 'I am now again inclined to think you are mad, unbalanced anyway. There is something vulgarly called being on the rebound. I think you are in a state of shock because of the ending – if it is the ending – of your long involvement with Jean. This together perhaps with finishing your book has temporarily unhinged you – this is the most charitable explanation of your tiresome and upsetting approach to me.'

'I did not mean to upset you – or rather I did – but not in an unpleasant way. I have always had a unique feeling for you, a unique sense of your being. Only two women have ever interested me. Jean was one, you are the other. I saw you before I saw Jean. I loved you before I loved Jean – No, let me go on. Of course this was a silent captive love, something inward and abstract. I had at once assumed you to be unattainable. Perhaps I was wrong –'

'Really –'

'I had the impression that you liked me. But I had not the courage to speak to you. I never expressed my love in any way. I regretted this later. I regret it now. Much later on I loved Jean, imagining that to be the only real love of which I was capable. Again I was wrong. My love for you had not died in captivity. But I never thought I could release it – until now – when I am brave enough to appear before you and ask you to believe me. Surely you can understand such a thing?'

'Please don't give me these explanations,' said Rose. 'You are half out of your mind because Jean is gone, and you want me to console you because you think you remember something you felt when you were twenty! A proposal of marriage in this situation is senseless.'

'I thought,' said Crimond, looking at her intently, 'that you were then, and are not now, indifferent to me.'

'I was, I am!'

'I thought this at our last meeting.'

'Our last meeting? You mean when I came to your house to find out –?'

'To find out if I was still alive. You were relieved.'

'Yes, but because of Jean, not because of you! And of course I didn't want to find you dead on the floor. I never cared for you, I find your ideas abhorrent –'

'Oh my ideas – but my person –'

The word 'person', sounding suddenly so archaic, almost made Rose laugh. 'Your *person* – are you suggesting –?'

'I mean my whole being. Look, Rose, don't be angry with me, and please forgive me for the suddenness, the shock – I couldn't do it any other way. We have neither of us been married, nothing prevents us from thinking in these terms. Love has to be awakened. I want to awaken yours. I think you are capable of loving me.'

There was a moment's silence. Rose said, 'I don't believe this stuff about the past, it's a fantasy, which occurred to you a few days ago, it's part of your own state of shock, and I'm sure, whether you admit or not, that this visit is really a revenge on Jean, and an attack on Gerard.'

They were silent for a moment, staring at each other across the table. Rose saw her hands trembling, and hid them on her knees.

Crimond murmured, 'It isn't so, it isn't so –' He went on, 'I felt it necessary to say what I have said. I hope you will, when you reflect, see how utterly serious it is, and must be. Naturally I don't expect any clear response from you now. Let us wait a while and talk of it again. I said at the beginning simply that I wanted to know you better. And I felt in honesty that I couldn't say just that without saying all the rest as well. But now that the rest is said, and I certainly do not and will not unsay it, let us return to that first idea. Please, let us know each other better. *That* cannot be an offensive idea. I suggest that we meet again in a week or so –'

'You persist in misunderstanding me,' said Rose, 'and you evidently don't listen to me!'

'Perhaps you find me rather – provincial – but –'

'Oh don't drag that in! If you think it's *class* –! It's perfectly simple, I don't like you!'

'I don't believe that,' said Crimond, and he flushed and drew back his thin lips to show his teeth. 'As for Gerard, what has he ever given you in return for your caring for him so –?'

Rose stood up and Crimond at once stood too. She was relieved to find herself more eloquently angry. 'How dare you speak like that of Gerard! You're envious of him, you're spiteful to him and insulting to me. You seem to imagine that I feel friendly, even warmly, towards you – I do not! And what your ridiculous "proposal" amounts to is that after being madly in love with Jean and wrecking her marriage you suddenly drop her and run to me in order to get your revenge on everybody, and – and you offer – you exhibit – some crazy feeling you have – it certainly isn't love – which consists of spite and vanity and sentimental nostalgia and inferiority complex – people thinking you're "provincial" – and you expect me to console you and – and *justify* you – oh, and what conceit, to imagine that I once cared for you and still do –'

'*It is* love,' said Crimond. '*You* are misunderstanding *me*.'

'When did you think of all this, three days ago? How can I take you seriously?'

'Of course you must be surprised, and perhaps you resent my direct approach, but –' Then he suddenly cried out loudly, 'Oh God, I could *explain* it all!' Then he said, quietly again, 'When can we meet – please –'

'I don't "resent" it,' cried Rose, 'I'm not *interested* enough to resent anything! I don't want to discuss your feelings. You are an enemy of people that I love, you are a person whom I utterly reject. I don't want to see you, I ask you to go and not to trouble me with any more of this nonsense. Now please go away, and understand that I don't want to see you again!'

She moved from the table and went to open the door. Looking back at him she saw his face for a moment blazing with emotion. The next moment, still flushed, he resumed his impassive expression. He walked as far as the middle of the room where he stopped, drew his heels together and bowed slightly. Then he went past her through the doorway, picked up his coat in the hall, and left the flat closing the door quietly behind him.

Rose stood still. His sudden departure, his *absence*, came to her as a strange shock. He was no longer there – and she was standing alone in the most terrible storm of her own emotions. How *could* he have come to say such a thing, to upset her so, to *hurt* her so! She felt, in that moment, dreadfully dreadfully *hurt*, wounded, as if he had rejected her, not she him. How could he so unfeelingly, so brutally, have put her in a situation where she was forced to behave as she had just behaved! I shouldn't have spoken like that, she thought, I lost my head, I should have been cool and collected and courteous, and not let him stay so long and say so much. I should have asked him to go away at the start. Of course I ought not to have let him come at all. I was too unkind, and it wasn't exactly what I felt either. I did like him then, at Oxford, I admired him, we all did. Oh I shall regret this so much, it will cause me so much pain later, that I behaved so stupidly, so badly.

Then she thought, I'll run after him. Then she thought, but it would be undignified and would give the wrong impression. Then she found herself dragging open the door of the flat and running down the stairs.

The air outside met her with a tidal wave of cold. She stood on the frosty slippery pavement and looked up and down. Had he come by car? Had he driven off already? He was not in sight. She ran to the corner and looked both ways along the next road. A car some distance away was just pulling out and disappearing. She ran back, past her house, slipping on the pavement and grasping the railings to prevent a fall. She scanned another road but could not see him. She walked slowly back and in again at the wide open door and up the stairs. She shut herself into the flat and leaned back against the door. She was gasping aloud. What was the matter with her? Why did it now seem the most important thing in the world to find Crimond and bring him back and talk to him and go on talking to him? Why ever had she let him go? Why had she spoken to him in such a crude cruel way? What could he be thinking of her now, he so proud a man, who had trusted her with so amazing an admission? He had said, surely she would understand such a thing. Yes, yes, she would, she did. She was deeply moved by that captive love which had never died. She believed him. She ought to have thanked him for loving her with such a love.

Rose began to walk about in her sitting room, up and down, up and down. The sun had gone, and she turned on the lights. Was it possible that somehow, within a period of minutes, she had *fallen in love* with Crimond? Why was I so aggressive, so final, she thought. Really, he has done me an honour – even if he only thought of me as a life-line. I was so haughty, so awful, so vulgarly conceited, talking of his insulting me by saying he loved me. I ought to have been grateful. I didn't have to reject him like that, to drive him away, to be so rude. I could have said I'd see him again. I ought to have done so anyway out of compassion. Why couldn't I even feel sorry for him, there would have been no harm in that. He looked so tired and so sad. I can still tell him, I can hear that *explanation* he said he could make. Only he won't forgive me for what I've said, he won't think I'm sincere. Oh what is happening to me, and what have I done!

Rose was aware, now, that she was intensely *flattered* by Crimond's homage. He, so fastidious, so aloof, had come to her as a suppliant. He said he loved her and had always loved her. Of course he is mad, she thought, I always believed he was mad. But how different that madness seemed now when it was expressed as love for her. I must see him again, she thought, I must see him *today*. I can't go on without seeing him. I'll ring him up, he may be home by now. She began to look in the telephone book, then remembered he had said he had no telephone. She thought, I'll drive to his house. But what could she say when she was there, what reason could she give, her appearance could only seem like a total surrender, and supposing he rejected her. Then I should go mad too, she thought, I *am* mad – but it's such a pain, I must relieve the pain somehow, oh why didn't I keep him here at least while I *thought* about it! I'll write him a letter and then run out and post it. I've got to do something or my heart will burst. I'll write a careful letter and suggest that we have another talk soon, I'll say I was sorry I was so rude, and I didn't mean to be, I'll say . . .

With a sense of relief she set out pen and paper and sat down at the table. She began hastily to write.

My dear David,

I am sorry I spoke so ungraciously to you today. What you had to say took me by surprise, it frightened me and I instinctively thrust it aside. I want now to thank you very much for the honour you have done me. I believe that you are sincere and I appreciate your feelings. I confess that you have disturbed me. I would like to see you again in order to efface the unpleasant impression which I must have made. I hope you will forgive me. It would, I think, be a good thing for both of us if we could talk together more peacefully and quietly. I will, if I may, write to you again shortly and suggest another meeting. With affectionate regards,

Yours,
Rose.

Rose read this through carefully, then crossed out the sentences about being disturbed and hoping to be forgiven, and wrote the letter out again. The writing of it relieved the pain. She was still looking at it when the telephone bell rang. Her immediate thought was, it's him, he feels just as I do, that we *must* meet again. She ran to the telephone, fumbling clumsily to pick it up.

'Hello, Rose, it's me,' said Gerard's voice.

Gerard. She had so completely forgotten Gerard's existence that she gave a little exclamation of surprise, and then was silent holding the instrument away from her. She could hear Gerard saying, 'Hello, Rose, is that you?'

She said, 'Could you hold on a moment, I must turn something off in the kitchen.'

She went away into the kitchen and looked at a row of matching red saucepans standing in order of size. She went back to the telephone.

'Yes?'

'Rose, what's the matter?'

'Nothing's the matter.'

'You sound very odd.'

'What did you want?'

'"What did I want?" What sort of a question is that? I'm just ringing you up! Are you ill?'

'No, no, I'm sorry –'

'I did want to ask you something actually, do you know when Jean and Duncan are coming back?'

Gerard? Jean and Duncan? Who were these people? Rose tried to concentrate. 'Very soon, I think, Tuesday or Wednesday, that's what Jean said when I rang her yesterday evening.'

'I'm so glad, I thought they might be afraid to show their faces in London. Look, could we have supper this evening, at your place, or I'll take you out?'

'I'm sorry, I can't.'

'Lunch then.'

'No, I've got to see someone –'

'Ah well – it's short notice, I'll try again. Darling, are you sure you're all right?'

'Yes, of course. Thanks for ringing. I'll give you a ring soon.'

Rose, who had no engagements that day, returned to the table. She thought, I am out of my mind. It is *impossible*, because of Gerard, because of Jean, for me to have any relation of any kind with Crimond. If I were to go round to his house now, which is what I want to do more than anything in the world, I am capable of falling into his arms, or at his feet. I ought to be locked up, I must lock myself up. This is dangerous insanity and I must get over it. Perhaps I could just send him the letter though – just the letter to take away that awful impression, to make peace somehow between us, otherwise I shall be in pain forever, thinking of what he must think of me. I could cut out the bit about seeing him again. But of course he might take the letter as encouragement, he might come again, simply turn up. Oh how I wish he would! She went back to the table and took up an envelope. Then she read the letter again and crumpled it up. Tears came into her eyes.

I pity him, she thought, that's what I must tell myself ever after. I love him, I love him, but it's no use. How can I make sense, how can something like this happen so quickly? But it has happened – and it's impossible, it's deadly, it must simply be stopped and killed, I must *drown* these thoughts. The least weakness could make a catastrophe, a desolation. No one must know. How could I live if Gerard knew? If anything were to happen – it could only go wrong – and that would break me, it would break some integrity, some dignity, some pride, something by which I live. I can't risk my life here. But, oh, what pain, a secret pain that will be with me forever. I must be faithful to my real world, to my dear tired old world. There is no new world. The new world is illusion, it's *poison*. God, I am going mad.

She went into her bedroom. She thought, and he wanted to *marry* me! She threw herself on the bed and wept bitterly.

During the short time when Rose was with them at Boyars, Jean and Duncan had kept up a pretence of some sort of instant recovery. Rose had been amazed at their calmness. At dinner that evening they were able to be almost like their old selves. This was not a prearranged 'act', it was an instinctive façade set up to make endurable Rose's embarrassing presence, her status as a witness who would eagerly report what she had seen in other quarters. It was necessary to 'impress' Rose before she could be got rid of. Rose was duly impressed and described their achievement to Gerard; at once however she and Gerard set to work to correct any misleading rosy impression which might have been made. They agreed that the 'calmness' was itself an effect of shock, the 'jollity' to be compared with the nervous cheerfulness of bereaved people at funerals, who then go home to weep. They sketched out many trials and difficulties, and wondered whether the reunion would work at all. Perhaps it might even collapse at once through Duncan's uncontrollable resentment, or Jean's flight back to Crimond. Rose and Gerard did not however try to imagine in detail what their friends were now up to, and did not continue their speculations beyond generalities; it was necessary to wait and see. Such temperance was characteristic of these two.

Rose had considered leaving Boyars at once, on the evening of Duncan's arrival, but thought it wise to wait until the next morning just to see a little how things were going on. She thought her presence, just at first, might be helpful, imposing a calming limiting formality. She had asked Annushka to make up a bed in the room at the back of the house which Duncan had occupied on the weekend of the skating. She said nothing about this and did not attempt to discover where he had spent the night. In fact Duncan had spent that night by himself in that room. After the first discovery that 'they did not hate each other', Jean and Duncan fell into an amazing shyness, a kind of mute fear, a time of not uncomfortable silences, when sitting in the same room was enough. They were soon aware, and as a short prospect this was a relief (so Rose was right), that they were simply waiting for Rose to go. At lunch, even at tea, there was an air of slightly crazy cheerfulness, but at dinner they were acting a part. They sat with Rose briefly after dinner, then disappeared saying, truly enough, that they were 'absolutely exhausted'. As soon as they were out of sight Rose *ran* to her bedroom up the back stairs so as not to pass Jean's room, noisily closed her door, and exhausted too, went early to bed and to sleep. The scene in Jean's room was brief too. Jean and Duncan wanted a rest from each other. They were aware too of the proximity of Rose. They hardly needed words to agree that tonight they would sleep apart. Duncan, also using the back stairs so as not to pass Rose's room, which lay between, tiptoed to his former bedroom, not surprised to find the bed made up and the room warm. Jean took one of Dr Tallcott's sleeping pills and went to sleep at once. But Duncan stood for a long time in the darkness at the window. At first he did not turn on his light because he was waiting for Rose to turn out hers. He could see the faint glow of her light on the lawn and on the curving wall of the turret. But when it went out he stayed there standing in the dark. He opened the window and let in the chill but moist air which even carried very faintly the smell of wet earth. The rain had ceased and a few stars were visible. He stood at the window uttering deep breaths like little soundless sobs. He felt the exalted anguish of a man in a spiritual crisis who is struck down by a sudden visitation, a mixture of shock, prostration, fear, and a weird painful joy. He was glad to be alone and able to tremble and gasp over it all. His irritable coldness to Gerard and Jenkin had not been entirely simulated. He had to stay cool, to stay cold, so as not to expect too much, not to expect anything, not to imagine the future at all; and he was, helpfully, annoyed by the gleeful faces of his friends bringing the good news and expecting him to be excited and grateful. He had inhibited his hopes, deliberately feared the worst, even nursed his old huge resentments, and did not know until he was actually in Jean's presence that he still absolutely loved her, and that she at least sufficiently seemed to love him. That was enough of a miracle to rest upon for one night at any rate.

Rose breakfasted early the next morning, and said goodbye to her guests who duly came down and seemed to be orderly and sane, and for whom Annushka's more elaborate breakfast arrangements were now waiting. The sun was shining upon the wet garden. They waved Rose off; but before the sound of her car had died away Jean broke down. She ran upstairs and locked herself in her bedroom. Duncan, outside, could hear her sobbing hysterically. At intervals he knocked and called. He was not impatient. He sat down on the floor in the corridor and waited. Annushka brought him a chair and a cup of coffee. As Duncan sat, listening to Jean weeping, a kind of resigned calm descended on him. He would have preferred to sit on the floor, but had to sit on the chair out of politeness to Annushka.

At last the door was opened. Jean unlocked it, then rushed back to the bed and lay there crying more quietly. Duncan looked round the familiar room, where the wood fire was blazing brightly. He noticed, which he had scarcely taken in yesterday, the demoted picture and the rectangle of blue paper. He picked up the octagonal table, decanted the books upon it onto the floor, put it beside one of the windows and placed two upright chairs beside it. Then he went to the bed, sought for Jean's two hands, pulled her up and led her to the table. They sat, half facing each other, half facing the sunlit view over little green hillsides, some distant village houses and the tower of the church. As soon as Duncan seized her Jean stopped crying. She sat now with her hands palm downwards on the table, her lips parted, her face wet, her hair tousled, looking away out of the window. She was still wearing Rose's tweed dress, but had taken the belt off. Duncan watched her for a while in silence. Then he drew out a handkerchief and leaned over and carefully dried her face. He drew his chair closer and began to caress her hands, and her arms, thrusting back the loose sleeves of the dress, then to stroke down her hair, combing it out with his fingers. Jean began to sigh quietly, bowing her head to the rhythmical movement of his big heavy hand.

After a while, moving away from her, he said, 'So the Rover is a write-off?'

'Yes.'

'What happened?'

'I was running away, too fast.'

'Will you run back equally fast?'

'No. That's smashed – too.'

'Aren't you still in love?'

Jean said, gazing out of the window, 'It's over.'

'I shall take some convincing.'

'I will convince you.'

'It'll take a long time, you know, to put us together again. Many tears. We must show all our wounds, tell each other the truth, abstain and fast. Time must pass. We do not know what we shall be or what we shall want.'

'But we'll be together.'

'I hope so.'

'You pity me.'

'I pity you very much, that is something you will have to put up with.'

'I am afraid of you.'

'Oh good – but, oh my darling, let us be happy at last.'

'Just when everything's going well, you spoil it all!' cried Lily.

'Sex is going well,' said Gulliver. 'Nothing else is. And don't say "what else is there". I'm tired of your smartness.'

'I'm not smart. I just try to be. You're hurting me deliberately. You've become mean and cruel. What's the matter with you?'

'I've told you what's the matter, I'm worthless.'

'That's what I say! So we're both worthless! So let's stick together!'

'No, you're real, you're something. I'm nothing. You've got money, that's something.'

'Then let's celebrate, let's go to Paris.'

'No. And you've got some inside, you've got courage, you're naive, that's something too, you've got being, you are un-educated and stupid, but you actually want to do things, you've got *joie de vivre*.'

'I wish you had. You've been a perfect misery for days. All you need is a job.'

'All I need is a job! How dare you taunt me! You despise me!'

'I don't. You're tall and dark and good-looking.'

'I shall never be employed again, never. Do you realise what it's like to face that? You don't care, you actually like doing nothing. I don't.'

'You can write can't you? You started writing another play.'

'It's no good. I can't write.'

'Couldn't we do something together, set up a small business, money could do that.'

'What sort of small business? Manufacturing ball-bearings or face cream? We haven't any skills. We'd just lose your money. Anyway, I'm through with your money.'

'Oh stop it, you bloody man! Can't Gerard get you a job? He tried before, didn't he?'

'Yes, and he's just tried again, he oh so kindly sent me to a man who ran a literary agency who told me to get lost! Gerard doesn't care. He only does fake good works to make people admire him.'

'That's not true. You said he led you on and dropped you! That's why you're against him!'

'He didn't even lead me on!'

'Gull, don't be so awful when things are getting better. *We're* better, Tamar's gone home, thank God, and she's back at work, Jean's come back to Duncan, it'll soon be Christmas –'

'Tamar's another damned soul who'll kill herself with drugs or cancer. And Duncan will kill Jean, he can't forgive her twice, he's just pretending, I bet she's scared stiff. One night when they're in bed she'll find him staring at her like Othello, and then he'll strangle her.'

'You'd better go to a doctor and get yourself seen to.'

'Why do you talk about *them* as if they cared about *us*? You're a snob. You'd like to belong to that horrible set, but they'd never regard you, or me, as one of them, not in a hundred years, so you needn't try so hard!'

'Oh shut up! Go and join the Foreign Legion!'

'I'm going away, I'm serious. I'm giving up my flat, I've sold the furniture to the next tenant, I've sold my books –'

'No!'

'Well, most of them, what do you think was in those boxes I asked you to store for me? I can't afford to live like that any more, and I'm not going to sponge on you. I'm going to the north.'

'To the *north*?'

'I want to be where people are really suffering and not just pretending to. I want to join the dregs of humanity, the bottom people, I want to be really poor. I've got to stop thinking I'm a bourgeois intellectual. If I can stop thinking that I can get a job. But not here, not with you lot, not with bossy Gerard and smarmy Jenkin and aristocratic Rose –'

'I'll come with you –'

'Don't be silly. You're another thing I've got to get away from, you're a bad symbol, you're an idle woman.'

'I think you hate women, I thought that when I first met you. I wish you'd let me do your horoscope.'

'And you're superstitious, and your grandmother was a witch, and –'

'Gull, do stop *terrifying* me, you're not yourself.'

'I have no self.'

'Now you're being smart. You don't mean all those horrid things you said about –'

'About *them*, no, all right, I didn't. But can't you recognise a man in *despair*?'

'Well, I'm in despair too, only I don't make such a fuss about it. All right, I've got some money, but I can't do anything with it or myself – then you turned up and I thought life made sense at last, and now you bother me with your bloody despair!'

'There comes a time when a man has to be *alone*, *really* alone.'

'Gull, please, won't you go and talk it over with someone, with Jenkin, I'll ring him up –'

'You won't. He's running away too, and I don't blame him, he's going to South America.'

'How did you know, did he tell you?'

'Marchment told me, that schoolmaster, I even went crawling to him for a job. Jenkin's fine, only he'd tell Gerard, and I don't want to go to South America.'

'I should hope not! You're *ridiculous*. Why not stay in London and live here with me? If you want to work with bottom people there are plenty in this city, I could work with you –'

'Lily, I don't want to work with people, like a social worker,

I want to be with people! It's no good, I'm through with compromises.'

'Gulliver, don't leave me. You're the only person who has ever really made me *exist*. We love each other, we agreed that the night before last. Let's get married, *please* let's get married.'

'No. I'm leaving.'

'Where do you imagine you're going to?'

'Leeds, Sheffield, Newcastle, I haven't decided. Everyone's unemployed up there.'

'You're mad – I'll tell Gerard to stop you –'

'If you do I'll never forgive you.'

'But you'll let me know where you are?'

'I'll write, probably, but not at once. Now please don't make a scene.'

Lily jumped up and began to cry. 'You'll never write, you'll disappear, you'll marry a girl in Leeds and get a job in a factory and I'll never never see you again!'

Jean and Duncan, now back in London, seemed to their anxious friends to be coming to terms with each other more easily than had been predicted. They were both *very tired*. They had been carrying heavy burdens and were glad now to lay them down, together, exhausted. There was a mutual agreement to tend themselves and each other. They were assisted here by a deep and determined hedonism, an early bond between them. With Duncan again, Jean soon rediscovered the pleasure principle. They made jokes about this. They fell over each other trying to invent consolations, gratifications, treats. They felt that, after surmounting mountainous difficulties to be together again, they deserved to be rewarded. Once they were known to be back they were showered with invitations.

The goal of being happy united them. The healing of deep terrible wounds was another matter. The question 'Can I forgive her?' had made, for Duncan, the concept of forgiveness so murky and complex that he ceased employing it. There were many other ways of handling the situation. They both referred to precedent; they had managed it last time, and hadn't they managed it fairly easily? It seemed so, but they could not remember too clearly. It had seemed, at the beginning, that they must simply *work* at their reconciliation by long talks about the past, telling the truth, showing every scar, probing every misunderstanding. But this comprehensive programme of mutual revelation proved difficult, and was felt by both, privately, to be dangerous. They did talk a great deal however, and told each other how valuable this was. They talked, selectively, about what had happened in Ireland. That first drama seemed sometimes closer, more real, more full of pictures, than what had happened more lately, over which so many clouds now hung. Duncan told Jean, for instance, what he had never recounted before, how, when he was in Wicklow, he had sat in a public house among the damned. This evocation of Duncan's state of mind seemed to have significance

423

for both of them. He had never told Jean, and certainly did not tell her now, of how he had found Crimond's hair on the floor of their bedroom. This detail, utterly revolting to Duncan, had with the years gathered all kinds of filth in his mind, and he had no intention of giving it more power and form by putting it into Jean's mind. Neither of course did he tell her about Crimond's blow and its long frightful sequel, the damage to his eye, the damage to his soul; of these terrible things he was bitterly ashamed. In fact, although they talked and reminisced a lot, and carefully handled a good deal of interesting material, neither of them had much to say about Crimond. It was as if, in that important central spot, there was a curious lacuna. They constantly talked round him but not about him. Well, was it really so important to talk about him? Duncan had wanted to be convinced, and Jean had engaged to convince him, that her relation to Crimond was finally over. But it became evident that this could not be done in any direct or simple way. Of course time would show. But how much time would be needed, perhaps the rest of their lives? Duncan watching her, thinking about her, could not but believe her still in love with Crimond. Such a passion could not suddenly vanish, it could only die of long starvation. Let it starve then. But he found it difficult to ask straight questions about this mystery. 'Telling each other everything' was to have included a long and detailed reliving of her whole relationship with Crimond, including the details of exactly how they came to part, so as to determine to the satisfaction of both of them that it was now at an end. This did not come about. A look of such misery came over Jean's face when he put certain questions that Duncan felt too sorry for her to proceed. He wanted to know what *exactly* they had said to each other which constituted 'an agreement'; but Jean was vague, made contradictory answers, changed the subject. Nor could he, talking to her, make any sense of the car crash, which on reflection seemed to have something odd about it. One subject after another was clumsily handled and postponed. Perhaps that was the only way to proceed and perhaps they were thereby making progress. In fact they did make progress, but not by the clarifi-

424

cation and truthfulness method. The 'fasting and abstaining' which Duncan had had in mind concerned or included sex. He had had, at Boyars, no idea of how, when, or whether, they could establish anything like their former sexual relation. He sometimes wondered whether it was *conceivable* that she could move from Crimond's bed to his, or that he could accept her with the aura of Crimond upon her. But a greater and more impersonal power, to which they both silently and readily submitted, brought it about that after a due time they found themselves in bed together again. This significant reunion was blessed and hastened by a sort of gentle tenderness with each other, an eagerness to please, which perhaps adequately took the place of showing wounds and telling the truth. They did not ask, 'Do you still love me?' But love was there, busily moving about inside what still seemed, at times, the awful mess of their damaged marriage.

The most important thing which Duncan did not tell Jean, and which he felt she did not guess, was the violence and ferocity of his hatred of Crimond. Of this he spoke to nobody. Of course it was taken for granted that Duncan loathed his rival. But as he and Jean gradually 'learnt' each other again, he felt that she, with enough to do struggling with her own darkened imagination, assumed that as Crimond receded from her, he receded from Duncan too. It was not so. Of course Duncan continued to wonder whether Jean had really left Crimond voluntarily, and whether, on any day, if he were to whistle she would run back. These were doubts and specula-tions which, constituting an intelligible pain, he had to live with. His hatred for Crimond was something else, obsessive, primaeval, poisonous, deep, living within him like a growing beast, living with his life, breathing with his breath. He continually rehearsed the defeat in the tower room, and his last sight of Crimond in that shameful encounter in the dark beside the river. The fall down the stairs, the fall into the river, awful images of his cowardly weakness and his stupid grace-less suffering. These things must be paid for. Of course he wanted to settle down again with Jean, and his 'let us be happy' had come from the heart. Sometimes *that* future was real, and he was pleased in her pleasure when they planned their treats and consolations. But at the same time there was another event in the future over which he brooded as over a precious dragon's egg, a dream which was becoming hideously like an intention, the moment when he would go to Crimond and kill him.

Meanwhile, in the ordinary world, the pursuit of pleasure was taking the form of plans. Duncan still went to the office and was soon to be promoted to a high place, though not so high as that which Gerard had rejected, some said funked. But Duncan had lately decided to refuse this 'plum', to quit Whitehall and go and live in France with Jean, as she had always wanted to do. They agreed, for they often found relief in discussing their friends, that Gerard had been a fool to refuse the offer of great power, since he could do nothing with his leisure and was idle and discontented. *They* were different, *they* would use *their* freedom to manufacture happiness. Much time was spent studying maps and house agents' brochures. They talked of old farmhouses to be restored and altered, of gardens and swimming pools and proximity to the sea. Meanwhile they 'went out' a good deal, to theatres and parties and restaurants. They ate and drank well. Jean bought jewellery, dresses. They saw a modest amount of Rose and Gerard, and one evening went to a dinner party at Gerard's house, organised by Pat and Gideon, where Rose and Jenkin were present and a man from Duncan's office and his wife. Gerard declared he had given up entertaining since Pat had taken over. Gulliver and Lily were invited, but Lily refused and Gulliver did not answer. Rose invited Jean and Duncan to lunch, but only Jean came, and talked about their recent weekend in Paris. Of course Duncan's old friends behaved with exquisite tact and intelligence, but they could not but seem to be inquisitive observers. At the dinner party Jenkin had mentioned Tamar, and said, without details, that she had been ill, but was better. This reference gave Duncan an uncomfortable feeling. Of course he had not forgotten that episode, but he remembered it only in the way in which one recalls something whose status is that of 'being forgotten'. He thought of it and instantly dismissed it. He had not told Jean about it. It remained put away as something he would tell her one day, in their new life, in France, telling it casually, diminished into the almost nothing which it essentially was.

Gulliver had got as far as King's Cross Station. It was nine o'clock in the morning and he had come to look at the timetables. He had fixed his departure for the following day. He had scrambled out of his flat the morning after his 'despair' session with Lily, fearing that she might turn up to dissuade him. Lily did in fact arrive just after he had left. He had now been staying for several days at a cheap lodging house, it could hardly be called a hotel, near to the station. He was encouraged to find how easily, *so far*, he was putting up with the being-no-one and having-nothing of this new state of affairs. He was frightened too of course. He had delayed his departure because of matters, not yet entirely complete, to be settled with his landlord, with the new tenant who had bought some of his furniture, with the man who had bought the rest of his furniture and some of his books. These latter transactions brought in a larger sum of money than he expected, so that, together with his still existent savings, he could at least start his new life without being penniless.

He tried not to think about Lily. He felt he could do nothing about the 'Lily problem' and it was partly from that that he was running away. He had said sincerely that he loved her, he was exceedingly touched that she said she loved him. But he was dismayed by the talk of marriage. How could he marry somebody like Lily, generally thought to be rather ridiculous, a 'rich tart'? He could not bear to be, and be seen to be, financially dependent on her. He could not bear not having a job, especially when 'hanging around' with Lily, and in the proximity of Gerard whose attempts to get work for him had so consistently failed, and who perhaps blamed Gull for this lack of success. He felt again his old childish feeling of being the outsider, the misfit, the nonentity. He was indeed truly 'in despair', 'at the end of his tether', and *had* to get out of London to somewhere quite else where perhaps his luck would change. Gulliver was serious in his resolve to embrace his misfit role and 'be no one', yet all the same he could not help glimpsing himself in the future as *someone*, however poor and obscure, using his talents and making a romantic marriage. Perhaps his pictures of himself as a retarded Dick Whittington did not exclude the 'girl in Leeds' to whom Lily had referred. The mention of Leeds had brought up the problem, then not yet solved, of where he was actually going. Coming to King's Cross was itself an act of decision. (In the interim he had considered France, Spain, India, Africa, America and Australia.) He had decided to go to Newcastle, influenced by the idea of being, where he had always wanted to be, beside the sea. His plans were not now quite as selflessly empty as they had been at first, he had stopped enacting his departure as if it were his death. What would he do when he emerged from the station in Newcastle, a town which he had never visited before? Of course he would have to find some cheap digs where he could leave his suitcases. He had reluctantly left a lot of clothes behind, not with Lily but at a bookshop he used to frequent. It had been *agony* choosing which to leave. Well, then he would go to the local employment exchange, and then, or perhaps first, ferret out where the little theatres were, the theatre workshops, the pubs which put on 'protest' shows. His Equity card was in his pocket. People content with very little pay can sometimes turn up at theatres and get jobs. If he could get even a quarter of such a job he might also earn money as a waiter or a cleaner. All these extremities, which he had certainly considered, would have been psychologically much more difficult to face in London where he cared about appearances and had Lily to run to. In the north he could be, what he had essentially become, a poor man looking for a job, an unemployed person among others, a man in a queue. And if he was prepared to take anything surely he would find something.

It was extremely cold in the station, but Gulliver was wearing his best thick winter overcoat, an expensive garment designed to last forever, which he now regarded as a prime piece of his equipment. Looking away beyond the vaulted roofs where the rails led on into the grey and recent daylight, he saw that it was beginning to snow. He walked a little way along one of the platforms to inspect the snow and was reminded of Boyars and the skating party and 'well done our side'. If only that beautiful triumphant Lily could be the *whole* of Lily! But he knew that love was not supposed to work like that. A huge diesel engine moved slowly past him and he watched the line of carriages, people at the windows, people, people, off to the north, off to the north. A child waved excitedly to him and he waved back. The station with its sombre yellow brick and its dimmed lights beneath its high arches was like a cathedral. It was also, it occurred to him, like a huge stable where the engines, with their long yellow noses and their sad dark green eyes looked like big gentle beasts. Yet they were lethal beasts too who would guarantee a man sudden and certain death. Gull hurried back to the timetable boards. There was a good selection of trains, and he noted down some early ones. Grantham, Peterborough, York, Darlington, Durham, Newcastle. Newcastle, Dundee, Arbroath, Montrose, Stonehaven, Aberdeen . . . Where might not that long-distance train carry him in the end? At any rate it was settled that tomorrow a particular train would take him away from his old life, perhaps forever. But I'm still in the old life now, he thought, I can't yet imagine that all these great intentions, those brave gestures like giving up my flat, are real choices. It's not too late, I can still go back, I can ring up Lily, we could have lunch together. Is my believing this what makes me able to look at a list of trains and choose one? It doesn't hurt yet like a real decision would. I'm still weighted down by my old London life. I suppose there'll be a moment when the balance begins to tilt the other way, and another scene and *other people* will be real, and London and Gerard and Lily will be a dream. When will it come? When I get on the train, when the train starts, when it arrives, when I stand in the station at Newcastle and look for the exit, when I walk out into the street and wonder which way to go? Or later when I talk to someone who *attends* to me, even if it is only a man in an office? Or when I find a friend? Ah, a friend . . . Perhaps it will take a long time for the balance to tilt from south to north – or perhaps it will happen very quickly. Perhaps I shall meet someone on the train who will change my life.

Underneath the sibilant hum of the trains and the loud announcements of departures and the clatter of luggage trolleys and the bird-like mutter of human talk and the purposive walking of many people there was a kind of silence like a clarity under a mist. Gulliver found a seat and after sitting motionless for a time began to feel a little dazed, almost sleepy. He thought, yes, this place is like a church, a place of meditation, or perhaps it's like a Greek orthodox church where you can walk around too and light candles. I wonder when the bar opens? He meditated for a while, watching his thoughts at first scampering, then drifting. He thought, perhaps I'm only just discovering what it's really like to be unemployed, when you're tired with trying and you give up and just sit about without any will to do anything or go anywhere. I suppose you'll be watching television if you can afford it. Gull became aware that someone was sitting beside him on the seat, a man. Gulliver and the man briefly inspected each other. The man, who had no coat, was wearing ancient blue jeans and a shabby lumpy jacket over a stained jersey. His face was thin, his hair was thin but still brownish, the stubble on his face and neck was grey. He held what appeared to be a cider bottle from which he took occasional gulps. He coughed. His hands, emerging from too short sleeves, were red and crabbed and swollen, they trembled. His eyes, blue as Gulliver saw when they turned towards him, were watery and rimmed with red as if his eyelids were turning inside out. Gulliver moved instinctively away from the man. He wanted to say something to him but could think of nothing to say. He felt upset and startled and annoyed.

At last the man spoke. 'Cold, in'it.'

'Yes.'

'It's the wind.'

'Yes, it's the wind.'

'Snowing too, in'it?'

'Yes.'

There was a silence.

'Do you believe in God?'

'No,' said Gulliver, 'do you?'

'Yes, but not in logic.'

'Why not in logic?'

'If there's God should be all O K, an'it? But it's bloody rotten. We're rotten. You and me, sitting here, we're rotten.'

'I don't think we're rotten,' said Gulliver. 'We're just unlucky.'

'Unlucky, you can say that again. No, I'm not unlucky, I'm a right bastard. That's why I believe in God.'

'Why?'

'What else? Got to. Sin brings you to it. I know all about *that*. If I didn't believe in God I'd jump under one of them diesels. Where you going, anywhere?'

'I'm going to Newcastle to look for a job.'

'Newcastle? You crazy? There ain't no jobs up there, just a lot of bloody Geordies, they'll knock your eyes out.'

'I suppose you haven't got a job either,' said Gull. Silly question, but he didn't like the man's tone, and he had thought about those Geordies too.

'Job? What's that? All I work at is where to spend the night.'

'Where do you live?'

'Live, is that what I'm doing? I do it here at the moment.'

'You mean –?'

'Here in this bloody station. I move about, see, 'cause they get to know you. Paddington, Victoria, Waterloo, they're all the same, they move you on and you have to walk about till something opens. Even the pubs won't let you in if you're filthy like me. And they call this place England!'

'Have you any family?' said Gulliver desperately.

'Family? They said "get lost", and I got lost! Once you start

431

going down you can't stop, you can't ever get back where you once were. And when you get to the bottom – it's black down there. Oh God. I'll die of cold soon and that'll be it. Do you believe in hell?'

'Yes. It's here.'

'You're bloody right.'

A deadly gloom settled over Gulliver. Why did he have to meet this awful pathetic man? You can't ever get back where you once were. Perhaps I shall be like that one day, he thought, perhaps sooner than I imagine, this must be my *alter ego*, something horrible and prophetic which had crawled out of my unconscious mind and is sitting beside me! Why should he fasten onto me? He's making me feel not only miserable but bad, *rotten*, like he said I was. That balance that was going to tilt toward something better, at least to a decent mediocre life, perhaps that's what it's tilting to, hating oneself not only in oneself but in other people! He may be as innocent as Christ, but I'm making him the cause that evil is in me. Why aren't I sorry for the bugger? I'm not, I can't be, and of course he's not innocent, he hates me, and I hate him. I'd like to push him under a train.

Then a terrible thought appeared in Gulliver's mind. *He ought to give this man his overcoat!* The thought, appearing suddenly, seemed like something planted by an alien force. Perhaps he was confronted by a demon in disguise. For the alien thought had nothing to do with goodness, it was an obsession, a superstition, a kind of blackmail. Unless he handed over his coat he would meet with every misfortune, he would never get a job, he would take to drink, he would end up in the pitiful condition portrayed by the hobgoblin at his side. Whereas if he gave his coat to the prophetic imp all would be well and he could live carefree ever after. The moment of choice had come. I *won't* give it to him, he thought, I don't care what happens to me! Of course I could buy another coat, but one like this would cost far too much now, far more than I can afford, besides I *like* this coat, it's *my* coat, why should he have it, he'd only sell it to buy drink! But then suppose he isn't a demon, or an *alter ego*, suppose he's Christ himself come to test me, or damn it, suppose he's just what he seems to be, a poor miserable unlucky sod like I might be one day, just himself, just a miserable accidental stranger? I wish I hadn't thought of giving him my coat, I wish I'd never set eyes on the wretch, but now I've thought of it haven't I got to do it?

Gulliver stood up and unbuttoned his overcoat. He put his hand inside into his pocket and drew out his wallet. He opened the wallet and drew out a five-pound note. He handed it to the man, who seemed to be expecting it, and said, 'Here, just a little present, good luck to you.' Then, replacing his wallet and buttoning up his coat, he walked briskly away. He was instantly consumed by misery and rage and fear. When he had walked some distance he looked back. The man had gone, probably to get some more drink somewhere and shorten his life a little more. Gulliver wished that he had given the man his coat, or rather he wished that in some other ideal life some Gulliver, who was certainly not himself, had been able to enact a good action spontaneously without degrading it into a superstition. He sat down on another seat and closed his eyes and buried his head in his hands.

After a while, retaining self-consciously the attitude of despair, he opened his eyes and looked miserably down through his fingers at a small area of the dirty concrete below him, covered with cigarette ends and chocolate papers. He stared at it for a while. Then he removed his hands and sat up a little. An odd little round thing about the size of a ping-pong ball was lying under the seat. Gulliver wondered what it was. Still sitting he stretched one hand in under the seat but could only touch the little thing with his fingertips. It rolled away. He thought, I'm bewitched today, I must get hold of that thing, what on earth is it? He got up and peered under the seat. The thing had moved again, perhaps accidentally kicked by one of the people passing by. Gulliver knelt down and tried to reach for it again, but now it was lying farther off, out in the open, likely to be stepped on at any moment. In an anguish of anxiety he pursued it, made a quick dart and seized it, then stood holding it in his hand. When he saw what it was he stared at it with disconcerted surprise.

Duncan was looking at a hammer. It was an old familiar hammer with a heavy head and a shortish thickish well-worn wooden handle. The grain-striped handle was unpolished save by the grip of many hands, and was splintered a little at the end. It was beautifully balanced. Duncan could remember his father using that hammer in a little workshop in the garden where he pursued his hobby of mending furniture. The hammer had travelled with Duncan, in his bachelor flats, later into his marriage, a friendly serviceable old hammer, always finding its modest place in a suitable drawer, always to hand, ready to tack a carpet, or hang a picture. Its head, with its substantial shining nose, was pleasantly rounded, as if worn, as if it had spent thousands of years in the sea, it looked like a dark glossy ancient stone. Duncan weighed the heavy head in his hand, testing its firmness, caressing it in his palm, then drew his fingers down the warm smooth wooden shaft. It was a good old tool with a friendly face, humble, faithful. He had gently rubbed the end of the handle with sandpaper. He laid it down on the kitchen table and looked at it. It had never before been for him an object of contemplation. It looked primitive, it looked innocent, a quiet symbol of unassuming diligent toil. He put it away in a drawer. He drew out of his pocket a letter which he had received two days ago and read many times. It was brief and ran as follows.

> *There is unfinished business between us.*
> *If you would like to deal with it come to*
> *this address next Friday morning at eleven.*
>   *D.C.*

This letter had arrived two days ago. Duncan had at once replied accepting the invitation. He had told no one. It was now Wednesday.

Jean had been present when, at breakfast time, he had

434

unsuspectingly opened the typed envelope. He had dissembled his emotion and pocketed the letter quickly. His first sensation had been fear, his second elation. He was living now in a state of extreme terrified excitement. He had of course considered every possible explanation, including the implausible one to the effect that Crimond wanted to bring about some sort of reconciliation. Such a project was contrary to common sense, but Crimond's brilliant crazy mind did not accommodate common sense. After all, he and Crimond had once been friends, even, in the context of the group, quite close friends, in those far off but eternally significant Oxford days. Perhaps Crimond had continued to like him, even felt, as man to man, sorry that they had been divided by a woman. Men who have loved the same woman can feel a bond over many years. Such a bond can have various foundations, of which contempt for the woman in question could be one. There is a relationship, which can also consist of chivalrous surrender on one side and grateful possession on the other. There can also be shared loss and romantic nostalgia mutually enlivened. Working along these lines, for of course he had thought in the interim of nothing else, Duncan could just imagine that what Crimond wanted was a cosy chat, a manly conversation, wherein they would both reminisce about their relations with Jean, and conclude that really, in the end, they were both satisfied with the situation as it was now and need no longer regard each other as enemies. They might even envisage the occasional meeting, a drink together, perhaps billiards or chess. However, distraught as he had become in the intervening days, Duncan was not quite mad enough to take this picture seriously. It was difficult enough to think of Crimond in this mood, it was even more difficult to believe that he might expect Duncan to fall in with it.

No. The invitation meant war, it signified confrontation. But of what kind? Could Crimond be considering some kind of belligerent self-justification? Was it just possible that he did not want to cut, in Duncan's vision of him, too bad a figure? He would not want Duncan to see him as a mean despicable rat, would want to explain, perhaps, how inevitable it had all seemed, how eloquently Jean had represented her marriage as unsuccessful, unimportant, virtually over in any case. This was also difficult to envisage and would involve a sort of denigration of Jean, a sacrificing of her in the interests of some kind of understanding with Duncan, which did not seem at all characteristic of Crimond. It was equally out of character to think of him as wanting to demonstrate to Duncan how little he cared that Jean had gone, how relieved he was, to explain perhaps that he had positively thrown her out, so as to efface any image of himself as a defeated man. Crimond was far too arrogant, also perhaps too much a gentleman, to descend to any such justification, however belligerent in tone. Duncan could not really imagine any conversation between them as likely to be possible. He was in any case determined not to let any such conversation begin, and felt sure that Crimond did not envisage it either. These exclusions left only the possibility of some sort of fight – but then again of what kind?

It was certainly possible that Crimond was testing his courage. If Duncan refused to come Crimond would despise him and Duncan would know that he was despised. If Duncan accepted Crimond might contrive to humiliate or terrify him. Duncan of course dismissed the undignified, indeed contemptible, idea of arriving with a bodyguard. This was man to man, and it was a safe bet that Crimond hated Duncan as much as Duncan hated Crimond. The detested, also the ridiculous, husband. Duncan remembered Jean's stories of Russian roulette, which she had described as being both tests of courage and elaborate charades. Jean had never believed that the guns were loaded, but it had also been clear that she was required to take the risk. From something which Jean had said, not of course in answer to any question from Duncan, it appeared that Crimond still played with guns, at any rate possessed them. Supposing in this case, the guns were loaded, supposing Crimond intended simply to kill Duncan and make it out to be an accident? Was not Duncan walking straight into a trap, offering himself gratuitously as a target to a man who loathed him? What was clear, was that whatever grim dramas he might imagine now, it was impossible to refuse the challenge. Supposing, later on, Jean were to discover somehow that he had funked it?

Duncan's inflamed mind went on to imagine a variety of outrageous and ingenious ways in which Crimond might intend to entrap and torment him. The most horrible prospect was that of humiliation, of being tied up, handcuffed perhaps, tortured till he begged for mercy. The room could contain traps, devices. Well, he would act rationally, he would not resist, he would not risk serious injury or extreme pain, he would capitulate and say and do whatever was required. As he imagined scenes of this kind Duncan writhed with misery and rage. After anything like that it would be impossible for Duncan to go on living without killing Crimond. Here he reverted to old familiar, now almost traditional, fantasies of how he would one day destroy his rival.

Duncan was well aware that Crimond had in him some sort of steely element, some pure mad self-indifferent recklessness, which Duncan, however strong his emotions, however fierce his hatred, simply lacked. Whatever the game was, Crimond was likely to win it; and Duncan even found himself relying, contemptibly, for the outcome, upon Crimond's rationality, or upon some hypothetical sense of decency which would preclude too brutal a treatment of the hated husband. And from here he would revert to discarded hypotheses about unimaginable conversations. One thing Duncan was determined to attempt was not to lose the initiative. Here the picture was not a very clear or well-omened one. A very little preliminary talk would make clear *what it was to be.* Then Duncan would hurl himself upon his adversary, as he had done in the tower, relying on his weight and a quick wrestling hold to frustrate whatever fiendish device Crimond seemed to be intending to bring into play. So, he would fight, but not under Crimond's rules. It was a function of this scenario that Duncan had, on the previous day, purchased a knife. He had posed as a bookbinder who wanted a long sharp knife with a narrow blade which could pass up the spine of a large book, a not too flexible knife with a sharp point, opening with a spring. He had considered and dismissed arming himself with a revolver.

437

It would not be easy to get one in the time available, and the weapon seemed to him otiose. A knife would be unexpected and at close quarters more effective. Close up against this imagined encounter Duncan found his thoughts dwelling not so much upon murder as upon grievous bodily harm. It was in this context that he then thought of the hammer. The smashed kneecap, the crushed right hand, the eye reduced to pulp, Crimond in a wheelchair, Crimond blind. Of course with *such* a Crimond still alive Duncan could never sleep secure. On the other hand, a murder charge could rest upon him, with its consequences which in his distraught state he was scarcely counting. The knife man would remember selling the knife. A few well-aimed hammer blows delivered with all his force could do irrevocable damage, and yet could also be passed off, by Crimond, later, discovered bleeding and alone, as some sort of accident; and here Duncan found himself, with another twist of the screw, relying upon something like Crimond's generosity! There was also Crimond's vanity, his pride, his unwillingness to appear so very publicly as the victim of the man he had wronged. As Duncan went about his work in the office and lived his quiet convalescent life with Jean, his mind crowded with these gory fantoms, he felt at times that he was going insane.

After a short time it began to seem to Duncan that Crimond's letter constituted a sign. It was fated, it came at its moment duly. This feeling was obscurely connected with what was still wrong, sometimes, he despairingly felt, irretrievably wrong, between himself and Jean. What was wrong was, it seemed, nothing obvious. With what was obvious they could deal. To say that he 'forgave' Jean was to use superficial language. Well, of course, he forgave her, but that was only a part or aspect of some enormous package, something as large as the world, which in being with her again he *accepted*. He accepted the pain, the wreckage of their lives, the desolation and the ruin in both their hearts, even the possibility that she might run away again. He accepted all the things he did not know and would never know about her relations with Crimond. It was like asking God to pardon the sins one has forgotten as well as those one remembers. He soon gave up the problem of whether she had left Crimond or whether Crimond had left her, it became like some piece of metaphysics finally seen to be empty. Perhaps Jean did not know, perhaps God did not know. He no longer tried to riddle out what exactly had happened on the night when Jean arrived at Boyars, crashing her car on the wrong road. He listened to the little that she said, and asked few questions. Jean was relieved and grateful, her love enlivened by relief and gratitude and by their world renewed. She was not happy, but, they both agreed, she was almost happy. She would become happy. He did not speculate too much now about her thoughts. He was not happy, but would become happy. All their talk about living in France, the books they opened and the maps they studied, were the symbol, not the substance of happiness to come. Sometimes he wondered whether they were wrong to want or expect to be happy, as they had once been; but *had* they been, perhaps their memory deceived them, or *that* was not what it was? Perhaps they had hold of the wrong concept. Perhaps all this thought, all this *analysis* in which they were both indulging, was simply a mistake, a substitute for some more substantial living in the present? Their living in the present so often seemed (and here too they tacitly agreed) like an *ad hoc* hedonism which put off the real issues into an elsewhere. This uncomfortable dualism seemed, after the first excitements, to intrude even into their renewed sexual relations which, though apparently so surprisingly satisfactory, took place inside a cloud of anxiety and dread. Of this, in kindness to each other, neither of them spoke. They thought that time would heal them, love would heal them, that love would heal itself, that just here was the place for faith and hope. At the same time he was conscious of something wrong which had not been put in the reckoning, a missing item which made the problem not only insoluble but unstatable. It was after the arrival of Crimond's letter that Duncan concluded that the missing item simply represented the fact that Crimond was still alive.

This was certainty not a simple matter. It was not, that is, simply to do with hypotheses about Crimond's appearance on the doorstep or Jean running back to him. It had more to do with falling down the stairs at the tower, even falling into the river. Yet again, it did not simply represent a desire for revenge. The whole world was out of joint and some radical adjustment was necessary. Rationally, Duncan did not imagine that if he killed Crimond 'things would be better'. If he actually committed just this murder, or this maiming, he would be in prison, or if he got away with it he would be consumed with guilt and fear. It did not appear to him as something owed to Jean; he was indeed aware that, just for this, Jean might hate him forever, and it was a measure of his obsession that he did not reflect much about this possibility. The requirement presented itself as a very pressing duty or the release of an agonising physical urge: something that *had to be done* about Crimond. When Crimond's letter came Duncan felt at once the appropriateness of the wording. 'Unfinished business' was precisely what there was between them; and *he* felt it too.

So it was that he looked forward to their meeting as to something fated and necessary, without at all seeing what it would be like. The hammer, the knife, were perhaps just blind symbols. He just had to pass the time somehow until Friday came.

On Thursday morning Jean had an unexpected visitor.

Often Jean felt very very tired. Among the things which she had not fully revealed to her husband were the continuing physical effects of the car crash. She had, on return, visited her doctor and the hospital. After all, she was told, you can't expect to turn your car over and just sprain your ankle! There was a jolt to the spine, a stiffening of the shoulder, nothing too serious, but needing prompt physiotherapy. Was she not in pain? No, mental anguish had for a time taken her out of her body, to which she now returned. She went to the hospital for heat treatments and to swim, as in a weird dream, in the warm hospital swimming pool. It's the pool of tears, she said to herself, but not to Duncan. She did exercises. The ankle mended, her shoulder felt better, but now she ached all over and errant pains crept about her body. She was too proud to mention these mundane matters to Duncan, except, for he knew that she went to the hospital, as a sort of joke. They talked laughingly of going to Baden-Baden, even to Karlsbad, when the spring arrived.

Meanwhile, upon that other plane, Jean too was experiencing the mutual incompatibility, yet necessary connection, between analysis and hedonism. She found some relief in both, but neither would relieve her of her deeper, spiritual, sickness, her love for Crimond, from which she had to try, and hope, day by day, hour by hour, to recover. She tried sometimes to remember what it had been like on the previous occasion. Had she really *tried* then – or had she simply kept the thing intact, hidden away like a virus or embryo, preserved alive in some mysterious jar in some secret cupboard? Would it be like this now, or did the thing at last face extinction, must it die, would it die? Like Duncan – for she was like him, had perhaps become like him, her mind like his mind, her talk and mode of argument like his talk and mode of argument – she sometimes wondered if she had misconceived the problem, had obscured its essence by a wrong concept. Why put the question at all? What mattered now was loving Duncan and being happy. In this light the loss of Crimond could seem almost like something mechanical, an inevitable happening, now past, which had not radically altered the flow of her life. In this mood she attached herself for support to certain memories, Crimond's repeated assertion that their love was 'impossible', and, which seemed to her particularly significant, his cry, upon the Roman Road, of 'take your chance!' Well, her chance had been his chance too, and she believed what he said. The brutality of his departure must have been intentional, a seal upon their separation. She was helped by her faith in his truthfulness. It was over and had to be over. There could be no resurrection now. He had needed his freedom and she must learn to need hers. But the illness was heavy and the healing was slow.

Duncan had gone to the office. He had not yet given in his resignation, that would happen soon. This time was an interim, a *breathing* space. Even the flat, which they planned to leave, knew it, although Jean tidied and cleaned it and made it almost as it had been before. There was something provisional about their present mode of life which they acknowledged, convincing each other that a move to somewhere else would rejuvenate them both.

Jean had been reading in a history of Provence about how they had found the skeleton of an elephant, which must have been one of Hannibal's elephants, when the bell rang at the door of the flat. She went to open the door. The person who stood outside was Tamar.

Jean had not seen, or indeed thought of, Tamar since her return to Duncan, though she remembered now that someone had told her that Tamar had been ill. She was glad to see her.

'Tamar! Come in, I'm so glad to see you! Are you better? Someone said you were ill. I'm so sorry I haven't asked you round. Duncan and I have been so busy. Come in, come in, sit down. Is it terribly cold out there? Let me take your coat. Thank heavens the snow has gone away. Would you like some coffee, or a drink? I can give you lunch if you'd like to stay.'

'No, thanks,' said Tamar, surrendering her coat. She dropped her handbag on the floor.

Jean saw at once that Tamar was different. She was leaner and looked paler and older, she even seemed taller. Her complexion, usually so delicately transparent, seemed thicker and more dull. Dark rings surrounded her large green-brown eyes. She was wearing her usual coat and skirt and a faded polo-necked jersey round the top of which her untidy hair stringily strayed. She stared about the room in an anxious irritable manner.

'Where's Duncan?'

442

'He's at the office,' said Jean. 'He'll be sorry to miss you. You must come again some evening soon when he's in. Please sit down and tell me how you are.'

Tamar sat down on the sofa near the fire and Jean sat opposite to her, experiencing the relief of one who, suddenly aware of another's troubles, forgets her own.

'Is Oxford term over? I'm so sorry, of course you've left Oxford. You've been ill?'

'Yes.'

'But you're better now? How is the job going? I believe you're back at work?'

'Yes. The job's all right.'

'Do let me give you something, coffee, sherry, biscuits?'

'No, thanks. Did Duncan tell you about me?'

'About your illness? No. But you'll tell me.'

'He didn't *tell* you?'

'Well – no – what do you mean?'

'Then I'd better tell you as he's bound to later.'

'Whatever are you talking about?' said Jean.

'Duncan and me – we had a love affair.'

'*What?*'

'Well, not a love affair, we had one night – not a night, an evening – one evening – and then I got pregnant – well, he doesn't know that, at least I think he doesn't unless it's got round – I didn't tell anyone of course, but Lily Boyne knows and I expect she's let it out, she's the sort of person who would –' Tamar uttered these words in a sing-song matter-of-fact rather irritated tone, looking here and there in the room as she spoke. At intervals she grimaced quickly and screwed up her eyes as at a spasm of pain.

'Wait a moment,' said Jean. Jean had immediately collected herself. She smoothed down her dress and folded her hands. She felt clear-headed and icy cold. 'Tamar, is this true? You're not imagining anything? You have been ill, you know.' Jean did not believe that Tamar was suffering from delusions, she simply wanted to check her and make her speak more plainly.

'Oh, it's true,' said Tamar, still in her nervous and rather

443

dreamy manner. 'I wish it wasn't. Only one night – evening. And I became pregnant. Wasn't that strange.'

'But you can't have done – Duncan can't –'

'Oh yes he can, believe me!' This was uttered in a sudden aggressive, almost raucous voice.

'You must be mistaken – *are* you pregnant?'

'No, it's gone, it's gone, I had it taken away.'

'Tamar, my dear, please, I'm not angry with you –'

'I don't care if you are,' said Tamar, 'I'm far beyond that.'

'You say you got rid of the child?'

'I had an abortion – double quick – it's gone – don't worry –'

'Will you please tell me this story right from the beginning? When did it start? You say you had a love affair?'

'No, I didn't – well, I said so, but that doesn't describe it – it all happened in a moment, just on that one occasion – I was trying to help, to *help* – I came to be kind to him – then I felt I loved him – and he was so unhappy he took me to bed – just for a, perhaps, an hour – he regretted it later.'

'How do you know?'

'He avoided me, he never spoke to me properly again.'

'You never told him you were pregnant?'

'No.'

'Why not?'

'Because it was *my business*,' said Tamar savagely.

'Are you sure the child was his?'

Tamar was silent for a moment, and cast one quick fierce look at Jean, whom she had not looked at since she entered the room. 'So you think I go to bed with lots of men, that I'm always doing it, perhaps every night?'

'I'm sorry. I'm very surprised by all this. I've got to get it clear.'

'I'm making it clear. Do you think I'd lie about the most important thing that ever happened to me? *Did* Duncan tell you?'

'*No*. But, Tamar, the child –'

'It's gone, it's dead.'

'We would have adopted it.'

Tamar jumped to her feet. She stood for a moment with her

444

mouth open and her head awkwardly on one side, one shoulder raised. Then she *screamed*. It was a loud deliberate scream, like a call. She picked up her coat and stood holding it. She said in an odd high-pitched voice, 'How very kind of you. But it was *my* child, mine to kill if I wanted to. I wasn't going to give it to *you* to love. It might as well have had no father. It was *mine*. I didn't need *your* permission! Everything was arranged for *you*, so that you and Duncan would be together, that's what everyone wanted, that's why they wanted *me* to go and see Duncan, as if I were your servant or your maid or something. I was supposed to *help*, and that was what happened, so I could tell nobody in case it spoilt *your* thing, and now you're back and I *had* to come and see you because I liked you so much once and I thought you *knew*, and I've been in hell –'

'*Please*,' said Jean, '*please* be calm – sit down –' Tamar's hysterical vibrating voice and what she had just said frightened Jean very much. The odd thing, and Jean reflected on this afterwards, was that when Tamar began her revelation Jean had taken the situation in instantly and had felt, in the midst of shock and dismay, a kind of pleasure at the idea that Duncan was to blame for something, that his life was imperfect too, he had deceived her and did not yet know that she knew. The sense of a mortal wound came later, her jealousy, her sense of Tamar's pain and, worse still, of Tamar's power to hurt. And then the lost child with its long revenge.

Tears were now streaming down Tamar's face. She stood holding her coat and her handbag. At one moment she mopped her face with her dangling coat sleeve. She uttered a low moaning sound as she wept.

Jean, near to tears herself, but still relentlessly controlled, said, 'Listen, Tamar, don't tell anyone else about this. It's better to keep quiet. I won't tell anyone.' Except Duncan, she thought. Or shall I *not* tell Duncan, *never* tell Duncan?

'I don't care who knows now,' Tamar wailed, 'I don't care about anything now. Oh it was so stupid of me to come here, I had to find out whether you knew, and now I've told you and you didn't know –'

'You did right to tell me.' Jean did not try to stop Tamar

who was making for the door. 'My dear – come back again soon – we'll talk again.'

'No, we won't. I hate you. I loved Duncan, I *loved* him – you left him and made him so unhappy – and now all this has happened and I'm ruined, my life is ruined, and I killed my child, and it's all *your* doing.'

'Tamar!'

'I hate you!'

She had opened the door and fled through it, carrying her coat and her bag. The door banged shut in Jean's face. Jean did not try to follow. She sat down and began to cry over the terrible damage, not yet assessed, which had been done.

It was Friday morning. Tamar was with Jenkin.

Jenkin had been up late on Thursday night. He had rushed round to Marchment's house in a state of wild excitement because Marchment had said that someone was going to lend him a typescript of part of Crimond's book. This promised treat did not materialise, but Jenkin then spent half the night arguing with Marchment and his friends. For some time now, ever since what Gerard ruefully called the 'arraignment', when Crimond had announced that it was finished, Jenkin's desire to see the book had been increasing until it was almost as if he were in love with the thing. He had dreams about it. The thought of holding it in his hands made him tremble. He did not dare to ask Crimond for news of it, fearing a rebuff.

Jenkin's present restlessness had also much to do with what he thought of, with a smile but soberly, as 'Gerard's proposal'. He had, since that meeting, been several times alone with Gerard, but neither of them had made any direct allusion to what had then been said. This reticence was, in different ways, characteristic of both. Gerard, too dignified to repeat himself,

446

was clearly prepared to wait indefinitely for Jenkin's response or indeed to do without any response except the one he had instantly received. Jenkin, afraid of giving, to someone so meticulous, so demanding of exactitude and truth, the wrong impression, thought it better not to blunder into words until he had something clear to say. But when would that be? Jenkin had been very *impressed*, more so even than he had realised at the time, by Gerard's statement. Jenkin preferred to think of it as a statement rather than as a suggestion. The statement had in fact already changed the world, and had in some ineffable sense been answered. Their meetings now, with no word uttered on the subject, were different, there was a new gentleness, a douceur, a closeness. They looked with a new calmness into each other's eyes. These were not 'meaningful' or 'questioning' looks. They were undemanding gazes which quietly fed their new sense of each other. They also laughed a lot, sometimes perhaps at an intuition of something harmlessly ludicrous in the situation. These communions made Jenkin feel extremely happy. It was like – well, it somehow *was* – being in love, and perhaps just *that* was what had been aimed at and achieved by the statement itself and nothing more had to be done. They had never, it occurred to Jenkin, actually *looked* at each other so much before.

However a query had been set up in his life by Gerard's prescient *démarche*. Was he going to go or to stay? Jenkin, in some pain, had gone over possible compromises and rejected them. If he did what he was intending to do he would be *getting right away* from Gerard and from his present 'world' altogether. He would be somewhere else, in another country with other people, doing new things, and as he saw it very absorbing and demanding and time-consuming things. Taking a plane to London for an occasional lunch with Gerard did not seem to fit into this picture; and such glimpses were likely to be more distressing than satisfying. Some comfort, some satisfaction, which belonged to his staying was just entirely incompatible with his going. If he went away he would lose, would never develop or regain, that peace which at times he now experienced and knew that Gerard experienced,

447

in their mutual presence, a sense of having come to rest in absolutely the right place. His departure would destroy that for ever. It was not at all that he imagined that Gerard would resent his decision and somehow cut him off, it was just that an almost continuous absence would make them into strangers. They might try to overcome this alienation but time and space would not be denied. Whatever happened Jenkin knew that Gerard's behaviour to him would be perfect. But such an absence would starve love of anticipations and treats and make of their old long friendship something smaller and different. The thought was agonising. Of course Jenkin had faced the prospect and felt the pain of it before but now what was to be lost had gained considerably in volume. The ideas of home and of peace which Gerard had trailed so temptingly before him did attract him deeply and did *surprise* him as things which he had never really thought he would achieve. He had, without reflection or regret, dismissed them as, for him, impossible, and so not objects of desire. He had had of course his own peace of mind which depended on his solitude. He had never even thought that he would ever get to know Gerard any better or come any nearer to him than what had been their splendid but static friendship of so many years standing. Now, if as Gerard had actually envisaged (and this still amazed Jenkin) they were to share a house this would involve what he had never in relation to Gerard dreamt of, a genuine *life together*. Jenkin had considered a shared life as, for him, out of the question, utterly not his lot, had not even, save in the vaguest way when he was very young, wanted it. His relations with women about which he had been so successfully secretive had never brought him at all near to notions of marriage; and he had settled down quite early in life to being cheerfully celibate and solitary, his only steady and important relationship being with Gerard and the set which had so long ago crystallised around him. Now this possible shared life with his oldest closest friend seemed immensely attractive to him and not only attractive but somehow in prospect easy, natural, appropriate, proper, fated. In this prospect problems about sex bothered Jenkin not at all. He had always since he first saw

448

him when they were both eighteen adored Gerard. The idea of being in bed with him had never occurred to him for an instant and would have seemed, and seemed now, actually comic. Jenkin in fact felt perceptibly *flattered* by Gerard's (evidently) not finding his old friend unattractive, though this too was immensely funny. Gerard's lovers had all been beautiful, Sinclair and Robin for instance, or formidably handsome, Duncan. But possible 'dramas' on that front were not part of his worries. Here again, whatever happened or more likely did not happen, Gerard would be perfect. Contemplating Gerard during their recent peaceful meetings Jenkin had even reflected that an old dog might still be taught new tricks; and this idea too made him laugh, afterwards. However all these tempting and beautiful thoughts, these deep tender desires, ran harshly up against Jenkin's equally deep resolution about the necessity of an absolute departure; and he felt uncomfortably that the voice of duty also spoke on that side. Jenkin did not want just yet to have that uncomfortable interview with duty. He was, he was aware, putting it off, being drunk upon the honeydew of Gerard's love.

Such thoughts were in his head when Tamar appeared at his door at about ten o'clock. He was not expecting her.

'Tamar, what luck, you've just caught me, I was just going out shopping. Come in, come in!'

He ushered Tamar into his sitting room and turned on the lights and lit the gas fire. It was cold and misty outside. He went to the kitchen and brought back a mug with holly in it and put it on the mantelpiece. He thought, when I'm in Spain at Christmas I shall get a sign. Tamar refused coffee, hot soup, toast. She kept her coat on. They sat down in the cold room, huddled near the fire.

'Not at the office?'

'I'm on sick leave again.'

'Well, how is it with you, my dear, and how are you?'

'I think I'm done for,' said Tamar. She spoke calmly and her face, still thickened and dulled as Jean had seen it on the previous day, was not jerking in spasms of pain, nor were her eyes straying about. She kept moistening her parted lips and

449

looked down steadily at the green tiles in front of the little spluttering fire. She breathed deeply.

'What's happened?'

'I've told Jean.'

'You mean about Duncan and the child?'

'Everything.'

Jenkin was dismayed to hear this. 'How did that come about?'

'I just couldn't bear not knowing whether Duncan had told her. He hadn't. But I went to her and blurted it all out, for nothing as it were. Now she'll tell him I've given him away and that he made me pregnant and the child is gone and so on.' She spoke slowly.

Jenkin's thoughts raced about in many directions. 'Jean and Duncan will survive. It won't wreck them all over again. You aren't afraid of that, are you?'

'No, I'm not.' Tamar went on with her terrible calmness, staring down at the green tiles. 'I'm not concerned about them. I'm concerned about myself.'

'What did Jean say?'

'She said she and Duncan would have adopted the child.'

'Oh –'

'That put me in a *rage*. It was as if they would have pushed past me and left me in the gutter and gone on together into the sunlight carrying my child away.'

'I understand.'

'I told Jean she had been horribly cruel to Duncan, and that I loved Duncan, and that I hated her.'

'But you don't hate her.'

'It doesn't matter. I shall never see her again. We shall be unable to bear each other. And Duncan will detest me. Everybody will detest me. But perhaps even that doesn't matter. I shall tell everyone now, I think.'

'Better wait a while,' said Jenkin. 'Absolute frankness sounds good, but it's not always the right policy.'

'I expect Lily Boyne had gossiped about it all over the place.'

'I feel sure she hasn't.'

'Jean will tell some version of it to someone. I'd rather tell my version straightaway.'

'Tamar, *wait*,' said Jenkin. 'We'll see. I feel rather confused about this and your head isn't exactly clear. Would you like me to go round to Lily and see her – and perhaps Jean too – would that help? I'm not sure –'

'I don't care. Perhaps I won't tell anyone. Let them hear anything they like and believe anything they like. I'm done for.'

'That's not true and it's wrong to say it. It's a way of trying to get out of trouble by pretending to give up, when you're dealing with trouble which you can't give up. You must *endure* this thing and *know* that it will pass and you will outlive it *in a good way*. There are all sorts of things, wise and unwise things, which you might do now and you've got to *think* about these – and they affect other people too.'

'Oh – other people! Actually there is something I can do, but it may be awful – *wicked* –'

'Tamar –'

'I just need help, *extreme* help –'

'What –?'

'I've decided to become a Christian.'

Jenkin was very surprised. 'Good heavens – do you really think –?'

'You, even you,' said Tamar in her quiet explanatory voice, 'do not at all understand how black and how destroyed my whole mind has become. That's what I meant when I said I wasn't concerned about Jean or Duncan or anybody, only about myself. I've got to be saved from destruction – I can't even say that I want to be, but somehow I must be, and I can't do it myself, and you can't do it either. I need supernatural help. Not that I really believe it's supernatural or there is any supernatural. But perhaps there is help somewhere, some force, some power –'

'But, do you believe –?'

'Oh you and your belief and your sincerity and so on, I knew you'd start on that, you all think that's so important! I don't. When you're drowning you don't care what you hold onto. I

451

don't care whether God exists or who Christ was. Perhaps I just believe in magic. Who cares? It's up to me, it's *my* salvation.'

'But, Tamar, who put all this –'

'All this nonsense into my head? Father McAlister. I've seen him several times. He wants me to be baptised and confirmed.'

The telephone rang in the hall and Jenkin got up to answer it.

Jean had not, on the previous evening, told Duncan about Tamar's visit or her revelation. The evening passed as usual except that Jean was more full of gaiety, jesting and laughing wildly. Duncan seemed in good spirits too. They had their customary pleasurable argument about Provence versus the Dordogne, and whether it might not be a good idea after all to live in north Italy. The following morning, Friday, Duncan went away at his usual time.

After he had gone Jean returned to the abominable task of thinking through in detail everything which Tamar had revealed. Jean could not comfort herself by imagining that Tamar was deluded or lying, or that the child was not Duncan's, or that the child was still alive. She felt sure that Tamar had told the truth. How was such an enormity to be thought about at all, how was it to be survived, what was the worst of it? Was there anything which could be in any way mended? Jean did not believe that this new horror could destroy her new relation, obscure as it still was, with Duncan. But it would wound it, perhaps change it in ways which were hard to foresee. There was the sheer surprise, the sense of the miraculous, that Duncan could after all produce a child; and there was the agony that it was not her child. And the separate and strange agony that the child was dead. There was also the particular shock of discovering that Duncan could go to bed (yet why ever not?) in her absence and do it so casually, with so young and vulnerable a creature. Wild peripheral considerations also tormented Jean. Told early that children were impossible, Jean and Duncan had not distressed each other by perpetual moaning about this. Jean had kept her own desire for a child as a secret sorrow. Perhaps Duncan had done the same. Together they were philosophical about it, even professing relief at being spared the horrors of parenthood. But now, since it appeared that Duncan *could* do it, would it not be possible to find a woman, any woman, who would bear his child and hand it over? Would Jean love such a child? Was it not, for both of them, *too late*? Then there was the awful question of whether she should tell Duncan at all? Was it true that the news was likely to 'get round'? The weird elation she had felt at first at having 'found him out' and 'knowing what he did not know' now appeared as a small nasty psychological oddity.

Tormented, walking up and down the room, Jean felt a piercing growing need to *do* something, anything, to relieve the pain of continuous reflection. Another form of distress came to her aid, a new hurtful hypothesis: perhaps during her absence Duncan had had many love affairs. Why should the escapade with Tamar be the only one? And perhaps it had not been by any means as brief, and on his side carnal, as she had suggested? Duncan had told Jean that he had not been near any woman during her absence and she had believed him. Evidently she had been naive.

Jean suddenly decided that there was one thing she could do, even if it were only to pass the time, she could search Duncan's desk. She went into his study and began carefully opening the small drawers and examining the papers. Almost at once she came upon Crimond's note. *There is unfinished business between us.* She looked at the date upon the note and at the time of the rendezvous. *Today.* She looked at her watch. It was ten thirty.

She put the note back in the desk and ran to the telephone and rang Duncan's office. He was not there. Was he at a meeting? No one knew. Then she thought. There could be no doubt about the meaning of the note, that it meant confrontation, not reconciliation or discussion. She at once thought of the games of Russian roulette which she had always taken to be charades. Could this be a charade, some sort of frightening or humiliating force – or the real thing? There had been the Roman Road . . . It could simply be a lethal trap. Whatever it was, there was no doubt in her mind that *Duncan would go*. He would never let Crimond vaunt, even in his mind, that Duncan was afraid.

Jean seized the telephone again and dialled Crimond's number. Of course this was crazy. On *this* morning Crimond would never answer. Besides what could *she* say to him? The number was unobtainable. Suppose she were to get out the car and drive there at once? Might not her presence enflame both men and make what might have been some harmless display into a murdeous fight? Jean rang Gerard's number. There was no answer. Then she rang Jenkin.

'Hello.'

'Hello, Jenkin, it's Jean. Look, this sounds mad, but I think Duncan may have gone round to Crimond's place to fight some sort of duel –'

'Oh – no –'

'At least, well, perhaps he hasn't, I'm not sure, he may have done, and I can't go round myself –'

'I'll go – when did he –?'

'Crimond asked him to go at eleven, I've just found the note – if you go at once you might arrive first – but oh hell you haven't got a car – and ours – I've just remembered it's at the garage, or I could drive you round, oh *hell* –'

'Don't worry, I can get a taxi, I can usually get one on Goldhawk Road and there's a taxi rank on the Green. Have you told Gerard?'

'He's not in. Oh Jenkin, I'm so sorry to trouble you, it may be *nothing*, now I come to think of it Duncan probably didn't go at all – he may have answered the note and – but *please* go at once, I feel if *you're* there nothing bad can happen. You know where Crimond lives, don't you, and the downstairs room –'

'Yes, yes. I'll go at once, don't worry –'

'And you'll ring me.'

'Yes – I'll fly now.'

Jenkin dropped the telephone and ran for his overcoat. He said to Tamar, 'I'm sorry, my dear, there's an emergency and I have to leave you for a while. Would you like to stay here till I come back?'

'Yes – yes, please – I'd like to stay.'

'I don't know how long I'll be, just stay and keep warm, I'd like to think you were here. There's lots to eat in the larder and you can rest on my bed – turn on the electric fire – I'm sorry I haven't made up the other bed.'

'I'll be all right, Jenkin, dear Jenkin.' She had risen and now threw her arms round his neck.

He kissed her. 'Stay here till I come back.'

Jenkin hurried along toward Shepherd's Bush Green. There were no taxis. He waited at the taxi rank.

As soon as Jean put down the telephone she thought, perhaps I ought to tell the police? Why didn't I think of that at once? Then she hesitated. Perhaps Duncan had decided not to go, perhaps he had replied suggesting another meeting place. This now seemed possible, even likely. She telephoned Duncan's office again. He was not there. She telephoned Gerard, and then Rose – no answer. Should she tell the police? If she did, whatever happened she would have to explain everything, it would all get into the papers. Even if it was a farce of some kind, Duncan might get into serious trouble and would be furious with her for interfering. And the police might be glad to have an excuse for picking on Crimond, and she might have to give evidence and this would involve her horribly with Crimond again just when she was trying to think that he did not exist. It then occurred to her that this sort of false frightening blackmail must be a part, perhaps only the beginning, of Crimond's revenge upon her. Unable to decide what to do she sat and wept.

Duncan had of course left Crimond's letter behind on purpose. If anything 'happened', if for instance Crimond were to do him some damage, he would like to have in a safe place, and not removed from his pocket by his assailant, the evidence that Crimond had, in an aggressive style, asked him to come. This could be important if Crimond were to plead self-defence against a hostile intruder. If Crimond did, Crimond must pay. Equally, if Duncan were to damage Crimond, it would be helpful to prove that Crimond had been asking for trouble. The idea that Jean might find the 'challenge' did not enter his head for a moment. Jean was not a searcher in desks, and he knew that she believed him when he had said there had been 'no one around' during her absence. This indeed was true, apart from the little incident with Tamar, which he would perhaps tell Jean about one day.

Since their car was being serviced Duncan took a taxi which put him down near his destination. His anxiety brought him there too early, and he had to walk about for some time round squares of little streets trying to keep warm. An appalled misery overwhelmed Duncan's heart. What on earth was he doing here walking about in these bleak squalid streets, with a hammer in his overcoat pocket? The hammer was heavy and jarred against his thigh. His hands inside his gloves were freezing. The cold made him feel weak and strengthless. He could not imagine holding, let alone using, any weapon. Why had he felt it impossible not to come when it would have been perfectly easy to ignore Crimond's ridiculous letter? It would have been better, it would have been *right*. Of course having said he would come, he had now to come. Yet why was that, what stopped him from going back to the office at once, where he *ought* to be, where important matters awaited his attention and decent ordinary work was to be done? Why was he walking about intending to kill somebody, if that was what he was doing – or gratuitously running the risk of being killed or maimed himself? And Jean – would she ever forgive him if he let Crimond wound him? Or – suppose he were to hurt Crimond, to hurt him badly? Would not this awaken Jean's sympathy, even perhaps reawaken her love? He was in a situation where he couldn't win, and had wantonly put himself there. Was there still a way out? He thought, I must keep my head, I'm imagining all sorts of improbable horrors. I'll be frank with bloody Crimond, I'll tell him I came to tell him there was no point in this farcical business, and that he could go to hell, I wouldn't co-operate with his play-acting, and he could keep out of my way and not communicate with me again. Surely nothing could stop him saying this and walking out, without letting Crimond start on whatever welcome he had contrived. This idea, with a rehearsal of its angry authoritative tone, cheered Duncan a little.

At eleven o'clock precisely Duncan mounted the steps to the door of Crimond's house. He pushed a bell which did not ring. He waited a moment. Then Crimond, who had evidently been waiting in the hall, opened the door.

It was not until that moment that it occurred to Duncan that, apart from what he had seen at the summer ball, he had not set eyes on Crimond since the meeting in the tower so many years ago. Yet oddly what shook him when he saw Crimond standing before him was how young he looked, and how like the quite different, far more distant person he had known at Oxford; and for an instant Duncan thought we *can't* fight – what on earth put the idea of a fight into my head at all! I'm mad. We are to *talk*, that's what this meeting is about. Perhaps it will end in reconciliation after all. And a glow of confidence and strength entered into him. Talking, conference, diplomacy, that was *his* subject. He would talk Crimond down.

Crimond was dressed in an old black corduroy jacket and trousers, and had obscured the neck of his shirt with a dark green knotted scarf. He looked at first sight dandyish, almost raffish. His hair was quite long, longer than at the dance, and, perhaps recently washed, a little fluffy. He was very thin and his pale eyes stared out of a face which seemed inordinately lengthened as in a caricature. His complexion, which in the summer had glowed with freckles, was sallow, and the skin strained over the bones as if ready to split. The only colour in his face was the extremely red, damp, rims round his eyes, and

457

a red area at the end of his long nose. His eyes in the staring face seemed alien, dry, like blanched stones. Duncan's second impression was that he was confronting a mad person. The sense of Crimond's youth had come from the slim figure, the corduroy, the scarf, the hair. Now he looked like a wraith.

Crimond said nothing, but moved his head to indicate that Duncan was to follow him. Duncan followed, closing the door behind him, across the icy hall and down some dark stairs into the long large basement room. This room was faintly warmer and smelt of a paraffin stove which was lurking somewhere at the far end. It was dark, very little light coming from outside, and only one lamp alight which was placed on the floor at the far end. The middle of the room was taken up by two long tables, placed longways opposite to each other, one at each end. There was a bed near the door, a great many books piled against the walls, two chairs, an open cupboard, a desk pushed into a corner near the lamp, no sign of activity upon it, the top swept clean. Otherwise the room was bare. As Duncan's eyes became accustomed to the dim light he saw the target. A contest of that sort? The lighting did not suggest target practice of any kind.

Duncan felt encouraged and ready to carry out his resolve to dominate the scene. Crimond closed the door. Duncan followed him down the room. Crimond picked up the lamp and put it on the desk. The lamp light fell on Crimond's hand which was trembling. Duncan felt calmer. He began to speak.

'Well, Crimond, as you see I've come in answer to your curious little note, but let me say this at once. I think I understand your wish, your craving perhaps to see me. Perhaps we both need to be convinced that we can be in the same room without the world coming to an end. You have done appalling damage to my life and to Jean's life and it would be ridiculous to talk here of forgiveness or reconciliation of any sort, which may conceivably, I say conceivably, have been in your head when you wrote that letter. What is perhaps worth proving for your, possibly also for my, state of mind is that we can look at each other, and this we have already managed to do. You may also have envisaged some kind of discussion. This, I must tell you, is entirely impossible. A crime of the magnitude of the one which you have twice committed does not allow of any place or topic for a meeting of minds. Do you really imagine that we are to sit down and have some sort of masculine discussion about Jean, or confess to each other that we are both sinners? You see that I have been able to mention her name in your presence and this is in itself remarkable, but is as far as we can go. I am sure you will agree. Your impertinent letter stirred me to anger. Having had time to reflect I see it in a different light. I suspect you yourself, in writing it, had no clear intention. I also suspect that in the interim you may have come to conclusions similar to mine. The meeting itself, what has happened in these last minutes, is the point. Of course my hatred, my detestation of you remains. One cannot magic such deep and just emotion away. But these things have to be lived with. Sometimes for one's own sake one must attempt to purge and calm one's imagination. If I were to spend the rest of my life in a state of crazed obsession that would be one more injury which you could boast of having done me. I don't want to have to think about you every day and wonder what would happen if we met. We have met and nothing has happened. There has been a release of tension, nothing to do with mutual understanding, just something automatic, almost physical. I am sure you understand. I suggest we leave this matter just as it is at this point, that is, we have looked at each other. What threats I might utter against you I leave to your imagination. I am certain that you will not willingly cross my path again. That is all I have to say.'

This extraordinary speech, quite unpremeditated, surprised Duncan very much. He had not, even when he was coming down the stairs, had any thoughts of this kind. But even as he spoke he saw both the good sense of what he was saying and also its immediate efficacy. Perhaps it arose too from the particular confidence which he derived from seeing Crimond's hand trembling. It *was* a vast relief to him, in a way he had not at all foreseen, to find that he could be in the same room with Crimond without some kind of terrible collapse or

459

explosion. He had intended, as 'talking him down', to utter some vague angry rhetoric. But what, as it happened, he had uttered actually had point, and constituted *an appeal to Crimond's intelligence*. He even felt that he had *impressed* Crimond. With his last word he turned to go, but not hastily. Crimond would certainly want to say *something*, and a brief coda would round off the event.

Duncan's speech, which he had not attempted to interrupt, had certainly held Crimond's attention. He even waited pointedly at the end of it in case Duncan did after all want to add anything. He stared intently at Duncan, raising his light reddish eyebrows whose long fine hairs were unusually il-lumined by the lamp. His face relaxed, and he was opening and shutting his hands as if to calm his body. He said in a quiet interested tone of voice, 'Oh, but it was not at all my idea to *discuss* anything with you, or, heaven forbid, to talk about Jean. There, I have mentioned her name too.'

It was at this moment that Duncan, with some sort of dismissive gesture, should have turned and walked away in a manner signifying: I don't care what your idea was, I've made my statement and I'm going. If he had done that Crimond would probably not have impeded him. But Duncan felt so full of power just then that he was tempted to indulge his curiosity. He made the mistake of asking, 'Well, what did you want us to do?'

'Fight, of course,' said Crimond, now giving a curious pained smile.

'Oh don't be a fool,' said Duncan, not yet alarmed but already being caught in the silken threads of Crimond's will. 'I'm not keen on theatre.'

'Why did you come?'

'I came to say what I said just now.'

'I don't believe you,' said Crimond. 'The rigmarole you uttered just now was something you thought of on the spur of the moment, it was empty rhetoric. What you said about hatred and anger was true though. You came because you *had* to come. Otherwise you could easily just have ignored my letter, which as you say was impertinent. You could have ignored it. I expected you to ignore it. I'm surprised that you're here. But since you *are* here –'

'I'm going,' said Duncan, now turning away with more determination.

'Oh no you're not.' Crimond moved quickly round Duncan, now standing between him and the distant door. He said, 'That door's locked, I locked it after I came in.'

Duncan stood where he was. In any case Crimond now represented a serious barrier. If he tried to move past, Crimond might touch him, seize hold of him. The idea of being *touched* by Crimond filled Duncan with a paralysing repulsion. Standing face to face with the man in this large cold dark room all Duncan's old vague furious ideas of hurling himself upon his enemy shrivelled up. No such lively impulses came to his aid. His concern now was simply to be able to leave with dignity. He felt that he had been able, for a time, to dominate Crimond, at least to silence him, and must try to do so again. But he was now in a position of weakness. He said in a firm voice, 'I'm not going to fight you. How can you imagine that to be possible? I haven't come here to humour your fantasy life.'

'Take off your coat,' said Crimond. 'You're going to stay here a while longer. I don't like to see you in that coat. Take it off.'

Duncan took off the overcoat which he had been wearing since his arrival. He did this because he now feared that Crimond might spring upon him and he did not want to be impeded by the coat. He also did it because he had begun to be afraid of Crimond. He thought, he's mad, he might do anything. He threw the heavy coat onto the desk where it overturned the lamp. Crimond returned from the door and set the lamp upright.

Taking refuge from fear in anger, Duncan said, 'This is false contemptible play-acting. You're mad with spite because Jean left you. She found you mean and cruel, she found you boring. That's what this is about.'

At this reference to Jean Crimond flushed, his pale face becoming suddenly crimson. But his expression did not alter. He said in a low voice, 'How can you! Not that, not that!'

'Open the door,' said Duncan.

'No, not yet,' said Crimond, who seemed suddenly breathless. He pulled at his neck and dragged off the green scarf and let it fall on the floor. He said in the tone of someone offering a helpful explanation, 'When I said "fight" I didn't actually mean like *that*, I mean like we did once. I just want you to play – that game. I felt it was – appropriate – and that you would think so too.'

'Game –?'

'Yes. Like this.' Crimond stepped forward. Duncan moved hastily back. But Crimond was reaching for an electric light switch. He turned the switch and the room was suddenly full of a cold clear light. Two neon strips across the ceiling flickered then lit again. Crimond opened a drawer in the desk to reveal two revolvers.

When he saw the guns Duncan understood the scene, he understood the significance of the two long tables set end to end. He felt a quick cold death terror, a heavy pain alienating his body. Then a weird excitement like a sexual stirring. He came forward almost with an air of curiosity. Crimond had placed the revolvers side by side on the table. He was pale again and put his hand to his throat, undoing another button on his shirt.

'Smith and Wesson,' said Duncan. 'I suppose you got these in America?'

'Yes.'

'Single action.'

'Yes.'

'Do you still collect automatic pistols too?'

'Not – collect –' Crimond went to close the open door of the cupboard.

As this conversation proceeded Duncan thought about the hammer which was in the pocket of his overcoat on the desk. This now seemed like a dream weapon, something transparent to be wielded in slow motion. What fantasy of revenge had made him bring the thing, what was he supposing he would do with it, take Crimond unawares, as for instance when he had been closing the cupboard door, and smash him between the shoulders? He could not do it. At the tower he could afford to let his anger carry him away. Now he was older, older, and Crimond seemingly as young as ever. There was no question of punching, wrestling. Yet was the dream hammer more unreal than what appeared to be happening now? He thought to himself, it's all make-believe, it must be. Jean said they did it for a joke with unloaded guns. Of course he wanted her to be frightened too. It's the same now. Anyway the weight of the cartridge always takes the loaded chamber down to the bottom so there's no risk, I've always known that. All the same, I won't do it. Of course the man is crazy, perhaps desperate.

'You see,' said Crimond in a low conspiratorial voice, 'what you said at the beginning wasn't entirely off the point. There is – between us – something to be done – something to be finished with – if we are not to go on obsessively thinking about each other for the rest of our lives, which I believe you would agree would be a sad waste of our time and energy. We want to be free of each other, yes? That was the psychology of duelling in the old days after all. Call what is necessary, if you like, an exorcism, a symbolic release. I want this, I need this, and I think that you, if you are honest, want it and need it too.'

'I'd like to kill you, if that's what you mean,' said Duncan. 'But I'm not interested in your symbolism. If it's symbolic it's not serious, and if it's serious it's not what I want either. I certainly don't want you to kill me! Why should I play your game? I won't.'

'You will,' said Crimond.

Duncan hesitated, actually wondering whether he had now the strength to walk to the door and rattle the handle until Crimond deigned to open it. Would that be what happened? Could Crimond force him to 'play' by making some awful humiliation the alternative? Could it happen like that a *third* time? Suppose he had to *beg* Crimond to let him go? Duncan, who had imagined all kinds of complicated traps, had let himself be caught in the simplest. Also however, and this dangerous thought strengthened his hesitation, he saw Crimond's point, and its meeting with his point. Something had to be done, to be *finished*, oh to *finish* with Crimond! Could this be done except by killing him? This was a question Duncan had often asked himself, but only as a rhetorical question commanding the answer no. Now common sense, suddenly entering through some amazing hole in the mad argument, informed Duncan that if he *did* ever actually kill Crimond he would be even, infinitely, more tied to him than he was at present. Duncan, in his 'speech', had suggested a symbolic solution to the problem, even that the problem was already solved. He had spoken impromptu under a particular emotional pressure and with an immediate end in view, to escape quickly from a situation into which he should never have entered. Whether he could believe that *that* solution would have worked seemed an academic question now that Crimond had proposed a far more radical, so perhaps more efficacious, cure. Would a symbolic killing, at the cost of exposing himself to Crimond's anger, bring about the desired freedom? Duncan was attracted, as Crimond had no doubt calculated that he would be, by Crimond's formulation. They were, as things stood now, bound to each other as men who, clasped together as each tries to drown the other, both drown.

Crimond, having pushed the guns aside, was now sitting on the table watching Duncan. He said, 'Yes?' It sounded almost like a sexual invitation.

'Describe your game,' said Duncan.

Crimond gave a long sigh.

Duncan, feeling himself entangled, indeed entangling himself, thought, as a rearguard support to what happened to be his decision, that of course Crimond, following the same chain of argument which Duncan had just followed, would not really want to kill Duncan! The extreme solution would not be a solution. What was required was an extreme symbolism. That's what made the Greeks write tragedies, Duncan found himself thinking. I'll tell that to Gerard one day. He also found himself thinking that if he left now, even if he were able to do so with dignity, he would regret this last chance for the rest of his life. Well, that was like sex too.

'It's very simple,' said Crimond, 'and traditional. Each gun has, out of six chambers, one loaded. We face each other, one at each end of the room, we spin and fire.'

'We fire at each other.'

'Of course, it's not a suicide pact. And of course we must aim to kill. It's not all that easy to be sure of killing someone even at this distance unless one is very experienced with firearms, which fortunately you are. You are familiar with this type of gun of course. Remember it's very light on the trigger.'

'Yes, yes. How many times do we fire?'

'I envisaged twice, that is assuming . . . But as many times as you like.'

'Twice, all right.'

'A shot which is not properly aimed is not counted.'

'Agreed.' He thought, we are both mad! What sort of conversation is this?

'Another thing, which I hope you will approve of. For absolute fairness the chambers must be of equal weight, otherwise, as we all know, the loaded one tends to descend. I have therefore tamped some spent cartridges with lead, making them the same weight as live cartridges, and put them in the other five chambers. Look.'

Crimond broke open one of the guns and thrust it towards Duncan.

'Fine, fine.' Duncan waved it away.

'Would you like to examine the guns?'

'No. Let's get on.' It would be indelicate to examine the guns especially if, as he was assuming, neither was loaded!

'We had better toss for position, though there's no difference in the light, and of course for who fires first.'

Duncan brought a coin out of his pocket and handed it to Crimond. Crimond said, 'Who wins has the target end.' Duncan said 'Heads.' Crimond tossed the coin, it fell heads. Crimond handed the coin back to Duncan. Duncan said, 'Who wins fires first.' Crimond said 'Tails.' Duncan tossed the coin, it fell tails. Crimond placed the guns on the tables, one at each end of the room.

After that they stood still, looking at each other. Duncan

could feel his heart beating, his hands sweating. He could hear his breath and Crimond's breath. Was this a moment at which perhaps . . . ?

Crimond said in the same soft silky almost ingratiating voice which he had used in the later part of their conversation, 'Of course, if we had seconds, which we have not, it would be their duty at this point to ask us both if the engagement was really necessary, if we could not agree, even at this late stage, not to fight. Should we not, in order to make this event crystal clear, act now as our own seconds?'

For a moment Duncan wondered: is this what it's all for? Did he mount the whole play in order to end it like this? He felt angry and also appalled at this sudden last-minute opening, when he had thought to be finished with decisions. 'That would amount to a reconciliation. No. Certainly not. You know that is impossible.'

'As you wish,' said Crimond, bowing his head slightly.

'Well, as you wish too, presumably?'

'Yes.'

'Then we need wait no longer.'

Crimond was staring at Duncan with a new intentness. He said, 'That left eye of yours, it's got an odd look. Is your vision all right?'

'With these glasses, perfect.' Duncan, who had been unaware of his glasses, suddenly took them off. He stared at Crimond with his vulnerable unassisted eyes and thought, we've been *looking* at each other, which we haven't done since *then*.

Duncan put on his glasses again. He took off his tie and his jacket and threw them on top of his overcoat on the desk, and unbuttoned the top buttons of his shirt. Crimond took off his jacket and dropped it on the floor. He undid another button on his shirt and felt about at his throat. We are undressing, thought Duncan, as if we were going to bed. It's all *mad, mad*. Oh would it were over.

He turned away from Crimond and walked to the far end of the room and stood beneath the target. Crimond placed a revolver in front of him on the table. Duncan thought, if either of us hits a live one it'll make a hell of a row. One can't use a gun like this properly with a silencer anyway. We haven't discussed what we're going to do if anything happens. Suppose one of us is horribly wounded. But nothing like that is going to happen. So there was no need for the discussion.

Crimond had reached the other end of the room. Duncan said, 'You can unlock the door now.'

Crimond unlocked the door.

Duncan stood without touching his gun. He rolled up the sleeves of his shirt. He saw Crimond outlined by the door. What am I going to do? I shall have to decide.

'Are we to begin then?' said Crimond.

'Yes. You first I believe.'

'Yes.'

There was a faint sound. Duncan realised that Crimond had instantly lifted his gun and spun the cylinder and pulled the trigger. Nothing there.

Duncan felt, with relief, an extraordinary euphoria, and a certainty that he would *be all right*, it was indeed a game, a ritual, an exorcism. He had been so wise not to ignore Crimond's invitation, not to funk the meeting, not to evade the rite. He lifted his gun, broke it and spun the cylinder, closed it. As soon as his hand touched the handle an old sensation, something he had not experienced for years, took possession of his whole body: a sensation of power and a demand for accuracy. He held the gun carefully in one hand and aimed it at the centre of Crimond's forehead. The very centre, the target. As he stood he could see also, to the right of Crimond's head, a sort of white mark on the door. The door was blue, the colour vividly emerging in the brilliant neon light. Crimond, motionless, was framed in the blue door. This is my first shot, thought Duncan, Crimond can shoot again too. Even if we wanted to kill each other it would be quite difficult. There can be terrible wounds which are worse than death. But wasn't that what I wanted when I brought that hammer with me? Suppose I were to aim at his right shoulder? For a second he kept the gun steady, holding the sights level at Crimond's forehead. With this gun and even at this distance there was no such thing as accuracy. Duncan felt a physical spasm and a sense of darkness as if he might faint. Simply in this second to hold Crimond at his mercy was the consummation of the ritual. Nothing more was needed. With the slightest movement he shifted the gun and aimed at the white mark on the door, tensing his fingers on the trigger.

Then, hearing it distantly as in a dream, Duncan heard the odd, the amazing, sound of someone's feet on the stairs outside. The sound of approaching feet and then a voice that cried out, 'David! David!' The door was flying open and instead of the blue rectangle Jenkin Riderhood stood there, emerged from the darkness of the stairs. Duncan, in the very moment of firing, adjusted his aim. The report, echoing in the enclosed room, was deafening. Another sound, a heavy thudding noise, was almost instantaneous. Duncan dropped the gun and put his hand to his head. Jenkin was not there, there was only the open doorway. Duncan walked slowly down the room. Jenkin was lying on the floor on his back. There was a neat red hole in the centre of his forehead in exactly the place at which Duncan had aimed when he was aiming at Crimond. Jenkin was clearly dead. His eyes were open and his face expressed surprise. Duncan closed the door.

Looking back later on what happened next Duncan was amazed at his own cold-blooded coolness. It was clear to him at once that, out of an unimaginable terrible, horrible catastrophe some things at least could be salvaged by swift intelligent action. A strange, weird, uncanny aspect of the situation – and Duncan recalled that he had felt it like that at a time when there were so many things to feel – was that Crimond began instantly, silently, to weep, and continued to shed streaming tears throughout the scene that followed.

Duncan *thought*, he *reflected*. He said to Crimond, 'We must explain this as an accident. Of course it *is* an accident. But how? What's the best story? Let's say we were shooting at the target and he got in the way. That's the best I can think of now, at least it's simple. Look, help me, we'll pull him down to the far end, near the target. Just as well there's so little blood.'

Duncan began to pull Jenkin's body by the legs. Crimond did not help, but walked beside him, weeping, as Duncan dragged the thing into position near the target. Crimond then went back to the bed and sat down on it and gave himself up to silent crying, his hands in front of his face.

Duncan pushed the two tables up against the wall. He even picked up some books and put them on the tables.

He said to Crimond, 'Shall I ring the police or will you?'

Crimond did not reply, continuing to shed tears. Duncan saw his tears, from his bent head, falling to the floor.

It was only at that moment that it occurred to Duncan that *he didn't have to stay there*. He could simply *vanish*.

Duncan picked up his jacket and his tie and put them on. He put on his overcoat, stuffing the gloves well down into the pockets. It took him a moment to realise what the hammer was when he touched it. He said to Crimond, 'You must telephone the police. I don't have to be involved. You understand? *I wasn't here*. You're the one who's got to explain. Just stick to the story, it was an accident, he got in the way. Do you hear, do you *understand*? I'm going, I was never here at all.'

Crimond did not respond. Duncan stood still, trying to *think*. What else must he do? Something about guns, fingerprints. He took out his gloves and put them on, then picked up the gun which he had fired, broke it, and poured out the contents of the cylinder onto the table. One spent cartridge and five duds. He replaced the spent cartridge in the blackened chamber, then carefully cleaned the handle of the gun with his handkerchief. He took the gun to Crimond and held it out to him, holding it by the barrel. Crimond automatically took it and laid it down on the floor. Duncan repeated the process. Crimond took the gun, held it a moment in his palm, then put it down. He paid no attention to Duncan, did not look up. Duncan decided to leave the gun on the floor near Crimond's feet. He turned his attention to the other gun, broke it and up-ended the cylinder. He shook it. Nothing came out. He looked at the gun. The chambers were all empty. He said to himself, I'll think about that later. He put the gun away in the cupboard, which also contained an automatic pistol. He thought, is that everything? No. The five dud cartridges were lying on the table. Crimond had made them carefully, cutting the lead and pressing it in, so that the contest would be *fair*. Duncan thought, he won't be able to explain those, I'd better take them with me. He put them in his pocket.

He went to Crimond and shook him, seizing him by the shoulders and pulling him violently to and fro. Crimond raised his head and put out a weak hand to push Duncan's grip away. Duncan *shouted* at him, 'I'm going now. I wasn't here. You shot him by accident, he got in the way. Just *think* what happened, *picture* it. Then ring the police, ring them soon. Do you understand me?'

Crimond nodded his head, not looking at Duncan, still trying feebly to push him away with a hand wet with tears.

Duncan went out, closing the door of the playroom, went up the stairs and quietly let himself out into the icy cold street. Cars were passing, people were walking. No one, evidently, had paid attention to a revolver shot. Duncan set off to walk to the Underground station, a taxi was too risky, anyway he would be unlikely to meet one. He turned up his coat collar and hunched his head down inside it and walked fast but not too fast. When he reached the station he heard the sound of a police car in the distance. Perhaps Crimond had pulled himself together and got his story ready and made the telephone call.

Duncan returned as quickly as possible to the office, amazed to find that he was able to arrive there before lunch time. No one seemed to have remarked his absence. Duncan rang Jean on some vague pretext. She sounded very glad to hear his voice. She said she had rung earlier, he said he was at a meeting. Duncan had lunch in the office canteen and chatted conspicuously with a number of people. He ate his lunch. On the way home he bought the evening paper as usual. There was a small confused item about an accident with a gun. The reporter had not even taken in who Crimond was. So brief is mortal fame, Duncan reflected, as he sat in the train going home.

PART THREE
Spring

Rose was standing at the window of her bedroom looking out at the sun shining upon the long wide lawn and the Italian fountain and the huge handsome chestnut trees and some fields full of black and white cows and some sloping woodlands and a receding horizon of hills. The funeral was over, the visiting mourners were gone. This was not the funeral of Jenkin Riderhood, now in the past, but the funeral of Reeve's wife, Laura Curtland. Rose was not at Boyars but at the house in Yorkshire. At Boyars the snowdrops were over, but here in the north a few clumps lingered in sheltered corners under still leafless trees and bushes. In the birch copse beyond the lawn the early double daffodils were coming into flower.

Laura Curtland, so long a *malade imaginaire*, had vindicated her status by suddenly dying. After maintaining for years that she had cancer when she had not, she developed a quick inoperable tumour and passed away. Perhaps, everyone said later, she had in some sense been right all the time. Laura's sudden departure caused a good deal of surprise, some dismay, and a certain amount of terrible grief. At Fettiston (this was the name of the house) grief, shared by the servants, prevailed. A few village people shed tears too. The relations, with the exception of Laura's husband and children, were calm. Rose, who had never particularly got on with Laura, found herself wishing that she had made more effort to get to know someone of whose good qualities she was now suddenly aware. Rose had felt that Laura was hostile, anxious to keep Rose at a distance. Perhaps, Rose now reflected, Laura had reasonably felt that Rose neglected them, found them dull, spent minimal time in Yorkshire, had made a rival 'family' for herself in London. Rose was moved, and deeply moved, by the evident, even frantic, anguish of Reeve and Neville and Gillian. The flowing tears of cook and maids, the bowed heads of sorrowing gardeners, also counted as evidence. From her *chaise longue* Laura has presumably not only organised that large house and garden, but aroused affection in those whom she directed as well as enjoying the absolute love of her nearest and dearest. Rose had been aware that Laura was not a fool, but in some way she had never taken her seriously, and no doubt Laura sensed this. Of course all these sensible reflections came too late.

Rose, who had come before the funeral and stayed on at the request of Reeve and the children, had now been at Fettiston for over two weeks. Rose was surprised later, though at the time it seemed natural and inevitable, at the speed with which it was *she* who, in the immediate management of the scene, took Laura's place. Reeve and Neville and Gillian, helplessly overwhelmed by grief, begged Rose to take charge and, without being told to, the servants all ran to her with their problems. The Vicar rang Rose about the funeral arrangements, and Rose extracted Reeve's wishes. Rose organised the 'party' after the funeral, and allotted bedrooms to relations who were staying the night. She also decided what, in the emergency, to delegate to Mrs Keithley, the extremely able cook. Of course Rose was glad to be of use; and a little more than that, she felt a certain ambiguous gratification at being suddenly important in a house where she had often felt she counted for little. Fettiston was a larger and far more beautiful house than Boyars. It was a pure simple unspoilt eighteenth-century house built in a local stone which varied in colour between a liquid brown and a faint rose. An ancestor who had visited Vicenza had adorned the balustraded roof with rows of statues, which had been removed to discreet places in the garden by Reeve's and Rose's great-grandfather. The house sat upon a wide terrace reached from the lawn by a fine narrowing stone stairway. Upon the lawn was the fountain, a rather more successful addition by the same ancestor. Beyond was the vista of English countryside, and farther away the slopes of the Pennines fading (today), outline against outline, into a blue distance which became the sky. Rose had never had any strong sense of 'family possessions' or indeed of family, beyond her parents and Sinclair. After they were dead she had settled to an idea of herself as having friends but, except in some formal or literal sense, no relations. She felt no belongingness to 'the Curtlands', no 'old Yorkshire family' bond, though the 'old house' had been in Yorkshire and all her forebears had lived there. (A local joke had it that when Curtlands referred to 'the wars', they meant the Wars of the Roses.) Rose was fond of Boyars, but would not have felt any great or special pang if she had had to sell it. Now, experiencing the Yorkshire house more intimately, she thought how odd it must be for Neville and Gillian, though perhaps after all they found it natural, to feel that this place was *their* place, to be entrusted to them and to their children and to their children's children, and filled with the pale strong presences of their ancestors, whose pictures, painted, unfortunately, by minor artists, hung (mostly) in the larger rooms, though some were banished to the bedrooms. On the wall of Rose's bedroom was a small awkward seventeenth-century picture of a rather touching lady, who had lived before Fettiston was built or thought of, who looked remarkably like Gillian.

The drama, for it was that among other things, of Laura's death had interrupted Rose's prolonged period of mourning for Jenkin. In a sad but understandable way it had come as an almost welcome interruption. It had removed Rose from the dark obsessive almost maddening atmosphere in London, to a place where her emotions were less deeply involved and where there were many practical things she could do. Her usual Christmas visit to Yorkshire, coming fairly soon after Jenkin's death, and before Laura's condition was diagnosed, had been a nightmare. Christmas at Fettiston was celebrated, as usual, with every extreme of jollity, log fires, Christmas trees, mountains of holly and ivy and mistletoe from the garden, carols, indoor games, excessive eating and drinking, and manifold exchanges of beautifully wrapped presents. Sleigh rides, skiing and skating were also hoped for, but a perverse period of warm weather made these impossible. Rose, hating every moment, got away as soon as she could. She had said nothing to her cousins about the terrible thing which had happened, and they made only perfunctory enquiries about her life elsewhere. Gerard, in so far as he had 'spent' or 'noticed' Christmas, passed it with Gideon and Patricia. It had been a notable occasion because, evidently persuaded by Gideon, Tamar and Violet had joined them. Jean and Duncan were in France as usual. Lily went to stay with her friend Angela Parke. Gulliver was said to be 'in the north', in Leeds or Newcastle. Rose had at first intended to stay in London with Gerard, but he had urged her to go to Yorkshire. In fact both Rose and Gerard felt a certain relief at being separated. They had spent too long grieving together and helping to make each other even more miserable. It was perhaps 'good for them' to be with people less affected, or unaffected, with whom they would have to behave in ordinary ways. Rose had become aware, after the appalling shock of his death, how much, how much more than she had ever realised, she had loved and depended on Jenkin. A slight haze had perhaps always, for her, rested upon him because of an old jealousy of Gerard's affection for him, a sense as if one day Jenkin might take Gerard away from her altogether. Now she remembered what a wonderful *presence* Jenkin had been in her life, he had indeed 'given a soul to all things'; and remembering his wisdom, his particular gentleness, his kindness to her, the unique charm of his physical being, it also seemed to her that he had perhaps loved her with some kind of special love. This thought made her particularly miserable, mingling her sorrow with remorse. Life without Jenkin seemed impossible, too much had been taken away. Her own mourning had of course blended with Gerard's much greater grief. Gerard's grief had appalled Rose, and wounded her the more because she could do nothing for it. Inevitably this death made them speak of Sinclair and renew their old sorrow. Rose had forgotten that Gerard could cry, and cry so terribly, sobbing and shedding wild tears as women do.

What, as time passed, they more and more discussed, and

made themselves more wretched thereby, was the extraordinary nature of that death, the circumstances, the accident. Here, after a while, they found themselves asking and saying the same things over and over again. Well, it *was* an accident, wasn't it, and accidents are bizarre. To the police and at the inquest Crimond had explained in the utmost detail what had happened, how he and Jenkin had been discussing Crimond's marksmanship, and had had a bet on his ability, how Jenkin had gone down near the target, how Crimond had told him to keep clear, and, concentrating upon his aim, had fired just as Jenkin turned and moved to say something to him, not realising he was in the line of fire. It was a simple, awful accident. The verdict was death by misadventure. Crimond's evident grief impressed the police and the coroner. Many reliable people were ready to testify that Crimond and Jenkin were friends, no one suggested they were dangerously close friends. Jenkin's golden character was attested by all. There was no suggestion of a sordid homosexual feud, nothing about jealousy, or about money, no shadow of any motive for foul play. If there was carelessness, it was on both parts. Crimond did get into trouble for possessing firearms without a licence, and was heavily fined. The police searched his flat but found nothing incriminating. He had never, in fact, even in his days of fame, been a terrorist suspect. He was now, so long had he been a recluse, scarcely news at all. No keen young reporter, apt to find out some hidden infamy, was sent to pursue the case. It did not seem to occur to anybody that there might have been a quarrel about politics. There was at that moment a great deal of 'news' around and plenty of far more scandalous and violent and sickening goings-on involving far more famous and important people. This odd little accident attracted small attention. Gerard did not expect, or receive, any communication from Crimond after the event, and of course neither Jean nor Duncan heard anything. The only person Crimond was known to have communicated with was Jenkin's schoolmaster friend, Marchment, who mentioned in the course of his testimony that Crimond had telephoned him from a call box just after Jenkin's death and immediately after he had rung the police, and told him briefly what had happened; and that Crimond had later told him the whole story in much greater detail. Gerard telephoned Marchment, then went to see him, and received the same account. So it was an accident. It was not possible, was it, that Crimond had murdered Jenkin? No, it was not possible. There was no conceivable motive. Surely it was not possible?

In all these rather horrible discussions Rose took part with a rather important reservation. She had, now, her own rather special view of Crimond, 'her Crimond', which must be henceforth and forever her darkest secret. Rose had, even before Jenkin's death, recovered from what now looked like the amazing, unique, inexplicable fit of insanity wherein she had felt herself to be madly in love with Crimond, during which Crimond from being nothing had become everything. Rose, who had at once told herself to 'return to reality', had managed reasonably well to do so within a few days of her 'seizure'. Gradually the lurid glow faded, her usual attachments regained their power, above all the agonising, tormenting sense of a possibility, a possible move, began to leave her; and she was able to be thankful that she had *not* found Crimond in the street when she ran down after him, had *not* written him a compromising letter whose existence would have disturbed her ever after. Of course she couldn't love Crimond! She loved Gerard, and could not, for thousands of reasons, love both of them. Moreover, she absolutely could not, for Jean's sake, have anything to do with Crimond. Crimond was a person she disapproved of, was perhaps even a mad person – what could have been madder than that sudden proposal? He was not someone with whom she could envisage spending time, let alone developing any close relation. One of her best comforts, in the early days of her recovery, was the thought that Crimond was actually a bit deranged and would have repented of his rash idea soon enough if Rose had shown any interest in it! All the same, and she realised this as soon as she was able to tell herself that it was over, something remained, and perhaps, Rose told herself with an odd mixture of sadness and pleasure, would always remain. There was some bond between her and that man, which was there even if, as was likely, he regretted his move and saw it as an aberration; and even if he now consoled himself by hating her for her graceless reception of him. Rose could not perceive exactly what this residuum was. No doubt it was something which would wear and change with time. It was partly that she was, in retrospect, so flattered, and so touched, by his suggestion. It is hard for a woman not to feel some kindness for a man who adores her. He, strange Crimond, whom people feared and hated, had been for a moment at her feet. How surprised everyone would be – but of course no one would ever know. But there was also another, and better, she felt, component. For a short time she had *loved* Crimond, her love, like a laser beam, had reached right into him, finding, however blindly, the real Crimond, the lovable Crimond, who therefore must exist. She did not allow herself to imagine that she would ever tell Crimond that she had loved him; and she could scarcely, even much later, apologise suitably for her rudeness without in some way hinting at those very different feelings. In that direction, there was no road. But her wish that somehow he could know remained as a point of pain, and she guarded her curious knowledge of him like the emblem of a forbidden religion.

This was her state before the news of Jenkin's death and its strange circumstances. The shock of this frightful blankly inexplicable disaster brought back to Rose her view of Crimond as something black and lethal. Rose and Gerard agreed that they could not and must not entertain the notion that their friend had been murdered. It was too incredible and too awful a charge to set up without a shred of evidence. 'We mustn't formulate this hypothesis, even to ourselves,' said Gerard. But they *had* formulated it, and were upset and sickened to find it being freely uttered by others, based simply upon malicious speculation. Here again Rose had her own private torment: it came into her mind that Crimond had indeed killed Jenkin, as an act of revenge against her, and against Gerard whom he might blame for Rose's rejection of him. This idea, when it suddenly appeared, caused her such agony that she felt she might go mad, even be mad enough to blurt out the whole thing to Gerard simply so that he could share her misery. She thought, so *I* am really responsible for Jenkin's death, if only I had been kinder to Crimond, if I hadn't been so cruel and scornful . . . Here however Rose's deep base of sanity eventually prevailed, her strong moral sense joined with her sense of self-preservation, and she judged this picture of the matter to be not only a crazy, but an evil fantasy.

Within a short space of time Rose had attended two burial services, both of them Anglican. Gerard, who had instantly taken it on himself to organise Jenkin's funeral, had decided that since Jenkin had latterly appeared to be something of a fellow traveller of the Christian faith, the solemn words of the Prayer Book, so sober and so beautiful, should bid him farewell. Jenkin had no family; but at the funeral a surprisingly large number of people whom Rose and Gerard had never seen before appeared and manifested their grief. Gerard decreed cremation, because he vaguely recalled Jenkin having approved of it, but chiefly because he could not bear the idea of his friend's body continuing to exist, rotting away in the earth. Better not to be. Laura of course was buried in the churchyard of the parish church in a place reserved for Curtlands. An argument about her tombstone was already going on. The two services were similar, except that the body of the departed was committed, in one case 'to the earth', in the other case 'to the fire'. Earth to earth, ashes to ashes, dust to dust.

Later that morning Rose was sitting in the library, where Reeve Curtland had been writing letters answering the numerous expressions of condolence upon Laura's death. The young people had departed, Neville to St Andrews where he was in his last year of studying history, Gillian to Leeds where she was in her first year of psychology. Both of them had failed to get into Oxford, but were proving it possible to flourish elsewhere. Reeve, who had also failed to get into Oxford had, as he often complained, passed a gloomy and profitless period at a minor London college. It had only lately occurred to her that Reeve, who was about her age, might have envied and perhaps disapproved of the golden times which Sinclair and the others were obviously having at the old university. Reeve had cheered up considerably, however, as uncharitable observers remarked, when his father inherited the title. The Curtlands were Anglicans, not Nonconformists or Quakers, but there was a puritanical streak which emerged at intervals. A Curtland had been an officer in Cromwell's army. Rose's Anglo-Irish mother had cheerfully tolerated Sinclair's homosexuality, but her gentle father had been quietly shocked. Of course Rose had never discussed these matters, or indeed anything of grave importance, with Reeve. Always searching for likenesses, she discerned in Neville's blond handsomeness a certain look of Sinclair. It was certainly clear that Neville, always nearly engaged to different girls, did not share his cousin's ambiguous propensities. Reeve bore no marked resemblance to any of his relations or ancestors, he certainly lacked the jaunty look which Curtland men seemed to have had, judging from the family portraits, a look which both Sinclair and Neville pre-eminently incarnated. He was not, like them, tall. He had mousy brown hair, not grey but balding a little, dark brown soft puzzled anxious eyes, a ruddy complexion and a much lined brow where the pitted rubbery flesh rose in little hillocks. His lips were anxious too. His eyebrows thick and furry. He somehow managed to look young. He was often shy and even *gauche* in conversation, unlike his son. He liked to stay at home all the time and work on innumerable jobs. He always wore a tie, even when out on the tractor. In spite of his awkwardness and sometimes maddeningly tentative approach to the world, he did not lack charm, perhaps the charm of some timid touching animal. As people also observed about him, he did in fact, for all his poor showing, manage his estate, and his investments, reasonably well. He also played the piano creditably and painted in watercolours.

'Reeve, I must go back to London,' said Rose, uttering words she had wanted to utter for some time.

'Oh no! Why? The children have gone but there's still me to look after! And how will the house run without you? You haven't anything to *do* down there. I've often wondered why you weren't with us oftener. You should regard this place as a second home.'

'Oh I do,' said Rose vaguely.

'Evidently you don't, as you're so mean with your time! You know how attached the children are to you, how much they depend on your advice.'

Rose could not recall ever having 'advised' Neville and Gillian, who were bouncily independent young people, though it was true that she had had some 'good talks' with them during this, exceptionally long, stay at Fettiston.

'How much they need you,' Reeve went on, 'and will – even more – in the future –'

Rose heard uneasily the slight weight which he put upon these words. She said, rather firmly, wanting now to be clear, 'I must get back. Gerard is in a rather unhappy state because a friend of his died in an accident.'

'Jenkin Riderhood.'

'Yes. I didn't know you knew –' Rose was surprised.

'Francis Reckitt told me, you know, Tony's son. Someone in London mentioned it to him quite recently and he remembered the chap's name. I met him with you once, years ago.'

'Of course, you met Jenkin, I'd forgotten.'

'Odd business – that man Crimond, wasn't it – that Communist or whatever –'

'Yes.'

'I'm sorry. I didn't say anything to you. I felt we had enough on our plate.'

'Indeed. Anyway – I feel I must go home – I'm sure you understand.'

'I think this is your home, but I won't argue! There aren't many of them left now, are there –'

'You mean –?'

'Gerard and his friends. He's living with his sister now, isn't he?'

'Yes.'

'Well, come back again soon. We do need you very much.

Things are going to be different now – and – Rose – *blood is thicker than water.*'

'A lot of things have happened since you went away,' said Gerard.

Rose had telephoned him on her return and he had come round at once.

'So you're living in Jenkin's house?'

'Yes. He left everything to me. I think I shall stay there.'

'So Patricia and Gideon got you out after all!'

'Yes. But I wanted to go. I'm tired of being surrounded by possessions. It's time for a radical change.'

'You mean you'll become like Jenkin?'

'Don't be silly.'

'Sorry, I'm being stupid. I feel terribly stupid just now.'

It was late evening. Rose professed to have had supper, though she had only had a sandwich. Gerard also said he had eaten. They were drinking coffee. He had refused whisky. The preliminaries of their conversation, so much looked forward to by Rose, had been awkward, almost irritable, as though they had both forgotten how to converse. She thought, he's angry with me for having stayed away so long. I hope it's only that.

Gerard looked different. His curly hair was dull and disordered, standing out in senseless directions, like the fur of a sick or frightened animal. His sculptured face, whose fine surfaces usually cohered so harmoniously, looked disunified and angular, even distorted. His mouth was awry, twisted in repose by a twinge of distress or annoyance. His normally calm eyes were restless and evasive, and he kept turning his head away from Rose in a sulky manner. Sometimes he became still and abstracted, frowning, as if listening. Oh he is

481

ill, he is not himself, thought Rose miserably, but it seemed that she could do nothing now but irritate him.

'You know Duncan's resigned from the office?'

'No.'

'Of course that's since you went away, you've been away such ages. He kept saying he'd resign, and now he's resigned. They're in France now looking for a house.'

'What part?' said Rose.

'I don't know what part!'

'I rang their number, I wanted to see Jean. So they're away. How are they?'

'Very cheerful, not a care in the world.'

'How are Gull and Lily? I hope *they're* all right.'

'Not very,' said Gerard with an air of satisfaction. 'You know Gulliver ran off to Newcastle? Yes, of course you know that. Lily hasn't heard from him.'

'I expect she thinks he's got a girl up there! I think she should go after him. So you've seen Lily?'

'No, of course not!'

'Perhaps he wants to vanish until he can return in triumph.'

'In that case he'll just vanish.'

'But you've seen Tamar?'

'You think I've seen everybody! Actually, I have literally seen Tamar, but not to talk to. My God, she's sleek, you wouldn't recognise her.'

'What do you mean, "sleek"?'

'Well, fit, in cracking form.'

'Really – how splendid!'

'I don't know whether it's splendid,' said Gerard, 'it doesn't seem real. I think she may be deranged or drugged or something.'

'I could never make out what was the matter with her – just Violet I suppose.'

'Do you know, I don't think Tamar cared at all – about – Jenkin –'

Rose said hastily, to cut off his emotion, 'I'm sure she cared. She's such an odd girl, she conceals things.'

'She's been seeing that priest, your parson.'

'Father McAlister.'

'She's been baptised and confirmed.'

'Good heavens! Well, if it's done her some good –'

'She's been stuffed full of a lot of consoling lies. Gideon's been looking after her too.'

'Gideon?'

'It seems so. I found her round at my – his – house twice lately. Of course I tried to see her, but she wouldn't see me.'

Rose thought, he's furious because Gideon is succeeding where he's failed. I must change the subject. 'Do you find you can work well in Jenkin's house? Are you writing something?

'No. I'm not going to write – anything. I've decided not to.'

'Gerard!'

'I haven't anything to say. Why write half-baked rubbish just for the sake of writing?'

'But you –'

'Crimond's book is being published by the Oxford University Press. I may be able to get hold of a proof copy from somebody who works there.'

As soon as Crimond's name was spoken it seemed as if the whole conversation had been simply steering towards it. Gerard, who had been looking away, now looked directly at Rose, he flushed and his lips parted, his face expressing a kind of surprise.

'Have you seen Crimond?'

'Of course not.'

As Rose was trying to think of something suitable to say Gerard got up. 'I must go. I've sold my car, that's another thing that's happened. I'll have to get a taxi. I can walk actually. Thanks for the coffee.'

'Wouldn't you like whisky, brandy?' Rose got up too.

'No, thanks. Rose, I'm sorry to be so – so – *hideous*.'

Rose wanted to embrace him, but he went away with a wave, without kissing her. The savour of that word *hideous* remained in the room. Rose could taste it upon her lips. She thought, he is sick, he is sick, he is *poisoned* by those thoughts, by those *terrible thoughts*.

Gerard, at home in Jenkin's parlour, was feeling wretched because he had not been able to communicate with Rose. He regretted what he had said to her. In conveying his news he had adopted a surly cynical tone, he had sneered at almost everyone he mentioned. He had behaved badly, he had lost his rational reticence, he had been deliberately hostile and hurtful to Rose. He thought, I am not myself, my soul is sick, I am under a curse.

Crimond was the name of the curse which Gerard was under. He could think of nothing and no one else and could not see how this degrading and tormenting condition could change. He thought every day of going to see Crimond, and every day saw how impossible this was. He dreaded seeing the book in case it was very good, equally in case it was not. Of course he thought continuously about Jenkin, but his mourning had been somehow taken over by Crimond, everything to do with Jenkin was misted over and contaminated by Crimond; and how terrible that was, and how *degraded* and *vile* Gerard had become to allow it to happen. Gerard was not even sure by now whether he found it conceivable that Crimond could have murdered Jenkin. It couldn't be true. And yet . . . Why had Jenkin been *there*? He said he didn't go to Crimond's house. Crimond must have invited him or lured him. Maybe it was an accident, but had not Crimond somehow made an accident possible, unconsciously as it were? Could this make sense? Another rumour that circulated, and which was mentioned to Gerard by a malicious acquaintance who added that of course he did not believe it, was that Jenkin and Crimond had been lovers, and it was a jealousy killing. This simply *could not* be true. Jenkin had never been close to Crimond, and would never have concealed anything of such importance from Gerard. He could not believe anything of the sort. And yet, perhaps, might not Jenkin and Crimond, possibly very long ago, have been very close friends or lovers, and would not Jenkin have felt bound to keep this secret? Perhaps there *had* been something – and such things can be timeless. Had Gerard's 'proposal' to Jenkin somehow – not of course by Jenkin telling Crimond – but by some perceptible change in

Jenkin's demeanour and plans, imparted to Crimond that 'something had happened', even that Jenkin was thinking of leaving his celibate state? Had Jenkin suddenly become, in some mysterious way, newly attractive? If so then in some sense Gerard was responsible for Jenkin's death. But this idea, awful as it was, was shadowy, and tortured him less than some very particular images of the hypothetical relationship, however long ago, between Jenkin and Crimond. And then he kept hearing Jenkin's voice, laughing, saying: 'Come live with me and be my love.'

On that day when Jenkin had left Tamar so hurriedly 'for an emergency' and had said, 'Stay and keep warm, I'd like to think you were here, stay here till I come back,' Tamar had waited, at first feeling a security in being alone in Jenkin's house, then after a while beginning to feel wretched and lonely and longing for his return. She went into the kitchen and looked into the refrigerator at bread, butter, cheese, she looked at tins of beans in the larder and apples on a dish. It was as if for her the food were contaminated, or seen in some future state mouldering away. She could not eat. She lay down on Jenkin's bed, but though she turned on the electric fire the room was cold. She shivered under a blanket, lacking the will to burrow deeper into the bed. The little infinitesimal spark of hope which she had gained simply from Jenkin's presence was extinguished. It was blackness again, ravaged, smashed, crushed, pulverised blackness, like the night after the earth-quake, only the dark was silent, there were no voices, no one was there, only herself, her vast awful smashed up self. Tamar, in running to Jenkin, had wanted simply to be saved from some sort of imminent screaming insanity. The speech she had

485

made to him about becoming a Christian and about magic and so on had been entirely impromptu, something wild, even cynical, said to startle Jenkin and perhaps herself. The words were hollow, another voice speaking through her. Of course she had listened, but with unabated despair, even with a kind of contemptuous anger to Father McAlister's talk about 'accepting Christ as her Saviour,' which seemed to her like the gabble of a witch doctor. Now, waiting for Jenkin to come back, she gave herself up to the old repetitive misery, and to waiting impatiently, then anxiously, for his return. After a while she started inventing excellent reasons why he had not come back, he had said it was an emergency, someone was seriously ill, or even more miserable than she was, or had attempted suicide, he was holding someone's hand, he was urgently needed, he was detained. During this time Tamar *had nothing to do*. She thought vaguely of cleaning the house, but the house was clean. She made herself a cup of tea, and washed up her cup and saucer, together with a mug which was beside the sink. After some time, after hours had passed, she could do nothing but feel very anxious, then very frightened, because Jenkin had not returned. She lay down and fell into a chilled coma, she got up, she cried for a while. About five o'clock she decided to go and started writing a letter to Jenkin which she then tore up. She put on her coat but could not make up her mind to return to Acton and to her mother. At last she rang up Gerard and asked if he knew where Jenkin was. Gerard told her he was dead.

Gerard had been one of the first people to learn of the event for a curious reason. The police had asked Crimond if he knew Jenkin's next of kin, or closest connection, and Crimond had given them Gerard's name and address. Gerard came back from the London Library to find the police on the doorstep. He was taken to a police station in South London where he was questioned about Jenkin, about Crimond, about the situation, about their relationship. It was partly, perhaps largely, Gerard's testimony which saved Crimond from being treated as a 'suspect'. Gerard was saved from having to identify his friend's body by the fact that Marchment had instantly, on

Crimond's 'phone call, made contact with the local police and made his own appearance on the spot in the role of best friend. The whole matter remained, during that day, in a state of confusion and coming and going, during which Gerard might well have come face to face with Crimond but did not. He got back home in fact just in time to receive Tamar's telephone call. Gerard asked her where she was. Tamar said she was in a telephone box. Gerard told her to wait there and he would fetch her by car. Tamar said, no, thank you, she would go home, her mother was waiting, and rang off, leaving Gerard to reproach himself for having, in his own shocked state, told her the news so bluntly. She went back to Acton, *said nothing to Violet*, listened to Violet's complaints, toyed with her supper and went to bed early. Her condition then, as she saw it afterwards, was the sort of suspended shock which enables a soldier whose arm has been blown off to walk, talk sensibly, even crack jokes, before quite suddenly falling dead. Tamar never told anyone, except Father McAlister, that she had been with Jenkin on that day. The idea of being questioned about it was intolerable. Anyway, that meeting was a secret between her and Jenkin. Tamar had not waited to be told by Gerard how Jenkin had died, it was sufficient to know that he was dead. Then after she had gone to bed that night and was lying in the darkness choking with grief, it occurred to her that, whatever might have happened to him, he had been killed *by the dead child*; and henceforth and forever anyone who came near to her would be *cursed* and *destroyed*. So she was responsible for Jenkin's death.

On the following day Tamar had an appointment to see the priest which she had intended to cancel but had forgotten to do so. She kept the appointment, and thereafter saw him at regular intervals. Father McAlister specialised in desperate cases. Over Tamar, he might positively have been said to gloat. His eyes sparkled but he did not underestimate his difficulties. His father had been a High Anglican clergyman, his mother a devout Methodist. Father McAlister could pray as soon as he could speak and the high spiritual rhetoric of the Bible and of Cranmer's Prayer Book was more familiar to him than nursery rhymes. His God was that of his father, but his Christ was that of his mother. He spoke the dignified and beautiful language of a reticent spirituality, but he breathed the fire of instant salvation. Beyond this felicitous amalgam lay Father McAlister's secret: he had by now ceased to believe in God or in the divinity of Christ, but he believed in prayer, in Christ as a mystical Saviour, and in the *magical power* which had been entrusted to him when he was ordained a priest, a power to save souls and raise the fallen. Herein, carefully judging her needs and her intelligence, he colluded with Tamar. He sought diligently in her despair for the tiny spark of hope which could be kindled into a flame. When she called herself evil he appealed to her reason, when she proclaimed disbelief he explained faith, when she said she hated God he spoke of Christ, when she rejected Christ's divinity he preached Christ's power to save. He sang both high and low. He promised strength through repentance, and joy through renewal of life. He exhorted her to remake herself into an instrument fit for the service of others. He used the oldest argument in the book (sometimes called the Ontological Proof) which, in Father McAlister's version, said that if with a pure passion you love God, then God exists, because He *has to*. After all, what your best self, your most truthful soul desires must be real, and not to worry too much about what it's called. To these arguments, this struggle, this as it were dance which she was executing with the priest, Tamar become addicted. She surrendered herself to him as to an absorbing task. She was moving, as it seemed to her, and thus it came to her also in dreams, through a vast palace where doors opened, doors closed, rooms and vistas appeared and vanished and she knew no way, yet there was a way, and the thing to do was to keep going forward. A great many different things had to fit together, *had to*, for her, for Tamar, for her salvation from despair and degradation and death. That breathless, precarious, often tearful, prolonged and ingenious 'fitting together' was perhaps the *cleverest* thing that Tamar had ever done. She

488

must live, she *must* be healed. This hope, appearing first as an intelligent determination, coexisted with the old despair, which now began to seem like self-indulgence, her sense that she deserved no happiness and no healing and was doomed. At this early period she recalled with bitter tears the time when she had felt innocent and was proud and pleased to be called an angel, and a 'good girl' who would always 'do people good'. Her fallenness from this state made her especially anxious to avoid Gerard who had done so much to build up this illusion. This shunning of Gerard, almost a resentment against him, was what gave Gideon his chance since he emerged as the only person with whom Father McAlister could discreetly cooperate. Here the priest found an eager, even too enthusiastic, ally; and hence the surprising appearance of Tamar and even Violet at the Christmas rituals.

At a certain point surrender almost seemed a matter of logic. When so much had clearly happened to her, been done for her and to her, must she not acknowledge the reality of the source? These formalities were important as symbols and assertions and promises. This belongingness would express a real bond and a real freedom. It was time for citizenship, for the initiation into the mystery. Tamar was moved by gratitude, by the loving diligence of her mentor, and by a liberal carelessness which was, she sometimes thought, a fresh, perhaps better, form of her despair. Why not? Had she not come to believe in magic? She wanted even to *brand* herself as having moved away from those whose opinions she had once valued so much, moved into a different house, a different world, which they would condemn in terminology which now seemed to her shallow and banal. There was a way and she must go on *moving forward*, she was not yet *safe*. The rites of baptism and confirmation took place on the same day. A godmother and a godfather were necessary. Tamar found her godmother, a Miss Luckhurst, one of her school teachers now living in retirement. Father McAlister provided a hastily introduced godfather in the person of an almost speechless young curate. Immediately after the ceremony she took communion. The magic, for which she was now ready, exerted its

489

power. Tamar could rest, her breath was quiet, her eyes serene. She put on the 'sleekness' of which Gerard had spoken and the tranquillity which had led him to say that she did not care about Jenkin's death. She was able to pray. The priest had talked much to her about prayer, how it was simply a quietness, an attentive waiting, a space made for the presence of God. Tamar felt that she made the space and something filled it.

Tamar was perfectly aware of her cleverness, was even ready to accuse herself of 'cheating'. She once used this word to her mentor who replied, 'My child, you *can't* cheat – here, and here alone, you cannot cheat. What you desire purely and with all your heart is of one substance with the desire.' He said this was a truth which had to be 'lived into'. Tamar did her best to live into it, at first simply in escaping from hell, later in practising what seemed an entirely new kind of calmness. Father McAlister was bold enough to speak of irreversible change. Tamar was not so sure. Was this religious magic or merely psychological magic? The priest dismissed this almost nonsensical doubt. Tamar could not believe in the old God and the old Christ. Did she really *believe* in the new God and the new Christ? Was she indeed one of the 'young' to whom belonged the 'new revelation', new, as revelation is renewed in every age? Were there many many people like herself, or was she alone with a mad priest? She had 'joined' because her teacher wanted her to 'belong'. In an empty church in Islington her face had been touched with water, in a crowded church in Primrose Hill her head had been touched by a bishop's hand. She now 'went to church' but as it were secretively, alone with God. She did not want to join a study group to discuss the Christian attitude. She was well aware of her teacher's immense tact, and that he had spent his holiday talking to her and enjoying every moment of it. Indeed they were, she sometimes felt, on holiday together. She had been, with him, self-absorbed, looking after herself, learning a religious mythology as she discovered hitherto unknown regions of her own soul. She was, to use his words, 'getting to know her Christ'. If Christ saves, Christ lives, he told her. *That* is the resurrection and the life. Tamar's reflections on this mystery did not dismay her, indeed she looked forward to pursuing them. Obviously religion rested on something real; she let her reason sleep on that. She went on long walks through London and sat in churches. Obediently, she read the Bible, Kierkegaard, St John of the Cross, Julian of Norwich. She felt light and weightless and empty, as if she were indeed living on white wafers of bread and sips of sweet red wine. She was, for the moment, her mentor warned her, being carried upon spiritual storm wind which would one day cease to blow, just as, one day, her meetings with her priest must become much less frequent, and much less intense. Then, Tamar knew, she would be forced to *test* the 'fitting together' and the 'having it every way', by which she had been saved from death and hell.

All this time Tamar carried around with her the horrors which had, in Father McAlister's words, 'driven her into the arms of the Almighty': the dead child, her faithlessness to Duncan, her cruelty to Jean, the shock of Jenkin's death in which she had felt so mysteriously involved, her awful relationship with her mother. Tamar, out of her old bitter godless strength, had been capable of saying nothing to Violet, on that evening, about Jenkin's death. She was also capable, in the ruthless reticence necessary for her 'recovery', of telling Violet nothing about what was happening to her and how she was spending her time. Relations between Tamar and her mother gradually and almost entirely broke down. Violet kept asking Tamar when she was going back to work, Tamar kept saying she was on leave. Violet said Tamar would lose her job, Tamar said she didn't care. Tamar tried to say 'kind things' to her mother, but it was as if, here, she simply did not know the language of kindness. Everything she said irritated Violet into spiteful replies. Later on they simply stopped addressing each other and lived in the house as strangers. Tamar was out all day, in churches, in libraries, or in the clergy house in Islington where her meetings with her teacher took place. Father McAlister, to whom she reported everything, kept saying that *that* problem would be solved later on; Tamar suspected that he had, at present, no idea how. About the other things she had gradually, as part of other changes in her reviving heart, begun to feel better, though not yet without fear of relapse. At times the old horrors still seemed like unassimilable matter, stones, darts, the poisoned heads of broken arrows. She had been able to rid herself of the insane irrational superstitious indeed wicked thought that she had 'brought about' Jenkin's death. She was able to feel a natural grief. Many frightful pains grew less, repentant regret, like a kind of knowledge, gradually replaced self-destructive self-hating remorseful misery and despair. There were differences and she understood the differences. She went on tormenting herself about Jean and Duncan, had Duncan told Jean about Tamar, had Jean told Duncan about the child? I gave away his secret, I cursed her. I must be hated and despised. Father McAlister said wise things about not worrying about other people's thoughts. Where one could see no way to mend matters, one must just keep them in mind, surround them with good reflections. The desire to mend was often a nervous selfish urge to justify oneself, and not a vision of how anything could be made better. He told her to wait patiently, to make abstention from action into a penance, not to meddle, to leave it to God. But Tamar doubted her patience and wanted very much to write a long emotional letter to Jean.

About the dead child Father McAlister, to his great satisfaction, was at last able to do something definitive. He had said all sorts of things to Tamar, he told her to keep the child with her, not touched, not agonised about, as a sad presence, lived with, not hated, not feared, not frenziedly yearned for. He told her to think of the child as the Christ child. Tamar found this difficult, the priest said it was a spiritual exercise. Then at last Father McAlister, alone with Tamar in a church in north London, performed a rite which he had never performed before, and which indeed he had largely invented, a kind of burial or blessing of the dead child, a formal affirmation of love and farewell, containing an act of contrition. He did not say so to Tamar, but he also thought of this performance as an exorcism, a propitiation of a potentially dangerous spirit: for he was not without his superstitions and had seen, in his time, very terrible demons emerging from the unconscious minds of his flock, or from whatever the places are where demons live.

Tamar murmured that she acknowledged her transgressions and her sins were ever before her, that she had been poured out like water and all her bones were out of joint, that she desired to be washed and to be whiter than snow, that a broken and contrite spirit might not be despised, that broken bones might after all rejoice, and she might put off her sackcloth and be girded in gladness. Father McAlister then blessed the poor nameless vanished embryo, desired it to repose in peace and be received by God into those heavenly habitations where the souls of them that sleep in the Lord Jesus enjoy perpetual rest and felicity, and that God might look upon Tamar's contrition, accept her tears and assuage her pain. Then was He to bless her and keep her, make His face to shine upon her and be gracious unto her, lift up the light of His countenance upon her, and give her peace. This rite, a mixture of old familiar words and his own pastiche, and thought of by the priest as a most holy farrago, gave him intense pleasure; and he was rewarded too by the sight of Tamar's face, tear-stained and radiant.

'You know what today is?' said Rose.

'Of course,' said Gerard.

They said no more. It was Sinclair's birthday. He would have been fifty-three.

Two nights ago Rose had woken in the night, hearing a dog scratching at the door of the flat. She had woken up thinking at once: It's Regent! He's come back! She put on the lamp beside her bed. The house was silent. Of course it was not Regent, it was a dream. All the same she got up and turned on all the lights in the flat, opened the door and turned on the lights on the stairs. She even went down and opened the door into the street in case there had been, somewhere, some poor dog, some real dog. But there was nothing. After that she could not sleep.

She recalled this now, sitting in the little sitting room of Jenkin's house, having tea with Gerard. This having tea together was a custom which they kept up intermittently, though the 'spread' had grown steadily smaller and less sumptuous as the passing years had somehow removed the substance from the idea of 'tea time'. At Boyars it retained some of its majesty for the sake of Annushka. But today, with Gerard, there had been no scones, no sandwiches, no bread, butter or jam, just some rather old biscuits and a fruit cake. Neither of them had eaten much. This was partly because Reeve was coming to pick Rose up and take her out to dinner at his hotel. This picking up had been Reeve's idea, he said he wanted to see Gerard, they had not met for so long; Rose rang Gerard, it seemed inevitable.

Gerard was angry that Rose had thought it conceivable that Reeve should come and pick her up. Of course he had said that he would be delighted to see Reeve, and he was concealing his annoyance from Rose, or trying to, but he could see her sad look, and cursed himself for not having vetoed the rotten idea, or at least now evidently not managing to dissemble enough to be a pleasant companion.

This living at Jenkin's place was not working, it had been a bad plan, based on an illusion. Whatever did I expect, Gerard wondered, that I could live a better life here as an ascetic hermit, that I could somehow *become* Jenkin? Did I think that? Or was I just trying to get away from Gideon and Pat? The house resisted him. At first he had tried not to alter it, then as that seemed wrong he made a few changes, a new sink in the kitchen, a larger refrigerator, a few of his watercolours brought over from the house in Notting Hill. Some of his furniture was still there, relegated to the upper flat, some was in store, some had been purchased by Gideon. His books were all over the place, at Notting Hill, with Rose, or here, not unpacked, as he had been unable to decide to touch Jenkin's books which still occupied the shelves. The house felt dead, it was senseless, it was becoming dusty and untidy. Rose had said she would come and clean it, but he had told her not to bother and she had not pursued the matter.

The tea things, Jenkin's teapot, Jenkin's milk jug, the cake on too small a plate, the biscuits on too large a one, were perched on a small folding table upon which Gerard had spread a flowery linen drying-up cloth, imagining it to be a table cloth. The cake, awkwardly cut, had spread its large moist crumbs upon the cloth, the biscuits, broken anyway, had deposited their smaller drier crumbs, and some crumbling mess upon the carpet was now being absently pushed by Gerard's foot onto the green tiles in front of the gas fire. Gerard was wearing slippers. He looked, Rose thought, tired and older.

Gerard was irritably aware of Rose's sympathetic stare. He felt tired and older. He had looked that morning, when shaving, for his familiar handsome face, so humorous, so ironic, so finely carved and glowing with intelligence, and it was not there. What he saw was a heavy fleshy surly unhappy face, dark-ringed wrinkle-rounded eyes, dulled extinguished skin, limp greasy hair. Rose had asked, tiresomely, as usual, whether he was writing. He was not. He was not reading either, although he sometimes gazed at the pages of some of Jenkin's books. He thought obsessively about Jenkin, about Jenkin's death, about Crimond. He kept imagining scenes in which Crimond shot Jenkin through the forehead. Through the forehead was what Marchment had said. Gerard could have done without that picture. Crimond had lured Jenkin there and murdered him. Why? As a substitute for murdering Gerard, as a revenge on Gerard for some crime, some slight, some contemptuous remark which Gerard had made to him and instantly forgotten, thirty or more years ago? So I am to blame for Jenkin's death, thought Gerard. My fault, my sin, brought it about. I can't live with this, I'm being poisoned, I'm being destroyed, and Crimond intended *that* too. He thought daily of going to see Crimond, but daily decided that it was impossible. When he was at his most obsessed he sought for help by recalling Jenkin laughing at him, and this sometimes worked, though it made him so deadly sad, and more often returned him to his loss and to the hell which he was inhabiting with Crimond. They were in hell together, he and Crimond, and sooner or later must destroy each other.

Of course Gerard did not reveal these thoughts to anybody, certainly not to Rose who still sometimes tried to draw him into speculations. In conversation with her he now quickly dismissed as unthinkable any notion that Jenkin's death could have been other than a simple accident. Nor did he reveal to her another obsessive pain which left him no peace and made of his present life a fruitless interim. His acquaintance at the Oxford Press had said that he would soon, he hoped, be able to lay hands on a proof of Crimond's book, and would send it to Gerard at once by special messenger. Gerard dreaded the arrival of this thing. He did not want to read Crimond's hateful book, he would want rather to tear it up, but he was *condemned* to it, he would *have* to read it. If it was bad he would feel a sickening degrading satisfaction, if it was good he would feel hatred.

Rose was looking older too, or perhaps it was just that, since he felt disturbed and irritated by her, he was at last looking at her, instead of regarding her as a nebulous extension of

496

himself, a mist presence, a cloud companion. He was suddenly able to see the parts not the whole. She had had her hair cut too close and too short, revealing her cheeks, the tips of her ears, her face looked unprotected and strained, her lightless hair was not grey but deprived of hue, like a darkened plant. Her lips looked dry and parched and scored with little lines, and she had dabbed too much powder on her pretty nose. Only her dark blue eyes, so like her brother's, her courageous eyes as someone had called them, were undimmed, looking at him now with some silent appeal from which he turned away. She was wearing a green silkish dress, very simple, very smart, with an amethyst necklace. It reminded him of the dress she had worn at the midsummer dance, when they had waltzed together, he even suddenly remembered the music and his arm round her waist and the stars over the deer park. Then he thought, she has dressed herself up for Reeve.

'Gerard, don't crush the crumbs into the rug.'

'Sorry.'

Rose straightened the rug. 'It's such a pretty rug.'

'I gave it to him.'

'I'll take these things away. Reeve will be here soon.'

So she's tidying the place up for Reeve. 'I suppose he'll want a drink. I'll get the sherry.'

'Reeve likes gin and tonic.'

'I'll get the gin and tonic. Don't fuss with the tea things.'

'We can't have them here. It won't take a moment.' Rose found the tray propped against the wall and started loading it.

'I haven't finished!'

The door bell rang.

'I'll let him in,' said Rose. She went into the hall, leaving the tray on the table. Gerard stood in the doorway of the sitting room holding his tea cup. Reeve came in, was welcomed, took off his coat, said there was an east wind blowing, that it was starting to rain, and was it all right to leave his car just outside the house. Gerard retreated with his cup, picked up the tray, sidled past Reeve who was entering the room, and searching for the gin in the kitchen heard Rose asking her cousin for news of the children.

Holding drinks, gin and tonic for Reeve and Gerard, sherry for Rose, they stood together awkwardly beside the fire like people at a party.

'Reeve says we mustn't stay long because of our table.'

Reeve, in an expensive dark suit, looked burly, broad-shouldered, his face weathered, ruddy, rosy-cheeked, his skin rough. The big broad nails upon his large practical uneasy hands were clean but jagged. He wore a wedding ring. His brown hair was carefully combed. He had probably combed it in the car, even standing at the door, before he came in. He peered up from under his softly lined brow and his projecting eyebrows at Gerard, expressing a sort of determined wariness. Of course they had often met over the years, they knew each other reasonably well, they liked each other reasonably well. Rose found herself for the first time anxious in case Gerard should seem to patronise Reeve, to condescend. So that was what he usually did, and she had never noticed it before?

Reeve was looking round at the little room, the faded torn wallpaper, the emergent patches of yellow wall. He could not conceal a little surprise.

'This is Riderhood's place?'

'Yes.'

'Rose says you live here now.'

'Yes, I do.'

'A sad business.'

'Yes. Sad.'

Reeve, leaning against the small mantelpiece, picked up the grey purple-striped stone which Rose had given to Jenkin years ago. 'I'm prepared to bet this stone came from Yorkshire.'

'Oh yes – yes!' said Rose. 'It came from that beach –'

'Yes, I know where.' They smiled at each other. Reeve continued to hold the stone.

'How's farming?' said Gerard.

'Awful.'

'I'm told farmers always say that.'

'Rose tells me the Cambuses are looking for a house in France. Everyone seems to be on the move.'

'Reeve is looking for a house in London,' said Rose.

'Really?' said Gerard, smiling pleasantly.

'Well, or a flat,' said Reeve apologetically. 'The children have been wanting one for ages.' He exchanged a glance with Rose.

The door bell rang.

Gerard went to the door and opened it onto the east wind, the rain, the dark street with distant yellow lamps reflected in wet pavements, Reeve's Rolls-Royce glittering in the light from the doorway. A youth was standing outside holding a parcel.

'Mr Hernshaw? I've got this for you from Oxford.'

'Oh, thank you – won't you come in? Is that your motor bike? Have you come all the way –?'

'Oh, all right – thanks. I'd better lock up the bike, I suppose I can lean it against the wall here.'

Gerard took the parcel, it was bulky and heavy. He put it on the chair in the hall. The boy, inside, slid off his mackintosh. He took off his crash helmet revealing a mass of blond hair.

'Come in – would you like a drink? Let me introduce, Rose Curtland, Reeve Curtland. I'm afraid I don't know your name?'

'Derek Wallace. No, I won't have any sherry, thanks. I wouldn't mind a soft drink.'

'He's ridden from Oxford on his motorbike in the rain,' said Gerard.

'Well, no, it's only just started to rain.'

'You'll have had the wind in your face all the way,' said Reeve, who thought about winds.

'I expect you'd like something to eat too?' said Rose. 'Or what about some hot soup?'

'No, really – just lemonade or Coke or something. I mustn't stay long, I've got to get back.'

'Are you an undergraduate?' said Gerard.

'Yes.'

'What college? What are you reading?'

Rose, in the kitchen, was fetching out orange juice, a tin of soup, bread, butter, cheese. She had seen the parcel in the hall and knew, for Gerard had told her he was expecting it, what it contained. She felt sick and unreal. The tall blond boy had a resemblance to Sinclair. She thought, Regent scratching at the door, and now this. Oh God. But it's nothing to do with Sinclair. We are surrounded by demons.

'Did that young chap remind you of anyone?' said Reeve, guiding his Rolls through the London evening traffic.

'Yes.'

'Of course, Neville's not so thin, and the nose and mouth – no, not really like –'

'Not really.'

Of course, thought Rose, they don't remember Sinclair, they don't recall what *he* was like. Do they ever look at photos of him? No, of course not. They have *unmade* him. Originally, they had to. Now he's just forgotten. They must have felt uneasy about that inheritance, not exactly guilty, but it must have been an awkward transition which they wanted to put behind them, to be as if it had always been *them* and not *us*. They had not wept at Sinclair's funeral, at that disposal of his broken body. They never knew Sinclair, they never really liked him. Perhaps that wasn't unreasonable. He had always treated them as country cousins. They did not have long to wait for the title, the father so soon followed the son into non-being. Another bit of luck. They could not but have been pleased when that accident happened. At the funeral they must have been concealing their delight at such a remarkable unexpected turn of events. Sad of course, but for them, lucky, splendid, for them and for their children and their children's children.

As Reeve, who was not used to driving in London, fell silent, preoccupied with the Shepherd's Bush roundabout where an unwary driver may suddenly find himself on the motorway, Rose was being assailed by terrible new fears. That boy, that *revenant*, what was he doing now, alone with Gerard, what was happening now? Had Gerard noticed the weird resemblance, how could he not have done? Supposing Gerard were to *fall in love* with that boy, that sudden sinister *intruder*, coming in out of the rainy dark and bearing such a fateful burden? People who so much resemble the dead may be demons, suppose the demonic boy were to kill Gerard, suppose he were to be found mysteriously dead, like Jenkin? Perhaps the mystery of Jenkin's death was but the forerunner, preluding that of Gerard? The hideous idea then occurred to her that perhaps the fateful figure was *Sinclair himself*, Sinclair returned after due time as an envious ghost or revengeful spirit, taking, through Gerard, revenge upon them all. For were they not all guilty of his death, for not preventing him from taking up that fatal sport, or not, on that day, proposing to him some other plan? Did we not bring about his death, she thought, we who loved him so much, by our negligence, by certain particular careless acts – and they, the others, the gainers, by their perhaps unconscious prayers? Rose knew that these were awful and *wicked* imaginings, brought about by all sorts of present accidents, by grief itself, old old grief and the torture chamber of fate. Yet she could not stop the swift work of her sick thought, the spinning out of awful pictures. The boy had brought *that book*, which was even now with Gerard, its proximity so dangerous to him, a vibrating ticking infernal machine. Perhaps Gerard, sitting up to read the book, would die mysteriously in the night?

Reeve, now safely in the Bayswater Road, the next hazard being Marble Arch, was saying, 'Of course no one can take the place of their mother, but they've always been so attached to you, ever since you were their Auntie Rose when they were little. And, you know, this change has been so terrible for us all – we have to think ourselves into a new era, make, really, a new beginning. Our life must have a different pattern – as of course it must anyway with the children almost grown up – well, some would say grown up, I suppose, but in so many ways they *are* still children, they're at a dangerous vulnerable age, they need love and care, they need a home with a centre. That's where you come in. We *must* see more of you – and my idea is this, and I hope you'll think it over, that you should come to live with us at Fettiston. Mrs Keithley can run the house, she practically does it now, and we're getting in another village woman, a sturdy soul. You won't have to be a housekeeper. What we want is your *being there*, and somehow as being *in charge of us*. You know how highly we think of you in every way. And of course we'll be in charge of you too. It's too early to talk of happiness, the children can't conceive of being happy again, but of course they will be – and I shall recover, I shall have to, and people do. And, dear Rose, I do see your being with us in that new way as something, for all of us, happy and good. We'll have a place in London, a big flat or a house, and we'd hope you'd live there too, or keep your present flat as well, we wouldn't monopolise you! But I can't help feeling your belonging more to us would be good for you too. We've often thought – well – how lonely you must be all by yourself. I know you have old friends like Gerard and Patricia, but they inevitably have other interests, and there's nothing like family. Anyway, think it over. I'm sorry to spring it on you in this hugger-mugger way, I didn't mean to say it in the car! The children have been at me for some time to make this little speech! I feel sure we'll persuade you – when you realise how much we need you, you'll want to come!'

Rose thought, Aunt Rose, the lonely ageing spinster aunt, so much needed, to take charge, to be taken charge of. Perhaps they had even discussed what to do with her in her old age. And why not, to all of it why not? It was not just the voice of common sense, it was the voice of love. She thought, perhaps after Jenkin's death all the old patterns are broken. I must stop mourning and yearning. She had missed Neville's and Gillian's childhood. Soon she could be baby-sitting for them, cherishing their children, holding them on her knee. (But I don't *like* children, thought Rose!) New duties were after all a source of life. Somebody needed her in a new way. And Gerard – perhaps even now she had already lost him, or lost, it was more just to say, her illusion of something *more*, something closer and more precious, which he had yet to give her.

'To talk of more frivolous matters,' Reeve was going on, 'we're planning to go on a cruise in the Easter vac, four whole weeks, and we want you to be our guest – please, please! It sounds marvellous, the Greek islands, then southern Russia. I've always wanted to be on the beach at Odessa! You will come, Rose dear, won't you?'

'I've got some engagements round about then,' said Rose, 'an old school friend is coming over from America –'

'I'll send you the details – do fit it in, your being with us would make it perfect – and let us know soon because of the booking.'

Rose was shocked at the speed with which she had invented the old school friend. Well, she knew how to lie. And all her old illusions, were they not lies too? She did not want to say yes to the cruise, yet she realised she did not want to say no either. Did she not at last – had it come to that – simply want to go where she was needed?

Reeve was silent now, manoeuvring round Marble Arch, finding the right street to turn into, following Rose's directions. There was the question of where to park the car. Did a yellow line matter at this time of night? The street was already crammed with parked cars. Would it not be best if he set Rose down to claim their table? He hoped to be back fairly soon! Rose got out of the car, waved goodbye to her anxious cousin, and saw the Rolls move slowly and uncertainly away. At least it had stopped raining. She hurried into the hotel and left her coat. After that, instead of going to the dining room, she found a telephone and rang Gerard's number. The 'phone rang several times, Rose could already picture herself in a taxi racing back to his house with death fear in her heart.

'Hello.'

'Gerard – it's me.'

'Oh – yes –'

'I'm at the hotel. Reeve is parking the car.'

'What is it?' He sounded remote and cold.

'Are you all right?'

'Yes, of course.'

'Is that boy still with you?'

'No, he had to go back.'

'Are you reading the book?'

'Crimond's book? No. I'm just going out.'

'Oh – where to?'

'To get something to eat.'

'Will you read the book tonight?'

'I shouldn't think so. I'll go to bed.'

'Gerard –'

'Yes.'

'I'll see you soon, won't I?'

'Yes, yes. I must be off.'

'The rain has stopped.'

'Good. Look, I must go.'

'Goodnight, Gerard.'

He rang off. Of course the telephone always irritated him. But if only he had said, 'Goodnight, Rose.' She could have lived a while on that, as on a goodnight kiss.

Gerard, already in his overcoat, looked at the large parcel which was still where he had put it down on the chair in the hall. Of course Gerard had noticed the resemblance which had struck Rose as so frightening. Gerard too, in a different way, could not help sensing a meaning in the fact that just *this* messenger had come bringing just *this* object. Close to the boy, as he filled his glass with orange juice, he had a very odd quick flash of memory, the *smell* of young hair. Or perhaps it was simply the colour of the hair, so painfully reminiscent, its particular blondness, its lively growth and sheen, which he was perceiving and seeming to smell.

Now, alone with the object, he could not help seeing it as a fatal package – fatal to him, fatal perhaps to the world. For a moment he thought that, if this were the only copy, he would feel it his duty to destroy it.

Oh let there be not hate, but love, not pity, but love, not power, oh not power, no power except the spirit of Christ, prayed Father McAlister as with clasped hands, after pulling down the skirt of his cassock and setting his feet neatly together, he sat and watched the battle raging to and fro.

Violet's flat had been invaded, Violet was at bay. Tamar had *invited* Gideon and Patricia and Father McAlister to *tea*. No one had said anything to Rose or Gerard. The decision to exclude these two had been a tacit one.

Pat was cleaning the kitchen. She had already been in Violet's bedroom and collected the mass of mouse-nibbled plastic bags into a sack, ready to be thrown away. The tea party had been taking place in Tamar's bedroom, where the lamps were switched on in the dark afternoon. Tamar had put a pretty cloth upon the folding table at which she used to study. Most of the tea things had been removed, even, by Pat, washed up. The ham sandwiches had attracted the priest, no one had touched the cakes. Gideon was in charge.

'Violet,' he was saying, 'you must give in, you must let us look after everything, you must let *me* look after everything. We've been pussy-footing around for long enough, it's time for drastic measures. Can't you see that things have changed, it's a new era? How can we stand by and see you sink?'

'I am not sinking,' said Violet, 'thank you! And nothing has changed except that Tamar has become cruel and has given up even trying to be polite to me. But that is *our* business. You and Patricia and this clergyman just walked in —'

'Tamar invited us.'

'This is *my* flat, not hers. I was not told or consulted —'

'You would have said no!' said Tamar.

'Evidently my views are of no account. I don't want to talk to you — I have asked you to go — I ask you again, please go!'

'They are my guests,' said Tamar, 'and they want to propose a plan, it's a *good* plan, so *please* hear it — you let us come to Notting Hill at Christmas time —'

'I was forced to come and I did not enjoy it.'

'Please understand, Mrs Hernshaw,' said the priest, 'that

we mean well, we mean, as Tamar said, something good, we come in peace –'

'What sickening rubbish,' said Violet, 'and bringing this sentimental parson along is the last straw. You are all violent intruders, you are thieves, assassins, you smash your way into my privacy –' Violet was controlled, eloquent, only her voice at moments slightly hysterical.

'There are, as I see it,' said Gideon, 'two main points. The first is that Tamar must go back to Oxford. I should be glad if we can regard this as settled.'

'I shall never allow Tamar to go back to Oxford.'

'Actually,' said Tamar, 'you can't stop me.'

Tamar was sitting on her divan bed, the others on chairs about the little table upon which now only the plate of sugary cakes remained. Father McAlister, who had wanted to eat a cake but had been prevented when the farce of 'tea' was ended by the acrimony of the discussion, wondered if he could take one now, but decided not to.

Tamar, dressed in a black skirt and black stockings and a grey pullover, was conspicuously calm. Gideon had been watching her with amazement. She had hitched up her skirt over her knees and stretched out her long slender legs in a manner which he could not believe was entirely unconscious. She had ruffled her fine silky wood-brown green-brown hair into an untidy mop. She dressed as simply as before, probably in the same clothes, but looked different, cooler, older, and even in this scene more casual, certainly detached. Something has happened to her, thought Gideon, she has *been through* something. She's strong, she thinks it's now or never and she doesn't care whom she kicks in the teeth. She's quite got over that depression or whatever it was. It can't be just this simple-minded priest. Perhaps she's got a really splendid lover at last.

'I explained to you,' Violet went on, looking at her daughter venomously, 'that there is no money. I am still in debt. This flat costs money. Your grant never covered more than half of what kept you in luxury in that place. I need your earnings, *we* need your earnings. If Gideon has said otherwise he is a wicked liar. You have no sense of reality, you have let these people put fancy ideas in your head –'

'I am going back to Oxford in the autumn,' said Tamar, fluffing up her hair and looking at Violet with a calm sad face. 'I've been in touch with the college –'

'I am certainly not going to pay for you!'

'Gideon will pay,' said Tamar, 'won't you, Gideon?'

'I don't want *charity* –'

'Certainly I will,' said Gideon, 'now, Violet, please don't shout. In fact Tamar is so economical that the grant will almost cover her needs, I will pay the rest, and I will also pay your debts. I have – wait a moment – another suggestion to make which is that you should sell this flat –'

'I think this flat is beyond help,' said Patricia standing in the doorway. 'It's only fit to be burnt.'

'And that you and Tamar should move into our house,' said Gideon, 'into the flat we used to occupy –'

'It's a lovely flat,' said Patricia.

'We want someone there anyway just to keep an eye on the place when we're away, we wouldn't charge you anything – wait, wait – this could be, if you like, an interim move while we all see what we want to do next – but while Tamar's at Oxford –'

'You come here and suggest burning my flat,' said Violet, 'well, you can burn it with me in it. I'd rather live in hell than in your house.'

'Perhaps you are living in hell now,' said Father McAlister.

'If I am it is nothing to do with you, you loathsome hypocrite, I know your type, peering into people's lives and trying to control them, breaking up families, smashing things you don't understand! You all want to take my daughter away from me.'

'No!' said Gideon.

'She's all I've got and you want to steal her –'

'No, no,' said Father McAlister.

'Well, you can have her! I *ask* her, I *beg* her, to stay here with me and do as I want – but if she doesn't she can go and I'll *never see her again*! I mean it! I hope you are pleased with your meddling now! Well, Tamar, what is it to be?'

'Of course I've got to go,' said Tamar in a matter-of-fact tone, 'but what you say doesn't follow.'

'Oh yes it does. Go then, *go* – and pack your things!'

'They are already packed,' said Tamar. 'You will change your mind.'

'I see, it's a conspiracy. It was all arranged beforehand. Wanting to help *me* was just a pretence!'

'No.'

'I am left to burn, I am left to die – you know that. For God's sake, Tamar, don't leave me, stay with me, tell those *wicked wicked* people to go away! What have they to do with us? You're all I have – I've given you my life!' The hysterical voice hit a ringing quivering piercing note which made everything in the room shudder. Patricia turned away from the door and hid her face.

Tamar did not flinch. She gave her mother a sad gentle look, almost of curiosity, and said in a low resigned tone, 'Oh – don't take on so – I'm going to Pat and Gideon – you'll come later – I'm sorry about this. I'm afraid it's the only way to do it.'

The original author of this scene, which as Gideon felt afterwards had a curiously brittle theatrical quality, was Father McAlister. Reflecting upon Tamar's situation and her future he had had the excellent idea of appealing not to Gerard but to Gideon. The priest saw, rightly, in Gideon, the mixture of self-confidence, ruthlessness, stage-sense and shameless money required to carry off what might almost, in the end, amount to an abduction. He had however envisaged the plan as unfolding more slowly and under his own guidance. He had persuaded Tamar, more easily than he had expected, to play her part, emphasising that the great change would actually, also, constitute the rescue, perhaps even the salvation of her mother. Father McAlister's very brief meetings with Violet had led him to a prognosis which was if anything grimmer than Tamar's own.

Gideon expected Violet to scream, and for a moment she

seemed likely to as she drew her breath in a savage gasp like a fierce dog. She clenched her fists and actually bared her teeth. She said in a low voice, 'So you won't do anything for me, any more?'

'I am doing something for you,' said Tamar, 'as you will see later. But if you mean will I do whatever you want, no. I can't do that – and at the moment probably I can't do anything at all for you – I can do – nothing for you.' Tamar then turned her head away, looking at the window where net curtains, grey with dirt, hung in tatters. Then she looked back, looking at Gideon with an alert prompting expression as if to say, can't we end this scene now?

Tamar had spoken so coldly, and now looked, as she ignored her mother and turned to Gideon, so ruthless, that a strange idea came into Father McAlister's head. Supposing it were all somehow false, the emotional drama, the passion play of salvation in which he and Tamar had been taking part? It was not that he thought that Tamar had been lying or play-acting. Her misery had been genuine, her obsession terrible. But in her desperation had she not *used* him as he came to hand, carrying out his instruction, as a savage might those of a medicine man, or as a sick patient obeys a doctor? Or why not simply say it was like an analysis, neurosis, transference, liberation into ordinary life, an *ordinary* life in which the liberated patient could snap his fingers at the therapist, and go his way realising that what he took for moral values or categorical imperatives on even the *devil* and the *eternal fire* were simply quirkish mental ailments such as we all suffer from, a result of a messy childhood, from which one can now turn cheerfully and ruthlessly away. Tamar had faced the devil and the eternal fire, he had seen her face twist with terror, and later, when he had exorcised the spirit of the malignant child, seen it divinely calm and bathed with penitential tears. Now Tamar seemed endowed with an extraordinary authority. Even Gideon, he could see, was startled by it. She was authoritative and detached and able, in this crisis with her mother, to freeze her feelings. It was her freedom she had wanted, perhaps all along, and now she could smell its proximity she was ready to trample on anyone. In this ritual of dismissal and liberation which he had been there to sanction, it was as if she had cursed her mother. The priest's 'bright idea' had envisaged a row, certainly, but with it an emergence of Tamar's genuine love for her mother, which he imagined he had discerned deep within her. He had not wanted to release his penitent from one demon to see her seized by another. Tamar's former obedience, the predominant importance she had given to her mother's states and her will, had had something bad about it. He kept telling Tamar about a true and free love of her, a love *in Christ*, which could heal Violet as she, Tamar, had been healed. The priest had, in his brief meetings with Violet, made her out as a monster. He could see, he thought, her terrible unhappiness, an unhappiness which made his sympathetic sentimental (she had used that word) soul wince and cringe, a black unhappiness, deeper and darker and *harder* than her daughter's, and he had seen too how her suffering had made her monstrous. He was not going to let his Tamar be any more this monster's victim. But must not, and by both of them, the poor monster be helped too? Now, as he looked at Tamar, who was brushing crumbs off her skirt and making the restless unmistakable shrugging movements of someone who is about to rise and depart, he wondered: is this new energy, this detachment, this authority, not perhaps simply a metamorphosis of an old deep hatred, which has been for so many years obediently kept in check? Have I liberated her not into Christ, but into selfish uncaring power? Have I perhaps simply created another monster? (In the very process however of unrolling these awful thoughts Father McAlister, by a gesture familiar to him, handed the whole matter over to his Master, knowing that it would be handed back to him later in a more intelligible state.)

Violet, who had been glaring at Tamar open-mouthed, her eyes suddenly seeming like blazing rectangular holes, rose suddenly to her feet, rocking the table and making Gideon hastily shift his chair. She fumbled for her glasses in the pocket of her skirt. Taken by surprise by the intrusion, she was, Gideon could see now, pathetically untidy, her blouse crumpled, her cardigan spotted with holes through which the colours of her blouse and skirt showed accusingly. She was wearing down-at-heel slippers one of which had come off. She looked down, stabbing at it angrily with her foot. Gideon moved the table. Violet went forward to the door. As she did so she composed her face. Patricia, who was standing in the hall, stood hastily aside. Violet entered her bedroom, banged the door, and audibly locked it.

As soon as Violet's departing back was turned to her, Tamar too rose, and saying, 'Let's go,' darted to a cupboard and began pulling out her suitcases.

Gideon said, 'Oh dear!' and rose to his feet. Father McAlister automatically picked up one of the sugary cakes, a pink one, and stuffed it whole into his mouth. They moved into the hall.

'Well,' said Patricia, 'you can't make an omelette without breaking eggs. Come on, let's get out, get Tamar away before she changes her mind.'

'She won't change her mind,' said Gideon.

'If only I'd got that sack out into the hall,' said Patricia, 'we could have taken it with us. I found such indescribable filth and mess in Violet's room, awful hairy decaying things under the bed, I couldn't even make out what they were.'

Patricia was putting her coat on. The priest picked up his. Tamar carried out three large suitcases and dumped them by the door. As she did so she looked at Father McAlister and an extraordinary glance passed between them. The priest thought, she has seen through me. Then: who has betrayed whom?

'I'm afraid the car's miles away,' said Patricia. 'Shall we all walk or shall I get it? We can carry the cases between us. I want to get out of here.' She said to the priest, 'Can I give you a lift?'

'No, thanks, I've got to see someone who lives nearby.'

Gideon said, 'You and Tamar get the car. There's no point in carrying the cases. We'll put them out on the landing. I'll wait here. Violet might even emerge.'

'She won't. O K. Come on, Tamar.'

Gideon and the priest looked at each other. The priest, raising his eyebrows, motioned slightly with his head toward the closed bedroom door. Gideon, expressionless, continued to hold the door open onto the stairs. He said, 'Thank you very much. We'll talk again.'

'Yes.' Father McAlister sighed, then with a wave of his hand set off down the stairs and into the street.

Gideon waited until he heard the front door close. Then he carefully closed the flat door and went to Violet's bedroom and knocked.

'Violet! They've gone. Come out now.'

After a short time Violet emerged. She had changed her clothes, combed her hair, powdered her nose, removed her glasses. She had evidently been crying, and elaborate powdering round her eyes had made the wrinkled skin pale, dry and dusty. She peered, frowning, at Gideon and he saw over her shoulder the chaotic room which had defeated Pat. She walked across to Tamar's tidy room, moved the table a little, then lifted the plate of cakes and offered it to Gideon. He took a cake. They both sat down on the bed. Gideon felt, for the first time for many years, a sudden physical affection for his old friend, a desire, to which he did not yield, to hug her and to *laugh*. He thought, somebody, a real strong person, a lovable, admirable person, has been *lost* here, *ruined*.

Violet's hair, like her daughter's, needed cutting but had been neatly combed and patted into shape. It was still brown, its lustre here and there embellished by single hairs of a pale luminous grey. Her nose was slightly red at the nostrils, whether from a cold or recent weeping. Her small mouth, now touched by lipstick, was at its sternest. She stroked down her fringe over her brow, over her indelible frown, moulding it into shape with a familiar gesture. She had, Gideon reflected, her higher civil servant look. She looked in no way like a defeated woman. In taking Father McAlister's gamble Gideon had feared, perhaps wanted, something rather more weak and pliable. It was a moment for Violet to surrender to fate, but she looked now unlikely to surrender to anything.

They had both been thinking, and each allowed a space for the other to speak first.

'They'll be back,' said Gideon, 'at least Pat will ring the bell and I'll carry down the cases. The car is a good way off. We've got ten minutes. But of course I'll come in tomorrow.'

Violet said, 'Why did you spring this loathsome charade on me? That creep McAlister was the last straw.'

'It was his idea,' said Gideon not entirely truthfully. The strategy had been the priest's, the tactics certainly Gideon's. 'It was a device, you understand.'

'To get Tamar away.'

'Yes.'

'But she could have gone any time, I wasn't keeping her a prisoner!'

'You know, in a way, you were. You had taken away her will. She had to have moral support –'

'*Moral* support?'

'To get out in a definite intelligible manner, with a reasonable explanation.'

'You mean sponging on you?'

'She couldn't just cut and run. There had to be a raid by a respectable rescue party.'

'It shows you think nothing of me, you think I'm not a person. That mob pushing their way in here without any warning! You wouldn't do that to anyone else. You feel contempt for me.'

'No, Violet –'

'All of you acting well-rehearsed parts.'

'You were acting too.'

'You think so? It was designed to humiliate me. All right, it was clever. My reactions could have been predicted, all my lines could have been written beforehand. It was like – it was – an attempt on my life.'

'I'm sorry,' said Gideon, 'but look, you don't really mind my paying a bit for Tamar at Oxford?'

'I don't care a hang –'

'Good, that's out of the way –'

'So long as I never see her again.'

'Then there's you.'

'I don't exist.'

'Oh shut up, Violet, *think*, you *can* think. McAlister thinks that Tamar really deeply loves you and –'

'She hates me. She's always been cold as hell to me, even as a small child. Obedient, but icy cold. I don't blame her. I hate her, if it comes to that.'

'I don't know about Tamar, I want to deal in certainties. Let's say I'm a person, possibly the only person, who not only knows you, but loves you. O K so far?'

Violet this time, instead of returning a cynical reply, said, 'Oh Gideon, thanks for loving me – not that I believe it actually – but it's useless – it's sour milk – only fit to be thrown away.'

'I never throw anything away, that's why everything I touch turns to gold. Let me help you. I can do anything. Just by sheer will power I drove Gerard out of that house in Notting Hill. Look, let's sell this flat, Pat's right, it's awful, it's haunted. Come and live at our place.'

'With Tamar? Being the housemaid? No thanks.'

'You and Tamar must make peace, you both need peace – never mind the details – you must live, you must be *happy* – what's money for after all?'

'It's no good. You're a happy person. Someone like you can't just manufacture happiness for someone like me. I'm finished. You can look after Tamar. That's what this is all about.'

The door bell rang.

'I'll come in tomorrow.'

'I won't be here.'

'Don't terrify me, Violet. You know I care for you –'

'Don't make me sick.' She went out into the hall, opened the flat door, then disappeared once more into her bedroom and locked herself in.

Gideon, hearing Pat call below, lifted the cases out onto the landing. He closed the door of the flat. He said to himself, she won't kill herself. I'm glad I said all those things to her. She'll *think* about those things.

In fact, although it was not tonight that Violet would kill herself, she was nearer to the edge than Gideon surmised. She had been frightened by Tamar's mysterious illness, not so much on her behalf as her own. She had seen in Tamar's death pallor and face wrenched by misery the picture of her own fate – her death, since she would never recover, whereas Tamar would recover, to dance on her grave. She was shaken by the new cruel self-willed Tamar, so unlike the cool but submissive child she was used to, and now dismayed by Tamar's departure, which she had not at all expected. After all she had needed, she had replied upon, Tamar's *presence*. She felt hideously lonely. Her sense of her own vileness, together with her chronic resentment, made any attempt at human society increasingly difficult. Soon it would be impossible. There were no pleasures. She hated all the plump glittering giggling people she saw on television. Even solitary drinking, which now occupied more of her time, was not a relief, more like a method of suicide. A sense of the unreality, the sheer artificiality, of individual existence had begun to possess her. What was it after all to be 'a person', able to speak, to remember, to have purposes, to inhibit screams? What was this weird unclean ever-present body, of which she was always seeing parts? Why did not her 'personality' simply cease to be continuous and disintegrate into a cloud of ghosts, blown about by the wind?

Later on, over the gin bottle, she thought, perhaps I *will* go to their place, to that flat. Tamar will move out. But they'll never get *me* out! I'll stay there and make their lives a misery.

Father McAlister, who had of course no one living nearby to see, was now concerned with getting back to his parish. He was sitting, in an unhappy state of mind, in an underground train. It was easier to set people free, as the world knows it, than to teach them to love. He often uttered the word 'love', he had uttered it often to Tamar. In the thick emotional atmosphere generated by frequent meetings between priest and penitent Tamar had declared that 'really' she loved her mother, and 'really' her mother loved her. It was what he expected, and induced, her to say. Was he however so much influenced by, so much immured with, images of the power of love that he could miss and underestimate the genuine presence of ordinary genuine hate? Was he too tolerantly aware of himself as a magician, pitting against an infinite variety of demonic evils a power, not his own, which must be ultimately insuperable? The case of Tamar had excited him because so much was at stake. He was sadly aware that much of his work in the confessional (and he was a popular confessor) consisted in relieving the minds of hardened sinners who departed cheerfully to sin again. At least they came back. But with Tamar it had seemed like life and death; if he could free her she would be free indeed. After so much experience he could still be so naive. Oh she had been brave, but what had made her brave? Had all that awful travail simply provided her with the strength required to leave her mother? Was there in the end nothing but breakage, liberty from obsession and nothing enduring of the spirit?

The priest recalled, as a sacred charm, the innocence of the children who had acted, under his direction, in the Nativity Play, always put on in the village church at Christmas time, the delight of the little children dressed up as Joseph and Mary and the Three Kings, and the Ox and the Ass (always favourite parts), the pride of their parents, the tears of joy shed by their mothers as they watched the little ones, with such natural tenderness and reverence, enact the Christmas Story. The crib containing the Child, the Saviour of the World, of the Cosmos, of all that is, became in that little cold church a glowing radiant object so holy that at a certain moment those who watched spontaneously fell on their knees. Could this be mummery, superstition? No, but it was also something of which he was not worthy, from which he was separated, because he was a liar, because a line of falsity ran all the way through him and tainted what he did. He said to himself, I don't believe in God or the Divinity of Christ or the Life Everlasting, but I continually say so, I have to. Why? In order to carry on with the life which I have chosen and which I love.

The power which I derive from my Christ is debased by its passage through me. It reaches me as love, it leaves me as magic. That is why I make *serious mistakes*. In fact, in spite of his self-laceration, a ritual in which he indulged at intervals, the priest felt, in a yet deeper deep self, a sense of security and peace. Behind doubt there was truth, and behind the doubt that doubted that truth there was truth . . . He was a sinner, but he *knew* that his Redeemer lived.

It was a long cold journey home. The heating in the train had broken down, but he managed to get a taxi from the local station to Foxpath instead of having to walk. When he had got inside his little cottage he closed the shutters and lit a wood fire. Then he knelt down and prayed for some time. After that he felt better and heated up a saucepan of stew which he had kept in the fridge. His Master, handing back the problem to him, had informed him that his next task was Violet Hernshaw.

Altogether elsewhere in the early spring sunshine Jean and Duncan Cambus were sitting together at a café restaurant in a little seaside town in the south of France. They both looked in good health. Their brows were clear; Duncan had lost weight. They had found, and bought, just inland from where they now were, exactly the old picturesque stone-built farmhouse for which they had been searching. Of course it needed a lot to be done to it, renovating it was going to be so exciting. At present they were staying in a hotel.

The sun was warm, but there was a chill breeze from the sea and they were wearing warm clothes, Duncan an old jacket of Irish tweed, Jean a vast fluffy woollen pullover. They were sitting out, under a budding vine trellis, on the *terrasse*, drinking the local white wine. Soon they would go inside and have a *long very good* lunch, with the local red wine, and cognac after. From where they sat they could see the little sturdy harbour with its short thick piers and wide quays, made of immense blocks of light grey stone, and broad gracious fishing boats full of rumpled brown nets, and the gently rocking masts of slim yachts.

Jean and Duncan were looking at each other in silence, as they often did now, a grave serene silence punctuated by sighs and slight twitching movements like those of animals luxuriously resting, pleasurably stretching their limbs a little. They had escaped. They were able to feel, now far away from them, superior to those who might have judged them or been impertinently curious about their welfare. Their love for each other had survived. This, which must be thought to be the most important part, indeed the essence, of their survival, was something they both thought about incessantly, but expressed mutely, in silent gazing, in shy sexual embraces, and in their *satisfaction*, in their new house, in being in France, in eating and drinking, in walking about, in being together. They constantly pointed out to each other what was interesting, charming, beautiful, grotesque, in what they daily saw; they made many jokes and laughed a lot.

An aspect of their silence was that neither of them had told the other everything. There were things which were too awful to be told; and for each, the possession of such dreadful secrets provided, besides intermittent shudders of fear and horror, a kind of deep excitement and energy, an ineffable bond. Jean had not told Duncan why her car had crashed on the Roman Road, nor about Tamar's revelations concerning her evening with Duncan, and the existence, then non-existence, of the child, nor about how Jean had found Crimond's note about the duel and telephoned Jenkin. So Jean knew what Duncan knew but did not know she knew, and also knew what Duncan did not know. Duncan had not told Jean about what happened that evening with Tamar, which she knew, nor had he told her about the circumstances of Jenkin's death, which she did not know. It did not occur to Jean that Duncan might have gone, after all, to see Crimond, nor to Duncan that Jean might have discovered Crimond's note. Jean thought it very unlikely that Tamar would ever decide to tell Duncan about the child. She believed that Tamar would wish to put the hideous experience behind her, and would be decent enough to spare Duncan a gratuitous pain. She was also certain that Crimond would never open his lips about what happened on the Roman Road. Duncan too thought it impossible that Crimond would ever reveal how Jenkin died. Crimond was someone pre-eminently able to keep silent, and who would take it as a point of honour not to seem to accuse Duncan of something of which he himself was more profoundly guilty. Crimond had set up a death-dealing scene and lured Duncan into it and thus occasioned Jenkin's death. For his own sake, as well as out of a proper regard for Duncan, he would keep his mouth shut. The fact that only one gun had been loaded was, very often, a subject of meditation for Duncan: of meditation rather than speculation. Duncan took the curious fact as an end point. Crimond had not planned to kill Duncan, he had planned to give Duncan a chance to kill him. Crimond had put the guns in place after the positions had been decided. Duncan dismissed the possibility of their disposal being left to chance. He recalled Crimond's saying, 'You have to be used to firearms to be sure of killing somebody even at close range.' Crimond was ready for it and wanted it properly done. Perhaps he reckoned he would win either way. If he died he would be rid of his life, which perhaps he no longer valued now the book was finished, and would leave Duncan to explain away what would look like a highly motivated murder. If he lived he would, according to some weird calculation made in his weird mind, have *got rid* of Duncan, made them eternally quits, and so henceforth strangers to each other. Duncan understood this calculation; indeed it had proved, it seemed to him, effective for him too. The unfinished business was finished. He even woke up one morning to find that he no longer hated Crimond.

In spite of all their motives for keeping off the subject, in an almost formal sort of way, as if it were a game they had to play not against each other but together, Jean and Duncan talked frequently about Crimond. This, they tacitly knew, was a phase they had to go through. Later on his name would not be mentioned. About Jenkin they thought a good deal but did not talk. It was a strange aspect of their mutual silence that they both blamed themselves for Jenkin's death. Jean's telephone call had sent Jenkin to the Playroom, Duncan's finger had pulled the trigger. This was an irony which they would never share.

'One trouble with Crimond was that he had no sense of humour,' said Jean. They always used the past tense when speaking of him.

'Absolutely,' said Duncan. 'He was terribly intense and solemn at Oxford. He and Levquist got on famously, Levquist had no sense of humour either. I think he got completely soaked in Greek mythology and never recovered. He lived all the time inside some Greek myth and saw himself as a hero.'

'Perhaps the Greeks had no sense of humour.'

'Precious little. Aristophanes isn't really funny, there's nothing in Greek literature which is funny in the way Shakespeare is. Somehow the light that shone on them was too clear and their sense of destiny was too strong.'

'They were too pleased with themselves.'

'Yes. And too frightened of the gods.'

'Did they really believe in those gods?'

'They certainly believed in supernatural beings. In a dignified way they were fearfully superstitious.'

'That sounds like Crimond. He was dignified and superstitious.'

'The first thing he published was on mythology.'

They were silent for a moment. When they talked of Crimond they never mentioned *the book*.

'When Joel comes over, let's go to Greece,' said Jean.

Joel Kowitz had discreetly, in his travels, and he loved travelling, avoided London during Jean's second 'Crimond period'. It was not that Joel held any theory about the permanence or impermanence of Jean's new situation. He knew when he was wanted and when he was not; he studied Jean's letters (for she wrote to him regularly during that time) waiting for a summons which would be sent the moment, the second, she really desired to see him again. Jean's letters made, to his loving eye, terrible reading. They were, almost, dutiful, saying she was well, Crimond was well, he was working, the weather was awful, she sent her love. They were, he thought, like letters from prison, like *censored* letters. He replied, tactfully, describing his doings in his usual witty style (he was a good letter writer), asking no questions. In fact he wanted very much indeed to visit, not only Jean, but Crimond, whom he regarded as a remarkable and extraordinary being, far more worthy and interesting than Jean's husband. There came a significant gap in communication. Then a quite different letter arrived. Jean was with Duncan again, they were going to live in France, she hoped he would come over soon. Joel, who thought and worried about his daughter all the time, gave a brief sigh for Crimond (if only she'd got together with that fellow at Cambridge), and rejoiced at the signs of life, of hope, of direct speech, in the new style.

'We must be sure the workmen know exactly what to do when we go away.'

'I still haven't chosen the tiles for the kitchen,' said Jean.

'Joel mustn't come here, I don't want him to see the house till it's finished. We could meet in Athens, just for a week or so, and go on to Delphi.'

'It would be lovely to be in Athens again.' Duncan was not so sure about going to Delphi. That dangerous god might still be around there. Duncan had his own Scottish streak of superstition. He did not want any more strange influences bearing on their life, he did not want Jean to be *disturbed* by anything. He felt for her health as for that of someone recovering from a fit of insanity.

'You put Rose off, I imagine?' said Duncan.

'Yes.' Jean and Duncan had stayed briefly in Paris with some old friends from diplomatic days, and from there Jean had, on a sudden impulse, written an affectionate letter to Rose. It had been a very brief untalkative letter, serving simply as a signal, a symbol or secret emblem, a ring or talisman or password, signifying the absolute continuation of their love and friendship. Rose replied at once of course, asking whether she might drop over. Jean and Duncan had left by then and Rose's letter, equally brief, equally significant, followed them to the south. Jean replied saying not to come. Of course their friendship was eternal. But she was not sure when and where she would want to see Rose again. They had survived Ireland and presumably would survive this. But Jean felt no desire for straight loving looks and intimate conversation. Later, of course, later on when their lovely house was ready, people would come. Rose and Gerard, their old friends – how few – their new friends, if any, their clever and amusing acquaintances.

Can we, with our souls so harrowed, find peace now, she wondered, is it all real, our house, Duncan sitting there so calm and beautiful, so like a lion, just as he used to be. Thank God he's drinking less, French food suits him. When the summer comes we shall swim every day. Will it be so? Have I really stopped loving Crimond? She asked herself this question often, not really in any doubt, but rather to insist upon the reality of her escape. It was sad, too, so sad. Jenkin's death had broken some link, killed some last illusion – or one of the last illusions. Of course Crimond didn't murder him. But he caused his death. Jean did not allow herself to brood upon that utterly impenetrably mysterious scene, something which, although she believed Crimond's account of the accident, remained a mystery. It was as if Crimond had killed himself. So in a sense Jenkin achieved something by dying, he died for me, she thought. Of course it's mad to say this, but all Crimond's surroundings are mad. And somehow too I killed him, not just by the telephone call, but because I failed to kill Crimond on the Roman Road. How strange to think how nearly I am not here. What did he intend? Would he have swerved at the last moment, did he think I would? Did he want to test himself by an ordeal he would be liberated by surviving? Was it just a symbolic suicide pact because he knew she would funk it and so bring their relationship to an end by the failure of her love, a way to be rid of her mercifully, a symbolic killing? If I pass the test I die, if I fail it he leaves me. Yet he might have died, perhaps he wanted to die, he offered himself to me as a victim, and I did not take him. He was really gambling, for him a gamble was a religious rite, an exorcism, he wanted to end our love, or end our lives, and left it to the gods to decide how. He had said often enough that their love was impossible – yet he had loved her in and through that impossibility. Sometimes she dreamt about him and dreamt that they were reconciled – and in the moment of waking when she knew it was not true her eyes filled with tears. When in that field he had said, go, *take your chance*, I shall not see you again, his love had spoken, his fierce love that had been ready to will both their deaths. Could such a love end? Must it not simply be metamorphosed into something quiet and sleepy and dark, like some small quiescent life form which could lie in the earth and not be known whether it were alive or dead. It is over, she thought, banishing these sad images, it is finished. I have a new life now under the sign of happiness. I never stopped loving Duncan – and now there is our house and I shall see my father again. Oh let our souls, so harrowed, find peace now.

Duncan was thinking, we are so quiet together, so peaceful –

but is that because we are both dead? Duncan could not make out whether he had survived it all better than would be expected, perhaps even, of all concerned, best of all, or whether he had simply been obliterated. He felt, often, as if he had been entirely broken, smashed, pulverised, like a large china vase whose pieces clearly, obviously, could never be put together again. More often he felt that a stump of himself had survived, a sturdy wicked ironical stump. What was left of him was not going to suffer now! Callousness would be his good. He had suffered so much because of Jean, now he would opt for no more suffering. Perhaps the world had already ended, perhaps it had ended with Crimond in that basement room, or on the night in midsummer when he had seen Jean and Crimond dancing. Perhaps this was an after-life. Vast tracts of his soul no longer existed, his soul was devastated and laid waste, he was functioning with half a soul, with a fraction of a soul, like a man with one lung. What remained was darkened, shrivelled, shrunk to the size of a thumb. And yet he could still plan and ruthlessly propose to be happy, and, necessarily, to make Jean happy too. Perhaps there had always been in him a wicked callous streak which had been soothed and laid to sleep by his love for Jean, his absolute love which had so seemed to change the world, and his *success* in marrying rich beautiful clever Jean Kowitz whom so many men desired. Perhaps it was this small parcel of vanity in his great love that he was paying for now? He loved Jean, he 'forgave' her, but his stricken vanity cried out to be consoled. Would he become, at the last, a demon set free? Oddly he sometimes felt Jean respond to it, this demonic freedom, unconsciously excited by it, as if taught by his new bad self.

At other times he was amazed at his calmness, his gentleness, his efficiency, his cheerfulness even. He loved his wife and was happy in loving her. He felt tired, but with a relaxed not frenzied tiredness. He was pleased with the new house and able to concentrate on the location of the swimming pool, even to think about it when he awoke in the night. Still he was aware of ghosts and horrors, black figures which stood beside him and beside whom he felt tiny and puny. Perhaps they would simply thus *stand with* him for the rest of his life without doing him any other harm – or would their proximity drive him mad? Could he go on existing knowing that at any moment . . . What did the future hold of intelligible misery? Would Crimond recur in his life, coming back relentlessly, inevitably after a period of years? Jean had even said to him – but she had said it, as she also told him, because she felt she must be able to *say anything*: 'Supposing I were to go off with Crimond again, would you forgive me, would you take me back?' 'Yes,' said Duncan, 'I would forgive you, I would take you back.' 'Seven times?' 'Unto seventy times seven.' Jean said, 'I have to ask this question. But my love for Crimond is dead, it is finished.' Was it true, could she know, would Crimond whistle and she run, Duncan wondered, but with a sort of resignation. Seventy times seven was a lot of times. If they were left in peace would he before long grow tired of worrying about Jean and Crimond? He had his house to think about, where he would sit and write his memoirs and Jean would create a garden and write the cookery book she used to talk about, and perhaps they would drive about the region and write a guide book, or travel and write travel books. He still thought but not obsessively, almost coldly, about what was known only to Crimond and himself, Jenkin's death. He felt not the slightest wish or obligation to inform anybody about what really happened. If people cared to think that Crimond had murdered Jenkin it was their affair, and not very far from the truth either. He had only lately performed a curious little ritual. When he had left Crimond to deal with the body and the police, he had carried away in his pocket the five dud leaded cartridges which he had removed from the gun with which he had killed Jenkin. He could not decide what to do with them. If ever connected with him, those odd little things could prove awkward and suggestive evidence. He had to get rid of them, but in London it had proved absurdly hard to decide on any really safe method. He took them with him to France and eventually, stopping the car in a wild place far from their farm house, while Jean was unpacking a picnic lunch, he strayed away and dropped them into a deep river pool. The feel of the smooth weighty objects in his hand made him think of Jenkin's body. It was like a burial at sea.

Yes, he understood why Crimond had had to summon him, responding to a nervous urge, an irresistible craving, like the toreador's desire to touch the bull. The woman had gone, the drama remained between him and Duncan. Crimond had always hated the idea of being in debt, he was a meticulous payer, he was a gambler, he feared the gods. The gesture of baring his breast was natural to him – it was a ritual of purification, an exorcism of something which, like a Grecian guilt, was formal and ineluctable, curable only by submission to a god. But why did Jenkin have to die? Crimond had offered himself as victim to Duncan, but Duncan had killed Jenkin. So Jenkin died as a substitute, as a surrogate, he had to die so that Crimond could live? Had some deep complicity with Crimond brought it about that Duncan could kill Crimond without killing Crimond? By not killing Crimond he had brought about Jenkin's death. Had he even in some sense brought it about deliberately? Duncan recalled daily the dark red hole in Jenkin's forehead and the sound of his body hitting the floor. He remembered the special warm feel of Jenkin's ankles and his socks, as Duncan pulled the body along the room, and how, afterwards, he had stepped to and fro over it in his frenzied hurry to tidy up the scene. He remembered Crimond's tears. He also, in the presence of these images, asked himself, retrieving it now from the depths of memory, whether perhaps he had not always, in his play with firearms, had a fantasy of shooting someone like that through the middle of the forehead? Perhaps an old sadistic fantasy, tolerated over many years, had been there to prompt him; and had found him ready because of other ancient things, such as an old jealousy of Jenkin surviving from Oxford days. After Sinclair's death it was to Jenkin, not to Duncan, that Gerard turned for consolation. That microsecond before he pulled the trigger: could it actually have contained a *decision*? Duncan had wanted to kill Crimond – but had found himself unable to – because he was afraid to – because he did not *really* want to – yet he had needed to take revenge on somebody, somebody had to die. It was as if, not strong enough to kill the man he hated, he had killed his dog.

'Your funny eye looks better,' said Jean, who had been staring at him. 'Well, I suppose it isn't actually different. Can you see better out of it?'

'I think so – or I imagine I can – the clever old brain has fudged things up, it often does.'

'It'll fudge things up for us,' said Jean.

They smiled at each other tired complicit smiles.

She went on, 'I can't remember when you first had that eye thing. You haven't always had it.'

'Oh years ago, I was developing it before we went to Ireland.' Something about this exchange made Duncan suddenly feel that it was a good time to tell Jean about the thing with Tamar. He would be relieved to get rid of it. 'I've got something to confess – it's about Tamar – I had a little momentary quasi-sex episode with her one evening when you were away and she came round to console me.'

'With Tamar!' said Jean. 'With that good sweet child! How could you!' She felt an unexpected relief at this sudden utterance by Duncan, as if even some partial shabbily doctored piece of truth-telling could somehow 'do them good'. 'I hope you didn't upset her?'

'Oh, not at all. Nothing happened really. She just threw her arms round me to cheer me up. I was feeling miserable and I hugged her. I was touched by her affection. No harm's done. There was nothing *else*.'

What a dear old liar he is, thought Jean. I certainly won't question him. 'I expect she was flattered.'

'Perhaps I was! She may not have thought it was anything at all. You're not cross with me?'

'No. Of course not. I'll never ever be cross with you. I love you.'

Jean thought to herself, if Tamar hadn't come round to tell me about Duncan and the child I would never have thought of searching Duncan's desk, and telephoned Jenkin and sent him to Crimond. If Duncan had not seduced Tamar Jenkin would be still alive. If I had not left Duncan he would not have seduced Tamar. Is it all my fault or his fault or Tamar's fault, or is it fate, whatever that means? Oh how tired I feel sometimes. It's as if Crimond devoured part of me which will never grow again. Perhaps that's my punishment for having left Duncan. Would the results of all these things ever reach their ends? And poor Tamar, and *that child*. Sometimes at night Jean thought about the child, Duncan's child, whom they might have adopted. So if Duncan could have children after all, there might yet be another child, not hers, but his, for them to cherish . . . But that way thoughts must not go, it was too late, it was too complicated, the time for mysteries and new beginnings and unpredictable adventures was over, their task now was simply to make each other happy.

The breeze had moderated, the sea which had been mildly disturbed and covered with flickering points of white had become calmer. The masts of yachts in the harbour were quiet. A fishing boat was moving out, its engine uttering little rhythmic muted explosions. The diffident lazy hollow sound came pleasurably to Jean and Duncan, as if it somehow united and summarised the scene, the harbour and the sea, so beautiful, so full of secure promise. The silky light blue unscored undivided sea merged at the horizon into a pale sky which at the zenith, cloudless, was overflowing with the blue sunny air of the south.

'It's time for lunch,' said Duncan. 'There are other pleasures!' Jean always argued that the most perfect time was that of the apéritif. He rose to his feet while Jean remained, listening to the parting boat and gazing at the sea.

As he got up Duncan put his hand into the pocket of his old tweed jacket and felt something in there, something round and very light and insubstantial. He drew it out. It was a small reddish ball of what looked like interwoven silk or thread. Duncan suddenly felt himself *blushing* violently. It was of course that ball of Crimond's hair which, such an infinitely long time ago, he had picked up from the floor of their bedroom in the tower in Ireland. He opened his hand and let the thing fall to the ground where it lay for a moment at his feet upon the pavement. The faint breeze moved it, rolling it very slowly against the iron leg of a coffee table. He had an impulse to pick it up again. Should something so fateful be allowed to vanish into the rubble of the world? It began to move away towards the road where it was swept into the wake of a passing car. After the car had passed he thought he could still see it lying in the roadway.

Jean was getting up. 'Let's go and look at those tiles after lunch.'

They went into the restaurant. Duncan felt pity for himself and wondered if he would soon die of cancer or in some strange accident. He did not feel unhappy, perhaps death, though not imminent, was indeed near; but it was now as if he and death had become good friends.

'We never found that Stone in the wood,' said Lily.

'What stone?' said Rose.

'The old standing stone, the ancient stone. I *know* it's there.'

'There's an eighteenth-century thing with a Latin inscription but it's quite small. I don't think there's anything prehistoric, if that's what you mean.'

'The Roman Road runs along a ley line.'

'Oh really?'

'That's why Jean's car crashed.'

'Why?'

'Ley lines are charged with human energy, like telepathy, so they collect ghosts. You know what ghosts are, parts of people's minds out of the past, what they felt and saw. Jean saw a ghost – probably a Roman soldier.'

'She said she saw a fox,' said Rose.

'People don't like to admit they've seen ghosts. They think they'll be laughed at – and they're *afraid* to – ghosts don't like to be talked about and if you see one you just know that.'

'Have you ever seen one?'

'No, I wish I had. There *must* be ghosts as Boyars.'

'I hope not,' said Rose, 'I've never seen anything.' She did not like this talk of ghosts.

'I always thought I'd see a ghost of James, but I never did.'

'James?'

'My husband – you know, he died and left me the money.'

'Of course you were married – I'm sorry –'

'I don't feel I was married. It was all over so quickly. And poor James was like a ghost when he was alive.'

'Do you often think about him?'

'No. Not now.'

Rose felt she could not pursue this any further. She said, 'So there's no news from Gulliver?'

'No,' said Lily, 'not a word. He's in Newcastle. Anyway that's where he said he was going. By now he may be anywhere, Leeds, Sheffield, Manchester, Edinburgh, Aberdeen, Ireland, America. He's given up his flat, he's *gone*. He's disappeared forever, that's what he wanted to do, he often said so, to go right away and leave no trace.'

'I expect he'll write soon.'

'No he won't. If he'd been going to he would have done already. He said it would be an adventure. He's probably met *someone else* by now. I've *lost* him. Anyway I don't want him any more, to hell with him. I'll make a wax image of him and drop it in the fire – like – like a guy I saw on Guy Fawkes day, it was like a real person, it lifted its arms up, oh it was awful –' Tears came into Lily's eyes and her voice gave way.

Rose and Lily were walking round the garden at Boyars. It was evening, a damp fragrant evening, almost a spring evening, though the weather was still cold. Low storm clouds, thick, bulging, dark and yellowish, with brilliantly white serrated edges, were moving towards the east, leaving behind a clear transparent reddish sunset. It had been raining most of the day, but now the rain had ceased. Rose and Lily were wearing overcoats and wellingtons. Lily had rung up Rose to find if anyone had heard from Gull (which they had not) and had been rather tearful over the telephone. Rose, sympathetic, had invited her to Boyars. It was not in fact a very convenient time. Annushka, suffering giddy spells, was in hospital for some tests. Mousebrook seemed to be ill too, or perhaps just moping; after all he was really Annushka's cat. Boyars had a deserted feeling, as if the soul of the house, filled with foreboding, had already fled. Perhaps it knew that Boyars would soon be empty, ruined, or changed into a quite different house with a different soul. Rose, walking about in it, had begun to wonder whether she had ever *really lived* there.

The daffodils were in flower, a pale patch on the edge of the shrubbery. The crows, after spending the day in warfare with the magpies, were cawing upon the highest branch of a still leafless beech tree, outlined against the radiant red sky. Rose and Lily were walking along in the wet grass beside one of the borders where early violets stained the earth beneath the budding shrubs.

'Tamar seems much better now,' said Rose, anxious to get Lily off the subjects of Gull and the supernatural.

The reference to Tamar did not seem to please Lily. Lily had been suffering pangs of conscience at the news of Tamar's 'depression' or whatever it was, because she felt she had *persuaded* Tamar to take that irrevocable step. She had enjoyed taking charge of Tamar, able to put her worldly wisdom, her specialised knowledge, her *money* at the disposal of the much praised little angel. Only later had she realised how grave the decision was which she had so blithely fostered. With that she began, as she never had before, to grieve over her own abortion, which had been such a happy relief to her mind at the time. She even reckoned up how old the child would have been if it had lived. She had lately received a note from Tamar enclosing a cheque for the amount which Lily had lent her. The covering note was brief, curt, no sending of love or good wishes or thanks. Perhaps Tamar now hated Lily for having persuaded her. Looking at the cold note, Lily felt near to hating Tamar for causing her so much regret and remorse.

'I don't care for all that religion she's got into,' said Lily. 'It's just a psychological trick, it won't last.'

Rose, who thought this too, said vaguely, 'Oh she'll be all right – she's a very strong girl really – she's brave.'

'I wish I was strong and brave and going to be all right,' said Lily.'

'Mind you don't step on the snails,' said Rose. 'There's a snails' dance going on after all that rain.'

The grass, illumined by the sunset light, was covered with glossy worms and wandering snails.

'I love snails,' said Lily, 'my grandmother attracted them, they came into the house. Of course snails do get in everywhere, I found one in my flat the other day. My grandmother could tame wild things, they came to her. She used the snails for telepathy.'

'How did she do that?' said Rose, who had heard quite a lot, indeed enough, about Lily's horrible grandmother who had the evil eye and whose name nobody dared to utter.

'To send a message to someone at a distance, each of you has a snail, and you tell your snail what you want to say, and the person with the other snail gets the message. You have to put a spell on the snails of course.'

Rose wondered how much of this nonsense Lily really believed. They went into the house.

They had supper in the kitchen at the big kitchen-table which Annushka had scrubbed so much that the grainy wood had become a pale waxen yellow. Rose let Lily cook. They had an omelette, and some spiced cabbage which Lily had felicitously improvised, then cheddar cheese, and Cox's Orange pippins whose wrinkled skins were now yellower than the table. During the two days which Lily had spent at Boyars they had eaten frugally, drinking quite a lot of wine however. Mousebrook, stretched out into a very long cat on the warm tiles at the back of the stove, watched them with his baleful golden stare. Rose pulled him out and set him on her knee, stroking him firmly, but he refused to purr and soon twisted away and returned to his warm shrine. His fur, usually so electrically smooth, had felt dry and stiffened. After supper they sat with whisky beside the wood fire in the drawing room. They were easy together. Rose felt increasingly fond of Lily, though her restlessness wearied her, and she was irked by Lily's continual attempts to prompt confidences. Lily had talked a lot to Rose about her childhood and about Gulliver. Rose had not reciprocated. But she was glad of Lily's company and touched by her affection. They retired to bed, at any rate to their bedrooms, early.

Alone in her room Rose stood at the window. A sick moon had risen among the rush of ragged clouds. A car was passing along the Roman Road, its headlights creating faint flying impressions of walls and trees. Then it was gone and clouds covered the moon and the countryside was pitch dark and silent. Rose switched on the electric fire. In winter the central heating, switched off in much of the house when there were no guests, made little impression on the draughty spaces. Rose could feel the proximity of empty unheated rooms. She had been able to chatter with Lily but felt now, as she walked up and down, that the gift of speech had left her, a recurrent sensation as if her mouth were filled with stones. She was cut off, dumb, alone. The image of her stone-obstructed mouth and weighted tongue reminded her that that morning, visiting the stables to fetch apples, she had picked up one of Sinclair's stones. It was on the dressing table, a flat black stone banded with white lines with a long crack on one side, as if it were bursting open, showing a glittering gem-like interior. She held the stone in her hand and inspected it carefully. There was so much dense individuality, so much to notice, in the small thing. Sinclair, on some very distant day, had chosen it out of thousands and millions of stones on some beach in Yorkshire, Norfolk, Dorset, Scotland, Ireland. The stone made her intensely sad as if it were demanding her protection and her pity. Was it glad to be chosen? How accidental everything was, and how spirit was scattered everywhere, beautiful, and awful. She put the stone down and put her hands to her face, suddenly frightened of the darkness outside and of the quietness of the house. Suppose Annushka were to die? Suppose she is already dead, and the house knows it? The house was creaking in the wind like an old wooden ship. There were presences, footsteps.

I'm losing my nerve, thought Rose, I'm losing my courage, I'm losing my people. Jean has stopped loving me. How do I know that? Can it be true? Will I ever talk to Jean again, with openness and love, looking into each other's eyes? She said I was living in a dream world where everyone was nice and good and every year had the same pattern. I have never been deified by love. I could have married Gerard if I'd really tried. Then, as it had been suddenly sharply uttered in the room, she heard Crimond's voice say 'Rose!' as he had said it and so startled her when she came to him from Jean to make sure he had not shot himself. We've neither of us ever been married, love has to be awakened. Supposing I lose Gerard, Rose thought, suppose I have actually lost him? *Can* I lose him, after so many years? This is what this is all about, this press of ghosts.

In the last weeks, especially in the last days, it seemed that her relations with Gerard had simply broken down. Reeve, now back in Yorkshire, kept ringing up, asking her to decide about the cruise. Rose kept giving evasive answers. Yet why should she, why did she feel she must consult Gerard's convenience, why should it matter to him if she were absent for four weeks with her family? Blood was thicker than water. But the thought of Gerard not minding what she did or where she was, touched her with deadly cold as if one of Lily's ghosts had brushed past her. Rose had not seen Gerard since the night when the book had been delivered. She had expected the usual chats by telephone, suggestions of a meeting. He must know how interested, how anxious, she must be about his reactions to the book. But Gerard had not telephoned, and when she telephoned him he had been cold and brief, not able to see her. She had not dared to ask him anything, about the cruise, about the book. Later his telephone did not answer, and she imagined him there frowning, letting it ring, knowing it was her. Supposing – oh supposing all sorts of things – supposing he had fallen in love with that boy who looked like Sinclair, supposing he were spending all his time with Crimond discussing the book, supposing . . . ? I've lost him, thought Rose. Yes, perhaps, I could have married him if I'd been a different person, if I'd had more courage, if I'd had more luck, if I'd understood something particular (I don't know what) about sex, if I'd become a god. But how much I love him and have always loved him and will always love him.

'Rose, please come on the cruise, you will, won't you?'

'Rose, do come, it'll make all the difference.'

'We'll have such fun, please!'

'All right,' said Rose, 'I'll come.'

She could no more resist the entreaties of Reeve and Neville and Gillian, and was extremely touched by their urgent wish that she should accompany them. She was extremely *grateful*.

It was nearly two weeks since Lily's visit to Boyars, and during this time spring had made its tentative appearance, glorifying London, even in its shabbiest regions, with smells of earth and flowers and glimpses of leaves and sunshine. Gideon Fairfax was giving a party in the house at Notting Hill. Leonard Fairfax was home from America, bringing his friend Conrad Lomas with him. Gideon had asked Reeve and his children, said by Rose to be in town, and Neville had brought Francis Reckitt, son of their Yorkshire neighbour, who had travelled down with them. Gideon's favourite New York art dealer, Albert Labowsky, from whom he had just acquired the coveted Beckmann drawings, was also present. Rose could hear the American voices, distinct like the cries of unusual birds. Tamar was there, and Violet, and some friends of Pat and Gideon unknown to Rose. Tamar was shepherding a Miss Luckhurst, a retired school teacher who wrote detective stories. There was also in tow a very thin very young man said to be not only a parson but Tamar's godfather. Rose was surprised to see Father McAlister, conspicuous in his black cassock. Pat was dispensing Gideon's special tangerine cocktail. Of course Gerard had been asked, but, although some people were already leaving, he had not appeared.

'What are you doing after this?' said Reeve. 'You'll have dinner with us, won't you?'

'Sorry, I can't. I'm tied up.'

'Then tomorrow you *must* come and see the flat!' said Neville.

'We can't give you lunch,' said Gillian, 'there's nothing in it except a tape measure and Papa's cap which he left behind! But there's a super Italian restaurant nearly next door.'

Reeve had just bought a flat in Hampstead.

'Thanks, I'd love to,' said Rose. She was troubled by an aching tooth.

Rose had no engagement that evening, but was hoping that Gerard would come, and would have dinner with her. She had still, in the lengthening interim since her time at Boyars, heard absolutely nothing from him. She rang his number less and less often. She wrote a letter and destroyed it. She did not dare to go round to his house. This faint-heartedness was a measure of how, after all these years, remote he had suddenly become: a dear friend, not a close friend, not an intimate. She had no idea at this moment where Gerard was or what he might be doing or thinking, and she dreaded asking anyone for news of him, thus admitting that *she* did not know what perhaps others did. Gerard might be out of the country, he might be in bed with someone, he might be in hospital or dead. He carried nothing which named *her* as closest.

Gideon, as master magician, watching his party fizzing on so well, had his chubby pretty look which annoyed Gerard so much. He had moved Gerard out of his house by playing on his weaknesses, his semi-conscious guilt feelings, his unhappiness which made him so unworldly, the sheer nervous irritability which suddenly made him want to get away from his sister and brother-in-law at any price. Gideon had completed the redecoration of the house, doing exactly what he wanted and not what Pat wanted. Pat's resistance had been minimal, so there was not much to crow about there. The drawing room, which under Gerard's regime had been an insipid spotty pinkish brown dotted with small pale English watercolours and full of dark dull conventional fat chairs, was now painted a glowing aquamarine adorned with a huge scarlet abstract by de Kooning over the fireplace and two colourful conversation pieces by Kokoschka and Motesiczky. The carpet was a very dark blue with pale blue and white *art deco* rugs. There were two very large white settees, and no other furniture. Gerard's hopeless kitchen had of course been completely reconstructed. Only the dining room retained its previous form and colour, exhibiting now upon its dark brown walls the pretty Longhis and the lovely Watteau. Even more pleasing to Gideon was the return from America, for good he hoped, of his beloved and talented son Leonard, now to study at the Courtauld Institute. What a team we shall be, thought Gideon, who had never dared to call himself an art historian, and what fun we shall have! Gideon could also look with some satisfaction upon his success (so far) with Tamar and Violet. After the abduction things had moved rapidly. Tamar had moved into the upstairs flat. Violet (surprising Pat but not Gideon) had suddenly moved in too. Tamar had moved out and now had a tiny flat in Pimlico. Violet's flat was up for sale. Violet was quiet, letting herself be looked after. What next, time would show, and meanwhile it was another one up on Gerard.

Patricia thought, Gideon's worked really hard to get hold of those two, I hope he won't regret it! He's too kind-hearted and of course he's a power maniac with delusions of grandeur. He's quite unscrupulous when he gets going like this. How on earth will we ever get Violet out? She's sitting there like a toad and playing the interesting neurotic, it could go on forever, I suppose we shall have to buy her out! My God though, she may be a mental case, but she's kept her good looks and her figure, it isn't fair! Patricia was well aware of Gideon's funny kinky affection for Violet, and it did not trouble her. She was in any case too happy at present, what with Leonard's return and the house to play with, to bear any ill-will to her unhappy cousin. As for Tamar, it looked as if they were adopting her after all. Perhaps that was what Gideon had always wanted. Surveying the scene Patricia had already noticed something else which gave her pleasure. Leonard seemed to be getting on very well with Gillian Curtland. Hmm, thought

Pat, a nice clever pretty girl, and she'll inherit a packet. When they come to live in Hampstead we'll invite them to dinner.

Violet's capitulation, which had occurred when Gideon arrived on the day after the abduction, was brought about by two kinds of consideration, one financial, the other emotional (Father McAlister would have used the word 'spiritual'). The latter was a special kind of despair which took the form of *missing Tamar*. Violet had been intensely and deeply shocked by the ruthlessness of Tamar's rejection of her. She realised that the docile spiritless girl she had known all her life was gone forever, and that she would never meet *that girl* again. With Tamar so utterly gone from it the flat was desolate, a cage without its little captive. Keeping Tamar prisoner had been far more important to Violet than she had ever realised. Whether this importance had anything to do with love was a question which did not now concern her; she needed help, she was ready to run, Gideon appeared. The financial consideration could be more clearly stated. Gideon announced, which Violet had anticipated, that Tamar had already given up her job. She wanted time to catch up with her studies. There were debts and bills and very little money. Gideon composed a rational argument. Violet had to face the facts and put her life in order. It made sense to sell the flat, which was a genuine asset, pay what was owed, and come and *rest* at Notting Hill, then get some sort of job (all right, not in his office) where she could use her wits, or anyway make a plan for a happier and more sensible life. She didn't have to stay on with him and Pat if she didn't want to, it could be an interim. Violet, who felt just then that the alternative was suicide, said yes with an alacrity which surprised Gideon, who had looked forward to a struggle, even a row, ending of course in victory. Gideon had given her money to buy clothes. She had accepted the money and bought the clothes. (Gideon, discussing it all with Pat, attached great symbolic significance to this surrender.) Now at the party she felt like some sort of wicked Cinderella. Albert Labowsky was talking to her as if she were an ordinary person. She could see Gideon looking encouragingly in her direction.

She had fallen into the hands of the enemy, the other race, who would now expect her to be grateful, even to become happy! Of course they had not expected her to share the flat with her daughter, the new Tamar. Gideon had bought a flat for Tamar before Violet moved in! What shall I do up there alone, thought Violet. Shall I quickly become ill, bed-ridden, have my meals brought up by kind people who will sit by my bed and chat? Perhaps even Tamar might come and sit, and look at her watch. Violet was experiencing a sudden total *loss of energy*, what a car must feel when there is no more petrol. She had not really lived, before, on pure unmixed resentment and remorse and hate, she had lived on Tamar, as a presence, as a vehicle, as something always expected and *looked forward to*. Through Tamar she had touched the world. Could she now live on a hatred for Pat and Gideon, which she did not yet feel, but might *have to* develop as a source of power? How she would detest their charity as the days went by, how she would loathe their kindness, their tactful sympathy, their gifts of flowers! But how *now* could she escape? Any relationship with the child who had rejected her seemed now impossible forever, one could only cast, in that direction, one's curse. Don't they *know*, thought Violet, that I'm not an ordinary person, that I'm dangerous, that I'll end by burning the house down? Now I'm a novelty. Soon they'll get nervous. I shall start to scream. They'll have foreseen this too. I shall go to a luxurious mental home and have electric shocks at Gideon's expense. If I leave now and go upstairs someone will be sent after me to see I'm all right. Soon they'll begin to be afraid of me. That at least will be something.

Father McAlister was looking forward to Easter. He had given up alcohol for Lent and the smell of the tangerine cocktail was inflaming his senses. Also of course he dreaded Easter. I do not know, I cannot tell, what pains He had to bear, I only *know* it was *for me* He hung and suffered there. The terrible particularity, the empirical detail, of his religion bore down upon him then as at no other time. He would endure it, he would purvey that story all over again, what else was he for? Without the endlessly rehearsed drama of Christ, His birth,

His ministry, His death, His resurrection, there was nothing at all, he, Angus McAlister, was a vanishing shadow, and so were the planets and the most distant stars and the ring of the cosmos. Others live without Christ, so why not I? must be a senseless question. *Nothing* can separate me from the love of Christ. How did Saint Paul *know*? Is it not upon *his* knowledge that the whole thing rests? Without Paul to carry that strange virus from land to land the gospels would have been lost forever, or rediscovered centuries later as local curiosities. So it was all an accident? That was *impossible*, for it was something absolute, and what is absolute cannot be an accident. Suppose there was nothing of Christ left to us but his moral sayings, uttered by some unknown man with not a fragment of history to clothe him? Could one love such a being, could one be *saved* by him? Could he come closer to one than oneself? Christianity spoils its believers as spoilt children are spoilt. The radiant master, the martyred man, the beautiful hero, the incarnate god, the best known individual in history, the best loved and most powerful: this is the figure Christianity has lived upon and may die of. That was not Father McAlister's business. He had his own certainties and his own paradoxes; he did not dare, as Easter approached, to call these his lies. It must surely be possible for him – in Christ – not to lie. Such a truth as ends all strife, such a life as killeth death. Christ on the cross made sense of all the rest, but only if he really died. Christ lives, Christ saves, because he died as we die. The ultimate reality hovered there, not as a phantom man, but as a terrible truth. Father McAlister could not dignify his beliefs by the name of heresy. He prayed, he worshipped, he prostrated himself, he felt himself to be a vehicle of a power and a grace which was given, not his own. But his terrible truth was never quite clarified, and that lack of final clarification troubled him on Good Friday as at no other time. This mysterious Absolute was what, during those awful three hours as he enacted the death of his Lord, he had somehow to convey to the kneeling men and women who would see – not what he saw, but something else – which was their business and God's business – only there was no God.

That the priest performed this task in agony, with tears, did him no credit. Rather the contrary.

Tamar had abandoned her brown and grey uniform and was wearing a midnight-blue dress with a jabot of frilly white silk at the neck. Her fine tree-brown tree-green hair had been cleverly cut into layers, she looked boyish and elfin and cool. Her face was slightly less thin, her complexion slightly less pale, she had lost her 'schoolgirl' look. She wore no make-up. Her large hazel eyes carried a wary self-consciously melancholy expression which was new. Conrad Lomas had, as he confided to Leonard, admired her for several seconds before recognising her. Tamar had let Gideon arrange her future, he typed letters for her and she signed them. What had seemed so impossible was fixed up easily and swiftly, what had seemed lost forever retrieved, no one seemed to be surprised, no one objected, her tutor, the college authorities, expressed calm pleasure at the prospect of welcoming her back. A van, conjured up by Gideon, brought to her all her remaining clothes, all her possessions down to the tiniest trinkets from her room. The awful old flat seemed gone from the earth, as if it had indeed been burnt, an image which haunted her. She bought books, acquiring again the works which her mother had made her sell and which she had parted from with such bitter tears. Though not without invitations, she remained solitary, as if, in a unique healing interim never to be repeated, she must fast.

The fervour of her religious conversion had, as the cynics predicted, worn off. It was amazing to her now to remember how she had *craved* for the sacrament. Had she really swallowed all those wafers of bread and all those sips of rich wine, more intoxicating by far than Gideon's cocktail? At present, she did not want this food. But the cynics (of whom she was well aware) understood very little. Tamar was indeed puzzled about herself. Father McAlister had constantly talked of 'new being'. Well, she had new being, she had been permanently changed. But what had happened? Was it simply that she had broken free from her mother, was that what her cunning psyche had, under the guise of other things, always been after?

She had been suddenly endowed with a supernatural strength. Like a trapped creature who, seeing a last, already vanishing, escape route, becomes savagely powerful, able to destroy anything which impedes its way. In that final scene, Tamar had felt ready to trample her mother into the ground, and had sensed with satisfaction her mother's apprehension of an irreversible shift of the balance of power between them. Was one, as a Christian, and a new Christian, allowed to take that much time off from the Gospel of Love? To say it was necessary, it is over, things will be better, there will be a fresh start seemed a shabby way of getting oneself off. Tamar had no idea what she had *done* to her mother. Tamar had not discussed these more recent problems with her mentor. She was, with his tacit consent, avoiding him. Later they would talk again – though never, perhaps, as they had talked once. She was sure of his concern, indeed, of his love. Only love, his or Christ's, his and Christ's, could have rescued her from that inferno of guilt and fear. She was also aware, with a half-amused irritation, of the way in which, when the priest apprehended her withdrawal, he 'transferred his affections' to her mother. Tamar and Father McAlister had of course talked a great deal about Violet, and he had visited her first with Gideon, later (as he told Tamar) by himself, brief and, as she understood, fruitless visits. However it took more than snubs and indications of the door to deter this connoisseur of hopeless cases. Tamar's teacher had insisted to his now, in this matter sceptical, pupil that her mother depended on her, really loved her, and really was loved by her. Before her escape Tamar was not ready to reflect on these theories. Now, reflecting on them, she made little progress. She had been told of, indeed had experienced, the transforming power of love, the only miraculous power upon this earth. Was it possible now for her to love Violet, or discover that she had always loved her? Tamar's new state placed her further from her mother than she had ever been, her liberation having been made possible by an anger which made her former submission seem more like weakness than love. Could she see more clearly now or less clearly? Had she always assumed that she loved her mother because that was what children did? The priest, who had seen and understood that sinful anger, had told her to banish it by thinking love, enacting love. Approach her! Do little things! She needs you! Tamar was not so sure. She had tried a little thing by bringing her flowers, accompanied by Pat, which had been a mistake. Violet had accepted them with a tigerish smile. Visible hatred terrifies. Tamar determined to try again soon.

Tamar had recovered from her obsessive guilt about the lost child. Magic against magic, she had been cured, relieved of evil pain, as her wizard put it, left with good pain. She had also stopped worrying about whether Jean had told Duncan or Duncan had told Jean. What did remain with her was a curious shudder which occurred whenever she saw a teapot. It was a strange feature of their recent tribulations which would have impressed her, and the priest even more, if they had known it, that Tamar, like the others, like Rose, like Gerard, like Jean, as well as of course like Duncan, felt that she had been responsible for Jenkin's death. Each one of his friends could enact responsibility. Tamar, the last of them to see him alive, a fact known only to her confessor, could not forget that when she arrived Jenkin had been about to leave the house. If she had not come he would not have received that mysterious telephone call. But what impressed her more was the idea that she had unloaded some sort of fatal evil onto Jenkin. She recalled an awful satisfaction it had given her to 'tell all' to Jean, and spatter her with her own misery, and hatred, and then to run to 'tell all' again to Jenkin. But she had not been destined to receive the hoped-for absolution. It was as if she had spread out all that evil filth before him and as he took it up and took it upon himself, she had made him vulnerable to some force, perhaps wicked, perhaps simply retributive, which had struck him instead of her. Her priest of course found the idea interesting, but condemned it as superstitious; and her persisting grief for Jenkin gradually ceased to terrify her as she recalled the long day during which she had waited for him to come back. Tamar did not believe in God or a supernatural world and Father McAlister, who did not believe in them either, had not troubled her with these fictions. What he had, in his fierce enthusiasm, wrestling for her soul, intended to give her, was an indelible impression of Christ as Saviour. Tamar was, in her privileged interim, prepared to wait and see what later on this radiant presence might do for her. She prayed, not exactly to, but in this reality, which turned evil suffering into good suffering, and might in time even enable her to reach her mother.

Patricia was taking pleasure in telling Rose about how Gideon had rescued Violet and Tamar.

'You mean Violet is here, and Tamar is going back to Oxford?'

'Yes! Gideon and Father Angus together were irresistible!'

Rose, who had never heard her parish priest called 'Father Angus' before, could not help feeling at once that it was all a conspiracy against Gerard! But of course it was wonderful. 'It's wonderful!' she said. Her aching tooth, which had been grumbling, suddenly set a sharp throbbing pain down into her lower jaw. Rose instinctively raised her hand, closing her fist two inches from her chin, as if to catch it. 'Pat, I think I must go, I've got a beastly toothache.'

'Can I give you an aspirin?'

Conrad Lomas was telling Tamar how awfully sorry he was that he had lost her at the dance, how he had searched and searched, now she owed him a dance, they must find one to go to, he would be in London till the fall.

Tamar, leaned over by the tall American, stepped back a little and cast an almost flirtatious glance in the direction of Father McAlister. They had not attempted to approach each other. The priest, looking grave, made a very faint movement of his head and eyes, as he had done to Gideon in Violet's flat, in the direction of her mother.

Francis Reckitt was now telling Rose that Neville, whom he admired, had decided to go into Parliament. 'He's a radical, you see,' Francis, a little drunk, kept repeating.

Gideon was saying to Reeve, 'It's quite easy really, you get some dry white wine and mix it with bitters and not too

544

little rum and some white port and pile in the peel of the tangerines.'

Violet, who had drunk quite a lot of the tangerine mixture, had decided it was time for her to go upstairs and rejoin the dark figure who waited for her up there, herself. She was alone for the moment leaning against a wall, looking about with an assumed air of amused contempt. Leonard Fairfax, who of course knew 'all about it', was feeling it was his duty to go and talk to her. He was forestalled however by Father McAlister. The priest, with a flurry of dark skirt, as if he had just noticed Violet, advanced. He took hold of her hand and held it, while uttering a flow of talk. Tamar watched this. The priest had, in all their encounters, never touched Tamar except at their first meeting and at the rite of baptism. This had impressed her. She watched his hand holding her mother's, wondering how long it would last. How handsome he looks today, she thought, perhaps he can put on handsomeness when he wants to! Gideon, looking over the shoulder of Rose, to whom he was now talking, also saw the hand-holding, and thought about animal magnetism. Gideon couldn't quite make Father McAlister out – a cynical fake, a charlatan, a mad saint or what? He's certainly a wizard, thought Gideon, I'll keep him around, he could be useful.

'Rose, don't go, I want to tell you my new idea, a *Tamargesellschaft!*

'A what?'

'I met Joel Kowitz in New York, we were talking about Crimond's book, and I thought, well now that's over, why not let's have a regular whip-round for Tamar, to see her through Oxford, Joel said he'd contribute, she can't live on that grant, she must have money to travel, to sail to Byzantium –'

'Oh I'll join,' said Rose, 'she must – yes – sail –'

Gideon, happy, was at his prettiest in a strawberry pink shirt, his dark curly hair cut short, shining with bronze and golden lights, his girlish complexion glowing with health and youth, his finely manicured fingers moving appreciatively over his delicately flushed cheeks and exquisitely smooth chin. He looked as young as his tall athletic son.

There was a sudden commotion near the door, laughter and something like a cheer. Lily had arrived accompanied by Gulliver Ashe. Lily, dressed in blue silk trousers and a golden jacket, was explaining to Conrad, and now to Gideon who had pushed his way towards her that, yes, Gull was back and he'd got a job, he'd met a man. 'Oh Rose, Rose, dear, he's back, he's back, it's all all right, I was such a misery about it, I'm so sorry, but everything is all right now!'

Rose kissed her and held her hot clutching hands, she kissed Gull. So Lily had got her man back after all.

'Rose, we're going to get married.'

'Oh, I'm so glad!'

'They're going to get married,' shouted Gideon.

Tears were in Lily's eyes. Tears flooded into Rose's eyes. Others pressed forward and she stepped back still sidling toward the door. Suddenly Reeve and Neville and Gillian were beside her. 'What's that about?' said Gillian.

'We haven't fixed about tomorrow,' said Reeve. 'We're off too actually, we'll take you.'

'They're going to get married,' said Rose, 'I always hoped they would.' Fumbling for her handkerchief she couldn't stop the tears. She said to Reeve, 'Oh, it's so touching, I'm so happy for them!' She felt, thinking of their joy, such a great shaft of sorrow which came down on her as if she had been struck from above, she almost reeled, she dropped her handbag. She had found her handkerchief and put it to her mouth.

Reeve held on to her, Gillian picked up her bag, and Neville patted her shoulder. 'Here's a map,' said Reeve, 'I've written it all down. We'll meet you at the flat at twelve thirty, and then we can have lunch after. Gillian, put it into Rose's bag.'

It was at that moment that Gerard appeared. The triumphant rout surrounding Gull and Lily had moved further into the room, leaving Rose at the doorway surrounded by her family. For a second Gerard found himself confronted by the Curtland phalanx.

He had left his coat outside near the front door and was neat in a dark suit, but he looked to Rose's eye very strange, very tired, a little mad. His hair hung in limp ringlets, his mouth drooped sulkily, his face looked puffy and soft, his glittering blue eyes glared down almost fiercely upon the group before him. At the next second all was adjusted. Reeve removed his hand from Rose's arm, Neville his from her shoulder, Gillian handed her her handbag into which she had thrust the instructions for tomorrow. Gerard's face reorganised itself into its usual set of hard surfaces and expression of pensive irony, and then relapsed into his usual inane disconcerting grin. They all moved out into the hall.

'Hello, Reeve,' said Gerard. 'What a row in there!'

Reeve, rather formal, said, 'How nice to see you. These are my children Neville and Gillian. I think it's some years since you've met them.'

'They've certainly grown!' said Gerard. 'Glad to meet you.' He held out his hand to Gillian, then to Neville. The children murmured something gracious.

'Well, we're off,' said Reeve. He turned to Rose. 'Can we drop you where you're going?'

'No, thanks, I can walk. I just want a word with Gerard.'

'See you tomorrow then.'

'Yes, tomorrow,' said Rose.

Neville, who had been smiling subtly throughout this encounter, said, 'We'll take you to Yorkshire.'

With waves they receded, leaving Rose and Gerard beside, now outside, the drawing room door. These two stood in silence not looking at each other while Reeve and his offspring disappeared into the dining room to find their coats. They emerged, looked back, waved again, and vanished through the front door.

Gerard said to Rose politely, 'Can I get you a taxi for your next appointment?'

'I have no appointment,' said Rose. She felt she was going to cry again, and walked past him to the dining room, picked up her coat, came out and began to put it on. Gerard helped her on with her coat.

Rose said, moving towards the front door, 'Goodbye then. By the way, Gull and Lily are getting married. They're in there.'

Leonard Fairfax came skidding out of the drawing room holding a glass which he put into Gerard's hand. He had adored Gerard all his life. 'I thought I heard your voice. I've been *panting* to see you.' Leonard resembled his father, with the same close-curling hair and pretty red-lipped mouth, but was taller and thinner.

'Hello, faun,' said Gerard. 'So you're going to the Courtauld, I'm so glad.'

'Just off, Rose?' said Leonard. 'Lovely to see you. Violet has gone upstairs with your parson!'

'Thanks so much,' said Rose. She opened the door. The new *art nouveau* lantern which Pat had installed illuminated the steps.

Gerard handed the glass back to Leonard. 'I'm just going to see Rose along.' He picked up his coat which he had thrown down in a corner by the door.

'Don't be long!' Leonard shouted after him. 'Dad wants to see you. Peter Manson's coming, he rang up looking for you. And I want to fix lunch with you tomorrow!'

Rose and Gerard walked away along the road. A slight unconvincing rain was falling, slanted by the east wind. Rose began to cry again, silently, covertly into her handkerchief.

Gerard said, 'Oh – damn –' Then, 'What's the matter?'

'Oh nothing. I've got toothache.'

'I'm sorry. Will you see the dentist?'

'Yes. Look, don't let me keep you.' She checked her tears and began to walk faster.

'So you're off again to Yorkshire tomorrow.'

'No, I'm not.'

'I thought Neville said so.'

'No. I'm having lunch with them. They've bought a flat in Hampstead.'

'How nice. So they're Londoners now.'

'Do go back, everyone's longing to see you. I can walk from here. I'll get a taxi in a moment anyway.'

'Where are you going?'

'Home. Look, there's a taxi. I'll say goodbye.'

'Oh, all right.' Gerard flagged down the taxi and opened the door.

Rose got in. 'Nice to see you. I'll give you a ring sometime.'

'What the hell's the matter with you?' said Gerard. 'Are you ill?'

Rose began to cry again. Gerard got into the taxi and slammed the door and gave the taximan Rose's address. He patted her shoulder but did not put his arm round it. They rode in silence. When they reached Rose's flat and Gerard had paid the driver they mounted the stairs in silence.

They dropped their coats, Rose pulled the curtains and put on the electric fire. She said, 'Would you like a drink?'

'Yes.'

'Sherry?'

'Yes.'

'Anything to eat?'

'No thanks.'

She poured out two glasses.

'What *is* the matter, Rose?'

'Nothing's the matter! Perhaps I should ask you what the matter is! You disappear for weeks. When I ring you say you can't see me, then you don't answer the 'phone, or else you're away God knows where and it hasn't occurred to you to let me know. Well, why should you let me know. I've got no special rights, I'm not part of your family –'

'And I'm not part of your family, if it comes to that. You've evidently decided to live in the north and be a mother to those bright young things! Well, why not. Blood is thicker than water.'

'That's what Reeve says.'

'You make it clear that you've got a home elsewhere!'

'Well, it doesn't affect you. I've never had a home here.'

'That's not true. It depends on what you call a home.'

'Yes, indeed! I never thought I'd see you being jealous and vindictive –'

'I never thought I'd see you behaving like a silly petty female! I'm not jealous. Why the hell should I be?'

'Why indeed. I realise that you have quite another life into

549

which I don't enter and when it suits you you vanish. How's Derek Wallace?'

'*Who?*'

'Derek Wallace. That boy who brought that – that proof copy – from Oxford.'

'Rose, are you crazy – or bloody-minded – or what?'

'What do you expect me to do when you disappear – or am I supposed not to think about you? If you *want* me not to think about you you're certainly going the right way about it.'

'Rose, do you really imagine –'

'Of course it's not your fault, it's my fault. You've always taken me for granted, that I'll always be there to be kind and useful. I shouldn't have hung around. Plenty of people advised me not to.'

'Well, why did you hang around?' said Gerard. 'I didn't demand it. Of course I took you for granted. I don't see what you're complaining about or why you're suddenly so angry with me.'

'And why do you say "damn" and "what the hell's the matter?" and turn up late at a party where you might have known I'd be there wanting to see you! Oh I'm a fool, a *fool*.'

'You said something about Gull and Lily getting married.'

'You're changing the subject.'

'It needs changing.'

'Yes, Gulliver's back from Newcastle – and he's got a job – and they're going to be married. And Gideon and Pat have adopted Tamar.'

'Have they?'

'Well, they're in charge, they've fixed everything, she's to go back to Oxford, there's to be a *Tamargesellschaft*, we'll all contribute to help her through –'

'Good. But who says so?'

'Gideon, he arranges things now. Tamar's got a flat of her own, Violet's living at Notting Hill, Tamar's happy, Violet's happy, all the things you might have done, only you hadn't time and didn't try –'

'I doubt if Violet's happy – but you're quite right that we didn't try enough –'

'Who's "we"?'

'Rose, just, please, be careful what you say.'

'It's come to that, has it, I have to "be careful what I say"! What about what *you* say? You accuse me of –'

'What have I accused you of except of being fond of your family?'

'I have no family. You are my family. That means I have no family. I've given you my life and you haven't even noticed.'

'You are talking nonsense which is designed simply to hurt me. Of course you have family. It looks to me as if Reeve is simply taking you over, he's leading you away like a little docile domestic animal.'

'You mean he's exploiting me, he want's a housekeeper?'

'Well, why shouldn't he? He counts on the conventions of family affection.'

'Why "conventions"? Those people need me and want me, which you have never done.'

'Rose, don't shout at me, you know I can't stand tantrums.'

'I'm not shouting. All right, I'm talking nonsense. It's all much simpler than that. I've always been in love with you and you can't be in love with me, which isn't your fault. But for some reason it's all suddenly become *unbearable*.'

'What am I supposed to do? Do you want me to go away, now?'

'You mean for ever?'

'Don't be silly. You seem to be finding me unbearable, you are certainly angry with me, I can't think why. It's not a good moment, you are overwrought, perhaps about something else, and I'm being no use here – it might be a sensible idea if I cleared off.'

'You mean someone is waiting for you, you are looking at your watch.'

'Rose, are you *drunk*?'

'All right, go then.'

There was a silence. Rose had unbuttoned the top of the brown corduroy dress she was wearing and pulled at the white collar of the blouse underneath it and clawed at her throat with one hand. She wondered, *am* I drunk? Why are these awful things happening? She had been walking to and fro as she spoke between the rosewood table on which she had put the untouched drinks and the desk where she suddenly noticed a letter to Gerard which she had started two days ago and not finished. She picked it up and crumpled it violently in her hand. She thought, is this the end of such a long road, shall I scream, shall I faint? He has forgotten that we were ever lovers. Well, it was a long long time ago and it didn't mean *that* even then. Now I am waiting for him to go, I shall not stop him, and if he goes everything will be different, we shall irrevocably become strangers to each other. Perhaps we are already strangers and I am only now beginning to notice it. She tossed the crumpled letter on the floor.

Gerard watched her. He was standing by the fireplace. He was upset and amazed by her sudden desire to wound him. For a moment he considered going away. But something else happened, which was that he suddenly felt overwhelmingly tired. He had plenty to be tired of and tired about, everything lately had been *too much*. He said, 'Oh God, I feel so tired!', and went to the table and picked up one of the glasses of sherry. As he did so he accidentally spilt some of the golden liquid on the table. Although the poor old table was already so stained Rose instinctively brought out of the pocket of her dress her hand-kerchief, still damp with tears, and mopped up the little pool. Gerard immediately put his hand down upon her hand and they stood quiet thus for a moment, not looking at each other. When the moment passed and he withdrew his hand and she lifted her head towards him he said, 'We mustn't quarrel, darling, *we* mustn't quarrel.'

Rose, who had been so tearless and fierce, now felt the tears about to come again, and with them a vast sensation of relief which was marked by a renewed consciousness of her tooth-ache, of which she had been oblivious. She felt so intensely glad, so thankful, so grateful that Gerard had not gone, that he had touched her and called her 'darling', and that she did not have to go on with her mechanical assault upon him which had hurt both of them so much. She said, as the tears rose, 'I must get another handkerchief, this one's soaked in sherry.'

'Here, take mine.'

She buried her face in his large white handkerchief, still stiff with its laundered folds, but already smelling of his pocket, warming it with her breath and wetting it with her tears. She had been let off some terrible fate, which had for a moment looked at her.

'Will you stay to supper?'

'Yes, of course,' said Gerard, 'but don't *make* anything.'

A little later after they had been in the kitchen together and Gerard had opened a bottle of wine and Rose had taken two aspirins and opened a tin of tongue and a tin of spinach and set out some cheese and apples and a plum cake, and they had talked a little about Gull and Lily, and Tamar and Violet, and Annushka who was thank God not seriously ill, they sat down at the round table, which Rose had covered with raffia mats, with the food and drink before them and confronted each other as for a conference. They were both very hungry however.

'Rose, you said that "for some reason" it's all unbearable. Can we get at the reason?'

'Do you think we should go on with that? I want to talk about you.'

'It's true that you haven't asked me how I am and what I've been doing, except for a ridiculous impertinent innuendo on the latter point.'

'I'm sorry. How are you and what have you been doing?'

'I *will* tell you, but I'd rather wait a bit.'

'Gerard, it's not anything awful?'

'Not exactly – awful – but – I'll tell you, only let's remove these other things first.'

'You mean the things I said?'

'And the things I said, and why we both – evidently – feel in a sort of crisis. Of course there are some obvious reasons.'

'You mean Jenkin –'

'Yes. That. As if the world has ended, and – for all of us it's the end of one life and the beginning of another.'

'For all of us,' said Rose, 'you mean for both of us.'

'I can't help feeling there are a lot of us still. Well, there's Duncan, but I don't know –'

'I think we've lost them,' said Rose.

'I hope not.'

'But what is it, this beginning of another life – isn't it just a sense of our own mortality, can it be anything else?'

Gerard murmured, 'There's work to do . . .'

'When Sinclair died we were young – we felt then, too, that we were to blame.'

'Yes. We felt we hadn't looked after them properly, either of them – but that's superstition. Guilt is one way of attaching a meaning to a death. We want to find a meaning, it lessens the pain.'

'You mean saying it's fate or –'

'Making it into some kind of allegory, dying young, the envy of the gods – or dying as a sacrifice, giving one's life for others, somehow or other, accepting their punishment, a familiar enough idea after all.'

'Oh – heavens –' said Rose, 'you've thought of that too – a perfect oblation and satisfaction –'

'Yes, but it won't do, it's a blasphemy, it's a corrupt kind of consolation – it's what feeling we're to blame leads to – I mean irrationally feeling we're to blame.'

'So that's not our new beginning.'

'A redemptive miracle? Of course not! It's the accidentalness we have to live with. I'm not sure what I meant by a new beginning anyway, perhaps just trying to live decently without Jenkin.'

'You said there was work to do.'

'Yes.'

'You don't think Crimond murdered Jenkin?'

'We must stop asking ourselves that question.'

'Would you ever – ask him?'

'Ask Crimond? No.'

'Because you *do* think it conceivable –'

'We've got to live with that mystery. But, oh Rose, it all hurts me so – you're the only person I can say this to – just

Jenkin being dead is so terrible, his absence. I loved him, I depended on him, so absolutely.'

Rose thought, I can never tell Gerard why I feel so particularly that Jenkin's death was my fault. But of course I'm *mad*. I *don't* think Crimond killed him. That's another – what Gerard called an allegory. Do I imagine that somehow the accident came about because of something in Crimond's unconscious mind, because of his resentment against me? Oh if only I'd behaved differently to him, more kindly, more gratefully. Gerard thought, I can never tell Rose just how much I loved Jenkin and in what special way I loved him, and how he laughed at me! That's a secret that isn't tellable to anyone. But it's a relief to mention his name to her. I shall often do that.

They were both silent for a while, Gerard intently peeling an apple, Rose dissecting her cheese into smaller and smaller pieces which she had no intention of eating. She was beginning to feel in a sad but calm way that the evening was reasonably, safely, over. Later, she knew, she would accuse herself of having said things, not unforgivable, for she knew they were already forgiven, but stupid and perhaps memorable. There had been no catastrophe. Yet were they not, these things and the sense in which they did not matter, proof of a distance between her and Gerard, of an impossibility which had always existed and of which she was only now becoming fully conscious? She was indeed a slow learner! Was she learning to be resigned, was that what being resigned was like, to shout and wave in the street as the prince passes, and realise he does not know or care whether you are cursing or cheering – and will smile his usual smile and pass on. What a ridiculous idea, thought Rose, I feel so tired, I must be falling asleep, that was almost a dream, seeing Gerard passing by in his coach! If only he would go now, I know I could go to sleep quickly. My toothache is better. She stared at him and her stare seemed to hold him, his strong carved face set out in light and shadow, the few gleaming lines of light grey in his curly hair. She felt her own face becoming heavy and solemn and her eyes closing.

'Rose, don't go to sleep! You haven't asked me an important question!'

'What question?'

'About the book!'

'Oh, the *book*.' Rose felt like saying, damn the book. She just wanted the book to be over, she had had enough of it. Perhaps that was resignation too.

'You haven't asked what I thought of it. After all, what do you imagine I've been doing all this time?'

'Well, what do you think of it? That it's no good, it's nonsense? Gerard, it doesn't *matter* now – that at least is finished with, isn't it?'

'Oh dear.' He said it ruefully, like a boy. 'Rose, let's have some whisky. No, don't get up, I'll get it. I say, let's get drunk, I want to talk to you so much, I want to talk and talk. Here, drink this, it'll wake you up.'

When Rose took a sip of the whisky she did suddenly feel more alert.

'You're the first person I've talked to, the first person I've seen since I finished it, that's why I haven't answered the telephone or been anywhere, I had to be by myself, to read it carefully and slowly, I just had to stay locked up with that book.'

'But is it any good? It must be a crazy book full of obsessions.'

'Yes, in a way it is.'

'I knew it – all that time and all that money to produce a madman's fantasy. It must have been dull, madmen's fantasies always are.'

'*Dull?* No, it nearly killed me. *It will* nearly kill me.'

'What do you mean? You're frightening me. I thought somehow it would hurt you –'

'Dangerous magic? Yes.'

'What do you mean *yes*?'

'Rose, the book is wonderful, it's *wonderful*.'

'Oh no! How awful!'

'Why awful? Do you mean I might die of envy? You know, I think I might have done, at the beginning, when I began to see how good it was, I had such a mean contemptible feeling of being disappointed!'

556

'You hoped you could dismiss it, throw it away – I wanted you to do just that.'

'Yes, yes, I felt put down – you know we got so used to thinking of him as crazy, unbalanced, and of course bad, unprincipled – *cruel*, like the way he treated Duncan at the dance.'

'You mean taking his wife?'

'No, I was thinking of his pushing Duncan into the Cherwell – that was something so ugly and gratuitous – not that we know what happened of course – Rose, do you remember how Crimond *danced* that night?'

'I didn't see him.'

'He was like a demon, it was like seeing a god dance, a destructive, creative *powerful thing*. We've all been so obsessed with closing our ranks because of the harm he did to Duncan – ever since the business in Ireland we've undervalued Crimond. We've thought of him as unsuccessful and shabby, and surly, like a dog prowling around outside – and then as our politics diverged so much, and that really did matter –'

'And still matters.'

'Yes, I'll come to that in a moment, we began to add up Crimond to be generally no good, wrong morals, wrong politics, irresponsible, vindictive, a bit dotty – How could such a person write a good book?'

'But you think he has.'

'Rose, it's an extraordinary book, I'm quite carried away – I'm sure I'm not wrong about it.'

'And not envious?'

'A bit, but that doesn't matter, admiration overcomes envy. One should be inspired by something good even if one disagrees.'

'So you disagree?'

'Of course I disagree!'

Gerard was not exactly tearing his hair but pulling his hands through it as if he wanted to straighten out its glossy curls lock by lock. His face, shining with light as it now seemed to Rose, was like a beautiful comic mask. She was touched, but

557

more deeply disturbed and frightened, by his emotion, which she could not yet understand.

'So it's good, and of course, you disagree, but at least it's *finished*. You've read it – and there we are.'

'No, we aren't there – not where you think –'

'I don't think anything, Gerard. Do calm down. Will you review it?'

'*Review* it? I don't know, I don't suppose anyone will ask me, that's not important –'

'I'm glad you think so. Have you told Crimond you like it, have you seen him?'

'No, no, I haven't been in touch with him. That doesn't matter, now, either.'

Rose felt some relief. She was disturbed by this excited talk about that dangerous book. All her old fears of Crimond were alert, that he would somehow damage Gerard, that the book itself would damage him, at the very least because he would be made unhappy by envious regrets. There was also, and she felt it now like the first symptoms of a fell disease, her fear of some amazing *rapprochement* whereby Crimond would revenge himself on her by making friends with his enemy and taking Gerard away. She wanted the book episode to be *over*; for Gerard, moved by his generosity from envy to admiration, to discuss the thing, and praise it, and then forget it, and everything to be as before, with Crimond, the surly dog, at a safe distance.

'I imagine not everyone will like the book.'

'No, they won't, some will hate it, some I'm afraid will love it.'

'You evidently don't hate it as it seems to excite you so! I can't believe it's all that interesting, a book on political theory. After all there are hundreds of them.'

'Rose, it's brilliant, it's all that we thought it might be when we decided it was worth financing it. It's all we hoped – it's also all we feared, later on that is. It will be immensely read, immensely discussed, and I believe, very influential. It's odd, I can remember now, which I'd somehow forgotten, what we felt about Crimond all those years ago when we thought what

558

a *remarkable* man he was and how he'd be able to speak for all of us, for *us*. Of course it isn't at all what we expected then, it's more than that, and it's not what we want to hear now, though we *have* to hear it.'

'I wish you wouldn't keep talking about "we" – just speak for yourself – you keep on imagining there's some kind of brotherhood, but we're scattered, we aren't a band of brothers, just solitary worried individuals, not even young any more.'

'Yes, yes, dear Rose, how well you put it –!'

'You're interested in the book because you know about it, because you know Crimond, because you financed the thing. If it was by someone you'd never heard of you'd ignore it. What's so good about this horrible book?'

'Why do you think it's horrible? You mustn't. It's not just another book about political theory, it's a *synthesis*, it's immensely long, it's about everything.'

'Then it *must* be a mess and a failure.'

'But it isn't. My God, the man's learning, his patience, what he's read, how he's thought!'

'You've read and thought too.'

'No, I haven't. Crimond said I'd stopped thinking, that what I'd been doing all my life wasn't thinking. And in a way he was right.'

'That's absurd, he's an absurd man. What will he do now the book's over, fade away? Go off to Eastern Europe?'

'Oh he won't go to Eastern Europe, he belongs here. Maybe he'll write another equally long book refuting this one! He's quite capable of it! But this volume will take a lot of digesting. I didn't know one of them could produce such a book now.'

'Who are "they"?'

'Oh Marxists, neo-Marxists, revisionists, whatever they call themselves. I don't know whether Crimond is "really" a Marxist, or what that means now, they don't know themselves. I suppose he's a sort of maverick Marxist, as their best thinkers are. The only good Marxist is a mad Marxist. It's not enough to be a revisionist, you've got to be a bit mad too – to be able to *see* the present world, to imagine the magnitude of what's happening.'

'Well, I always said he was mad,' said Rose, 'and if the book is entirely wrong-headed –'

'Yes, it is – but one has got to understand –'

'Crimond believes in one-party government – one doesn't have to go any farther than that.'

'Well, he does and he doesn't – his argument is much larger –'

'I should think,' said Rose, 'that there is nothing larger than that matter.'

'Oh Rose, Rose!' Gerard suddenly reached his hand across the table and seized hers. 'What a lovely answer.' She held onto his warm dear hand which mattered so much more than any book, more than the fate of democratic government, more than the fate of the human race. 'But, my dear Rose, we have to think, we have to fight, we have to *move*, we can't stand still, *everything* is moving so fast –'

'You mean technology? Is Crimond's book about technology?'

'Yes, but as I said it's about everything. He said to me ages ago that he just had to do it all *for himself*, to explain the whole of philosophy *to himself*, alone. And that's what he's done, the preSocratics, Plato, Aristotle, Plotinus, right up to the present, and Eastern philosophy too – and that means morality, religion, art, it all comes in, there's a splendid chapter on Augustine, and he writes so well, it's funny and witty, all sorts of people will read it –'

'But if it's all wrong that seems rather a pity!'

'Yes. It could enflame a lot of thoughtless smashers. He thinks liberal democracy is done for. He's a sort of pessimistic utopian. And of course we're right, all right I'm right, and he's wrong – but my rightness – needs to be changed – shaken, uprooted, replanted, enlightened . . .'

'I think this book will be a nine days' wonder,' said Rose, 'and then we can all relax! Even you may feel a bit more normal tomorrow morning. You're drunk on whisky and Crimond!'

'It may be that it's directed simply at *me.*'

'Surely you don't think –?'

'I don't mean literally. There may be a small number of people who will understand the book and be *ready* for it, and they are the people it is for – some will agree, some will disagree, but they'll have received an important communication. It may be like a signal by heliograph – there's only one point where it's received, and there it's dazzling.'

'It's dazzled you anyway. But if it's all about Plato and Augustine and Buddha I can't see it as a political bombshell.'

'It's not all about – it's an attempt to see the whole of our civilised past in relation to the present *and the future*, it's pointed, as it were, at the revolution.'

'Oh that! Oh really!'

'Rose, I don't mean the proletarian revolution out of old-fashioned Marxism. I mean the whole human global revolution.'

'I didn't know there was one. Neither did you. You've just picked it up out of Crimond's book!'

'My dear!' Gerard began to laugh crazily, pouring himself out some more whisky.

'*You're* drunk. You said I was. Now we both are.'

'My dear girl, yes, I'm drunk, and I didn't "pick up" out of Crimond's book something which of course I knew before, but which I now see in a new light.'

'It's an illusion. Everything is just a muddle. That's what liberal democracy means.'

'Rose, you see, you *understand*. But a popular illusion is a great force – and even the maddest prediction can reveal things one hadn't dreamt of which are really there.'

'What do you mean, technology, Africa, nuclear war –?'

'Many many things which seem separate but are connected or will connect. The foundations are shifting, we're about to see the largest, deepest, fastest change, the most shattering revolution, in the history of civilisation.'

'I don't believe those things connect,' said Rose, 'that's mythology. I'm surprised at you! We have a lot of different problems with different solutions. Anyway, dear Gerard, *we* shall not see this exciting cataclysm. I hope and believe that in what remains of my lifetime I shall still be able to go out and buy half a pound of butter and a copy of *The Times*.'

'Who knows? Think what's happened already in our lives.'

'Hitler?'

'Yes, unpredictable, unimaginable things. Space travel. We are surrounded by a future we can't conceive of. We're like those natives in New Zealand who just went on fishing because they *couldn't see* Captain Cook's ship – there it was in the bay, but they couldn't conceptualise it.'

'I like that. But what you can't know you can't know.'

'Rose, human life is too short, not just that it's sad to spend so little time at the play, but it's too short for serious thinking – thinking needs a long training, a long discipline, a long concentration – even geniuses must have felt they were tiring too soon, giving up when they'd just *begun* to understand – philosophy, perhaps human history, would be quite different if we all lived to be two hundred.'

'Our lives are quite long enough to have some fun, do some work, love a few people and try to be good.'

'Yes, yes, but we've got to, some of us have got to, try to *think* about what's happening, and to *fight* –'

'Against what?'

'Against – how can I put it – against *history*. All right, this sounds crazy – Rose, it's so difficult, I can't even pick it up yet – I feel like I felt in my first term of philosophy at Oxford, as if I were crawling round and round a slippery sphere and couldn't get inside.'

'Why bother to get inside? That might have been worth trying when you were a student, but why bother now?'

'You mean – well, yes, I was too young then – perhaps I'm too old now – that thought hurts terribly.'

'I don't mean to hurt you.'

'You're pouring on cold water, buckets and buckets of it, but that's right, one must be cool, one must be cold –'

'I don't understand. Is Crimond on the side of history?'

'Yes. History as a slaughterhouse, history as a wolf that

wanders outside in the dark, an idea of history as something that *has to be*, even if it's terrible, even if it's deadly.'

'I thought Marxists were optimists who thought the perfect society would soon emerge everywhere as the victory of socialism.'

'They used to be. Some still are, others are haggard with fear but hanging on. Crimond thinks we must purify our ideas with visions of utopia during a collapse of civilisation which he thinks is inevitable.'

'And looks forward to, no doubt! He's a determinist, as they all are.'

'He's a black determinist, that's the most dangerous and attractive kind. Marxism as despair, and as the only possible instrument of thought, the only philosophy that will be *ready* to *look after* a period of unavoidable authoritarian government.'

'And as the ark carrying the new values. All the old bourgeois ones will be extinct.'

'He's trying to grasp the whole problem – Of course I don't agree –'

'I don't think there is a whole problem, or that we can imagine the future, no one in the past managed it.'

'I can't convey it, the book is a huge interconnected *argument*, and it's not just pessimistic – it's very utilitarian, that's always been the nicest part of Marxism! It's about everything – there's a lot about ecology and kindness to animals –'

'Suitable for women!'

'Rose, it's a very *high-minded* book, about justice, about suffering –'

'I don't believe it. He wants to liquidate the bourgeois individual, that is the individual, and bourgeois values, that is values! He believes in the inevitability of cruelty.'

'It's a comprehensive attack on Marxism by a very intelligent Marxist, an attempt to think the whole thing through – you'll see –'

'I won't. I might look up ecology in the index, and animals, kindness to –'

'Rose, please don't just mock –'

'You seem to be overwhelmed because the book looks like

"what the age requires", a new synthesis and all that, but if it's just Marxism rules the world and utopia beyond, that's not new, it's just the old dictatorship of the proletariat in modern dress – and it's everything that *you* detest anyway, so why are you so impressed? I don't believe in Crimond's ark, his boat which is going to shoot the rapids.'

'Well, what do you believe in?'

'I think we've got to protect the good things that we have.'

'But really – ahead – what do you see? Catastrophe? *Après nous le déluge.*'

Rose was silent. Gerard had got up and was leaning over the back of his chair, his face illumined by a glare of excitement which seemed to Rose something comic, an intensification of his usual zany smile. At last, unwilling to say yes, she simply nodded.

Gerard turned away and began to walk up and down the room. 'Rose, have you got any of those chocolate biscuits?'

'The dark ones, those very dry ones? Yes, I'll get them.'

The table still carried their plates covered in fragments, the cheese and the plum cake, the apples in a pretty bowl.

'I'm still hungry. I'll have some of the cake too. Is it Annushka's?'

As Rose, in the kitchen, found the tin with the chocolate biscuits, she reflected that what was enlivening her in this argument with her old friend was physical desire, the debate was, for her, sex, her urgent agonising wish to be in bed with him transformed into repartee, as he said into mockery, just that, and not the future of civilisation!

Gerard was eating the plum cake, now the biscuits, now attacking the cheese, walking about and dropping crumbs on the carpet. Watching him trampling in the crumbs Rose said in exasperation, 'You keep praising this book, but you say it's all wrong! If it's Marxism it must be. Isn't that the end of the matter?'

'No – no – it's the *beginning*. When you read it –'

'I'm not going to read it! I think it's a detestable book, I wish it didn't exist.'

'You've *got* to read it.'

'Why?'

'For reasons I'll explain in a minute. In a way I wish it didn't exist, it will encourage fools and knaves and have a lot of bad results, yet I'm glad it exists too, it will *force* its opponents to think, it shows that people can have, just in this crucial area, new thoughts.'

'Books of new thoughts are published every week.'

'No they aren't, not pointed at just this spot.'

'The revolution, the greatest in human history. It's just sensationalism, all it will stir up is all our old ideas.'

'Then we must have some new ones.'

'We *can't*. Oh Gerard I'm so *tired*.'

'Darling, sorry, don't get sleepy again – I want to tell you –'

'I'm going on a cruise with Reeve and the children, a *long* cruise, a *world* cruise.'

'Oh.' This arrested Gerard. 'When?'

'At Easter. Well, not a world cruise, but longish, weeks – I can't remember.'

'Oh. That should be nice.'

'I'm going to see *much* more of them, I'm going to change my life, I'm going to sell this flat and go and live in Yorkshire.'

'Rose! You're not to!'

'Why ever not? Who's to stop me?'

'I am. Look, all right go on this damn cruise, see your family if you want to –'

'Thanks!'

'But just *listen* to what I'm going to say.'

'All right, all right!'

'*Wake up.*'

'I am awake. I'm sorry to be so dismissive about Crimond's book, I'm sure it's no good, though it certainly seems to have done something to you, but you'll get over it, it's nothing to do with us.'

'We financed it.'

'That was an accident. You'll soon forget it. It hasn't changed your life.'

'It has, actually – this is what I want to explain. This book must be answered, and it can be answered, point by point.'

'All right, review it – only you said you wouldn't.'

'It deserves more than a review.'

'What then?'

'An equally long book.'

'Who will write that?'

'I will.'

Rose stooped and picked up some crumbs from the carpet and dropped them on the table. She felt, not yet comprehensible to her, a sense of doom, as of a death sentence written in a foreign language. She said wearily, 'Oh don't – don't do that.'

'Rose, I must. It's my duty.'

'Gerard, it's *vanity*, wanting to do this, it's simply *vanity*. You can't start a long book now, you haven't time.'

'I've got to – for Jenkin – for Sinclair – for all of us.'

'Don't be so romantic – sentimental –'

'Crimond's book is deep, and it's fizzing with ideas – some of it's partly right, much of it's absolutely terrifyingly wrong.'

'You'll write a commentary on it.'

'No! I must write *my own book*. I see how to do it now. It will mean a vast amount of reading, and *thinking* till one *screams* – but I feel now, nothing else matters – that book must not go unanswered –'

'Funny,' said Rose, scraping the apple parings and the minutely chopped cheese from her plate onto Gerard's and placing his plate on top of hers, 'I used to think that at some time, perhaps when you retired, you and I might have some sort of different happiness together, I don't mean anything special, just like going to Venice or something. I even thought we might have some fun together. Poor Rose, she wanted to be happy, but alas it was not to be. Yes, it's time I went to Yorkshire. I'll go riding over the dales with Reeve and Neville and Gillian.'

'Look, I shall need a research assistant.'

'Try Tamar.'

'I thought of you, we could work together.'

'Gerard –'

'That's why you've got to read that book, you've got to *study* it – and why you mustn't leave London. We might live close to each other, next door, even share a house – why not? I've thought –'

Rose began to laugh. 'Share a house?'

'Why ever not? I think it's a good idea. We needn't be in each other's pockets. But we could meet every day –'

Rose went on laughing helplessly. 'Oh – Gerard – you and I – share a house –'

'Well –?'

'No, no, it's out of the question.'

'All right,' said Gerard, picking up his coat, 'and you don't care for the research assistant idea?'

'No, I don't!'

'Well, maybe it was a silly idea. I'll find someone. You're tired. What the hell are you laughing at?'

Rose, sitting at the table, was laughing hysterically, covering her wet mouth and eyes with Gerard's fine white handkerchief. 'Oh just – you – or history – or – something!'

'I'll say goodnight then,' said Gerard rather stiffly, putting on his overcoat. 'Thank you for supper. I'm sorry I made those absurd, as you evidently think them, suggestions.'

'Wait a minute!' Dropping the handkerchief Rose darted to him, she seized the sleeves of his coat, still damp from the rain and shook him, pulling him for a moment off his balance so that they both nearly fell to the floor. 'Don't be such a *fool*, do you understand *nothing*? Of course I'll be your research assistant, and of course we'll share a house or live next door or whatever you want – but if this happens we've got to have a pact – it must be like getting married, I mean *like* getting married, I'm tired of having *nothing*, I want *something* at last, we must be *really* together, I must have some sort of *security* – I'll read the book, I'll do anything you want, but I must feel at last – or is it hopeless – oh that book – you're not going to marry Crimond, are you?'

'Rose, are you going mad?'

'You'll want to be with him, to discuss the book.'

'I don't want to see him yet, perhaps not for ages, he may not want to see me, I suppose we'll meet sometime, but we can't be friends – because –'

'You're not going to go away – and marry someone else – we'll be together –'

'Yes, yes, and you can go on your cruise, but you're not to go and live in Yorkshire.'

'Because you need a research assistant.'

'Because I need *you*.'

'I'm making you say these things.'

'Rose, don't be so exasperating, you know I love you.'

'I *don't* know, I know *nothing*, I live on the edge of *blackness* – if you follow this book idea I'll go with you – but I must have some sort of security.'

'You have security! You're Sinclair's sister, you're my closest friend. I love you. What more can I say?'

Rose released him. 'Indeed. What more can you say. And you remember – well, why should you remember. So we'll live together, or next door, or nearby, and see each other *often* –'

'Yes, if you want it.'

'You suggested it.'

'Because I want it.'

'All right then. Now go home. I really am tired.'

'Rose, don't be so –'

'Go now. I'm all right. I'll help you with your book.'

'Goodnight, darling. Don't be angry with me, dearest Rose. I really do love you. I'll make you believe it. We may even go to Venice.'

After he had gone Rose cried quietly, soaking the white handkerchief and dropping her tears onto the stained rosewood of the table. She thrust the plates away and poured out some more whisky. Oh the tears she had shed for that man, and they were certainly not yet at an end.

She felt exhausted, aware that something large had happened, but not sure what it was, whether it was something to her advantage, or a terrible mistake, the throwing away of her last card. How impeccably, she felt, she must have behaved all these years, so many of them now, to be thinking of her behaviour tonight as such an outrageous display of emotion!

She felt remorseful and ashamed, she had shouted at him, she had said what she thought. She had said that she loved him and that she had got nothing in return, which was not only not true, but definitely not good form. She had seen Gerard wince at her tone and at the crudity of her formulation. These were old griefs, often privately rehearsed, concerning which she had never, that she could remember, exclaimed so to their innocuous author. What she regretted most bitterly however about the recent scene, and what left her now so limp with apprehension, was that she had actually revealed to Gerard what she had so often thought, that what she wanted from him was a *promise*. What of all things was more likely to alienate him, to make him cautious and aloof, than such a *claim* made upon him by a hysterical woman? It was just what he would dislike most that she had so thrust against him. Oh how imprudent, how perhaps fatally unwise.

It was true that what had occasioned her indiscretion was Gerard's own suggestion that they should share a house, his use of these words which evoked what, in her modest way, she had always hoped for! He had, more precisely, said live near each other, live next door or share a house, separate flats no doubt, not in each other's pockets. It was she who had then made conditions, demands for 'security', and in a turbulent manner most likely to make him tactfully withdraw. She pictured now the coolly grateful way in which she should have greeted his idea! In any case, the notion of proximity had come up as a matter of convenience, of having one's research assistant close at hand! What on earth would that collaboration, if it came to it, be like? Would she be capable of such a demanding and such a protracted task? Would she be able to study and understand that difficult book whose 'wrong-headedness' she would hate and fear, settle down to hard and perhaps uncongenial work, living with the continual possibility of disappointing and displeasing Gerard? Suppose she tried it for six months and was then replaced by a competent young woman? Oh the traps and miseries which dog all human desires for happiness, one ought not to desire it! Now Gerard was excited by the book, it filled him with new life and strength, but later perhaps, defeated by it, unable to write his great 'reply', it might bring him down into humiliation and despair. She might have to witness that. The whole situation was fraught with possibilities of new and awful pain, now that she was no longer young and wanted rest and peace. This wish for peace, she realised, had been wafted to her by Reeve and his children, had come to her at Fettiston, moving towards her, over the moors, out of that quiet well-remembered landscape. She was, she realised, very much looking forward to the cruise! Well, Gerard had given her leave to go. But as she became, if she became, more involved in his work, more necessary, she would increasingly disappoint her newly discovered family, who were kind enough to need her, would be bound to neglect them and hurt their feelings by being seen to be the property of Gerard. But had she not always wanted just that, to be the property of Gerard? I am a wretch, she thought, I am luckier than almost anyone in the world but I have always made myself discontented by an obsession which I ought long ago to have controlled or banished.

Rose had drunk some more whisky and eaten some more of Annushka's rich plum cake. She had begun to feel she would have to sit up all night in a state of painful excitement going over and over these pictures of the recent past and the near future. As, to encourage herself to go to bed at last, she kicked off her shoes and undid her stockings she began to think about Crimond. She had wanted the book to be over, to be an ending, something drifting away at last and taking its author with it. Now of course, if Gerard was right about it, there would be reviews, discussions, controversies, photographs of Crimond in the papers, his voice on radio, his face on television. *Crimond would be famous.* This was something they had not imagined during that long time when the 'surly dog' had been wandering around somewhere outside in the dark. If only she could believe that there was something which would pass, pass away, like the publication date of the book itself. If only she could believe now, as she believed before, even hours ago, that they, she and Gerard, had really finished with Crimond, that he would become a name of someone who had published a book which no one read or noticed. What was now seeping into her troubled consciousness like a dark dye was the thought that Crimond could not thus belong to the past. He belonged, perhaps hugely, like his book, to the future. Gerard had said he had no plans to see Crimond. But in the nature of things, in the nature precisely of his own enterprise, he would have to. They would be drawn together. At some point, surely, he would long to argue with Crimond, to question, to persuade, to try out his own ideas upon so strong an opponent. Perhaps it was even, half-consciously, the prospect of this combat face to face which was making Gerard so excited and so passionate. Or could she believe that Gerard would cool, see the book as ordinary and his own enthusiasm as a passing mania? Did she *want* to believe that Gerard would calm down and lose interest and that all that ardour, that great intent, would come to nothing after all?

Rose found that, as she continued slowly to undress, pulled off her brown corduroy dress and her white blouse, she was breathing deeply, almost sighing. She got into her long night-dress, settling it over her raised arms, seeking comfort in the familiar gesture. So there would be a future Crimond. If Gerard wrote, or even began to write, his book, if Rose was helping him, even if she were in any way, even as she had always been, close to him, she was bound to meet Crimond again. As she felt this she began, with the automatic swiftness of thought, to rewrite in her mind the letter of – what was it – apology, retrieval, reconciliation, which she had written to Crimond when he had just left the house on that amazing day after his proposal of marriage. My dear David, please forgive me for my graceless words. Your disclosure took me by surprise. Let me say now how grateful and how moved I am. I ran after you but you had gone. You said that we should meet again. Please let us do so, let us get to know each other. Perhaps I could love you after all. I am mad, thought Rose. Do I not remember how relieved I was, so soon after, that I had not sent that reckless compromising letter, a letter which, however little it said, would have brought Crimond back to me with every expectation? I would have had to send him away a second time, and how painful and significant that second parting would have been for both of us. Even the existence of that letter in Crimond's hands would have bound me to him in some sort of terrified servitude as if he were to blackmail me with it. How much I would have feared that Gerard might find out that, however briefly, even for seconds, I had felt like that. So, these are the rights over me which I give to Gerard. But supposing . . . *I assumed you to be unattainable, perhaps I was wrong. Rose, don't be angry with me, please forgive me. Love has to be awakened, I want to awaken yours. You are capable of loving me.* If I had written at once, she thought, I could have got him back, I could at least have erased that dreadful impression. By now he will have digested my arrogant words and decided to hate me. What treatment I gave to that proud man, and how I may yet be made by him to suffer for it.

Those thoughts, condensed into a moment of complex vision, flashed in Rose's mind like some terrifying aerial explosion. She said aloud, 'I don't really think this.' She began to carry the remains of the supper into the kitchen, throwing away the fragments on the plates, wrapping up the cheese, putting the cake into one tin and the biscuits into another. She remembered, then felt, her toothache, but it was less acute. She took two more aspirins. She was exhausted, her desire to sit and think all night had left her, she felt now, and was grateful for it, simply the need to become unconscious. She told herself, come back to reality. I did the only right thing, though I did it so ungraciously and badly. The hurt is to my vanity. We shall go on thinking about Jenkin and whether the impossible was possible. Gerard said that they would never be friends – but they are sure to meet, and one day I too shall see Crimond again, and we shall tremble with shock and then be cool and ordinary ever after; and he will never tell, never, even under torture would he tell, not only for his own sake, but for mine. So there is a strange sad bond between us that will always hurt us both.

She thought, I wonder if Gerard meant it about our sharing a house, and if it could ever happen? Somewhere perhaps there really is a house where Gerard and I will live together ever after as brother and sister. Then as she got into bed she began to wonder to herself where that house might be. Perhaps beside the river. She had always wanted to live by the river. She turned out the light and fell asleep and dreamt she was in Venice with Marcus Field.

Gerard, feeling unusually drunk, had decided to walk all the way back from Rose's flat to the Goldhawk Road. The timid rain had ceased, and a fuzzy mad moon had risen. The east wind was moving steadily across London. He had brought no gloves and kept putting his hands into his pockets, finding this uncomfortable and taking them out again. The east wind was jerking his hair about and icily fingering his scalp.

What a state Rose had been in, so unusual, what language she had used, words like 'unbearable'. Had they managed later to sort that out, had they sorted anything out, or just created some sort of superfluous unintelligible confusion? Of course they were friends, their friendship, their bond, was absolute, and she must know that as well as he. Had he somehow done wrong, been lacking in consideration, did she really need reassurance? Perhaps she did, she had less to think about than he had, more time to brood. He felt now that he had given Rose less than she wanted, said less than he was tempted to say, been ungenerous and cautious. Perhaps she had been struck by a difference between the pressing attentions of the Curtland gang and the way in which he, Gerard, 'took her for granted'? 'I've given you my life and you haven't even noticed.' That was a very extreme thing to say. But surely it expressed a mood and not any deep resentment? How could he not take her for granted, was not that in itself a proof of something absolute? How strange, almost embarrassing, that she had actually spoken of needing a 'pact', something like a promise. It only then occurred to him that Rose had been demanding from him exactly what he had demanded from Jenkin! Poor human beings, he thought, always wanting security, but unwilling to provide it! Jenkin had laughed. Rose had laughed too but, as it were, in the wrong place. Why had she laughed so when he suggested sharing a house, and then later said that this was just what she wanted? Rose was usually so rational and calm. Of course she was annoyed about the book, even jealous of it, but that was another thing. Had the bloody Curtlands been getting at her? Gerard recalled the cunning look on Neville's face when he had said they were taking her to Yorkshire. Was that a thrust of some kind, a preliminary to a battle? There could be no battle. Rose belonged to him, she had always done. He was responsible to her and for her. Of course she could tend her Curtlands. But Gerard was her real family, there could be no doubt about *that*! He thought, I'll reassure her, I'll look after her, perhaps I haven't tried enough to make her happy, but I will now.

He was, as he came near to Jenkin's house, beginning to feel very damp and cold. He had, in coming to live in the little house, intended something, perhaps symbolic but also marking some deep change in his mode of existence, some giving up of worldly goods, some kind of liberating simplification. He had indeed sold many of his possessions, while reflecting ironically that it is not exactly asceticism to sell what you have and put the money in the bank. He had lately begun to feel false in Jenkin's house, as if he were playing at something. The neighbours knew it, perhaps the house knew it too. It was not even a part of his mourning, seeming sometimes even a desecration of it. There was a kind of futile unmanageable pain in living with Jenkin's things when Jenkin was dead. He had not intended to speak to Rose of a house, though the idea had been for a short time in his head. Now he began to feel an interest in living, not where he had been before, but not here either. He needed to create some entirely new scene, and he did not have to play at austerity now he had suddenly acquired such an awesomely demanding aim in life. He did not think that he had overestimated Crimond's book, but whether he had or not he now had to write his own. He could now, thanks to Crimond, *see* the book that he had to write. He thought, I may indeed be carried away, but I must try my damnedest to *get it all clear*. As he thought this he suddenly thought of Levquist, of what it had been like to *get clear* some appallingly difficult piece of Greek, and recalled, and felt now in his guts, that almost sexual shudder with which, arriving at Oxford, he had found himself confronted with an impossibly high standard. He recalled too some words of Valéry which Levquist used to quote: a difficulty is a light, an insuperable difficulty is a sun. Well, more often no doubt an insuperable difficulty is an insuperable difficulty. In attempting now to 'answer' Crimond he must be prepared for what he wrote to seem, perhaps even to be, merely a commentary on someone else's book. Perhaps indeed all that awaited him was a long and final failure, a dreary fruitless toil, wasting his energy and his remaining time to produce something that was worthless. The words of Augustine quoted by Father McAlister came back to him: before the countenance of God my soul shrivels like a moth. Perhaps he would have nothing in the end but a broken heart, not even contrite!

As he reached the little house it was beginning to rain again, and as he pressed the key into the lock he experienced a feeling of intrusion, as of making an unexpected and perhaps unwelcome visit. The house was extremely cold. Jenkin had never entertained the idea of central heating. Gerard turned on the lights and pulled the velveteen curtains and lit the gas fire in the sitting room. He decided he was still hungry, he had been too excited to eat properly with Rose, too anxious to tell her of something great. Of course he had quite failed to convey the book, how right it is, how wrong it is. He thought, it's right because it's about suffering, it's wrong because it's about being *true* to a *future good* society. That's the main idea, what the book depends on really – but there's no such thing. Truth can't reach out into the future in that way, as Rose said, we can't imagine the future – and there can never be a perfectly good society – there can only be a decent society, and that depends on freedom and order and circumstances and an endless tinkering which can't be programmed from a distance. It's all accidental, but the values are absolute. That's the simple point about human life with the long explanation.

575

Suppose Rose's 'cold water' were just the beginning of a general dismissal of Crimond's book? Of course nothing that happened to *that* book could affect *his*. But Gerard realised that though he would be annoyed if Crimond got only good reviews he would be dismayed if he got only bad ones! He went out to the kitchen and poured a tin of soup into a saucepan. He found some sliced bread and buttered it while the soup was heating, then brought soup and bread back into the sitting room where Crimond's galley proofs were piled high on the sideboard guarded by the Staffordshire dogs. He put the plate and the mug of soup on the green tiles by the fire, and as he turned to close the door he saw some letters lying on the mat in the hall. He recognised Duncan's writing. He brought the letters in, tearing open Duncan's envelope.

My dear Gerard,

You will have seen Levquist's obituary in the Times. *Whoever wrote it didn't praise him enough. That kind of greatness is not the fashion these days I daresay! I felt extraordinarily sad and felt I must write to you. I know you saw him at that terrible dance last summer, and maybe you have seen him since. He was a kind of saint of scholarship, a special kind of example. Perhaps his life ending made me wonder what I've made of mine. What a mess it's all been, and how short the business is really, a topic I've heard you mention. I conclude that what really matters is friendship, not that overrated love business, but one's close friends, the really close people who are one's comforters and one's judges. You have always been both to me. May I express the hope that, in all the recent shambles, we haven't lost each other. It seems, here, infinitely far from London. We have bought a house, but address at present is this hotel. I hope you are writing something. I've given up thought.*

Yours
    Duncan

Gerard had not seen the *Times* obituary. So Levquist was gone. He recalled the long room, the big desk covered with books, the window open to the summer night, Levquist's great grotesque beautiful head, Levquist saying 'Come again, come and see the old man.' He had not been again. He had never kissed Levquist's hands and said he loved him. Levquist saying, 'I saw young Riderhood. He was quite stumped by that piece of Thucydides!' 'Oh God, oh *God*,' said Gerard aloud, and sat down in one of the uncomfortable chairs by the fire and hid his face in his hands. A cloud, a *presence*, of dark unhappiness was suddenly beside him. That was the night when his father died. Levquist, who had also been his father, was dead too. And Jenkin was dead; and the presence in the room was that of Jenkin, Jenkin sad, Jenkin as sadness, Jenkin as incurable torturing grief. Why did you have to die, when I loved you so? Gerard said to Jenkin. And it was terrible, terrible to him, as if the shade of Jenkin were weeping and holding out its strengthless hands. It wasn't my fault, said Gerard to the shade, forgive me, forgive me, I am bereaved, I am punished, I am poisoned. Why are you weeping these awful tears? Is it because you were murdered and I have befriended your murderer? Oh Jenkin, how can we have so lost each other, how can we be so changed, you an accuser and I paralysed by a poisonous drug!

Gerard stood up and actually looked around the room, searching for something, some *little* thing, for that was what the awful accusing shade had now become, something like a little box or a black mechanical toy. There was nothing but the room itself, awkward and graceless and accidental and empty. With a sudden gesture Gerard hit the pile of neatly stacked proofs knocking them onto the floor. As they fell they took one of the Staffordshire dogs with them. The dog was broken. Gerard picked up the pieces and put them on the sideboard.

He thought, I'm poisoned all right, I'm haunted, I'm cursed, I'm mad. The destruction of the dog had brought tears to his eyes at last. How can I write this book, he thought, when I can't help thinking that Jenkin was murdered? What do Crimond's thoughts matter? Why did I talk to Rose about a house or being together? Let her go to Yorkshire. I'm under a curse, I'm condemned to a haunted solitude. Crimond's book made me feel I had some thoughts, but it was an illusion. Levquist said I had no hard core, Crimond said anything I wrote would be beautified and untrue, Rose said it was vanity. I haven't got the *energy* to write a long book. I see now it's *not*

577

important. I'll get out of here though. I don't want company any more, whether it's humans or ghosts. Oh God, I'm getting old. I've never felt this before. I'm *old*.

He picked up the plate and the mug from the tiles beside the fire and took them back to the kitchen. He put on the kettle for his hot water bottle. He had forgotten to switch on the electric fire in the bedroom and the room was icy. He switched it on and pulled the curtains. The wind, now filled with rain, was lashing at the window panes which were rattling and admitting cold streams of air which were agitating the curtains. He said to himself, of course I'm drunk, but that's how it is. The curse I'm under is the one we're all under. The Oxford colleges and Big Ben can't buy us off now. The time when we could talk on this planet of controlling our destinies is finished for good – the short short time. Rose is right, it's no use trying to *think* any more. The party's over. *Après nous le déluge*.

The kettle boiled and he filled the bottle and put it in the bed which seemed to be inhabited by some cold damp fungus. He took his pyjamas and went back to the sitting room to undress before the fire. Crimond's galley proofs were all over the floor and he thrust them into a heap with his foot. He took off his tie which he had put on hours ago to go to the Fairfaxs' party, where he knew he would see Rose, and where he had arrived late because he had been unable to tear himself away from that damnable book.

As he unbuttoned his shirt he saw Duncan's letter open upon the chair. He would reply of course, but he felt no urgent desire to see Duncan. Later perhaps. I feel *discredited*, he thought, these deaths have knocked the stuffing out of me. I'd be *ashamed* before Duncan. It's all right for *him* to have a woman and a house. Duncan could manage his life, even his bad luck, he was never 'high-minded', like Jenkin, like Gerard, like Crimond. Gerard remembered that he had used that term to Rose to describe Crimond's book. But Jenkin's high-mindedness was not like Gerard's or like Crimond's. Gerard recalled how Levquist had snubbed him when he had suggested that Jenkin hadn't 'got anywhere'. 'Riderhood doesn't need to get anywhere. He walks the path, he exists where he is. Whereas you –' Yes, thought Gerard, Jenkin always walked the path, with others, wholly engaged in wherever he happened to be, fully existing, fully real at every point, looking about him with friendly curiosity. Whereas I have always felt reality was elsewhere, exalted and indifferent and alone, upon some misty mountain peak which I, among the very few, could actually see, though of course never reach, and whose magnetism thrilled in my bowels (that was Levquist's phrase) while I enjoyed my superior vision, my consciousness of height and distance, the gulf below, the height above, and a sense of pleasurable unworthiness shared only by the elect – self-satisfied Platonism, Augustinian masochism, Levquist called it. Why didn't I go back and see him and talk about all that, I could have gone any time. Now I feel, I *feel* at last alone – and the mountain and the mountain peak, that hanging on, that looking up, was it all an illusion? Can I live without thinking of myself, and of *it*, in just that way? Perhaps it was the loss of *it* which I felt just now when I realised how poisoned I am by that murderous doubt, when I thought it's too high, it's too far. Just when I meet with the insuperable difficulty which I've so much desired I find I have no strength left. I shall shrink and shrink and creep into a crevice. What I thought was the top of the mountain was a false summit after all – the summit is far higher up and hidden in cloud and as far as I'm concerned it might as well not exist, my endurance is at an end.

He thought, I'll go right away and hide somewhere. I'll buy a flat and lock it up and *go*. I won't tell anyone where I am. Who cares anyway, except Rose, and she's got her own family now. What a lot of nonsense I talked to her tonight, it was probably the drink, I'm not used to it. I'll tell her not to tell anyone I had that daft idea. Well, she won't tell anyone, she wants it to go away, she probably knows it's bound to. How I wish I could talk to Jenkin. Perhaps this visitation of awfulness is really knowing at last that Jenkin is dead and *isn't anywhere*. He put Duncan's letter back in its envelope and put it on the mantelpiece, and began to glance at the other letters which he had dropped on the floor. There were two letters for Jenkin. There had been many of those to begin with, now there were fewer. These two were advertisements and he put them in the wastepaper basket. One was the gas bill which he put in his pocket. Then he suddenly felt something like a massive electric shock, a jolt, which for a moment he could not account for and imagined he had actually been touched by some stray wire which had sent a current through him. Or perhaps he was ill, something had given way in his brain. He found he was looking down at the last of the letters which was lying on the floor at his feet. It was the writing on the envelope which, darting its message into his unconscious mind, had produced this strange shock, and even now, after Gerard had realised that this writing was portentous, perhaps terrible, he did not immediately recognise whose writing it was. Handwriting can tell a tale of joy or of fear well before it is connected with a name. It was Crimond's writing. It was many years since Gerard had received a letter from Crimond, but the script somehow, like a sinister hieroglyph revealed by torchlight in a tomb, took him back many more years, to Oxford, to something, some event, some feeling, too deep now to be uncovered, far away in the dark depths of his mind, and from which the frightening portent derived its original power. Even as Gerard was returned to his present self he felt a sick terror at the sight, a disgusted loathing, and was tempted to tear the unopened letter up into small pieces. He even turned his back upon it and went out to tidy the kitchen, to wash his mug and plate under the hot tap and turn off the light. Then he returned to the sitting room and picked up the letter and opened it. At any rate it was not a long letter. It consisted of only one line. *It was an accident. D.*

Gerard now took another interval. He went out into the hall, he even opened the front door and found that the rain was less, the wind as ill-tempered as ever. He closed the front door and instinctively bolted it, though he did not always do this. Then he returned to the sitting room and sat down beside the fire and read the note again several times. He sat very quiet while a storm of mixed emotions filled his head, then flew round his head, then filled the room as if with a mass of dark silent swift birds. Human thought is easily able to break the rules of logic and physics, and at that moment Gerard was able to think and feel a very large number of vivid, even clear, things at the same time. He thought chiefly about Jenkin, Jenkin's death and the accident which had caused it, and this presented itself as a topic which he could now discuss with Jenkin. At any rate, as he put it to himself, now Jenkin doesn't have to be a ghost, he can be himself, only in the past. His being remains absolute. He didn't suffer, Gerard thought, I can really say this to myself now, it was sudden, he didn't know. Gerard had been unable to look at the brief newspaper reports which described a freak mishap, but he had received an impression from hearing people talk. He felt now no urge to go further than that impression. I won't ever ask him, he thought (meaning Crimond), I don't want to know exactly what happened, because it doesn't matter now. At no point did it occur to Gerard to doubt that Crimond's sentence told the truth. To doubt it would have been to consent to soul-destroying madness, the whole of the rational world cohered with Crimond's truth-telling. He could not write such a letter and it not be true. As Gerard took all this in he not only felt the *energy* which had seemed to forsake him flooding back in great calm generous waves, he also felt as if, in some way he could not yet master, the whole world had pivoted around him, being the same yet offering him all sorts of different views and angles. As he began to consider these Gerard rose and collected up the scattered sheets of Crimond's book and replaced them in a neat pile on the sideboard. He walked to and fro across the little room, and it was as if the dark bird-thoughts which had been tearing round and round like swifts had begun to settle quietly on the furniture and regard him with their bright eyes.

He sat once more and looked at the note. It was evident that Crimond had been deeply disturbed, perhaps tormented, by wondering what Gerard was thinking about his friend's death. He had *had* to remove that terrible image from Gerard's mind. He had, equally, had no doubt that Gerard would believe him.

It had evidently taken him some time to decide to write however. Perhaps he felt an interval was necessary, perhaps he had been unable to decide what exactly to say. He got it right, thought Gerard. The signature too was significant. Not C. or D.C. but D. Gerard allowed himself to be moved by this and stowed it away in his mind for later inspection. He was now able too, for the first time, to pity Crimond for the terrible thing which he had unwittingly done, and must live with ever after. At least Crimond, by writing to him, had liberated himself from one extra horror, and with that had, and much more, liberated Gerard. The liberation was something huge, but also painful, bringing back in a purer and sadder form his mourning and his loss. Here there recurred in his mind the idea, which had so much tormented him, that, perhaps in a remote past, Crimond and Jenkin had known each other better than he had ever suspected. But this speculation was now to be seen as idle and empty, it had gained its poisonous force from that other poison, which was at last utterly gone from him.

Gerard took off his shirt and trousers and gradually enclosed himself in his pyjamas. There was also the question of how to reply to the missive. That would require some reflection. Crimond would have mitigated his distress by sending it. But he would also expect an acknowledgement. An interval would be necessary, then an equally brief note. I'll think about that tomorrow, thought Gerard. And he said to himself, of course I *will* write that book, I was pretending something to myself when I imagined I wouldn't, I was sick then, I've *got* to write it. Of course I'll be fighting not only against those insuperable difficulties, but also against time. Even to get to the *start* will be a long struggle. But I'll do it, I mean I'll attempt it with all my heart. I'll do it for Jenkin, now things are clear between us, I can say that too. Christ, how I shall miss him as I go on alone upon that way. I'll start reading Crimond's book again tomorrow and I'll remember all the things Rose said about my being 'bowled over' and 'carried away' and how if I hadn't known the author I wouldn't have noticed the book. I don't think she's right, but even if she is a bit right it won't matter now, because I see what *I* have to do, what *my* job is. And that's certainly thanks to Crimond.

As he sat on his bed he thought too, and the thought was disturbing: one day I shall see Crimond again. Certainly not soon. There is a strict decorum which must be kept between us. There is Jenkin's death, of which we will not speak, and there is the book. *Of course* I shall want to talk to Crimond about the book, and what I have to say will interest him too. Or will he have forgotten the book, even rejected it? People who write long learned remarkable books sometimes reject them, do not want to discuss them or even hear them mentioned, not necessarily because they now think them no good, but just because quite other matters now obsess them. Crimond is certainly capable, as I said to Rose, of writing another long book to refute this one, or of writing equally passionately, equally learnedly, upon some totally other subject! Still, I shall see him again, some time – and when that time comes he will expect me.

He thought, I'll look after Rose too, I won't let her drift away into Curtland land, I'll make her happy. Rose is happiness – only it's never worked out like that. I can't do without her. He got into bed and turned out the light. He thrust his feet and the hot water bottle down into the icy nether regions of the bed. The wind was blowing in gusts and tossing the drops of rain like little weak pebbles onto the glass. In the dark, as sadness swept over him again, he began to think about his father, and what a gentle, kind, patient, good man he had been, and how he had given way, out of love, to his wife, sacrificing not only his wishes but sometimes even his principles. All that must have caused pain, and his children too, never quite in tune with him, must have grieved him as the years went by. I didn't try enough, thought Gerard, I didn't visit him enough or ask him to stay, I never seemed to have time for him. I should have made him a part of my life. And my mother – but he could not see his mother, that sad shade signalled to him in vain. He thought, they are dead, my father, my Sinclair, my Jenkin, my Levquist, all dead. And then it occurred to him for the very first time to wonder if, really and truly, Grey were dead too. Parrots live longer than we do, and Grey was a young bird then. But parrots in cages are helpless, they depend on the kindness of humans, and there are other ways they can die before they are old, by neglect, by illness, they can be forgotten in empty houses, they can starve. The thought that Grey might have starved to death was so terrible to Gerard that he suddenly sat bolt upright, and there flowed into him, as into a clear vessel, a sudden sense of all the agony and helpless suffering of created things. He felt the planet turning, and felt its pain, oh the planet, oh the poor poor planet. He lay back, turning on his side and burying his face in the pillow. He let the moment pass. He thought, I've got to go on, or rather, if I can, *up*, because I'm not going to abandon my life-image, not for Levquist, not even for Jenkin. *It is* up there, solemn and changeless and alone, indifferent and pure, and, yes, I feel its magnetism more strongly at this moment, perhaps, than ever before, and, yes, there is an awful pleasure in that sense of distance, of how high and unattainable it is, how alien, how separated from my corrupt being. I shrivel before it, not as before the face of a person, but as in an indifferent flame. I have seen the false summit, and now as the terrain changes I glimpse more terrible cliffs and peaks far far above again. Yes, I'll attempt the book, but it's a life sentence, and not only may it be no good, but I may never know whether it is or not. Thoughts at peace: could thoughts ever be at peace again? This was the moment before the beginning. Tomorrow, he thought, he would have to begin, to start his pilgrimage toward where Jenkin had once spoken of being, out on the edge of things. Yes, beyond that nearer ridge there was no track, only a sheer cliff going upward, and as he gazed upon that vertical ascent Gerard paled as before a scaffold.

He thought to himself now, I'll never get to sleep. I'd better get up and do something. I wonder if I could mend that Staffordshire dog? It's not too badly broken. But he was already drowsy and beginning to dream. He fell asleep and dreamt that he was standing on that mountainside holding an open book upon whose pages was written *Dominus Illuminatio Mea* – and from far far above an angel was descending in the form of a great grey parrot with loving clever eyes and the parrot perched upon the book and spread out its grey and scarlet wings and the parrot was the book.

Lily Boyne was walking, with slow haste, along a shabby decrepit street in South London. Her haste was slow because her heart was beating violently and her mouth was open and she was panting with emotion and felt as if she might soon faint or at least have to sit down. Only there was nowhere to sit except on the kerb. She was anxious to arrive, yet afraid of arriving. Although she so much looked forward, she wished it was over and she was going home. When she went home would she be going in one piece or mangled? Was she sane now and would be mad later, or mad now and would be sane later? Or had madness entirely taken her over?

Lily was going to see Crimond. She had not seen him or sent him any communication since the awful occasion of the midsummer ball. The baneful memory of that night haunted her, sometimes tormented her, although she did not really imagine that, for her, it could have been different. Well, perhaps she did imagine a little, could not altogether banish beautiful painful fantasies of how on that evening Crimond could at last have 'found himself' in realising how much he cared for her. She had felt, still a little felt, with a kind of pride and a kind of terror, that it was 'all her fault', because it was she who had brought Jean and Crimond together. If she had not told him of the dance he would not have manifested himself in that kilt, radiant with godlike power. Although she had told no one about her own crucial role in that drama, she could not help feeling that someone or something would punish her for it – perhaps fate, perhaps Crimond. Yet also it was a bond, she had played the part of Love's messenger, and it was not because of her that Love had been, so mysteriously, vanquished. One of her present terrors, as she walked along the ragged street, was that Crimond might think that she had come to *sympathise* with him! This idea made her feel ready to destroy herself. In fact she knew nothing, and it seemed that nobody knew anything, about the reasons for Jean and

Crimond's second parting. The fact was that Crimond was once more alone, and no woman had yet enabled him to 'find himself'. Of that Lily felt sure. She was going to see him because she had to.

As she neared the house and her knees were as water she began to ask herself again (for she had gone over it in detail many times during the last weeks) whether in spite of her intuitions she might be entirely wrong about Crimond, and have been wrong all along? Her impression of him as solitary could be entirely accidental and fallacious. Perhaps the 'Jean business', about which Gerard and company were so solemn, was just one of an endless stream of adventures? Suppose a woman were even now in possession, in the house, ready to open the door to Lily and sneer at her? It seemed madness to make this gratuitous unheralded excursion which could end with some new and more awful humiliation by which she would be scarred forever. But there was upon her a fiercer and more awful imperative, issuing from the depths of her prescient and frightened soul. She might regret having come, but would surely much more terribly regret not having come.

The sun was shining and, even in this cluttered and ramshackle part of London, there was the sense of a spring day. Windows which had long been closed were open and people, hatless and gloveless, had put on lighter and brighter clothes. In tiny front gardens bushes were budding and grass actually beginning to grow. There were, here and there, trees, slightly hazy with green, which shed an aura, even a fragrance of new life. A fresh cold sunny light announced the start of the long English spring. Of course Lily had given careful thought to what she was to wear. She had considered and rejected various smartish but simple dresses, even the black and white one with the velvet collar which was so subtly becoming. She decided on dark brown, very narrow, trousers, of unobtrusively expensive tweed, with a lighter brown leather jacket and a blue cotton shirt and a silk scarf with a blue and pink abstract design. In spite of attempts to put on weight, she was as thin as ever, her face that morning, as she put on discreet make-up, looking almost gaunt, the tendons of her long neck sturdily in view, her collar bones protruding under the soft cotton of the shirt. Her melted-sugar eyes were clear and bright, but the wrinkles increasingly massed round them collected the face powder conspicuously onto their ridges. Her thin lips, without lipstick, were almost invisible, her mouth a slit. She had unwisely washed her scanty unconvincing hair the previous night, and it was now, however much she combed it down and tucked it in behind her ears, standing up on end in dry senseless wisps. She had given up the much-advertised hair oil. She had wrapped the silk scarf carefully round her neck and that at least stayed in place. Over this gear she had put on her long green coat, and her trousers were tucked into black boots.

At last Crimond's house was near, then in view, and Lily hurried her pace so as to preclude any sickening last-minute hesitation. She mounted the stone steps. The big door, which looked like a modern painting, patchily coloured and scribbled over with cracks, was closed. Lily tried it. It was not locked and she entered into the familiar shabby hallway, dark and smelling of old dirt and neglect. She paused in the darkness, blinded after the hard clear sunlight, and inhaled the atmosphere of silence and anticipation and fear which she knew so well. She listened. She thought, he's out, he's moved. She stepped forward and tripped against the bicycle and stood still again after the sound. She opened the door leading to the basement and tiptoed down the stairs. Here she listened again. Silence. She turned the handle noiselessly and slowly opened the door a little and looked through the opening into the Playroom.

She saw, as in a familiar picture, the familiar scene, the murky room, the lighted lamp, the figure at the desk writing. It was like a dream, indeed she had often dreamt it. The window onto the area, untouched by the sun's rays, gave near the door a little dead illumination, but the other end of the room was dark except for the lamp. Crimond, his head bowed, unaware of his visitor, continued to write, and Lily inserted herself quietly into the room and sat down on a chair near the door. She breathed deeply, hoping that she was recovering and not becoming more unnerved. There was for a moment a trance-like peace as if she had been granted a timeless vision, a scene transfigured by a ray from beyond, falling upon it accidentally like the shadow of an aeroplane upon a landscape.

Suddenly Crimond lifted his head and stared down the room. He said in a sharp tone, 'Who's that?'

Lily thought, he thinks it's Jean. She said, 'It's Lily.'

Crimond stared a moment, then lowered his head again and continued to write.

Lily came slowly forward carrying her chair. She set it down, not up against the desk, but a little way in front of it, as if she were a candidate about to be interviewed. She took off her coat and sat down. She noticed that the target, which had been on the wall behind Crimond, was gone. She waited.

After about two minutes Crimond looked up again. He was wearing rather thicker glasses of a different rounder shape with dark rims which altered his appearance. He took off the glasses and looked at Lily. 'Well?'

'Forgive me,' said Lily. 'I just wanted to see you.'

'What about?'

Lily was ready for this question. 'I just wondered if I could do any typing for you. Someone said you had nearly finished your book.' In fact Lily knew quite well that the book was finished, as Gulliver had told her some time ago.

'Thank you,' said Crimond, 'the book has been typed. I don't need any assistance.' However he did not seem to expect her to go, but continued to stare at her. He waited for her to speak again.

'So it's finished?' said Lily.

'Yes.'

'So what are you writing now?'

'Another book.'

'Is it like the first one, a sequel?'

'No. It's quite different.'

'What's it about?'

Crimond did not answer this question. He rubbed his long nose where the new spectacles had made a red line on the bridge. Then, not looking at her, he busied himself cleaning the spectacles with a handkerchief, then refilling his fountain pen at an ink pot and wiping it on a piece of blotting paper. She thought, feeling a little calmer now, that he looked older, his pale face a little puffy, his faded red hair a little thinner.

Lily said, 'What else are you doing?'

'Learning Arabic.'

'Why Arabic?'

'Why not.'

'So that's what *that* is. I thought it was shorthand.' Some handwriting at the edge of the desk had caught her eye. She moved her chair forward.

Crimond, who had given her his attention for a moment, was now looking down at the loose-leaf book in which he had been writing when she came in. The Arabic was in an open exercise book. Lily peered at it. 'Did you write this?'

'Yes.'

'Is it difficult?'

'Yes.'

There was a moment's silence. Crimond then said, 'As we have nothing more to discuss, and I am very busy, perhaps you could go away.'

Lily suddenly blushed. She could feel the blush running up her long neck and through her cheeks to her brow. She felt that she must now say something striking or be banished forever. It was like the moment in the fairy tale when one must answer the riddle or die. Unfortunately Lily could not think of anything striking. She said lamely, 'I very much want to help you.'

'I need no help, thank you.'

'I could help you in your political work –'

'No.'

'I could type, I could run errands, I could fetch books, I could do anything.'

'No.'

'I know you're a lion and I'm a mouse, but a mouse could help a lion. There's a story of a lion who's kind to a mouse, and the mouse says I'll help you one day, and the lion laughs and then the lion is caught in a trap and the mouse gnaws through all the ropes and sets him free.'

This little speech at last showed some sign of amusing Crimond and attracting his attention. He said, but unsmiling, 'I don't like mice.'

'Then I'll be anything you like,' said Lily. 'That's what I came to tell you. I love you. I've always loved you. I know I'm a little worthless person, but I want to be in your life. For all I know you have hundreds of Lilies, little people who want to serve you, all right, but I'm me, and I exist for you and I know that I do. I told you about that dance last year. Whatever happened you know I meant well. I feel I'm a sort of messenger in your life. After all I've known you a long time. I'd do anything you wanted, I'd be your slave, I want to give myself to you as a total present, I don't care what might happen, all I want is to know that you accept me as someone you could rely on for ever and use in any way you pleased. I feel this as a vocation, as if I'd been told by God, you are an absolute for me, I can't do anything but give myself. If you can only accept me I'll be silent, I'll be invisible, I'll be as quiet as a mouse – sorry, you don't like mice – but I just want to be *there*, like something in the corner of the room, waiting for anything that you want me for –'

Crimond, who had been listening to this with a slight frown, holding his spectacles against his lips, said, 'I don't like this stuff about little people and your being a little worthless person. You are a person, not a little person. I don't like that terminology.'

Crimond seemed to be making a general point, and nothing to do with her personally, but she said eagerly, 'I'm glad you don't think I'm worthless – I'd study, you could teach me –'

'Oh Lily, just get back to reality, will you.'

'You are my reality.'

'You know you're talking idle nonsense, just something that you want to get off your chest even if it makes no sense. Now you've said it perhaps you'll kindly go away.'

'I can't go away,' said Lily. She had been talking fast and eagerly, but calmly. Now her voice sounded in her ears with that dreadful hysterical edge to it. 'I won't go away. I'm sure you have some special feeling about me. You must be kind to me. Can't you even be kind when I love you so much? How can there be so much love and it simply go to waste? I must have something from you, like a pact, a kind of status, anything, even a very very small thing, which is between us for always.'

Crimond, his gaze straying from her as if wearily, gave a sigh. 'Lily, I can't attach any sense to what you ask. You speak as if I could easily give you something very valuable –'

'Yes, yes, easily, you could, you could!'

'But I haven't got this thing, this special feeling, I don't want you as a slave –'

'Then I wouldn't be –'

'Or an invisible object in the corner of the room, or a mouse, I don't *like* things like that, I couldn't have such a person near me, and I can't give you any sort of "status" as you put it, I just don't have any special feeling for you or any special role for you – I'm sorry.'

Lily, controlling tears, got hold of her coat which had been lying on the floor and pulled it up onto her knees. 'All right. I understand. I'm sorry. I *had* to see you and I *had* to say what I've said.'

'Now do get back into real life. What are you doing now in the real world?'

'I'm getting married. To Gulliver Ashe. Tomorrow.'

Crimond did then actually smile, in fact he laughed. 'Oh Lily, Lily – so you were ready to run even from under the wedding crown?'

'Yes.'

'Or would I have had to put up with a married slave?'

'No, no – if you'd wanted me none of that would have happened, none of that would have existed.'

'Oh you silly – silly – girl.'

Lily smiled through tears then dashed the tears away and stood up and put on her coat. She said, 'I can see you though, sometimes in the future, call in, you won't say never?'

'Not never, but I've got nothing for you.'

'Then I'll come for nothing.'

'For Christ's sake, Lily,' said Crimond, 'just clear off and be *happy*, can't you, and make someone else happy, and forget all this dream stuff. Go on, go away, get out and be happy!'

'Rose and Gerard have invited us to dinner, for after when they came back from Venice,' said Lily.

'At their new house?' said Gulliver.

'No, silly, they've only just bought it, at Rose's place.' Rose and Gerard had bought a house in Hammersmith near the river.

'I thought Gerard would never stick it out in Jenkin's foxhole,' said Gull, 'it's definitely not his scene.'

'What about our scene?' said Lily. 'I think we should buy a house soon, a nice small one in Putney or somewhere, with a garden. The children will like that.'

'The *children*?!'

'Now you've got a job and I've got a project we can afford it. I believe I've still got some of that old money left too, God knows what happened to most of it.'

'Let's not be in a hurry,' said Gulliver. 'I like it here. And we aren't even married yet!'

'We will be this time tomorrow!' It was evening, late evening, of the day of Lily's visit to Crimond, and Gull and Lily were still sitting at the table after a lengthy celebration dinner including numerous toasts in vodka, wine and later cherry brandy, wishing themselves happiness and success in the future. They were both drunk but feeling exceptionally alert, clear-headed, argumentative and witty.

'We will be,' said Gulliver, 'unless one of us funks it – or both of us!'

'Running away from under the wedding crown.'

'That's a phrase out of Dostoevsky,' said Gull, 'I thought you hadn't read him.'

'Oh. I thought it was just a general expression. I heard it somewhere.'

'Well, *I* won't run away!' said Gulliver. 'Look, here's the ring!' He showed Lily the golden ring nestling in its little furry velvet box. He also, in an instant, pictured the dreadful goings-on in that Dostoevsky novel. What a business it was to deal with women. One just had to take the risk.

'You've told Leonard what to do?' Leonard Fairfax was to be best man, and Angela Parke, Lily's old art school friend, was to be bridesmaid.

'At a registry office, there's nothing to it!' said Gull. 'I'll give Leonard the ring so he can give it me back at the crucial moment. I bet most people don't bother even with that. Anyway, you've done it before!'

'Yes but – there wasn't a ring – I can't remember –' Lily had refused to wear a wedding ring. It seemed incredible now that she had once been married. Gulliver didn't want to hear about her shadowy husband, and she could not now remember his face – poor James, oh poor James. 'I do like a bit of ritual.'

'It'll all be over in four minutes.'

'My God. Then we'll be stuck for life!'

'I certainly hope so. Maybe we can arrange a match between Leonard and Angela?'

'I doubt it,' said Lily. 'Angela's older than me and she's got fat. Anyway Leonard seems to be getting off with Gillian Curtland. Now *she's* an eligible girl.'

'She's awfully pretty,' said Gulliver, quickly banishing the image of that eligible nineteen-year-old.

'I still can't decide what to wear.'

'I'm going to wear my pale grey check suit with the pale pink over-check. You won't wear trousers, will you, please?'

'Of course not. I think I'll wear that black and white dress with the velvet collar.'

'So we just invite Angela and Leonard back here afterwards? It's almost a clandestine wedding! I forgot to tell you I saw Tamar round at Leonard's place. Conrad Lomas was there and that trendy priest from Boyars.'

'All religion did for her was get rid of her mother.'

'I don't know,' said Gull, 'I think it was something deep.

Anyway she and the priest were having a jolly good laugh together! And Violet's rumoured to be happy.'

'That's impossible, she can't be happy.'

'Well cheerful or gleeful or something. Pat and Gideon don't know what to do with her, Leonard says she's eating them!'

'They're not edible,' said Lily, 'not like Tamar was. Gideon will pension her off.'

'I say, look at us, we're gossiping about our friends just like in real life.'

'Are they our friends, have we friends?'

'Yes, and we'll have lots of new ones too, and we'll invite them to dinner, just like ordinary real people do!'

'But do we want to be ordinary real people?'

'Are we capable of it?'

They both looked doubtful.

'I wonder if Gideon will invest in our Box Shop?' said Lily.

Lily and Angela Parke had decided to set up a shop, well to begin with a stall, selling matchboxes. It had been Angela's idea, though Lily had supplied the managerial enthusiasm and financial backing. It was, according to Lily, bound to succeed. Every tourist will buy a pretty matchbox, the cheapest and most picturesquely 'typical' of all gift souvenirs. From matchboxes the idea spread to other boxes, hand-painted wooden boxes in the Russian style, carved boxes with Celtic designs, boxes charmingly decorated with images and designs stolen from museums and art galleries all over London, attractive arty stuff not pretentious and not kitsch. Angela was sure she could collect together a lot of unemployed talents. 'Art students aren't all grand,' she said, 'they don't all think it's beneath their genius to make pretty things!'

'I hope so!' said Gulliver in answer to Lily's question. He had not yet met the formidable Angela Parke, and he feared that 'the project' would simply swallow up the rest of Lily's money. As soon as they were married he would see Lily's accountant, he would 'go into the matter' and if necessary 'put his foot down'. After all, he had to play the husband! 'I look forward to meeting Angela!'

'Yes, and I'll meet your miracle-working Newcastle friend, Mr Justin Byng!'

This was a young American stage-designer who had promised Gulliver a job in a stage design studio he was hoping to set up in London, where Gulliver was to be his secretary and guide to the London theatre. 'You still haven't told me how you met him,' said Lily, 'or what really happened in Newcastle. We've been in such a state since you came back.'

This was a moment which Gulliver had been putting off. He was suddenly full, choked, with all the fears which the excitement of his new relation with Lily, much of which had taken place in bed, had temporarily eclipsed. Lily would lose her money, Gulliver would lose his job, he was tomorrow to *take on* a wife whom he would have to *provide for*; and there was now the more immediate anxiety about how Lily would receive what he was about to tell her.

'Lily, I've got to tell you something. I never went to Newcastle.'

'*What?*'

'I didn't get farther than King's Cross station.'

'Then *where were you* all that time?'

'To begin with in a cheap hotel near King's Cross, and then – staying with Justin Byng.'

'Oh *God*,' said Lily, '*that's* started already!' She got up from the table and marched to the mantelpiece where she picked up a jade tortoise, considered throwing it across the room and decided not to. Gull was looking so attractive tonight, recent events had improved, even beautified him. He was wearing his pale brown corduroy trousers, resplendently cleaned after the skating disaster, with a new aquamarine sweater from Simpson's, and new dark brown leather boots.

'Don't be so bloody,' said Gull, 'nothing's started! Justin lives with a beautiful girl from Michigan who's married to him! He took me in out of kindness and because he wanted to work with me. And I didn't tell you sooner because I wanted to be sure it was all real and I really had a job.'

'All right, go on, tell me, and tell me *everything*.'

'A most extraordinary thing – well, an odd thing –

happened to me at King's Cross station. I know this is absurd, but this is how it is. I found a snail.'

'A *snail?*'

'Yes. Wasn't it peculiar? Well, I suppose snails are everywhere but one doesn't expect to find one in a London main-line station.'

'Good heavens! Go on.'

'I was just checking the trains to Newcastle and I saw this thing on the ground, it was rolling about, someone must have kicked it, I didn't know what it was, I thought it was something quite peculiar, I picked it up. Of course the little fellow was well back inside his shell, but I assumed he was alive and I sat down with him on a seat, and sure enough after I'd been holding him in my hand for a moment he came right out and unrolled his eyes and started waving his front part about and I put him on the back of my hand and he walked and – do you know – he *looked* at me.'

'Oh Lord!' said Lily.

'What's the matter? Anyway I didn't know what to do with him. I couldn't just leave him there, or keep him in my room at the hotel and take him with me to Newcastle, and as I'd developed this sort of personal relationship with him I felt I had to look after him properly. I'm sorry, this sounds daft –'

'It doesn't,' said Lily.

'So I set out with my snail, I felt by then he was my snail, to find somewhere safe to put him. But, honestly, round about King's Cross –'

'I can imagine.'

'I walked about a lot of streets looking for a decent park or garden but I couldn't find one. So I went back to the station and took the tube to Hyde Park Corner.'

'Well done.'

'I put the snail inside my handkerchief in my trouser pocket and I kept my hand over him all the time, fortunately the train wasn't crowded. Anyway I set off into the park – but you know, even there, at that end of the park it's all great vistas of trees and grass and I couldn't just put him down in the open

597

where a blackbird might scoff him, so – I was pretty obsessed by this time – I went on walking until I came into Kensington Gardens. I knew it was no good in the flower-beds where he'd be unpopular with gardeners. I thought of the Peter Pan area but of course lots of people come there to feed the ducks and there are a lot of birds about. So I fixed on a place beside the Serpentine, nearer the bridge, you know, where there's a low railing, and I got over the railing and started looking about to find a really bushy place to hide him. Well, while I was ferreting about among the shrubs, holding the dear old snail in my hand, a tall chap stopped on the path and started watching me, he couldn't think what on earth I was doing. Then he got over the railing and came down and asked me. And then, there was really no other way of explaining it, I told him the whole story. And do you know, he was so nice, he was so amused and quite delighted, he said he cared about little animals too. Then he helped me to find the absolutely ideal spot and we left the snail there with our best wishes and went back to the path and began to walk toward the bridge.'

'That was Justin Byng.'

'Yes. I'd told him I was just going to Newcastle to look for a job and he asked what sort of job and did I know anybody there and where was I living now and lots more questions, and then we went and had a drink at the Serpentine restaurant, and then we had lunch and he told me the story of his life and I told him a lot of mine, and then he insisted I forget about going north and get out of my mouldy lodgings and come and stay with him and Martha while we discussed the job –'

'And one day you suddenly turned up here and said you'd been in Newcastle!'

'I never said I'd been in Newcastle,' said Gull, 'I let you think so. I'm sorry. It was a kind of lie. But I was in such a daze and I wanted to be *sure* about the job before I – and then we –'

'Yes, yes.'

'I'm sorry. I hope it doesn't make you feel I'm no good – you were a bit romantic about my going all the way to Newcastle and coming back with a job.'

'What you've told me,' said Lily, returning to the table, 'is far far more romantic and far more to the point. But this Byng sounds too good to be true.'

'Well, you see he's a Baptist.'

'A what?'

'A Baptist. You know what that is. So is Martha. He's a good egg, he's one of the nicest men I've ever met, he's very high-minded.'

'We seem to attract high-minded people, I hope he can make money too. Does he know that I exist?'

'Of course, I've told him all about you.'

'Oh! What did you say?'

'I said there was a girl I wanted to ask to marry me as soon as I got a job.'

'Oh Gull – Gull –' Lily wiped confused tears from her eyes, tears of laughter, of joy, and of some deeper mystical emotion. 'I can imagine how touched Justin was! Of course you didn't do it on purpose.'

'No, I didn't – but naturally he was interested, and so was Martha. She keeps referring to you as my bride.'

'They'll be disappointed,' said Lily. 'They probably think I'm a fresh young thing!'

'I've told them you're eccentric.'

'Thanks!'

'But, Lily, they're so nice. They're not frightening people at all! You'll like them and they'll like you. And isn't it strange, it all depended on an extraordinary series of coincidences, if the snail hadn't been there, if I hadn't seen it, if I hadn't failed to find anywhere to put it, if I hadn't gone exactly to that place in Kensington Gardens, if Justin hadn't happened to be passing at exactly that moment – Chance is really amazing!'

If it *was* chance, thought Lily to herself. 'So,' she said aloud, 'we shall have some new friends to show off to our old friends – when we are married – after we are married – tomorrow.'

Gulliver was thinking, it's all worked out marvellously. All the same, I wish I *had* been to Newcastle, as I pretended to Lily I had. It was such a brave exciting idea, and *anything* might have happened up there, awful disasters or else wonderful things, even better than Justin, if one could see the future.

My God, there's the future too! I wonder if I'll ever regret meeting that dear old snail? That idea of just walking out and going away meant a lot to me, it was a kind of ordeal, a trial of strength, a test of courage which now I'll never have – not that particular one anyway – and I was ready for it. Of course I didn't funk it, it was all an accident, that I didn't go, and that I'll never know. I might even have met a girl up there . . . But Gulliver soon checked this treacherous and disturbing line of thought. Then he thought, well, I never got to Newcastle and poor Jenkin never got to South America. Were these good dreams that we had or bad dreams, I wonder? And what about that man at King's Cross station, where is he now, and will I have to go and look for him?

Lily was reflecting that Gulliver might have told her everything but she had not told him everything! She had not revealed that that very morning, when she had said she was going shopping, she had run to offer herself body and soul to another man. She had indeed never revealed to him, or to anyone, that she loved Crimond. He might have gathered, she thought, that I was proud of knowing Crimond, but I'm sure it never occurred to him that I was mad about him. And I was mad about him at the start, and then I cooled down and he was simply the most important person in the world, and then just now I've become mad again, I've fallen in love again because – because of Gull and because of marriage and the marriage bond and that sense of an irrevocable change. As soon as I saw *that* ahead of me, as soon as I had settled down to loving Gull, I realised how terribly much and differently I loved someone else. Perhaps that often happens to people. I had to go to him, I had to try. If I hadn't gone to him on my last day of freedom I would have regretted it ever after. I'd have grieved forever thinking how perhaps, after all, he might have needed me and wanted me, and I'd been afraid to try. Other people are so mysterious, and who knows? As it is . . .

As it was, she felt that a great weight had been taken off her mind, and that she had been liberated into a new space of peace and freedom, which was also a serene surrender to fate. Now what would be, would be, and she could hope to meet it bravely and without mean remorse. Of course Crimond must remain for her, as she had told him, an absolute, and for his sake she would perhaps carry round her neck a little painful amulet. But she knew, even now, that it was a harmless dream object which would fade with the years, and that she had received a freedom which only he could give her. Now it was time to become real and be happy. I think I'm happy, she thought, but am I real? Anyway Gull is real and I really love him, so I suppose that's a good start.

As for that extraordinary story about the snail: could that be just a chain of coincidences? Why not, were not human lives just chains of coincidences? But really it was too odd. Lily too had, as she had told Rose on the evening of the snails' dance at Boyars, found a snail in an unusual place, inside her flat, in fact walking upon her dressing table. As she took it out into the garden, worrying about Gull, she had mumbled to it some words from an old snail-charm which her grandmother used to recite. Of course telepathy was something real, but how could one snail instruct another snail –? I'll swear there's something in it, she thought, something strange happened and I brought it about! How utterly mysterious the world is! She was on the point of telling her thoughts to Gull but decided not to. It sounded too mad. Besides, in the vicissitudes of family life, a little extra secret power might come in handy sometimes; and as her grandmother had told her, power depends on silence. I'm a witch, I'm a witch! thought Lily – grandma did say it was hereditary! But somehow I know that if this was a trick, it worked through love, and if I ever have any magic it will only work through love, and I'll be *that* kind of witch. Oh what a mysterious world we live in!

'Gull darling, look at the time, it's our wedding day! Here's to us – and to snails!'

'To us – and snails, God bless them!'